IN SYSTEM

THE ILIAD

THE ILIAD

Homer

Translation, Introduction, and Notes
by
Barry B. Powell

Foreword
by
Ian Morris

New York   Oxford
OXFORD UNIVERSITY PRESS

Oxford University Press is a department of the University of Oxford.
It furthers the University's objective of excellence in research,
scholarship, and education by publishing worldwide.

Oxford   New York
Auckland   Cape Town   Dar es Salaam   Hong Kong   Karachi
Kuala Lumpur   Madrid   Melbourne   Mexico City   Nairobi
New Delhi   Shanghai   Taipei   Toronto

With offices in
Argentina   Austria   Brazil   Chile   Czech Republic   France   Greece
Guatemala   Hungary   Italy   Japan   Poland   Portugal   Singapore
South Korea   Switzerland   Thailand   Turkey   Ukraine   Vietnam

Copyright © 2014 by Oxford University Press

Published by Oxford University Press
198 Madison Avenue, New York, New York 10016
http://www.oup.com

Oxford is a registered trademark of Oxford University Press

Library of Congress Cataloging-in-Publication Data

Homer.
  [Iliad. English]
  The Iliad : a new translation / Homer ; translated by Barry B. Powell.
    pages. cm.
  Includes bibliographical references and index.
  ISBN 978-0-19-932610-5
  I. Powell, Barry B. II. Title.
  PA4025.A2P69 2013
  883'.01--dc23
                                        2013005120
Printing number: 9 8 7 6 5 4 3 2 1

Printed in the United States of America
on acid-free paper

To Sanford Dorbin, poet, friend, athlete

Table of Contents

List of Maps and Figures

Maps

Figures

Foreword

Born in an age of expansion and out of a mood of melancholy, the *Iliad* is the off-spring of a world very different from our own. But although the era that created it has long since vanished, the poem itself has lived on. Dictated by Homer to a scribe writing on papyrus, for ninety generations it was copied and recopied onto parchment and paper. In the last generation or two it has been spread even further by radios, the cinema, and the Internet. It has inspired painters, more poets, sculptors, and screenwriters; and now Barry Powell, one of the twenty-first century's leading Homeric scholars, has given us this magnificent new translation.

The *Iliad* is a riddle, wrapped in a mystery, inside an enigma. The hard truth is that we know next to nothing about its poet. In the nineteenth century some classical scholars even suggested that Homer had never existed at all; the poem, they argued, was the creation of an editorial committee, stitching together shreds and patches of verse composed by wandering minstrels whose names are now lost. After reading this translation, though, you will see why this has always been a minority view. The *Iliad's* unity of theme, form, and language speaks clearly of a single creative genius, whom ancient writers always called Homer.

Homer probably lived in the eighth century BC, in the very years during which Greeks were adapting a writing system used in Phoenicia (roughly the same area as modern Lebanon) to create a script from which all modern alphabets descend. Writing had been around for a very long time by this point, going back all the way to 3300 BC in what we now call Iraq, but—as Barry Powell has forcefully argued in a series of books and essays across the last twenty-five years—this new Greek script was highly unusual.

Most methods of writing began their lives as accounting systems, used to keep business and bureaucratic records, and only gradually acquired the flexibility to record literature. The Greek alphabet, by contrast, seems to have been linked to literature from its earliest days. Whoever designed the Greek alphabet set aside certain signs to represents vowels. Hardly any other scripts did this, because separate signs for vowels were not necessary for bookkeeping; but for recording the sounds and quantities of poetry, they were essential.

This seems not to have been an accident. Greek is almost unique among ancient scripts in that most surviving examples from the first generation or two of its use are fragments of poetry, not managers' tallies. It is hard to avoid the conclusion that Greeks created their alphabet in the eighth century primarily to write down poetry; or even, as Professor Powell proposed in his groundbreaking book *Homer and the Origin of the Greek Alphabet* (1991), that they created it specifically to write down Homer's poetry.

Homer seems to have been the greatest of the oral poets of eighth-century Greece, composing epics as he performed, much like modern jazz, blues, and rock guitarists compose their music as they perform. Around 800 BC, some genius—Powell calls him "The Adapter"—decided to modify the writing system currently in use in

Phoenicia, adding vowels to make it better suited to recording poetry accurately. In recording sessions that must have gone on for months, the Adapter had Homer dictate his inspired poetry and used the new alphabetic technology to immortalize first the *Iliad* and then the *Odyssey*.

These extraordinary events were only possible because Homer and the Adapter lived in an age of expansion. Around 850 BC, the wobbles and tilts in the earth's axis as it rotates around the sun began pushing the world into a new era of climate, moving from what geologists call the Sub-Boreal period into the Sub-Atlantic. The Sub-Atlantic was slightly cooler and wetter, producing stronger winter winds that carried more rain off the Atlantic and into the Mediterranean Basin. Because the biggest problem facing farmers in the ancient Mediterranean was always that rainfall was low and unreliable, this shift was generally a good thing, and by 800 BC population was growing rapidly.

The number of people in Greece probably doubled during the eighth century, with dramatic consequences. There was more fighting, of the kind we see in the *Iliad*, as towns squabbled over land; more effective governments took shape, to resolve leadership meltdowns like the quarrel of Achilles and Agamemnon; and hungry Greeks began trading further and further afield, having the kind of adventures that Homer sang about in the *Odyssey*. Trade brought Greeks into the East Mediterranean Sea and Phoenicians into the Aegean Sea, and in one (or both) of these settings Greeks learned about the Phoenician script, which, thanks to the Adapter, ultimately made our text of the *Iliad* possible.

But if the *Iliad* was the child of an age of expansion, it was also born out of a mood of melancholy. Homer grew up and learned his craft in a landscape dotted with the ruins of a better, vanished age. Five hundred years before his own time, Greece had been filled with glorious palaces. Their rulers had exchanged gifts with the pharaohs of Egypt, fought with bronze spears from swift-moving chariots, and overseen the economies of broad kingdoms.

Around 1200 BC, however, the great palaces—Mycenae, Pylos, Tiryns, Knossos— all burned to the ground. Despite more than a century of scholarship, we still do not know why. It is one of history's greatest mysteries. Earthquakes, climate change, migrations, and new kinds of war might all have been involved. Whatever the cause, Greece's great kings disappeared after 1200 BC, taking their sophisticated armies, bureaucracies, and artists with them. The population of Greece shrank by at least half. The impoverished survivors clustered in the shadows of the burned palaces or migrated to islands and mountaintops that seemed to offer safety. A Dark Age set in.

No written records from before 1200 BC survived for Dark Age Greeks to read, and at some point—we will never know exactly when—Greeks stopped thinking of the men who had built the mighty walls that now stood in ruins as regular, flesh-and-blood people. By the eighth century BC, the shift in ideas was complete: Greeks now reimagined the long-lost lords who had ruled the ruined palaces as *hêrôes*, semidivine supermen who had communed with the gods and been bigger, faster, stronger, and above all angrier than the mortals of today.

A great cycle of legends grew up. Some tales probably did reflect fairly accurate memories of the warriors of yesteryear, while others were surely entirely fictional. Singers who knew all the stories and could perform them at feasts and festivals were in great demand, and over time they raised their craft to the level of artistry that we see in the *Iliad*. Gradually, the web of tales of the Heroic Age expanded to weave every town and village in Greece into a seamless story, stretching from the origin of the universe to the great wars at Thebes and Troy in which the *hêrôes* destroyed themselves.

Since the Trojan War, Greeks concluded, it had all been downhill. "Would that I were not among the men of [the following] generation," the poet Hesiod lamented around 700 BC, "for now is truly a race of iron. Men never cease from work and sorrow by day or from death at night, and the gods lay harsh troubles on them." And things, he added, would only get worse. All too soon, he explained, the goddesses Shame and Indignation, "their sweet bodies wrapped in white robes, will flee this earth with its wide roads and forsake man for the company of the deathless gods. Bitter sorrows will be left for mortal men, and there will be no help against evil."

The Greeks of the eighth century BC became obsessed with the lost Heroic Age. When they accidentally disturbed ancient tombs, they left offerings in them. They set up shrines to honor the *hêrôes* of legend, worshiping them and giving them rich gifts. Odysseus received sacrifices in a cave on Ithaca, Menelaos and Helen enjoyed a shrine just outside Sparta, and even Agamemnon got his own cult center at Mycenae. And when truly great men died in the late eighth century, they might be buried in styles that mimicked the funeral of Patroclus in the *Iliad*, complete with sacrificed horses, funeral mounds and stelai, and bronze urns to hold their cremated bones.

Historians argue endlessly over just why interest in the *hêrôes* exploded like this in the eighth century BC, but the most plausible theory may be that the upsurge of interest in the legendary past was a reaction against the pace of change in the eighth-century present. Claude Lévi-Strauss, the most famous anthropologist of the modern era, once remarked that other societies are "good to think with," meaning that spending time among the very alien cultures of the Amazonian rainforest helped him see his own homeland, of France, in entirely new ways. Perhaps the Heroic Age worked much like this in eighth-century BC Greece: By reflecting on the causes of the Trojan War or on why Achilles rejected Agamemnon's gifts, Homer and his audiences reached a deeper understanding of the traumatic events of their own age.

We will never know for sure. But whatever it was that drove Homer to dictate the sixteen thousand lines of the *Iliad* and the Adapter to write them down, between them they created a classic in the fullest sense of the word. The poem spoke first and foremost to the expansive, melancholic concerns of eighth-century Greeks, but its appeal has proved timeless. Although thousands of years have passed since the little city-states of Greece disappeared and hundreds more since the Industrial Revolution swept away the agricultural lifestyles that Homer took for granted, we still care about the fates of swift-footed Achilles, man-killing Hector, long-dressed Helen, and Odysseus of the many turns. And now, thanks to Barry Powell's extraordinary translation, we can enjoy them all afresh.

Ian Morris
Palo Alto, California

Preface

In 1956 in Sacramento, California, when I was a teenager, I saw a movie called *Helen of Troy* about some war that took place long ago—but when? where? who were these people, and what where they fighting about? The movie excited in me a burning desire to learn the answers to these questions. Looking back, I see the story had something to do with a beautiful blonde, that was clear, but what I remember best is a warrior running across the plain and suddenly an arrow piercing his throat in a wondrous image of terrible violence. What was this war anyway?

From that moment I conceived my lifelong passion for what turned out to be the Homeric poems. I drifted away to other interests, but in college I came back to the story I then knew to be based on Homer's *Iliad*. I learned Greek, wrote a doctoral dissertation on the *Odyssey*, and for years taught Homer in college. I wrote several books on Homeric problems. But never did the force of these early questions disappear: When did this war really take place? Did it ever take place? What were they fighting about? Did Achilles ever live? What about Helen of Troy? The answers were by no means obvious and are still hotly debated today.

Yet despite the interest of such historical questions, what matters most are the poems themselves, the stories they tell and the language they are told in. Without them we would have no Trojan War, no Helen or Achilles, or Ajax, or Paris, nor the tragedy of Hector. The poems are the thing, and when Charles Cavaliere of Oxford University Press suggested to me rather out of the blue that I translate the *Iliad*, I welcomed the opportunity. When I told friends about this project, they said, "But hasn't Homer already been translated many times?" Yes, sure, I tried to explain, but not by *me*—here was a chance to put into English what the Greek had come to mean to *me*, how it sounded, what the words meant, what was their power that had, indirectly, entranced me as a youth through the medium of film. Too often in modern translations the translator tries to impose a modern sensibility on the style, as if in this way Homer can be made "relevant." I have avoided such affectations, trying always to communicate in a lean direct manner what the Greek really says, to put in English how Homer in Greek might have sounded to a contemporary listener.

Probably because of the film *Helen of Troy* (Warner Brothers, 1956), I've been interested in my career in how the *Iliad* was represented in art in the ancient world, the distant antecedent of our own cinema. After all it was the Greeks who first told stories in art, and they did so inspired by the Homeric and similar poems. *Helen of Troy* is only a modern cinematic version of this ancient tradition. In my translation I want to show some of these images, selecting two or three pictures from ancient art for each book to show how the Greeks and Romans visualized Homeric events. This translation is unique in being illustrated by ancient art.

I've also written an *Introduction* that summarizes scholarship on the Homeric poems, a digest of over fifty years of reflection. About Homer there will always be somebody somewhere who thinks absolutely anything, but in the notes to my translation I have attempted to give common-sense answers to problems of Homeric interpretation. The reader's experience with the Iliad is further enriched by a companion website, www.oup.com/us/powell, which includes audio files of key passages that I read aloud (indicated in the text by an icon placed in the margin), overviews and plot summaries for the poem's twenty-four books, and PowerPoint slides that include outlines and all the maps and photographs in the translation.

Homer's *Iliad* is a very odd poem, so difficult to comprehend in its astonishing range and complexity. I hope that this translation will open to many its beauty and glory, a song about a war fought long ago. There is always war, and the issues are always the same: anger, glory, honor, hate, love, death, terror, violence, and forgiveness. The *Iliad* is about all these things. It is about ourselves. That is why it is so interesting.

Santa Fe, 2013

Acknowledgments

My thanks to Sandy Dorbin, who read the entire manuscript and made more suggestions than I can count. John Bennet, William Aylward, Richard Janko, Ian Morris, Margalit Finkelberg, and William Johnson read the Introduction and translation and saved me from many indiscretions. Finally, my wife Patricia suffered through the whole thing with characteristic good cheer.

I also wish to thank the following readers, in addition to those who wished to remain anonymous, who read early samples of the translations. Their advice was excellent, for which I am very grateful, and I have attempted to make use of their many fine suggestions: Jonathan Austad, Eastern Kentucky University; Michael Calabrese, California State University, Los Angeles; Joel Christensen, University of Texas at San Antonio; Susan Gorman, Massachusetts College of Pharmacy and Health Sciences; William Johnson, Duke University; Erin Jordan, Old Dominion University; Rachel Ahern Knudsen, University of Oklahoma; Carolina López-Ruiz, The Ohio State University; Lynn Wood Mollenauer, University of North Carolina–Wilmington; Nicholas D. More, Westminster College; Clementine Oliver, California State University, Northridge; Joseph Pearce, Ave Maria University; Andrew Porter, University of Wisconsin, Milwaukee; J. Aaron Simmons, Furman University; Richard L. Smith, Ferrum College; Nancy St. Clair, Simpson College; Paul Scott Stanfield, Nebraska Wesleyan University; Dr. Eric Waggoner, West Virginia Wesleyan College; Carolyn Whitson, Metropolitan State University

Many have helped in the production of this book, but I would like to thank especially John Challice, vice president and publisher of Oxford University Press, who supported the book from the beginning; Marianne Paul, the production editor, who did so much to insure a good product, and for which I am very grateful; Kim Howie, who devised an outstanding design; and Michelle Koufopoulos, who has been helpful in many ways. Above all, I want to thank Charles Cavaliere, whose notion it was in the first place to bring out a new translation of the Iliad. He inspired the project, then guided it with diligence and imagination.

About the Translator

BARRY B. POWELL is the Halls-Bascom Professor of Classics Emeritus at the University of Wisconsin–Madison, where he taught for thirty-four years. He is the author of the widely used textbook *Classical Myth* (8th edition, 2014). His *A Short Introduction to Classical Myth* (2001, translated into German) is a summary study of the topic. *Homer and the Origin of the Greek Alphabet* (1991) advances the thesis that a single man invented the Greek alphabet expressly in order to record the poems of Homer. *Writing and the Origins of Greek Literature* (2003) develops the consequences of this thesis. Powell's critical study *Homer* (2nd edition, 2004, translated into Italian) is widely read as an introduction for philologists, historians, and students of literature. *A New Companion to Homer* (1997, with Ian Morris, translated into modern Greek) is a comprehensive review of modern scholarship on Homer. Powell's *Writing: Theory and History of the Technology of Civilization* (2009, translated into Arabic and Greek) attempts to create a scientific terminology and taxonomy for the study of writing. *The Greeks: History, Culture, Society* (2nd edition, 2009, with Ian Morris, translated into Chinese) is a complete review, widely used in college courses. The recent textbook *World Myth* (2013) reviews the myths of the world. Powell has also written novels, poetry, and screenplays. He lives in Santa Fe, New Mexico, with his wife and cats.

Maps

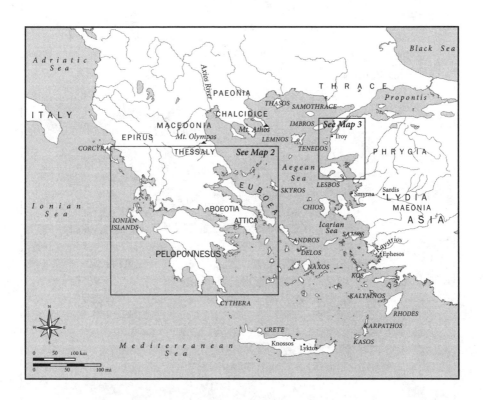

MAP 1   The Aegean

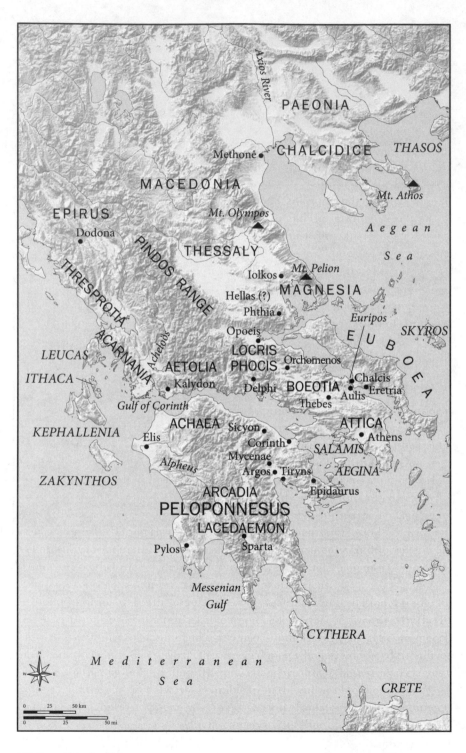

MAP 2   Mainland Greece

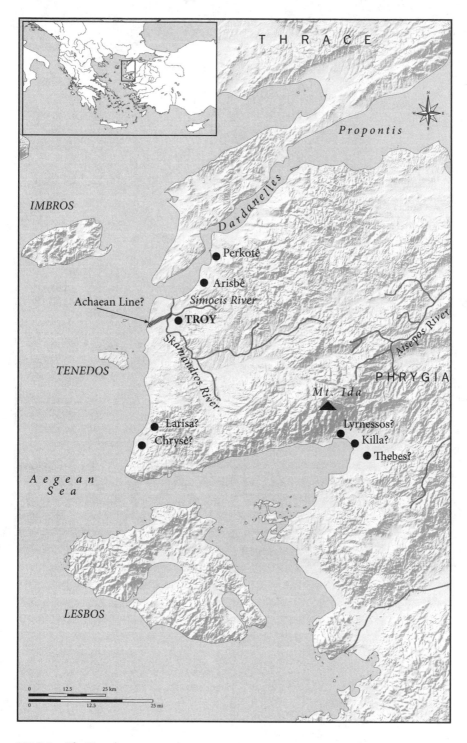

THRACE

Propontis

IMBROS

Dardanelles

● Perkotê

● Arisbê

Simoeis River

Achaean Line? →

● **TROY**

Aïsepos River

PHRYGIA

TENEDOS

Skamandros River

Mt. Ida ▲

● Larisa?

● Lyrnessos?

● Chrysê?

● Killa?

● Thebes?

*Aegean
Sea*

LESBOS

| 0 | 12.5 | 25 km |
| 0 | 12.5 | 25 mi |

MAP 3   The Troad

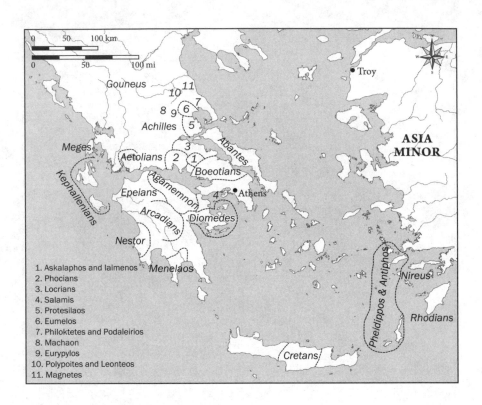

Troy

ASIA
MINOR

Gouneus

11
10 7
8 9 6
5

Achilles

Meges

Aetolians

3
2 1

Boeotians

Abantes

Epeians

Agamemnon

4

Athens

Arcadians

Diomedes

Kephallenians

Nestor

Menelaos

1. Askalaphos and Ialmenos
2. Phocians
3. Locrians
4. Salamis
5. Protesilaos
6. Eumelos
7. Philoktetes and Podaleirios
8. Machaon
9. Eurypylos
10. Polypoites and Leonteos
11. Magnetes

Pheidippos & Antiphos

Nireus

Rhodians

Cretans

0 50 100 km
0 50 100 mi

MAP 4   The Catalog of Ships

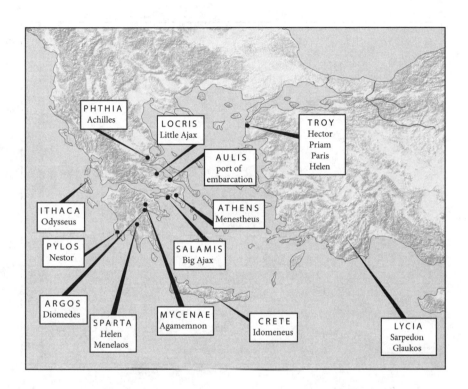

MAP 5 Origins of Heroes

MAP 6   The Trojan Catalog

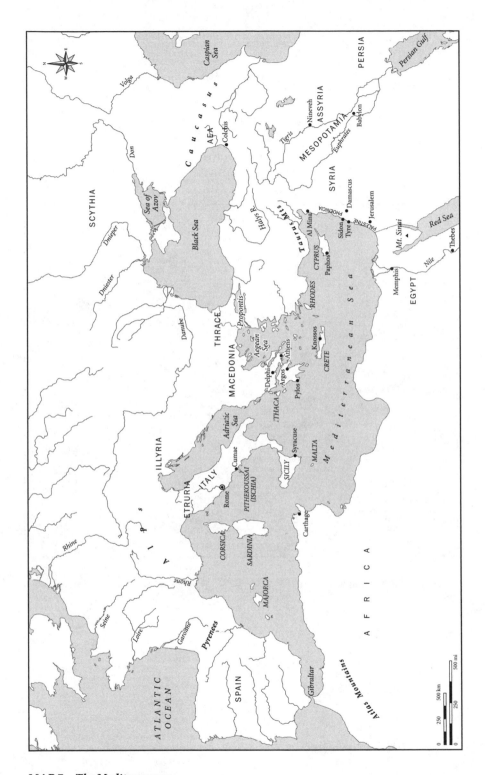

MAP 7   The Mediterranean

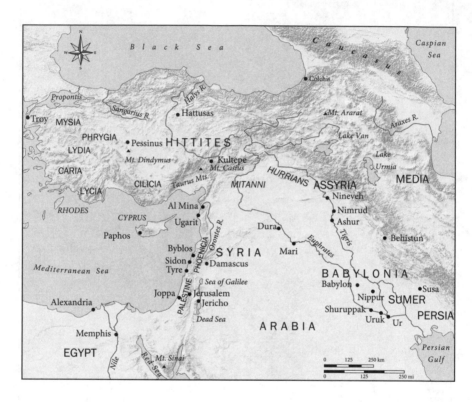

MAP 8 The Ancient Near East

Homeric Timeline

c. 1200 BC	Fall of Troy
c. 800 BC	Dictation of the Homeric poems
	Invention of Greek alphabet
from 566 BC	Panathenaic festival
c. 450 BC	Herodotus
c. 200 BC	Alexandrian Vulgate
c. AD 950	Venetus A
c. AD 1500	First printed edition of the *Iliad*, in Italy
from AD 1598	Chapman's English translation of Homer
AD 1715–1720	Translation by Alexander Pope
AD 1788	Publication of Venetus A by Villoison
AD 1795	Wolf's *Prolegomena ad Homerum*
AD 1871	Heinrich Schliemann digs at Troy
c. AD 1930	Milman Parry
AD 1991	Connection of invention of alphabet with recording of Homeric poems

Introduction

In 1928, Bruce Rogers (1870–1957), probably the greatest American book designer, and his associates in England contracted with the famous Lawrence of Arabia (1888–1935), writing as T. E. Shaw, to do a translation of Homer's *Odyssey*. Lawrence's military glories were in the past, and he was soon to die in a motorcycle accident. He began work in 1928, but it took much longer than he expected. Here Lawrence is explaining to Rogers in a letter why he is taking so long:

> I see now why there are no adequate translations of Homer. He is baffling. Not simple, in education; not primitive, socially ... There's a queer naivety in every other line: and at our remove of thought and language we can't say if he's smiling or not ... I have tried to squeeze out all the juice in the orange; or what I thought was the juice. I tried to take liberties with the Greek: but failed. Homer compels respect.
>
> I must confess he has beaten me to my knees. Perhaps if I did much more I might be less faithful. The work has been very difficult: though I'm in a Homeric sort of air; a mud-brick fort beset by the tribes of Waziristan, on a plain encircled by the hills of the Afghan border. It reeks of Alexander the Great, our European forerunner who also loved Homer.
>
> But, as I say, it has been difficult.[1]

Though Lawrence was unsure of the quality of his translation of the *Odyssey*, the backers of the project were enthusiastic. They went on to produce Lawrence's *Odyssey* in November 1932, one of the most handsome books ever manufactured.

THE DIFFICULTY OF HOMER

Lawrence was right: Homer *is* baffling. Everything about him defies expectations. He knows about too many things. It is often impossible to be sure what tone he intends. What are these gods doing here? Is he being funny? What is the joke? Why is this passage here? Where do all these names come from? Or he is savage, or sad, or beautiful.

The *Iliad* and the *Odyssey* are alternate realities. You can slip into this world of Homer and taste his food and smell his fires and endure his sufferings and enjoy his

---

1 Quoted in Joseph Blumenthal, *Bruce Rogers: A Life in Letters, 1870–1957* (W. Thomas Taylor, Austin, TX, 1989), pp. 130–131.

humor and never be afraid that it is going to end, because it seems to go on forever. It is a complete world—engulfing, like life itself, but somehow more real.

Achilles comes to question the bases for action that his society takes for granted, the heart of the story of the *Iliad*. But the *Iliad* is just as interested in the long boasting speeches of its heroes and in sudden gruesome death on the battlefield as in any moral dilemma. Some five thousand lines or fully one third of the poem consists of descriptions of battle: 318 heroes are killed, 243 of them named. It is all set in a coherent world where the relationships between the characters are clearly drawn, including relationships with the gods, who are powerful characters in their own right.

But you cannot just sit down and read the *Iliad* and the *Odyssey* cold without guidance about their historical, geographical, and literary background. This I provide in the form of notes, which explain unusual usages and sometimes points of plot and character or obscure references. The purpose is to make Homer approachable, understandable.

It is a strange world, far removed in ethics and in expression from our own. It is huge, vast. It is a world certainly of long ago, but in every way recognizable, both socially and psychologically. It is a world in which the problems that men and women face are similar to those we ourselves experience. In a sense the men and women in Homer are ourselves, living in a world torn by violence, sexual passion, and revenge. Sometimes we live in such worlds, too. It is this odd mix of the alien and the familiar that gives Homer his charm. For thinkers and poets in the ancient world, Homer was always the touchstone, the inspiration and model for thought and expression. But Homer is baffling, and one has to wonder how he ever became a classic.

In Greek, the language is extremely odd. As a student I was told constantly that Homer was easy to read, at least in comparison with other Greek authors, but Homer is by no means easy to read. Every ninth line occurs a word that never appears again in Homer, or in many cases in the whole range of Greek literature. There are all kinds of unparalleled forms, driven by the unusually complex meter. The illusion that Homer is easy to read comes from the fact that there are many phrases and whole lines that are repeated again and again, but he is nonetheless not easy to read.

He composes in a complex meter called *dactylic hexameter*. Dactylic hexameter consists of six strong beats, each followed by either another strong beat or two weak beats, and looks like this in a standard scheme:

$$-\smile\smile \mid -\smile\smile \mid -\smile\smile \mid -\smile\smile \mid -\smile\smile \mid --$$

"Dactylic" comes from the Greek *daktylos* meaning finger, because it has a long joint and two short joints. Hexameter means that there are six of these fingerlike units per line. But the last unit is always strong-strong (——), probably because the poet feels the end of the line.

Because Greek is naturally iambic—a short beat followed by a long—it is not clear how dactylic hexameter verse can have come into being in Greek. Once it was thought to be taken from a preGreek language, but this now seems uncertain. In any event, the complicated demands of dactylic hexameter, which go against the natural rhythm of the language, seem to account for many of the puzzling and unprecedented grammatical forms found in Homer. This analysis of the Homeric meter depends wholly, however, on a written text. As an oral poet—someone who created his song without the aid of writing—Homer himself would not have been conscious of the meter, except as a feeling. (For the whole issue of oral poetry—what it was and how it worked—see below.)

You can never be free with the meaning of the Greek, as Lawrence says, because Homer casts a spell over you, compelling obedience. He beats you down. It is all very odd.

WHO WAS HOMER?

Absolutely nothing is known about the historical Homer, but he certainly existed. He composed the *Iliad* and the *Odyssey* and maybe other poems. His name looks like it means "hostage," and all sorts of fantastic biographical details have been wrapped around this etymology, and other etymologies, too. In fact we are not sure what the name *Homeros* means. Presumably it was the poet's name. Otherwise why was it attached to his poems?

By "Homer" in this book I mean the composer of the *Iliad* and the *Odyssey*, the oldest poems in alphabetic writing in the world. In the ancient world poems other than the *Iliad* and the *Odyssey* were attributed to Homer, including a lost *Thebaïd* on the war at seven-gated Thebes. A group of lost poems, some anonymous, built around the saga of the Trojan War, were called the Cyclic Poems, because they were thought to be told in a circle (*kuklos*) around the *Iliad* and the *Odyssey*. We have summaries of their content. The Cyclic Poems explained what happened before and after the Trojan War and appear to have been composed later than the *Iliad* and the *Odyssey*. They were short, widely circulated and performed, and inspired the majority of illustrations with Trojan themes that appear on Greek pots from the seventh to the fourth centuries BC, some of which are included in this book. Such illustrations are one way we have of reconstructing what those lost poems said. It must be that the *Iliad* and *Odyssey* were too massive, and too rarely performed *in toto*, as compared with the very much shorter poems of the cycle that found a far wider circulation.

Other poems in a similar style were also attributed to Homer. A collection dedicated to the gods called the *Homeric Hymns* has survived, but except for the hymn to Aphrodite they appear to have been composed mostly later, and we do not know who the poets were. The *Iliad* and the *Odyssey* survived entire, in spite of their inordinate length, because they were the oldest poems in the Greek alphabet, and they were the best poems, as everybody knew.

Many places claimed to be Homer's birthplace, but the AEGEAN islands of CHIOS and Ios and the nearby settlement of SMYRNA on what is today the coast of Turkey were especially popular candidates (*see* Map 1: places found on any of the maps will be indicated by SMALL CAPS the first time the name appears). Old handbooks say that he was an Ionian poet—that is, he lived in IONIA on the coast of central ASIA MINOR (in modern Turkey). The main reason for thinking this is that his language is mostly in the Ionic dialect, a form of speech spoken in Ionia, in the central Aegean islands, and on EUBOEA, the long island off the east coast of Greece.

But there are many forms in Homeric language that come from another dialect called Aeolic, spoken north of Ionia in Asia Minor (including Smyrna), on the island of LESBOS, and on the mainland in THESSALY. Evidently the tradition of poetry that Homer inherited came through Thessaly, the homeland of Achilles, and was passed down into Euboea, where Ionic was spoken. Several features of Homeric language tie it to the West Ionic branch of the dialect, spoken on Euboea, rather than to its East Ionic branch, spoken on the coast of Asia Minor. From dialect alone the island of Euboea is the most likely location of Homer's creative activity, wherever he was born, and there are other strong reasons for placing Homer on Euboea, where his poems were probably written down.

Homer, however, was certainly familiar with Asia Minor, and even with the site of Troy. For example, he knows that you can see the peak of SAMOTHRACE over the island of IMBROS from the Troad. In similes he shows a familiarity with MOUNT MYKALÊ on the west coast of Asia Minor, with the KAYSTRIOS river that flows near EPHESUS (Maps 1, 6). Homer's geographical knowledge is wide. He knows about the northern Aegean, including the islands of IMBROS, Samothrace, Lesbos, and TENEDOS, and he speaks about the HELLESPONT (or DARDANELLES) and inland PHRYGIA, and regions south to LYDIA and far south to LYCIA (Maps 1, 3, 6), and even to SIDON in PHOENICIA (in modern Lebanon). He also knows about the central Cycladic island of DELOS, CYPRUS, CRETE, and EGYPT (Maps 7, 8). In the *Odyssey* he seems to have firsthand knowledge of ITHACA and the surrounding islands and mainland THESPROTIA, and ELIS, and Nestor's kingdom of PYLOS (Map 2).

Homer knows about all these places. He seems to have lived at the time of aggressive Greek sea travel out of the settlements of CHALCIS and ERETRIA on the island of Euboea in the eighth century BC. Chalcis and Eretria lay across a plain and fought the earliest *historical* war in Greece, in which many overseas communities were involved, even as in the *Iliad*. The Euboean port was at AULIS, on the mainland across the very narrow EURIPOS strait. The Achaean expedition to Troy was launched from Aulis, according to Homer, not a logical port for a story in which the Greek commanders come from the Argive plain far to the south, but logical for a Euboean audience.

In the early eighth century BC the Chalcidians and Eretrians were the wealthiest and most adventurous of all the Greeks. They began the tradition of Greek colonization (although other cities were involved), sailing to CHALCIDICE in northeast Greece (named after Chalcis; Map 1); evidently to an emporium at a place called AL MINA at the mouth of the ORONTES RIVER in northern SYRIA (Map 8), where their ceramics are found and local inhabitants used West Semitic (that is, Phoenician) writing; and in the other direction to far-off ITALY. There, on the island of ISCHIA in the bay of Naples, then called PITHEKOUSSAI ("monkey island"), they were involved in a multi-ethnic trading enclave in c. 800–775 BC, from which the earliest Greek colony at CUMAE on the mainland across the bay was founded, apparently named after a settlement on the east coast of Euboea (Maps 2, 7). The natural audience for the *Odyssey*, which describes dangerous sea travel in the far West, were Euboeans who had actually made that journey, evidently in search of iron and copper ores. "Chalcis" means copper or bronze; "Eretria" means city of rowers.

Around 800 BC or slightly before someone invented the alphabet on the basis of the preexisting Semitic syllabary—a writing system whose symbols indicate only whole syllables (discussed later). This invention seems to have taken place on Euboea, probably in Eretria, where Semitic speakers were living side by side with Greeks. There we find a mixture of inscriptions in West Semitic, on the one hand, and in the oldest alphabetic writing in Greece, on the other, dated c. 775–750 BC. Other very early fragmentary inscriptions come from a nearby site called Lefkandi, which may have been an earlier settlement of the Eretrians. These short inscriptions consist of only a few letters. Recently inscriptions from the late eighth century, some metrical, have been found at METHONÊ in Macedonia, an Eretrian outpost. From Ischia in Italy, from about the same time, we also find Semitic writing mixed with Greek, and c. 740 BC one of the earliest Greek alphabetic inscriptions of more than a few words, including two perfect hexameters and an apparent reference to the cup of Nestor in *Iliad* Book 11 (see Figure 11.2). Among the earliest surviving alphabetic writing in the Greek world is a literary reference.

Here is the puzzle of the Homeric poems: You cannot have Homer without the alphabet, but in Homer's world there is no writing. He does refer to writing once, but seems not to understand what it is.

THE TEXT OF HOMER

Investigation into the origin of the text of Homer constitutes the famous "Homeric Question" (from the Latin *quaestio*, "investigation"), a central topic in the humanities for over two hundred years. When did these two very long and complex texts come into being? Where and why? How and by whom? What did those texts look like?

The Homeric poems are improbably long—the *Iliad* around sixteen thousand lines and the *Odyssey* around twelve thousand. The *Odyssey* takes place later than the *Iliad* and knows the *Iliad* intimately: No stories told in the *Iliad* are repeated in the *Odyssey*, but several events foretold in the *Iliad* are described in the *Odyssey*, for example, the death of Achilles. The poet seems to be finishing various stories in the *Odyssey* that he began in the *Iliad*. Perhaps the only element of Homeric criticism that all scholars agree on is that the *Odyssey* came after the *Iliad*. From a time in which there was no reading public, it is impossible than any poet could have been so familiar with the *Iliad* unless he were himself its composer. Both poems are by the same man—Homer—as tradition always maintained.

In spite of much speculation, no one has been able to offer a persuasive model for the circumstances of the performance of the complete *Iliad* and the *Odyssey*, although portions of the poems were presented at the Panathenaia in Athens in the sixth century BC, nearly two hundred years after their composition. In the seventh and sixth centuries BC, the heyday of Greek lyric poetry, written texts were prompt books for memorized reperformance. They were studied in the schools but never "read" for pleasure, as we read Homer today. This is true of Pindar, too, from the early fifth century BC. He sold written copies of his poems, some of which survive, to clients around the Mediterranean, who performed them to the accompaniment of song and dance. Herodotus and Thucydides from the mid-fifth-century BC still produced works to be listened to as someone read them aloud, as far we can tell. If Homer belonged to the eighth century BC—he was always said to be Greece's oldest poet—his poems, or parts of them, could have been memorized for reperformance, but we must admit that we have no idea what these poems were for, what purpose they originally served. They appear as if from nowhere, wrapped in mystery.

THE ALEXANDRIAN VULGATE

Homer has been the object of curiosity and study since the sixth century BC when a Greek living in southern Italy named Theagenes (whose works are lost) is reported to have explained the battles of the gods in the *Iliad* as allegories for natural phenomena. It was not until the third and second centuries BC in Alexandria, Egypt, that the first real inquiry arose on the Homeric texts. There, in the *Mouseion*, the "temple to the Muses," librarians tried to establish an official text from the many variant versions. Our text goes back to this "official" Alexandrian text and is, practically speaking, identical with it.

It is a remarkable situation. The Ptolemies, Macedonian descendants of a general of Alexander the Great (356–323 BC), ruled Egypt as a personal possession. They were rich beyond dreaming. To prove the cultural superiority of the Greeks over the subjugated Egyptians, with all their exaggerated claims to cultural achievement, the Ptolemies funded, on foreign soil, the world's first comprehensive library of alphabetic texts. Using their power and prestige, the Ptolemaic librarians bought and otherwise obtained texts of all the famous poets of the past, including Homer. They seem to have amassed around 500,000 texts.

The Ptolemies obtained Homeric texts from various cities, from Marseilles in France to Sinopê on the Black Sea, the so-called "city texts," and also from individuals. A third textual tradition is called the "common" (*koinê*) text, perhaps a generic text in common circulation, but we are not really sure. There is reason to think, on the basis of the way some words are spelled in the Athenian style, that the "clean text" the Alexandrians prepared is based on a text retrieved from Athens. This might also accord with the tradition that something was done to the text of Homer in Athens in the sixth century BC (discussed later).

Homer is strongly represented in Egyptian papyrus finds that come from this time (c. third to first centuries BC), although there are many more fragments from the *Iliad* than from the *Odyssey*. Some of these papyri were once used to mummify crocodiles! Many fragments seem to be from school editions. They sometimes vary from the standard text in having different forms of words and alternate phrasings and sometimes extra or "wild" lines. The wild lines almost invariably repeat other lines or are made up from other lines. They never add to the narrative. The origin of the wild lines seems to be scribal in nature: A scribe copying the text inadvertently adds lines or repeats other lines that he knows.

The Alexandrian scholars Zenodotus of Ephesus (active c. 280 BC) and Aristophanes of Byzantium (c. 257–c. 180 BC), and especially Aristarchos of Samothrace (active c. 220–240 BC) somehow established a text that did not have the wild lines.

The wild lines disappear from the papyrus fragments around 150 BC. From this time on there is a fixed number of lines to the poems.

Perhaps the librarians at Alexandria exerted so much prestige that after their editorial work copyists brought the book industry into line with the scholarly exemplars, but it is not at all clear how work in the library governed the book trade; there must have been some connection. This clean text that the Alexandrians prepared we call the *vulgate*, the basis for all medieval and modern texts. We do not have it directly, but we infer it. There is no extra-Alexandrian textual tradition for the Homeric poems.

In addition to throwing out the wild lines, the Alexandrian librarians went on to question many other lines in Homer, placing a mark beside a line when they thought it suspicious, the origin of our word *athetesis*. So began the venerable tradition of wondering about the real meaning of many words in Homer and whether this or that line was "genuine." But though the Alexandrians marked lines as being suspicious, they seem never to have prepared a text that actually omitted such lines.

We might contrast the situation of Homer's text with that of the very long epic, the Sanskrit *Mahabharata*, the "great story of the Bharata dynasty," the longest epic poem in the world with over ninety thousand verses, long passages in prose, and 1.8 million words. According to tradition, it was composed by one Vyasa, who supposedly also composed various sacred texts. We cannot date Vyasa accurately, although he may belong to the time when writing was introduced into India about 600 BC. He was presumably a man who had something to do with fixing the Hindu epic poem in writing, but the *Mahabharata* contains demonstrably much later material and in fact exists in many versions. The poem did not settle down into something like its modern form until AD 400, one thousand years after Vyasa.

The *Iliad* and the *Odyssey*, unlike the *Mahabharata*, exist in single versions, not in many. Early papyri of Homer, and early quotations and misquotations, do not represent different versions of the poems. There is a single text undergoing occasional corruption in the usual manner.

BEFORE AND AFTER THE VULGATE

Unfortunately, we know very little about the condition of the text of Homer's poems from the time of their composition, c. 800 BC, to the Alexandrian version, c. 150 BC. The Alexandrian version is pretty much the same as a modern text, but what went before?

Evidence from Greek art, mostly paintings on pots, suggests that the *Iliad* and the *Odyssey* were widespread in the Greek world beginning c. 675 BC. We cannot, however, always be sure whether such illustrations depend on literary exemplars or on lost oral songs. In any event it is clear that Homer had become a cultural yardstick by the late sixth and early fifth centuries BC, especially in the city of Athens, where most of our information comes from. From the fourth century, Plato (424–348 BC) and Aristotle (384–322 BC) and other authors quote Homer frequently, but they are careless in their quotations, and their text often differs from ours. It is not clear that such writers are looking at a manuscript of Homer so that the quotations are evidence for the *text* of Homer at this time. More likely such writers are quoting from memory. Greek education consisted of memorizing passages of Homer and other poets. Every literate Greek had Homer somewhere in his head.

We cannot penetrate beyond the veil of the stabilization of the text by the Alexandrian scholars. Their text of Homer is *our* text—what seemed right to them is what we have. The *original* text of Homer cannot be recovered. It existed, but it cannot be found.

In the fifth century AD, knowledge of Greek disappeared from Western Europe and did not return until Italian bibliophiles brought Greek manuscripts from Constantinople in the fourteenth and fifteenth centuries. The learned Dante Alighieri (AD 1265–1321) knew about Homer and the Trojan War, but he knew no Greek. While we do not have the edited text of the Alexandrian scholar Aristarchos of Samothrace (third century BC), the oldest surviving complete text of the *Iliad* incorporates many marginal commentaries from his writings, called *scholia*. This text is now kept in Venice and called *Venetus A*.

Venetus A seems to have appeared in Italy sometime in the fifteenth century. It is a large, beautiful, and extremely expensive vellum (calf's hide) manuscript written in the tenth century AD in Constantinople. The manuscript also has a summary of the lost poems of the so-called Cyclic Poems. *Venetus A* was forgotten until 1788, when a French scholar (Jean-Baptiste Villoison) published an edition of the text and the previously unknown scholia—a publication that began the modern era in Homeric scholarship.

The scholia seemed to prove that the Alexandrians had created our modern text, but, still, what was the ultimate origin of this text?

THE HOMERIC QUESTION

Previously, the universal assumption by scholars was that Homer had created his poems in a fashion similar to Vergil and Dante and Chaucer, all direct heirs to the technological revolution of the invention of the alphabet, about which early scholars knew absolutely nothing. Homer had taken a pen to paper and composed his poetry, just as had Vergil, Dante, and Chaucer.

After the publication of *Venetus A*, a German scholar, Friedrich August Wolf (AD 1759–1824), revolutionized Homeric studies in his famous *Prolegomena ad Homerum* of 1795. Wolf was the creator of the modern science of "classical philology," the careful study of language to reveal the truth about the classical past. He presented drastic evidence about the poems that shocked his contemporaries and directly contradicted Aristarchos' conviction that the poems had a unity and a unified origin.

Wolf noticed that nowhere in Homer is there any reference to writing, except in the story of the hero Bellerophon's exile in *Iliad* Book 6, when Bellerophon carries tablets bearing "ruinous signs" (*sêmata lugra*) to his host in Lycia. But in later Greek, "writing" is never referred to as "signs" (*sêmata*). Evidently Homer is reporting a story that contained a detail he did not understand.

Homer must come from a time when there was no writing in Greece, Wolf argued, otherwise he would in some place have mentioned it. In fact there are several passages that cry out for the use of writing, if Homer knew about it. Because it is quite impossible to memorize twenty-eight thousand lines of poetry, what appears to be the unity of the *Iliad* and the *Odyssey* is in reality a compilation of short, oral songs capable of being memorized, Wolf thought.

There were reports in various ancient writers that the Athenian tyrant Peisistratos (d. 527 BC) or his son Hipparchos (d. 514 BC) had brought "the Homeric epics" to Athens and ordered the *rhapsodes*, in their performances at the Panathenaic Festival, "to go through them in order," each taking up where the last left off. The implication is that the various episodes were accustomed to be performed out of sequence. It must have been at this time, in Athens, that the *Iliad* and the *Odyssey* were created by unknown editors from earlier separate, short, orally preserved songs capable of memorization, Wolf thought. The poems had been "stitched together" (based on a popular but inaccurate understanding of *rhapsode* as meaning "song-stitcher"). This hypothetical event came to be known in Homeric scholarship after Wolf as the *Peisistratean Recension*.

Wolf formalized the point of view, already old, that the Homeric texts must be anonymous compilations. This view is known in Homeric criticism as *Analysis*: the theory that the poems were created by different poets at different times. The theory was modeled on contemporary eighteenth-century biblical criticism, which had discovered different layers to the certainly edited first five books of the Bible (Pentateuch).

Analysis was predominant in the nineteenth century, especially in Germany, and well into the twentieth and is still embraced by some scholars. For generations scholars subdivided the poems, and even the lines, into this or that layer, ignoring or ignorant of the material conditions that would make such editorial activity improbable. There were no desks in Homer's world, or studies, or libraries, or a reading public. There was no scribal class dedicated to protecting a religious vision, nor record of the people, nor a bureaucratic state. If there was so much editorial interference going on, we would expect more than a single version of the *Iliad* and the *Odyssey*, as we get with the Indian *Mahabharata*. But all evidence testifies to a single version.

Analysis was opposed by the minority *Unitarian* view, which held that the poems were the creation of a single intelligence at a single time. Whereas the Analysts made use of narrative and logical inconsistencies (of which there are a good number) to establish the lines of demarcation between allegedly originally discrete poems, the Unitarian position looked past such flaws in a theory of unitary composition, although accretions and alterations were probable. Everything about the poems betrays careful design, they argued—not always the design that will pass a modern scholar's muster, but an intelligent design all the same. You never forget when reading Homer that a single personality stands behind the plan of the plot and its arresting expression.

The Unitarians also complained that if the poems are made up of separate parts, or if they began as a core that was expanded, then why is there no agreement on where the divisions lie between the originally separate songs? And if someone makes up extra lines, or changes words, how do such additions and changes enter the textual tradition? Someone bent on interpolation must recopy the entire poem, or the portion he is altering, and then that copy must somehow become the canonical version—the one that everybody else copies, in direct ancestry to the text that the Alexandrians inherited, the vulgate.

No doubt the poems suffered various distortions in their transition between an archaic orthography to a modern one, but to copy the complete *Iliad* and *Odyssey* is no mean feat, requiring many months of sustained daily labor. It is extraordinary that after two hundred years of argument, not one single line of Homer's poems, the *Iliad* and the *Odyssey*, can be *proven* to be an addition to the original text (which in any event cannot be reconstructed).

The Unitarians tended to be poets, such as Goethe and Schiller, the Analysts to be scholars. The Analyst position held all the prestige in this argument.

THE ORAL-FORMULAIC THEORY

Throughout the debate, no attention was paid to how a written text comes into being or to the nature of the writing system that made the Homeric poems possible. With surprising naiveté, scholars assumed that Homer was like the professors themselves, toiling away in a dim light, crossing out words, improving the expression, adding favorite lines and incidents. Somehow, poems once oral became written poems, for unclear reasons; these were then manipulated further, for unclear reasons.

MILMAN PARRY AND ALBERT B. LORD

This discussion was turned on its head by the writings of a young American scholar, Milman Parry (1902–1935), who studied the creation of oral poetry in Bosnia-Herzegovina in the early 1930s. Milman Parry was born in Oakland, California, and studied classics at the nearby University of California in Berkeley, where he earned a BA and MA.

Parry became interested in the Homeric Question as an undergraduate. How did these poems really come into being? What does the trail look like that extends backward from *Venetus A* to a manuscript that touched the poet's hand? Parry's remarkable discoveries were to revolutionize Homeric studies as well as the study of many other literatures.

When Parry began his work, the prevailing view was the Analyst position—that the poems were the result of a long period of accretion and editorial redaction. In early academic studies Parry showed how the formulaic style, which all commentators on Homer had noticed, was not compatible with the theory that Homer's poetry had been created in writing. Parry was interested in such noun-epithet combinations translated as "Achilles the fast runner" and "wine-dark sea" and "Hector of the flashing helmet" that are so striking to a reader. An epithet is a descriptive term accompanying a noun. Epithets occur again and again and with little respect to the context. For example, Achilles is described by the epithet "fast runner" even when he is sitting down.

In meticulous fashion, Parry showed how the epithets vary not in accordance with the demands of the narrative but in accordance with the position of the name in the metrical line. So different epithets are attached to the same name in accordance with where in the metrical line the name appears—at the beginning, middle, or end.

Not only does the system show *extension*, in which there are different epithets for many characters for different positions in the line, but it shows *thrift*, because usually there is but a single epithet for a single position in the line. Such stylistic features are impossible, and in fact are unknown, in poems created in writing. Hence Homer's poetry was created without the use of writing.

In 1924 Parry traveled to Paris and enrolled at the Sorbonne, where he studied under the great linguist Antoine Meillet (1866–1936). In 1923 Meillet had written the following (quoted in Parry's first French thesis, 1925):

> Homeric epic is entirely composed of formulae handed down from poet to poet. An examination of any passage will quickly reveal that it is made up of lines and fragments of lines which are reproduced word for word in one or several other passages. Even those lines of which the parts happen not to recur in any other passage have the same formulaic character, and it is doubtless pure chance that they are not attested elsewhere.

Meillet thought that such features might be distinctive of orally transmitted epic in general and suggested to Parry that he observe a living oral tradition. In 1933–35 Parry traveled with his assistant Albert B. Lord (1912–1991) to Bosnia-Herzegovina. There Parry made original studies of many illiterate, mostly Muslim singers, who spoke Serbo-Croatian, a southwest Slavic dialect.

Parry made many recordings on primitive recording equipment, and he took down poems by dictation, several as long as the *Odyssey*. His and Lord's collection of oral documents is still today the largest ever made in the field. He discovered that although his informants claimed that they could reproduce a song word for word at different times, in fact their songs were always different. There was no fixed text, because of course a fixed text depends on a written version.

Until the fieldwork of Parry and Lord, the theory of the oral origins of the Homeric texts had depended on Parry's rigorous analysis of the language of the text, but the theory was supported by Parry and Lord's unprecedented experiments in the contemporary world. Parry argued that Homer, like the Serbo-Croatian poets, composed orally by means of "formulas" instead of "words." Parry defined a formula as "a group of words that is regularly employed under the same metrical conditions to express a given essential idea." For example, such phrases as "dawn with her rosy fingers" or "wine-dark sea" occupied a certain position in the metrical line and enabled the singer (in Greek *aoidos*) to compose rapidly. Because of formulaic thrift— one formula with a certain metrical pattern occupying a certain place in the line—such a system could not be the creation of one man. It must depend on a *tradition* to which the singer had access. An oral tradition (from Latin "hand over") is a system of transmission of cultural material from generation to generation through vocal utterance without the assistance of writing, in this case of stories about heroes.

Of course the formulas in oral traditional speech did allow internal substitutions and adaptations in response to narrative and grammatical needs, and eventually Parry fixed on the notion of a "formulaic system" that contained both constant and variable elements.

The purpose of such a system of ready-made diction was to enable composition in performance so that the traditional features of Homer's language became proof of its oral origins: *The poems are not memorized, but created anew in performance from traditional material and diction every time the songs are sung.* Parry's thesis seemed to explain the highly unusual "artificial language" (German *Kunstsprache*) in which Homer composed, the so-called "epic dialect" that no Greek ever spoke. Basically, the dialect is Ionic (spoken on the central west coast of Asia Minor, on the islands, and on the island of Euboea), but as we have seen, it incorporates features from other dialects (especially Aeolic). Parry thought this epic language must have emerged over a long period of time through exposure to various dialectal forms that proved useful in the construction of the poetic line. Such features could only have come into being through generations, as a collective inheritance of many singers.

Parry died before he could systematically compare the technique of South Slavic poetry with Homer's. His work attracted little attention until the publication in 1960 of *The Singer of Tales* by his assistant Albert B. Lord, the most influential work of literary criticism of the twentieth century. Lord summarized his teacher's discoveries, made original contributions of his own, and examined other non-Greek poems to discover their oral features. Lord also wrote about the singer's apprenticeship. He described the study of an aspiring illiterate singer as a young boy under an illiterate master up until the time of his mastery of the craft. Lord went on to describe other features of oral-traditional style, for example the story patterns that governed whole epics, and the building blocks of individual epics, the type scenes.

Type-scenes are blocks of words in which typical events are arranged in the same order and often with the same words. Typical type-scenes in Homer include *Arming, Battle, Travel, Speeches, Sleeping, Dreams, Divine Visitation, Conference, Assembly, Supplication, Dressing, Oath-Taking, Bathing,* and *Seduction*—and there are others.

For example, in an arming scene the warrior first puts on his shin guards and breastplate, then he takes up his sword, shield, helmet, and spear—always in that order. When somebody arrives for a feast there is always a seating of the guest; a servant brings water for washing; a table is placed before the guest; a servant provides bread and other foods; and a carver hands around meat and gold cups. Then:

> They put forth their hands to the good things set ready before them.
> But when they had cast off all desire for drink and food ...

All such type scenes can be fleshed out or compressed in accordance with the dramatic requirements of the narrative. They are common in the South Slavic epic that Parry studied, as well as the theme of Withdrawal and Return that determines the overall story of the *Iliad*, a theme also attested in the traditions of medieval England, Russia, Albania, Bulgaria, Turkey, and Central Asia.

The theory of oral composition was used to explain the various narrative inconsistencies of which Analysts had made so much, for the dictating poet has no way to go back and correct "errors," nor any interest in doing so. It also explained the use of such out-of-context epithets as "blameless Aigisthos" to describe the murderer of Agamemnon, or "Achilles the fast runner" while he sits calmly in his chair. It also could explain the inordinate length of the Homeric poems, because when an oral poet dictates his text released from the exigencies of a live performance, free to elaborate his tale at will, the songs can become very long. The *Iliad* and the *Odyssey* are far longer than ordinary oral poems and were probably never performed as we have them. When Parry took down texts by dictation, the process gave the informant time to think, to expand, to add, just as we find in the *Iliad* and the *Odyssey*. Neither Homer nor his audience cared about the various inconsistencies that so troubled the Analysts. After all, there was no written text to check up on, and who cared anyway? Inconsistencies, repetition, and formulas or formulaic phrases were signs of the oral style.

The thrust of the Parry-Lord school is that Homer was like the Serbo-Croatian singers. He was illiterate. He composed the *Iliad* and the *Odyssey* at some early time, and his words were taken down by somebody who understood how to write down Greek. The Parry-Lord model has become orthodoxy in a modern understanding of the genesis of Homer's poems.

Oral Theory was initially criticized because it appeared to make the fount and origin of Western culture a slave to a mechanical system. Where was there room for the genius of poetic invention if the lines were made up of preset expressions? and preset events? The contribution of individual creativity appeared to be submerged in a collective poetic tradition. However, the units of expression that Parry and Lord identified in oral verse are no more restrictive to expression than is the large but finite store of "words" (conventionally understood) in literate traditions. The oral-formulaic language is just that: a language, subject to the morphological and grammatical restrictions of any language, which in this case happens to include metrical expression.

This is why scholars were unable to define clearly what was meant by a "formula." Noun-epithet formulas were easy to find, but other formulaic expressions slipped away as one tried to pin them down. That could have been the only outcome, just as the attempt to define a conventional "word" has proved impossible. Language is a flexible medium depending on invisible templates that generate the form on the surface. Language is not mechanical but a human faculty whose origins and functioning are poorly understood.

We think of poems as being made up of words, but linguists cannot define a "word" except as something found in dictionaries. The concept "word" is a product of literacy. For the illiterate singers of Bosnia-Herzegovina, a "word" is a unit of meaning, not a typographical convention that depends on the technology of writing. Further questioning of the Serbo-Croatian bards revealed that by "word" the singer could mean several lines, a scene, or even a whole poem. Any spectrograph reveals that speech is a continuous *stream* of sound, with peaks and valleys, a wave, not a sequence of separable sounds. So Homer's song was a continuous stream of sound, roughly reconstructible from a system of written symbols that crudely encode aspects of the phonology of this sound.

What Parry/Lord did not explain is how a dictated oral song became a text, a stream of symbols on a piece of papyrus.

HOMER AND THE ALPHABET

The eastern coast of the Mediterranean—modern Lebanon and northern Syria—was a mosaic of coastal city-states like TYRE and SIDON (MAP 8), whose inhabitants spoke a West Semitic dialect belonging to the same language family as Hebrew and Arabic. They traded with the Euboean Greeks in the late ninth and eighth centuries BC, in Syria at AL MINA, on the Greek mainland, and in ISCHIA in Italy, and no doubt in such other places as southern SPAIN, SARDINIA, and NORTH AFRICA and with other groups, like the peoples of ETRURIA. They used a writing often called the "Phoenician alphabet," but these Semites did not call themselves Phoenicians, nor was their writing alphabetic. It was a sort of syllabary of around twenty-two signs, each of which represented a consonant, with an implied vowel to be supplied by the speaker. No doubt some western Semitic speakers intermarried with the illiterate Greeks, and their children were bilingual speakers of Greek and Semitic dialects. In Ionia, the founder of Greek philosophy Thales (seventh–sixth centuries BC) was said to be the child of an Examyes and Kleoboulinê, both Phoenician nobles.

THE INVENTION OF THE ALPHABET

The western Semites had a tradition of taking down texts by dictation, which may explain why all the elements in their system of writing are phonetic—that is, they have a sound attached. This is not true of the earlier Egyptian and cuneiform systems, which contained many nonphonetic elements. There is a clear example of creating a poetic text by means of dictation in a note attached to a poem on Baal written c. 1400 BC in the earliest attested use of West Semitic writing, from the emporium of UGARIT (in so-called Ugaritic cuneiform, not in West Semitic script), on the coast in North Syria (Map 8). The appended note remarks on the names of the priest who dictated the text and the scribe who took it down.

Evidently somebody—his name may have been Palamedes according to Greek tradition—knew the West Semitic writing and was heir to the tradition of taking down a poetic text by dictation. If for unknown reasons he tried to do this with an extremely famous poet named Homer, he soon discovered that West Semitic syllabic writing was unable to preserve the rhythm of the Greek in which the poetry resided (Semitic poetry works on different principles). If you applied the West Semitic system to write down the first line of the *Iliad* and separated the words by dots as the Phoenicians did, in Roman characters it would look something like this:

MNN·D·T·PLD·KLS

or for the Greek alphabetic:

MENIN AEIDE THEA PELEIADEO AKHILEOS

You cannot pronounce a text written in West Semitic writing unless you are a native speaker because the sound of the spoken word is never given—only hints about its sound. West Semitic writing could not, and did not, encode Homer's poetry, which was so rich in vowel sounds and subtle rhythms.

It was the meter's dependence on the alternation of vocalic qualities that gave the adapter, our Palamedes, his idea. He redesigned the West Semitic system into a system consisting of two different kinds of signs: one group pronounceable, the five vowels signs; and one group unpronounceable, what we call consonants. The inventor added the inviolable spelling rule that *a sign from the long unpronounceable group must always be accompanied, before or after, by a sign from the short pronounceable group.* Only in this way do you get a pronounceable syllable, though not one accurately reflecting what we think of as "long" and "short" syllables, which the vowels signs did not distinguish. The adapter also added three new signs to the series of unpronounceable signs: φ, Χ, and ψ.

The adapter's spelling rule revolutionized human culture. It is the writing that we use every day of our lives, but its initial purpose seems to have been to make possible a written record of poetic song. To judge from very early and unexpected inscriptional finds in hexametric verse on baked clay and stone, the Greek alphabet was from the beginning used for just this purpose, to notate the rhythms of the Greek hexameter.

We must be talking about the poems of Homer, for otherwise it is hard to explain the coincidence of the sudden appearance of a writing that encoded the approximate sound of the voice, capable of encoding dactylic hexameter, with the sudden appearance of a poetry that depended on just those sounds. As F. A. Wolf noticed in 1795, alphabetic writing is not referred to a single time in Homer, who wrote verse that delights in the description of everyday life. This is because Homer lived at a time when alphabetic writing was unknown or known only to a few. Apparently the few who possessed alphabetic technology in the eighth century BC were applying its power to record the songs of *aoidoi*. Hesiod, very close in time to Homer and also an oral poet, seems to have been the second singer whose songs were recorded—the *Theogony* and the *Works and Days* and, a poem that only exists in fragments, *The Catalog of Women*. It only occurred to someone, perhaps in the seventh century BC, that you can create poetry from scratch *in writing* by using this same technology.

Homer comes like a shot out of the blue, at a time when most of Greece was an impoverished backwater. Instead of temples and pyramids, the decorated pot was their greatest cultural contribution. There was no state, no scribal class. Suddenly there are 28,000 lines of complicated verse inscribed on expensive papyri—more, in fact, when you count the poetry of the near contemporary Hesiod and the Cyclic Poems that soon followed.

The invention of the Greek alphabet c. 800 BC was the third most important invention in the long history of the human species after the discovery of fire in the primordial past, and the invention of writing itself c. 3400 BC in Mesopotamia. The Greek alphabet was the first writing that could be pronounced by a nonnative speaker. It is a technology that allows the re-creation of a rough phonic equivalent of speech, even if you do not know the language. The Greek alphabet was the first system of writing capable of preserving Homer, and it seems to have been designed for this very purpose. Attempts to place Homer later than the early eighth century on the basis of archaeological data are inconclusive; on balance, we must place Homer at the time of the alphabet's invention in the early eighth or late ninth century.

It is wrongheaded to be concerned with the elegance or crudeness of expression, as many commentators are, when to the composer and those who heard him sing it is all a continuum of rhythmical sound. The poet must carry his listeners along on the path of song, and nothing else matters. Palamedes' epoch-making invention transformed Homer's poems from an oral version to a cold, roughly phonetic abstraction. Gesture, intonation, and musical accompaniment, so essential to oral song, are lost—they are not part of the alphabet. So we should not imagine that we "have the poems of Homer": We have a symbolic representation of some of the phonetic aspects of the language of Homer.

WHY HOMER IS IMPORTANT

In circumstances almost unimaginable today, probably on the island of Euboea, in Eretria, among the very wealthy Euboean international traders where alphabetic writing first appears archaeologically, we should suppose that two men, the poet and his scribe, worked together for many months to create the *Iliad* and the *Odyssey*. We must remember that after the recording of the poems, only one man in the world, the adapter, could read them. Nothing is known directly about Homer because he lived in a time when there were no records of any kind: no libraries, no readers, no records. There were only the Homeric poems and, later, the poems of Hesiod. They were the object of study for, at first, a tiny, then a rapidly growing literary and social elite, men who understood the rules of alphabetic writing well enough to memorize portions of these poems for representation as entertainment at the feast.

At first Euboeans were this elite, leaders in wealth and international trade. Early Greek inscriptions present a remarkable unprecedented use of writing. In the East, "literacy"—the ability to manipulate a system of symbols with partial ties to speech— is entirely in the hands of a scribal class, special men who have devoted their lives to the mastery of the symbolic system. The power and wealth of these scribal classes was very great, and they are not always separable from the ruling elite themselves.

In Greece, by contrast, "literacy" is in possession of amateurs without connection to the power structure of a state, which scarcely exists. These amateurs are interested in poetry and never in business. As far as we know, Greek alphabetic writing was never used for economic purposes of any kind until about 600 BC, two hundred years after its invention. It was used preeminently for poetic expression, to judge from the inscriptional finds.

But we should be surprised that Homer ever became *the* classic. His poems are much too long, and sometimes it is hard to retain the narrative thread in them. The expression is exaggerated, with wild and improbable similes, strong emotion directly expressed, and a seemingly inexhaustible taste for gore. Yet the *Iliad* and the *Odyssey* are by far the most studied of ancient texts, then as now. Only the intersection of the invention of the Greek alphabet, the technical means that made Homer's poems possible, and the greatness of Homer himself can explain this oddity.

From the beginning of alphabetic literacy—from the beginning of the Western world—the Homeric poems have been at the core of Western education. They, or portions of these poems, were the books that one read when learning to read. Still today, every course in Western Civilization begins with the *Iliad* and the *Odyssey*. The invention of the Greek alphabet in order to record the poetry of Homer, and then Hesiod, is the single most important event in the history of the Western world. That is why Homer is important.

THE FIRST TEXT OF HOMER

Texts of the Homeric poems are easy to find, in print constantly since the first printed edition in Florence in 1488. Because it is a material thing, a text has a certain appearance, not only the texture and color of the paper or leather, but also the conventions by which the signs are made. Early printed editions of the *Iliad* were set in typefaces made to imitate Byzantine manuscripts, with its many abbreviations and ligatures (in which more than one letter is combined into a single sign). No ancient Greek could have read such a text, nor can a modern scholar do so without special training, not even a professor who has spent an entire life reading and teaching Greek.

In the nineteenth century, modern typefaces and orthographic conventions replaced typographic conventions based on manuscripts handwritten in Byzantium before the invention of printing, but in no sense did such modern conventions attempt to recreate the actual appearance, or material nature, of an ancient text of Homer. For example, the forms of the Greek characters in T. W. Allen's standard Oxford Classical Text, first published in 1902 (the basis for this translation), imitate the admirable but entirely modern Greek handwriting of Richard Porson (1759–1808), a Cambridge don important in early modern textual criticism. Complete with lower- and uppercase characters, accents, breathing marks, dieresis, punctuation, word division, and paragraph division, such Greek seems normal to anyone who studies Greek today. Here are the first few lines of the *Iliad* from the Oxford Classical Text:

μῆνιν ἄειδε θεὰ Πηληϊάδεω Ἀχιλῆος
οὐλομένην, ἣ μυρί᾽ Ἀχαιοῖς ἄλγε᾽ ἔθηκε,
πολλὰς δ᾽ ἰφθίμους ψυχὰς Ἄϊδι προΐαψεν
ἡρώων, αὐτοὺς δὲ ἑλώρια τεῦχε κύνεσσιν
οἰωνοῖσί τε πᾶσι, Διὸς δ᾽ ἐτελείετο βουλή,

ἐξ οὗ δὴ τὰ πρῶτα διαστήτην ἐρίσαντε
Ἀτρεΐδης τε ἄναξ ἀνδρῶν καὶ δῖος Ἀχιλλεύς.
   Iliad 1.1–7

If you study Greek today and take a course in Homer, you will be expected to be able to translate such a version. You are reading "the poems of Homer." In fact the orthography is a hodgepodge that never existed before the nineteenth century. A full accentual system, only sometimes bearing meaning, does not appear until around AD 1000 and is never used consistently. The distinction between upper and lower cases is a medieval invention. Porson's internal sigma is drawn [σ], but in the classical period the sigma was a vertical zigzag Σ (hence our "S"), and after the Alexandrian period always a half-moon shape c (the "lunate sigma"); the shape σ appears to be Porson's invention. The dieresis, two dots over a vowel to indicate that it is pronounced separately (e.g. προΐαψεν), is a convention of recent printing. Periods and commas are modern, as is word division, unknown in classical Greek.

The Oxford Classical Text would have mystified Thucydides or Plato. The much earlier first text of the first seven lines of Homer, if we take account of inscriptional evidence from the eighth and seventh centuries BC, seems to have looked something like this:

In this earliest form of Greek alphabetic writing there is no division of words (giving rise to many later false divisions), nor other diacritical devices, such as capitalization or

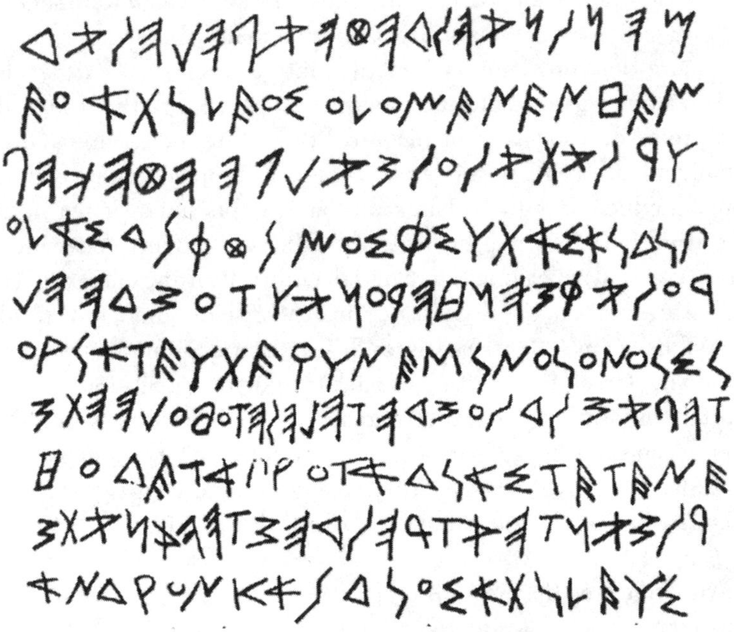

FIGURE 0.1   **The first seven lines of the *Iliad*.**   This reconstruction is based on what we know about the earliest Greek orthography.

periods, to indicate the function of a word in a sentence. In fact there are no words, but a continuous stream of symbolic signs to match the continuous stream of sounds. There is no Homeric word for a discrete "word" (the Homeric *epea*, from which comes *epic*, means an utterance, as in "may I have word with you"). There are only five vowel signs, which do not indicate "length" (as the later *omega*, "long o," was distinguished from *omicron*, "short o"). Doubled consonants are written as single consonants. The writing was *boustrophedon*, "as the ox turns," that is, it went from right to left, then left to right, imitating both the plowing of a field and the endless road of song. There are no accents.

In reading such a text in an archaic alphabet, the exchange of meaning from the material object to the human mind takes place in a different way than when we read Homer in English or Greek today. The Greek reader of the eighth century BC decoded this writing by the *ear*, whereas we read by the eye. First the reader heard the sounds behind the signs, then he recognized what was being said. One thousand years after Homer the Greeks still did not divide their words.

When we read Greek (or English), by contrast, we are deeply concerned with where one word begins and another ends, and how the word is spelled. The *appearance* of our texts carries meaning, as when a capital letter says "a sentence begins here" or a period says "a sentence ends here" or a space says "a word ends here." Our text is directly descended from an ancient Greek text, yes, but the alphabetic text works for us in a different way.

When modern editors attempt to recover an original text of Homer, they never mean that they are going to reconstruct a text that Homer might have recognized. Rather, they mean that they are going to present an interpretation of how an original text might be understood according to modern editorial bias. What appears to be orthography in a modern text, "the way something is written," is really an editorial comment on the meaning and syntax. If editors gave us Homer as Homer really was, no one could read it.

THE GRAPHIC REPRESENTATION OF ORAL SONG

Earlier criticism approached the text of Homer with little understanding that it is the dim mirror in alphabetic writing of a once continuous stream of sound with its own internal logic, with little respect for what we term the rules of grammar or the rules of metrics. The alphabetic representation of this stream of sound is only approximate because the relationship between systems of writing and speech are approximate. The song is like a stream, but the alphabetic signs are like buckets.

We examine with intense interest the grammar and the style and the "words" of the Homeric text, but they prove surprisingly slippery. In the Greek of Homer there are constantly grammatical constructions that make no sense, and words of mysterious formation, and words whose meaning is never clear. To interpret the "language" of Homer is regularly to find reasons for exceptions to the rules—exceptions in scansion, construction, and meaning.

A tradition of textual exegesis that explains forms and usages and discusses alternatives is now over 2300 years old, but it is based on a misunderstanding of the relationship of the original text to the oral song that underlies it. The text is *not* the song, but a symbolic representation of the phonetic aspect of the song. The many "rules of Homeric scansion" are a form of special pleading: In fact Homer only scans roughly, as with all oral poetry, and such "rules" only attempt to find regularities in a sea of flexibility.

In the very many grammatical and other irregularities of the Homeric vulgate we glimpse behind the text the continuous stream of highly stylized sound that came from the poet's mouth. And we glimpse the many, many inaccuracies in the scribe's efforts to reduce the sound of the song to a phonetically symbolic representation. Thinking that Homer was like us, that he wrote down his big poems as Vergil wrote the *Aeneid*, laboring over every word and scene, earlier scholars were led into a labyrinth of false speculation. To him the poem was a continuous stream of sound, with a rhythmical feeling behind the sound. He did not have time to think about refined effects.

For this reason it is easy to find places in the poem that are "not very good," that do not follow the rules of grammar or scansion, or even logic. Homer is telling a story as vividly as possible within a conventional medium that evolved as a means of public storytelling. This medium, the technique of oral composition, exists for a single purpose: to tell a riveting story.

HOMER AND HISTORY

In the *Iliad* Homer sings a tale set in the days of the Trojan War, and the *Odyssey* records its aftermath. Naturally, one wonders if there was ever a Trojan War, and if so, when, and what was it about?

GREEK HISTORY

Intensive study of the archaeological and literary evidence in the last 150 years has revealed a good deal about historical periods in ancient Greece. In rough terms, the third and second millennia BC (3000-1000 BC) are the *Bronze Age* and the first millennium (1000 BC-) is the *Iron Age*, named after the metals commonly used, but we may break the schema down further.

In the late third millennium BC, the earliest European civilization arose on the island of Crete, called the Bronze Age *Minoan Civilization* by its discoverer, Arthur Evans (1851–1941), after the legendary King Minos. The ethnic affinities of the Cretans are unknown, but they are often thought to come from Anatolia (modern Turkey). They certainly were not Greek-speakers. They built palaces of astonishing elegance and size, decorated with frescoes of beauty and charm. They administered their kingdoms with the help of a writing system called Linear A, inspired by writing in Mesopotamia but independent of such systems. The writing has not been deciphered, but the signs seem to represent syllables, not alphabetic letters.

The heyday of the Minoan Civilization was from about 2000 to 1400 BC, when dwellers on the Greek mainland, the Mycenaean Greeks, appear to have conquered them or to have moved in after some natural catastrophe. The Greeks' arrival on the mainland from somewhere to the east may have been around 2300 BC, and they reached a height of power between c. 1600 and 1150 BC—the Bronze Age *Mycenaean Period*. They had a system of syllabic writing called Linear B, a modification of the earlier Minoan Linear A. Linear B is preserved on a large number of clay tablets. The writing, now deciphered, is an early form of Greek, but the clay tablets record only administrative accounts and no literature of any kind. Sometimes names known from Homer appear in the Linear B writings. From early in this period come the royal burials at Mycenae discovered by Heinrich Schliemann (1822–1890) in 1876, which contained pristine burials with intact skeletons and a huge amount of treasure in the form of gold masks, vessels, and weapons of astonishing sophistication and beauty (see Figure 4.1). Agamemnon, ruler of Homer's Greeks in Homer's *Iliad*, came from Mycenae, which Homer calls "rich in gold," and in fact Schliemann was looking for Agamemnon's stronghold.

Then about 1200 BC a catastrophe of unknown nature befell the whole area around the Aegean (but not Mesopotamia or Egypt) that lasted for about four hundred years—the Iron Age *Dark Ages*. Linear B writing disappears along with the palaces that it served. The catastrophe is somehow connected to marauding bands of seafarers called the Sea Peoples, who devastated the entire east Mediterranean and attacked Egypt around 1200 BC. Some think that the famous Philistines of Palestine were Mycenaean Greeks from Crete who belonged to the coalition of Sea Peoples and who settled in the Near East at this time; in fact Philistine pottery bears a striking resemblance to Mycenaean pottery.

The invention of the Greek alphabet c. 800 BC ended the Dark Ages and began the *Archaic Period*, which lasted about three hundred years, until the Persians attacked Greece in 490 and 480 BC. Both epic and lyric poetry flourished during this period, but little survives except the poems of Homer and Hesiod. The Persian invasions began the *Classical Period* in Greek culture. The great figures of Greek alphabetic culture who lived during the Classical Period include Aeschylus, Sophocles, Euripides, Socrates, Plato, Aristotle, Pericles, Herodotus, Thucydides, and others. The death of Alexander the Great in 323 BC marks the end of the Classical Period and the beginning of the *Hellenistic Period*, when, thanks to Alexander, Greek culture became world culture. The death of Cleopatra in 30 BC is usually taken as the end of the Hellenistic Period and the beginning of the *Roman Period*.

SCHLIEMANN'S TROY

If there ever was a Trojan War, it must have taken place in the late Mycenaean Period, where, in fact, ancient commentators always placed it (as if they had any way of knowing). The Dark Ages were too backward and impoverished to have sponsored an undertaking of this magnitude. Homer could have known about such a war through the oral tradition, which is continuous and could easily reach back over the four hundred years of the Dark Ages to the Mycenaean Period. After all, Mycenae was a village c. 800 BC, but in 1200 BC it was the center of unimaginable power.

Heinrich Schliemann was a German businessman who set out to find Troy against the certain views of scholars who dismissed the war as folklore, no more real than the poet Homer himself. Impoverished as a youth and poorly educated as a young man, Schliemann earned a fortune in Europe and then in Sacramento, California, where in 1851 he was a banker during the gold rush. He had a talent for languages and learned fourteen of them during his life, including Turkish and Arabic. Because he was in California when it became a state, Schliemann became an American citizen.

After the gold rush, Schliemann moved to Russia (where he had lived earlier) and greatly increased his wealth through international trade. At one time he controlled

FIGURE 0.2   Sophia Engastromenos wearing the Jewels of Troy.   Having divorced his first wife in an Indiana divorce court, Schliemann married seventeen-year-old Sophia Engastromenos (1852–1932) in 1869, despite the thirty years difference in age. Here she is shown wearing jewelry that Schliemann found in 1873 in a level of the city that we now know is much too early for the Trojan War, c. 2400 BC. Schliemann called the cache "Priam's Treasure." Schliemann smuggled the jewelry out of Turkey and gave it to the University of Berlin. Feared lost after the Russian sack of Berlin in 1945, the jewelry emerged at the Pushkin Museum in 1994, but who owns it remains a matter of international dispute.

the trade in indigo, a dye. Schliemann retired in 1858 at age 37 and thereafter devoted his life to proving the historicity of the Homeric poems, a driving passion conceived in early childhood.

Schliemann searched in northwest Asia Minor for a likely site until he met a British expatriate named Frank Calvert, whose family owned half of a promontory at a place called Hissarlik, about five miles from the Dardanelles. Hissarlik is Turkish for "fortress." Calvert, who worked as a consul for the British and the Americans, was interested in the problem of the site of Troy. He was convinced that the mound at Hissarlik held its ruins, where earlier in the century others had looked for Troy. Calvert had conducted modest excavations there but had not discovered much.

Schliemann began work on Hissarlik in 1870 and continued until 1873. With his superior resources, he dug deep into the hill, uncovering massive walls and thousands of artifacts: diadems of woven gold, rings, bracelets, earrings, necklaces, buttons, belts, brooches as well as anthropomorphic figures, bowls and vessels for perfumed oils, daggers, axes, and jewelry (See Figure 0.2). He declared that he had discovered Priam's Troy. Schliemann conducted later excavations at Troy between 1878 and 1890, when he died.

Though Schliemann had misdated his finds on Hissarlik, the identification of Hissarlik with the Troy of Greek legend fits fairly well with Homer's own descriptions, and in fact with ancient tradition. The first Roman emperor, Augustus (63 BC–AD 14), established a city called New Ilium that encompassed Hissarlik, a fact established even before Frank Calvert and Heinrich Schliemann. After 150 years of debate, a consensus has emerged that Hissarlik is in fact Homer's Troy. Schliemann wrote many books, he warred with the professors, and he sometimes lied about his achievements; after all, he had been a trader in a turbulent time. But he discovered the Greek Bronze Age, about which nothing was known formerly.

WAS THERE A TROJAN WAR?

There are nine separate settlements on Hissarlik, one of the most complicated archaeological sites in the world. "Priam's Treasure" (Figure 0.3) belongs to the second city, evidently destroyed by fire around 2250 BC—much too early, on balance, for mythical chronology. Probably Homer's Troy was the sixth city, which had astounding walls, or an early phase of the seventh city, apparently destroyed by enemy action around 1190 BC (See Figure 0.4).

The site may be referred to in tablets from the Hittite capital near Ankara where it is called Wilusa, that is, Ilion, the usual name for Troy in the *Iliad*. In 1995, in the level of the seventh city, the only example of writing ever found at Troy was discovered: a biconvex bronze seal with the parts of two names written in a special Hittite writing (called Luvian "hieroglyphs")—one the name of a scribe and the other the name of a woman.

But what do we mean by "Trojan War"? If we mean a war caused by a queen's infidelity, avenged by an outraged husband whose brother in the ninth year of the campaign came into conflict with his best fighting man, we must confess that

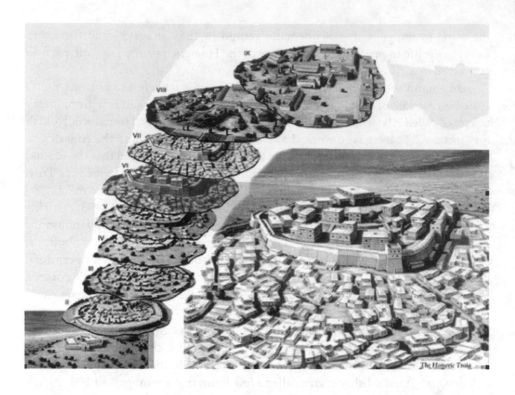

FIGURE 0.3 The superimposed settlements of Troy, from c. 3000 BC to c. AD 100.
The enlarged illustration shows Troy VI, c. 1300 BC. (After drawing by Christof Haussner)

the question is not a historical one. We can never know whether such behavior motivated a campaign or not. Homer lived four hundred years after the event, evidently, and had no concept of history. In the study of oral traditions throughout the world, it is clear that patterns of folktale quickly overlay the reporting of actual events, so that "what really happened" soon becomes irrecoverable. We have in the *Iliad* a tale about the anger of a man whose honor was slighted. The *Iliad* is a story about anger and its devastating consequences, as the first lines of the epic make clear. The Trojan War is simply background to this moral tale.

There is an oral tradition in which one singer teaches another and so passes on old songs. The Homeric tradition seems to have centered on the Boeotia/Euboea/Thessalian circuit. The Boeotian entry in the Catalog of Ships (Book 2) is by far the longest. Alphabetic writing was invented on Euboea, where Ionic was spoken. Achilles is from Phthia in Thessaly. Aulis is the Boeotian/Euboean port from which overseas expeditions to southern Italy were launched in the early eighth century BC. The Homeric formulaic language has an underpinning of the dialect spoken in Thessaly, as if the singers who carried this tradition had once been from Thessaly before their song was taken over by Ionic speakers. A tradition of stories about the Thessalian hero Achilles, the best of the Achaeans, has fallen under the spell of a probably older cycle of stories about a war fought against an overseas mercantile center of power,

FIGURE 0.4 The walls of Troy. The translator standing before the walls of the sixth city at Troy.

Troy. This other cycle of stories, with heroes from Argos in the Peloponnesus leading an Argive campaign, must go back to the time of the Trojan War itself. No one sings about glorious deeds performed in an imaginary war.

So there was a Trojan War, that is, an Argive campaign launched against the city of Troy sometime in the Late Bronze Age. Some of the names of the fighting men may be historical, but we can know nothing of the details of the war. The story Homer tells is in any event older than any historical war, going back to Mesopotamian song and the story of Gilgamesh and his friend Enkidu, whose death Gilgamesh indirectly caused, as Achilles indirectly caused the death of his friend Patroklos. Every once in a while details from this far-distant past peer through, but the *Iliad* is certainly not a poem about the Bronze Age. Together with its companion the *Odyssey*, it is a poem that appealed to the interests of the adventurous, wealthy, seafaring Euboean Greeks of the early eighth century BC.

HOMER'S WORLD

There are two parallel worlds in the *Iliad*, each imagined with breathtaking vividness. One is the world of the everyday, told best in the similes and in the description of Achilles' shield (Book 18). The other is the world of heroic valor, where all armor is made of bronze (Homer lived in a subsequent age of iron) and there is a kind of glitter hanging over everything. In the heroic world the gods are just around the corner, at the edge of vision, or standing right in front of you in the appearance of a mortal.

THE HUMAN DILEMMA

Achilles' mother was a goddess, Thetis. Aeneas' mother was a goddess, Aphrodite. Zeus stole Ganymede, a son of Tros after whom Troy was named, because of his great beauty. Aphrodite snatched Paris from the battlefield and placed him in Helen's boudoir. Achilles' horses talk, telling him he soon will die. The god Hermes drives Priam's chariot to the camp of the Greeks. Homer works hard to suppress the fairy-tale, any-wondrous-thing-can-happen side of his story, but it keeps creeping in.

Homer has inherited, no doubt from the Near East, stories filled with fantastic goings-on, but his hardheaded rationalist sensibility—or rather, that of his audience—makes him constantly suppress such elements. Still, the story begins with a plague that an angry god sends against the Greek camp. Patroklos, Achilles' friend, dies when Apollo strikes him on the back and his armor flies off so that he stands naked before Hector and the Trojans. Athena takes on the form of Deïphobos, Hector's brother, and makes Hector think he has a helper when he has none. The gods are ridiculous parodies of men and women, but they are behind all that happens. Nothing happens by chance in this heroic world. Humans occupy a kind of middle ground. Humans know that they are plaything of the whimsical gods. Humans can only take on a certain attitude: I'm going to die anyway, so I might as well live courageously while I'm alive. The gods are behind everything that happens, except the choices you make in a crisis.

GLORY, PRIZE, AND HONOR

To be a man you must earn *kudos*, "glory," and *timê* (**tē**-mā) "honor." Then you achieve *aphthiton kleos*, "undying fame." You defeat your enemy, the evil fate of death, by achieving this fame, this *kleos*. Everything in this world of fighting men is *kudos* and *timê* leading to *kleos*.

You get *kudos*, glory, by killing an enemy. You take his bloody armor, his power, his own glory, and now it is yours. The armor becomes your *geras*, your "prize." Everybody admires you in the possession of your prize and it gives you *timê*. *Timê* means what you are worth, your value. It is the modern Greek word for "price."

Achilles is the best there is: at killing other men and taking their armor, and at sacking cities and taking all the prizes within, the women and the loot. Surely he has earned *aphthiton kleos*, "undying fame." There is a confusion between *kudos*, glory; *geras*, prize; and *timê*, honor. They are inextricable, really one and the same thing. The *Iliad* is a study in the hazards of making the pursuit of *timê*, honor, the goal of human life.

CHERCHEZ LA FEMME

Thucydides (c. 460–c. 300 BC), in his realistic analysis of the Trojan War (Thuc. 1.3–12), notes that in the time of the war there was no common name for the Greeks, later called the Hellenes. Homer calls them indifferently "Achaeans," "Danaäns," and "Argives." Achaeans and Danaäns are probably tribal names, and

Argives refers to their origin on the plain of Argos, which surrounds the great Bronze Age site of Mycenae (see Map 2). Thucydides takes the lack of a common name for the Greeks as proof of the lack of unity of the Greeks in early times, as no doubt it does.

Thucydides also notes that, being camped on one spot for ten years, the Achaeans were in constant need of supplies and needed to divide their otherwise overwhelming force by raiding nearby communities. Perhaps this is the reason that Achilles has raided the village of THEBES (no connection with mainland THEBES) somewhere at the foot of MOUNT IDA, in the Troad behind TROY (Map 3), though Homer does not give any reason for the raid. As we later learn, Achilles killed King Eëtion, the ruler of Thebes at that time, and, it turns out, six of his sons, brothers of Andromachê, Hector's wife, who came from Thebes. He also took the woman Chryseïs captive, who for some reason was in Thebes at that time.

Chryseïs was not a native of Thebes but came from the town of nearby CHRYSÊ (**krī-sē**). Chryseïs just means "daughter of Chryses," because girls did not necessarily have their own names, but were named after their fathers. Chryseïs' father, Chryses ("he of Chrysê"), seems to take his name from the town. Perhaps Chryseïs was married to someone in Thebes and that is why she was there when Achilles sacked the town.

Similarly, in a raid on another town nearby, LYRNESSOS, Achilles has taken captive a second woman, Briseïs, "the daughter of Briseus." Lyrnessos, we later learn in an odd detail, was inhabited by Cilicians. CILICIA is far away, in today's central coastal region of Turkey opposite CYPRUS (Map 8), and so we do wonder about this.

Apparently the custom was to gather all the spoils taken in a raid and divide it equally. Every man then got his *geras*, his prize, which also established his *timê*. According to custom, the man who actually captured the city and its wealth did not distribute the spoils, but the community of fighters, the "sons of the Achaeans," awarded the booty, and hence determined a man's *timê*. The sons of the Achaeans had awarded Chryseïs to Agamemnon and Briseïs to Achilles.

Women have little intrinsic value outside sexual and other domestic service, but they are the external, visible testimony to the fighting man's *timê*. Achilles repeatedly claims as his right to Briseïs the division by "the sons of the Achaeans," not the fact that he had captured her in the first place.

THE PLOT: THE RAGE OF ACHILLES

Chryeïs' father Chryses is a priest of Apollo with special influence where it counts. The poem begins when Agamemnon rudely sends the priest Chryses away from camp, although he has come to offer a fair ransom for his daughter Chryseïs. In retribution Chryses reminds Apollo of what the god owes him. Apollo hears Chryses and sends a plague on the Achaean camp.

To appease the god, Agamemnon absolutely must now give up the girl, that is clear. But he must obtain another *geras* somehow or else he will lose *timê*, and a king without *timê* is a contradiction in terms. Agamemnon has the most power, and therefore he must have the emblems of that power.

THE DOUBLE BIND

In a few lines Homer creates the impossible situation at the heart of a great plot. Agamemnon is caught in a double bind. No matter how he acts, he is going to lose. But he must act, even though only evil can result from his action, and there is nothing he can do about it. Agamemnon must act arbitrarily in his own interest and by his action subtract from a fellow warrior's *timê*. By his act he must therefore commit an injustice, but not to act would be unjust too. What is justice anyway? This is the central question of Greek philosophy, here foreshadowed in the *Iliad*.

Agamemnon has come into this desperate position through his brutish and stupid exercise of power. He should never have sent the father Chryses away. He should have taken the face-saving ransom, an opportunity to be generous with his power; he would have survived the affront. Instead, he flaunted his lust to the father's face and bitterly insulted him, careless of the consequences to himself and all his men.

The direct result of Agamemnon's peremptory and unpopular behavior is disease. Now that the Achaeans are dying of disease, in addition to being worn down by the daily grind of war, the chance for face-saving is over. The prophet Kalchas instructs that the girl go back *without* ransom, and with an offering besides. Agamemnon's back is to the wall. He snarls like a mad dog. He feels the trap and lashes out, saying he will take someone else's prize, if she must go back, even that of the hothead Achilles.

And so begins the rage, the first word of the poem (*mênin*)—the emotion that drives the plot. Rage can be a wonderful feeling, and highly useful on the field of battle, but when it is turned against one's compatriots, it brings only destruction.

Achilles draws his sword halfway from its sheath when Agamemnon makes his threat. He wants to kill Agamemnon, as Agamemnon fully deserves, but Athena catches Achilles by the hair and restrains him.

Here is a problem of the chain of command, of authority. Agamemnon claims the greatest authority because "he rules over more people." But he also claims to derive his authority from Zeus himself, as exemplified by the scepter that Agamemnon carries. The scepter was made by Hephaistos, then delivered to Zeus, then given to Hermes, who brought it to the mortal line of Pelops and his two sons Atreus and Thyestes, and finally to Atreus' son Agamemnon. Odysseus uses this very scepter, snatching it from the inept hands of Agamemnon when, later in the poem, Odysseus calms the host and forces them back to their seats. The scepter is magical, it has power. It was made by the gods and deserves respect, and Agamemnon clings to it in his argument with Achilles.

Agamemnon claims to be "best of the Achaeans" because of his pedigree as son in a line of Zeus-fostered kings. This claim is the legitimation of his power. But Achilles denies the claim, saying that the title "best of the Achaeans" belongs to the man who is best in war, that is, to himself. "Achilles always wants to put himself above all others," Agamemnon complains.

Achilles' advisor Athena tells him that if he relents, if he does not kill Agamemnon, then three times as many prizes will come to him later, and the *timê* that comes with them. On that understanding, Achilles relents.

THE EMBASSY TO ACHILLES

Chryses may love his daughter, but in refusing the ransom Agamemnon has taken away Chryses' *timê*. The whole motive for the Trojan War is the harm done to the *timê* of Menelaos and Agamemnon when Paris took Helen, as Achilles takes care to remind Agamemnon in an angry speech. Here is irony, Achilles notes—they are camped on the windy plain, dying from war and disease, trying to restore *timê* to the sons of Atreus, lost when Paris took Helen. Now Agamemnon is taking *Achilles'* girl, depriving Achilles of his own *timê* in the very same way!

Achilles stalks to his tent. He calls to his mother Thetis. He asks that she claim a favor from Zeus. Zeus must oversee the slaughter of Achilles' fellow Greeks by the Trojans in revenge for the outrage that Agamemnon has done to Achilles' *timê*, an insult unprotested by his fellow captains. For this, they deserve to die.

Thetis does as her son asks, Zeus agrees, and in the next eight books of the *Iliad* we are treated to the exploits of various Greek heroes. Although the Greeks are supposed to be driven back through the will of Zeus, they are, in fact, winning on the battlefield. Homer seems to have better narrative resources for Greek victories than Trojan ones. In the whole poem more than three times as many Trojans are killed as Greeks. Nonetheless, several of the captains finally are wounded, and in Book 9 the Greek leaders, desperate, send an embassy to Achilles to beg him to return to the war, which they are losing without him. Agamemnon says he is sorry. He offers Achilles all the prizes that anyone could ever want, plus many women, including Briseïs, whom Agamemnon says he has never touched. Agamemnon also offers Achilles marriage with one of his own daughters.

To everyone's surprise, Achilles turns down the offer flat. He scorns the gifts and the chance to marry into the house of Atreus. Prizes are there for the taking, but once death comes upon you, there is no going back. What is the use of honor on such a basis? "I have no need of this honor (*timê*)! I think that I am honored in the allotment of Zeus," Achilles says.

With this claim, Achilles explicitly rejects the ethical system on which the heroic code is based, its code of values. He knows that he is a good man, in fact "best of the Achaeans," and Zeus knows it too. He does not need the esteem of his compatriots, who can go to hell as far as he is concerned. He has the inner certainty of his own righteousness.

In rejecting the social values of the world he lives in, Achilles sets himself up for unimaginable loss.

THE RESOLUTION OF THE PLOT

When Hector attacks the wall that protects the Achaean camp and burns one of the ships, Achilles' friend and aide Patroklos complains that Achilles is too hard in his anger toward Agamemnon. Achilles therefore allows Patroklos to relieve the Greek forces, wearing Achilles' own armor, as if Achilles himself had returned to the fight. But Hector falls on Patroklos under the walls of Troy and kills him.

In regret and sorrow for the loss of his beloved friend, Achilles forgets his anger toward Agamemnon, based on slighted honor, and transfers it to Hector, based on the lust for revenge. In an astounding display of energy and power, he kills Trojans left and right, and in a surrealistic scene even fights the river Skamandros. At last he corners Hector and kills him.

Though Achilles drags Hector's corpse around Patroklos' bier daily, his heart is not at peace. The gods are offended by Achilles' impious behavior, and at Thetis' instruction Achilles releases the corpse to Priam, whom the god Hermes, in disguise, has led to Achilles in the night bearing ransom. In a forgiving spirit, Achilles sees in Priam the plight of his own father Peleus, who will soon lose his only son (himself!), and he understands that all humans are united in their suffering. Achilles gives up his rage. Priam returns the corpse to Troy, the women lament it, and the Trojans bury Hector, tamer of horses. The story is over.

SHAME CULTURE, GUILT CULTURE

The moral realm of the Greeks in Homer's *Iliad* is familiar enough. The world is a violent and dangerous place. Everywhere is rapine—rape, enslavement, and death in horrible ways. All social power is in the hands of the men, who organize to protect their own helpless women and children. First they build walls, then they subscribe to a moral system wherein every man strives for honor and the good opinion of his fellows. Unafraid of death, which is inevitable, they never turn away from the enemy but fight to the end of their lives.

Anthropologists call this a "shame culture," similar to Japanese society where the sanctions of shame are called *bushido*, "the way of the warrior." During World War II American and British soldiers learned to their sorrow the power of this code. Shame comes from falling short of an ideal pattern of social conduct. Opposed to it is a "guilt culture," such as our own, in which guilt is the consequence of transgression against the laws of God. The sanctions of shame are external ("prize," *geras*). The sanctions of guilt are internal (feelings of remorse).

The enemy has come for the Trojans in their black ships. The Achaean raiders have no families to protect. They live by the same warrior code as the Trojans and are determined to destroy the city and take everything in it. In this dangerous and violent world, Achilles alone sees the emptiness of heroic values, that they lead nowhere. It does not matter what others think of you. To Achilles the sanctions of right action are internal; he gets his honor from Zeus. But he is a man alone, without anyone with whom he can share his superior moral vision.

Tragedy is a literary genre, but as a *type* of story it is one in which the protagonist becomes ever more isolated from the society around him, until at last in death he is completely alone. The *Iliad* is often called a tragedy because it follows the pattern of the progressive isolation of the protagonist. Achilles' crisis plays out against the backdrop of a doomed city. He knows that his own death must soon follow Hector's. Everything is sadness and gloom.

PLOT AND THE *ILIAD*

Homer seems to have been the inventor of plot in literature: There are no true plots in the older literary traditions of Mesopotamia, Canaan, and Egypt. In the stories from these Near Eastern cultures, first one thing happens, then something else, then something else, in an inorganic sequence. The earliest example of plot as we understand the term today is in the *Iliad*.

As Aristotle (384–322 BC) observed, a plot has three elements. As the first element, a scene is set, a situation. Then something happens to turn the plot in a certain direction. In the second element, the consequences of what has happened are worked out. Sometimes there is a midpoint, a crisis of some kind. In the third element, something else happens which brings the story to its resolution.

In the *Iliad* the first element is the situation in the Greek camp. Then something happens to change everything: Achilles withdraws from the war. In the second element, the war rages and many are killed. As a midpoint, an embassy is sent to Achilles to beg his return, but he refuses (if he had agreed, it would have ruined the plot!). The fighting resumes as before. Then the story turns again as Patroklos is killed. Achilles returns to exact his revenge on the Trojans. The plot is resolved when Achilles accepts Priam's ransom and abandons his anger, seeing in the old man—his bitter enemy—the community of suffering that unites all humans. The plot is resolved with this moral vision.

THE POWERS BEYOND

The power of the warriors who live by the heroic code is challenged by another group of men: the priests, specialists in dealing with the irrational spirits who stand behind the horrible things that surround us. Hector is the exemplar of the warrior, defending his city and women and children within it. Kalchas and Chryses exemplify the priests, whose power does not correspond with the warriors' power and often opposes it. "Prophet of evil, never have you said a word pleasing to me! You only like prophecies of evil! Never have you uttered a word of good, nor brought a good thing to pass," Agamemnon says to Kalchas when Kalchas orders that Agamemnon return Chryseis.

In his prayer to Apollo to destroy the offending Greeks, Chryses appeals to the religious principle "I give, that you might give" (Latin *do ut des*). He burned thighpieces to the god and roofed his shrine. Therefore Apollo owes him and should send plague to the Greek camp. When the gods show so much displeasure at Achilles' treatment of Hector's corpse that they command that he relinquish it, it is because in life Hector always burned the thigh bones of oxen to them: He gave to them, now they give back to Hector.

FATE

Hector's sacrifices did not, however, forestall his death because his death was *fated*. The usual Greek word for fate is *moira*, which means a "portion," evidently the portion of meat that one is given at the division of the meat (another Greek word is *aisa*, which means the same thing). This usage must come from a time of food shortage when it mattered a lot what cut of the sacrificed animal one received.

Everyone has a *moira* that "spins the thread" of one's fate, the day of death. Achilles' great complaint in the embassy to him is that "*Moira* is the same for one who hangs back as for one who is a strong fighter." When Hector is about to go into battle, he says to his wife Andromachê that no man will send him to Hades before the fated day: "But no man, I say, has escaped *moira*, neither coward nor brave man, once he has been born."

Moira determines all outcomes and even Zeus is powerless against it. When tempted to spare his son Sarpedon and, later, Hector "beyond fate," Hera and Athena remind Zeus that "a man being mortal, has long ago been doomed by fate (*aisa*)." As modern warriors say, "every man has a bullet with his name on it." You will die when you are destined to die, not before and not after.

Because one's day of death is already appointed, and even Zeus cannot change it, it is useless to complain or attempt to change *moira*. One can only live like a man and face death like a man. There is a prophecy about Achilles that he tells to the embassy: His goddess mother has told him that he can choose between two fates—to live either a long pedestrian life or a short glorious one. Achilles makes a good rhetorical point when he repeats this prophecy, but, given his nature, he has only one choice, that is pretty clear.

THE GODS

The gods have complex origins. So Zeus is the "cloud-gatherer" because in origin he is the god of storm who clings to the top of mountains, where clouds gather and where there were many shrines to Zeus. He has an invincible weapon in the thunderbolt. He is the strongest of the gods. The quality of a nature god always attaches to Zeus, but we know him in Homer as the head of a royal household, his power somewhat beleaguered by a covey of conspiring women who are always trying to outwit him. It is true that Zeus could suspend Hera from the sky with ankles tied to her feet, as he threatens (Book 8), but, still, she is getting her way in the inevitable destruction of Troy, a city that Zeus loves. The city is doomed, and even Zeus cannot save it.

The court of the Olympians is like an aristocratic court on earth. There is a headman, who supposedly has all the power, but his female consorts conspire to diminish it. So Hera schemes to prevent Zeus from doing what Thetis wishes, another persuasive female. Homer undoubtedly excited admiration and hilarity from his eighth-century audience of aristocratic males when Zeus threatens to lay his heavy hands on Hera to bend her to his will. This is what they would like to do to their own wives.

The gods once revolted against Zeus's power, we learn, a plot thwarted only by Thetis, Achilles' mother, whose importance as a goddess must have once been very high. That is why Zeus owes Thetis a favor, in this case to bring about the destruction of the Greek army. The story about Thetis saving Zeus from binding by Hera, Poseidon, and Athena is unknown elsewhere and is related to the "myth of the war in heaven," so prominent in Greek and Near Eastern myth. The sea-spirit Thetis must be a very old goddess, going back to the primordial Tiamat of Babylonian myth, who represents the waters from which the world was made.

The whole picture we get of a family of squabbling gods, modeled after a human family of quarrelsome adults, derives from Mesopotamia. It is a poetic fiction colored occasionally by cult practice, but Homer's gods by no means reflect the actual practice of Greek religion. We cannot be sure of the origin of this Mesopotamian poetic fiction, but it is already very old when it first appears in Sumerian documents from around 2500 BC, nearly two thousand years before Homer.

In the Mesopotamian version the gods are not as clearly defined as in Homer, but they inhabit similarly restricted spheres of action. The sky-god controls the storm; the sex goddess governs sex and, in Mesopotamia, war (Athena takes over this function in the Greek tradition). The water god is clever and can sneak things by one, a function split off into Hermes in the Greek tradition, the wayfarer god. Death is a goddess in Mesopotamia, and Persephone or Hades in Homer, though Homer has little interest in these figures.

The gods are thoroughly involved in the action of the *Iliad*, always part of the picture. The gods sponsor certain warriors in their triumphs, as when Athena stands beside Diomedes and guides his missiles to their mark (Book 5). The gods' power to determine outcome in battle makes possible such improbable, and comical, events as Paris disappearing from the field in a mist cast by Aphrodite. He turns up in Helen's boudoir and makes love to her as her husband snorts around on the plain! The gods' behavior is often meant to provoke a laugh, as in the ludicrous Battles of the Gods in Books 5 and 21, but at other times the gods' interaction is deadly serious, as when Athena takes on the appearance of Hector's brother to give Hector false confidence in the final duel with Achilles.

Apollo, the son of Leto and Zeus, is a complex god who favors the Trojans, along with his mother and sister, Artemis. He is the second god to appear in the *Iliad* after Zeus. As the bringer of plague, Apollo motivates the action of the *Iliad* from the start. The priest of Apollo, Chryses, calls him Apollo Smintheus, seeming to mean "he of the mouses," because mice bring plague. Remains of a temple to Apollo Smintheus have actually been found in the Troad, probably inspired by this opening passage. Before modern times, almost yesterday, the origin of disease was always thought to be an invasion from the other world, probably by the spirits of the dead. That is why Apollo "shoots from a long ways off." His arrows are the arrows of disease: invisible, mysterious, deadly, coming from nowhere. In the family of gods he serves the same role as the *aoidos*, the "singer" or "oral poet" in human society, entertaining by singing and plucking his lyre.

Apollo's reasons for favoring Troy are never clear, as are those of his divine rivals Athena and Hera, whom Paris scorned in the Judgment of Paris, when he gave the prize for being the fairest to Aphrodite. In fact King Laomedon of Troy cheated Apollo and Poseidon when he did not pay them for building the walls of Troy. Logically Apollo, like Poseidon, should be against the Trojans—but he is not. The etymology of Apollo's name is unclear, but he may be related to a Hittite god. His association with Troy may go back to some historical reality.

Athena, who favors the Greeks, constantly opposes Apollo, even in small things, as when Apollo knocks the whip from Diomedes' hand in the chariot race at Patroklos' funeral games. Athena darts in, picks it up, and hands it back. Athena is mentioned more times than any other god in the *Iliad* except Zeus. She is constantly rousing warriors to the fight, and in Book 5 dons a full suit of armor to fight against her fellow gods. She is also the inspirer of cultural productions, of handicrafts and arts of all kinds. She stands behind the *aristeia*, or "moment of glory," of Diomedes, who wounds Aphrodite in a famous scene in Book 5.

Aphrodite, the goddess of sexual (usually illicit) passion, is alternately powerful and weak. She flees to her father for comfort when wounded, but it is Aphrodite who has set off the war by bringing Paris and Helen together. Hera, as sponsor of marriage through her role as queen of the gods, is Aphrodite's natural enemy, though she makes use of Aphrodite's services when Hera wishes to seduce her own husband in Book 14. Aphrodite has given up the war-like attributes of Inanna/Ishtar, her Mesopotamian model, but is a lover of the war-god Ares according to the *Odyssey*. Aphrodite has an affection for Trojans: for Anchises, father of Aeneas; for her son Aeneas, whom she saves from the battle; and for Paris, who awarded her the prize in the Judgment of Paris, whom she saves in his duel with Menelaos.

Aphrodite's lover Ares, probably "he who brings harm," is a minor god, the most despised of all Olympians by Zeus. Often his name is just a metaphor for "battle" or "slaughter," as when warriors are said to "stir up Ares" or "glut Ares with blood" when they die.

Though in later Greek myth Hermes is a thief, stealing secretly through the night, in the *Iliad* he is a herald and guide, leading Priam's chariot and wagon through the Greek forces in the last book of the *Iliad*, a scene reminiscent of a descent into the underworld. The gods do propose that he "steal" away the corpse of Hector, but then they reject their own proposal. He is a proper "soul-guide" (*psychopompos*) in the last book of the *Odyssey*, where he leads the breath-souls of the dead suitors into the House of Hades. We might think of him as a trickster god who presides over boundaries.

Poseidon is a major figure in the *Iliad*, a son of Kronos and Rhea, and younger brother to Zeus and Hades. Once, we are told, the three brothers split up the world among them: Zeus took the sky, Poseidon the sea, and Hades the underworld. Poseidon's name might mean "husband of the Earth," though "Earth" in his name is very doubtful. He is god of the sea, over which he rides in his chariot, and as god of earthquakes he is called the "earth-shaker." For some reason he is also a god of horses, from which his epithet "dark-maned" may derive. He and Apollo are the only gods who strike dignified postures in the comical Battle of the Gods (Book 21).

Poseidon is unashamedly pro-Achaean, giving as reason that Laomedon had not paid him (or Apollo!) for building the walls of Troy. Normally he obeys Zeus's commands, but in Books 13 and 14 he goes against Zeus's explicit prohibition against divine intervention. His antecedent in Mesopotamian stories is the storm-god Enlil, represented in the Greek stories by both Zeus and Poseidon, but Poseidon is characteristically Greek; the lives of the ancient Greeks were dominated by travel on the dangerous, storm-riven seas, an opportunity for experience unknown to the land-encircled Mesopotamians. His name is attested in Linear B inscriptions from Pylos.

Hephaistos is the god of fire and all the wondrous things that fire makes possible: exquisitely made handicrafts and, in the *Iliad*, the magical shield of Achilles. There are intelligent robots living in his chamber that move by themselves. Hephaistos is lame because real blacksmiths often were lame, and he is the bumbling butt of laughter. Yet he made the shining houses in which the gods live, and they could not do without him. It is Hephaistos who calms the quarrel between his mom Hera and his dad Zeus in Book 1.

The story about Hephaistos being thrown from heaven is told twice in the *Iliad* (Books 1 and 18), with significant variation. It is the only time in all of Homer that we are given two versions of a myth. Either his father Zeus threw him from heaven, and so made him lame, because Hephaistos took Hera's side in an argument, or Hera threw him from heaven, horrified that he had been born lame.

Artemis, the huntress, the lady of wild beasts who rejoices in arrows, is on the Trojan side, along with her brother Apollo and her colorless mother Leto. Artemis plays little part in the action but is often referred to as the cause of death among women. When a woman died for no apparent reason, she was said to have fallen to the arrows of Artemis, as a man fell to the arrows of Apollo.

Hades is more a place than a god. The House of Hades is where you go when you die. And yet, as one of the three sons of Kronos, Hades shared control over the world with his brothers Zeus and Poseidon.

The gods are like humans, only grander, more beautiful—and much more powerful. In one characteristic they differ: They will never die. Hence their activities lack seriousness and their behavior is often comical. Achilles knows that he will die; there is nothing funny about that.

HOMER'S AUDIENCE

We can tell a lot about Homer's original audience, the men he would ordinarily have sung to. The *Odyssey* presents several descriptions of singers in action, and we can extrapolate from them that Homer's audiences were all male; only one woman is ever present, a queen, at a song in the *Odyssey*. His audiences were older men rather than younger men, who knew what it is like to fight in hand-to-hand combat. They are warriors and seafarers. They have a taste for gore and moral conflict. They are preoccupied with male issues of honor and nobility. They have a taste for the rhetorical, which is why we get so many fancy speeches in the *Iliad*—one half of the *Iliad* consists of speeches.

Homer's audience loves long and detailed descriptions of ordinary procedures, as when Homer describes the yoking of Priam's wagon and chariot (Book 24), or when he describes how Odysseus built a raft to leave the island of Kalypso (*Od.* Book 5). Homer's audience has plenty of time and enjoys a leisurely pace. To judge from descriptions in the *Odyssey*, there really is no other form of entertainment in this world, only the song of the *aoidos*, the singer, who always performs after a banquet. The audience wants the song to go on and on so they do not have to face the hardships and tedium of everyday life. King Alkinoös in the *Odyssey* begs Odysseus to continue with his tale, though it is late at night (*Od.* Book 12).

Homer's audience has a strongly developed sense of humor and finds the behavior of the gods absurd and quite funny. They are monogamous but resent the institution, hence the constant complaints about Hera's henpecking of her poor husband Zeus. (Mesopotamian society, by contrast, was polygamous.)

When the pompous Agamemnon makes a fool of himself by urging his men to go home, supposing they will oppose his cowardly suggestion and shout, "No, no, we must fight on!" but instead they all rush pell-mell to the ships—this story appeals to men who have actually been at war, who know abject fear and terror. Evidently Homer has set up this whole scene, which does not advance the narrative, simply as a means to get a laugh.

No doubt Homer's audience were the "captains" (*basileis*) who had a proper contempt for those not of their class. Thersites, in Book 2, is the model for all that the *basileis* despise. His physical ugliness testifies to his worthlessness. Most of the words used to describe his ugliness are unknown elsewhere. Thersites is the parodic opposite of Achilles. Thersites makes the same complaints against Agamemnon that Achilles does: Agamemnon has plenty of bronze and women in his tents, he always takes his pick, and he is a greedy boor. Yet without Achilles' stature as a warrior, lacking Achilles' good looks and fine upbringing, Thersites' complaints are the thoughtless complaints of a little man whose power to do evil must be nipped in the bud. Thus does Odysseus whip him with Agamemnon's Zeus-descended scepter, to the laughter of Homer's aristocratic audience.

ON TRANSLATING HOMER

The audience can absorb only so much information so fast, but the singer cannot stop his delivery, he cannot be silent for long. His task is to replace the listener's thoughts with his own words, and so the words must come constantly. Thus in Homer an audience always "listens and obeys," and when characters speak, "he spoke and he addressed them." The pervasive use of such amplified expression, and of epithets, enhances the audience's comprehension.

To enjoy our modern Homer, we must teach ourselves to accept this repetitive, formulaic style, evolved in order to help the poet create his rhythmic line on the fly in oral composition.

THE REPETITIVE STYLE

Not only are many lines repeated somewhere, but sometimes whole passages. For example, when in the poem a message is given, the listener knows that it will be repeated word for word when delivered. The fixed epithets attached to heroes and gods lengthen the line and slows the rate of the delivery of information while reminding the audience what this character is best known for. The epithet puts the character in context. Hence "Achilles the fast runner" or "resourceful Odysseus" takes longer to say than "Achilles" or "Odysseus" while reminding us of what sort of men these are. The epithet is part of the meaning, a capsule biography. And there is something evocative about "wine-dark sea" that "sea" alone does not convey.

The translator faces the temptation to ignore these epithets entirely and translate "Achilles the fast runner" simply as "Achilles." This would produce a translation that is not very fair to the poet-singer, obscuring the reality of the origin of these poems as oral compositions. Another strategy is to always translate the epithets in a different way, for example "swift-footed Achilles" or "Achilles the fast runner" (for the Greek *podas ôkus*, "swift as to his feet"), again hiding the origin of the text as an oral poem.

I have followed a middle way: using the epithets, thus making clear that this poem is composed in an oral style, but sometimes allowing a different wording, or ignoring the epithet altogether, in accordance with modern taste. Still, we have to adjust to the repetitive style if we want to read a translation of Homer. Homer is an oral poet and he is singing in an oral style, a style utterly practical but grounded in the practicalities of oral presentation.

A STYLIZED WORLD

Homer's world is a stylized world. Emotions are exaggerated or expressed in concrete imagery that strikes us as strange. Gods and goddesses zip in and out of the story with perfect credibility. Eating is highly ritualized, and Homeric heroes do a lot of eating. Everything is strange about this world, yet recognizable. A translation must acknowledge this strangeness.

The extraordinarily long and often unexpected similes relieve the tedium of carnage and open a window into another world, giving a different point of view, often pastoral or peaceful. The similes are odd, because the poet feels as if he can create alternate worlds in the midst of his original alternate world. They abound with beautiful images from the natural world, especially of magnificent predators to whom the warriors are compared. But they also delay the progress of the narrative.

Such is a hallmark of Homer's oral style, to stretch things out by interposing all kinds of delaying tactics. He inserts episodes and diversions of every kind to put off what must come. Evidently Homer was encouraged when dictating the *Iliad* and the *Odyssey* to make the songs as long as possible for reasons we can only imagine. Milman Parry seems to have had a similar experience with Avdo Mejedovich

(c. 1870–1955), his best singer, who at Parry's encouragement sang *The Wedding of Smailagich Meho*, about as long as the *Odyssey*.

Words have a different range of meaning in Greek than in English, especially those referring to feelings. The Greek does not distinguish between emotional and mental categories as we do, so we must seek parallels in English that correspond to the nuance in the Greek. For example, there are several words that indicate the things that go on inside a person's chest, but Homer is very imprecise in his use of these words, and they must constantly be translated in different ways.

So *thumos* means something like the air that you breathe in, but it comes to mean the heart, as in grieved "at heart" or "in spirit," as in "he was troubled in his spirit." But at other times *thumos* means the life, the breath-soul that departs from the body when you die, like the *psychê*, really "breath," the air or "breath-soul" that leaves a dead inert body. But *thumos* can also be the seat of thought. The word *kêr* probably means the organ the "heart," but it is also commonly used to designate the place where decisions are made, like *thumos*. The word *phrên*, or in the plural *phrenes*, may also designate a specific internal organ, but whether this is the lungs or the liver or something else is never clear, and often *phren(es)* can mean "heart," like *thumos* or *kêr*. The word *êtor* is another word that refers to the place of feeling in the chest, not thinking, as in "grieving at heart."

The meaning of these vague terms varies according to the context, but it is clear that the Homeric Greeks saw the basis for thought, decision, and action as taking place in the chest. After all, it is emotion, not thought, that drives men to behave in certain ways, just as emotion lives in the stomach and in the heart even today. And it is emotion that drives the story of the *Iliad*.

Translations reflect the taste of their times. Since the seminal translation of George Chapman (1559–1634) in iambic heptameter (seven feet, all iambs), published in full in 1616, there have been around 131 translations of Homer's poems into English. Alexander Pope (1688–1744) took 11 years (1715–1726) to complete his translation in rhymed couplets, which suited the prevailing conviction that *rhyme* was what characterized poetry, raising it above pedestrian prose.

In modern poetry, rhyme is avoided as something that stands in the way of direct expression. But Homer seems wrong as prose—after all, it is a poem composed in dactylic hexameter. Again, I have chosen a middle way, adopting a rough five-beat line in this translation. My focus is on the meaning of Homer's words and how they would sound today in contemporary English.

Homer's style may be strange, but it is always simple, direct, and sensual. I have tried to reproduce these qualities in this new English translation. Flexibility within accuracy has been my principle. I have often added personal names to replace pronouns, because Homer's use of pronouns can be very unclear.

Translating the meaning of the text does not necessarily imply a word-for-word rendering. After all, Homer's thoughts are rendered in a different language with very different habits of expression. Still, I hope to convey the sense of each word and phrase in the Greek, without prettifying or embellishing. I am not concerned with sounding "poetic," or beautiful, or clever, because that would be to falsify the plain style of the original Greek. Yet much of the stylistic beauty of Homer's poetry comes from his use of words in unexpected or startling ways, a feature I try to preserve.

TRANSLITERATION AND PRONUNCIATION OF NAMES

There are two traditions in transliterating classical names, the Latin and the Greek. The Latin spellings come through the Latin language and impose traditional rules of Latin spelling. In Greek spellings, the names are transliterated more or less as they are written in Greek, but using Latin characters. The Latin tradition lies behind English dictionary usage, because Latin was once the language of the educated classes in England and the United States. So in dictionaries the names are "Achilles," "Priam," "Helen," and "Ajax." In the 1950s, however, a fashion began of using the Greek spellings, so that it is "Akhilleus," "Priamos," "Helena," and "Aias." The trouble with using the Greek forms, however, is their lack of familiarity. The trouble with using all Latin forms is that they look too fussy, old-fashioned.

In this translation I have followed the practice in transliteration of the excellent *The Homer Encyclopedia*, edited by Margalit Finkelberg (Wiley/Blackwell, 2011). "Achilles," "Priam," "Helen," and "Ajax" are too familiar to be changed, but except for these major players, and for place names, I give the names of subordinate characters in the Greek spelling: "Kalesios" not "Calesius."

Two other conventions are observed: Where the upsilon in Greek is pronounced in English as /i/, I have transliterated the upsilon as [y], not [u]. I have used a dieresis, two dots over a vowel [ï], to indicate when adjacent vowels are to be pronounced separately: Eëtion, Alkathoös. I have transliterated the Greek [Χ] as [ch]. When the *final vowel* of a name is to be pronounced, I write it with a caret on top: Niobê, Astyochê. Final *es* is also pronounced, as in Achill*ēs*.

There is a fair amount of uncertainty as to how to pronounce Greek names in English, and even professionals can be unsure. Moreover, Greek names are pronounced differently in, for example, England and the United States. Certainly an ancient Greek would be puzzled at the ordinary English pronunciation of his or her name. There is little agreement on how to pronounce the vowels, so one hears the name of the Athenian playwright Aeschylus pronounced as *e*-schylus or *ē*-schylus or sometimes *ī*-schylus. Is the famous king of Thebes called *e*-dipus or *ē*-dipus? With many names, however, there is a conventional pronunciation, which I give in parentheses in the Pronunciation Glossary at the back of the book.

Another problem is the accent—where to stress the word. Greek relied chiefly on pitch and quantity, whereas English depends on stress. Because of the influence of Latin on Western culture, the English accent on proper names follows the rule that governs the pronunciation of Latin: If the next-to-last syllable is "long," it is accented; if it is not "long," the syllable before it is accented. For many it will be easiest simply to consult the Pronunciation Glossary, where the syllable to be accented is printed in **bold** characters.

BOOK 1. *The Rage of Achilles*

The rage° sing, O goddess, of Achilles, the son of Peleus,
the destructive anger that brought ten-thousand pains to the
Achaeans and sent many brave souls of fighting men to the house
of Hades and made their bodies a feast for dogs
and all kinds of birds. For such was the will of Zeus.   5

Sing the story from the time when Agamemnon, the son
of Atreus, and godlike Achilles first stood apart in contention.
Which god was it who set them to quarrel? Apollo, the son
of Leto and Zeus. Enraged at the king, Apollo sent an
evil plague through the camp, and the people died.   10
For the son of Atreus had not respected Chryses, a praying
man. Chryses had come to the swift ships of the Achaeans
to free his daughter. He brought boundless ransom, holding
in his hands wreaths of Apollo, who shoots from afar,
on a golden staff. He begged all the Achaeans, but above all   15
he begged the two sons of Atreus, the marshals of the people:°

"O you sons of Atreus, and all the other Achaeans,
whose shins are protected in bronze, may the gods who
have houses on Olympos let you sack the city of Priam!
May you also come again safely to your homes. But set free   20
my beloved daughter. Accept this ransom. Respect
the far-shooting son of Zeus, Apollo."

                                 All the Achaeans
shouted out that, yes, they should respect the priest
and take the shining ransom. But the proposal was not
to the liking of Agamemnon, the son of Atreus.   25
Brusquely he sent the man away with a powerful word:
"Let me not find you near the hollow ships, either

---

1   *rage:* The Greek word is *mênis,* an archaic word used only of Achilles and the gods. It is the first word in the
    poem and defines its theme.

16 *marshals of the people:* That is, Agamemnon and his brother Menelaos, the leaders of the expedition. Menelaos
    was married to Helen before her elopement with Paris, but the injury done by her behavior hurts the whole
    family, and Agamemnon has become the supreme leader of the expedition.

hanging around or coming back later. Then your scepter
and wreath of the god will do you no good! I shall not
30 let her go! Old age will come upon her first in my
house in Argos, far from her homeland. She shall
scurry back and forth before my loom and she will
come every night to my bed. So don't rub me
the wrong way, if you hope to survive!"

So he spoke.
35 The old man was afraid and he obeyed Agamemnon's
command. He walked in silence along the resounding
sea. Going apart, the old man prayed to his lord
Apollo, whom Leto, whose hair is beautiful, bore:
"Hear me, you of the silver bow, who hover over
40 Chrysê and holy Killa, who rule with power
the island of Tenedos°—lord of plague!° If I ever
roofed a house of yours so that you were pleased
or burned the fat thigh bones of bulls and goats,
then fulfill for me this desire: May the Danaäns° pay
45 for my tears with your arrows!"

So he spoke in prayer.
Phoibos° Apollo heard him, and he came from the top
of Olympos with anger in his heart. He had on his back a bow
and a closed quiver. The arrows clanged on his shoulder
as he sped along in his anger. He went like the night.

50   He sat then apart from the ships. He let fly an
arrow. Terrible was the twang of the silver bow. At first
he attacked the mules and the fleet hounds. Then he
let his swift arrows fall on the men, striking them
with piercing shafts. Ever burned thickly the pyres
55 of the dead.

---

41 *Chrysê ... Tenedos:* See Map 3: The first time that a place name on one of the eight maps appears in a Book,
the name will be in small caps. "Chryses" is simply "the man from "Chrysê."

41 *lord of Plague:* In the Greek, Chryses calls Apollo "Smintheus," seeming to mean "he of the mice," that is,
god of plague because that is what mice or rats bring (rats are "big mice" in modern Greek). Remains of a
temple to Apollo Smintheus have been found in the Troad. Apollo "shoots from afar" because his arrows are
the arrows of disease: invisible, mysterious, deadly.

44 *Danaäns* (**dān**-a-anz): Homer indifferently calls the invaders "Achaeans," "Danaäns," and "Argives," never
"Greeks." The first should mean "the men of Achaea," perhaps a general name for Greece (though later a
territory located in the northwestern Peloponnesus), or it is a tribal name; the second is a tribal name; the
third should mean "the men from the city of Argos" in the Peloponnesus.

46 *Phoibos:* An epithet of uncertain origin and meaning, though often interpreted as meaning "pure, radiant."

For nine days he strafed the camp with his
arrows, but on the tenth Achilles called the people to assembly.
The goddess with white arms, Hera, had put the thought
in his mind, because she pitied the Danaäns, when she saw
them dying.

When they were all together and assembled,
Achilles, the fast runner, stood up and spoke: "Sons of Atreus,   60
I think we are going back home, beaten again, if we
escape death at all and war and disease do not together
destroy the Achaeans. So let us ask some seer or
holy man, a dream-explainer—dreams are from Zeus!—
who can tell us why Phoibos Apollo is angry.   65
Is it for some vow, or sacrifice? Maybe the god
can accept the scent of lambs, of goats that we kill,
perhaps he will come out to ward off this plague."
So speaking he took his seat.

Kalchas arose, the son of
Thestor, by far the best of the bird-seers, who knows   70
what's what, what will happen, what has happened.
He had led the ships of the Achaeans to Ilion° by his seership,
which Phoibos Apollo had given him. He spoke to the troops,
wishing them well: "Achilles, you urge me, you whom Zeus
loves, to speak of the anger of Apollo, the king who strikes   75
from afar. Well, then I will tell you. But first you must
consider carefully. You must swear to me that you will
defend me in the assembly and with might of hand. For I'm
afraid of enraging the Argive who has the power here, whom
all the Achaeans obey. For a chief has more power against   80
someone who causes him anger, a man of lower rank.
Maybe he swallows his anger for a day, but ever
after he nourishes resentment in his heart, until he
brings it to fulfillment. Swear then, Achilles, that you will
protect me."   85

The fast runner Achilles answered him:
"Have courage! Tell your prophecy, whatever you know.
By Apollo, dear to Zeus, to whom you yourself
pray when you reveal prophecies to the Danaäns—not so
long as I am alive, and look upon this earth, shall anyone

---

72 *Ilion*: Another name for Troy.

90 of all the Danaäns lay heavy hands upon you
beside the hollow ships, not even if you might mean
Agamemnon, who claims to be best of the Achaeans."

The seeing-man, who had no fault, was encouraged,
and he spoke: "The god is not angry for a vow, or sacrifice,
95 but because of the priest whom Agamemnon dishonored
when he would not release the man's daughter. He would not take
the ransom. For this reason the far-shooter has caused these pains,
and he will go on doing so. He won't withdraw the hateful disease
from the Danaäns until Agamemnon gives up the girl with
100 the flashing eyes, without pay, without ransom, and until he leads
a holy sacrifice to Chrysê. Only then might we succeed in
persuading the god to stop."

So speaking, he sat down. The heroic
son of Atreus, Agamemnon whose rule is wide, then stood up,
deeply troubled by the words of Kalchas. His black heart
105 was filled with a tremendous rage, and his eyes shone
like blazing fire. First he addressed Kalchas, his eyes filled
with hate: "Prophet of evil, never have you said a word
pleasing to me! You only like prophecies of evil! Never have
you uttered a word of good, nor brought a good thing to pass.
110 And now you say in your 'prophecy' before the Danaäns that
the far-shooter causes us sorrow because I refused to take
the shining ransom for the daughter of Chryses! Because I prefer
to keep her in my house! In fact I like her better than Klytaimnestra,
my wedded wife. She is no inferior in beauty, in looks,
115 or in character, or in her skills in handwork. Nonetheless, I am willing
to let her go, if that is best. I'd rather that the folk prospered than
it perished. But you'd better get another prize for me. It's not right
that I alone of all the Argives be without a prize!
It is not right, for you see that my prize goes elsewhere."°

120   Then answered him Achilles, the fast runner, like a god:
"Son of Atreus, most honored sir, most *greedy* of all!
How are the Achaeans, who are generous, going to give you a prize?
We have no wealth stacked in a warehouse, but everything
we've taken in our raids has been given out a long time ago.
125 We can't gather this stuff up again. Look—give up

---

119 *prize goes elsewhere*: The Greek word is *geras*, which determines a warrior's *timê*, "honor," really "value." The woman, or *geras*, is the external and visible testimony to *timê*, without which life is not worth living.

the girl to the god. Then the Achaeans will give you three
or four times as much loot, if Zeus grants us to sack the high-walled
city of Troy."

     King Agamemnon answered as follows:
"Don't Achilles—though of good birth and 'like to a god'—
don't try to trick me with your mind! You will not get past me,   130
and you will not persuade me. Do you want to stand there,
yourself with a prize, while I sit without one? Do you order me
to give up this girl? If the great-hearted Achaeans will give me
a prize, fitting it to my heart, so that it will be of equal
value … but if not, I will *myself* take your own prize!   135
or I will go to Ajax and take his, or I will go to Odysseus
and take his prize. The man will be angry, no matter who.
But let us think this over at some later time. Come,
let us draw a black ship into the shining sea.
Let us get together appropriate rowers and load up   140
a sacrifice, and let us place Chryseïs of the lovely cheeks
within.° Let one man who knows what to do be the leader,
either Ajax, or Idomeneus, or brilliant Odysseus—or *you*,
son of Peleus, most ferocious of men. Then with our sacrifice
we might calm the far-shooter."   145

     But Achilles, the fast runner,
glowered from beneath his brows and said: "Shameless fool!
Greedy, how now can your speech gladly persuade any
of the Achaeans either to go on an ambush or to fight
in the hand-to-hand? *I* at least did not come here to war
because of the Trojan spearmen. They have done nothing   150
to me. They have not taken my cattle, nor horses.
Not in Phthia° with its very rich plowlands,
the nurse of men, have they laid waste the harvest.
For many are the shadowy mountains that lie between us,
and the echoing sea. No, we followed you—you dog   155
without shame!—that you might be happy, that you
might win honor from the Trojans for Menelaos—
and for yourself! Dog! You don't ever think about that,
do you? Are you troubled by that? You threaten yourself

---

142 *Chryseïs*: Chryseïs means simply "daughter of Chryses," just as Briseïs is "daughter of Briseus." Girls did
     not necessarily have their own names but were named after their father. *Chryses* is the father; *Chrysē* is the
     place; *Chryseïs* is the daughter.

152 *Phthia*: Phthia (**thī**-a) is the homeland of Achilles in southern THESSALY, through which the Spercheios
     river flows. See Map 2.

160 to take *my* prize, for which I labored sorely?
The sons of the Achaeans gave her to me. I never
get a prize equal to yours, when the Achaeans take some
populous city of the Trojans, though I myself
bear the hard brunt of the fighting. When the spoils
165 are divided, your prize is always bigger. *I* get
some small, little darling thing and slouch off
to my ships, worn out with the war.
"Okay, I'm off
to Phthia. I think it's better to head away in my beaked ships
than to hang around here and pile up endless wealth
170 for you, while I remain without honor!"

The king over men,
Agamemnon, then said in reply: "Go then, if that's what you
want to do. Don't stay on my account. There are plenty who
will honor me, and Zeus above all, whose wisdom is great.
You are most hateful to me of all the god-reared chieftains!
175 You ever love contention and war and battle. If you are strong,
that is because some god gave you the gift. Go home with
your ships and your companions. Rule over the Myrmidons! \
I don't like you, I don't care if you are angry.
"But I tell you what
I'm going to do. Just as Phoibos Apollo takes away Chryseïs—
180 and I'll send her in a ship with an escort—even so
I will myself come and take the high-cheeked Briseïs,
your prize, that you might know how much stronger I am
than you, and so that any other may think twice
before saying that he is my equal and liken himself to me
185 to my face!"

So he spoke. A great hurt arose inside
the son of Peleus, and his heart within his shaggy
breast was divided in two ways, either to draw his sharp
sword from his thigh, break up the assembly, then kill
the son of Atreus, or whether he should stop his anger,
190 bridle his tumult. While he pondered in his heart and in his spirit,
he drew out the great sword from its scabbard, but Athena came
from heaven—the goddess Hera of the white arms sent her
because she loved and cared for both men equally.

Athena stood behind him and she seized the son of
195 Peleus by his light-colored hair. Only he could see her.

FIGURE 1.1 The rage of Achilles.   The seated Agamemnon holds the scepter of authority and sits on a throne, his lower body wrapped in a robe. Achilles, in "heroic nudity," pulls his sword from its scabbard ("heroic nudity" is an ancient artistic convention of unclear meaning, whereby heroes are shown without clothes). Athena seizes Achilles from behind by the hair. Roman mosaic from Pompeii, c. first century AD.

He was amazed. He turned around, and right away he recognized
Pallas Athena.° Her eyes shone with a terrible light. He spoke
to her words that went like arrows: "Why have you come,
daughter of Zeus who carries the goatskin fetish?°
200 To see the insolence of Agamemnon, son of Atreus?
But I will tell you this, and I think it shall come
to pass—through his insolence he will quickly lose his life!"

Flashing-eyed Athena° answered him: "I have come
from heaven to stop your anger, if I can persuade you.
205 White-armed Hera sent me, because she loves
and cares for both of you. So come, let go
of this contention. Unhand your sword. Abuse him
with words. Tell him how things will be. For I promise you
that this will come to pass: You shall one day have
210 three times as many gifts because of this violence.
Hold back, trust us."

Achilles, the fast runner, answered:
"What can I do but obey the two of you, goddess,
even though I am seething? It is better that way. The gods
listen to him who obeys." And he stayed his heavy
215 hand on the silver sword-hilt, and back into the scabbard
he thrust the great sword, not disobeying the word of Athena.
She went off to Olympos to the house of Zeus who carries
the goatskin fetish, to be with the other gods.

But the son of Peleus again spoke violent words
220 to the son of Atreus. In no way had he abandoned his anger:
"Drunkard, dog-eyes, with a deer's heart—you don't arm with
your people and go out to war, nor dare in your heart to go on
an ambush with the best of the Achaeans. To you that is death!
Much better to take your ease in the broad camp of the Achaeans
225 and steal the gifts from whoever opposes you. Devourer

---

197 *Pallas Athena*: The "Pallas" is sometimes explained as from a Greek word meaning "to brandish," so the
meaning would be "[spear]-brandishing Athena." But probably it is preHellenic, not a Greek name.

199 *... fetish*: The Greek is *aegis*, which means "goatskin," maybe in origin either a shield, or a "medicine"
bag containing power objects. In Homer, the *aegis* is an object that offers divine protection or inspires
terror. In works of art from a period somewhat later than Homer, the *aegis* is a cloak with snake-head
tassels and a Gorgon's head in the center, worn more by Athena than Zeus. Apollo also carries the *aegis*
(see Figures 7.1, 24.1)

203 *Flashing-eyed Athena*: The Greek is *glaukôpis* but is hard to say whether it means "flashing-eyed," "owl-eyed,"
or "gray-eyed." I have chosen "flashing-eyed" as the most likely interpretation.

of the people, 'king,' you rule worthless men. Otherwise
this would be your last act of insolence, O son of Atreus!

   "But I will tell you, and swear a great oath: By this scepter,
which will never grow leaves or shoots since first it left
its stump in the mountains. It won't again grow green. The bronze   230
has stripped its leaves and bark, and now the Achaeans
hold it when they judge, when they guard the laws given
by Zeus—this oath will be mighty among you! One day
the longing for Achilles will be great among the sons of the Achaeans!
But you will not be able to ward off evil, though your sorrow   235
is great, when many fall dead at the hands of man-killing Hector.
You will gnaw your hearts that when angry you did not honor
the best of the Achaeans!"

              So spoke the son of Peleus,
and he threw the scepter on the ground, fitted with nails
of gold. Then he sat down. But the son of Atreus on his side   240
still steamed with anger when Nestor stood up, whose voice
was sweet, the clear-voiced speaker of the men of Pylos,
from whose tongue flowed a sound sweeter than honey.
Two generations of mortals had passed away in his time,
men begotten and raised with him in sandy Pylos, but now   245
he was king in the third generation. He hoped to calm things
down: "Alas, I think a big sorrow has come to the land
of the Achaeans. If Priam and his sons and the other Trojans knew
about you two quarreling, they would greatly rejoice—you two,
best in counsel and best in battle! Listen—you are   250
both younger than I. When I was young, I mixed with men
more warlike than you. They never looked down upon me.
I have never seen such men since, nor shall I, men such as
Peirithoös and Dryas, the shepherd of the people, and Kaeneus
and Exadios and Polyphemos, like a god, and Theseus, the son   255
of Aegeus,° a likeness of the deathless ones. Most powerful of men
raised on the earth were these men. Most powerful they were.
They warred with the wild beasts° in the mountains and destroyed
them. I came from Pylos, far, far away, to mingle with
these men who had summoned me. I fought to the best of   260
my ability. I say that no one today who walks the earth

254–256 *Peirithoös … Aegeus*: The first names are princes of the Lapith tribe, who lived in Thessaly. Theseus,
son of Aegeus, is from Athens. According to the story known elsewhere, at the wedding of Peirithoös
the savage Centaurs tried to rape the bride and her attendants. A great war broke out in which Theseus,
a friend of Peirithoös, took part.

258 *wild beasts*: That is, the Centaurs, but it is not clear that Homer understood them to be part horse, part man.

could have fought these men. They listened to my advice,
and believed it. So you believe it too. It is better that you do.
  "You, Agamemnon, though strong, do not take this girl,
265 but let it go—the sons of the Achaeans first gave her to him.
And you, son of Peleus, do not wish to contend head-on with a king.
A chief who bears the scepter holds a special honor,
one to whom Zeus has given glory. If you are a stronger
fighter, and your mother is a goddess, yet he is more powerful
270 because he rules more men. Son of Atreus, you stop your anger.
I beg you—let go your wrath at Achilles, who is like a
huge wall to the Achaeans in the midst of destructive war."

  King Agamemnon answered him as follows:
"You have spoken as is fit, old man, everything you say.
275 But this man wants to be over everyone. He wants
to be king over all, to rule every man, and to boss
everyone around. But there is someone who is not persuaded!
Just because the gods who live forever made him a spearman,
do they also egg him on to go around casting insults?"

280   But shining Achilles broke in and said: "Surely
I would be called a coward and of no account if I were
to yield to you in everything that you say. You may give others
your commands, but give no orders to me. I don't think
I will obey you. And I will tell you something else.
285 Think it over. I shall not come to blows over the girl,
neither with you nor with anyone else, the girl whom
you have and now take away. But of my other
possessions laid up beside my swift black ship,
you shall carry away not a thing against my will.
290 Go ahead and try it!—then these too will know.
Swiftly your black blood will run down my spear!"

  And so these two struggled with savage words.
They stood up. The assembly dissolved beside the ships
of the Achaeans. The son of Peleus made his way
295 to the huts and his well-proportioned ships. He went with
Patroklos, the son of Menoitios, and his companions.

  But the son of Atreus dragged a swift ship to the sea.
He chose twenty oarsmen. He loaded a sacrifice for the god.
He placed high-cheeked Chryseïs in the boat.
300 Odysseus, the devious man, went along as leader.
They mounted the boat and sailed the watery paths.

Now the son of Atreus urged the people to purify
themselves. They purified themselves and threw the waters
they washed with into the sea. Then they sacrificed to Apollo
perfect bulls and goats beside the shore of the sea   305
that grows no crops. The scent spun, twisting in the smoke,
to heaven. And so they labored throughout the camp.

But Agamemnon forgot not the quarrel in which he
first threatened Achilles. He called to Talthybios and Eurybates,
his heralds and busy comrades in arms: "Go to the tent of   310
Achilles, son of Peleus. Take the high-cheeked Briseïs
by the hand and lead her here. If he won't give her,
I will myself go there with a large band of men and take her.
This will be shivery for him!"

                    So speaking he sent
the two men forth, and he laid on a solemn command.   315
They walked in silence along the sea that grows no crops.
They came to the tents and ships of the Myrmidons. They found
him sitting beside his tent and black ship. Achilles
was not happy to see them. The heralds stood there terrified,
in awe of the king. They did not speak nor ask questions.   320

But Achilles knew in his heart, and he said the following:
"Greetings, heralds of Zeus and the messengers of men.
Come closer. It's not your fault, but Agamemnon's, who sent
you forth on account of the girl Briseïs. But come,
Patroklos of Zeus's line, bring out the girl. Give her   325
to them to take away. And may these two men
be witnesses before the gods and before all men who die,
and before that arrogant king—if ever in time to come
you need me to ward off a destructive fate from the troops …
Why, the man is mad! He does not know how to   330
look before and after so that the Achaeans may fight
in safety beside the ships."

                    So he spoke. Patroklos
obeyed his companion and brought high-cheeked Briseïs
from the tent and delivered her to the men. Again they walked
along the ships of the Achaeans, and the girl went with them   335
unwilling.

But Achilles burst into tears, and he withdrew
apart from his companions. He sat on the shore beside

FIGURE 1.2   The Taking of Briseïs.   Achilles sits in a chair holding his spear while Patroklos, his back turned to the viewer, a sword slung over his shouder, hands over Briseïs to Agamemnon's men. To the far left stands Talthybios with his herald's wand. Achilles' tutor Phoenix stands behind his chair. Four armed warriors stand at the back against the wall of the tent. Roman fresco from Pompeii, c. first century AD.

the gray sea. He stared over the huge deep.
He raised his arms and prayed to his dear mother:
"Mother, because you bore me to a short life, Olympian   340
Zeus, who thunders on high, ought to have put honor
in my hands. But he has given me no honor at all. For the
son of Atreus, whose rule is wide, has dishonored me.
He has come and taken my girl."

              Thus he spoke, tears
streaming down his face. His revered mother heard him   345
as she sat beside her aged father in the depths of the sea.
Swiftly she came forth like a mist from the gray sea. She sat
down before him, as he wept. She took him by the hand
and she spoke his name: "My son, why do you weep?
What sorrow has come to your heart? Tell me, don't hide it,   350
that we both may know."

              Then, groaning heavily spoke
Achilles, the fast runner: "You know! Why do I need
to tell the whole story when you already know? We went
to THEBES, the sacred city of Eëtion.° We burned it to the ground
and took everything. The sons of the Achaeans then divided the loot   355
among themselves. For the son of Atreus they chose
Chryseïs, whose cheeks are beautiful. Chryses then came
to the fast ships of the bronze-shirted Achaeans, a holy man,
a priest of Apollo the far-shooter. He wanted
to free his daughter, and he brought boundless ransom,   360
holding the wreaths of Apollo the far-shooter
around a golden staff. And he begged all the Achaeans, and
above all the two sons of Atreus, the leaders of the people.
All the Achaeans shouted we should respect the holy man
and accept the shining ransom. But Agamemnon, the son   365
of Atreus, did not like this, and he roughly sent the man
away, and he lay on a strong word. Angry, the old man
went off. Apollo heard him as he prayed,
because he was dear to the god, and he sent an evil
shaft against the Argives. The people died like flies.   370
The missiles of the god fell everywhere through the broad
camp of the Achaeans. A knowing prophet explained
the doing of the god who strikes from a long way off.

---

354 *Thebes ... Eëtion*: Not of course the Thebes in Greece or Egypt; see Map 3. Eëtion (ē-**et**-i-on) was king of
the Thebes in the Troad. Because Chryseïs was taken in Thebes and not in Chrysê, perhaps she was married
to someone in Thebes. It is not clear why Thebes is "sacred," but cities often are, especially Troy.

Straightaway I was first to insist that we appease the god,
375 but anger seized the son of Atreus. He stood straight up
and lay down a threat, which now has come to pass.
The bright-eyed Achaeans are taking Chryseïs in a fast ship
to Chrysê, and they have gifts for the god. As for the other girl,
Briseïs, the heralds have taken her from my tent,
380 she whom the sons of the Achaeans gave to me.
      "But you, if you can, protect your son. Go to
Olympos and beg Zeus, if ever you have pleased him
in word or in something you've done. For I often heard
you boast in my father's halls that you alone
385 of the gods fended off disaster from the son of Kronos,
he of the dark clouds, when the other Olympians
wanted to tie him up—Hera and Poseidon
and Pallas Athena. But you went to him and set him
free from the bonds, having swiftly called to high Olympos
390 the hundred-hander whom gods call Briareos, but men call
Aigaion. He was stronger than his father.° He sat
down beside the son of Kronos, glorying in his power.
The blessed gods were frightened of him and did not bind Zeus.°
      "Remind him of this incident. Sit by his side.
395 Seize his knees—to see if he might help the Trojans
pen the Achaeans by the prows of their ships, their backs
to the sea. May they die like dogs! Thus may all share
in the wisdom of their chief, and Agamemnon, the wide ruler,
may know that he went insane when he dishonored
400 the best of the Achaeans."

                  Thetis answered him, pouring
down tears: "O my child, why ever did I bear you,
born to sorrow? I wish that you might have stayed
by the ships without weeping, without pain, since your life
is fated to be all too short. As it is, your fate is soon
405 upon you. You are more wretched than all men.
Therefore I bore you, in our halls, to an evil life.

---

391 *his father*: Briareos means "strong"; Aigaion, "of the sea," may refer to Poseidon, presumably the father of
      this Hundredhander, the personification of the power and roar of the sea. The significance of alternate
      names among men and gods is unknown. It occurs several times in the *Iliad*.

393 *bind Zeus*: The story about Thetis saving Zeus from imprisonment by Hera, Poseidon, and Athena is striking.
      Unknown elsewhere, it is related to the myth of the war in heaven prominent in Greek and Near Eastern
      myth. But why should Thetis have summoned the Hundredhander to Zeus's aid, one of Zeus's mighty
      allies against the Titans (according to the story told by the 8th century BC poet Hesiod)? The sea-goddess
      Thetis must be very old, going back to the waters from which the world was made, the primordial Tiamat
      of Babylonian myth (perhaps the names are related). Her role in saving Zeus from a divine conspiracy
      shows her to be more powerful than we expect from being merely the mother of Achilles.

"I will make your request of Zeus, who delights
in the thunder. I will myself ascend Olympos, clad in snow,
to see if I can persuade him. You stay here, nursing
your anger, beside the swift ships. Don't fight any more.   410
Yesterday Zeus went to Ocean, to the Aethiopians who do
no wrong, to a feast, and all gods went with him. On the twelfth day
he will return to Olympos. Then I shall go to the bronze-tiled
house of Zeus. I will take him by the knees and I think I will
persuade him."   415

         So speaking, she went off. She left Achilles
there in his rage on account of the slim-waisted woman,
whom Agamemnon took away by force, against his will.

But Odysseus came to Chrysê with the sacrifice.
When they got inside the deep harbor, they folded up the sail
and placed it in the black ship. They quickly loosened   420
the ropes and let down the mast into the mast-holder. They rowed
to a good mooring. They threw out the anchor stones and bound
up the stern with cables. They went forth on the shore
of the sea, driving before them the sacrifice to Apollo,
who shoots from a long way off. Chryseïs got out   425
of the sea-going boat. Leading her to the altar, the clever
Odysseus placed her in the hands of her father and said:

"O Chryses, the king of men Agamemnon has sent me here
to give to you your child and to perform holy sacrifice
to Phoibos on behalf of the Danaäns, who would like to appease   430
the lord, who brings agonizing pain to the Argives."

So saying he placed her in Chryses' arms. The father
received his dear child with joy. The men quickly set up
the sacrifice around the altar, made of dressed stone.
They washed their hands and took up the barley grains.°   435
Chryses raised his hands on their behalf and prayed
in a loud voice: "Hear me, you of the silver bow,
who hover over Chrysê and sacred Killa and are king
with power over the island of Tenedos. You already
heard me when I prayed to you, and you gave me honor.   440
You mightily struck the Danaäns! So fulfill for me now

---

435   *barley grains:* Grains of barley were sprinkled on the sacrificial victim as part of the religious ritual, perhaps
      because of barley's association with fruitfulness.

my new request: Let go from these Danaäns the destructive
plague!"

So he spoke in prayer. Phoibos Apollo
heard him. When they had prayed and sprinkled the barley,
445 they first drew back the heads of the cattle, then they cut
their throats. They skinned them out. They cut out the bones
of the thighs, covered them in two layers of fat, and placed
raw meat on top. The old man burned them
on splinters of wood. He poured out shining wine
450 on top. The young men beside him held out their forks
with five prongs. When he had burned the thigh bones
and they had tasted the guts, they cut up the rest
and spitted the pieces. They roasted the meat with care.
Then they drew it from the spits. When they were done
455 with their work and had prepared their meal, they ate.
Nor did their hearts lack for anything in the equal feast.°

When they had put aside their desire for drink and food,
the young men filled the mixing bowls to the brim
with wine. They poured libations from every cup,
460 then distributed the wine all around. They beseeched
the god with song, singing the Apollo-hymn,
the young men of the Achaeans, singing a hymn to the god
who works from far away. And he was delighted
to hear them.

Then the sun went down and darkness came.
465 They slept by the sterns of the ships. When dawn came,
spreading her fingers of rose, they set out for the broad
camp of the Achaeans. Apollo who works from a long way
off sent them a favorable breeze. They raised
the mast and spread the white sail. The wind filled
470 the middle of the sail. The purple waves roared around
the keel of the ship as it went. She ran over the waves,
making her way forward. When they arrived at the broad camp
of the Achaeans, they dragged the black ship high on the sand
of the shore. They fitted long props beneath. The men
475 scattered to their tents and their ships.

But the Zeus-nourished
son of Peleus, Achilles, the fast runner, continued to nurse

---

456 *equal feast*: In an equal feast everyone receives an equal portion so that no one's honor is slighted.

his anger, sitting beside the fast ships. He never went
to the place of assembly, where men win glory, nor ever
to the war. He wasted away in his heart, remaining idle,
though he longed for the cry of war and the fight.   480

When twelve days had passed, all the gods, who live
forever, went in a band to Olympos, with Zeus in the lead.
Thetis did not forget the request of her son. She arose from
the wave of the sea. Early in morning she went up
to heaven and Olympos. She found the son of Kronos,   485
who sees things from far off, sitting apart from the others
on a steep peak of Olympos, which has many ridges. She sat
down near him and took hold of his knees with her left hand,
while with her right she gripped him beneath the chin.
Beseeching, she spoke to Zeus the king, the son of Kronos: 490

"Zeus, our father, if ever I have helped you among the
immortals either in word or in something I did,
fulfill for me this desire. Give honor to my son
who, more than others, is born to a quick death.
But as it is, now the king of men Agamemnon   495
has not given him honor. He has taken away his prize.
He holds it! But give him honor, O Olympian, counselor Zeus.
Give power to the Trojans until the Achaeans honor my son
and increase his honor." So she spoke.

                                  The cloud-gatherer
Zeus said nothing, but sat in silence for a long time.   500
As Thetis had clasped his knees, so now she held him
close, and asked again: "Make me this firm promise,
bow your head to it—or turn me away. You have nothing
to fear, so that I may know how of all the gods I have
the least honor …"   505

                    Zeus, who assembles the clouds,
was deeply disturbed. He said: "This is a bad
business. You will set me on to quarrel with Hera, who
will anger me with her words of reproach. Even as it is
she is always on my back among the deathless gods, saying
that in the battle I help the Trojans. So leave   510
now or she may notice something! Yes, I'll take care
of this. I'll bring it to pass. Here, let me bow
my head to you so that you will believe me,
for this is the surest sign I give among the immortals—

515 I will never take it back. It is no illusion. It will always
come to pass, whatever I nod my head to."

Then the son of Kronos nodded with his brows,
dark like lapis lazuli, and his immortal locks fell all around
the head of the deathless king. Olympos shook.

520 After the two took counsel together in this fashion,
they departed, Thetis descending from shining Olympos
into the deep sea, and Zeus went to his house. All the
gods stood up from their seats when he entered. No one
dared to await his coming, but they all stood up.

525 So he sat there on his throne, but Hera
knew he had made a deal with Thetis of the
silver ankles, the daughter of the Old Man of the Sea.°
She spoke to Zeus at once, the son of Kronos,
with mocking words: "Who, my clever fellow,
530 have you been making deals with? You just love that,
to stand apart from me and make judgments about things
that you have decided in secret. Nor do you ever
bother willingly to tell me what you have been up to."

The father of men and gods said the following:
535 "Hera, don't hope to know all my thoughts! It will be
the worse for you if you do, although I sleep with you.
What you should know, you will know before all other gods
or men. But what I wish to devise apart from
the gods, don't ask about it. Make no inquiries!"

540 Hera, with eyes like a cow, the revered one,
then said to him: "O most dread son of Kronos!
What a thing you have said! In the past I have never asked
you about your affairs, nor made inquiry, but you
fancied anything you like. But now I greatly
545 fear in my heart that silver-ankled Thetis has led you
astray, the daughter of the Old One of the Sea.
She came this morning and sat beside you and gripped
your knees. I think you promised her that you would give

---

527 *Old Man of the Sea*: Nereus.

honor to Achilles, that you would destroy a multitude
beside the ships of the Achaeans."   550

               Zeus, who assembles
the clouds, then replied: "You bitch! You have your ideas,
and nothing gets past you! Nonetheless, there is nothing you can do
about it. You will only drift further from my heart, which will
be the more shivery for you. If this is what I'm thinking,
I must like it. So shut up and sit down! Obey my word,   555
or all the gods in Olympos will do you no good as I close
in and lay upon you my powerful hands!"

               So he spoke,
and the cow-eyed revered Hera took fright. In silence
she took her seat, curbing the impulse of her heart.

    The Olympian gods in the house of Zeus were troubled   560
by what had happened, when Hephaistos, known for his craft,
said this, bringing kindness to his dear mother Hera
of the white arms: "Surely this will be a nasty turn,
scarcely to be born, if the two of you quarrel like this
over men who die. You bring squabbling into the midst   565
of the gods. There will be no pleasure in the feast, when trouble
has the upper hand. I advise my mother, whom I know to be
sensible in her own right, to be kind to our dear father, so that
he does not tangle with her again and stir up trouble at the feast.

    Why, what if the Olympian, master of the lightning, wished to blast   570
us from our seats? For his strength is much the greater.
So—please calm him with gentle words. Then the Olympian
will be kind to us."

             So he spoke, and leaping up he placed
a two-handled cup in his mother's hand, and said to her:
"Courage, my mother! Hang on, though you are irritated,   575
or else I may see you beaten with my own eyes.
You are so dear to me, but though grieving you may be unable
to do anything about it. The Olympian is not someone
you want to go up against. Why, I remember the time
that I was eager to save you and he grabbed me by the foot   580
and threw me from the divine threshold. I fell all day.
When the sun was setting, I landed on the island of LEMNOS,

barely alive. There, after my fall, the Sintian men
quickly cared for me."°

                So he spoke, and white-armed
585 Hera smiled, and, smiling, she took in hand the cup
from her son. Then Hephaistos, moving from left to right,
poured out wine to all the gods, drawing sweet nectar°
from the mixing bowl. An unquenchable laughter
arose among the blessed beings when they saw Hephaistos
590 puffing along through the palace.

                    So they dined all day
until the sun went down. They did not lack for anything
in the equal feast, not the lovely lyre that Apollo
played, and the Muses sang in beautiful response.°
But when the bright light of the sun had disappeared,
595 they went to lie down, each to his own house,
where for each one the lame god, famous Hephaistos,
had made a palace with his cunning skill. Zeus,
the Olympian, the master of lightning, mounted his own bed.
There it was always his custom to rest, where sweet
600 sleep came to him. He went up and fell asleep,
and Hera of the golden throne slept beside him.

---

584   ... *cared for me*: For Lemnos, see Map 1. The Sintians are the native inhabitants. The story about Hephaistos
being thrown from Heaven is told again (Book 18) with significant variation, the only time in the Homeric
corpus that a single myth is told twice.

587   *nectar*: The wine of the gods; its etymology is unknown.

593   *response*: Apollo sings for the gods just as singers (*aoidoi*) like Homer sang for human courts. Hephaistos
is lame because real blacksmiths often were lame, and he is the bumbling butt of laughter. Yet he made the
shining houses in which the gods live, and they could not do without him.

BOOK 2. *False Dream and the Catalog of Ships*

The other gods and the chariot-charging men slept the whole
night through, but sweet sleep came not on Zeus. He wondered
in his heart how to honor Achilles and destroy many beside
the ships of the Achaeans. This seemed to him the best plan,
to send to Agamemnon, the son of Atreus, a destructive dream.   5

So he spoke to Dream words that sped like arrows:
"Go on, go, O Destructive Dream, to the fast ships of the
Achaeans. When you come to the tent of Agamemnon,
son of Atreus, tell him exactly what I tell to you:
Order him swiftly to arm the Achaeans with long hair,   10
for now he can take the city of Troy with its broad roads.
The deathless gods, who live on Olympos, are no more
of two minds about this matter. Hera, with her pleading,
has persuaded the gods to allow the destruction of Troy."

So he spoke, and Dream went off at Zeus's   15
command. He soon arrived at the swift ships of the Achaeans.
He went to Agamemnon, son of Atreus. He found him
asleep in his tent, a godlike sleep upon him. He stood
over his head and, looking like Nestor, son of Neleus,
whom of all old men Agamemnon trusted the most,   20
he said, this dream from heaven:

                              "You are sleeping, O son
of Atreus, wise tamer of horses. But you ought not,
a man of counsel, sleep the whole night through, one
to whom the people turn, you who have many troubles.
But listen: I come from Zeus. Although far away,   25
he cares greatly for you, and he pities you. He orders
you swiftly to arm the Achaeans with long hair,
for now you can take the city of Troy with its broad roads.
The deathless gods, who live on Olympos, are no more
of two minds about this matter. Hera, with her pleading,   30

has persuaded the gods to allow the destruction of Troy.°
Zeus has condemned the Trojans to destruction!
Now remember this, and do not forget it when honeyed
sleep lets you go."

           So speaking, Dream departed.
35 He left Agamemnon with a thought of things that would
never come to pass. For Agamemnon thought that on
that day he would take the city of Priam—what a fool!
He never knew what Zeus intended, how he was
going to cause, through grievous battle, pain
40 and agony among the Trojans and Danaäns alike.

    Agamemnon woke up. The divine voice sounded
all around him. He sat up straight on the edge of the bed.
He put on his soft shirt, a beautiful new one, then put
on his great cloak. Beneath his feet he bound
45 his beautiful sandals, and over his shoulders he cast
his great sword with silver nails. He took up his scepter,
a family heirloom—deathless, lasting forever!—
and he walked along the ships of the Achaeans, clothed
in bronze.

       The divine Dawn went to tall Olympos
50 to proclaim the light to Zeus and the other deathless ones,
while Agamemnon ordered his clear-voiced heralds to call
to assembly the Achaeans with long hair. They called,
and the army gathered in haste. But first Agamemnon
summoned the wise old men to gather beside the ship
55 of Nestor, the chief of PYLOS. Having brought them together,
he devised a clever plan: "Hear me, my friends! A dream
of the gods came to me while I slept, during the immortal night.
The Dream looked like goodly Nestor in form and height
and build. He stood right near my head and spoke:
60 'You are sleeping, O son of Atreus, wise tamer of horses.
But you ought not, a man of counsel, sleep the whole
night through, one to whom the people turn,
you who have many troubles. But listen: I come
from Zeus. Although far away, he greatly cares
65 for you, and he pities you. He orders you swiftly

---

31 *destruction of Troy*: It is typical of oral style for messages to be repeated word for word.

to arm the Achaeans with long hair, for now you can
take Troy with its broad roads! The deathless gods,
who live on Olympos, are no more of two minds
about this matter. Hera, with her pleading, has persuaded
the gods to allow the destruction of Troy. Zeus   70
has condemned the Trojans to destruction! Now
remember this, and do not forget it when honeyed
sleep lets you go.'
                    "So speaking, the Dream flew away,
and sweet sleep released me. Come then, let's arm
the sons of the Achaeans! But first I want to test   75
the men in speech, as is right. I will urge them to flee
in their ships with many benches, then you, from all sides,
must hold them back with your words!" So speaking,
he sat down.

            Nestor stood up before them, the king
of sandy Pylos. Wishing them well, he spoke to them: 80
"My dear friends, leaders and counselors of the Argives,
if anyone else told us this dream, we would say it
is false. We would have nothing to do with it.
But as it is, the best of the Achaeans has had this dream!
Let us therefore arm the sons of the Achaeans."   85

    So speaking, he led the way from the council.
The scepter-bearing chieftains got up and followed
the shepherd of the people. But all the while the people
were hastening on. Just as the tribes of swarming
bees pour forth from a hollow rock, and in bunches   90
hover above the spring flowers, some in clusters here,
some over there—even so the many tribes from the ships
and the huts along the deep sea-beach were arranged
in order at the place of assembly, lined up in companies.
And in their midst burned Rumor, urging them on,   95
the messenger of Zeus.

                    The Argives gathered. The place
of assembly was in turmoil. The earth groaned beneath
the people as they took their seats. The din was terrific.
Seven heralds, hollering, held them back—"If you
 stop the hullabaloo, you can hear the god-nourished chieftains!"   100
With haste the people sat down. They arranged themselves
in rows and ceased from their clamor.

FIGURE 2.1 Nestor. Gray-haired, he had already seen three generations of men. He wears no armor and holds a staff of authority, appropriate to his role as advice-giver. On an Athenian red-figure vase, c. 450 BC.

King Agamemnon stood up,
holding the scepter that Hephaistos had made. Hephaistos
gave this scepter to Zeus, the son of Kronos, the king,
and Zeus gave it to the messenger Hermes, the killer   105
of Argos.° Hermes, the king, gave it to Pelops,
driver of horses. Pelops gave it to Atreus, shepherd
of the people. When Atreus died, he left it to Thyestes,
rich in sheep, and Thyestes left it to Agamemnon°
to bear, to rule over many islands and all of Argos.°   110

Now leaning on this scepter, Agamemnon spoke   🔊
to the Argives: "My dear fighting-men, you Danaäns,
you servants of man-devouring Ares—Zeus, the son
of crooked-counseled Kronos, has bound me in a crazy
madness—he is a hard god! At first he promised me,   115
and nodded his head to it, that we would sack Ilion
with its wonderful walls and then go home. But he
only contrived a wicked deception! Now he urges me
back to Argos after losing so many men to war!
I suppose this is what Zeus wanted, whose power   120
is paramount. He has loosed the crown of many cities,
and he will loosen others in future times. For his strength
is overriding. But it is shameful to learn, and will be for
generations, how we led to war so many people, and of such
quality, against far fewer men—all for nothing!   125
    "There is no end in sight. Why, if Achaeans
and Trojans made a sacrifice and swore an oath, and did
a head count, and all the Trojans who have hearths in the city
were gathered together, and the Achaeans were divided in groups
of ten, and every group should choose one Trojan to serve   130
the wine at the drinking-party—then many groups
would go without. So many more are we sons
of the Achaeans than the Trojans who live in the city.
    "But alas, they have many allies who use the spear,
who constantly strike me and will not let me take   135

---

106 *killer of* Argos; The Greek is Argeïphontes (ar-jē-i-**fon**-tēz), probably "the killer of Argos," a monster with
      500 eyes, though there are other interpretations. It is a standard epithet of Hermes.

109 *Agamemnon*: Many famous stories were later told about Pelops, Atreus, and Thyestes. Pelops came from
      Asia and gave his name to the Peloponnesus, "the island of Pelops." Atreus and Thyestes committed vile
      crimes of murder, cannibalism, rape, and incest, and Agamemnon was heir to the house.

110 *Argos*: Argos means "plain" and probably here refers to the city of Mycenae and surrounding territories, for
      Diomedes, according the Catalog of Ships (see below), ruled the nearby city of Argos (Maps 2, 4).

this populous city of Ilion, though I desire it. Nine years
of great Zeus have passed. The planks of the ships
are rotten and the ropes are frayed. Our wives and little
children sit waiting for us in our halls while the task
140 for which we came lies undone. So let's all obey
what I say: Let's sail out of here! Let us return to the land
of our fathers. We will never take Troy with its broad streets!"

So he spoke, and through the multitude he aroused the spirits
in their breasts—of as many men who were not at the council.
145 The assembly was stirred like long waves of the Icarian Sea°
that East Wind and South Wind have stirred, driving on from
clouds of Zeus the father. Or as when West Wind riffles
the towering fields of wheat, coming roughly on, and the ears
of wheat are bowed—even so was the assembly stirred.

150 With a Huzzah! they raced to the ships° and the dust
flew into the air from beneath their feet. They shouted
to each other to take hold of the ships and drag them
into the shining sea and to clean out the slipways.
The roar of the men desiring to go home reached to heaven,
155 and they laid hold of the props under the ships.

Then would
the Argives have defeated fate in their homecoming, but
Hera spoke to Athena: "Good grief, daughter of Zeus
who carries the goatskin fetish, you who are tireless—
the Argives are about to flee to their native earth
160 on the wide back of the sea. Priam and the Trojans
will boast that they possess Helen of Argos, on whose
account many Achaeans have died at Troy, far
from their dear native land. But go now among the Achaeans
clothed in bronze. Hold them back with your gentle
165 words, don't let them drag the ships, with oars
on both sides, into the sea."

So she spoke
and flashing-eyed Athena obeyed. She went in a rush

---

145 *Icarian Sea*: Between the central Cyclades and Asia Minor (Map 1).

150 *raced to the ships*. Homer has gone a long way to set up this joke: Agamemnon is such a fool that he thinks
by suggesting to his men that they depart without victory they will all protest, "No, we want war!" Instead
they race to the ships, "Let's get out of here!" The scene is sheer slapstick (there is no slapstick in the
Odyssey). The joke, sure to raise a laugh from Homer's audience of male aristocratic warriors, appeals to
the knowledge that war is not always fun.

down from the peaks of Olympos. Soon she arrived
at the ships of the Achaeans. She came up to Odysseus,
standing there equal to Zeus in his counsel. He had not   170
gripped his many-benched black ship, because agony had come
to his heart and his spirit.

                  Coming nearby, flashing-eyed
Athena said: "God-nurtured son of Laërtes, Odysseus,
skilled at ingenious devices, are you thus all falling
into your ships, anxious to flee homeward to your native   175
land in your many-benched ships? Priam and the Trojans
will boast that they possess Helen of Argos, on account
of whom many Achaeans have died at Troy
far from their dear native land. But go now
among the Achaeans clothed in bronze. Hold back   180
each man with your gentle words, don't let them drag
their ships, with oars on both sides, into the sea."

   So she spoke, and he knew the voice of the goddess
as she spoke. He made ready to run. He threw off
his cloak, which Eurybates° the Ithacan picked up,   185
who waited on him. He went straight to Agamemnon, the son
of Atreus. He seized from him the heirloom scepter—
deathless, forever!—and with it he ran through the ships
of the Achaeans clothed in bronze. Whenever he came
on a chief or a man in some way outstanding, he tried   190
to hold him back, standing beside him and addressing him
with pleasing words: "Surely, it is hardly right
to frighten you, as if you were a man of no account,
but please sit down and make the rest of your folk
do the same. Believe me, you don't know what the son   195
of Atreus really means. Why, he is only testing you.
Soon he will smash the sons of the Achaeans! It is true
that not all of us heard what he said in the council. Be careful
he does not grow angry and do harm to the sons of the Achaeans.
Big is the spirit of the god-nurtured chieftain—their honor   200
is from Zeus! Zeus, who counsels wisely, loves them."

   But if he came on a man of the people shouting away,
he struck him with the scepter and called him out: "Sit down
and be still! Listen to the words of others who are better.

---

185 *Eurybates*: Odysseus' herald. He accompanied Agamemnon's herald, Talthybios, at the taking of Briseïs.

205 You are worthless for war and a weakling. You are of no
account in the contendings, nor in the council. We can't
all be chiefs. Rule by the many is not good!
We want one boss, one chieftain, to whom the son
of clever Kronos gave the scepter and the laws, that he might
210 give good advice." Thus like a master did he range
through the army. And again they surged into the place
of gathering away from the ships and the huts, always chattering,
as when a wave of the resounding sea thunders
on the broad beach and there is a roar from the deep.

🔊 215   The others sat down, all except brawling Thersites,
who went on scolding, whose mind was filled with disorderly
words to condemn the chiefs, all for nothing, hardly in good form,
but he said whatever he thought would raise a laugh among
the Argives. Thersites was the most disgusting man who went
220 to Troy. His legs were bowed, one shorter than the other,
and his shoulders curved inwards over his chest. His head
was pointy and a scant tuft of hair grew on top.
Achilles especially hated him, but also Odysseus,
for Thersites constantly reviled these two men.

225   At the moment, however, he attacked goodly Agamemnon
with his sharp words, for the Achaeans were furious with
Agamemnon and blamed him in their hearts. In a loud voice
Thersites insulted him now: "O son of Atreus, what
is wrong? What do you lack? Your tents are filled, I think,
230 with bronze. You have fine women in your tents,
which we Achaeans gave to you as first pick whenever
we attacked some town. Or maybe you still lack gold,
which a horse-commanding Trojan has brought from Troy
as ransom for his son? Maybe I bound him and led him away,
235 or some other Achaean ... or is it a pretty young thing
for you to bed, whom you will keep to yourself?
You've got no business as our leader to bring
us to pain, the sons of the Achaeans. Sad fools,
miserable pathetic things, you are no men
240 but like the ladies of Achaea! Let us go home
in our ships and leave this man here in Troy
to ponder his prizes. Then he may know if we
are any good to him or not—he who dishonored
Achilles, a far greater man than he! For he took
245 that man's prize and he holds it. Achilles must know
no anger in his heart. He must have set it aside.

Otherwise, O son of Atreus, this would be
your last outrage!"

        So spoke Thersites, abusing
Agamemnon, the shepherd of the people. But Odysseus
quickly came up to him, and glowering beneath his   250
brows he put him in his place with a savage word:
"Be still, Thersites, fancy with words, clear-voiced
speaker—don't try and argue with the chiefs, alone
as you are! No one worse than you ever came to Troy
with the sons of Atreus. So don't go around with 'chief'   255
lightly on your lips, despising them, saying we should all
sail home. No one knows how this will all turn out,
or whether the sons of the Achaeans will return in victory
or defeat to our homes. You stand there insulting Agamemnon,
shepherd of the people, because the Danaän spearmen give   260
him many gifts. You rail on and on—but let me tell you
something, which surely will come to pass. If again
I find you playing the fool as you do now, then no
longer may my head sit on my shoulders, or I
be called the father of Telemachos, if I don't seize you   265
and strip off your clothes, your cloak and shirt that covers
your privates, and drive you wailing out of the assembly
to the fast ships in a rain of shaming blows."

   So he spoke, and with the staff he struck Thersites'
back and shoulders. Thersites bent over. A hot tear   270
rolled down his cheek. A bloody welt rose up
on his back beneath the golden scepter. He sat
down, deeply alarmed, in pain, with a helpless
look on his face. He wiped away a tear.

        The Achaeans,
though they suffered, laughed merrily at his plight.   275
One would say, glancing at his neighbor: "Well, I think
that Odysseus has done a thousand good things in the council
and leading us in battle, but now he has done the best
thing of all among the Argives, who has shut up
this foul loud-mouth and stopped his prattle. I don't   280
think the proud spirit of Thersites will again urge him on
to speak ill of the chiefs with his insults."

        So spoke
one common man. But Odysseus, the despoiler of cities,

stood tall, still holding the scepter. Beside him appeared
285 flashing-eyed Athena, looking like a herald. She urged
the people to be quiet so that the Achaeans, both near and far,
could hear his words and consider his counsel.

With the best
of wishes, Odysseus addressed the troops: "Son of Atreus—
who are king—it looks like the Achaeans now wish to make you
290 the most despised of mortals, and to reject the promise
they made when they sailed from Argos with its horse
pastures, to sack high-walled Troy before returning home.
Like children or widowed women they complain that they want
to go home. Sure, there is trouble enough to make anyone
295 *want* to go home. A man away for a month from his wife
wishes to return in his well-benched ship, a man whom
wintry storms shuts in and a high sea. But we've been
here nine years! So I don't blame the Achaeans
for their anger beside the high-beaked ships. Still,
300 it's a thing of shame to stay so long, then sail home
empty-handed. So persevere, friends, wait for awhile.
Let us learn whether Kalchas has made a true prophecy
or not. For this we well know, all here are witness
to it—at least those whom the darkness of death
305 has not swept away.
                    "Why, it was only yesterday, or the day
before, when the ships of the Achaeans were gathered in
AULIS, ready to bring evil to Priam and the Trojans.
We were gathered around a spring, placing on the holy altar
a perfect sacrifice to the deathless gods. There was
310 a lovely plane tree above, from which flowed shining
water. Then a wondrous sign appeared—a serpent
with a blazing scarlet back, awesome. The Olympian
had sent him into the light. Sliding from beneath
the altar, it darted toward the tree. A sparrow's nestlings,
315 little babies, hid beneath the leaves on the topmost branch—
eight little babies and the mother who hatched them made nine.
The serpent ate them as they squealed pitifully. The mama
flew around, shrieking for her dear little babies. Coiling,
the serpent grabbed her by the wing as she screamed
320 around him. When he had eaten the babies and the mother too,
the god who sent him made a clear sign: The son
of clever Kronos turned him to stone! We stood there,
amazed at what had happened.

"When the awesome sign broke in
on the sacrifice to the gods, Kalchas immediately made
a prophecy: 'Why have you all fallen silent, Achaeans   325
with the long hair? The wise Zeus has made this great sign
clear. Though slow to come, the tale of this achievement
will never die. Just as this serpent has devoured the eight
little babies, and the mother who bore them makes nine,
even so we will fight for as many years, and on   330
the tenth we will take the city with its broad streets.'
That's what Kalchas said. And now all is coming to pass.
So hang in, all you Achaeans with your fancy shinguards,
until we take the great city of Priam!"

So he spoke,
and the Argives moaned aloud, and around the ships   335
arose a great roar as the Achaeans shouted, thrilled
with the advice of godlike Odysseus.

Then Nestor of Gerenia,°
the horseman, spoke to them: "You know you seem
to me like little children. You gather here, and have
no thought of war. Where are the oaths we took?   340
We might as well throw all the plans we made into the fire,
and the oaths we swore with unmixed wine° while we clasped
our hands, in which we placed our trust. It is useless to wrangle
with words. That way leads nowhere, although we spend
forever arguing. You, Agamemnon, continue to hold   345
to your unbending purpose, as you always have, and lead
the Argives in their terrible struggle. Those one or two
of the Achaeans who sneak off by themselves and plan
to go home to Argos before we discover if the promise
of Zeus, who carries the goatskin fetish, is right   350
or not—they can go to hell! You'll get nothing from them
anyway. I tell you that the son of Kronos, supreme in power,
nodded in our favor on that day when the Argives sailed
in our swift-traveling ships, bringing death and doom
to the Trojans. There was lightning on the right, a sign of success.   355
So don't be anxious to sail home before you sleep with a Trojan

---

338 *Gerenia*: Gerenia is apparently a place with which Nestor is associated, near Pylos in the southwestern
Peloponnesus.

342 *unmixed wine*: Ordinarily wine was mixed with water for drinking, usually in a ratio of two parts wine to
three parts water.

woman in payment for your trouble and the pain caused
by Helen. And if someone wants so much to sail
home, let him take hold of his black many-benched ship—
360 then in the sight of all may he die and meet his fate!
   "But my king, think well on this—believe another!
Don't cast aside the word I speak. Separate the men according
to tribes, Agamemnon, and clans so that one clan may
support another, and the tribes too. If you do this, and the
365 Achaeans follow you, then you will know who among
the captains is a coward, and who of the army, and who is
brave. For the clans will compete with each other. You will
know if it is because of the will of the gods that you can't
take the city, or whether because of your men's cowardice
370 and ignorance of war."

          King Agamemnon then answered him:
"Yes, again, old man, you have proven your excellence
in speaking, above the other sons of the Achaeans. By Zeus
the father, and Athena, and Apollo, I wish only
that I had ten such counselors among the Achaeans.
375 Then would the city of King Priam soon bow its head,
taken and sacked at our hands. But the son of Kronos,
Zeus who wields the goatskin fetish, has caused
me a lot of woe. He casts me into the midst of strife
and quarrels. For Achilles and I have fought over a girl,
380 speaking vile words. It was I who first got mad.
Could we only see eye-to-eye, then there would be no
putting off of evil—no, not for a second.
                              "But for now,
let every man eat a meal and prepare for war.
Sharpen your spears, get ready your shields, feed
385 your horses, the fast runners. See to your cars,
that they are ready for the fight, so that all day long
we may contend in hateful war! There'll be no break
in the fighting, not even a short one, until the coming
of night puts a stop to the anger of men. The strap
390 on his wrap-around shield will drip with sweat as it hangs
around his breast, and his hand will grow weary holding
the spear. The horse of every man will be wet with sweat
as it pulls the polished car. But if I find someone
hanging around the beaked ships, longing to go home,
395 I will give his body to the dogs and the birds!"

So he spoke, and the Argives roared aloud, as when
South Wind, driving on, raises a wave against a towering cliff,
a headland against which every kind of wind drives
waves constantly as they come from every direction.
The men stood up and scattered among the ships. They made   400
fires in the huts and took their meal. Every man prayed
to his own god who never dies, asking that he escape death
and the work of Ares. And Agamemnon, the king of men,
killed in sacrifice a fat bull, five years of age, to the son
of Kronos, superior in power.   405

            Agamemnon gathered
to him the elders, the best of the Achaeans: first of all Nestor,
then King Idomeneus, and also the two Ajaxes and the son
of Tydeus,° and as the sixth came Odysseus, the equal
of Zeus in counsel. Menelaos, who shouted loud in war,
came without being asked, for he knew in his heart   410
what his brother was going through. They stood around
the bull and took up the grains of white barley.

   The good King Agamemnon spoke among them
in prayer: "O Zeus, most glorious, greatest, lord
of the dark cloud, dwelling in heaven—may the sun not set,   415
and the darkness come before I throw to the ground the hall
of Priam, blackened with soot, and burn the doorways
with consuming fire, and split the shirt of Hector
around his breast, ripping it with bronze, while many
of his close companions, lying in the dust, bite the earth   420
with their teeth!" So he spoke, but the son of Kronos
did not grant him his wish. He accepted the sacrifice,
but he gave Agamemnon dreadful sorrow.

            When they had prayed
and sprinkled the grains of barley, they pulled back the victim's
head, cut its throat, and flayed off the skin. They cut out   425
the thigh bones and covered them with a layer of doubled fat.
On top they placed raw flesh. Then they burned everything

---

408   ... *Tydeus*: Idomeneus is the leader of the Cretans. The two Ajaxes are Ajax, son of Telamon, from the island
of SALAMIS; and Ajax, son of Oïleus, from the territory of LOCRIS northwest of Boeotia; they are
unrelated but are always called the "two Ajaxes" or "Big Ajax," son of Telamon; and "Little Ajax," son of
Oïleus. The son of Tydeus is Diomedes, one of the greatest fighters at Troy, as we will soon see.

on splints from which the leaves were removed. They spitted
the guts and held them over the flame of Hephaistos.°
430   When the thigh bones were burned and the innards eaten,
they cut up the rest and placed the meat on spits. They cooked
the meat thoroughly, then drew it off from the spits.
When they had ceased from their labor and prepared
the meal, they ate. No one went without his fill
435   of food, equally distributed.

                    When they had their fill
of food and drink, Nestor from Gerenia began
to speak: "O son of Atreus, most glorious, king
of men, Agamemnon, let us no longer be gathered here,
nor let us longer put off the work that the god
440   places in our hands. So come, let's have the heralds
of the Achaeans, clothed in bronze, go through the ships
and summon everyone together. Let us go too in a bunch
through the broad camp of the Achaeans to swiftly stir up
the sharp work of war."

                    So he spoke, and King Agamemnon
445   obeyed. Immediately he ordered the clear-voiced heralds
to summon to battle the Achaeans with their long hair.
They did summon them, and quickly the army assembled.
The chiefs around the son of Atreus, divinely nurtured,
ran through the crowd and organized them into gangs,
450   and among them went Athena with the flashing eye,
holding the goatskin fetish, of exceeding value—
ageless, deathless! From it hung a hundred tassels
of solid gold, every one of them finely woven,
every tassel worth a hundred cattle. With it she raced
455   like lightning through the mass of the Achaeans,
urging them to go forth. She roused strength in the heart
of each man to fight and do battle without end. Instantly
war became sweeter to them than to sail away
in their hollow ships to the beloved land of their fathers.

460   Just as when a consuming fire ignites the endless
forest on a mountain top, and from a distance the gleam
is clear, even so the dazzling shining of the wonderful
bronze of the men as they came on reached heaven
through the sky. Even as the many tribes of winged birds,

---

429 *Hephaistos*: As the god of smiths, he became equated with fire.

of geese, or cranes, or long-necked swans in the meadow of ASIA,   465
around the streams of the KAYSTRIOS,° flying this way and that,
thrilling in the power of flight they settle with loud cry
ever onward, and the meadow resounds—even so
the many tribes poured forth from the ships and the tents
onto the plain of SKAMANDROS.° And the earth resounded terribly   470
under the tramp of feet and the feet of their horses. They took
their stand in the meadow of flower-bound Skamandros, without
number, as many as there are leaves and flowers in their season.

Or as the many tribes of swarming flies that buzz
around the shepherd's yard in the season of spring,   475
when milk moistens the pails—so many of the Achaeans
with flowing hair took their stand in the face
of the Trojans, longing to tear them in pieces.

Even as when a goatherd easily picks out
his own goats scattered wide in the pasture, so did   480
the leaders organize the tribes on this side and that,
ready for battle, and among them King Agamemnon,
his eyes and head like Zeus who thrills to the thunderbolt,
his waist like Ares, his chest like Poseidon. Even as
a bull in the herd is by far the greatest of all—   485
for he stands out among the cattle as they gather together—
such did Zeus make the son of Atreus on that day,
outstanding among many, chief among the fighting men.

Tell me now, you Muses who have houses on Olympos,
for you are divine, you are at hand, you know everything while   490
We hear only the sound about things.° We know nothing.
Who were the leaders of the Argives? Who were their captains?
I could never tell the masses, or name them all, not with
ten tongues and ten mouths and my voice unbroken and my heart
within made of bronze, if the Olympian Muses,   495
the daughters of Zeus who carries the goatskin fetish,
did not remind me of how many there were of those who went
beneath Ilion with its high walls.

465–466 *Asia … Kaystrios*: Asia vaguely designates an inland territory comprising part of LYDIA and lands
          further south (Map 1). From this once restricted use the word has acquired its modern reference to
          a continent. Kaystrios is a river that flows into the AEGEAN near EPHESOS (Map 1).

470   *Skamandros*: One of the two rivers crossing the plain of Troy (Map 3).

491   *sound about things*: Homer appeals to the Muses, who embody the oral tradition, at critical junctures.
          He perceives his power of song to come from outside him.

Now I will name the captains
of the ships and all the ships themselves.° Peneleos
500 and Leïtos led the BOEOTIANS, and Arkesilaos and Prothoënor
and Klonios, who lived in Hyria and rocky AULIS, and Schoinos
and Skolos and high-ridged Eteonos, and Thespeia and Graia
and Mykalessos with its broad dancing places, and those
who lived in Harma and Eilesion and Erythrai, and those
505 who held Elea and Hylê and Peteon, Okalea and Medeon,
a well-made fortress, and Kopas and Eutresis, swarming
with pigeons, and Thisbê, and those who held Koroneia
and grassy Haliartos, and Plataia,° and those who lived
in Glisas, and those who lived beneath the well-made
510 citadel of THEBES,° and sacred Onchestos with its brilliant
grove of Poseidon, and those who possessed Arnê with its rich
vineyards, and those who held Mideia and sacred Nisa,
and Anthedon, the furthest land. From these places
sailed fifty ships. In each were 120 young men.°

---

499   *the ships themselves:* Here begins the famous Catalog of Ships. Catalogs have little appeal to modern
literary tastes, but they were of great interest to Homer's audience. There are several catalogs in the *Iliad*,
but the Catalog of Ships is by far the longest. It contains many puzzles. It begins with BOEOTIA instead
of Agamemnon's realm in the Peloponnesus. Boeotia receives an exceptional emphasis: With 29 entries,
when around seven is usual, Boeotia has by far the most names. After moving onto the territories
bordering on Boeotia—PHOCIS, EUBOEA, ATHENS, and SALAMIS—the Catalog then descends into the
PELOPONNESUS. It does not begin with Agamemnon's realm as one might expect, but with that of
Diomedes, ruler of ARGOS. Oddly, in the Catalog's account of the distribution of power Agamemnon's
realm is cut off from the Argive plain, over which Diomedes rules. Various areas in the Peloponnesus
are then listed, but some are left out entirely, especially in the south and west. After the Peloponnesus,
Homer lists places in AETOLIA across the GULF OF CORINTH, then goes to the IONIAN ISLANDS,
including ITHACA, then drops down to the Aegean but mentions only CRETE, RHODES, and several islands
along the coast of ASIA MINOR. Finally, the Catalog returns to THESSALY from which it derives no less
than nine contingents with a total of ships greater than for central Greece! Furthermore, two of the
Thessalian contingents are landlocked and so could have had only little experience of the sea.
   All in all it is a strange compilation. Why does Homer begin with Boeotia? Why does he omit certain
areas entirely, for example the central coasts of Asia Minor and the CYCLADES? Few of the names can be
identified with known sites, but the Catalog supports the theory that the poet was active in the area of
Boeotia/Euboea; Of course the Euboean port of AULIS is in Boeotia just opposite Euboea. Thessaly, just
north of Euboea, receives strong emphasis no doubt because Homer's tradition of orally composed heroic
verse came through Thessaly: Achilles is a Thessalian hero.
   The Catalog is a showy set piece, demonstrating, in case anyone should doubt, that the poet is remark-
able in his knowledge of the Greek world and the places that men inhabit there, even if it is not a compre-
hensive account. See Maps 1 and 2 for the location of places in small caps; Map 4 for the location of peoples
mentioned in the Catalog, also in small caps; Map 5 for a summary of the homes of the heroes.

508   *Plataia:* In southern Boeotia, site of the celebrated battle of the Greek allies against Persian invaders
in 479 BC.

510   *citadel of Thebes:* Homer seems to imply that the upper citadel, Thebes proper, no longer exists, no doubt
because of the war of the Seven Against Thebes.

514   *young men:* This is the largest number given for a ship's crew, again reflecting the prominence give to the
Boeotians in the catalog.

Askalaphos and Ialmenos were the leaders of those who   515
lived in Aspledon and ORCHOMENOS of the Minyans,°
sons of Ares, whom Astyochê bore in the house
of Aktor, son of Azeus, the modest young girl, conceived
of mighty Ares when she entered into the upper chamber.
For he slept with her in secret. Thirty hollow ships   520
lined up with these men.

              But Schedios and Epistrophos,
sons of generous Iphitos, the son of Naubolos, commanded
the PHOCIANS, who lived in Kyparissos and rocky Pytho°
and rugged Krisa and Daulis and Panopeus, and those
who lived around Anemoreia and Hyampolis, and those   525
who lived beside the bright river Kephisos, and those who
occupied Lilaia at the spring of Kephisos. These men
forty black ships followed.

              The commanders of the Phocians
busily arranged the men in ranks, and they armed
them for battle hard on the left of the Boeotians.   530
The swift son of Oïleus, the Little Ajax, led the
LOCRIANS, by no means so great as Ajax son of Telamon,
but much the less. He was small and wore a linen
corselet, but with the spear he surpassed all the Hellenes°
and the Achaeans, those who lived in Kynos and   535
Opos and Kalliaros and Bessa and Skathê and lovely
Augeia and Tarphê and Thronion along streams
of the Boagrios. Forty black ships of the Locrians,
who live opposite sacred EUBOEA, followed Ajax.

Then there were the raging ABANTES who held Euboea   540
and CHALCIS and ERETRIA and Histiaia with its fine vineyards,
and Kerinthos on the sea and the steep citadel of Dios,
and those who held Karystos and those who lived in Styra—
the leader of these men was Elephenor, descended from Ares.

---

516 *Orchomenos of the Minyans:* Impressive ruins from the Bronze Age are found there, and Orchomenos must
     have been a great power in the Mycenaean period.

523 *Pytho:* That is, Delphi.

534 *all the Hellenes:* Apparently by "Hellenes" Homer here means, uniquely, "all the Greeks," a meaning "Hel-
     lenes" had acquired by the Classical Period (fifth–fourth centuries BC). When "Hellenes" is used in the
     Myrmidon entry (line 688), it means only "those people who live in Hellas," a small territory near Achil-
     les' home in Phthia in Thessaly (Map 2). It is unknown why "Hellenes" was universalized to mean "the
     Greeks," but perhaps through a desire to be connected to Achilles.

545 His father was Chalkodon. He led the Abantes, of generous
spirit. The swift Abantes followed him, who tied their long
hair at the back, spearmen longing to smash with their
outstretched ash spears the corselets on the chests of the enemy.
Forty black ships followed him.

                    Then those
550 who live in the well-built citadel of ATHENS, the land
of great-hearted Erechtheus, whom Athena raised, the
daughter of Zeus, whom the bountiful earth gave birth to,
and she made him dwell in Athens in her rich shrine.
There the young men of the Athenians, as the years roll on,
555 try to win his favor by the sacrifice of bulls and rams.
The son of Peteos led the Athenians, Menestheus.°
There never was a like to him upon the earth
for arranging chariots and the men carrying shields.
Only Nestor was his rival, for he was the older man.
560 Fifty black ships followed Menestheus.

                         Big Ajax led twelve
ships from SALAMIS. He stationed them beside the gangs
of the Athenians.

            And they who held ARGOS and TIRYNS
with its fine walls, and Hermionê and Asinê, embracing
a deep gulf, and Troezen and Eïonai and vine-clad
565 EPIDAURUS, and those youths of the Achaeans who held AEGINA
and Mases—the leader of these men was Diomedes, good
at the cry, and Sthenelos, the son of famous Kapaneus.°
With them came Euryalos as the third commander,
a man like a god, the son of the chieftain Mekisteus,°
570 the son of Talaos. But Diomedes, good at the war cry,
led them. Eighty black ships followed these men.

      Those who held the well-founded citadel of MYCENAE,
and rich CORINTH, and well-founded Kleonai, and who lived
in Orneiai and in lovely Araithyrea, and SICYON,
575 where Adrastos first was king, and those who lived

---

556 *Menestheus:* The great Athenian hero Theseus has previously died.

567 *Kapaneus:* Who died in the war of the Seven against Thebes. The Theban war took place one generation
     earlier than the war at Troy.

569 *Mekisteus:* Also one of the Seven in the war against Thebes.

in Hyperesia and steep Gonoëssa and those
who held Pellenê and those who lived around Aigion,
and through all Aigialos, and around broad Helikê—
over all these ruled King Agamemnon, the son
of Atreus, with 100 ships. Much the largest mass   580
of men followed him, and good ones too.
Among them he put on his shining bronze, proud
like a lord, and he stood out among all the fighting
men because he was the best, and he led
the most men.   585

　　　　And those who held the valley
of LACEDAEMON, cut by ravines, and Pharis and
SPARTA, and Messê with its many doves, and Bryseiai
and lovely Augeiai, and those who held Amyklai
and the citadel of Helos hard by the sea, and those
who held Laäs and lived around Oitylos—his brother   590
Menelaos led them, good at the war cry, with sixty
ships. They were arranged apart. He himself
went among them, confident in his eagerness,
urging them on to war, for he especially wanted
to avenge the turbulence and the pain that Helen   595
had caused him.

　　　　And those who lived in PYLOS and lovely
Arenê and Thryos, the ford of the Alpheius, and well-founded
Aipu, and those who lived in Kyparisseïs and Amphigeneia
and Pteleos and Helos and Dorion, where the Muses
encountered Thamyris from THRACE and put an end   600
to his song as he was coming from Oichalia, from the house
of Eurytos, the man of Oichalia. He boasted he would beat
the Muses themselves in the song, the daughters of Zeus
who carries the goatskin fetish. In their anger they made
him a cripple, then they took away divine song and   605
he forgot how to play the lyre. Nestor from Gerenia
led them, the horseman. Ninety hollow ships
were lined up for him.

　　　　And those who held ARCADIA
under the steep mountain of Cyllenê, beside the tomb
of Aipytos, where there are men who fight in close;   610
and those who lived in Pheneos, and who held Orchomenos°

---

611 *Orchomenos*: Distinct from Boeotian Orchomenos.

with its many sheep, and Rhipê and Stratia and windy
Enispê and Tegea and lovely Mantinea, and those
who held lovely Stymphalos and lived in Parrhasia—
615 the son of Ankaios, Lord Agapenor, led them,
with sixty ships. In each ship embarked many
Arcadian men, knowing in the fight. Agamemnon,
the king of men, had himself given them ships
with good benches to cross the wine-dark sea,
620 because they knew nothing of the sea.

And those who
lived in Bouprasion and shining ELIS,° all that Hyrminê
and furthest Myrsinos and the rock of Olen and Alesios
encloses within—of these there were four captains
and ten swift ships to each, and many Epeians
625 piled on board. Amphimachos and Thalpios led
some of them, descendants of Aktor, one the son of
Kteatos and the other the son of Eurytos.° Powerful
Diores, the son of Amarynkeus, led the others,
and the fourth band godlike Polyxeinos led, son of
630 King Agasthenes, the son of Augeas.

And those from
DOULICHION and the Echinai, the holy islands that lie
across the sea opposite Elis—Meges the equal
to Ares was their leader, the son of Phyleus. Phyleus
the horseman, whom Zeus loved, was his father,
635 but angry with his father he had gone to live in Doulichion.
Sixty black ships followed Meges.

Odysseus led
the great-hearted Kephallenians, who held ITHACA
and Neritos, covered by forest, and lived in Krokyleia
and rough Aigilipa, and those who held ZAKYNTHOS
640 and lived in Samos, and those who occupied the mainland
and the shores opposite the islands—these men Odysseus
led, like Zeus in his cleverness. Twelve ships, with red
prows, followed him.

---

621 *Elis*: Probably here the territory around the city of Elis. The Epeians are the inhabitants of this territory.
Pisa was in Elis, in the Classical Period the site of the Olympic Games.

627 *Eurytos*: Kteatos and Eurytos are the Aktorionê, the twin "sons of Aktor." In postHomeric tradition, they
were Siamese twins, joined at the waist, whom Herakles killed in a savage duel.

FIGURE 2.2 A typical Greek warship.   Although this illustration is from the sixth century BC, its features are the same as earlier ships from Homer's day. The steersman sits on a kind of platform at the rear of the ship, to the right, and steers with a large double-oar. The many rowers are represented as black circles, their shields affixed to the side. At the front of the ship, on the left, at the water line, is a ram for penetrating enemy craft, and, above, a chair for the captain (here unoccupied). The sail (not visible here) is attached to a mast that can be lowered into the belly of the craft on a kind of hinge when not in use. Ropes hold it in place. There is no jib so that such ships could only run before the wind; for this reason, much travel is by rowing. On an Athenian black-figure wine-cup, c. 530 BC.

Thoas led the men of AETOLIA,
the son of Andraimon, who lived in Pleuron and Olenos
645 and Pylenê and Chalkis close on the sea, and stony
Kalydon. The sons of great-hearted Oineos were
no more, he himself was dead, and light-haired Meleager
too had died, on whom it was established that he
would have full power among the Aetolians.° Forty
650 black ships followed Thoas.

          Idomeneus, famous for
his spear work, ruled over the Cretans, those who
hold KNOSSOS and Gortyn with its fine walls,
and Lyktos and Miletos and Lykastos with its white chalk,
and Phaistos and Rhytion, well-populated towns, and all
655 those who lived in CRETE with its 100 cities, these
men did Idomeneus lead, famous for his spear work,
and Meriones, the equal to Enyalios,° the killer of men.
Eighty black ships followed these men.

          Tlepolemos,
a son of Herakles, brave and tall, led nine ships
660 of the noble Rhodians from RHODES, those who lived
on the island of Rhodes in three communities—
Lindos and Ialysos and Kameiros, with its white chalk.
Tlepolemos led them, famous for his spear work, whom
Astyocheia bore to the might of Herakles, a woman he
665 had led forth from Ephyrê, from the river Selleïs,° when he
sacked many cities of the god-nourished fighting men.
When Tlepolemos was raised to manhood in the
well-built hall,° he soon killed his father's uncle, aging
Likymnios, in the line of Ares. Hastily he built ships,
670 gathered a great mass of people, and fled over the sea.
Other sons and grandsons of Herakles threatened him.
He came to Rhodes in his wanderings, suffering much,
and he founded three settlements according to tribe.
Zeus, who rules the gods and men, loved them and the
675 son of Kronos poured out wondrous wealth on them.

---

649 *Aetolians*: Seemingly a reference to the myth of the Kalydonian Boar Hunt, as a result of which Meleager
was killed.

657 *... Enyalios*: Meriones is the fine Cretan archer, aide to Idomeneus. "Enyalios" is another name for Ares.

665 *Ephyrê ... Selleïs*: In northwest Greece, near Aetolia.

668 *well-built hall*: In Tiryns.

Nireus led three nicely-balanced ships from SYMÊ,
the son of Aglaïa and Charops the king. He was the most
handsome man among the Danaäns who went under Ilion
after Achilles, the fearless son of Peleus. However,
he was good-for-nothing and few followed him.°   680

And those who possessed Nisyros and KARPATHOS
and KASOS and COS, the city of Eurypylos, and the
Kalydnian islands°—these Pheidippos and Antiphos led,
the two sons of King Thessalos, a son of Herakles.
Thirty hollow ships followed them.°   685

                               And those who inhabited
Pelasgian Argos,° who lived in Alos and Alopê and Trachis,
who inhabited PHTHIA and HELLAS with its beautiful women.
They were called Myrmidons and Hellenes and Achaeans.°
Achilles was leader of their fifty ships. They did not,
however, concern themselves with wretched war,   690
for there was no one to lead them into the ranks.
Shining Achilles, the fast runner, lay among the ships,
angry because of Briseïs, whose hair is lovely. He had
captured her in LYRNESSOS at great effort, when he
savaged Lyrnessos and the walls of THEBES,° and he   695
overthrew Mynês and Epistrophos, who raged with
the spear, the sons of King Euenos, Selepos' son. Angry
about her, Achilles lay idle, but soon he would rise again.

And those who hold Phylakê and flowery Pyrasos,
the holy ground of Demeter, and Iton, mother of flocks,   700
and Antron, close on the sea, and Pteleos bedded
in grass. The warrior Protesilaos led these men
when he was alive, but before now the black earth held

---

680   *followed him*: One of the strangest of the entries. Nireus, who comes from an obscure island near Rhodes
        and leads a small contingent, is never mentioned again.

683   *Kalydnian islands*: Probably KALYMNOS and some other nearby islands.

685   *ships followed them*: Now the Catalog leaves its cursory review of the islands, not venturing north to SAMOS
        and CHIOS nor going west to the Cyclades, and returns abruptly to Thessaly in the mainland.

686   *Pelasgian Argos*: "Pelasgian" always means "aboriginal," that is, in this case belonging to the preGreek
        peoples. The famous Argos was far south in the Peloponnesus.

688   *Achaeans*: "Achaeans" is surprising because in Homer we usually take the word to refer to all the Greeks;
        here it refers to the neighbors of Achilles.

695   *Thebes*: Thebes in the Troad: see Map 3.

him fast.° His wife, her twin cheeks torn with grief,
705 was left behind in Phylakê, his house only half complete.
A Dardanian killed Protesilaos as he leaped from his ship, by far
the first of the Achaeans. But his men were not without
a leader, though they longed for their commander. Podarkes,
of the blood of Ares, put them in order. He was the son of Iphiklos,
710 who had many flocks, the brother of great-hearted Protesilaos,
though younger. The warrior Protesilaos was the older
and the better man. So the people did not lack a leader,
but they longed for the noble one they had lost. Forty
black ships followed Podarkes.

Then those who lived
715 in Pherai beside Lake Boibeïs, and in Boibê and Glaphyrai
and well-built IOLKOS—Eumelos the beloved son of
Admetos led them, with eleven ships. He was the son of
Admetos and Alkestis,° a wonder among women, the most
beautiful of the daughters of Pelias.

And those who lived in
720 Methonê and Thaumakia, and who held Meliboia and rough
Olizon, Philoktetes was their leader, a great archer,
with seven ships. Fifty men went in each, all of them
mighty archers. But he lay on the holy island
of LEMNOS in terrible pain where the sons of the Achaeans
725 left him suffering an evil wound from a deadly water-snake.
There he lay in pain. But soon were the Argives
beside their ships to think of Philoktetes the king.°
Still, they did not lack a leader, though they missed
their commander. Medon, the bastard son of Oïleus,°
730 put them in order, the son of Rhenê and Oïleus,
sacker of cities.

And those who held Trikka and craggy
Ithomê, and those who held Oichalia, the town of Oichalian
Eurytos—their leaders were the fine doctors Podaleirios

---

704 *held him fast*: Protesilaos was celebrated as the first man to die at Troy.

718 *Alkestis*: Whose self-sacrificing death is the subject of Euripides' (480–406 BC) famous play, *Alkestis* (438 BC).

727 *Philoktetes the king*: Because the Greeks needed the bow of Philoktetes in order to take the city, the subject of Sophocles' (497–405 BC) play *Philoktetes* (c. 409 BC).

729 *Oïleus*: Thus the half-brother of Little Ajax, also the son of Oïleus. Medon is killed in Book 15.

and Machaon, the sons of Asklepios. Thirty ships were arranged
in a row for them.   735

          And those who held Ormenion, and the fountain
Hypereia, and Asterion, and the white peaks of Titanos—
Eurypylos the brilliant son of Euaimon was
their leader. And forty black ships followed him.

     And those who held Argissa and lived in Gyrtonê,
and Orthê, and Elonê and the white city of Oloösson—   740
Polypoites led them, a staunch fighter, the son of
Peirithoös, the son of deathless Zeus. Hippodameia
conceived him by Peirithoös on that day when he took
vengeance on the wild beasts and drove them off
MOUNT PELION to the Aithikes.° He was not alone,   745
but with him went Leonteus of the stock of Ares,
son of high-hearted Koronos, the son of Kaineus.
Forty black ships followed him.

               Gouneus led twenty-two ships
from Kyphos. With him followed the Enienes, staunch
in battle, and the Peraiboi, who had set up their houses   750
near wintry DODONA. They lived in the plowed land
near the desirable Titaressos, which pours its beautiful flow
of water into the Peneios, but it does not mix with the silver-swirling
Peneios, but slips on over the water like olive oil. The Titaressos
is a branch of the terrible Styx, the river of oath.°   755

Prothoös, son of Tenthredon, led the MAGNETES,
those who lived in Magnesia near Peneios and Mount Pelion,
covered with quivering forest. Swift Prothoös
led them, and together went forty black ships.°

Such were the leaders of the Danaäns and their commanders.   760
But who were the best of them—tell me this, Muse!—of the men
and of the horses, who followed the sons of Atreus?

---

745   ... *Aithikes*: Peirithoös was famous because of the war between his Thessalian tribe of Lapiths and the
      wild Centaurs (see Figure 2.3). The Aithikes were a tribe in the PINDOS RANGE in central Greece; Mount
      Pelion, where the Centaurs had lived, is in MAGNESIA east of IOLKOS.

755   *oath*: A god's oath sworn on the underworld river Styx can never be broken.

759   *black ships*: The Achaean catalog ends here. We have heard the names of 44 men, 10 of whom will die in
      later fighting. There are 1,186 ships with an apparent average of 50 men per ship, so 60,000 men. This is far
      more than the number of warriors who seem to be fighting later, but these figures are formulaic.

FIGURE 2.3   Lapiths and Centaurs.   In this relief from the Parthenon in Athens a bearded Centaur seizes the hair of a Lapith youth and prepares to kill him. Homer calls the Centaurs "wild beasts," and it is not clear that he thought of them as half-horse, half-man, as they were always later portrayed. The Lapith is "heroically nude," though he does wear a cloak around his shoulders. This is one of the Parthenon *metopes*, or carved panels, that surrounded the temple high above the line of sight. Marble, c. 430 BC.

Of the horses by far the best were the mares of the son
of Pheres, which Eumelos drove, fast like birds,
like-colored, of the same age, of exactly the same height.   765
Apollo, whose bow is silver, raised them in Pieria,°
both mares, bearing the panic of war. As for the men,
Big Ajax, son of Telamon, was best, so long as
Achilles continued his rage. For he was much stronger,
as were the horses that bore the unequaled son of Peleus.   770
But he lies among his beaked sea-faring ships, enraged
at Agamemnon, shepherd of the people, the son of Atreus.

   Achilles' men made fun along the shore of the sea
by throwing the discus and the javelin and by shooting
the bow. The horses stood beside their cars and munched lotus   775
and parsley raised in the marsh. The well-covered cars
themselves were placed in the tents of their owners.
The men, longing for their captain, whom Ares loved,
wandered here and there through the camp. They did not fight.

   And so they marched as if the whole earth were scorched   780
with fire. The earth groaned beneath them, as beneath Zeus
who thrills in the thunderbolt when in anger he lashes the land
around Typhoeus in the country of the Arimi, where they say
is the couch of Typhoeus.° Even so did the earth groan
greatly beneath the feet of the men as on they came.   785
And swiftly they crossed the plain.

                    To the Trojans speeded Iris,°
her feet like the wind, as a messenger from Zeus who carries
the goatskin fetish, with a sorrowful message. The Trojans
were holding an assembly at Priam's gate, all gathered
together, both young men and old men. Speedy Iris   790
stood near them and spoke. She made her voice like

---

766 *Pieria*: In southern MACEDONIA, north of MOUNT OLYMPOS.

784 *couch of Typhoeus*: Where this was, no one can say; but perhaps the Arimi are the Aramaeans, the
     inhabitants of ancient Damascus and surrounding territories. In Homer's day they were a powerful and
     influential people. The local Semitic dialect, called Aramaean, was the international language and script of
     the Assyrian Empire. The story of Typhoeus is Near Eastern in origin and comes into Greece from Greek
     forts along the Orontes River in northern Syria in the Late Iron Age (c. 900–800 BC). Damascus is inland
     from these forts.

787 *Iris*: The "rainbow." Personified, she is the messenger of the gods. She appears in this capacity ten times in
     the *Iliad*, but never in the *Odyssey* where Hermes plays the role of divine messenger.

the son of Priam, Polites, who was posted on lookout
trusting to his rapid feet, on the top of the tomb
of old Aisyetes,° waiting until the Achaeans should pour
795 forth from their ships. In his likeness, spoke speedy Iris:
"Old sir, always do you love endless talk as if this
were a time of peace. But relentless war is upon us.
I have entered many times into the battles of men,
but never have I seen such an army, so fine, and of so great
800 an extent. They are like leaves, or sand, as they march
across the plain to war against the city.
                                        "Hector, I lay
this command on you especially, and please do as I say.
There are many allies in the great city of Priam.
'Different are the tongues of different peoples scattered
805 abroad.'° So let each man pass on the word
to those whom he commands, then let him lead
forth the men of his city, once he has put them in order."

     So she spoke. Hector recognized the goddess,
and swiftly he dissolved the conference. They rushed to find
810 their armor. All gates were opened. The army rushed out,
the footmen and the charioteers. A great roar rose up.

     Now there stands before the city a high mound far out
on the plain, with an open space on either side, which men call Batieia,
but the deathless ones call the tomb of skipping Myrinê.
815 There on this day the Trojans and their allies were organized
into companies.°

               Great Hector, the son of Priam, whose helmet
flashed, led the Trojans. With him armed the most and the best
of the army, raging with the spear. The brave son

---

794 *Aisyetes*: Never mentioned again.

805 *... abroad*: A proverbial statement.

816 *companies*: Here begins the Catalog of the Trojans and their allies. It is much shorter than the Catalog of
Ships. It shows an erratic knowledge of western Asia Minor beyond the Troad. We hear nothing about
Ephesus or Smyrna on the middle coast, early Greek settlements. Little is known of the interior. The size
of the contingents are never given, and of course there are no numbers of ships. The places in the text in
small caps are found on Maps 3 and 6.

of Anchises led the Dardanians,° Aeneas, whom Aphrodite
bore to Anchises after sleeping with him in the meadows of Ida,   820
a goddess with a mortal man. But Aeneas was not alone.
Together with him were the two sons of Antenor, Archelochos
and Akamas, skilled in every kind of fight.

                          And those
who lived in rich ZELEIA on the lowest foothills of IDA
drinking the black water of the AISEPOS, Trojans°—   825
these men Pandaros led, the son of glorious Lykaon,°
to whom Apollo himself gave the bow.

                          And they who held
Adrasteia and the land of Apaisos, and who held
Pityeia and the sharp mountain of Tereia—Adrastos led
them and Amphios, who wore linen armor, the two sons   830
of Merops from PERKOTÊ. Merops was superior to all

---

819 *Dardanians*: The Dardanians are one branch of the House of Troy. Aeneas gives the history of the royal
     family in Book 20. We can reconstruct the family tree as:

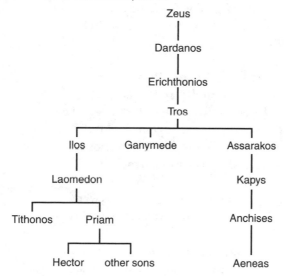

     Dardanos founded a place called Dardaniê on the slopes of Mount Ida, where his descendants
     remained—the Dardanians. Dardanos' great grandson Ilos founded Ilion, the city in the plain, also called
     Troy after Tros, Ilos' father. So the whole Trojan force consists of Trojans, Dardanians, and allies.

825 *Trojans*: Because they have such close relations with the city of Troy they are called Trojans, though they
     are actually from Zeleia.

826 *Lykaon*: No connection with the Lykaon son of Priam, slaughtered by Achilles in Book 21.

others in foretelling the future. He would not allow
his sons to go to man-destroying war. But the two men
were not at all persuaded, for the fates of black death
835 drove them on.

     And those who lived around Perkotê
and Praktios, and who held SESTOS and ABYDOS and shiny
ARISBÊ—Asios, the son of Hyrtakos, was their leader,
a leader of men. His large tawny brown horses
had brought him from Arisbê, from the river Selleïs.
840 Hippothoös led the tribes of Pelasgians, mad with the spear,
who lived in LARISA° with its deep soil. Hippothoös
led them, and Pylaios, of the blood of Ares, the two sons
of Pelasgian Lethos, son of Teutamos.

     And Akamas
and the warrior Peiroös led the THRACIANS, all those
845 whom the powerful stream of the HELLESPONT encloses
Euphemos was leader of the CICONIANS, spearmen,
the son of Troezenos, nurtured by Zeus, the son of Keas.
Pyraichmes led the PAEONIANS with curved bows,
from a long way off, out of Amydon from the wide-flowing
850 AXIOS—the Axios whose water is the most beautiful
that flows over the earth.

     Shaggy-hearted Pylaimenes°
led the PAPHLAGONIANS, from the land of the Eneti.
The race of wild mules comes from there. These were they
who held Kytoros and lived around Sesamon, and who
855 had their famous houses beside the river Parthenios,
and who held Kromna and Aigialos and high Erythinoi.

   Of the HALIZONIANS, Odios and Epistrophos were
the leaders, from a long way off, from Alybê, where silver was born.

   Chromis led the MYSIANS, and Ennomos the bird-seer.
860 Yet with all his bird-seership he did not avoid black fate,
but he fell at the hands of Achilles, the fast runner,

---

841 *Pelasgians … Larisa*: The Pelasgians were, in this case, the preTrojan inhabitants of the land. There were
   fourteen Larisas in Greek lands!

852 *Pylaimenes*: Famous in Homeric studies because he is killed in Book 5, then is alive again in Book 13.
   Probably "shaggy-hearted" means a man whose chest is hairy.

when he slaughtered Trojans and others at the river. Phorkys
led the PHRYGIANS from a long way off, and Askanios, like a god,
from Askania. They were eager to fight in the hugger-mugger of war.

Mesthles and Antiphos led the MAIONIANS, the two   865
sons of Talaimenes. Their mother was the LAKE GYGAIA.
They led the Maionians, who were begotten beneath MOUNT TMOLOS.

Nastes led the CARIANS, who spoke a foreign tongue
and lived in MILETOS and the mountain of Phthires, with its dense
leafage, and the streams MAIANDROS and the high peaks of MYKALÊ.   870
Amphimachos and Nastes were the leaders—Nastes and
Amphimachos, the wonderful children of Nomion. He came
to the war all decked out in gold, like a girl—what a fool!
The gold was of no use to him in fending off deadly destruction,
for he fell at the hands of Achilles, the fast runner, and glorious   875
Achilles carried off the gold.

Sarpedon and outstanding Glaukos
led the LYCIANS from faraway LYCIA, from the whirling XANTHOS.

BOOK 3. *The Duel Between Menelaos and Paris*

But when they were arranged, the opposing companies came
together with their leaders—the Trojans with a clang and a shout,
like birds when the clamor of the cranes fills the sky as they flee
before the winter and the endless rain and with a clanging
5 sound they fly to the streams of Ocean, bringing death
and destruction to the Pygmies.° Early in the morning
they bring to them the rough fight.

                           But the Achaeans came
on in silence, breathing fury, eager in their hearts each
to help the other. As when South Wind lets down a mist
10 on the peaks of a mountain unfriendly to the shepherd,
for theft better than the night, and you can see as
far ahead as you can throw a stone, so did the dust
arise beneath their feet as on they came.

                                Swiftly they
crossed the plain. When, advancing together, the two armies
15 came near, Alexandros,° like a god, appeared wearing
a panther skin on his shoulders, and his curved bow,
and his sword. Shaking in his hands two spears° tipped
with bronze, he called out to all the best of the Argives

---

6 *Pygmies*: The origin of this odd tale of the war between the cranes and the Pygmies is unknown, but it is
sometimes thought to be an Egyptian folktale. It was a fairly popular subject in Greek art.

15 *Alexandros*: Greek "defender of the city" is another name for Paris, appearing in the *Iliad* about four times
more frequently than Paris. The names are used indifferently. The name Paris is not Greek whereas Alexan-
dros certainly is Greek. Hittite tablets from c. 1300 BC, which speak of a place called *Wilusa*, that is, Ilion,
refer to an "Alakshandush" living there, and some think that this must be our Paris. It certainly is odd that
the Hittites associated a Greek name with Troy.

17 *two spears*: In hoplite warfare of the Classical Period, the fighter was armed with a single thrusting spear
that he held at his side while marching in a line against the enemy. The spears of Paris are javelins, meant to
be thrown, and he has two, one as backup. This is usual for Homeric combat, although sometimes the poet
seems to be thinking of combat with the single thrusting spear. Most Homeric fighting revolves around
single heroes at the forefront, more a clash of individuals than one army against the next.

to meet him in dread combat. When Menelaos, whom Ares
loves, saw him coming forth from out of the crowd,   20
striding long, even as a lion rejoices when he chances
on a carcass when he is hungry, either finding a horned
stag or a wild goat and greedily the lion devours it,
although fast dogs and brave young men assail him—
even so Menelaos rejoiced when he saw Alexandros,   25
like a god, with his own eyes. He thought that the criminal
was caught. On the instant he jumped from his chariot, fully
armed, to the ground.

But when Alexandros, like a god,
saw him among the foremost fighters, his heart collapsed,
and he shrank back into the crowd of his companions, avoiding death.   30
Just as when a man sees a snake in the wilds of the mountain
and he jumps back and his limbs tremble and a whiteness
suffuses his cheeks, even so did godlike Alexandros
slip into the crowd of lordly Trojans, fearing the son of
Atreus.   35

When Hector saw him, he reproached
him with words that put Paris to shame: "Little
Paris, nice to look at, mad for women, seducer boy—
I wish you had never been born! I wish that you had died
unwed. That's what I wish. That would be better than
being an outrage, as you are, the object of everyone's   40
contempt. I think that the Achaeans, who wear their hair long,
would laugh aloud thinking that we have chosen as champion
someone just because he was good-looking, while in his heart
there was no strength or power. Was it in such a spirit
that you sailed across the sea in your sea-faring ships, taking   45
with you your friends? You went to an alien people.
You brought back a beautiful woman from a faraway land.
She was the daughter of spear-bearing men, a sorrow
to your father, and to the city, and to the people. To your
enemies it was a joy, but to you a scandal. You don't want   50
to face off against Menelaos, beloved of Ares? You would
soon see what sort of man is he whose ripe wife you
possess! Your lyre will be worthless to you, and the gifts
of Aphrodite—your fancy hair and good looks when you
are mixed with the dust! The Trojans are meek—or long ago   55
you would have donned a shirt of stones for all the evil
you have done."

And godlike Alexandros answered him:
"Hector, yes, you reprove me rightly. You are not
out of order—but your heart is unyielding, like an ax driven
60 through a beam of wood by a man skilled in cutting
timber for a ship,° and the ax increases his power. Thus is
your mind in your chest never afraid. But please don't
throw in my face the splendid gifts of golden Aphrodite!
Not to be spurned are the wonderful gifts of the gods,
65 whatever they give, which you could never get by wanting them.

     "Anyway, if you want me to go to the war, let the Trojans
sit down and all the Achaeans too. Put me in the middle
along with Menelaos, dear to Ares, so that we can
fight over Helen and all the treasure. Whoever
70 is victorious, whoever proves the greater, may he take
all the treasure and take the woman home. Then
may all you others swear oaths of friendship and seal it
with a sacrifice. Then may you live here in the land
of Troy with its deep soil and let the others sail off
75 to Argos where they pasture horses, and to Achaea,
the land of beautiful women."

                So he spoke, and Hector
was happy to hear his words. He went out in front
and held back the ranks of the Trojans by grasping
his spear in the middle. They all sat down. The Achaeans,
80 with their long hair, fired their bows at him and tried
to hit him with their arrows, and they threw stones.

    But Agamemnon, the king of men, shouted
aloud: "Hold your weapons, Argives! don't shoot,
you Achaean youth! Hector, whose helmet flashes,
85 is behaving as though he wants to say something."

    So he spoke, and they held back from battle.
Immediately they fell silent. Hector spoke between
the armies: "Hear, O Trojans and Achaeans with your
fancy shinguards, the speech of Alexandros. On his account
90 this quarrel has arisen. He urges the other Trojans and all
the Achaeans to lay aside their beautiful armor on the rich earth.
He will come forth into the middle and so will Menelaos,

---

61 *for a ship*: Similes are characteristic of Homer's style, but usually they are in the mouth of the narrator, not a
    speaker within the text. Hector's hard heart is like an ax in the hands of an expert carpenter.

whom Ares loves. Then they will fight for Helen and
the treasure. Whoever is victorious, whoever proves
the greater, may he take the treasure and take the woman   95
home. Then let all the rest swear oaths of friendship,
and seal it with a sacrifice."

        So he spoke, and everyone fell
into a deep silence. Menelaos, good at the war cry,
spoke to them: "Now listen to me. Above all the pain
has afflicted my *own* breast. I think that Argives   100
and Trojans should separate. You have suffered a great
deal of evil through the quarrel that Alexandros began.
For whichever of us two death and fate is appointed,
let that man die! And may all the rest of you
be parted as soon as possible.   105

       "So bring in two lambs,
one white, the other black, to Sun and to Earth. For Zeus
we will bring in another. Bring here the majesty of Priam
so that he might himself swear an oath sealed with a sacrifice.
Why, his sons are overbearing, faithless! That way no one
will go too far and violate the oaths of Zeus. I'm afraid   110
that the minds of the young are many times floating in air!
But in whatever an old man chooses to take part,
he looks ahead and he looks behind so that it works out
much the better for both parties concerned."

       So he spoke.
And the Achaeans and the Trojans were glad, thinking that   115
they would soon cease from bitter war. They pulled up
their cars in the ranks, and out they leaped and took off
their armor. They placed it on the ground in close order,
and there was little space between. Hector sent
two heralds running to the city to bring back the lambs   120
and to summon Priam. Lord Agamemnon sent Talthybios
to the hollow ships, and he ordered him to bring a lamb.
Talthybios did not disobey the noble Agamemnon.

   But Iris came as messenger to Helen of the white arms
in the likeness of Alexandros' sister, the wife of the son   125
of Antenor whom the lordly Helikaon, son of Antenor,
had as wife—Laodikê, the most beautiful of the daughters
of Priam. Iris found Helen in her chamber weaving
a purple garment of double thickness on her large loom.

130 In it she embroidered the battles of the horse-taming Trojans
     and the Achaeans with shirts of bronze, which they endured
     on her account at the hands of Ares.

                                  Standing nearby, Iris spoke,
     the swift messenger: "Come here, dear lady, so you can see
     the wonderful actions of the horse-taming Trojans and
135 the Achaeans who wear shirts of bronze. They who earlier
     waged tearful war against each other on the plain, longing
     for death-dealing war—now they are seated in silence.
     War is ended. They are leaning on their shields. Their spears
     are fixed in the ground. Alexandros and Menelaos, dear to Ares,
140 will fight with their long spears—for you!° You will be called
     the wife of whoever is victorious."

                                  So she spoke. The goddess placed
     in Helen's heart the sweet desire for her former husband
     and her city and her parents. Right away she wrapped herself
     in brilliant linen and went forth from the chamber. She wept
145 a gentle tear. She did not go alone, but with her
     went two servants, Aithra the daughter of Pittheus,°
     and Klymenê, with cow-eyes. They came to the Scaean Gates.°
     Priam and his advisors—Panthoös and Thymoites
     and Lampos and Klytios and Hiketaon, of the stock of Ares,
150 and Oukalegon and Antenor, wise men both—they sat
     at the Scaean Gates, the elders of the people. Because
     of old age they had ceased from war, but they were fine
     speakers, like cicadas in the forest who sit on a tree and send forth
     their voice graceful as a lily. Even so did the leaders of the
155 Trojans sit in the tower.

---

140 *for you*: But the duel between Paris and Menelaos belongs to the opening days of the war. By such scenes
     Homer is trying to give the illusion of the passage of time during which Achilles' anger takes effect.

146 *Pittheus*: According to postHomeric accounts, Aithra the daughter of Pittheus, king of Troezen in the Pelo-
     ponnesus, was the mother of Theseus, Athens' greatest hero. Theseus abducted Helen from Sparta when she
     was prepubescent and left her with his mother Aithra near Athens until Helen was old enough for sexual
     relations. But the Dioscuri, Helen's brothers from Sparta—Kastor and Polydeukes—saved the young girl
     while Theseus was in the underworld with his friend Peirithoös, king of the Lapiths (Peirithoös wished to
     marry Persephone, queen of death!). At this time the Dioscuri abducted Theseus' mother and made her
     Helen's slave, and she went with Helen to Troy. But Homer betrays no knowledge of these traditions.

147 *Scaean Gates*: "the left-hand gates," but to the left of what? It could mean the "unlucky" gates because the
     left hand is the unlucky hand; it is here that Achilles will fall in the postHomeric tradition. Many fateful
     events in the war take place before these gates. Homer also refers three times to the "Dardanian Gates," but
     whether or not these are the same as the Scaean Gates is not clear.

When they saw Helen
coming up the tower, softly they spoke to one another,
sending forth words like arrows: "It's no reproach
that Trojans and Achaeans with their fancy shinguards
should have suffered so long for such a woman.
Why, she resembles a deathless goddess to look on her!   160
All the same, though she is beautiful, let her be gone
in the ships. Let her not be a curse to ourselves and to
our children who shall come!"

So they spoke, but Priam called
Helen over to him: "Come here, my dear ... sit here
in front of me so that you can see your former husband   165
and your brothers-in-law and your friends.° It's not your fault,
my dear. It's the doing of the gods who have brought this tearful
war of the Achaeans to me. But tell me, who is that huge man,
this Achaean man so bold and so tall? Others are bigger
but I've never seen such an imposing man, nor one so stately.   170
He looks like a chieftain all right."

Helen answered him,
like a goddess among women: "I revere and am in awe of you,
dear father-in-law. Would that I had chosen foul death
instead of following your son, abandoning my bridal-chamber
and my family, and my late-born daughter, and my lovely companions   175
of girlhood. But that was not meant to be ... So do I melt
away with weeping. But I will tell you, because you ask me.
This man is the son of Atreus, wide-ruling Agamemnon,
both a good chief and a powerful spear fighter. He was
my brother-in-law—slut that I am, if ever there was one!"   180

So she spoke. The old man was amazed, and he said:
"O happy son of Atreus, child of fortune, blessed
by heaven ... I see that many are the youths of the Achaeans
who are your subjects. Once I went to Phrygia
covered in vines where I saw multitudes of the Phrygians   185
riding their horses with glancing eyes, the people of
Otreos and godlike Mygdon, who at that time were
camped on the banks of the SANGARIUS. Because I was

---

166 *your friends*: This famous scene is called the "View from the Wall." It too belongs to the early days of the
war. Priam acts as if he had never before seen the leaders of the Achaean fighters.

FIGURE 3.1 Helen and Priam.   The scene is not from the *Iliad* but inspired by it. Helen is inside—note the column on the left—and pours out wine into a special dish, from which Priam will pour a drink offering. The buxom Helen wears a gown covered by a fine cloak. She pulls the veil away from her face, perhaps to speak. Priam is an old man with a white beard who holds a staff in his other hand. Above him a shield hangs from the wall with a lion blazon, and a sword. Interior of an Athenian red-figure wine cup, c. 460 BC.

their ally, I was numbered among them on that day
when the Amazons came, the equals to men. But not so   190
many were they as the Achaeans with their glancing eyes."

    Next, seeing Odysseus, the old man asked:
"Well, tell me who is this other fellow, my dear child.
He's shorter than Agamemnon, the son of Atreus, but
broader in shoulder and chest to judge by looking. He's put   195
his armor on the rich earth, but he himself, like the leading
sheep in a flock, goes through the ranks of men
like a ram with thick fleece going through a large flock
of white lady sheep."

                    Helen, sprung from Zeus,
answered: "This man is the son of Laërtes, resourceful   200
Odysseus, who was raised in the land of Ithaca, a rugged place.
He knows every kind of trick and cunning device."

    Wise Antenor then answered her: "O my lady,
you have said that aright! He came here once, the shining
Odysseus, on an embassy on your account, with Menelaos,   205
dear to Ares. I received them in my halls and entertained them.
I got to know their nature and their clever tricks.
When they mingled with the Trojans, gathered together,
Menelaos' broad shoulders overtopped Odysseus,
but when they were seated, Odysseus seemed more   210
prepossessing. When they wove the web of speech and counsel
in the presence of all, Menelaos spoke fluently, not many
words though well put—a man of few words who didn't ramble.
He was the younger. But when many-minded Odysseus arose,
he stood stock still and looked down with fixed eyes.   215
He moved the scepter neither back nor forwards, but held it
motionless like a man without sense. He seemed like
a surly man, a fool! But when he let forth the powerful
voice from his chest, and his words fell like wintry
snowflakes, then might no other man equal Odysseus.   220
Then did we not so wonder at the way he looked."

    Old man Priam then asked: "Who is this other Achaean,
brazen and tall, standing out among the Argives
both for his height and his broad shoulders?"

    Helen, who wore a long gown, answered him,   225
like a goddess among women: "This man is Ajax, a huge wall

for the Achaeans. Idomeneus stands right next to him,
like a god among the Cretans, and the leaders of the Cretans
are gathered around him. Full often Menelaos, dear to Ares,
230 welcomed him in our house when he came from Crete.
But now I see all the other of the bright-eyed Achaeans,
whom I could easily recognize and name. But I cannot
see the leaders of the people, Kastor, a tamer of horses,
and Polydeukes, a fine boxer, my brothers, born of the same
235 mother. Either they did not follow from lovely LACEDAEMON,
or they came here in sea-faring ships but now do
not want to enter in the battles of men, fearing
the words of shame and the insults set against me."

So she spoke, but the life-giving earth held them
240 in Lacedaemon, in their dear native land.° Meanwhile,
the heralds carried through the city the offering to establish
a trust-oath to the gods—two lambs and wine that gladdens
the heart in a goatskin sack, the fruit of the earth.
The herald Idaios carried a shining bowl and golden
245 cups. He stood by old man Priam and roused
him, saying: "Rise, O son of Laomedon! The chiefs
of the horse-taming Trojans and the Achaeans dressed
in bronze summon you to come down into the plain
where you can swear a trust-oath with a sacrifice.
250 Alexandros and Menelaos, dear to Ares, will battle
it out with the spear over the woman. Whoever
is victorious will take the woman and the treasure. Then
may all you others swear oaths of friendship and seal
the oath with a sacrifice. Then may we live here in Troyland
255 with its deep soil, and the others may sail off to Argos where
they pasture horses, and to Achaea, land of beautiful women."

So he spoke, and the old man shivered. He ordered
his companions to yoke up a team. Quickly they obeyed.
Priam mounted. He drew back the reins. Beside him
260 Antenor stepped into the supremely beautiful car.
The two of them went through the Scaean Gates and onto
the plain, drawn by their fast horses. They rode out into

---

240   *land*: Kastor and Polydeukes had been killed on a cattle raid, according to later tradition. The brothers were
     not known as the Dioscuri, "the sons of Zeus," protectors of horseman and sailors, until the late
     fifth century BC.

the area between the Trojans and Achaeans. They stepped
onto the bountiful earth. They went into the middle
of the Trojans and the Achaeans. Immediately the king of men,   265
Agamemnon, stood up, and Odysseus of many minds.

The noble heralds prepared the trust-oath with a sacrifice.
They mixed wine in a bowl. They poured out water
over the hands of the chiefs. The son of Atreus
drew with his hand the knife that always hung beside   270
his sword-scabbard. He cut a lock of hair from the heads
of the lambs. Then the heralds apportioned it among the chiefs
of the Trojans and the Achaeans.

                         Agamemnon raised his hands
and he prayed in a loud voice: "Father Zeus, who rules
from Ida,° most glorious, most great—and Sun, who sees   275
all things and hears all things—and Rivers and the Earth,
and you who beneath the earth take vengeance on men
who have died,° whoever has sworn a false oath—be you
witnesses, protect these trust-oaths. If Alexandros kills
Menelaos, then let him have Helen and the treasure too,   280
and let us sail away in our sea-faring ships. But if
light-haired Menelaos kills Alexandros, then may
the Trojans give up Helen and all the treasure and pay
a suitable recompense, one such as men not yet born
will speak of. If Priam and the children of Priam do not   285
want to pay the recompense when Alexandros falls,
then I will myself fight on because of the recompense,
staying right here until I find an end to the war!"

He spoke and cut the throats of the sheep with the
terrible bronze. He placed the sheep on the ground, gasping   290
for breath. The bronze had taken their strength. They took
wine in their cups from the big bowl and poured it out.
They prayed to the gods who last forever. One of the Achaeans
or the Trojans would say: "Zeus most glorious, greatest,
and all the other deathless gods—whichever of the   295

---

275 *from Ida*: The Mount Ida in the Troad, not the Mount Ida in Crete near which Zeus was born.

278 *who have died*: Presumably he means the Furies, or Erinyes, but nowhere else in Homer do we find the notion
      that the ordinary human's sinful behavior in this world is punished in the next (the fates of such great sinners
      as Tantalos in the underworld of *Odyssey* Book 10 are unique and do not apply to the average person).

two parties should first do harm against these oaths,
may their brains flow forth onto the ground, just as this
wine, not only their own brains but those of their children.
May their wives be the prey to others!" So they spoke,
300 but the son of Kronos did not grant them fulfillment.

   Priam, the son of Dardanos, then spoke in their midst:
"Hear me, Trojans and Achaeans with the fancy
shinguards—now I shall go back to windy Ilion, for
I cannot bear to see with my own eyes my dear son fight
305 with Menelaos, dear to Ares. But Zeus and the other
deathless gods know on which one is fixed the doom
of fate and death."

              He spoke and the godlike man
placed the sheep into the car. He went up himself
and pulled back the reins. Antenor got into the exceedingly
310 beautiful car beside him and the two men went back
to Ilion. Hector, the son of Priam, and shining
Odysseus first measured out a space. Then they took lots
and shook them in a bronze helmet to determine who
would first throw his bronze spear. The people prayed.
315 They raised their hands to the gods. Thus would one
Achaean or Trojan say: "Father Zeus, ruling
from Ida, most glorious, greatest—whichever one brought
these troubles on both peoples, grant that he
may die and enter the house of Hades, but to us
320 may there come friendship and trust-oaths."

◀◉   So they spoke. Great Hector, whose helmet flashes,
shook the helmet while looking backward. Swiftly the lot
of Paris flew out. The men sat down in ranks according
to where they had hitched their high stepping horses.
325 They set down their inlaid armor. Shining Alexandros put on
his gorgeous weaponry around his shoulders, the husband
of Helen with the lovely hair. First he placed the fine-looking
shinguards around his shins, fitted with silver anklets.
Next, he placed the breastguard of his brother Lykaon
330 around his breast, and he fitted it to himself.°

---

330 *to himself*: As an archer, Paris has no breastguard. Achilles later murders Paris' brother Lykaon in a pathetic
     scene on the banks of the Skamandros River (Book 21).

He cast a sword with silver rivets around his shoulders,
a bronze one, and then a shield, big and strong.
On his powerful head he placed a well-crafted helmet
with a horse-hair crest. The crest was awesome as it
nodded down. He took up his sturdy spear, fitted   335
to his hand. Then in the same way Menelaos, a man
of war, put on his own armor.

                    When they had armed themselves
on either side of the throng, they went forth glaring dreadfully
into the middle space between the Trojans and Achaeans.
Everyone was amazed when they saw them, both the horse-taming   340
Trojans and the Achaeans in their fancy shinguards. The men
stood near each other in the space marked off. They shook
their spears in anger. Alexandros threw his spear with
its long shadow, and he struck the shield of the son of Atreus,
perfectly round, but the bronze did not break through.   345

   The point of the spear was bent against the strong shield.
Then the son of Atreus, Menelaos, rushed on him
with his spear, praying to Zeus: "Zeus, king, allow me
to take revenge on the man who first wronged me, noble
Alexandros! Subdue him beneath my hands so that anyone   350
of those yet to be born may shudder to harm his host,
one who has extended friendship!"

                    He spoke, and brandishing
his spear with its long shadow he threw, and he struck
the perfectly round shield of the son of Priam. The powerful
spear went through the light-reflecting shield and through   355
the ornately decorated breastguard. The spear tore through the shirt
and slipped beside the flesh over the ribs. Paris bent away
and just escaped black death. The son of Atreus
then drew his sword with silver rivets and, raising
it high, brought it down on the ridge of Paris' helmet.   360
The sword broke in three or four pieces and fell from his hand.

   The son of Atreus groaned and looked into the broad heaven:
"Father Zeus, there is no god more harmful than you!
Here I thought that I'd take vengeance on Alexandros
for his wicked ways, but now the sword in my hand   365
is broken and my spear is flown from my hands, for nothing!
I did not hit him!"

FIGURE 3.2   The duel between Menelaos and Paris.   On the left, Helen, holding a piece of yarn (?), stands behind Menelaos as he draws his sword and attacks Paris, just as Homer describes. Paris holds a spear in his right hand and runs away, but Artemis—with her emblem, the bow—not Aphrodite, stands behind Paris, perhaps because Artemis always favors Trojan affairs. The warriors are dressed as typical fifth-century BC hoplites with breastplate and helmet, except that they do not have shinguards (*greaves*). Their shields have a strap for the arm and a handgrip, never found in Homer, where shields are suspended over the shoulder by a baldric (*telamon*); some shields are as large as the whole body (see Figure 4.1). The artist is recreating the scene to include elements he remembers from Homer's story, but he is careless about details: Helen favored Menelaos; Paris ran away; the gods supported Paris. All the figures are labeled except for Helen. Athenian red-figure wine cup found in Capua, Italy, c. 480 BC.

He spoke, and rushing in
he seized Paris by the helmet, by its thick horsehair.
Whirling him around, he dragged him toward the Achaeans
with their fancy shinguards. The embroidered strap   370
beneath Paris' tender throat, which stretched tight
beneath his chin to hold the helmet, choked him.

And now would Menelaos have dragged Paris away,
and earned undying glory, if Aphrodite, the daughter of Zeus,
had not been quick to see. To Menelaos' harm, she broke   375
the strap made from a slaughtered ox. The helmet came away
in Menelaos' powerful hand. He spun it around and threw
it into the crowd of Achaeans with fancy shinguards
and his trusted companions gathered it up. He sprang back,
eager to kill with his bronze spear,° but Aphrodite   380
easily snatched Paris up. She covered him with a thick
mist and placed him down in his fragrant, sweet-smelling
chamber. She herself went to call Helen.

                              Aphrodite found her in
the high tower, surrounded by Trojan women.
With her hand she took hold of Helen's fragrant gown   385
and tugged at it, looking like a very old woman, a comber
of wool who had worked the beautiful wool when Helen
lived in Lacedaemon—and Helen loved her very much.

In the likeness of this woman the divine Aphrodite spoke:
"Come with me! Alexandros calls you home. He's in   390
his chamber on the inlaid couch. He shimmers with beauty.
He is dressed in beautiful clothes. You would hardly say
that he came from warring with an enemy, but rather that he
was about to go to a dance, or that he sits there as if
he'd just come from a dance."   395

                              So she spoke, and she aroused
the spirit in Helen's breast, who recognized the exquisite
throat of the goddess and her lovely breast and her flashing
eyes. Helen was amazed and addressed her by name:
"Great lady, why do you want to fool me so? I suppose
you would now lead me further, into the dense cities of Phrygia   400

---

380   *bronze spear*: It is not clear where he got this spear, since he seems to have begun with one spear, which he
      has already cast.

or lovely Maeonia,° if perhaps there is someone there
among mortal men who is dear to you. For as it is,
Menelaos has overcome the noble Alexandros and he wants
to lead me—hateful as I am!—home with him.
405 For this reason you have come here with your treacherous
thoughts. But go to him—sit by his side. Give up the way
of the gods! Let your feet no longer carry you to Olympos.
You can fuss over Paris and guard him until he either
makes you his wife—or more likely his concubine!
410 I will not go there. That would be a subject for reproach,
to bed with him now. All the Trojan women will blame me
after. This pain in my heart has no end."

                                                        In anger the divine
Aphrodite answered: "Don't provoke me, you little hussy!
I may abandon you in my anger. For I may hate you even
415 as I now love you fully. I may construct a destructive hate
shared by Trojans and Danaäns alike.° You would then suffer
a vicious fate."

                    So she spoke, and Helen, of the line
of Zeus, was afraid. She went in silence, covering herself
in a bright luminous cloak. The Trojan women did not
420 notice her. The goddess led the way. When they came
to the fine house of Alexandros, the slaves quickly
turned to their duty while Helen went into the high-roofed
chamber, a goddess among women. Aphrodite, who loves
laughter, took a chair for her and placed it opposite
425 Alexandros. There Helen sat down, looking the other way,
the daughter of Zeus who carries the goatskin fetish.

     She rebuked her husband with this word: "You've come
from the war. Would that you had perished there,
overcome by a stronger man, who used to be my husband.
430 Once you boasted that you were stronger in hand and better
with the spear than Menelaos, dear to Ares. Well,
go then and call out Menelaos, the war lover, to fight
you again in the hand-to-hand! … but no, don't do that,

---

401   *Phrygia or lovely Maeonia*: See Map 6.

416   *Trojans and Danaäns alike*: That is, a mutual hatred for Helen, when she might be killed by the Trojans as an
      adulteress.

don't go up against Menelaos, don't be so foolish as to fight him,
or likely he will kill you with his spear ..."   435

                              Paris answered her:
"Do not rebuke me with your rough words. For now
Menelaos has beaten me with the help of Athena, but some
other time I will beat him. We have gods on our side too.
But come, dear, let us now make love, and lie down together,
for never has so much desire so enfolded my soul,   440
not when I first carried you from lovely Lacedaemon
and sailed away in my sea-faring ships, and on a rocky
island I made love to you—as I long for you now in love,
and delicious desire seizes me."

                              He spoke. He led her to
the bed and his wife followed. And so the two of them   445
made love on the bed, whose mattress was made
of cords. But the son of Atreus wandered through the crowd
like a wild animal, to see if he could see the godlike
Alexandros somewhere.° But no one of the famous Trojans
or their allies could show Alexandros to Menelaos, whom   450
Ares loves. Not for affection did they hide him, if someone
had seen him, for they hated Paris like black death.

    The king of men, Agamemnon, spoke then: "Hear me
Trojans and Dardanians and allies! Victory seems to belong
to Menelaos, dear to Ares, and you must therefore give up   455
Helen and the treasure along with her, and you must pay a
suitable recompense, which those still not born will speak of."
So spoke the son of Atreus. And the Achaeans applauded.

---

449 *somewhere*: The scene is more slapstick. Menelaos is looking everywhere for Paris who at that very moment
     is having sex with Menelaos' wife!

BOOK 4. *Trojan Treachery, Bitter War*

The gods, seated beside Zeus, held assembly in the chamber
with the golden floor. The queenly Hebê° poured out
nectar among them. They drank to one another as they looked
out over the city of the Trojans.

Suddenly the son
5 of Kronos tried to provoke Hera with jeering words,
speaking slyly:° "Menelaos has two helpers in the
goddesses, Argive Hera and Alalkomenian Athena.°
They take pleasure in sitting apart and looking in on the action
while Aphrodite, who loves to laugh, always goes beside
10 Prince Paris and pushes away fate. Why just now
she saved him when he thought he was going to die!
Anyway, Menelaos, dear to Ares, won the match.
Let us therefore consider how things will be. Shall
we rouse up wicked war and the horrible din of battle,
15 or shall we sponsor friendship between the two sides?
If friendship seems right, and a sweet thing to all, then
might the city of King Priam still exist, and Menelaos
can carry Helen of Argos home."

So Zeus spoke,
and Athena and Hera murmured among themselves.
20 They sat side by side, devising trouble for the Trojans.
Athena was silent and said nothing, though she was furious
with her father, and a divine anger had seized her. But Hera's
breast could not contain her anger and she said:
"Most august son of Kronos, what a word you have
25 spoken! You only want to make my labor useless and
without effect, and the sweat that I sweated, and the two
horses worn out with the effort of bringing the people

---

2 *Hebê:* "Youth," a child of Zeus and Hera and wife of Herakles after he ascended to Olympos.

6 *slyly:* Zeus needs to get the fighting going again so that he can fulfill his promise to Thetis.

7 *Alalkomenian Athena:* The obscure epithet seems to mean "defender."

together to do evil to Priam and his sons° ... Go ahead!
But the other gods are not going to like it."

                                    Zeus, who assembles
the clouds, was angry with her, and he said: "Strange   30
goddess, how has Priam and the sons of Priam done you
such harm that you relentlessly rage to destroy the well-founded
city of Ilion? Maybe if you went inside the gates and
the high walls and devoured Priam *raw* and the sons
of Priam and the other Trojans—maybe then you would   35
assuage your anger! But do what you wish. I don't
want this quarrel to be a cause of discord between the two
of us in times to come. And I'll tell you something else,
and you pay careful attention. When the day comes
that I am eager to destroy a city whose inhabitants   40
are dear to you, don't get in the way of my anger!
Let it go! For I agreed with you on this, but against
the desire of my heart. For of all the cities inhabited
by mortal men beneath the sun and the starry heaven
holy Ilion is most honored in my heart, and Priam and the   45
people of Priam with the strong ash spear. For my altar has
never lacked in the equal feast, or in the offerings of wine,
or in the scent of burned flesh. We take it as our due."

   Queenly Hera with cow eyes then answered:
"Well, there are three cities that are much the dearest to me— 50
ARGOS and SPARTA and MYCENAE with its broad roads.
Go ahead, destroy them whenever they are hated by your heart.
I shall not stand before them, nor give them great importance.
Even if I don't want to give them to you, and don't want
to allow you their destruction, I shall not succeed,   55
because you are much the stronger. Still, all my labor
should not be for nothing. For I am a god too!
I have the same begetting as you do. Clever Kronos
begot me as the eldest of all his daughters.
I have my own status because I am the oldest   60
and because I am your wife, and you are king
of all the gods.
                "But let us yield one to the other—
I to you and you to me. The other deathless

---

28 *sons*: Hera bases her complaint on the effort she and her horses expended in gathering the Achaean host,
    now threatened by Zeus's suggestion that they make peace.

gods will follow. You speedily dispatch Athena
65 into the terrible din of battle between Trojan and
Achaean. Let her contrive that the Trojans first begin
to harm the arrogant Achaeans, against the terms
of the oath."

So she spoke, and the father of men
and gods did not disobey. Immediately he addressed Athena
70 with spoken words that went like arrows: "Quickly
go to the armies, into the midst of Trojans and
Achaeans, to attempt to contrive that the Trojans first
begin to harm the arrogant Achaeans, against
the terms of the oath."

So speaking he stirred Athena
75 to act, who was eager even before he spoke.
She darted down from the peaks of Olympos, just as
when the son of crooked-counseling Kronos sends
forth a star, a sign to sailors or to the broad host of
an army, a shining thing from which many sparks fly—
80 like that did Pallas Athena dart to the earth. She leaped
into the middle of them. An amazement fell on all
when they saw the portent, both the horse-taming Trojans
and the Achaeans with fancy shinguards. One would turn
to his neighbor and say: "Watch out, there will be hateful
85 war again and the terrible din of battle! Either that or
Zeus will set up a friendship between the two sides.
After all, he dispenses battle among men." So would
one of the Achaeans or Trojans say to his neighbor.

Athena entered the crowd of Trojans in the likeness
90 of Laodokos, a son of Antenor,° strong in the spear-fight.
She sought out Pandaros, who was like a god. She found
the strong and noble son of Lykaon. He was standing there
surrounded by powerful ranks of fighters with shields,
who had followed him here from the waters of the AISEPOS.°

95 Standing close, she spoke words that went like arrows:
"Will you now be persuaded, wise son of Lykaon? Be daring!
Let fly a swift arrow at Menelaos. You will then earn

---

90 *Antenor*: One of the most prominent of the Trojan elders, an adviser to Priam.

94 *Aisepos*: The Aisepos River is in the foothills of Mount Ida about 70 miles east of Troy (Map 3).

the thanks of the Trojans and glory from them, and above all
from chief Alexandros. You would then earn splendid
gifts from him before others if he should see the warrior   100
Menelaos, the son of Atreus, overcome by your shaft
and thrown on the grievous fire. So come, shoot your
arrow at the glorious Menelaos. Make a vow to Apollo
the wolf-god,° famous for his bow, that you will perform
a magnificent sacrifice of yearling lambs once you   105
get home to your city of sacred ZELEIA."°

                    So spoke
Athena, and she persuaded his thoughtless mind. Immediately
Pandaros uncovered his polished bow, made from
the horn of a full-grown wild goat that he himself
had struck beneath its breast as it came forth from a rock.   110
Lying in ambush, he hit it in the chest and it fell
backwards into the rock. From its head grew horns
four feet long. These the hornworker fashioned and fitted
together. He smoothed the whole thing carefully and fitted
to it a tip of gold.°   115

            Pandaros placed the bow down well
against the ground, and he stretched it, bending it backwards.
His noble companions held their shields in front of him
so that the fighting sons of the Achaeans would not leap up
before he struck the warrior son of Atreus. He opened
the lid of the quiver. He took out a feathered arrow   120
that had never been shot, the support of black pain,
and quickly Pandaros fitted the terrible shaft to the string.
He vowed to Apollo, the wolf-god, famous for his bow,
that he would perform a magnificent sacrifice of yearling
lambs once he got home to his city of sacred Zeleia.   125
He drew the bow, gripping at the same time the notched arrow
and the string made of ox sinew. He pulled the string

---

104 *wolf-god*: The meaning of the Greek *lukêgenês* is uncertain, either deriving from *lukos* "wolf" or from *Lycia*, a place
     near the Troad with which Pandaros is associated (not the better known Lycia in southern Asia Minor).

106 *Zeleia*: Northeast of Troy (Map 6).

115 *tip of gold*: Homer seems to be describing a "composite bow" made from horn, wooden staves, and sinew.
     The horn is inlaid on the inside of the wooden staves and the sinew is laminated to the backside, making a
     weapon with considerably more power than if just made of wood. The tip serves to catch a loop in the end of
     the string attached to the other end of the bow. Nomadic warriors and hunters on the plains of Asia seem to
     have invented the mighty composite bow in the second millennium BC.

FIGURE 4.1 **The "Lion-hunt" dagger from the shaft graves of Mycenae, c. 1600 BC.**
Discovered by Heinrich Schliemann in the late nineteenth century, many scholars find remote
echoes of this kind of fighting in Homeric accounts, preserved in the oral tradition. Here the shields
are "like towers" and are carried by a strap around the neck, the *telamon*. On the far left a man wields
a Cretan-style figure-of-eight shield, made of a convex frame covered by cowhides (unfortunately,
no examples survive). The man wears no armor. He carries the single thrusting spear. Next is a
bowman without shield. In the middle, the man's shield is rectangular-shaped. The man to his
right uses his figure-of-eight cowhide shield as protection against the lion, which he threatens with
a single spear. In front him lies the body of a companion, killed by the lion. The companion also
carried a rectangular tower-like shield, which stans upright. Gold, bronze, and niello, sixteenth
century BC, from Tomb IV, Mycenae.

to his breast and the iron arrowhead° to the bow.
And when he had bent the great bow into a circle, the bow
twanged, the string cried aloud, the sharp arrow leaped, 130
longing to fly through the crowd.

But the blessed gods did not
forget you, my Menelaos!° Above all, the booty-bringing
daughter of Zeus, who stood before you and brushed aside
the piercing shaft. Why, Athena brushed away the arrow
from the flesh as a mother brushes aside a fly from her child 135
when he lies in sweet sleep. She directed it to where the golden
clasps of the belt were fastened and the chest-protector doubled.
The bitter arrow fell on the clasp and was driven through
the fancy belt, and through the highly worked chest-protector
and the belly-protector too, which he wore as a screen and guard 140
for his flesh against any arrow, a main line of defense.°
Yet even through this the arrow pierced and scratched
the outermost flesh of the man. Immediately the dark blood
flowed from the wound. It was as if when a woman from MAEONIA
or CARIA stains ivory with Phoenician scarlet to be a cheek-piece 145
for horses. It lies in a chamber, though many horsemen
pray that they can wear it—a delight for the king,
both a decoration for his horse and a boast for the driver—
like that, my Menelaos, were your handsome thighs stained
and your legs and the beautiful ankles beneath. 150

Agamemnon,
the king of men, shivered when he saw the black blood
run down from the wound. The warrior Menelaos shivered
too. But when he saw that the sinew and the barbs were outside
the flesh, then his breath-soul was gathered back into his breast.

With a heavy moan King Agamemnon spoke, holding 155
Menelaos by the hand, and his companions moaned too:
"Dear brother, it is your *death* I swore with the oath and sacrifice,
setting you out alone before the Achaeans to fight with
the Trojans. Now the Trojans have shot you and trampled
down the trust-oaths! But not for nothing are Oath and the blood 160

---

128 *arrowhead*: Ordinarily, weapons in Homer are made of bronze and everyday implements are made of iron, but here the arrowhead is iron.

132 *my Menelaos*: Homer sometimes addresses his character directly, mostly Menelaos (seven times) and Patroklos (eight times, all in Book 16), as if he felt a special sympathy for the character.

141 *line of defense*: We cannot reconstruct exactly what Homer means by these pieces of armament.

of lambs and the drink offerings of unmixed wine, and handshakes
in which we place our trust. Even if at the moment the Olympian
does not bring all to fulfillment, in the end he does,°
and that man pays a heavy price not only with his own life
165 but with the lives of his wife and children. For I know
this in my heart and soul: The day will come
when sacred Ilion will be destroyed and Priam
and the people of Priam with their fine ash spears.
Zeus, Kronos' son, from his high throne, dwelling
170 in the upper air, will shake his dark goatskin fetish over all,
furious because of this deception. Surely these things
will come to pass.
              "But O Menelaos, a terrible grief will
you bring if you die and fill out your allotment of life.
Most despised would I then return to thirsty Argos.° Right away
175 the Achaeans would remember the land of their fathers, and we
would leave to Priam and the Trojans Argive Helen,
something to boast about. The earth will rot away your bones
as you lie in the land of Troy, your task unfinished.
And thus will one of the haughty Trojans say
180 as he leaps on the tomb of brave Menelaos: 'Thus did
Agamemnon fulfill his anger! He led an Achaean army
here to no purpose—he has gone home to his dear native land
with empty ships, leaving the good Menelaos.' So he
will speak in times to come. But on that day may the broad
185 earth open for me!"

              But light-haired Menelaos spoke
cheeringly to him: "Courage, don't panic the Achaeans.
The sharp arrow is not fixed in a mortal place. The belt stopped
it before it could penetrate through, and the flashing
skirt beneath, and the belly-protector and chest-protector
190 that the bronze workers made."

              King Agamemnon answered him:
"May that only be true, dear Menelaos! But the doctor will have
a look—he'll apply a poultice that will stop the black pain."

---

163 *in the end he does*: The first expression in Greek literature of the powerful dogma that Zeus punishes wrong-
     doing in the end.
174 *Argos*: Agamemnon does not mean the city of Argos, which belongs to Diomedes, but to the Peloponnesus
     in general.

Immediately he spoke to his godlike herald, Talthybios:
"Talthybios, call over Machaon right away, the son
of Asklepios,° a good doctor, so that he can have a look   195
at the warrior Menelaos, the son of Atreus. Somebody
skilled in archery has shot him with an arrow, a Trojan
or a Lycian. Glory for him, but gloom for us!"

                             So he spoke,
and his herald obeyed him. He went through the army of bronze-shirted
Achaeans, looking everywhere for Machaon. He saw him standing   200
there in the midst of the powerful ranks of shield-bearers
who had followed from Trikê,° a land that nourishes horses.
Standing near, he spoke words that went like arrows: "Get up,
son of Asklepios, King Agamemnon is calling for you to have a look
at the warrior Menelaos, captain of the Achaeans. Somebody   205
skilled in archery has shot him with an arrow, a Trojan
or Lycian. Glory for him, but gloom for us!"

     So he spoke, and he stirred up the spirit in Machaon.
Machaon went through the crowded army of the Achaeans.
But when he came to light-haired Menelaos, wounded,   210
and around him were gathered in a circle the head chieftains,
the godlike man stood in their midst and right away
withdrew the arrow from the clasped belt. The sharp
barbs bent back as he withdrew the arrow. He loosed
the sparkling belt and, underneath, the belly-protector   215
and the chest-protector that the workers in bronze had made.
When he saw the wound where the sharp arrow had struck,
he sucked out the blood and with sure knowledge spread out a healing
poultice, which once the beneficent Cheiron° had given
to his father.   220

             While they busied themselves around Menelaos,
good at the war cry, the ranks of the shield-bearing Trojans
came on. The Achaeans put on their armor too, watchful
of war. Then you would not have seen the godlike
Agamemnon asleep, or cowering, or not wanting to fight—
he wanted to enter the battle where glory is won!   225

---

195 *Asklepios*: In Homer Asklepios and his sons appear to be ordinary mortals, but later Asklepios is of divine descent, the Greek god of medicine.

202 *Trikê*: In THESSALY.

219 *Cheiron*: Cheiron, "hand," was the "most just of the Centaurs," expert in medicine and the other civilized arts. In later tradition he was Achilles' tutor too (see Figure 11.3).

But he let go his horses and chariot inlaid with bronze.
His driver Eurymedon, son of Ptolemaios, son of Peiraios,
held the snorting animals to the side. Agamemnon gave out
a stern instruction to have them at hand whenever fatigue
230 should overcome him as he gave orders through the multitude.

He went on foot through the ranks of men.° And whenever
he came on Danaäns who were eager with their swift horses,
he stood beside them and roundly encouraged them:
"Argives, don't ever give up your angry valor!
235 Zeus will not help liars! Those who first broke
the oaths will pay when vultures devour their tender
flesh! We will carry away the Trojan wives and
their little babies in our ships, once we take the city!"

But whenever he came across someone holding back
240 from the bitter war, he gave them a mighty reproof
in furious words: "Argives who rage with the bow,
wretches, have you no shame? Why do you stand
around, dazed like fawns who are worn out running
over the wide plain? Who stand still and there is
245 no strength in their hearts? Even so you stand around
dazed and do not fight. I suppose you are waiting for the Trojans
to come to where the ships with their elegant sterns are dragged
up on the shore of the gray sea, to see if the son of Kronos,
the cloud-gatherer, will stretch his hand over you?"

250   So he ranted through the ranks of men, giving commands.
He came to the Cretans as he moved through the crowd of men.
These were arming themselves around the wise Idomeneus.
Idomeneus was among the forefighters like a wild boar
in strength, and Meriones was spurring on the rearmost battalions.
255 The king of men Agamemnon rejoiced when he saw them,
and right away he addressed Idomeneus with words
like honey: "Idomeneus, I honor you above all the Danaäns
with their fast horses, in war and in other matters, and at the feast
when the captains of the Argives mix in a bowl the gleaming
260 wine of the elders. Although the others of the long-haired Achaeans
drink an allotted portion, your cup is always full,
just as mine is, to drink whenever you are so inclined.

---

231 *ranks of men*: The following section is called "The Tour of Inspection" (*Epipolesis*), rather like Helen's "View
from the Wall" (*Teichoskopia*) of Book 2 because it gives us information about the Achaean leaders. It is
also part of Homer's scheme of delay as he puts off the fighting one more time.

But rouse yourself for battle. Be now such a one
as once you claimed to be!"

               Idomeneus, the Cretan leader,
made this reply: "Son of Atreus, I will be a trusted   265
companion to you, even as at first I promised and pledged.
But urge on the other of the long-haired Achaeans that we go
at once into battle. The Trojans have wrecked our oaths!
Death and all future pain to them! They were first
violent in defiance of their oaths."   270

               So he spoke. The son
of Atreus moved down the line, feeling pleasure in his heart.
He came to the two Ajaxes as he moved through the crowd
of men. The two of them were putting on their armor.
Around them was a mass of foot soldiers. As when a man
herding his goats sees a cloud from a place of outlook   275
scudding over the sea under a blast from West Wind—
to him, being a long way away, the cloud seems black
like pitch as it passes over the sea, and it stirs up a huge
whirlwind; he shivers when he sees it and drives his herd
into a cave—even so were the thick battalions   280
of god-reared young men around the two Ajaxes, stirred
to go to savage war, bristling with shields and spears.°

  King Agamemnon greatly rejoiced when he saw them,
and he spoke words that went like arrows: "You two Ajaxes,
leaders of men who wear shirts of bronze, the two of you— 285
well, I don't need to urge *you* on! I have no command
for you. You yourselves stir up the people to fight with zest.
I'd ask Father Zeus and Athena and Apollo that a similar
spirit could be found in the breasts of all. Then would
the city of King Priam soon bow its head, taken   290
and raped!"

        So speaking, he left them there and went
onto others. He found Nestor, the clear-voiced speaker
of Pylos who was organizing his companions and rousing them
to the fight. Their captains were Pelagon and Alastor and Chromios
and Lord Haimon and Bias,° the shepherd of the people.   295

---

282 *spears:* The two Ajaxes drive on their troops like a herdsman who, facing a storm, drives on his flocks.

295 *Bias:* These are generic names that recur in the poem but refer to different people. Curiously, Homer omits
      Antilochos, son of Nestor and important later in the poem.

In the lead he placed the charioteers with their horses and cars.
Behind them he placed the foot soldiers, many and noble,
a bulwark in the battle. The cowards he drove into the middle,
where they would have to fight whether they wanted to or not.

300   On the charioteers Nestor laid this command: to keep
the horses in hand and not to drive in a tumult among the crowd:
"Nor let any man trust so in his horsemanship and in
his valor that he desires to fight alone before the others
against the Trojans. But don't hold back—you will be
305 the feebler. If from your car you come on another car,
strike forth with your spear. It is better that you do so.
In this fashion did earlier men destroy cities and walls,
having such a mind and spirit within their breasts."

Thus the old man urged them on, wise in battle
310 from of old, and Agamemnon rejoiced when he saw him.
He spoke to him words that flew like arrows: "Old man,
I wish that your knees were as nimble as your spirit is great,
and that your strength were resolute. But old age, the equalizer,
wears you down. Would that someone else had
315 your years, and you were among the youths."

Then Gerenian Nestor, the horseman, answered:
"Son of Atreus, I wish that I were as I was
when I killed the good Ereuthalion. But the gods do not
give all things to men at one time. I was a young
320 man then, but now old age is my companion.
Yet even so will I remain among the charioteers.
I will encourage them with advice and counsel. That is what
you do when you get old. The young men will wield
the spears, younger than I am and confident in their strength."

325   So he spoke, and the son of Atreus passed on,
rejoicing in his heart. He came on the son of Peteos,
Menestheus the driver of horses, standing there,
and around him the Athenians, makers of the war cry.
But the clever Odysseus stood nearby, and with him
330 stood the ranks of the Kephallenians, hardly weaklings.°
The people had not yet heard the cry of war.

---

330 *weaklings*: The Athenians and Kephallenians are oddly paired. Athens is on the southern mainland,
    whereas the Kephallenians come from the Ionian Islands generally, including Ithaca, far to the west.

The battalions of horse-taming Trojans and Achaeans had only
just stirred themselves to action. They stood waiting
until another battalion, like a tower, should advance and take
on the Trojans and begin the fight.   335

                        When he saw them,
the king of men Agamemnon reproached them, and he spoke
words that went like arrows: "O son of Peteos,
a god-reared chief, you are skilled in evil deceit!
You have a crafty mind. Why do you stand aside
cowering and wait for others? The two of you ought   340
to take a stand among the foremost to face blistering
battle. You are first to hear of my feast when the Achaeans
prepare a banquet for the elders.° Then it is fine
to eat roast meat and to drink wine as sweet as honey
from the cup for as long as you please. But now you would   345
be glad to see ten battalions of the Achaeans, like towers,
fight with pitiless bronze in front of you!"

                        But many-minded
Odysseus, looking with an angry glance from beneath his brows,
said: "Son of Atreus, I don't understand what you just said.
How can you say that we hold back in battle? The Achaeans   350
rouse keen war against the horse-taming Trojans. You will see
if you want, and if you are concerned with such matters,
the father of Telemachos mix it up with the foremost fighters
of the horse-taming Trojans. Your words are empty, like wind."

    When Agamemnon saw that Odysseus was angry,   355
he smiled and took back his words: "Well, Zeus-nurtured
son of Laërtes, Odysseus of many devices, I do not need
to reprove you nor to urge you on. I realize that
the spirit in your breast knows only kindly thoughts.
You and I are of like mind. But come, let us work   360
this out later, if something ill has been said. May the gods
make all like air!"

                        So saying he left them there and went
on to the others. He found the son of Tydeus, the brave
Diomedes standing among his horses and cars. Next to

---

343   *elders*: In fact, Menestheus is not one of Agamemnon's privileged dining companions and is not included
       among the select diners in Book 2.

365 him stood Sthenelos, the son of Kapaneus.° King Agamemnon
reproached Diomedes when he saw him, and he spoke to him
words that went like arrows: "Oh no, son of Tydeus,
the wise tamer of horses, why do you cower? Why are you
staring at the bridges of war?° It was never the way of Tydeus
370 to cower like this but to fight far in front of his warlike
companions. At least that's what they say who saw him
in action. For I never met him or saw him. They say
he was the greatest of all.
            "Once he came to Mycenae,
not as a hostile, but as a guest, together with godlike
375 Polynikes, to gather the people. In those days they were
warring against the sacred walls of Thebes, and they
made a strong request for glorious allies.° The men
of Mycenae were willing to grant their request, and at first
they assented. But Zeus changed their minds by sending bad omens.
380 And so the expedition departed. When they had gone forward
down the road, they came to the grassy banks of the Asopos,°
deep in reeds. There the Achaeans sent forth Tydeus
on an embassy. He went and found the many sons of Kadmos
dining in the house of mighty Eteokles. Though a stranger,
385 Tydeus was not afraid, but he was alone among
the many Kadmeians. He called them out to feats
of strength and easily overcame them in every contest.
    "Such a friend he had in Athena! The horse-goading
Kadmeians grew angry and led out a strong ambush as Tydeus
390 made his way back, of fifty youths. Two were their leaders,
Maion the son of Haimon, like the deathless ones,
and the son of Autophonos, Polyphontes, who holds out
in the fight. Tydeus let lose on them an ugly fate,
killing them all.° One alone he released to go home—

---

365 *Kapaneus*: Who died blasted by Zeus's thunderbolt in the war of the Seven Against Thebes when he
     climbed the wall and shouted that not even Zeus could stop him.

369 *bridges of war*: Apparently referring to the open spaces between the groups of combatants.

377 *allies*: In the background story of the Seven Against Thebes, Polynikes and Eteokles were sons of
     Oedipus, who killed his father and married his own mother. When Oedipus was driven from the throne,
     the sons agreed to rule in alternate years, but after one year of rule Eteokles refused to turn over the throne.
     Polynikes gathered allies in the Peloponessus to attack the city in the war of the Seven Against Thebes,
     seven heroes meeting enemy heroes at the seven gates of Thebes.

381 *Asopos*: South of Thebes.

394 *them all*: The story of Tydeus among the Kadmeians is paralleled by Odysseus' adventure among the Phaeacians
     (*Odyssey* Books 6–8): A stranger appears before a court, challenges the host to various contests, and shows them
     he is the better man. On Ithaca, too, Odysseus comes as a stranger among many enemies and kills them all.

trusting to portents from the gods, he sent forth Maion.   395
Such was Tydeus the Aetolian. But he fathered a son
worse in battle, though better in the council!"

                                So Agamemnon
spoke. Strong Diomedes did not answer, respecting
the reproof from the king whom he revered.° But Sthenelos,
the son of bold Kapaneus, did answer: "No need,   400
son of Atreus, to lie when you know how to speak clearly!
We are far better men than our fathers. We took
seven-gated Thebes when we led a smaller army
beneath a better wall, trusting in the portents of the gods
and in the help of Zeus.° Those men died from their own   405
reckless folly. Please don't place our fathers in like honor
with us."

    But strong Diomedes, glancing from beneath
his brows, said: "My friend, keep quiet! Listen to my word.
I do not hold it against Agamemnon, shepherd of the people,
that he urges on the Achaeans to the fight. Great glory will come   410
to this man if the Achaeans destroy the Trojans and take
the sacred city of Ilion, but great sorrow if the Achaeans
are destroyed. So come then, let us pay attention
to our furious valor."

                       He spoke, and leaped down from his car
in full armor to the ground. The bronze rang terribly around   415
the chest of the chief as he moved. Even one steady in heart
might have been terrified. As when on a resounding beach
the swelling of the sea rises, wave after wave,
driven by West Wind—at first the sea forms a crest
out on the deep, then breaking on the land it makes   420
a huge sound like thunder as around the headlands,
swollen, it rears its head and spits out a foam
of brine—just so the battalions of Danaäns moved
forward, wave after wave, ceaselessly, to the war.
Each captain gave orders to his own men, but the rest   425

---

399 *revered*: It is no more clear why Agamemnon has criticized Diomedes than why he criticized Odysseus.

405 *Zeus*: Sthenelos refers to the successful campaign of the Epigoni, "the Descendants," the sons of the Seven who
fought and died at Thebes in the first unsuccessful campaign. Homer is well informed about the Theban cycle
and a lost poem about the Theban war, the *Thebaïd*, may even have been Homer's composition.

went forward in silence. You would not think that so great
a people had any voice in their breasts, marching in silence
from fear of their commanders, each man flashing the inlaid
armor that he wore.

                But the Trojans were like ewes in the court
430 of a rich man, who stand numberless waiting to be milked
of their white milk, bleating when they hear the voice of their
lambs. Even so arose the clamor of the Trojans throughout
the broad army. For their speech was different, they did not speak
the same language, their tongues were mixed. They were a folk
435 summoned from different places. But Ares urged them on,
while Athena stood behind the Achaeans, and Terror and Fear
and Eris° that rages without end, the sister and companion
of man-killing Ares. At first Eris rears her head
just a little, but then she fixes her head against
440 the sky while her feet bestride the ground, then she casts
dreadful strife into the midst, striding through the crowd,
increasing the groanings of men.

                When the warriors had come
together into one place, they dashed together their shields
and spears in the rage of men who wears shirts of bronze.
445 The bossed shields came together and a great din arose.
Then was heard the agony of the wounded and the boast
of victory as men killed and were killed, and the earth ran
with blood—as when winter rivers run down from the mountains
from their great springs to a basin, and they join their mighty
450 flood in a deep gorge, and the shepherd hears the roar far off
in the mountains—even so did a cry go up, and there was
work as the two sides came together.

                First Antilochos°
killed a man of the Trojans with horse-hair helmet,
a nobleman who fought among the forefighters, Echepolos,
455 son of Thalysios. Antilochos struck him on the ridge

---

437 *Eris*: "strife," "contention." According to later tradition, the goddess Eris was not invited to the wedding of
      Thetis and Peleus, Achilles' parents, but Hera, Athena, and Aphrodite were. So Eris rolled a golden apple
      across the floor, saying it was for "the fairest" of the three goddesses. Paris was to decide in the famous
      Judgment of Paris, briefly alluded to in Book 24 of the *Iliad*. Paris chose Aphrodite, and Helen was his
      reward, so causing the Trojan War.

453 *Antilochos*: First mentioned here, he is the son of Nestor and the first Achaean to kill an enemy in the
      Iliad. He is an important fighter, oddly not mentioned as one of the Pylian leaders in the list earlier given
      (Book 2). He will play a major role in the chariot race of Book 23.

of his helmet with its crest of horse hair, then drove the spear
into his forehead. The bronze point passed inside the bone
and darkness clouded his eyes. Echepolos fell like a tower
in the savage conflict. Prince Elephenor grabbed him by the foot,
the son of Chalkodon, captain of the great-hearted Abantes.° 460
He tried to drag him out from under the rain of weapons,
hoping speedily to remove his armor, but his effort
did not last long. Big-hearted Agenor° saw Elephenor
dragging the corpse and he stabbed him with his spear
of bronze in the ribs where, as he stooped, his shield left 465
the flesh exposed. Elephenor's limbs went loose
and the breath-soul left his body, and over him Trojan
and Achaean made grievous labor, leaping like wolves
upon one another, man grappling with man.

Then Ajax the son of Telamon struck Anthemion's son 470
Simoesios, in the full bloom of youth. His mother bore him
on the banks of the SIMOEIS,° having come down from MOUNT IDA
after following her parents there in order to look after the sheep.
For this reason they called him Simoesios. But he did not pay back
to his parents the trouble of his rearing. Short was his life 475
beneath the killing spear of great-hearted Ajax.
Ajax hit him as he strode through the foremost fighters,
in the chest beside his right nipple. The bronze spear
went straight through the shoulder and he fell to the ground in the dust,
like a poplar that has grown up in the hollow of a great marsh, 480
with a smooth stem, except at the very top there are branches.
The chariot-maker has cut the poplar down with the gleaming
iron so that he might make a wheel for his very beautiful car.
and it lies drying beside the banks of a river. Even so
did Ajax, of the race of Zeus, kill Simoesios the son 485
of Anthemion.

Now Antipos, whose chest-protector gleamed,
a son of Priam, threw his sharp spear into the crowd.
He missed Ajax, but hit Leukos, a noble companion
of Odysseus, in the groin as he tried to pull the corpse
of Simoesios to the side. Leukos fell on top and the corpse 490
slipped from his grasp.

---

460   *Abantes*: From Euboea, the long island to the east of Athens, where alphabetic writing was invented.

463   *Agenor*: The son of Antenor, the prominent Trojan elder and adviser to Priam.

472   *Simoeis*: One of the two rivers on the Trojan plain (Map 3).

FIGURE 4.2   Greek against Greek.   From three hundred or so years after Homer, both men are armed as hoplites, but the warrior on the left is in "heroic nudity," except that he wears shinguards (*greaves*). The design on the shield of the naked warrior is probably a tripod, a metal object of high value. The warrior on the right wears bronze shinguards, a chest-protector (*cuirass*), and a helmet with horse-hair crest. Both fighters use the single thrusting spear. Athenian red-figure painting on a wine-cup from c. 450 BC.

Odysseus was very angered
because of his dead companion, and he strode forth
among the foremost fighters, armed all in shining bronze.
He went up close and took his stand. Glancing
all around him, he cast his bright spear. The Trojans   495
shrank back as Odysseus threw, and not in vain did it fly.
He hit the bastard son of Priam, Demokoön, who had come
at Priam's call from his farms of swift steeds at ABYDOS.°
Odysseus got him with his spear in the temple, angry
because of his companion. The bronze spear point came out   500
the other side and darkness covered his eyes.
He fell with a thud, his armor clanged.

                              Then the foremost
fighters and glorious Hector yielded ground, and the Argives
gave a great shout as they pulled away the corpses
and advanced far further onward. Apollo was outraged,   505
looking down from Pergamos,° and he called out with a shout:
"Get going, you horse-taming Trojans! Don't give ground
to the Argives! Their skin is not made of stone or iron
to withstand the flesh-slicing bronze when they are hit.
Besides, Achilles, the son of Thetis is not fighting   510
among them, but he ripens his bitter rage beside the ships."

    So spoke from the city the terrible god. But the glorious
daughter of Zeus, Athena Tritogeneia,° went among
the crowd of Achaeans with shirts of bronze to urge them on,
whenever she saw a slacker.   515

                    Then fate caught Diores,
son of Amarynkeus, in its snare. A ragged stone
hit his right ankle, thrown by a Thracian captain,
Peiros, the son of Imbrasos who came from AINOS.°
The pitiless stone utterly smashed both the tendons
and bones. He fell backwards in the dust, spreading out   520
both his hands towards his dear companions as he gasped

---

498 *Abydos*. On the Hellespont (Map 6).

506 *Pergamos*: The upper citadel, the acropolis, where Priam and his sons had houses and Apollo had a temple.

513 *Tritogeneia*: Apparently "Triton-born," or "Thrice-born," but Athena has nothing to do with the sea (Triton is a sea-god) and was not born several times. Probably it is a non-Greek name applied for unknown reasons to Athena.

518 *Ainos*: See Map 6.

for breath. Then he who had struck him ran up, Peiros,
and stabbed him by the navel with his spear. All his guts
ran onto the ground and darkness covered his eyes.

525   But as Peiros sprang back, Thoas from AETOLIA hit him
with his spear in the chest above the nipple. The bronze was fixed
in the lung. Thoas moved in and he pulled out the heavy spear.
He drew his sharp sword and stabbed Peiros in the middle
of his belly. Peiros breathed out his breath-soul, but Thoas did
530 not take the armor because Peiros' top-knotted Thracian
companions stood with their long spears, and they drove him back
from them, though Thoas was large and strong and brave.
Thoas was shaken, he retreated. Thus two corpses
were stretched in the dust next to each other, captains,
535 the one of them Thracian, the other a bronze-shirted Epeian.°

       Many others died around them. From that point on
no one might make light of the work of war, even should
he move through the crowd unscathed by arrow or the thrust
from the cutting bronze, and Pallas Athena should be leading
540 him on, holding his hand, protecting him from the rush
of missiles. For many were the Trojans and Achaeans who on
that day lay stretched out beside one another in the dust.

---

535 *Epeian*: A tribal name designating the people who lived in Elis, in the northwestern Peloponnesus, here
referring to Diores.

BOOK 5. *The Glory of Diomedes*

Well then, Pallas Athena gave Diomedes, the son
of Tydeus, strength and boldness, so that he might
stand out among all the Argives and so that he might win
high praise. She lit on his helmet and shield
an unwearying fire, like the harvest star that shines   5
above all others once it has bathed in Ocean.° Just such
a flame did she kindle from his head and his shoulders,
and she sent him into the thick of it where most men
were camped.

         There was among the Trojans a certain
Dares, rich and blameless, a priest of Hephaistos.   10
He had two sons, Phegeus and Idaios, both of them
experienced in every kind of battle. These two
separated from the throng and went after Diomedes.
The two men drove their car, but Diomedes went on foot
on the ground. When they got near, advancing against   15
each other, Phegeus threw his long-shadowed spear first.°
The point of the spear went over the left shoulder
of the son of Tydeus and did not hit him. Then the son
of Tydeus threw his bronze. Nor did the weapon fly
in vain from his hand, but struck Phegeus on the chest   20
between the nipples. He dropped him from the car.

   Idaios sprang back and quit the very beautiful
chariot, not daring to stand over his dead brother.
Nor would he himself have escaped black fate,
except Hephaistos saved him. Hephaistos hid him   25
in night so that their aged father might not be ruined
by grief, but the son of magnificent Tydeus drove off the horses
and gave them to his companions to take to the hollow ships.

---

6 *Ocean*: The harvest star is Sirius, called in Book 20 "Orion's dog." Ocean is the river that surrounds the
    earth. When Sirius is not visible, it is said to bathe in Ocean.

16 *first*: Typically the weaker warrior casts first and fails, then is killed.

When the big-hearted Trojans saw that one of the sons
30　of Dares had run off and the other was dead beside the car,
panic struck. But flashing-eyed Athena took mad Ares
by the hand and spoke to him: "Ares, Ares—
murderer of men, blood-stained stormer of walls,
ought we not now to leave the Trojans and the Achaeans
35　to fight?° Zeus can give glory to whichever side
he chooses. But let us withdraw and avoid the anger
of Zeus."

　　　　So speaking, she led mad Ares from the battle.
She sat him down on the banks of the sandy SKAMANDROS.
The Danaäns turned the Trojans into flight. Each man
40　of the captains got his man. First the king of men, Agamemnon,
knocked down the leader of the Halizones, the great Odios,
who had turned to flee. The spear got him in the back
between the shoulders, and the shaft drove through his chest.
He fell with a thud and his armor clanged about him.

45　　　　Now Idomeneus took down Phaistos, the son of Boros
the Maeonian, who had come from deep-soiled Tarnê.° Idomeneus,
famous for his spear, pierced him with the long shaft
as Phaistos mounted his car. Idomeneus struck his right
shoulder and Phaistos tumbled from the car. Hateful darkness
50　encompassed him. The followers of Idomeneus stripped the body.

　　　　Then Menelaos, the son of Atreus, hit the son of Strophios,
Skamandrios, cunning in the hunt, with his sharp spear.
Artemis had taught Skamandrios how to strike down
all the wild animals that the forest nurtures in the mountains.
55　But Artemis, who pours forth arrows, was no good to him then,
nor was his archery of use in which he earlier excelled.
Menelaos, the son of Atreus, famous for his spear,
stabbed him in the back with his spear as he ran away
before him, right between the shoulders. He drove it through
60　to the other side. Skamandrios fell on his face
and his armor clanged around him.

35　*to fight*: In Book 4, Ares had roused the Trojans, Athena the Achaeans. Now Athena wants Ares off the field
so that Diomedes can show his brilliance. Ares, with typical dullness, complies.

46　*... Tarnê*: Idomeneus, from Knossos, kills Phaistos, the name of a rival Cretan town! The location of Tarnê
is unknown.

Next Meriones killed Phereklos,
the son of Harmonides the carpenter. Phereklos knew how
to make all kinds of delicate things with his hands,
for Pallas Athena loved him above all men. Phereklos
had made the well-balanced ships for Alexandros,   65
the beginning of harm, which became an evil for all the Trojans
and for himself. For he did not know the oracles of the gods.
Meriones pursued Phereklos and when he got close
Meriones hit Phereklos in the right buttock. The spear
went through to the bladder beneath the bone. Phereklos groaned   70
and fell to his knees and death concealed him.

                    Now Meges°
killed Pedaios, a son of Antenor. Although he was
a bastard, the excellent Theano° raised him with care
as if he were her own child, to please her husband.
Meges, famous for his spear, came up close and struck   75
Pedaios with his sharp spear on the back of his head.
The bronze went straight through the teeth and cut off his tongue.
He fell in the dust, seizing the cold bronze with his teeth.

     Eurypylos,° the son of Euaimon, then killed the good
Hypsenor, son of the brave Dolopion, who was   80
made priest of Skamandros. He was honored like a god
by the people. Eurypylos, the brilliant son of Euaimon,
struck Hypsenor on the shoulder with his sword as that man
ran before him, rushing from behind. Eurypylos cut off
the heavy arm. Blooded, the arm fell to the ground. A purple   85
death came over Hypsenor's eyes and overpowering fate
seized him.

          And so it went as they labored in the relentless
contendings. As for the son of Tydeus, you could not say
which side he was on, whether he was the fellow of the Trojans
or the Achaeans. For he raged across the plain like a winter river 90
in flood that in its swift flow wears away the embankments.
The embankments, though tightly packed, cannot withstand
the water's force, nor can the walls of the fruitful gardens
as it comes roaring along, when the rain of Zeus drives it on,

---

72 *Meges*: The leader of a contingent from the island of Doulichion, near Ithaca (Book 2).

73 *Theano*: A priestess of Athena, as we later learn in Book 6.

79 *Eurypylos*: A leader from a town called Ormenion in Thessaly who came to Troy with forty ships. He is mentioned eighteen times in the *Iliad*, so is an important fighter.

95 and many are the handsome works of men brought to ruin—
even so were the thick ranks of the Trojans driven in rout
by the son of Tydeus. The Trojans did not await him,
even though they were many.

But when Pandaros, the good
son of Lykaon, saw Diomedes raging across the plain and driving
100 the Trojan ranks before him, he stretched the curved bow
and aimed it at Diomedes. He hit him in the right shoulder
as he rushed onwards, on the plate of his bronze chest-protector.
The bitter arrow flew through the plate, it went straight
on its way, and the bronze chest-protector was drenched in blood.

105 Then the glorious son of Lykaon boasted over him:
"Get up and go, you great-hearted Trojans, goaders
of horses! I have wounded the best of the Achaeans. I don't
think he can long endure the powerful shaft if in truth
the king, the son of Zeus, sent me forth when I came
110 from Lycia."° So Pandaros said, boasting.

But the sharp arrow
did not subdue Diomedes. Pulling back, he took his stand
beside his horses and his car. He spoke to Sthenelos, the son
of Kapaneus: "Come down, son of Kapaneus, from the car
and draw this arrow from my shoulder." So he spoke, and Sthenelos
115 jumped to the ground from the chariot. He stood beside him
and drew the sharp arrow all the way through the shoulder.
The blood spurted up through the supple shirt.

Then Diomedes,
good at the war cry, prayed: "Hear me, unwearied one,
the daughter of Zeus who carries the goatskin fetish—
120 if ever with good thoughts you stood beside my dear father
in the fury of war, Athena, then now be kind
to me. Grant that I take my man, that he come
within the cast of my spear, whoever it was who hit
me on the sly and now boasts of his blow. He doesn't
125 think I shall long behold the sunlight."

So Diomedes spoke
in prayer, and Athena heard him. She made his limbs

110 ... *from Lycia:* The "king" is Apollo, archer-god and sponsor of archers such as Pandaros. This "Lycia" is
northeast of Troy, not in the far southeast where the major fighter Sarpedon comes from (as we will see).

to be light, and his feet and hands too. Standing
near him, she spoke words that went like arrows:
"Have the courage to go up against the Trojans now!
For in your breast I have placed the strength of your father   130
who never turned aside, such as the horseman Tydeus had,
wielder of the shield. I have removed the mist from your eyes
that lay upon them, so you can recognize who
is a god and who a man. If any god comes here to make trial
of you, don't attack the deathless being—unless it is the daughter   135
of Zeus, Aphrodite, who comes to the war—then stab
her with the sharp bronze!"

        So speaking, flashing-eyed Athena
went away. The son of Tydeus went back and tangled with
the foremost fighters. Although before he was eager to fight
the Trojans, now three times the rage came upon him, like a lion   140
that a shepherd guarding his wooly sheep in the field has wounded
as it leaped over the wall of the sheepfold, but he did not kill him.
The shepherd has roused the lion's might and gives up his defense,
lurking between the outbuildings, and the flock having no
protection tries to flee. But the sheep are heaped in piles   145
next to each other while the lion in his rage springs up
from the high-walled courtyard°—even with such fury did
the powerful Diomedes tangle with the Trojans.

        To begin,
he killed Astynoös and Hypeiron, shepherd of the people.
The first he hit above the nipple, striking with the bronze spear.   150
The second he struck with his great sword on the collar bone
beside the shoulder, and he cut away the shoulder from
the neck and from the back. He let them go and went after
Agas and Polyeidos, sons of Eurydamas, the old man who
prophesied from dreams. But he interpreted no dreams for their   155
homecoming, for the powerful Diomedes killed them.

    Then he went after Xanthos and Thoön, both of them
sons of Phainops,° born late in his life. Now Phainops was worn

---

147   *courtyard*: Pandaros is like the shepherd who wounds the lion, then is overwhelmed by the enraged beast,
       except the lion's strength is increased by the wounding, whereas Diomedes receives his strength from
       Athena, not the wound Pandaros has inflicted.

158   ... *Phainops*: Homer has inherited a large store of names to use in designating minor actors. Mostly these
       names do not reappear or, when they do, refer to different minor characters.

down by grievous old age and fathered no other sons
160 to make his heir. Diomedes killed the sons, he took
away their dear lives, both of them, and he left to the father
moaning and pain, for he did not receive them alive returning
from battle. The near of kin divided the inheritance.

Then he took two sons of Priam, a descendant
165 of Dardanos, in a single chariot, Echemmon and Chromios.
Just as a lion leaps among a herd of cattle and breaks
the neck of a calf as the herd grazes in a woodland
pasture, even so did Diomedes drive the two of them
helter-skelter from their car, quite unwilling. Then he
170 took their armor. He gave the horses to his companions
to take to the ships.

Aeneas saw Diomedes throwing into chaos
the ranks of men and went through the battle and the tumult
of spears looking for godlike Pandaros, to see
if he could find him somewhere. At last he found him,
175 blameless and strong, and Aeneas stood before him and spoke:
"Pandaros, where is your bow and your winged arrows
and your fame? No man here dares compete with you
in this, nor does any one in Lycia boast that he
is better than you. But come now, lifting your hands
180 to Zeus, fire an arrow at this man who is doing such
violence and ferocious harm to the Trojans. He has loosed
the knees of many noble young men. Maybe it is a god
angered with the Trojans because of some sacrifice!
The wrath of a god can be harsh."

The fine son of Lykaon
185 then answered him: "Aeneas, good counselor to the Trojans
who wear shirts of bronze, this man looks like the valiant son
of Tydeus to me. I can tell from his shield and his helmet
with its crest, and his horses. Of course I don't know
if it is a god. If this is the man I think, the valiant
190 Diomedes, it is not without some god's help that he rages,
but some one of the deathless ones who live on high Olympos
must stand near him, shoulders hidden in a cloud.
This god turned aside the sharp shaft as it made
its way to the mark, for I have already fired a shot. I hit him
195 in the right shoulder and the arrow went straight through
the plate of his bronze chest-protector. I thought that I had cast
him down to the house of Hades, but I did not subdue him.

"It must be some angry god! I have no horses
and no car that I could mount, though in Lykaon's halls
there are eleven brand-new chariots, just made. Cloths   200
cover them. Beside each stands a yoke of horses
munching on white barley and wheat. The old spearman Lykaon
ordered me again and again before I set off to the war
from my well-built house—he commanded me to mount
horse and car and to lead the Trojans° through the bitter   205
conflicts. But I wouldn't listen. It would have been better
if I had! I spared the horses. I was afraid that they
would lack feed in the midst of so many men
when they are used to eating their fill. So I left
them and came to Troy on foot, trusting to my bow,   210
which was to do me no good at all.
                             "Already I have fired
at two captains, the son of Tydeus and the son of Atreus.
From both I drew true blood when I hit them,
but that only excited them the more. With bad luck I took
my curved bow from its peg on that day when I led   215
my Trojans to lovely Ilion, bearing pleasure to shining
Hector. If I return home and see with my own eyes the land
of my fathers and my wife and my high-roofed house,
may some utter stranger cut off my head if I do
not smash this bow with my hands and cast   220
it into the blazing fire! It is worthless to me,
like the wind!"

        Aeneas, a Trojan captain, answered:
"Don't talk like that. Things will be no different until
we go up against this Diomedes with horse and car
and take him on in our armor. So come, get in my car   225
so that you might see what sort of horses are these
horses of Tros.° They know full well how to pursue
swiftly, and to retreat in any direction over the plain.
They will carry us safely to the city, if Zeus again
grants glory to Diomedes, the son of Tydeus. But come,   230
take the whip and the shining reins. I will descend

---

205   *Trojans*: That is, his own people, the inhabitants from around Zeleia on the slopes of Mount Ida northeast
      of Troy, who are called "Trojans."

227   *Tros*: This divine breed of horses was begun by Aeneas' ancestor Tros, to whom Zeus gave horses in
      recompense for Zeus's snatching of Tros's son Ganymede, a beautiful prince of the house of Troy.

from the car in order to fight him.° Or you can attack him,
and I will care for the horses."

         The good son of Lykaon
then answered: "Aeneas, you hold onto the reins yourself
235 and keep control of your own horses. They will better pull
the car made of bent rods when they recognize who is holding
the reins, if we have to flee from the son of Tydeus.
I am afraid that they may panic and run wild
and be unwilling to bear us out of the war
240 because they miss your voice, and I fear that the son
of Tydeus might then waylay and kill us both
and drive off the single-hoofed horses.° So you must
drive your own car and control your horses. I'll take
Diomedes on with my sharp spear as he comes at me."

245   So speaking they mounted into the ornate car.
Eagerly they turned the swift horses against the son
of Tydeus. Sthenelos, the fine son of Kapaneus, saw them,
and at once he spoke to the good Diomedes with words
that flew like arrows: "Diomedes, son of Tydeus, dear
250 to my heart, I see two powerful men eager to fight you,
men with boundless strength. One is Pandaros, a straight
shot with the bow. He boasts of being the son of Lykaon.
The other is Aeneas, who claims he is the son
of blameless Anchises, with Aphrodite for a mother.
255 But come, let us withdraw in the car. Don't rage in this
way among the frontline troops or you may lose
your life!"

        Powerful Diomedes glowered beneath his
brows and said: "Don't speak of flight! I don't think you will
persuade me. It is not in my blood to fight by running
260 away, nor to squat cringing. My strength is still steadfast.°
I am not going to mount a car, but I will go against them
just as I am. Pallas Athena will not let me be afraid.
As for these two, their swift horses will not carry them back
from us again, even if one or the other gets away.

---

232 *fight him*: That is, they will ride into the battle and Aeneas will dismount when they are close to Diomedes. Chariots in Homer are ordinarily used as transportation and not as fighting machines, no doubt reflecting actual practice in Greece in Homer's day. Chariots confer prestige and social power on their owners.

242 *single-hoofed*: Apparently to distinguish them from the cloven hoofs of cattle, sheep, and goats.

260 *steadfast*: Even though Diomedes has been wounded.

"I'll tell you something else, and please pay attention to   265
what I say. If wise-counseling Athena gives me the glory of killing
both these men, then you hold back our swift horses
by wrapping their reins around the rail. And remember to rush
upon the horses of Aeneas and drive them from the Trojans to the
Achaeans with their fancy shinguards. For they are of the race   270
that Zeus, whose voice reaches far, gave to Tros as recompense
for his son Ganymede. They are the best horses beneath
the dawn or sun. The king of men Anchises° stole from this line
when, unknown to Laomedon, he had them cover his mares.
From these were born a stock of six in Anchises'   275
halls. Four of these he raised himself at the stall,
and he gave two to Aeneas, the deviser of rout.
If we can capture these horses, we will gain a handsome
reputation."

        So Diomedes spoke to Sthenelos just as
the Trojans came near, driving their swift horses. The good son   280
of Lykaon spoke to Diomedes first: "Son of lordly Tydeus,
stalwart and wise, I guess my sharp arrow did not
finish you off, that bitter shaft! Now I will try to hit you
with my spear, to see if I can take you down!"

    So Pandaros spoke. He balanced his long-shadowed spear   285
and cast. He struck the son of Tydeus on his shield. The bronze
spear-point went straight through and reached the bronze
breast-plate. The good son of Lykaon shouted aloud over him:
"Got you, right through the belly! You won't last long!
You've given me great glory!"   290

                        Without fear powerful Diomedes
answered: "But you missed the mark. You did not hit me.
I don't think that you two will be done before one or the other
gluts Ares with his blood, the warrior-god who carries
the shield!"

    So speaking, Diomedes cast. Athena
guided the missile onto Pandaros' nose next to the eye   295
and it pierced his white teeth. The unyielding bronze cut the tongue
off at the root and the point came out beside the lower part

---

273 *Anchises*: Anchises, Aeneas' father, was also descended from Tros through his mother Themistê, a daughter
     of Ilos (a son of Tros). The breed of horses was inherited by Laomedon, Themistê's brother and the father of
     Priam.

of the chin. Pandaros tumbled from the car. His armor
clanged about him—bright, flashing—and the swift-footed
300 horses turned aside. His breath-soul and his strength
were loosened.

          Aeneas jumped down with shield and long spear,
fearing that the Achaeans would snatch the corpse from him.
He hovered over Pandaros like a lion trusting in its might.
He held his spear and shield before him, well-balanced
305 and round, impatient to kill whoever should come
against him, and he screamed terribly.

                              The son of Tydeus
picked up a boulder in his hand, a mighty deed,
a stone that two men might carry such as mortals
are today, but he easily hefted it by himself.
310 With it he struck Aeneas on the hip where the thigh
bone rotates on the hip bone—they call it the "cup."
The stone smashed the cup, and it smashed the two tendons.
The jagged stone peeled away the skin. Then the warrior
Aeneas fell on his knees and he stayed there. He rested
315 his thick hand on the earth. Black night enclosed his eyes.

      And now Aeneas, the king of men, would have died
if the daughter of Zeus, Aphrodite, had not caught sight
of him—his mother, who bore him to Anchises when he was
herding cattle. Aphrodite placed her pale forearms
320 around her beloved son. She covered him with a fold
of her shining dress, spread before him as a protection
in case any Danaän with swift horses should throw the bronze
into his chest and take away his breath-soul.
She then carried her beloved son out of the war.

325   But the son of Kapaneus, Sthenelos, did not forget
the agreements he had made with Diomedes, good at the war cry.
He held back his own single-hoofed horses from the fray,
lashing their reins to the rail. He ran up to the horses
of Aeneas with beautiful manes and drove them out
330 from the Trojans to the Achaeans with fancy shinguards.
He gave them to Deïpylos to drive to the hollow ships,
his dear companion, whom he honored above all his age-mates
because they were likeminded. Then Sthenelos mounted
his own car and took the glinting reins. Swiftly

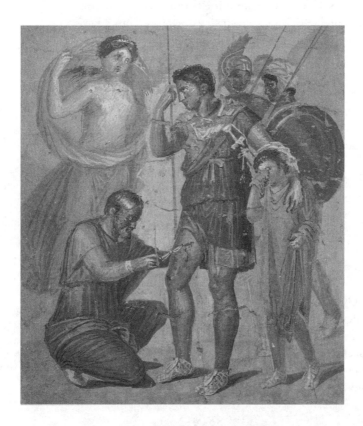

FIGURE 5.1 The wounded Aeneas.   The bare-breasted Aphrodite stands to the left, her cloak around her head in a gesture typical of Roman gods. The physician Machaon cuts the missile from Aeneas' leg, who stands stoically holding his spear, his sword at his side, dressed in a breastplate. The boy would be his son, Ascanius (or Iulus), famous from Vergil's *Aeneid* (c. 19 BC). Other Trojan warriors stand in the background. Fresco from Pompeii, first century AD.

335 he drove the horses with strong hooves, eagerly seeking
the son of Tydeus. But Diomedes had gone in pursuit
of Kypris° with his pitiless bronze, recognizing that she
was a god without strength, not one of those who dominate
in the war of men—no Pallas Athena, nor city-sacking Enyo!°

340   When he came upon her, pursuing through the immense
crowd, he thrust with his sharp spear as he leaped upon her.
The son of great-souled Tydeus pierced the skin on Aphrodite's
delicate hand. Immediately the spear went into the flesh,
passing through the deathless clothes that the Graces°
345 themselves had made, injuring the wrist above
the palm. Immortal blood flowed from the goddess,
ichor, which flows in the veins of the blessed gods.
For gods do not eat bread or drink the shining wine.
Thus they are without blood and are called deathless.

350   With a loud cry Aphrodite let her son Aeneas
fall from her. Phoibos Apollo took Aeneas in his arms
from a dark cloud so that no one of the Danaäns
with their fast horses might throw the bronze into his chest
and kill him.

        Over Aphrodite Diomedes, good at the war cry,
355 shouted aloud: "Get out of here, daughter of Zeus,
leave this battle and the war! Isn't it enough that you deceive
strengthless women? If you are going to enter into battle,
I think you will shudder soon even to hear the word 'war,'
even should you hear it at a distance!"

        So he spoke,
360 and she left, beside herself and much distressed.
Wind-footed Iris took Aphrodite and brought her out
of the throng, wracked with pain. Her beautiful skin
turned black. She found mad Ares on the left of the battle,
sitting down. He had leaned his spear against a cloud
365 and his swift horses were there.

---

337 *Kypris*: Another name for Aphrodite because she was born on Cyprus and had a shrine at Paphos on
     Cyprus. For unknown reasons she is called "Kypris" five times in this book and never again in the *Iliad*.

339 *Enyo*: A war-god, by this time identified with Ares; also called *Enyalios*.

344 *Graces*: In Greek they are the *Charites*, goddesses of feminine charm who often accompany Aphrodite. In
     the *Iliad* Hephaistos is married to a singular *Charis*, "grace."

Falling on her knees, Aphrodite
fervently begged her dear brother for his horses with head-pieces°
of gold: "My beloved brother, save me! Give me your horses
to go to Olympos and the seat of the deathless ones. I am much
pained because of a wound that a mortal man has given me,
the son of Tydeus, who now would fight even with father Zeus."   370

So she spoke, and Ares gave her the horses
with golden head-pieces. She got in the car, much distraught
at heart. Iris got in beside her and took the reins
in her hands. She lashed the horses to drive them on.
The two sped onward. Quickly they arrived at steep
Olympos, the seat of the gods. There wind-footed Iris   375
stayed the horses and set them free from the car
and cast before them immortal food.

But divine
Aphrodite threw herself on the knees of her mother Dionê,°
who held her daughter close and stroked her with her hand.   380
Then Dionê said: "Dear child, who of the heavenly ones
has foolishly done this to you, as if you were doing something
evil in full view?"

Laughter-loving Aphrodite answered her:
"The bold Diomedes, the son of Tydeus, has wounded me,
because I rescued my own beloved son from the war,   385
Aeneas, who of all people is by far the most dear to me.
The dread battle is no longer between Trojans and Achaeans,
but now the Danaäns fight against the deathless ones."

Then Dionê, the great goddess, answered her:
"Endure, my child, and hold up for all your suffering. Many   390
of those who live on Olympos, in bringing dire pain
to one another, have suffered from men. Ares suffered
when mighty Otos and Ephialtes, the sons of Aloeus,

---

366   *head-pieces*: Decorations that fell over the horse's brow.

379   *Dionê*: But according to the account in Hesiod, a contemporary of Homer, Aphrodite was born from the foam
      that gathered around the severed genitals of her father, Ouranos (*Theogony* 188 ff.). "Dionê" is the feminine
      form of Zeus, "Mrs. Zeus." She, not Hera, was the consort of Zeus at the oracular shrine of Dodona in north-
      west Greece, referred to in the *Odyssey* (Map 2). Presumably Dionê was a consort of Zeus before the Greeks
      came into the Balkans, bringing Zeus and his consort with them. At this time, Hera, a local mother-goddess
      replaced Dionê as the consort of the male storm-god. There are many Near Eastern parallels: The Mesopota-
      mian god of the sky Anu had as consort a female counterpart, Antu, the feminine form of his name.

bound him in powerful bonds.° He lay tied up in a bronze
395 jar for thirteen months. And Ares, insatiate for war,
would have died if their very beautiful stepmother
Eëriboia° had not told Hermes, who stole away Ares,
already much worn down, for the harsh bonds had overcome him.
Hera suffered when Herakles, the powerful son of Amphitryon,
400 wounded her in the right breast with a three-barbed arrow.
Incurable pain overcame her. Monstrous Hades
too suffered the sharp arrow when that same man,
Herakles, the son of Zeus, the cloud-gatherer, hit Hades
in Pylos among the dead and gave him over to pain.°
405 Hades went to the house of Zeus and to high Olympos,
lamenting in his heart and pierced with pains, for the arrow
had fixed in his strong shoulder and distressed his spirit.
Paiëon° applied a pain-killing poultice and healed him—
for Hades was not made to die. Scoundrel, doer of violence!
410 Herakles cared not if he did evil! With his arrows he caused pain
to the gods who possess Olympos.
                        "Now flashing-eyed Athena
has set this man upon you—the fool! Diomedes
knows not in his heart that he who goes up against
the gods does not last. His children do not call him
415 'papa' as they hover about his knees when he returns
from the war and the dread battleground. For all that
Diomedes is mighty, let him take care that he not go up
against someone stronger than you, or for sure the wise
Aigialeia, daughter of Adrestus, will wake from sleep.
420 She will rouse with her wailing all those in her house,
crying for her wedded husband, the best of the Achaeans—
even she, the strong wife of Diomedes, tamer of horses."

---

394   *powerful bonds*: Iphimedeia was married to Aloeus but bore Poseidon twin sons. They were of monstrous
size, over 50 feet tall at age 9! In addition to their attack on Ares, they threatened to pile the Thessalian
mountains Ossa on Olympos, then Pelion on Ossa so as to reach heaven and attack the gods. Apollo killed
them before they reached maturity.

397   *Eëriboia*: Eëriboia was the granddaughter of Hermes (her father was Hermes' son, one Eurymachos) and
the second wife of Aloeus, hence the stepmother of the monstrous Otos and Ephialtes. It was she who
informed Hermes of Ares' plight.

404   *to pain*: It is unknown why or under what circumstances Herakles shot Hera in the breast. Herakles'
wounding of Hades in Pylos is equally obscure, as well as the mention of Pylos (which could mean "in the
gate" instead of the settlement at Pylos—the gate of the realm of Hades?).

408   *Paiëon*: A healing god known from the Bronze Age syllabic Linear B tablets; he appears only in this book
and in Book 4 of the *Odyssey*. Paiëon or Paian eventually became a title of Apollo as healer. A *Paiëon*
(*paean*) is a song to Apollo.

So Dionê spoke and with both her hands she wiped away
the *ichor*. The arm was healed and the pains were lessened.

When Athena and Hera saw Aphrodite, they thought   425
to irritate Zeus, the son of Kronos, with mocking words.
The flashing-eyed goddess Athena began to speak among them:
"Father Zeus, I wonder if what I will say will make you angry?
It seems to me that Kypris has been urging *someone* of the Achaean
women to follow after the Trojans,° a people she loves so much ...   430
and while stroking a certain one of the Achaean women,
who wear fine gowns, she has scratched her delicate hand
against a golden brooch!"

So Athena spoke. The father
of men and gods smiled. He called to golden
Aphrodite and said: "The works of war are not   435
for you, my child. Follow after the lovely works
of marriage. Let all these other things be the concern
of swift Ares and Athena."°

And so they conversed with one
another, but Diomedes good at the war cry leaped on Aeneas,
though realizing that Apollo himself held his two arms   440
over Aeneas. But Diomedes had no regard
for the great god. He was eager to kill Aeneas
and to strip off his famous armor. Three times he leaped
on him, desiring to kill him—three times Apollo
beat back his shining shield. But when for a fourth time   445
Diomedes rushed on him like a god, Apollo,
who works from a long way off, said, shouting
terribly: "Only think, son of Tydeus, and withdraw!
Don't wish to be like the gods. The races of immortal
gods and men who walk the earth are not the same."   450

So he spoke, and the son of Tydeus withdrew a little
backward, avoiding the anger of Apollo, who strikes from afar.
Apollo set Aeneas apart from the crowd in sacred

---

430   *Trojans*: That is, Helen.

438   *Athena*: This passage was to spawn a whole genre of ancient poetry, especially Roman, where the lover
         insists that his battlefield is the bed, not the field of war. The wounding of Aphrodite may enhance
         Diomedes' prowess, but is humorous in showing off Aphrodite's weakness against a mortal's violence.
         In spite of Dionê's warning, Diomedes comes to no harm through his attack on the gods. In fact nothing
         is known of the death of Diomedes, son of Tydeus.

Pergamos, where his temple was built. Leto and Artemis,
455 who showers arrows, healed him in the great sanctuary,
and they glorified him. But Apollo of the silver bow made
a phantom of Aeneas, just like Aeneas himself and wearing
the same armor. Around that image the Trojans and the
good Achaeans struck their shields made of bull's hide,
460 which protected their breasts, both rounded shields and long ones
with feathers attached.°

                Then Phoibos Apollo spoke to
mad Ares: "Ares, Ares, murderer of men, blood-stained
stormer of walls—will you not go into the battle
and withdraw this man, Tydeus' son, who now
465 would fight even with Father Zeus? First in a close fight
he wounded Kypris on the hand at the wrist, and then he
leaped on me as if he were a god!"

                    So speaking he sat down
at the top of Pergamos while deadly Ares went among
the ranks of the Trojans and urged them on. He took on
470 the likeness of Akamas, the swift leader of the Thracians.
He urged on the sons of Priam: "O sons of Zeus-nurtured
King Priam, how long will you let your people
be slaughtered by the Achaeans? Are you waiting
until the fight is at the foot of the finely crafted gates?
475 A man lies here whom we honor as we honor good Hector,
Aeneas, the son of generous-hearted Anchises. But come,
let us save our fine comrade from the fight!" So speaking
he roused up the strength and spirit in each man.

    Then Sarpedon° sternly reproved good Hector:
480 "Hector, where has that strength gone that once you had?
You said that without armies and allies you would hold the city
alone with your brothers-in-law and your brothers. But of these
I am unable to see or note anyone! They cower like dogs
around a lion.° We do the fighting, who are but allies
485 among you. I myself come as an ally from very far off.

---

461   *with feathers attached*: They are fighting over a phantom, whereas the real Aeneas is in the temple of Apollo.
      The meaning of the Greek in the description of the shields is not, however, clear.

479   *Sarpedon*: Sarpedon, a son of Zeus and a woman named Laodamia, was king of Lycia in Asia Minor.

484   *lion*: In fact two sons of Priam have recently been killed (lines 156–157).

For LYCIA is far, along the eddying XANTHOS,° where I left
my beloved wife and my infant son and my many
possessions, which anyone who lacks will covet. Still I urge
on the Lycians and I long myself to fight my man,
although there is nothing here of mine that the Achaeans   490
wish to drive off or take. Yet there you stand!
You do not urge your people to hold their ground
or defend their wives. Beware you do not become a prey
and a spoil to your enemies as if caught in the meshes
of a net that ensnares all! They soon will sack your well-populated   495
city. These cares should weigh on you day and night.
You should beseech the captains of your far-famed allies
to hold their ground without flinching, and so put aside
all strong criticism of your command."

                    So spoke Sarpedon
and his words stung Hector to the heart. At once Hector leaped   500
from the chariot in full armor to the ground. Brandishing his two
sharp spears, he went everywhere through the army, urging
the Trojans to fight. He roused the dread din of battle.
They rallied and took their stand opposite the Achaeans.

    The Argives waited for them in gangs, they did   505
not flee. Even as the wind carries the sacred chaff across
the threshing floor and the men as they winnow, which light-haired
Demeter separates with a driving wind, the grain from the chaff,
and the chaff grows white in piles—even so were the Achaeans
whitened in the upper part of their bodies with dust that   510
the hooves of the horses kicked up between them to the
bronze-colored heaven, as again they contended in war.°

    The charioteers wheeled around. They bore straight forward
the strength of their hands. Mad Ares covered the battle
with the veil of night to help out the Trojans. He went   515
everywhere. Thus he accomplished the command of Phoibos Apollo,
he of the golden sword,° who urged Ares to enliven

---

486 *Xanthos:* Not the Lycia from where Pandaros comes, but in southwestern Anatolia (Map 6).

512 *in war:* As the winnowers toss up the wheat and chaff with their winnowing fans, the winds blow the pale
     chaff to one side where white heaps form. This is like the white dust that covers the men, driven up by the
     horses' hooves. As often in Homer, the simile evokes a peaceful scene against the terror of war.

517 *sword:* An odd epithet for a god whose typical weapon is the bow. It recurs only once (in Book 15) and is
     the name (*Chrysaor*) of the figure who, traditionally, sprang from the severed head of Medusa, along with
     Pegasus.

the spirit of the Trojans when he saw that Pallas Athena
had left the field of battle, who had been helping the Danaäns.

520   Apollo himself sent forth Aeneas from his very rich sanctuary,
and Apollo put courage in the breast of the shepherd of the people.
Aeneas° took his place among the companions. They rejoiced when
they saw him coming back alive and whole and with an abundant
courage. They asked no questions. Another sort of labor
525   prevented them that he of the silver bow roused up, and Ares
the destroyer of men, and Eris who rages without end.

On the other side, the two Ajaxes and Odysseus and Diomedes
stirred the Danaäns to the fight. They did not fear the ferocity
of the Trojans, nor their pursuit, but they held their ground,
530   like clouds that the son of Kronos in quiet weather has placed
motionless on the tops of mountains at a time when North Wind
is asleep, and the other violent winds that blow and scatter
the shadowy clouds with their shrill blasts—even so
the Danaäns held their ground and did not flee.

535   Agamemnon, the son of Atreus, went through the crowd
giving many orders: "My friends, be men! Show a strong heart!
Have shame before one another in the ferocious battle.
Of men with shame, more are saved than perish. Of those
who flee, there is no fame, no use."

He spoke
540   and Agamemnon quickly hurled his spear. He hit
a leading fighter, a companion to Aeneas, Deïkoön,
son of Pergasos, whom the Trojans honored like the sons
of Priam. He was eager to fight among the foremost.
King Agamemnon struck him on the shield with his spear.
545   The shield did not stop the spear but the bronze passed
straight through. He drove it through the belt into
the lower belly. Deïkoön fell with a loud thud
and his armor clanged around him.

Then Aeneas killed two
of the best men of the Danaäns, the sons of Diokles, Krethon
550   and Orsilochos, whose father dwelled in well-built Phemê,
rich in substance. He came from the line of the river

---

522 *Aeneas*: We hear no more about the phantom image of Aeneas that Apollo had earlier made to distract the
Achaeans.

ALPHEUS, which passes through the land of Pylos,° broad
in its flow. Alpheus bore Ortilochos as a king ruling many.
Ortilochos bore Diokles, great of heart, and from Diokles
came the twin sons, Krethon and Orsilochos, experienced   555
in every kind of battle. When the two came of age, they followed
the Argives on the black ships to Ilion with its fine horses,
to bring honor to Agamemnon and Menelaos, the sons of Atreus.
There the end of death concealed them. Like two lions on the peak
of a mountain who are raised by their mother in the thickets   560
of a deep forest—they snatch cattle and fine sheep and make havoc
of the farms of men until they are killed at the hands
of men wielding sharpened bronze—even so did these two
men fall at the hands of Aeneas, like fir trees.

                         As they fell
Menelaos, beloved of Ares, took pity on them. He stalked   565
through the foremost fighters decked out in splendid
bronze, shaking his spear. Ares roused up the bravado
of Menelaos, thinking he would fall to Aeneas. Antilochos,
the son of Nestor, saw Menelaos, and he stalked
through the forefighters. He feared greatly for Menelaos,   570
that something should happened to him and all their effort
be for nothing. Menelaos and Aeneas held out their hands
and their sharp spears against one another, eager to do battle,
when Antilochos stood close to the shepherd of the people.
Aeneas backed off, though he was a swift warrior, when he saw   575
that two men were holding their ground, side by side.

   So Menelaos and Antilochos dragged the corpses
to the Achaean side. They placed the luckless two men in the hands
of their companions, then themselves turned back to fight
in the forefront. The two of them killed Pylaimenes,°   580
the equal to Ares, leader of the great-hearted Paphlagonian
shield-men. Menelaos, Atreus' son, famous for his spear,
thrust at Pylaimenes as he stood, hitting him in the collarbone.
Antilochos hit Mydon, Aeneas' charioteer, the noble
son of Atymnios, as he was turning the single-hoofed   585
horses. He hit him with a stone smack on his elbow.
The reins, white with ivory, dropped from his hands

---

552 Alpheus ... Pylos: See Map 2. The Alpheus was the largest river in the Peloponnesus, linking the regions of
     Arcadia and Elis in the western Peloponnesus.

580 *Pylaimenes*: But alive again in Book 13, "standing fast at the gate"!

to the ground in the dust. Then Antilochos jumped on the car
and drove his sword into Mydon's temple. Gasping
590 for air, Mydon fell from the well-built car headlong
in the dust on his forehead and shoulders. He stood propped
there for a long time, for he had fallen into deep
sand. Finally the horses kicked him and he fell
to the ground in the dirt. Antilochos drove the horses
595 into the army of the Achaeans.

                    Hector saw them
through the ranks. He rushed on them, screaming.
The strong battalions of the Trojans followed, Ares
in the lead and revered Enyo, who brought with her
Kydoimos,° shameless in carnage. Ares wielded in his hands
600 an enormous spear, going now before, now behind Hector.
Diomedes good at the war cry shivered when he saw him.

        As when a man crossing a vast plain stands helpless
at the edge of a swift-flowing river, flowing to the sea,
and he sees it seethe with foam and he starts back,
605 so did Diomedes draw back, and he spoke to his people:
"My friends, how we marveled at the good Hector
for being a spearman and a brave fighter! Ever by
his side is one of the gods, who wards off ruin. And now
Ares is at his side in the form of a mortal man.°
610 Let's back off, keeping our faces to the Trojans.
Don't take on the gods in your rage!"

                    So he spoke as
the Trojans closed in. Hector killed two men experienced
in war, in a single car, Menesthes and Anchialos. As they
went down, the great Telamonian Ajax took pity
615 on them. He went up close and cast his shining
spear, and he struck Amphios the son of Selagos,
who lived in Paisos,° rich in possessions, rich
in wheat land. But his fate led him to come to the aid
of Priam and his sons.

                    Telamonian Ajax hit him
620 on the belt. The far-shadowed spear penetrated his

---

599 *Kydoimos*: "uproar," an allegorical figure.

609 *mortal man*: Athena gave Diomedes the power to tell the difference between men and gods earlier in this book.

617 *Paisos*: Location unknown.

FIGURE 5.2 Ares. On the handle of the famous François Vase, Ares crouches on a stool. His name is written before him ("ARTEMIS" belongs to the figure behind him). He is fully armed as a sixth-century BC hoplite warrior: Shins and chest protected by bronze, he wears a helmet with horse-hair crest and kneels before his shield. He clings to his single thrusting spear with its point downward. He seems to hold some kind of scepter in his left hand, which he touches to his beard. His genitals are exposed in accordance with conventions of "heroic nudity." The extraordinary François Vase, found in Italy, is covered with mythical images, some inspired by the *Iliad*. Athenian black-figure wine-mixing bowl by Kleitias, c. 570 BC.

lower belly. He fell with a thump. The glorious Ajax
ran up to strip the armor. The Trojans poured
their spears on Ajax, sharp, gleaming. Many spears
struck his shield. Ajax planted his heel on Amphios
625 and drew out the bronze spear, but he could not take
the handsome armor from Amphios' shoulders because
missiles oppressed him. Ajax feared the powerful defense
of the Trojans, who opposed him in great numbers,
standing nobly, their spears aloft, driving Ajax back,
630 though he was tall and strong and brave. Ajax reeled
and retreated.

       And so they labored in the savage strife.
But a strong fate urged Tlepolemos,° the son of Herakles,
valiant and tall, to go against Sarpedon, like to a god.
When they came near to each other, the son and the grandson
635 of Zeus who gathers the clouds, Tlepolemos was first
to speak: "Sarpedon, adviser to the Lycians,
why do you skulk around, being a man with little
experience of battle? They lie who say you are
a son of Zeus who carries the goatskin fetish,
640 for you are far inferior to those men who were begotten
of Zeus in the old days, among men of former times.
But they say that mighty Herakles was a different kind of man,
my father, who never gave up, whose heart was like a lion.
Once he came here because of the horses of Laomedon
645 with only six ships and fewer men. He sacked
the city of Ilion, he emptied the street.° But you have
the heart of a coward. Your people are dying. I don't think
your coming here from Lycia will prove a defense for
the Trojans, not even if you are very strong, but overcome
650 by my hand you shall pass the gates of Hades!"

                    Sarpedon,
captain of the Lycians, answered him back: "Tlepolemos,
truly Herakles destroyed holy Ilion through the folly
of the good Laomedon, who insulted one who had done him

---

632 *Tlepolemos*: "enduring in war," a leader of the Rhodians and a son of Herakles. Herakles himself had sacked
Troy in an earlier generation.

646 *street*: Troy was threatened by a sea-monster to whom Hesionê, a daughter of Laomedon, was offered as
a sacrifice. Herakles bargained to kill the monster and free the girl in exchange for the divine horses that
Zeus had given to Tros. Herakles killed the monster, but Laomedon would not surrender the horses, so
Herakles returned with an army and destroyed the city. He killed Laomedon and all his sons except Priam,
who was "ransomed" by Hesionê ("Priam" looks like it means "the ransomed one").

a favor, and Laomedon did not relinquish the horses on account
of which Herakles had come from afar. As for you, I expect   655
that my hands will fashion death and black fate. Conquered
by my spear you will be a boast for me, and your breath-soul
will belong to Hades, famous for his steeds!"

                              So spoke
Sarpedon. Tlepolemos raised his spear made of ash.
The long missiles sped at the same time from their hands.   660
Sarpedon's hit Tlepolemos full on the neck and the terrible
point went through. Dark night fell over his eyes.
But Tlepolemos had hit Sarpedon on the left thigh with
his long spear. The point eagerly went through the flesh
and grazed the bone, but his father Zeus warded
off death. The good companions carried out Sarpedon,   665
like a god, from the war. The long spear caused him much pain
as they dragged him along, for no one thought or noticed
in their haste to draw out the ashen spear from his thigh
so he could walk. They were having a lot of trouble
taking care of him. On the other side, the Achaeans dragged   670
the dead Tlepolemos from the fighting.

                              Odysseus saw
what was happening, and, having an enduring spirit,
his heart raged within. He wondered in his breast
and in his spirit whether he should pursue Sarpedon,
the son of thunderous Zeus, or whether he should take   675
the lives of more Lycians. But it was not allotted
to big-hearted Odysseus to kill the mighty son of Zeus
with his sharp bronze, and so Athena turned
his mind to the numerous Lycians.

                              He killed Koiranos
and Alastor and Chromios and Alkandros and Halios   680
and Noëmon and Prytanis.° And the good Odysseus
would have killed more of the Lycians had not great Hector
of the sparkling helmet been quick to understand the situation.
He stalked through the foremost fighters, armed in shining
bronze, bringing terror to the Danaäns.   685

---

681   ... *Prytanis*: The name of Sarpedon may in fact be Lycian; the other names are Greek and many recur, later
       applied to other minor characters. They are mostly "speaking" names referring either to battle—Alastor,
       "eternal foe"; Chromios, "thunderer"; Alkandros, "strong man"—or to social ranking—Koiranos, "ruler";
       Noëmon, "adviser"; Prytanis, "leader." Halios is "the man of the sea."

Sarpedon, the son of
Zeus, was cheered when Hector came up, and he spoke a
pathetic word: "Son of Priam, don't let me lie here a prey
to the Danaäns, but help me. May life leave me in your city,
because I can not return home to the dear land
690 of my fathers, to delight my own wife and my infant son."

So Sarpedon spoke, but Hector of the sparkling helmet
did not answer him at all. He hastened past,
anxious to drive back the Argives as soon as possible,
to take the lives of many. His good companions
695 placed Sarpedon, like a god, beneath a most beautiful
oak of Zeus who carries the goatskin fetish. Able Pelagon,
a dear companion, forced the ashen spear out of
Sarpedon's thigh. The breath-soul left his body, a mist
700 poured over his eyes. Then he revived, and the breath
of North Wind brought him back to life, blowing on him who
had painfully breathed forth his spirit.°

The Argives
did not turn back to the black ships before the attack
of Ares and Hector armored in bronze, nor did they
705 hold out in the fight, but always they edged backward
when they heard that Ares was with the Trojans. Well, then,
who first and who last did Hector, son of Priam,
and brazen Ares kill? Teuthras, who was like a god,
and then Orestes, driver of horses, and Trechos, the Aetolian
710 warrior, and Oinomaos and Helenos, son of Oinops,
and Oresbios° with his flashing belly-protector, who lived
in Hylê where he took good care of his great wealth
on the edge of the Kephisian lake.° Nearby lived
other Boeotians on a land that is exceedingly rich.

715 Now the goddess white-armed Hera saw the situation,
how the Argives were being destroyed in the terrible combat.
Right away she spoke words to Athena that went like arrows:
"Alas, O daughter of Zeus who carries the goatskin fetish!

---

702   *his spirit*: The next time around Sarpedon will not be so lucky (despite Zeus's temptation to save him), when Patroklos kills him in Book 16.

711   *Teuthras … Oresbios*: No name in this list of minor characters occurs again in the poem.

713   *Kephisian lake*: The large Lake Copaïs in northern Boeotia.

Unwearied one, I think that we spoke to no purpose when we
promised Menelaos that he would sail home after sacking   720
Ilion … if we permit this ruinous Ares to rage in this way.
But come let us two think of furious valor!"

So Hera spoke, and the flashing-eyed Athena, divine,
did not disobey her. Hera went back and forth harnessing
her horses with head-pieces of gold. Hebê quickly   725
fitted the curved wheels to either side of the car.
The wheels were made of bronze with eight spokes,
and the axle was made of iron. The rim was imperishable
gold and on top of it were fitted tires of bronze, a marvel
to behold. The hubs were made of silver, spinning   730
around on either side. The body was woven
of gold and silver strips. Two rails ran around it.
The pole was made of silver and from its tip
Hebê bound a beautiful golden yoke and cast
on the yoke handsome breast-collars. Beneath the yoke   735
Hera led horses with lightning feet, eager
for strife and the cry of war.

But Athena, the daughter
of Zeus, let her soft embroidered gown fall
to her father's floor. She herself had made it
with her own hands. She put on the shirt of Zeus   740
who gathers the clouds. She armed herself for tearful war.
Around her shoulders she cast the tasseled goatskin
fetish, an object of terror, crowned by Rout, while
inside is Eris, inside is Valor, inside is freezing
Attack, and inside is the head of the dreadful   745
monster Gorgon, hideous and awful, a wonder
of Zeus who carries the goatskin fetish. On her head
Athena placed a helmet with ridges on either side and four
golden plates, fitted with foot soldiers of a hundred cities.°
She stepped into the flaming chariot. She took up the spear—   750
heavy, large, powerful!—with which she overcomes
the ranks of men, of warriors with whom she is angry,
she of the mighty father.

---

749   *hundred cities*: Apparently emphasizing the helmet's enormous size, but the Greek is obscure.

Swiftly Hera touched
the horses with the lash. The gates of heaven
755 groaned open. The Horai° keep them, to whom are
entrusted the great heaven and Olympos, whether to throw
open the thick cloud or whether to shut it up. There
through the gates they drove their horses, tolerant
of the goad.

They found the son of Kronos sitting apart
760 from the other gods on the topmost peak of Olympos,
which has many ridges. Staying the horses,
the white-armed goddess Hera questioned Zeus,
the exalted son of Kronos: "Zeus, father,
don't you resent Ares for his violent acts?
765 To my sorrow he has destroyed a great and good
army of the Achaeans, recklessly and not according
to the right order of things. In the meanwhile, Kypris
and Apollo of the silver bow, free from care, take delight
in having sent down this mad god without respect for law.
770 Zeus, father, will you be angry if I give Ares a good cuffing
and chase him from the battle?"

Zeus the cloud-gatherer
answered: "Well then, rouse up Athena, the gatherer of loot.
It's *her* habit most to inflict on Ares intolerable pain."

So he spoke, and the white-armed goddess
775 Hera did not disobey. She applied the lash.
The two horses, not unwilling, flew between
the earth and the starry heaven. As far as a man
can see into the misty distance, sitting on a place
of outlook and looking over the wine-dark sea,
780 just so far did the high-whinnying horses leap in a
single bound. But when they came to Troy and the two
flowing rivers, where the Simoeis and the Skamandros
join their streams, there white-armed Hera stayed
the horses, loosing them from her car, and she
785 poured about them a thick mist. Simoeis sent up
ambrosia° for them to graze on.

---

755 *Horai*: The "hours" or "seasons," a personification of time, here as the gatekeepers of heaven. See Figure 5.3.

786 *ambrosia*: The word means "immortal," a special food of the gods, but with many other uses, here said to grow on the banks of the Simoeis and to feed the divine horses.

FIGURE 5.3 Spring.   One of the four Horai or "hours, seasons," Spring is shown as a young woman picking flowers and holding a basket of flowers. Her body is turned in the S-curve long favored by Greek sculptors. Fresco from a Roman private house in Stabiae, Italy, c. AD 60.

                          The two goddesses
went like nervous pigeons in their walk,
anxious to help the Argive men. But when
they came to where the most and best men stood,
790 crouched around powerful Diomedes tamer of horses—
like lions who eat raw flesh, or wild boars,
hardly weaklings!—there white-armed Hera
stood and shouted in the likeness of greathearted Stentor.°
His voice was like bronze and so loud it was like fifty men
795 shouting: "Shame on you Argives, a bitter reproach,
good only to look at! So long as Achilles came into
the battle, the Trojans did not come forth before
the Dardanian Gate. They feared his powerful spear.
But now they fight near the hollow ships far from the city."

800   So speaking she excited the strength and spirits of every man.
The flashing-eyed goddess Athena leaped to the side
of Tydeus' son. She found Diomedes beside his horses and his car,
cooling the wound he had received from the arrow of Pandaros.
The sweat poured beneath the strap of his round shield.
805 He was bothered by it and his arm grew tired. He raised up
the strap and wiped away the dark blood.

                          The goddess lay
hold of the yoke of his horses and said: "Surely Tydeus
begot a son very little like himself! Tydeus was short
in stature, but a fighter. Once I would not let him
810 fight or shine forth, when he went alone as a messenger
to Thebes among the many Kadmeians. I urged
him to dine, to be cheerful in the halls, but having his strong
spirit, as of old, he challenged the youths of the Kadmeians
and he easily defeated them. I was such a helper to him.
815 As for you, I stand at your side and protect you
and I am glad to urge you to fight against the Trojans. But either
too many assaults have drenched your limbs in weariness
or a spiritless fear possesses you. You are no son of Tydeus,
the wise son of Oeneus!"

                    The mighty Diomedes
820 answered her in this way: "I know who you are,
goddess, daughter of Zeus who carries the goatskin fetish.

---

793 *Stentor*: Although he was later proverbial (we say that someone speaks in a "stentorian voice"), this charac-
ter never again appears in the *Iliad*.

And so I will happily tell you my thoughts and I will not
conceal it. No spiritless fear possesses me, nor any
unwillingness to engage. But I am always mindful
of the instructions that you laid upon me. I am not to fight   825
face to face with the blessed gods, unless the daughter
of Zeus, Aphrodite, should come into the battle—
her I should wound with the sharp bronze! For this reason
I have withdrawn from the fighting and urged the other Argives
to assemble. For I see that Ares is lording it over the battlefield."°   830

Then the flashing-eyed goddess Athena answered him:
"My Diomedes, son of Tydeus, darling to my heart,
don't be afraid of Ares nor any other of the deathless ones,
so powerful a helper to you am I going to be.
So come, turn your single-hoofed horses right away   835
against Ares. Fight him in the hand-to-hand!
Have no respect for this great mad Ares—this raving one,
this evil made to order, this good for nothing. Just now
he was telling me and Hera that he was going to fight against
the Trojans and give aid to the Argives, but as it is   840
he's mingling with the Trojans, and the others are forgotten."

So speaking, she drew back Sthenelos with her hand
and shoved him from his car to the ground. Speedily he jumped!
She got in the car next to good Diomedes, a goddess
anxious for battle. The great axle, made of oak, groaned   845
beneath the burden, for it carried a goddess and the best
of men. Pallas Athena took up the lash and the reins
and right away she headed the horses toward Ares.

He was just then stripping the armor from the huge Periphas,
by far the best of the Aetolians, the fine son of Ochesios.   850
Ares, dripping with blood, was stripping the corpse,
but Athena put on the cap of Hades so that powerful
Ares could not see her.

When the murderous Ares saw
the good Diomedes, he let huge Periphas lie where he was,
where Ares had killed him, setting free his breath-soul,   855
and he headed straight for Diomedes, the tamer of horses.
When they came near, advancing against one another,

---

830   *battlefield*: But we've just been told that Diomedes withdrew from the fighting in order to cool his wound!

first Ares stabbed over the yoke and the reins of Diomedes'
horses, eager with his bronze spear to take away
860 the other's life. But the flashing-eyed goddess Athena
caught his spear in her hand and thrust it above the car,
making it fly away in vain. Next Diomedes, good at
the war cry, thrust at Ares with his bronze spear. Pallas
Athena sent it into his lower belly near the buckle
865 of the belly-protector. Diomedes wounded him and cut
the beautiful skin, then he pulled out the spear.

Brazen Ares bellowed as much as nine thousand
or ten thousand men yell in battle when they join
in the contendings of Ares! A trembling took hold of
870 the Achaeans and Trojans, they were afraid, so loudly
did Ares roar, insatiate of war. Even as when a black
air appears from the clouds after a heat wave,
when a blustery wind arises—even so the brazen
Ares appeared to Diomedes, son of Tydeus,
875 as he went together with the clouds into the broad sky.°

Soon he arrived at the seat of the gods, steep Olympos,
and he sat down next to Zeus, the son of Kronos,
pained at heart. He showed him the immortal blood
running down out of the wound, and with a wailing
880 he spoke words that went like arrows: "Zeus, father,
doesn't it anger you to see these violent acts?
Always we gods suffer shivery things from the devices
of one another, whenever we show favor to men.
We are all at war with you! You gave birth to that insane
885 and destructive daughter, always concerned with evil acts.
All the gods who are in Olympos obey you
and are subject to you. But you pay no attention to her,
whether in word or in deed, but you encourage her—
because you yourself begot this destroying child!
890 Now she has set Diomedes, high of heart,
the son of Tydeus, to rage against the deathless gods.
First he wounded Kypris in the close fight on the hand
near the wrist, but then, like a god, he raged against
me myself! Luckily I was able to run away.

---

875 *sky*: Ares' rising into heaven is compared to a tornado which is black in color and after descending rises
      rapidly into the sky. The scene of the wounding of Ares is more slapstick. The gods behave like clownish
      humans, provoking a laugh in Homer's all-male audience of men who were themselves warriors, who knew
      the dangers and rewards of battle.

Otherwise I would have suffered pains there for a long time   895
amidst the vile heaps of the dead, or I would have been alive,
but without strength from the blows of the bronze."°

Zeus answered him, glowering beneath his brows:
"Ares, don't sit beside me and whine, you good for nothing!
You are most hated to me of the gods who inhabit   900
Olympos. Always dear to you are strife and wars
and battles. You have the mind of your mother
Hera, intolerable, unyielding! I can scarcely control
her with words. Therefore I think that you
are suffering these things because of her suggestions.   905
Nonetheless I will not let you continue to endure
these agonies. You are of my blood. Your mother bore
you to me. If you were born of any other god, destructive
as you are, then long before now you would be lower
than the Ouraniones!"°   910

            Zeus spoke and he asked Paiëon
to heal Ares. Paiëon spread a poultice over the wound
and healed him, for surely Ares was not made to be mortal.
Even as the juice of the wild fig quickly makes to grow
thick the white milk that is liquid, but soon curdles as a man
stirs it, even so swiftly did Paiëon heal mad Ares.   915
Hebê bathed him and placed lovely clothes upon him.
He sat beside Zeus, the son of Kronos, exulting
in his glory.

            Back to the house of great Zeus went
Argive Hera and Alalkomenian° Athena, having put
an end to man-killing Ares' murderous rampage.   920

---

897   *bronze*: The rather stupid Ares seems impossibly confused in his fears for what might have happened to him.
910   *Ouraniones*: The "heavenly gods," not here the Olympians but Kronos and the other Titans, the children of
      Ouranos whom Zeus imprisoned in underworld Tartaros, according to the story told in Hesiod's *Theogony*.
919   *Alalkomenian*: A title meaning "defender."

BOOK 6. *Hector and Andromachê Say Goodbye*

The dread strife between Trojans and Achaeans was left
to itself. The battle surged over the plain, now to this side,
now that, as they aimed their bronze-tipped spears between
the SIMOEIS and the XANTHOS rivers.°

                      Big Ajax, the son
5 of Telamon, the bulwark of the Achaeans, first broke the ranks
of the Trojans. He set out a light of deliverance for his companions.
He hit a man who was chief among the Thracians, Akamas,°
a son of Eüssoros, rough and tall. He hit him first
on the ridge of his helmet with its thick horsehair, then
10 he drove his spear into the forehead. It went through the bone,
the spear point of bronze. Darkness shut Akamas' eyes.

    Diomedes with a fearful war cry then killed Axylos,
the son of Teuthras, who lived in well-built ARISBÊ,°
a man rich in the necessities for life, beloved of all.
15 He offered entertainment to all, living in a house
on the high road. Of all these there was not one to meet
the enemy and ward off hateful destruction. Diomedes
took the breath-souls of the two of them, Axylos and
his aide Kalesios, who drove his car. The two of them passed
20 beneath the earth.

             Then Euryalos° killed Dresos
and Opheltios.° Then he went after Aisepos and Pedasos,

---

4 *Xanthos:* "yellow-colored" is another name for the Skamandros River.

7 *Akamas:* An inconspicuous figure, but Ares assumed his form in Book 5.

13 *Arisbê:* Perhaps on the Dardanelles (Map 6).

21 *Euryalos:* His father Mekisteus was one of the Seven Against Thebes. Euryalos was one of the Descendants (*Epigoni*) and third in command of Diomedes' contingent, according to the Catalog of Ships (Book 2).

21 *...Opheltios:* Dresos appears only here. Another Opheltios turns up on a list of Hector's victims in Book 11.

whom once the water nymph of Abarbarea bore
to the excellent Boukolion.° Boukolion was the son of the good
Laomedon, his oldest born, but the mother bore him
in secret.° When Boukolion was herding his flocks, he slept 25
with the nymph. She conceived and bore twin sons.
From both twins did the son of Mekisteus take away
the strength from their shining limbs. Then he stripped
the armor from their shoulders.

              Polypoites, stalwart
in the fight, then killed Astyalos. Odysseus took down 30
Pidutês of PERKOTÊ with his bronze spear. Teucer
took down the good Aretaon. Antilochos the son
of Nestor destroyed Ableros with his shining spear.
Agamemnon, the king of men, killed Elatos,
who lived on the banks of the fair-flowing Satnioeis, 35
in steep Pedasos. Leïtos the fighting man took
Phylakos as he ran away. Eurypylos killed Melanthios.°

   Menelaos good at the war cry then took Adrastos
alive.° His two horses had run in terror over the plain
after becoming entangled in a tamarisk bush, breaking 40
the curved car at the end of the pole. They ran
to the city, where others fled in panic. Adrastos was thrown
from the car beside the wheel, in the dust, on his mouth.
There beside him stood Menelaos, the son of Atreus,
holding his far-shadowing spear. 45

              Adrastos seized
his knees and begged him: "Take me alive, son of Atreus,
take a worthy ransom. There are many treasures
in the house of my father, bronze and gold and iron
worked with great labor. From this my father would grant
you boundless ransom, if he should learn that I 50
am alive at the ships of the Achaeans."

---

23   ... *Boukolion*: Aisepos is the name of a river on Mount Ida (Book 2), Pedasos the name of a nearby town
(see line 36). Nothing further is known of Abarbarea, a puzzling name. Boukolion is "cow-man."

25 *in secret*: That is, he was illegitimate.

37   ... *Melanthios*: Polypoites is a leader of the Lapith tribe from Thessaly, prominent in Books 12 and 23. Leïtos
is a Theban commander. Eurypylos is from Thessaly, an important minor fighter referred to by name
eighteen times. The Trojan victims all have Greek names (except the odd Ableros).

38–39 *Adrestos alive*: Adrestos is an all-purpose name; we never learn where he is from or who his father was.

So he spoke,
and he tried to persuade the heart in Menelaos' breast.
And in truth Menelaos was about to give him to his assistant
to take to the swift ships of the Achaeans, when Agamemnon came
55 up running and he spoke a word of reproof: "Hold on, Menelaos,
why do you care so much for these men? Have good things
come to your house from the Trojans? Let none of them
escape complete destruction at our hands, not even
the man-child that the mother bears in her womb, let not
60 even him escape. Let them all die in Ilion, unmourned
and unnoticed!"

So spoke the fighter, and he changed the mind
of his brother, saying what must be. Menelaos thrust away
the fighting man Adrastos with his hand. Lord Agamemnon
struck him on the side and he fell backwards. The son
65 of Atreus put his foot on his chest and pulled out the spear
of ash.°

Nestor shouted aloud to the Argives, and called
to them: "My friends, fighting men of the Danaäns, servants
of Ares, let not anyone stay behind longing for spoil, so that
he might carry off the most to the ships. Let us kill men!
70 Then in peace you can strip the dead bodies of their armor."

So speaking, he stirred the strength and spirit of each man.
Then the Achaeans, dear to Ares, would have driven the Trojans
back to sacred Ilion, overcome by their weakness,
if the son of Priam, Helenos, best of the bird-prophets,°
75 had not come up to Aeneas and Hector. He stood
beside them and said: "Aeneas and Hector, because you
more than others must bear the labor of the Trojans
and the Lycians°—for you are the best in every undertaking
in war and in the counsel … Well, hold your ground! Go back
80 and forth before the army. Stop those before the gates
from falling in flight into the arms of their wives, a joy
to the enemy. And when you have aroused all our battalions,

---

66   … ash: Only Trojans are taken prisoner in the *Iliad*, and they are invariably killed, usually after a supplication.

74   *bird-prophets*: Helenos could tell the course of events by watching the flight of birds. In the next book, he mysteriously knows the thoughts of the gods.

78   *Lycians*: Helenos must mean the allies in general.

we will stay here and fight the Danaäns, though we are
having great difficulty. For necessity drives us on.

"But Hector, you go into the city. Speak to your mother   85
and mine. Tell your mother to gather together the aged wives
in the temple to flashing-eyed Athena on the acropolis of the city.
Have her open the doors of the sacred house with her key.
Have her then select the robe that seems most precious
and largest in the house, one that she values above all others.   90
Have her place it on the knees of the goddess with the lovely hair.
Promise her that you will sacrifice in her temple twelve cattle,
one-year old, that have never been goaded,° if Athena
will pity the city and the wives of the Trojans and the little
children. Perhaps she will keep away from sacred Ilion the son   95
of Tydeus, that wild spearman, the powerful maker
of rout, whom I think has become the strongest of the Achaeans.
We never feared Achilles like this, the leader of men,
whom they say was begotten of a goddess.° This man
rages too much, but none can rival him in power."   100

So he spoke, and Hector did not disobey his brother.
Immediately he leaped from the car to the ground in his armor,
and shaking his two sharp spears he went everywhere
throughout the army urging them to fight. He stirred
up the terrible din of battle. And so they rallied   105
and took their stand facing the Achaeans. The Argives
gave ground, they stopped the slaughter. They thought that one
of the deathless ones had come from the starry heaven
to assist the Trojans and that's why the Trojans rallied.

Hector called out to the Trojans, shouting aloud: 110
"High-hearted Trojans, and allies famed from afar,
be men, my friends! Remember your brute valor!
I must go into the city and tell the aged advisors
and our wives that they should pray to the gods
and promise sacrifice."   115

So speaking, Hector of the flashing
helmet went off. The dark skin of his bossed oxhide

---

93   *goaded*: That is, they have never served as farm animals, pulling the plow.

99   *goddess*: The only time in the poem where the superiority of Achilles is questioned.

shield at either end struck his ankles and his neck,
the rim that ran around the outside.°

                            Glaukos,° the offspring
of Hippolochos, and Tydeus' son came together in the space
120 between the two armies, eager to fight. When they came
near to one another, Diomedes, good at the war cry,
was first to speak: "Who are you, mighty one among
mortal men? I never saw you in the battle where men win glory
until this day.° But now you come out much ahead of the others
125 in your boldness, and you challenge my long-shadowed spear.
They are the children of wretched men who face my power.
If you are one of the deathless ones come down from the sky,
well, I would not fight with the heavenly gods.°
No, strong Lykourgos, the son of Dryas, did not last long,
130 he who contended with the deathless gods. He drove down
over holy Mount Nysa° the nurses of raging Dionysos.
All together they let their wands° fall to the ground, struck
by the ox-goad of man-killing Lykourgos. Dionysos fled
and was submerged under the wave of the sea. Thetis
135 received him, terrified, in her lap, for a commanding fear
had seized Dionysos from the threats of Lykourgos. The gods,
who live in ease, were then supremely angry with Lykourgos,
and the son of Kronos made Lykourgos blind. He didn't
last long after that, for all the gods hated him.°

---

118   *outside*: Homer seems to be talking about a Mycenaean "figure of eight" shield, or a "tower" shield (see
Figure 4.1), remembered in the oral tradition, not the smaller round "buckler" shields that most Homeric
warriors carry. The "boss," a knob or protuberance at the center of the shield, belongs to the buckler type,
so Homer has confused the two shields. The body shield, suspended by a strap or *telamon* around the
shoulder, went out of use probably around 1200 BC.

119   *Glaukos*: Earlier mentioned only as Sarpedon's second-in-command (Book 2).

124   *until this day*: Unlikely, unless Diomedes is insulting Glaukos.

128   *heavenly gods*: Diomedes seems to have lost his power to distinguish between men and gods; the mist that Athena
removed must again have descended. Also, he does not mention that he has just fought against Aphrodite and Ares!

131   *Mount Nysa*: There were many mountains with this name in the ancient world, but probably here is meant a
mountain in Thrace because Thetis lived in an underwater cave between the islands of SAMOTHRACE and
IMBROS near THRACE (Book 24).

132   *wands*: These would be the *thyrsi* of the Maenads, the ecstatic followers of Dionysos. *Thrysi* were phallic
sticks entwined with ivy and surmounted by a pine cone.

139   *hated him*: According to Sophocles (*Antigone* 955), Lykourgos was king of the Edonians in Thrace, with which
Dionysos had close associations (as well as with PHRYGIA). References to Dionysos are few in Homer: once
more in the *Iliad* (Book 14), where his mother Semelê is the topic, and twice in the *Odyssey* tangentially in
connection with Thetis and Ariadnê. The cult of Dionysos may be Mycenaean (his name appears on the Linear
B tablets), but Homer has little interest in this unheroic god. The myth of Lykourgos is the oldest of the many
myths of resistance to Dionysos that were popular later in Greek history, especially in Euripides' celebrated play
the *Bacchae* (405 BC).

"No more do I want to fight with the blessed gods.   140
But if you are a man who eats the fruit of the field, come closer
so that you might more quickly arrive at the bounds
of death."

Glaukos, the son of Hippolochos, answered
him in this way: "Son of Tydeus, great of heart, why
do you ask about my lineage? As are the generations of leaves,   145
so are the generations of men. Some leaves the wind
blows to the ground, but the forest burgeons and puts forth
new leaves when the season of spring comes. So it is
with the generations of men—one grows while the other withers
away. But if you really want to hear about these things,   150
so you will know my background—and many know it—
there is a city called Ephyra° in a corner of ARGOS,
which nourishes horses. That was the home of Sisyphos,°
the most clever of all men, Sisyphos, son of Aiolos.
He had a son whose name was Glaukos,° and Glaukos   155
was father to the good Bellerophon. To him the gods gave beauty
and a lovely manliness. But King Proitos devised evil things
in his heart, and because Proitos was far the stronger he drove
Bellerophon from the land of the Argives—Zeus had made them
subject to his rule. Now the fair Queen Anteia, Proitos' wife,   160
went mad for Bellerophon, longing to mingle in secret love,
but she could not persuade the wise-hearted Bellerophon,
who always wanted to do what was right. She lied to Proitos,
the king, saying: 'Either die yourself, Proitos,
or kill Bellerophon, who wanted to mingle with me   165
in love, against my will.'°
                    "So she spoke. The king was angered
to hear this word. He was reluctant to kill Bellerophon,

---

152   *Ephyra*: An old name for CORINTH, where Bellerophon tamed Pegasos (hence the flying horse was the
        symbol of Corinth on her coins).

153   *Sisyphos*: Punished in the underworld in the *Odyssey* (Book 11) for his many crimes by being compelled to
        roll a boulder up hill, which would roll back just as he neared the top.

155   *Glaukos*: The namesake and grandfather of the Glaukos who is speaking.

166   *against my will*: This is the folktale type called "Potiphar's wife" after the biblical story (c. 500 BC), of the
        Pharaoh's general Potiphar, whose wife tried unsuccessfully to seduce Joseph, then said he had raped her.
        It is the oldest recorded folktale in the world, appearing in the much earlier Egyptian "Story of the Two
        Brothers" from about 1200 BC. The Greeks liked the story too: It is the subject of Euripides' *Hippolytos*
        (c. 428 BC) in which Theseus' wife Phaidra falls in love with her stepson Hippolytos, propositions him, then
        kills herself when she is turned down.

for he had respect in his heart,° so he sent him to LYCIA.°
Proitos gave Bellerophon ruinous signs scratched
170 on a folded tablet, many and deadly.° Proitos told Bellerophon
to show these to his wife's father, so that he might be killed.
He went to Lycia under the blameless escort of the gods.
When he came to Lycia and the river XANTHOS, the king
of wide Lycia honored him with a ready heart.
175 For nine days the king entertained Bellerophon. He sacrificed
nine cattle. But when the tenth Dawn came, whose fingers
are of rose, then the king questioned Bellerophon. He asked
to see the tokens from his daughter's husband, Proitos.
When he had received the evil tokens of his daughter's husband,
180 first he ordered Bellerophon to kill the invincible Chimaira.
She was of divine lineage, not of the race of men,
in the front a lion, in the back a snake, and in the middle
a she-goat. She breathed the terrible strength of shining fire.
He killed her, trusting in the portents of the gods.° Second
185 he fought against the stalwart SOLYMI.° He said this was
the hardest fight of men he ever entered. Third, he killed
the Amazons, the equals of men. When he came back,
the king wove another clever deceit. He set an ambush,
choosing from broad Lycia the best men. They never
190 came back home, for the blameless Bellerophon killed
them all.°
      "But when the king saw that Bellerophon
was the noble offspring of a god, he kept him there
and he gave him his daughter.° The king gave Bellerophon

---

168   *respect in his heart*: That is, respect for the conventions of *xenia*, the unwritten rules that govern hospitality:
      You do not kill a guest, and a guest does not sleep with his host's wife. The Trojan War was caused by Paris'
      taking Helen from her home, a violation of *xenia*.

168   *Lycia*: In southwest ASIA MINOR (Map 6).

170   *deadly*: The only reference to writing in Homer. Tablets, recessed and coated on the inner side with wax,
      were common in the ancient Near East (but not EGYPT); one survives from a shipwreck c. 1400 BC. We
      cannot say what Homer means by *sêmata lugra*, "ruinous signs," but he does not refer to alphabetic writing,
      which is never called *sêmata*, "signs." Homer has heard of writing but does not know what it is exactly. The
      signs here are "deadly" because they mean "kill the bearer" or the like.

184   *... gods*: Such monsters of mixed type are otherwise unknown in Homer (except perhaps the Centaurs).
      Homer curiously suppresses any mention of Pegasos.

185   *Solymi*: A Lycian tribe (Map 6).

191   *killed them all*: This is similar to the ambush set against Tydeus when he went up to THEBES (Book 4),
      a common folktale.

193   *... daughter*: So that Bellerophon is now the brother-in-law of Anteia, who slandered him!

FIGURE 6.1 Bellerophon. Riding the winged horse Pegasos, wearing a traveler's hat, the hero prepares to stab the Chimaira ("she-goat"). A monster with a snake's tale, a goat's head growing from its back, and a lion's body, the Chimaira is perhaps an invention of the Hittites, who dominated central Anatolia around 1400–1180 BC, and later northern Syria around 900 BC. Pegasos sprang from the blood of the Gorgon when Perseus cut off her head, along with a mysterious Chrysaor, "he of the golden sword" (Apollo has this epithet in Book 5 of the *Iliad*). From the rim of an Athenian red-figure *epinetron* (thigh-protector used by a woman when weaving), c. 425–420 BC.

half of all his royal honor, and the Lycians cut him
195 out a territory better than all, a beautiful orchard
land and plowland, just for Bellerophon. The king's daughter
bore three children to wise Bellerophon: Isandros
and Hippolochos and Laodameia. Zeus the counselor
slept with Laodameia, who bore Sarpedon,
200 like a god, armed in bronze.° But when even Bellerophon
came to be hated of all the gods, he wandered
alone over the Aleian plain,° devouring his own soul,
avoiding the paths of men. Ares, insatiate of war,
killed Isandros, his son, as he warred against the glorious
205 Solymi. Artemis, whose chariot reins are golden, grew
angry with Bellerophon's daughter and killed her.
Hippolochos fathered me, and from him do I say
I have come into being. He sent me to Troy
and he laid on me a strict order: always to excel
210 and to be superior to the others, and not to put to shame
the race of our fathers, who were by far the noblest
in Ephyra and in broad Lycia. Such is my background,
my bloodline, from which I am sprung."

So he spoke, and Diomedes,
good at the war cry, rejoiced. He planted his spear in the
215 much-nourishing earth. With gentle words he spoke to the shepherd
of the people: "Glaukos, you are a guest-friend of my father's
from long since! For Oeneus° once hosted the blameless
Bellerophon in his halls, entertaining him for twenty days.
They gave beautiful friendship-tokens to one another.
220 Oeneus gave a belt shining with scarlet, Bellerophon
a golden double cup which I left in my house when I came here.
I do not remember Tydeus, since he left when I was just
a boy, when the army of Achaeans was destroyed at Thebes.
So now I am a dear guest-friend to you when you
225 are in the midst of Argos, and you will be mine

---

200   *... bronze*: Therefore, Glaukos is the nephew of Sarpedon, because his father is Hippolochos, brother of
Laodameia.

202   *Aleian plain*: The "plain of wandering," a mythical place perhaps invented for this story. According to other
traditions, Bellerophon offended the gods when he attempted to fly to heaven on Pegasos. He fell off and
was killed.

217   *Oeneus*: "wine-man" is the grandfather of Diomedes, father of Tydeus, and king of KALYDON in the south-
western portion of mainland Greece.

when I arrive to the land of your people. Let us avoid
one another's spears even in the thick of battle. For there
are many Trojans for me to kill, and their far-famed
allies too, whomever a god will give me and my feet
to overtake. And there are many Achaeans for you to kill,   230
whomever you can. Let us now exchange armor
with one another so that these other men might know
that we are guest-friends from the days of our fathers."

So speaking, leaping from their chariots, they took each
other's hands and gave each other assurances. Then Zeus,   235
the son of Kronos, took away the good sense of Glaukos
who exchanged with Diomedes, the son of Tydeus, golden
armor for bronze, the worth of a hundred oxen as against nine!°

When Hector came to the Scaean Gates and the oak tree,°
the wives and daughters of the Trojans ran up to him, asking   240
about their sons and brothers and relatives and their husbands.
He urged them to pray to the gods, all of them and in order.
But sorrow was fixed on many.

                When Hector came to the beautiful
house of Priam built with dressed stone porches—
in it were fifty chambers of polished stone built near   245
one another, where the sons of Priam slept with their wedded
wives, and on the other side, just opposite inside the courtyard,
were twelve chambers of the daughters of Priam, roofed
in dressed stone built near one another, where the sons-in-law
of Priam slept with their chaste wives°—there his bountiful   250
mother came toward him accompanied by Laodikê, the most
beautiful of her daughters, and she clasped him by hand and spoke
to him and said his name: "My child, why have
you left the fierce battle and come here? Surely the sons

---

238   *against nine*: No commentator, ancient or modern, has been able to explain this bizarre incident. In Book 8
      Hector tells *his horses* that Nestor has a shield of gold, but otherwise golden armor in unknown. Nothing
      is said about the armor when the conversation begins, and golden armor is hardly practical. Evidently
      the conventions of folktale, with its exaggerated, improbable, and miraculous developments has for some
      reason influenced Homer's narrative, creating a break in the narrative as Hector goes into the city.

239   *oak tree*: A landmark on the battlefield near the Scaean Gates, first mentioned in Book 5 and several times
      later.

250   *... wives*: We cannot really get a picture of the layout of the palace from this description, and it is hard to see
      how twelve chambers can face fifty in a courtyard.

255 of the Achaeans—a curse on their name!—are wearing you down
fighting around our city. Your heart has impelled you to come
here to raise up your hands to Zeus from the summit
of the city? But let me pour some honey-sweet wine for you.
First pour out some of it to Zeus and the other gods,
260 then you yourself might have its benefit, if you will drink.
Wine increases the great strength in a tired man,
and you have been exhausted defending your companions."

    Then great Hector, whose helmet sparkled, said:
"Dear mother, do not bring me honey-sweet wine,
265 or you may sap the strength in my limbs and I
may forget my valor. And I am reluctant to pour
out flaming wine to Zeus with unwashed hands,
nor is it right to pray to Zeus of the dark cloud
spattered with blood and gore. But you go gather
270 together the older women. Take offerings to be burned
to the temple of Athena who gathers the spoil. Select
the robe that seems most precious and largest in the house,
one that you value above the others, and place it
on the knees of the goddess with the lovely hair.
275 Promise that you will sacrifice in her temple twelve cattle,
one-year old, that have never been goaded, if she
will pity the city and the wives of the Trojans and the little
children, in hope that she will hold off from sacred Ilion
the son of Tydeus, that wild spearman, the powerful
280 deviser of rout. So go to the temple of Athena
who gathers the loot while I go to see Paris
and call him out, if he is willing to listen to me.
May the earth swallow him where he stands! The Olympian
has raised him to be a pain to the Trojans and to big-hearted
285 Priam and his sons. If I should see that man going down
to the house of Hades, I would think that my heart
had forgotten its joyless sorrow!"

               So he spoke, and she,
going toward the hall, called out to her attendants.
They gathered together the older women throughout the city.
290 She herself went down into the fragrant storage-chamber
where were the finely wrought robes of Sidonian women,
which godlike Alexandros himself had brought from Sidon
when he sailed over the broad sea, on the trip when he abducted

well-born Helen.° Hekabê took one of them as a gift
to Athena, the most elaborately embroidered and largest,   295
and it shone like a star. It lay at the bottom of the pile.
Then she went her way and the many elderly ladies
hurried after.

          When they came to the temple of Athena
at the top of the city, Theano of the beautiful cheeks,
daughter of Kisseus, the wife of horse-taming Antenor,   300
opened the doors for them. The Trojans had made her
the priestess of Athena. With a cry they all raised their hands
to Athena. Theano took up the robe and placed it
on the knees of Athena who has fine tresses. With vows
she prayed to the daughter of great Zeus: "Revered Athena,   305
guardian of this city, divine goddess, break the spear
of Diomedes and cause that he fall down on his face in front
of the Scaean Gates so that we may sacrifice in your temple
twelve cattle, one-year old, that have never been goaded,
if you will take pity on the city and the wives of the Trojans   310
and the little children." So she spoke in prayer, but Pallas
Athena rejected the request.°

          Hector went to the beautiful
house of Alexandros, which he himself had built with
the best builders in deep-soiled Troy, who made
for Paris the chamber and the house and the hall   315
close to Priam and Hector at the top of the city.°
There Hector came, the beloved of Zeus, and in
his hand he held a spear sixteen feet long. Before him
blazed the bronze point of the spear, and around it ran
a ferrule of gold.   320

---

294   *Helen*: Evidently Paris was blown off course in returning to Troy and, improbably, ended up in Phoenicia
      on the coast of the eastern Mediterranean in modern-day Lebanon. Sidon was the most important of the
      Phoenician ports. The Sidonians made a precious purple cloth. The purple dye, the most valuable in the
      ancient world, was made from a shellfish found there in abundance. Probably *Phoinikes* means in Greek
      the "red-handed ones," named from the dye; the term was never used by these coastal dwelling Semites to
      describe themselves.

312   *request*: It is odd that the Trojans should pray to Athena when she is resolutely on the Achaean side. The
      Trojans must not see it this way.

316   *city*: Homer appears to describe a late Bronze Age settlement, such as Mycenae or Athens or Troy itself
      (that is, Troy VI or VIIa, whose ruins are thought to be Homer's Troy). Iron Age settlements, by contrast,
      never had monumental secular structures.

Hector found Paris in the chamber
polishing his beautiful armor, his shield and chest-protector,
and handling his curved bow. Argive Helen sat among
the women attendants and gave orders to her maids
about the famed handicraft.

                When he saw him, Hector
325 rebuked Paris with shaming words: "What has come over you?
It is not right that you nourish this anger in your heart.°
The people perish in their fight around the city and
the high wall. It is on *your* account that the din and war burn
about the city. *You* would quarrel with anyone you saw
330 holding back in the hateful war, so get up or soon
you will see the city ablaze with consuming fire."

    Godlike Alexandros then answered him: "Hector,
you reprove me rightfully, and not without good reason.
I will tell you then: Please consider what I say,
335 and hear me out. It is not so much because of anger
or indignation against the Trojans that I sit in my chamber.
Rather, I want to give myself over to sorrow. Even now
my wife has tried to turn my mind with gentle words, urging
me to go to the battle, and this seems to me too
340 to be better. Why, victory shifts from man to man!
But come now, just wait. I'll put on my armor of war. Or go,
and I will come after. And I do believe I'll overtake you!"
So he spoke, but Hector of the sparkling helmet
said nothing.

           Then Helen addressed Hector with
345 honeyed words: "My brother—brother to a scheming, icy bitch!—
I wish that on the day my mother first bore me an evil
wind had come along and carried me away to the mountains
or beneath the wave of the loud-resounding sea, where
the wave could snatch me away before any of these things
350 happened. But since the gods have made such horrible
things come to pass, I wish that I could be the wife
of a better man, one that could feel the hostility of others
and their many insults. This man here—his mind
is not stable, nor will it ever be. Someday he will

---

326 *heart*: Hector must mean Paris' anger at the Trojans for wanting to hand him over to the Achaeans when
    the duel with Menelaos ended as it did.

reap the fruit, I think. But come now, come in,   355
sit on this stool, my brother, for the trouble falls
most on your spirit because of me—a bitch!—
and on account of the madness of Alexandros. Zeus
has placed a dark fate on us so we might be the subject
of song for men who come later."°   360

                   Great Hector, whose helmet
sparkles, answered her then: "Don't make me sit, Helen,
though you love me. You won't persuade me. Already
my spirit urges me to defend the Trojans, who want me
back among them. But you rouse this man to get going
by himself so that he overtakes me while I am still   365
in the city. Now I am going to go to my house to see
the servants and my dear wife and my little baby.
For I do not know if I will again return, or whether the gods
will kill me at the hands of the Achaeans."

                     So speaking, Hector
of the sparkling helmet went off. Quickly he arrived   370
at his house, a lovely place to live. He did not find
white-armed Andromachê in the halls, but she stood even then
by the wall with her child and her maid with the nice gown,
moaning and filled with sorrow.

                 Hector, when he saw
that his beloved wife was not within, stopped on the threshold   375
as he went out, and he spoke to the women slaves:
"Come now, women, tell me straight out: Where has
white-armed Andromachê gone from the hall? Has she gone
to the house of one of my sisters or one of my brother's wives,
whose robes are fine, or has she gone to the house of Athena   380
where the other Trojan women with woven tresses are beseeching
the dread goddess?"

                 Then a harried attendant said:
"Hector, since you strongly enjoin us to tell the truth,
she has not gone to the house of your sisters or of your
brothers' wives, who wear nice robes, nor to the house   385
of Athena where the other Trojan women, with fine tresses,
beseech the dread goddess. She has gone to the great tower
of Ilion. She heard that the Trojans are hard pressed,

360   *come later*: As here, in Homer's *Iliad*.

FIGURE 6.2   Hector and Andromachê.   Hector bids farewell to Andromachê and Astyanax. Andromachê, seated in a fancy chair unlike in Homer, wears earrings, a bracelet in the form of a serpent, and a necklace. The boy, wearing an ankle bracelet in the form of a serpent and a headband, stretches to touch his father's helmet. A beardless Hector, naked from the waist up, holds in his left hand a spear and shield. From a south Italian red-figure wine-mixing bowl, c. 370–360 BC.

that the power of the Achaeans is great. She went to the wall
in haste, like a mad woman. With her a nurse carries the child." 390

So spoke the woman attendant. Hector hastened from
the house, back the same way through the well-built streets.
When he came to the Scaean Gates, passing through the great city
from which he was about to go forth onto the plain,
there his wife with the generous dowry came running to him, 395
Andromachê, the daughter of great-hearted Eëtion, who had lived
beneath wooded Plakos, in THEBES under Plakos, ruling over the men
of Cilicia.° It was Eëtion's daughter that bronze-harnessed
Hector had to wife. She met him then, and with her
came a maid holding the tender-hearted boy, just a little baby, 400
like to a beautiful star, the beloved son of Hector.
Hector called him Skamandrios, but the others Astyanax,
because Hector alone protected Ilion.°

Hector smiled
when he glanced at his son in silence. Andromachê stood
beside him weeping. She clasped his hand and spoke 405
and called him by name: "My darling, your strength will destroy you,
nor do you take pity on your speechless babe and luckless me,
who will soon be a widow. For quickly the Achaeans will rush
upon you and kill you. For me it would be better to go
under the earth if I lose you. Never will there be 410
comfort for me when you have met your fate, but only sorrow.
I have no father and no revered mother. My father
Achilles killed when he sacked the city of the Cilicians,
high-gated Thebes. He killed Eëtion, but he did
not despoil him, for in his heart he respected him. 415
He burned Eëtion in his fancy armor, and he heaped
up a tomb. The nymphs of the mountains planted elm trees
all around it, the daughters of Zeus who carries the goatskin
fetish. I had seven brothers in my halls who went

---

398 *of Cilicia*: Eëtion is Andromachê's father and mentioned several times. His name is non-Greek. Achilles
sacked nearby LYRNESSOS when he captured Briseïs, and Thebes, when he captured Chryseïs after killing
Eëtion and his seven sons (Map 3). Andromachê had earlier married Hector and at the time was safe in
Troy. In the loot taken from Thebes is Achilles' lyre, which he plays in Book 9, and his horse Pedasos. Plakos
seems to be a southern spur of MOUNT IDA. These Cilicians are distinct from the Cilicians in southeast Asia
Minor—unless they migrated here. Similarly, Pandaros' Lycians lived in the Troad and are not the Lycians
from southwest Asia Minor.

403 *... Ilion*: Skamandros is the main river of the Troad; the child must be named after the river. He is called
Skamandrios only here; elsewhere he is always Astyanax, "defender of the city," named for his father's role.
Odysseus will throw Astyanax from the tower after the sack of Troy, as Homer's audience knew.

420 into the house of Hades all in a single day.
The good Achilles, the fast runner, killed them all
as they tended their lumbering cattle and white-fleeced sheep.
As for my mother, who was queen in wooded Plakos,
they brought her here with the other possessions. Quickly
425 Achilles took abundant ransom for her and let her go,
but Artemis the archer shot her down in the house of her father.
    "But Hector, you are my father and my revered mother
and my brother. You are my strong husband. So come, have pity
and stay here at the tower so that you do not make your son an orphan
430 and your wife a widow. Station your army near the fig tree,°
where the approach to the city is easiest and the wall is vulnerable.
Three times the best fighters have come here and tested the wall,
those who follow the two Ajaxes and famous Idomeneus
and the two sons of Atreus and the brave son of Tydeus.
435 Some prophet told them about it, or their own spirit urges them
on and encourages them."

                    Great Hector, whose helmet sparkled,
then answered: "Yes, I am troubled about this, woman,
but I feel a terrible shame before the Trojans and the Trojan
women with their trailing robes, if like a coward I skulk
440 apart from the war. Nor does my spirit permit it, because
I have learned always to be valiant and to fight with the foremost
fighters of the Trojans, winning fine fame for my father
and for myself. For I know this well in my heart and in my soul:
The day will come when sacred Ilion will be destroyed
445 and Priam and the people of Priam with his good spear of ash.
But not so much does the grief of the Trojans in times
to come trouble me, nor of Hekabê herself, nor of King Priam,
nor of my brothers, who though many and brave shall fall
in the dust at the hands of hostile men, as does
450 your grief when one of the bronze-shirted Achaeans shall lead
you away in tears, taking away your day of freedom.
Then in Argos you will work your loom at another's
command, and you will carry water from Messeïs or Hypereia,°

---

430 *fig tree:* The fig tree, like the oak tree, is one of the fixed points on the Trojan plain, apparently near the walls
   but not near the Scaean Gates, as is the oak.

453 *Messeïs … Hypereia:* Messeïs, "middle spring," and Hypereia, "upper spring," are generic names that cannot
   be located specifically. According to postHomeric tradition, after the sack of Troy Andromachê first
   became the wife of Neoptolemos, the son of Achilles; then after Neoptolemos was murdered at Delphi, she
   became the wife of Helenos, Hector's brother, who survived the war and migrated to northwest mainland
   Greece.

much unwilling, but a powerful necessity will compel you.
And someone will say who sees you weeping: 'This   455
is the wife of Hector, the best of the horse-taming Trojans
in war, in the days when they fought around Ilion.'
So will they say. To you will come fresh grief
in your lack of a man to ward off the day of slavery.
But let the heaped-up earth hide me, dead,   460
before I hear your cry as they drag you away."°

    So speaking, shining Hector reached out his arms
to his son, but his son shrank back, crying, into the bosom
of the fair-belted nurse, amazed at the sight of his father,
and fearful of the bronze and the horsehair crest, seeing   465
it nodding terribly from the top of his father's helmet.
The father laughed, and his august mother did too. Shining
Hector at once took the helmet from his head and he placed
it gleaming on the ground. He kissed his dear son
and held him in his arms, and he spoke in prayer to Zeus   470
and the other gods: "Zeus and you other gods,
grant that this my son, like me, may prove to be outstanding
among the Trojans, and great in strength, and that he might
rule Ilion with power. Then someday one might say
that he is much better than his father, when he returns   475
from war. May he possess the blood-stained spoils of a gallant
man he has killed, and may he gladden the heart of his mother."

    So speaking he placed his son in the arms of his dear wife.
She took him into her fragrant bosom, laughing through her tears.
Seeing her, her husband was moved with pity. He stroked her   480
with his hand and spoke to her: "My darling Andromachê,
I beg you, don't grieve too much for me in your heart.
No man will cast me into the house of Hades beyond
my fate. I don't think that any man can escape his fate,
neither a coward nor a brave man, when once he is born.   485
Go home now and busy yourself with your own tasks,
the loom and the distaff,° and urge your attendants to do
their work. War is for men, for all men but especially for me,
of all those who live in Ilion."

---

461   ... *away*: Hector emphasizes the work at the loom and the fetching of water, a slave's duties, and omits the
       violent rape that awaits the women of the city.

487   *distaff*: A distaff was a stick held beneath the arm, pressed to the woman's side, that held a mass of unspun
       wool at its tip. From this mass the woolworker spun the thread. In genealogy, a family's "distaff side" is the
       female ancestry.

So speaking shining Hector
490 took up his helmet with the horsehair crest. His dear
wife went off home, continually turning around,
weeping warm tears. Soon she came to the well-peopled
house of man-killing Hector. She found there her many
attendants. She roused among them all a wailing. They
495 lamented Hector while still alive, in his own house,
for they did not think that he would again return from war,
fleeing the strength and the hands of the Achaeans.

Paris did not stay long in his high house. He put on
his glorious armor, worked in bronze. He hurried
500 then through the city, trusting in his fleet feet,
as when a horse confined to a stable has fed his fill
of barley at the feeding trough, then breaks his bonds
and runs stamping across the plain exulting—for he is accustomed
to bathe in the fair-flowing river. He holds his head high,
505 and his mane streams around his shoulders. Trusting
in his splendor, his legs easily bear him to the haunts
and pastures of mares—even so Paris the son of Priam
came down from the summit of Pergamos brilliant in his armor,
like the blazing sun, laughing out loud, and swiftly
510 his feet bore him on.

Quickly he overtook his brother
Hector just as he was about to turn from the place
where he conversed with his wife. Godlike Alexandros
was the first to speak, saying: "My friend, surely
my tardiness holds you back when you wish to rush out,
515 and haven't I come as you you commanded?"

Hector of the flashing helmet answered him:
"You're an odd fellow. No one who is of sound mind
could disrespect the work you do in battle, for you
are brave. But you willfully hold back and do not care.
520 My heart is grieved in my breast when I hear shameful words
about you from the Trojans, who because of you labor much.
    "But let us go. We will make all this right in the time
to come, if Zeus will allow us to set up a bowl of freedom
to the heavenly gods that live forever, once we have driven
525 from Troy the Achaeans with their fancy shinguards."

So saying, shining Hector rushed out of the gates,
and with him went his brother Alexandros. In
their hearts both were eager to go to war, to fight.
As when a god sends a breeze to sailors who long
for it, who are tired driving the sea with their highly   5
polished oars of fir, and their limbs are exhausted,
so did the two of them appear to the Trojans,
who longed to see them.

        Then Paris killed the son
of king Areithoös, Menesthios, who lived in Arnê,°
whom the maceman Areithoös fathered and Phylomedousa,   10
who had cow eyes. Hector struck Eïon with his sharp spear
on the neck beneath his helmet, made of fine bronze,
and his limbs were loosened. Glaukos, the son of Hippolochos,
captain of the Lycians, hit Iphinoös, the son of Dexios,
on the shoulder with his spear in the ferocious   15
conflict, as he was climbing into his car drawn by swift
horses. Iphinoös fell from his car, and his limbs
were loosened.

        When flashing-eyed Athena saw Trojans
killing Argives in the savage conflict, she descended from
the peaks of Olympos in a rush to sacred Ilion. Apollo rushed   20
to her when he saw her from Pergamos, for he wished victory
for the Trojans. They met one another beside the oak tree.
Apollo, the son of Zeus the king, addressed her first:
"Why, O daughter of great Zeus, have you come so eager
from Olympos? Why has your great spirit urged you on?   25
So that you can grant to the Danaäns the conquest that turns
the tide of battle? You have no pity for the Trojans

---

9 *Arnê*: A town in Boeotia (according to the Catalog of Ships).

when they are destroyed! But if I can persuade you, this will be
much the better: Let us now cease from the war and the fighting
30 for this day. Later they will fight until they put an end
to Troy, since the utter destruction of this city is so dear
to you goddesses!"

The goddess flashing-eyed Athena answered
him: "So be it, you god who works from a long ways off.
With just this in mind I have come from Olympos into the midst
35 of the Trojans and Achaeans. But you want now to stop
the fighting of warriors?"

Apollo, the son of Zeus
the king, answered her as follows: "Let us rouse
the mighty strength of Hector, tamer of horses,
so that he challenges some one of the Danaäns to fight
40 one-on-one in the dread combat. Then the Achaeans
with bronze shinguards, indignant, will rouse up someone
to fight good Hector, one-on-one."

So he spoke,
and flashing-eyed Athena did not disobey him. Helenos,
the son of Priam, put together the plan of the gods in his heart,
45 which had pleased them in council.° He went to Hector
and stood beside him and he spoke to him this word:
"Hector, son of Priam, like Zeus in council, listen
to me, for I am your brother. Let all the other
Trojans sit down and all the Achaeans too. You
50 yourself challenge who is the best of the Achaeans to fight
one-on-one in the dread contest. For it is not fated
that you die and meet your doom. I have heard this from
the gods who last forever."

So Helenos spoke. Hector
rejoiced greatly when he heard these words. Going
55 into the center of the Trojans, he held back the battalions,
grasping his spear by the middle. All of them sat down,
and Agamemnon made the Achaeans sit too.

Athena and Apollo
of the silver bow sat in the likeness of vultures at the top

---

45 *council*: Helenos is a prophet and somehow knows the will of the gods.

of the oak tree of their father Zeus, who carries
the goatskin fetish, taking joy in the warriors, who sat   60
in close rows, as their shields and helmets and spears
shimmered. Just as the ripple of West Wind, newly arisen,
is spread out over the sea, and the sea grows black
beneath it, even so were the ranks of the Achaeans and Trojans
in the plain.   65

      Hector spoke, standing between the two
sides: "Hear me, Trojans and Achaeans who wear
fancy shinguards, so that I may speak what the heart
in my breast bids me. The son of Kronos, who weighs
the balance on high, did not bring the oaths to completion,
but with malicious intent decrees an evil time for both sides,   70
until either you take Troy with its well-built towers, or you
be destroyed beside your sea-faring ships.° With you are
the captains of all the Achaeans. Now let whoever's heart
bids him fight against me come forth from all of you to be
a champion against good Hector. Thus do I declare   75
my word. May Zeus be our witness. If that man should beat
me with his long-edged bronze, may he strip my armor
and carry it to the hollow ships, but give back my body
to my home so that the Trojans and the wives of the Trojans
may give me the allotment of fire in death. If I conquer him,   80
and Apollo grants me glory, I will strip his armor and carry it
to sacred Ilion. I will hang it up on the temple of Apollo
who strikes from a long way off. I will give up
the corpse to the Danaän ships so that the long-haired
Achaeans may bury him and heap up a barrow near the broad   85
HELLESPONT. Then one might say of the men who
are yet to be born, sailing on the sea, dark as wine,
in a ship with many oars: 'This is the tomb of a man
who died a long time ago. Shining Hector once killed
him at the height of his power.' So will someone say,   90
and my fame will never die."

---

72 *ships*: The oaths were those taken by Agamemnon (and Odysseus) and Priam in Book 3, that if Paris killed
Menelaos, then Helen was to stay in Troy and the Achaeans were to depart immediately; if Menelaos
killed Paris, then the Trojans were to hand over Helen and the property stolen at the time of her abduc-
tion and pay appropriate reparations. However, the duel ended in an unforeseen manner without a clear
decision. Hector does not mention the treachery of Pandaros and makes it seem as if the whole situation
were an act of God. But this second duel in the poem, between Hector and Ajax (after that of Paris and
Menelaos), is poorly motivated: It is Homer's way of further delaying the action while Achilles mourns in
his tent.

Thus Hector spoke.
All fell into silence, ashamed to refuse the challenge,
and they feared to meet him. At last Menelaos stood up
and spoke with reviling words, and deeply did he groan
95 in his heart: "Boasting braggarts, women of Achaea,
not men!—this will be a loathsome, a dire humiliation,
if no one of the Danaäns will go up against Hector.
But become water and earth, all of you, sitting here!°
Each man with no heart, undeserving of fame! Well,
100 against this man I will myself take up arms. From on high
are the issues of victory, given by the immortal gods."

So speaking he put on his beautiful armor. Then,
my Menelaos, would have appeared the end of your life
at the hands of Hector, because he was much the stronger,
105 but right away the captains of the Achaeans leaped up and took
hold of him. The wide-ruling Agamemnon himself
seized Menelaos' right hand and spoke to him and called
his name:

"You are mad, god-reared Menelaos! You have
no need of this madness! Hold off, though you are aggrieved.
110 Don't wish from rivalry to fight against a better man—Hector,
son of Priam. Others beside you abhor him. Even Achilles
shudders to meet this man in battle where men win glory,
and he is much better than you. But go now and sit down
among the tribe of your companions. The Achaeans will
115 put up another champion against this man. Hector
may be fearless, insatiate of battle—still, I think
he will gladly bend his knee in exhaustion, if he can
escape the terrible battle and the dread conflict."

So saying, Agamemnon persuaded the mind of
120 Menelaos, speaking what was right, and his brother obeyed him.
Gladly attendants took off the armor from his shoulders.
Nestor then stood up among the Argives and spoke: "Well, I think
that a great sorrow has come on the land of the Achaeans!
The old man Peleus,° a driver of chariots, would groan

---

98   *sitting here*: Apparently a proverbial expression, meaning "you might as well be the impassive elements of
     water or earth" for all the initiative you show.

124 *Peleus*: Achilles' father Peleus of course lives in Phthia, a province of Thessaly in northern mainland
     Greece. Peleus rules the Myrmidons, which for some reason means "ants." Nestor is from a long way off in
     Pylos, in the southwestern Peloponnesus.

aloud, the noble counselor and orator of the Myrmidons.   125
Once he questioned me in his own house, and he rejoiced
when I told him the lineage and birth of all the Argives.
If he were to hear that all these now cower before Hector,
he would raise up his hands to the immortal gods and pray
that his spirit leave his limbs and descend into the house   130
of Hades!
     "O father Zeus and Athena and Apollo,
would that I were young as when beside the swift-flowing
Keladon the Pylians and the Arcadians, mad with the spear,
gathered together to fight beside the walls of Pheia
on the banks of the Iardanos.° As the champion of the Arcadians,   135
Ereuthalion stood up, a man like a god, having the armor
on his shoulders of King Areithoös, the good Areithoös,°
whom men, and their wives with beautiful belts called
the 'maceman' because he fought not with bow and arrow,
or with the long spear, but with an iron mace.   140
He broke the battalions. Lykourgos killed Areithoös
by a trick, not by might, in a narrow road where his iron
mace was useless to save Areithoös from destruction.°
Lykurgos got to Areithoös first and pierced him through
the gut with a spear, and backward he fell on the earth.   145
Lykurgos stripped the armor of Areithoös,
which brazen Ares had given him. This armor
Lykourgos wore thereafter in the melée of Ares,
but when Lykourgos grew old in his halls, he gave it
to dear Ereuthalion, his aide, to wear.   150
            "Having
the armor of Lykourgos, Ereuthalion called out all
the best fighters, who trembled and were afraid,
and no one dared. But my much-enduring heart
egged me on to fight him in my boldness, though I
was the youngest of all. And I fought Ereuthalion,   155
and Athena gave me glory. Ereuthalion was the tallest
and strongest man that I ever killed. As a sprawling hulk
he lay stretched out this way and that.
           "I wish that I were
as you, and my strength were as firm. Then would Hector,
whose helmet sparkles, soon find he had a fight on his hands.   160

---

135   ... *Iardanos*: The location of all these places (except PYLOS and ARCADIA) is unknown.

137   *Areithoös*: Paris just killed his son Menesthios earlier in this book.

143   *destruction*: Because the way was too narrow for him to swing the club. This Lykourgos is distinct from the
     Thracian Lykourgos who opposed Dionysos (Book 6).

As for you who are the captains of all the Achaeans,
no one wants with a ready heart to take on this Hector."

So the old man complained, and then nine men
rose up. First by far was the king of men Agamemnon
165 and after him the mighty Diomedes, the son of Tydeus.
Then the two Ajaxes, clothed in ferocious valor, then
Idomeneus and the companion of Idomeneus, Meriones,
the equal to Enyalios, the killer of men. Then Eurypylos,
the brilliant son of Euaimon. Then up sprang Thoas,
170 the son of Andraimon, and the good Odysseus. All
of them wanted to fight the able Hector.

Gerenian Nestor,
expert with horses, spoke to them: "Now may you shake
the lot in turn, to see who wins. This man will profit
the Achaeans, who wear fancy shinguards and he will
175 raise his own spirit, if he escapes from ruinous war
and the dread conflict."

So he spoke, and each man put
his mark on a lot and threw it into the helmet of Agamemnon,
son of Atreus. The people prayed, they raised their
hands to the gods. Thus would one say, looking
180 into the broad heaven: "Father Zeus, may Ajax win
the lot, or the son of Tydeus, or the king himself
from Mycenae rich in gold."

So they spoke. Gerenian
Nestor, expert in horses, shook the helmet and out
from the helmet sprang the lot of Ajax, just what everybody
185 wanted. A herald carried the lot everywhere through
the crowd, from left to right, showing it to all the captains
of the Achaeans, but they did not recognize it.°
Every man denied it until he arrived, going everywhere
through the crowd, to the man who had marked it and thrown
190 it into the helmet, glorious Ajax. Then Ajax
reached out his hand. The herald stood near and placed

---

187 *recognize it*: The marks on the lots are not writing because each man recognizes only his own "sign," the
same word used for the "ruinous signs" on the letter of Bellerophon in Book 6. This incident indicates the
absence of writing in Homer's world. Probably the lots were pieces of pottery.

the lot in his hand. Ajax recognized the sign
on the lot. When he saw it, he rejoiced in his heart.
He cast the lot on the ground beside his foot and said:
"My friends, surely this lot is mine. I am happy   195
in my heart. I think that I will take down the able Hector.
But come, while I put on my warrior's armor, you pray
to Zeus, the son of Kronos, the king, in silence, by yourselves,
so that the Trojans learn nothing of it—or in the open
if you want, because we fear no man. For by force shall no one   200
drive me in flight of his own will, and in despite
of my will—no, nor by skill. I don't think I was raised
in SALAMIS as a man without skill!"

                    So Ajax spoke. They prayed
to Zeus, the son of Kronos. Thus would one of them say,
looking to the broad heaven: "Father Zeus who rules   205
from MOUNT IDA,° most honored, greatest, give victory to Ajax!
May he gain shining glory! But if you love Hector and care
for him too, grant a like strength and glory to both."°

    So they spoke. Ajax dressed in gleaming
bronze. When he had clothed his flesh in armor,   210
he rushed forth like giant Ares, who goes forth to war
among men whom the son of Kronos has cast together
in the fury of consuming strife. Even so Ajax,
the huge bulwark of the Achaeans, rushed forth,
his terrible face smiling. He went with long strides of his feet   215
beneath him, brandishing his long-shadowed spear. When
the Argives saw him, they rejoiced, but a fearful trembling
took hold of the limbs of every one of the Trojans, and Hector's
heart beat fast in his breast. But he could not run away
or fade back into the crowd of the people. He had himself   220
made the challenge through his will to fight.

                    Ajax moved in
close, carrying his shield like a tower, bronze, made
of seven ox-hides, which Tychios had fashioned

---

206 *Mount Ida*: Zeus sometimes perches on Ida to watch what is going on at Troy, as we will see in the next book.

208 *to both*: It is hard to explain why they would pray for Hector to be equal to Ajax, unless the poet is setting up the draw that actually comes.

for him with a lot of labor, by far the best of the workers
225 in hides. Tychios lived in Hylê,° and made for Ajax
the flashing shield of seven ox-hides of sturdy
bulls, and as an eighth layer he added one of bronze.

Carrying it before his breast Telamonian
Ajax stood close to Hector, and he threatened him:
230 "Hector, now you will clearly learn in the hand-to-hand
what sort of men are the captains of the Danaäns, even after
the lion-hearted Achilles, the smasher of men. He stays
now among the beaked sea-faring ships, angered
at Agamemnon, the shepherd of the people. But we
235 are not afraid to face you, yes, many of us. But come,
let us close for battle and war!"

Then Hector of the flashing
helmet answered him: "You Ajax, son of Telamon,
begotten of Zeus, captain of the army—don't test me
as if I were a puny boy, or a woman who knows nothing
240 of the facts of war! I know battle well and the killing of men.
I know how to wield the seasoned shield to the right,
to the left. That is what I call real shieldmanship!
I know how to rush into the melée of swift horses.
I know how to dance the dance of furious Ares
245 in the hand-to-hand. But I do not want to strike you,
eyeing you in secret, because of who you are, but openly,
if I might get at you ..."

He spoke and, brandishing
his long-shadowed spear, he cast it. He struck Ajax's
fearsome tower shield of seven ox-hides and the outermost
250 of bronze, the eighth layer of the shield. The tireless bronze
cut through six layers, but it stuck in the seventh hide.

Then Zeus-nourished Ajax threw his long-shadowed
spear and he struck the shield of the son of Priam,
well balanced on every side. The powerful spear
255 went through the shining shield and forced its way
through his highly decorated chest-protector. The spear
cut through his shirt at his side, but Hector turned

---

225 *Hylê*: Evidently the Boeotian town mentioned in the Catalog of Ships (Book 2), though Ajax is from the
island of Salamis in the harbor of Athens.

and avoided black death. The two men at the same time withdrew
their long spears with their hands and fell upon one another,
like flesh-eating lions or wild boars whose strength   260
is enormous.

       The son of Priam then struck with his spear
the middle of Ajax's shield, and the bronze did not break,
but the point was turned.° Ajax leaped on Hector and pierced
his shield. The spear went straight through and pounded
Hector in his fury. It reached his neck and gashed it.   265
Black blood spurted.

       But even so Hector of the sparkling
helmet did not let off the battle. Stepping back
he picked up with his strong hand a stone lying
on the plain, black, jagged, and large. He threw it
at Ajax's dread shield of seven ox-hides, striking   270
it in the middle on the boss. The bronze rang.

Then Ajax picked up a much larger stone and spun
and threw at Hector, and he put immeasurable force
behind it. He broke the shield inward with his cast of the rock,
like a mill stone. Ajax beat down Hector's knees.   275
Hector stretched out backwards, crumpled under his shield,
but Apollo immediately set him upright.

       And now
they would have wounded each other in a close fight,
if the heralds, messengers of Zeus and men, had not
interfered, the one a Trojan and the other a bronze-clad   280
Achaean, Talthybios and Idaios, both prudent men.

They held scepters between the two, and Idaios,
skilled in wise counsel, spoke a word: "My dear sons,
fight no more. Give up the battle. For Zeus who gathers
the clouds loves both of you. You are both spearmen,   285
that we all know. Night has come. It is good to obey the night."

Ajax, the son of Telamon, then answered:
"Idaios, ask Hector to say these things. For it was he

---

263 *turned*: The outermost layer of bronze on the shield was not penetrated, but the point of the bronze spear
    was bent by the impact.

FIGURE 7.1   The duel between Ajax and Hector.   Behind Ajax, on the left, stands Athena,
protector of the Achaeans. She wears a helmet and the goatskin fetish (*aegis*) around her shoulders.
With her left hand, she touches Ajax's helmet, giving him strength, and holds a down-turned spear
in her right hand. Ajax is dressed as a fifth-century hoplite, including shinguards, but is barefooted.
He holds a hoplite shield (not a "tower shield"). Behind Hector on the right stands Apollo with his
bow and a quiver over his shoulder, protector of the Trojans. Hector is shown in "heroic nudity." He
wears a helmet, a hoplite shield, and holds a sword. Wounded in the chest with blood streaming out,
Hector leans back to avoid the point of Ajax's spear. Between the two figures, above Ajax's shield, is a
large stone, standing for the rocks the fighters threw at each other. The figures are labeled. Athenian
red-figure wine-cup, 490–480 BC.

who in his will to fight called out our best fighters.
Let him begin. I will obey even as he says." 290

Great Hector of the sparkling helmet then answered:
"Ajax, because a god has given you stature and strength and wisdom,
and you are best of the Achaeans with the spear, let us cease
from our fight and contention for this day. Later we will fight
again until a spirit decides between us, and gives victory 295
to one or the other. Night is upon us. It is good
to obey the night, so that you bring joy to all the Achaeans
beside the ships, especially to your relatives and companions,
those that you have. And I will bring joy to the Trojans
and the Trojan wives with their trailing robes throughout 300
the great city of King Priam. Praying for me, the king
will enter the sacred place of assembly. Come, let us both
give notable gifts to each other so that one of the Achaeans
or Trojans may say: 'They fought in soul-consuming strife,
but they departed in peace after making a compact.' " 305

After speaking in this fashion, Hector presented a sword
with silver studs in a scabbard with a well-cut strap. Then Ajax
gave a belt shining with purple. So parting, the one went into
the Achaean army, the other went to the gathering of the Trojans.
The Trojans rejoiced when they saw that Hector was alive 310
and sound, having escaped the might and invincible hands of Ajax.
And they brought him to the city, scarcely believing that he was safe.

The Achaeans, who wore fancy shinguards, from their side
brought Ajax to the good Agamemnon, who rejoiced in the victory.°
When they came to the huts of the son of Atreus, the king 315
of men Agamemnon sacrificed a five-year-old bull to the son
of Kronos, supreme in power. They flayed and prepared
it and divided the meat into all its parts. They skillfully
sliced up the meat and spitted it and roasted it carefully
and drew everything from the spits. When they had ceased 320
from their labor and had made ready the feast, they ate,
nor did their hearts lack in the equal feast. The warrior
wide-ruling Agamemnon, the son of Atreus, gave Ajax
the backbone with ribs attached as a sign of honor.

---

314 *victory*: Because Ajax survived unscathed.

325   But when they had cast from themselves all desire
       for drink and food, old man Nestor first began to weave
       a plan for them. His advice had appeared in earlier
       times to be best. With good intention he spoke and addressed
       them: "Sons of Atreus and you others who are best
330 of all the Achaeans—many of the long-haired Achaeans
       have died, whose black blood the sharp Ares has spilled
       along the broad-flowing SKAMANDROS, and their breath-souls
       have gone down into the house of Hades. For this reason it is best
       to interrupt the war of the Achaeans. Let us gather in order
335 to wheel here on carts drawn by cattle and mules the bodies
       of the dead. We will burn them a little way from the ships
       so that every man can carry home the bones of the dead
       when we return to the land of our fathers. Let us heap up a tomb
       around the fire, bringing in soil from the plain for all alike.
340 In addition let us speedily build a high wall, a defense
       for the ships and for ourselves.° Let us place well-fitted gates
       in the wall so that there may be a road for chariots through it.
       Outside, but close, let us dig a deep trench that will stave
       off their cars and their army, swarming everywhere, so that
345 the war of the massed Trojans might not press so upon us."

       Thus he spoke and all the champions agreed.
       At the same time a gathering of the Trojans took place at the top
       of the city of Ilion, a gathering ferocious and tumultuous,
       outside the doors of Priam's house. The wise Antenor° began
350 to speak: "Listen to me, Trojans and Dardanians and allies,
       so that I might speak what is in my heart. Come now,
       let us give Argive Helen and the treasure taken with her
       back to the sons of Atreus to carry away. As it is,
       we fight after cheating on our oaths of faith.°
355 I have no hope that anything of benefit will come to us
       if we do not do this."

                    After speaking he sat down.
       The good Alexandros rose up among them, the husband
       of Helen who has lovely hair. Speaking words that shot

---

341 *ourselves*: Like Helen's View from the Wall, this episode properly belongs to the earliest days of the war.

349 *Antenor*: Priam's chief adviser. He had hosted Menelaos and Odysseus when they came to retrieve Helen at the beginning of the war (Book 3).

354 *oaths of faith*: Antenor is referring to the oaths sworn before the duel between Paris and Menelaos.

like arrows, he said in reply: "Antenor, you no longer
speak to my pleasure. You can think of something better!   360
But if in truth you speak in earnest, then the gods themselves
have ruined your brain. But I will speak to the horse-taming
Trojans: I absolutely refuse to give up the girl! However,
the treasure I brought from Argos to our home, I am willing
to give it all back and to add more from my own house."   365

     So speaking, he sat down. Dardanian Priam rose up
among them, an advisor equal to the gods. Wishing
them well, he spoke and addressed them: "Listen to me,
Trojans and Dardanians and allies, so that I may speak
what is in my heart. For now, take your dinner   370
throughout the city, just as before. Keep the watch!
May each man stay awake. At dawn let Idaios
go to the hollow ships to tell Agamemnon, the son
of Atreus, and Menelaos, the proposal of Alexandros.
It is on Alexandros' account that this conflict has arisen.   375
Let him speak, too, this word of wisdom, if they are willing
to let off this painful war until we burn the dead.
Later we will fight again until a spirit decides
between us, and gives victory to one or the other."

     Thus Priam spoke. Readily they listened to him and obeyed.   380
They took their dinner throughout the army in companies.
At dawn Idaios went to the hollow ships. There
at the place of assembly he found the Danaäns, the followers
of Ares, beside the prow of the ship of Agamemnon.
Standing in their midst, the herald spoke to them in a loud   385
voice: "O son of Atreus and you other captains of all the Achaeans!
Priam and the other noble Trojans have urged me to relay
the proposal of Alexandros on whose account this conflict
has arisen, to see if it be pleasing and sweet to you.
As for the treasure that Alexandros brought in his hollow   390
ships to Troy—I wish he had died before all this happened!—
he is willing to give it all up and to add more
from his own house. But he says that he will not give up
the lady wife of glorious Menelaos, though the Trojans
urge him to. Furthermore, they have asked me to say   395
this word, in case you are willing to let off from the painful
war until we can burn the dead. Later we will resume
the fight until a spirit decides between us and gives
victory to one or the other."

So he spoke and they all
400 fell into silence. Finally Diomedes, good at the war cry,
spoke to them: "May no man accept the treasure
from Alexandros, nor Helen. Even a fool knows that
the cords of destruction are now made fast about the Trojans!"

So he spoke, and all the sons of the Achaeans shouted
405 aloud. They applauded the advice of Diomedes, the tamer
of horses. And then King Agamemnon spoke to Idaios:
"Idaios, you have yourself heard the word of the Achaeans,
how they answer. It is my own pleasure too. As for the burning
of the dead, that is apt. There is no sparing, in the matter
410 of dead bodies, of a quick consolation with fire. May Zeus
be our witness to these oaths, the loud-thundering husband of Hera."

So speaking he raised up his scepter to all the gods,
and Idaios went back once again to sacred Ilion. The Trojans
and the Dardanians were together in the place of assembly,
415 all gathered together, waiting until Idaios should return. He came
and gave the Achaean response, standing in their midst.

They quickly readied themselves to gather both
the bodies of the dead and wood for the pyre. The Argives
on their side rose up from the ships with many benches
420 to begin the gathering. The sun just then struck the fields,
rising up from the deep streams of peaceful Ocean,
rising to the heavens. The two armies met. It was difficult
to identify every man, but they washed away the bloody
gore with water and lifted the bodies into the wagons,
425 weeping hot tears. Great Priam would not allow them
to lament, so in silence they heaped the corpses on the pyre,
sore at heart. When they had burned them in the fire,
they returned to sacred Ilion.

In the same way, on the other side,
the Achaeans with their fancy shinguards heaped the corpses
430 on the pyre, sore at heart. When they had burned them in fire,
they went back to the hollow ships. It was still not dawn,
but the half-light of the night, when a chosen gang of
the Achaeans gathered around the pyre. They built a single
barrow over it, bringing in soil from field for all alike.

435 They built nearby a wall and high towers, a defense
of the ships and the men. They placed well-fitted gates

in the wall so that there might be a road for chariots through it.
Outside, but close, they dug a deep trench, wide and great,
and in it they fixed sharpened stakes.

So the long-haired
Achaeans labored. But the gods, seated next to Zeus,   440
the master of lightning, marveled at the great work
of the bronze-shirted Achaeans. Poseidon, the earth-shaker,
began to speak: "Father Zeus, is there any one of the mortals
on the boundless earth who will declare to the deathless ones
his mind and intention? Do you not see that now again   445
the long-haired Achaeans have constructed a wall to defend
their ships and driven a ditch before it, and have not
given glorious sacrifice to the gods? The fame of this wall
will reach as far as the dawn spreads its rays. People
will forget the wall that Phoibos Apollo and I built   450
with so much effort for the warrior Laomedon."°

Zeus, who gathers the clouds, groaned and said:
"Alas, you shaker of the broad earth—what words you
have spoken! Another god might fear this thing,° much weaker
than you in his hands and might. But your fame will reach   455
as far as the dawn sheds its rays. Come, after the long-haired
Achaeans have returned with their ships to the land
of their fathers, smash down the wall and wash
it all into the sea. Cover the great beach with sand
so that the great wall of the Achaeans may be wiped out."   460

They said such things to one another. The sun went down
and the task of the Achaeans was finished. They killed oxen
throughout the tents. They ate dinner. Many ships
were at hand from LEMNOS bringing wine, which Euneos
the son of Jason had brought, whom Hypsipylê bore to Jason,   465
shepherd of the people.° The son of Jason gave a thousand

---

451 *Laomedon*: A grandson of the early King Tros and a son of Ilos, Laomedon—Priam's father—contracted
with Poseidon and Apollo to build the walls of Troy, then refused to pay them. Herakles destroyed these
walls when Laomedon refused to give him the horses of Zeus in return for Herakles' saving of Laomedon's
daughter Hesionê from a sea-monster. Laomedon never paid his debts.

454 *this thing*: That the Achaean wall will eclipse the wall that Apollo and Poseidon built, famous in legend.

466 *shepherd of the people*: According to later tradition, when Jason and his crew stopped on the island of Lemnos
en route to the BLACK SEA to capture the Golden Fleece, they discovered the island populated only by
women, who had killed their husbands years before in a bitter dispute. The sex-starved women welcomed
the Argonauts, who remained a year. The queen of the Lemnian women, Hypsipylê, slept with Jason and
conceived Euneos. The saga of the Argo is mentioned only here in the *Iliad* and once in the *Odyssey* (Book 12).

measures of wine to be brought to the sons of Atreus
alone, Agamemnon and Menelaos. From these ships
the other long-haired Achaeans bought wine, some
470 by paying in bronze, others with shining iron, others
with hides, others with the cattle themselves, others
with slaves. They made a fat feast.

                                Then all night long
the long-haired Achaeans feasted. The Trojans and their allies
did the same in the city. All night long Zeus the counselor
475 devised evil for them,° thundering terribly. Pale fear
took hold of both sides. They poured on the ground wine
from their cups, nor did anyone dare to drink before
pouring an offering to the all-mighty son of Kronos.
Then they all lay down and took the gift of sleep.

---

475 *evil for them*: Presumably evil for the Achaeans, in fulfillment of Zeus's promise to Thetis. But both sides
seem to be terrified of the thunder.

BOOK 8. *Zeus Fulfills His Promise*

Dawn in her saffron robe spread out over all
the earth. Zeus, who delights in the thunder, called
an assembly on the highest peak of Olympos, which has
many ridges. He himself held forth, and all the gods
listened: "Hear me, all you gods and goddesses,   5
so that I may say what the spirit in my chest recommends.
None of you female gods, nor any of you male gods,
are to attempt to circumvent my word! I want you all
to agree, so that I may accomplish these things as soon
as possible. If I catch any of you wanting to go to help   10
the Trojans or the Danaäns, he'll not come back to Olympos
without getting smacked around. Or I'll grab him and throw him
into murky Tartaros far, far away, where is the deepest
gulf beneath the earth, where the gates are made of iron
and the threshold is bronze, as far beneath Hades as the heaven   15
is from the earth—then you'll know how far I am the strongest
of all the gods! Go on—try it! So that you all
may know. Hang a golden chain from the heaven,
then all you gods and goddesses grab hold and tug.
You could not drag Zeus the counselor, the highest,   20
out of heaven to the ground, no matter how hard you try.
But if I wanted with a ready heart to drag you all up,
then I would do so, and bring up the earth and sea too.
And then I would tie the rope around a spur of Olympos,
so that everything should hang in the air. By so much   25
am I above the gods and men."

                    So he spoke, and all
the rest fell into silence, amazed at his word, for he had
spoken with great power. At last flashing-eyed Athena
spoke: "O our father, son of Kronos, highest of all lords,
we all know very well that your power is unyielding, but still   30
we pity the Danaän spearmen, who will perish fulfilling
an evil fate. Nonetheless let us stay out of the war,
just as you command. We will give the Argives some advice
that will profit them, so that all do not perish from your wrath."

35   Smiling upon her, Zeus, who gathers the clouds,
        said: "Be of good cheer, my daughter, Tritogeneia.
        I'm not really serious ... I want to be kind to you!"

        So speaking, he ordered his horses with bronze hoofs,
        very fast, to be harnessed beneath his car, their golden manes
40   flowing. He donned his golden clothes and took up his golden,
        finely crafted whip. He stepped up into his car. He touched
        the horses with the whip to rouse them. And not unwilling
        they flew off between the earth and the starry heaven. They came
        to Gargaros° on Ida with its many fountains, the mother
45   of wild beasts, where is Zeus's sanctuary and its smoky
        altar. There the father of men and gods stationed
        his swift horses. He set them free from the car,
        and he cast a thick mist around them.° He himself sat
        on the peak, rejoicing in his glory. He could see the city
50   of the Trojans from where he sat, and the ships of the Achaeans.

        The long-haired Achaeans took a hasty dinner throughout
        the huts. Afterwards they put on their armor. The Trojans,
        on their side, put on their armor too in all parts of the city,
        but there were fewer of them. Nonetheless, they were
55   eager to fight in the battle, compelled by necessity,
        for they fought for their children and their wives.

                                                The Trojans
        opened the gates. Their army rushed forth, the foot soldiers
        and the charioteers. A huge clamor arose. When they had come
        together into one place, they thrust together their shields
60   and spears in the frenzy of men who wear shirts of bronze.
        The bossed shields came together. A great din arose.
        The agony of the wounded and the boast of victory were heard
        as men killed and were killed, and the bountiful earth
        ran with blood.

                        So long as it was dawn and the sacred
65   day still waxed, for so long the missiles of either side
        struck home, and the warriors fell. When Helios
        reached the middle of the sky, then the father lifted
        on high the golden scales. He placed on it two fates

---

44 *Gargaros:* The highest peak of Mount Ida.

48 *around them*: To conceal them.

of bitter death, one for the Trojans, tamers of horses,
the other for the Achaeans, who wear shirts of bronze. He held $\qquad$ 70
the balance in the center. Down dropped the day of doom
for the Achaeans. The fates of the Achaeans were settled
on the much-nourishing earth, but the fates of the Trojans rose up
to wide heaven.

      Zeus threw down a great bolt of thunder—
he sent a blazing flash into the midst of the Achaeans! 75
Seeing it, they were amazed and a white fear took hold of all.
Then Idomeneus no longer dared to resist, nor Agamemnon,
nor the two Ajaxes, the servants of Ares. Only Gerenian
Nestor, who watched over the Achaeans, held out,
not because he wanted to, but because his horse was wounded. 80
The good Alexandros, the husband of Helen with the lovely hair,
had hit the horse with an arrow on the top of its head,
where the mane of horses first grows on the skull. There
is the deadly spot. The horse leaped up in agony.
The arrow went into its brain, throwing the other horses 85
into confusion as it writhed around the bronze arrowhead.
While Nestor leaped out of the car and cut away the trace-horse°
with his sword, the fast horses of Hector came on into
the rough tumult, carrying a bold charioteer—Hector!

    And then old man Nestor would have died if Diomedes, 90
good at the war cry, had not seen what was happening.
He shouted a terrible shout, urging on Odysseus:
"Zeus-begotten, devious son of Laërtes, Odysseus—
where are you running to with your back turned to the enemy,
like a coward in the crowd? I hope nobody spears you 95
in the back while you are running away! But let us drive
away this wild man from old man Nestor."

          So he spoke,
but the enduring good Odysseus did not hear him
as he raced by, heading to the hollow ships of the Achaeans.
The son of Tydeus, therefore alone, advanced into 100
the forefight and took his stand before the horses
of the old man, Nestor, the son of Neleus.

---

87 *trace-horse*: The chariot was drawn by two yoked horses, but some chariots had one or two "trace-horses."
    It is not clear what their function was, or if Homer even understood it. The trace-horses were apparently
    attached to the car by means of a strap; they were not yoked and did not pull the car. Only two horses die in
    the *Iliad*, one here and one in Book 16, both trace-horses.

Diomedes spoke to him
words that went like arrows: "Say old man,
I see that younger fighters are wearing you down.
105 Your strength is loosened, your old age weighs heavy
upon you. Your aide is a weakling, your horses are slow.°
Come, get up into my car so that you may see what sort
of horses are these of Tros, who know well how both
to pursue across the plain, and how to flee. I captured
110 them from Aeneas, the maker of mayhem. Let your two
aides take care of your horses—with these we will ride
against the Trojans so that Hector will see how my spear
rages in my hands!"

So Diomedes spoke. Gerenian Nestor,
the horseman, quickly obeyed him. The two aides,
115 the strong Sthenelos and the kind Eurymedon, took care
of Nestor's horses.

Nestor and Diomedes mounted
into the car of Diomedes. Nestor took the shining reins
in his hands. He lashed the horses. Quickly they closed
in on Hector. As Hector charged straight at them,
120 the son of Tydeus cast his spear.° He missed Hector,
but hit his charioteer, Eniopeus, the son of high-hearted
Thebaios, in the flesh of his chest beside the nipple
as he held the horses' reins. He fell from the car
as the swift horses swerved aside. His breath-soul
125 and his strength were undone.

A terrible pain afflicted
the heart of Hector for his charioteer. But he left him
to lie there and, though sorry for his companion,
sought out another bold charioteer. Nor did his horses
for long lack a master. Quickly Hector found the brave
130 Archeptolemos, son of Iphitos.° Hector made him
mount up behind the swift-footed horses and gave him
the reins.

---

106 *slow*: He says nothing about the dead horse.

120 *spear*: Here the warriors fight from chariots instead of dismounting first, an unusual procedure.

130 *Iphitos*: Presumably Hector has dismounted in order to find a new charioteer. Archeptolemos appears only here and when he is killed later in this Book (line 315). His father Iphitos was a son of Eurytos of Oichalia, probably on the island of Euboea. Iphitos gave Odysseus the bow that Odysseus uses to slaughter the suitors in the *Odyssey*.

Then would ruin have come and matters
beyond fixing. The Trojans would have been penned up in Ilion
like sheep, if the father of men and gods had not been quick
to see. He thundered terribly and threw down his white   135
thunderbolt, right to the ground in front of the horses
of Diomedes. A terrible flame burst up of burning sulfur.
The two horses took fright and cowered beneath the car.°

'The shining reins fell from Nestor's hands.
He was afraid in his heart, and he spoke to Diomedes: 140
"Son of Tydeus, turn our single-hoofed horses
in flight! Don't you see that victory from Zeus is not coming?
Zeus the son of Kronos has given glory to Hector on this day.
Maybe some other time, if he wills it, he will give
us victory. A man cannot overturn the plan of Zeus,   145
not even a strong man, for Zeus is stronger still!"

Then Diomedes, good at the war cry, answered him:
"Yes, old man, you have spoken aptly, what is right.
But this savage pain comes to my heart and spirit when I know
that Hector will one day say, speaking to a gathering   150
of the Trojans, 'The son of Tydeus went to the ships
fleeing from *me*.' So will he boast. Then may the broad
earth open for me!"

        Gerenian Nestor then answered him:
"O my son of wise-hearted Tydeus, what a thing you've said.
Hector may say you are a coward and without strength,   155
but I don't think he'll persuade the Trojans and Dardanians
and the wives of the great-hearted Trojans, bearers
of shields, whose hot husbands you have cast into the dust!"

So speaking, he turned the single-hoofed horses in flight,
back again through the melée. The Trojans and Hector   160
with a wondrous shout threw their groaning missiles at them.
Hector of the sparkling helmet shouted aloud to Diomedes:
"Son of Tydeus, the Danaäns who have fast horses
respected you with the seat of honor and with fine
cuts of meat, and with a full cup. Now they will dishonor you.   165
You are no better than a woman! So go away, you coward.
You puppet! Not through any flinching of mine will you climb

---

138 *beneath the car*: It is not clear how this is possible.

our walls and carry our women away in your ships.
Before that I will give you your doom!"

                         So Hector spoke.
170 The son of Tydeus turned his mind in two ways,
    whether to wheel his horses and fight head on or ...
    Three times he turned this over in his breast and in his spirit,
    three times Zeus the counselor boomed from the peaks
    of Ida, showing a sign to the Trojans of the victory
175 that turns the tide of battle.

                         Hector called to the Trojans
    and he spoke loudly: "Trojans and Lycians and Dardanians
    who fight in close! Be men, my friends! Have a thought
    for reckless valor! I see that with a ready heart
    the son of Kronos has given me victory and great glory,
180 but to the Danaäns only pain. They are only fools
    who have devised these walls, weak and of no account.
    They will not stop my power! Our horses will easily jump
    over the ditch that they've dug. And when I come
    amidst the hollow ships, let someone remember
185 to bring the devouring fire so I can burn the ships
    and kill all those Argives who stand by the ships,
    confused by the smoke."

                         So speaking, he called out to his horses
    and addressed them: "Xanthos and Podargos and Aithon
    and good Lampos, it is time that you two° paid back for the
190 provisions that Andromachê, the daughter of great-hearted
    Eëtion, placed before you in abundance—honey-hearted wheat,
    mixed in wine when the spirit urged her. She took better care
    of you than me, who am supposed to be her strong husband!
      "But hurry up in pursuit so we can take the shield of Nestor,
195 whose fame reaches the heavens—the shield made entirely of gold,
    both the handgrips and shield itself. And let us snatch from the shoulders
    of Diomedes, the tamer of horses, his highly-wrought chest-protector,

---

189 *you two*: There seems to be something wrong with the Greek, because nowhere else in the *Iliad* do four
     horses draw a chariot (the one or two trace-horses do not actually pull the car), and after naming four
     horses (Xanthos = "tawny"; Podargos = "swift of foot"; Aithon = "fiery"; Lampos = "bright") Homer
     switches to the dual number, speaking of only two horses. Perhaps Hector has two trace-horses that are
     here named along with the yoke-horses, and then he addresses just the yoke-horses.

which Hephaistos made for him.° If we take these two pieces
of armor, I would believe that the Achaeans will flee tonight
on their swift ships!"°   200

        So he spoke, boasting, but the revered
Hera was most indignant. She shook herself on her throne,
and high Olympos quaked° as she spoke directly
to Poseidon, the great god: "Well, wide-ruling shaker
of the earth, your spirit has no pity for the Danaäns
as they perish, though at Helikê and Aigai° they brought you gifts,   205
many and dear. You used to wish them victory. If we only
were willing—all of us who support the Danaän cause—
to push back the Trojans and to hold back Zeus, whose voice
is heard from afar, then he would be sorry sitting
there on Ida all by himself!"   210

        Groaning mightily,
Poseidon, the earth-shaker, said: "Hera, you have spoken
a word that should never be spoken. It is not I who would want
to see us all fight against Zeus the son of Kronos,
for he is much stronger."

        Such things they said to one another.
And now was all the space filled—as much as the ditch   215
enclosed on the side of the ships away from the wall—
with horses and shield-bearing men, huddled together.°
It was Hector who huddled them there together, the son of Priam,
the equal to Ares in speed, now that Zeus gave him glory.

    Now Hector would have burned the balanced ships with blazing   220
fire, if the lady Hera had not placed in the heart of Agamemnon
the thought that he should bestir himself and swiftly rouse up
the Achaeans. So Agamemnon went through the huts and along
the ships of the Achaeans carrying a large purple cloth

---

198   *... made for him*: We never again hear of Nestor's improbable golden shield. The highly wrought chest-
protector of Diomedes, the gift of Hephaistos, is not the gold one he got from Glaukos (Book 6).

200   *swift ships*: It is hardly likely that the Achaeans would depart if Hector were to capture these two odd pieces
of armament. Hector is admirable, but not always very smart.

202   *quaked*: Probably humorous.

205   *Helikê and Aigai*: Towns in ACHAEA in the northeast Peloponnesus that had shrines to Poseidon.

217   *together*: Apparently Hector has driven the Achaeans over the ditch and trapped them in the space between
the ditch and the wall, but the Greek is very obscure.

225 in his thick hand.° He stood on the black ship of Odysseus
with its huge hull, because it was in the middle so one could shout
to both ends, both to the tents of Ajax, the son of Telamon,
and to those of Peleus' son, Achilles. They had drawn up their
balanced ships at the very ends, trusting in the manly strength
230 of their hands.

          Agamemnon uttered a piercing shout,
calling to the Danaäns:° "Shame, Argives, and reproach!
You are only good to look at! Where's all your boasting now?
When we said we were the best? What about the hollow boasts
that you spoke in Lemnos while eating the abundant flesh
235 of straight-horned cattle and drinking bowls brimful of wine—.
you said that every man could take on one hundred Trojans,
yes, two hundred in battle! As it is, we are not equal
even to one, this Hector, who will soon burn our ships
with blazing fire!
          "Father Zeus, was there ever a mighty king
240 that you blinded with a blindness such as this,° and took away his glory?
I say that never did I pass by one of your most beautiful altars
in my ships with many benches, coming here, but on all I burned
the fat of bulls and their thigh-bones in my desire to sack
Troy with its wonderful walls. But Zeus, fulfill for me
245 at least this desire: Let us escape and avoid death! Don't leave
the Danaäns to the Trojans to be squashed like this!"

     So Agamemnon spoke, and the father took pity on him
as he wept. Zeus agreed that the Argives would be saved
and not destroyed. At once he sent down an eagle,
250 the surest of bird-signs. The eagle held a fawn
in its talons, the offspring of a swift deer. It dropped
the fawn—kerplop!—beside the most beautiful altar of Zeus,
where the Achaeans were used to sacrifice to Zeus, the source
of all omens.°

---

225 *hand*: To attract attention as a speaker.

231 *Danaäns*: If the Achaeans are huddled outside the walls between the ditch and wall, it is not clear how they
can hear Agamemnon's speech, unless we are to imagine the boat with its "huge hull" as taller than the wall
and Agamemnon is speaking over it.

240 *blindness*: The word for "blindness" is *atê*, an untranslatable word that Agamemnon uses eleven times. *Atê*
is the force that leads one to act in ways that bring bad results, but may refer to the disaster itself. Here
Agamemnon's *atê* is to have thought that by making appropriate sacrifice, Zeus would favor him.

254 *omens*: This altar is never heard of again.

FIGURE 8.1   Zeus and his emblem, the eagle.   Zeus sits on a throne dressed in an elaborately embroidered cloak. His hair is long and braided and his beard full. Spartan black-figure wine cup, c. 550 BC.

When the Achaeans saw that the bird
255 was from Zeus, they leaped again on the Trojans, remembering
their love of battle. But none of the many Danaäns
could claim that they turned their swift horses faster than
Diomedes, the son of Tydeus, to drive them across the ditch
and to fight in the hand-to-hand. Diomedes was the first one
260 to strike a man in armor, Agelaos, son of Phradraon.
In flight Agelaos turned his horses. As Agelaos wheeled
around, Diomedes hit him right in the back between
the shoulder blades. Diomedes drove the spear
through his breast and Agelaos fell from the car, his armor
265 clanging around him.

Afterwards came the sons
of Atreus, Agamemnon and Menelaos; and then the
two Ajaxes, cloaked in war madness; and then Idomeneus
and the companion of Idomeneus, Meriones, the equal to
Enyalios, the killer of men; and then Eurypylos the noble son
270 of Euaimon. As ninth came Teucer,° stretching his back-bent
bow. He crouched beneath the shield of Ajax, the son
of Telamon. Ajax would move the shield away from him
while the warrior Teucer, taking aim, would loose an arrow
and strike someone in the crowd, who fell and gave up
275 his life. Then Teucer, like a child snuggled by his mother, would
duck back toward Ajax, who protected him with his shining shield.

Whom first did blameless Teucer kill? Orsilochos
first, then Ormenos and Ophelestes and Daitor and Chromios
and godlike Lykophontes. Then Amopaon, the son of Polyaimon,
280 then Melanippos.° One after another he brought them to the bountiful earth.

Seeing him, Agamemnon, the king of men, rejoiced
that Teucer razed the ranks of the Trojans with his powerful bow.
Agamemnon went up to him and stood beside him and spoke
as follows: "Teucer, dear fellow—son of Telamon, captain
285 of the people, go on, shoot! Maybe you can be some kind of a light
to the Danaäns, and to your father Telamon who raised you when

---

270   *Teucer*: Half-brother to Telamonian Ajax. According to post-Homeric accounts, Teucer was the bastard son
of Hesionê, the daughter of Laomedon, and Telamon. There was an early Trojan king named Teucer, so this
Greek warrior bears a *Trojan* name (his mother Hesionê was after all a Trojan). Teucer, son of Telamon, was
a king of the island of Salamis in the harbor of Athens. Probably by the "two Ajaxes" Homer confusingly
sometimes means Ajax and *Teucer*, not Ajax the son of Telamon and *Ajax the son of Oïleus*.

280   ... *Melanippos*: Though some names later reappear, these victims are made up for the occasion.

you were a baby, and although you were a bastard took care
of you in his own house. Well, move him towards honor,
though he is far away. And let me tell you something
that I think will come to pass. If Zeus who holds   290
the goatskin fetish and Athena ever grant it to me—
I mean the sacking of the well-built citadel of Ilion—
I will place first in your hand a reward of honor—
after myself, of course! Either a tripod, or two horses
with a car, or a woman who can go up into your bed."   295

The blameless Teucer answered him: "Son
of Atreus, covered in glory, why do you urge me on
when I am already eager? I go at them to the limits
of my power. From the time when we first drove
them towards Ilion, from that moment I lay in wait   300
and killed men with my bow. I have fired eight
long-barbed arrows and all have fixed in the flesh
of youths swift in battle. Only I cannot hit this mad dog!"

He spoke and loosed another arrow from his string
straight at Hector. His heart longed to hit him. He missed,   305
but he hit with his arrow the blameless Gorgythion,
a brave son of Priam, in the chest, whom his wedded mother
bore, the beautiful Kastianeira from Aisymê,° alike
in her appearance to a goddess. Like a poppy Gorgythion
bowed his head to the side that in a garden is weighed   310
down with seed and spring rain—just so he bowed
his head to one side, weighed down by his helmet.

Teucer fired a second arrow from his string straight at Hector.
His heart longed to hit him, but he missed because Apollo
made the arrow swerve. Instead he hit Archeptolemos,°   315
Hector's bold charioteer, hurrying into battle.
He hit him in the chest next to the nipple. He fell
from the car, and his swift-footed horses veered off.
There his breath-soul was loosed and his strength.

A terrible pain for his charioteer clouded the mind   320
of Hector. Then he let it go, though sorry for his companion.

---

308 *Aisymê*: Perhaps in Thrace. Gorgythion is not heard of elsewhere.

315 *Archeptolemos*: Earlier sought out as Hector's replacement charioteer for Enipeus, killed by Diomedes'
     spear throw.

He ordered Kebriones, his brother, standing nearby,
to take the reins of the car. When Kebriones heard,
he quickly obeyed.

           Hector himself, all-shining,
325 jumped from the car to the ground with a terrible yell.
He took a stone in his hands and ran straight at Teucer,
for his heart urged him to snuff him out. Teucer
had drawn a bitter arrow from his quiver, and he placed
it on the string, but Hector, whose helmet flashes, rushed
330 upon him and struck him on the shoulder where the collarbone
separates the neck from the chest, the most vulnerable spot.
Hector struck him there with the jagged stone as Teucer
aimed at him eagerly. Hector broke his bow string.
Teucer's hand went numb at the wrist. He fell to his knees
335 and stayed there and the bow dropped from his hand.

    Ajax saw that his brother had gone down. He ran over
to him and hid him with his shield. Two faithful companions,
Mekisteus, the son of Echios, and the good Alastor stooped
beneath him and carried Teucer, groaning miserably,
340 to the hollow ships.

              Once again the Olympian raised up might
among the Trojans, and they drove the Achaeans straight
toward the deep ditch. Hector ran ahead among
the foremost fighters, glorying in his strength. Just as
when some swift-footed hound chases a wild boar
345 or lion and the trailing hound snatches at sides and buttocks
as the prey maneuvers to avoid the deadly fangs—even so
Hector pressed on the long-haired Achaeans, always
killing the laggards. The Achaeans were driven in rout.

    But as the Achaeans went through the stakes
350 and the ditch in their flight, many fell at the hands of the Trojans.
Then the Achaeans halted and stayed beside their ships,
The Achaeans called out to one another in dismay.
They raised their hands to all the gods, and every man
prayed mightily.

             Hector wheeled his horses with the beautiful
355 manes this way and that. His eyes were like those

FIGURE 8.2 **Trojans and Achaeans fighting hand to hand.** In this carving on a Lycian Tomb, Trojan and Achaean warriors fight in the hand-to-hand. The warrior on the left has just speared his opponent, who falls dead. The figures are dressed as contemporary hoplites with round shields, horse-hair crested helmets, and shinguards. The Lycians, who lived in the southwest of Asia Minor, were not Greeks but were deeply influenced by Greek art and culture, and in Homer's *Iliad* they are the most important Trojan allies. They used the Greek alphabet to record an unknown language and on this tomb carved many scenes from the fighting at Troy. Limestone relief on the tomb of a Lycian prince, from the west side of the Heroön of Goelbasi-Trysa, Lycia, Turkey, c. 380 BC.

of the Gorgon° or of murderous Ares. Seeing them, the goddess,
white-armed Hera, took pity. Right away she spoke words
to Athena that flew like arrows: "How, O daughter of Zeus
who carries the goatskin fetish, how shall we two
360 not care for the Danaäns when they are being ruined,
even at this last moment? They perish fulfilling
an evil fate, all because of the attack of one man—
Hector, son of Priam, who rages out of control.
He is wreaking mayhem!"

Flashing-eyed Athena
365 answered her: "How I wish that Hector would lose
his strength and spirit at the hands of the Argives, destroyed
in the land of his fathers. But my father rages with
an evil mind. Wretch, always the rogue, thwarter of my plans!
Zeus remembers not at all how I often saved Herakles
370 when he was being abused by the contests of Eurystheus.
Truly, he would cry out to heaven, and from heaven Zeus
would send me to save him. If I had known this in the wisdom
of my heart, when Eurystheus sent Herakles to the house of Hades,
the great gate-fastener, to retrieve from Erebos the hound
375 of hateful Hades, Herakles would not have fled the steep
waters of Styx.° Now he hates me, and he fulfills the desires
of Thetis, who kissed his knees and took his chin
in her hand, begging that he honor Achilles, the sacker
of cities. But the time will come when he again calls me
380 his 'little flashing-eyes' ...
                    "But now please ready the single-hoofed
horses for us, so that I can go to the house of Zeus
who carries the goatskin fetish and attire myself
in armor appropriate for war. Soon we will know
whether the son of Priam, Hector of the sparkling helmet,
385 will be happy to see us appear on the bridges of war!
I think that many Trojans will glut the dogs and the birds
with fat and flesh, fallen at the ships of the Achaeans!"

---

356 *Gorgon*: Any one who looked into the Gorgon's eyes was turned to stone.

376 *waters of the Styx*: The labors or "contests" (*athloi*) of Herakles were not yet standardized as ten or twelve
     tasks. In this task the cowardly Eurystheus, Herakles' cousin who held power over him, compelled the hero
     to descend to the underworld and bring back Cerberus, who protected the gates to the house of Hades. The
     waters of the Styx, "hateful," surround the underworld.

So Athena spoke, and the goddess white-armed Hera
quickly obeyed. She went to and fro harnessing
the horses with golden head-pieces, Hera, the queenly 390
goddess, the daughter of great Kronos.

But Athena,
the daughter of Zeus who carries the goatskin fetish, let drop
her delicate, embroidered gown on the floor of her father.
She herself had made the gown and worked it with her hands.
Athena put on the shirt of Zeus who gathers the clouds 395
and put on the armor for tear-making war. She walked
out to the fiery car, took up her spear—heavy, huge, strong!—
with which she overwhelms the ranks of fighting men,
with whomever she is angry, this daughter of a powerful father.
Hera quickly touched the horses with the lash,° and heaven's gates 400
groaned open by themselves that the Hours control,
and to whom the sky and Olympos are entrusted, whether
to throw open the thick cloud or to close it in. Through
these gates they drove the horses, tolerant of the goad.

But when Zeus the father saw them from Ida, he became 405
greatly vexed, and he sent forth Iris with the golden wings
to make an announcement: "Up, go, fast Iris!
Turn them back! Do not let them come against me!
This war will not be a pretty one. I will say this,
and I think it will come to pass: I will maim their swift 410
horses yoked to the chariot! I will cast them out of the car!
I will smash it! Not in ten years will their wounds heal
when the thunder hits them. Then maybe the flashing-eyed one
will know what it is to fight against her own father.
I'm not so annoyed by Hera, nor so angry—she always 415
opposes what I say!"

So Zeus spoke, and storm-footed
Iris went off to proclaim his word. She went from
the hills of Ida to high Olympos, at the outside
of the gates of Olympos with its many folds, where she met
the goddesses and held them back. Iris spoke the word 420
of Zeus: "Where are you going? Have your hearts
gone mad in your breasts? The son of Kronos does not
permit you to go to the aid of the Argives. The son of Kronos

---

400   *lash*: Hera has joined Athena in the chariot.

has made this threat, which will come to pass: that he will
425 maim the swift horses beneath your chariot, and that he will cast
you out of the car and he will smash it. Not in ten years will
your wounds heal when the thunder hits you. Then maybe
the flashing-eyed one will know what it is to fight
against her own father. But he's not so annoyed by Hera,
430 nor so angry—she always opposes what he says!
But you are an awful bitch and fearless if truly you dare
to lift your huge spear against Zeus."

                Thus swift-footed Iris
spoke and, so speaking, she went away. But Hera said this
to Athena: "My dear, I can no longer permit the two
435 of us to wage war against Zeus on the account of mortals.
Let this one live, let that one die, just as it happens.
Leave Zeus to have his own ideas and to judge between
Trojans and Danaäns, as is fit."

              So speaking Hera turned
back her single-hoofed horses. The Hours unyoked
440 the horses with beautiful manes for them and tethered
the horses at their food-bins filled with ambrosia. Then Hera
leaned the car up against the sidewall of the bright vestibule.
The goddesses sat down on golden thrones in the midst
of the other gods, aggrieved in their hearts.

                Then Zeus
445 the father drove his well-wheeled chariot and horses
from Ida to Olympos. He arrived at the meeting of the gods.
Poseidon, the famous earth-shaker, unharnessed the horses
for Zeus and placed his chariot on a stand, then spread
a cloth over it. Zeus, whose voice reaches afar,
450 then took his seat on the golden throne, and great Olympos
quaked beneath his feet. Only Athena and Hera sat apart
from Zeus. They did not speak to him, nor ask him
any questions.

          But Zeus knew in his heart and he said:
"Why are you so upset, Athena and Hera? Are you tired out
455 through destroying the Trojans, against whom you hold a bitter
hatred, in the battle where men win glory? In any event,
such are my strength and my irresistible hands. I could not
be turned aside by all the gods in Olympos. As for you two,
a shaking took hold of your glorious limbs before you even

glimpsed the war and the horrendous deeds of war. I will   460
tell you this, and I think it has already come to pass:
You would not have returned upon your car back to Olympos,
the seat of the gods, when it was blasted by thunder!"

    Thus Zeus spoke, and Athena and Hera murmured.
Despite sitting near him, they still devised evil for the Trojans.   465
Athena fell silent and would say nothing, so furious was she
with her father Zeus. A wild anger had taken hold of her.
Hera, too, could not contain her anger, and she said: "O most
dreaded son of Kronos, what words you say! Now we begin
to understand that your strength is immense. Nevertheless we feel   470
sorry for the Danaän spearmen who perish, accomplishing an evil
fate. But we will have done with the war, if you order it.
Only we shall give to the Argives some advice, in hope
to help them, so that not all die, thanks to your wrath."

    Zeus, who assembles the clouds, then answered her: 475
"And at dawn you will see the most mighty son of Kronos
destroying, if you wish, O revered Hera with the cow eyes,
a far greater portion of the army of the Achaean spearmen!
For the powerful Hector will not cease from the war before things
are made right with Achilles, the fast runner, beside the ships   480
on that day when they fight at the sterns of the ships
over the dead Patroklos. For it is so ordained!° Nor do I give
a fig for your anger, even should you go to the lowest bounds
of earth and sea where Iapetos and Kronos sit and take
no joy in the rays of Helios Hyperion, nor of the breezes,   485
and deep Tartaros is all around.° Not if you go
there in your wandering do I care a bit about your anger,
for there is no greater bitch anywhere than you!"°

---

482 *ordained*: Because that is the story that Homer inherited, according to which Troy did fall, and not even
the gods can change that. Zeus is powerless before Fate, though he claims that he could overrule Fate if he
wished (he never does). Homer here summarizes the story of the *Iliad*—the wrath of Achilles that results
in the deaths of Patroklos and Hector—to remind his listeners and himself.

486 *around*: Zeus imagines Hera going to Tartaros—the roots of earth, sea, and sky—where Zeus imprisoned
the Titans, represented by the Titan Iapetos (the biblical Japeth), the father of Prometheus, and the Titan
Kronos, the father of Zeus himself. Earlier in this book Zeus threatened to send to Tartaros any god who
disobeyed him (line 13). "Helius Hyperion" means the "sun who goes across." After Homer, Hyperion was
said to be an independent Titan, the father of Helius.

488 *than you*: Zeus's exaggerated resentment of his wife parodies the monogamous woes of the warrior elite
who were Homer's audience. The origins of monogamy are not clear, but in the classical world only Greeks
and Romans were monogamous.

So he spoke, and white-armed Hera did not answer him.
490 The bright light of the sun fell into Ocean, dragging
with it black night over the rich plowland. The Trojans
were unwilling to see the sun set, but to the Achaeans
the dark night was welcome, yes, three-times prayed for.
Glorious Hector called an assembly of the Trojans,
495 leading them away from the ships to the banks of the swirling
Xanthos, in a clean space where there were no corpses.
They dismounted from their cars to the ground to hear the word
of Hector, who was dear to Zeus. In his hand he held
the sixteen-foot spear, which before him gleamed with its bronze tip.
500 Around it ran a ferrule of gold.

                Leaning on this, Hector
spoke to the Trojans: "Hear me, Trojans and Dardanians
and allies! I thought to destroy the ships and all
the Achaeans now and then to go back to windy Ilion.
But before I could, darkness came on, which has saved
505 the Argives more than anything, and their ships on the shore.
Nevertheless, let us obey the dark night and make ready
our dinner. Let us unyoke the horses with beautiful manes
and give them fodder. Bring oxen and sheep from the city quickly.
Bring honey-sweet wine and bread from the halls. Gather
510 cords of wood so that all night long, until the light
of dawn, we might burn many fires, and the light will reach
to heaven so that the long-haired Achaeans do not hurry to flee,
even during the night, over the broad back of the sea. Let them not
board their ships at their ease and without trouble, but let
515 many of them contemplate some weapon, struck by an arrow
or sharp spear as they leap onto a ship. This shall be a lesson
to anyone who thinks he can bring dread war against the Trojans!
    "Let heralds, dear to Zeus, go through the city and announce
that the young children and old men with white hair should camp
520 on the walls built by the gods.° And may the women, every one
of them, build great fires in their halls, but let them always be wary
of an ambush coming into the city while the army is outside.
    "May it be so, O great-hearted Trojans, as I say.
This is my advice, which is sound and good. At dawn
525 I will speak again to the horse-taming Trojans. I hope

---

520 *built by the gods*: They camp on the walls, built by Poseidon and Apollo for Laomedon, in anticipation of the
great fight to come at dawn.

by praying to Zeus and to the other gods we shall drive out
of here these dogs carried by the Fates, those whom the Fates bore
on their black ships. For this night we will take care of ourselves,
but in the morning at break of dawn let us arm ourselves
and make dread battle at the hollow ships. I will know   530
if the son of Tydeus, strong Diomedes, will push me
back from the ships against the wall, or whether I will overcome
him in the fight and carry away his bloody armor. Tomorrow
he will come to know his valor and if he will wait for my spear.
Many of his companions will fall around him too   535
as tomorrow's sun rises. I wish that I were deathless
and ageless for all my days, and that I were honored as Athena
and Apollo, so surely as now this day brings evil
to the Argives!"°

      So Hector spoke, and the Trojans gave assent.
They loosed the sweating horses from beneath their yokes.   540
They tethered them with thongs, each man standing near his own car.
They brought cattle and sheep from the city, quickly, and honey-sweet
wine, and bread from the halls, and they gathered much wood.
The winds bore the smoke from the plain into the heaven.
Thus the Trojans with high hearts stayed all night long   545
along the bridges of war. The fires burned in their multitudes.

    As when in the heaven stars around the brilliant moon
appear shining, when the air is breathless, and easily seen
are the mountains and the high headlands and the forests
and clearings, and from heaven breaks open the infinite air,   550
and all the stars are clear, delighting the heart of the shepherd—
just so many, between the ships and the waters of Xanthos,
did the fires of the Trojans appear before the face of Ilion.

    A thousand fires burned on the plain, and next to each
sat fifty men in the glow from the blazing fire.   555
Their horses, eating white barley and wheat, stood next
to the chariots and waited for Dawn on her beautiful chair.

---

539 *Argives:* That is, as surely as he would like to live forever, and be honored as a god, just as surely will the
    Achaeans be defeated.

BOOK 9. *The Embassy to Achilles*

Thus the Trojans kept watch, while a tremendous panic,
the companion of icy fear, fixed on the Achaeans.
An unbearable anxiety settled on all the captains.
As when two winds stir up the fishy sea, North Wind
5 and West Wind blowing suddenly out of THRACE,
and immediately a dark wave crests, pushing
a line of seaweed along the shore—even so
the hearts of the Achaeans were torn in their breasts.°

The son of Atreus, struck in his heart by a great sorrow,
10 went here and there commanding his clear-voiced heralds to call
secretely every man by name to the place of assembly—but not to
shout too loud. Agamemnon himself worked amidst the foremost.°

They sat down, much troubled, and Agamemnon rose,
pouring tears like a spring of black water that over
15 a rocky cliff rains down its dark water—even so,
groaning, he spoke to the Argives these words: "Friends,
leaders and advisers of the Argives, Zeus the son of Kronos
has bound me in a deep blindness°—the wretch!—who once
promised me and agreed that I would sail home after sacking
20 the high-walled city. But now he has devised a wicked
deception, and enjoins me to return in shame to Argos
after having lost many warriors. Well, such is the pleasure
of almighty Zeus, who has loosed the crowns of many
cities, and will of still others to come. For his power is the highest.

25 "But come, let all obey what I say: We shall flee
on our ships to the beloved land of our fathers. We shall never
take Troy of the broad highways!"

---

8 *Achaeans*: In this unusual simile the visible, tangible waves on the sea are compared with the invisible, intangible feelings of the men. Usually storm similes accompany furious warfare. The Achaeans seem to have retreated to inside the earthen wall, though Homer never says this.

12 *foremost*: That is, to gather the assembly.

18 *blindness*: The Greek word is again *atê*: doing things whose consequences you did not foresee, and the disaster itself that follows.

So he spoke, and the company
fell into silence. For a long time they remained silent,
sorrowing, the sons of the Achaeans, but at last Diomedes,
good at the war cry, spoke: "Son of Atreus, I will   30
first disagree with you in your foolishness, as is right,
my king, here in public assembly.° So don't get mad.
My valor you did first insult among the Danaäns,
saying I was not a man of war, and without courage!°
Both young and old of the Achaeans know that this is what happened.   35
The son of cunning Kronos gave you a two-edged gift:
Above all he granted that you to be honored by the scepter,
but he did not give you valor. There's the greatest authority!
    "If your spirit enjoins you to sail home, then go!
The road is open. Your ships stand near the sea,   40
they followed you from Mycenae in vast numbers.
But the other long-haired Achaeans will remain until
we take Troy. And if they too wish to flee in their swift ships
to the beloved land of their fathers, then I and Sthenelos°
will fight on until we win the goal of Ilion. We have come   45
with divine approval."° So he spoke and all the sons
of the Achaeans assented, applauding the words of horse-taming
Diomedes.

        Then Nestor the horseman arose and spoke:
"Son of Tydeus, you are powerful in the fight, and in council
you are the best of your peers. Not one Achaean will make light   50
of what you say nor deny its truth. But you have not
said all there is to be said. For you are still young.
You might even be my son, the youngest born.
And you speak sense to the chiefs of the Argives, for you
have spoken in accord with the way things seem.   55
But come, I, who am older than you—I will explain
all, I will clarify every issue. Nor will any

---

32 *assembly*: The assembly is a type-scene that by convention always sets in motion a new sequence of events, in
    this case, the embassy to Achilles.

34 *courage*: In Book 4, in the marshaling of the chieftains, Agamemnon for no good reason reproached
    Diomedes, but he did not say that he was "not a man of war" nor that he was "without courage."

44 *Sthenelos*: The son of the Theban-fighter Kapaneus and one of the commanders of the contingent from
    Argos, according to the Catalog of Ships. After this reference he drops from sight until the funeral games for
    Patroklos in Book 23.

46 *approval*: Because in violating the laws of hospitality (*xenia*) Paris has guaranteed divine disapproval. For
    this reason even Zeus cannot save Troy, although he loves the city (also, Troy is fated to fall.).

man scorn my word, not even the ruler Agamemnon.
Without attachment to clan, without law, without a hearth
60 is the man who loves icy war among the people.°
    "But let us obey black night and make ready our dinner.
Let there be sentinels posted along the ditch beyond
the wall. I hereby command the young men to do this—
and you, son of Atreus, lead! For you are most kingly.
65 Make a meal for the old men. It is suitable, it is not unsuitable.
Your tents are filled with wine that the ships bring daily
over the broad sea from Thrace. You have every kind
of entertainment, and you rule over many. When we get many
together, you will follow that man who proposes the best plan.
70 I think we Achaeans have a great need for some good and
intelligent counsel, seeing that the enemy is kindling many fires
close to the ships. Who could be happy about this?
This night will bring ruin to our army, or save it."

    So Nestor spoke, and everybody listened and took heed.
75 The sentinels in their armor hastened around Nestor's son
Thrasymedes, shepherd of the people—Askalaphos and Ialmenos,
sons of Ares, and Meriones and Aphareus and Deïpyros,
and the son of Kreon, the good Lykomedes.° These were
the seven leaders of the sentinels, and with each one went
80 one hundred young men. They sat down in rows, holding
long spears in the middle ground between the ditch and the wall.°
There they built a fire, and each man prepared his meal.

    But the son of Atreus brought the elders of the Achaeans
in a body into his tent, and before each man he placed
85 a satisfying meal. They put forth their hands to the good cheer
set ready before them.

---

60 *people*: The "people" being Agamemnon and his warrior Diomedes. Nestor is trying to calm the potentially
    explosive situation, similar to that with which the poem began. He sees that Agamemnon could again be
    forced into a corner by a hothead warrior, Diomedes, taking a moral stance. He defuses the situation by
    recommending a private council.

78 *... Lykomedes*: Thrasymedes' brother Antilochos, the first Achaean to kill someone in the poem (Book 4)
    and active later, is curiously not mentioned. Askalaphos dies accidentally in Book 13; Askalaphos and
    Ialmenos are mentioned in the Catalog of Ships as captains from Orchomenos. Meriones is the Cretan archer,
    friend, companion, and aide to Idomeneus. Aphareus is killed in Book 13 by Aeneas. Deïpyros is killed by the
    Trojan Helenos, also in Book 13. Lykomedes is mentioned in three more books: Lykomedes' father Kreon
    was king of Thebes and brother to Epikastê, the queen who married (and gave birth to) Oedipus.

81 *wall*: For some reason hard to imagine the Achaeans have built the ditch a fair ways away from the wall, not
    at its foot. Earlier Hector penned the Achaeans in this space.

But when they had cast off all
desire for drink and food, old man Nestor, whose past
advice had always seemed best, first of all began
to weave a plan. Wishing them well, he rose
and addressed them: "Most glorious son of Atreus,   90
the king of men, Agamemnon, with you will I end, with you
I begin,° because you are king of many and Zeus has given
you the scepter and good judgment so that you might take counsel
for the people. Therefore it is proper that you deliver a superior
plan, but that you listen too, and that you fulfill for another   95
what his heart impels him to say if it is to our advantage.
What we finally undertake depends on *you*.°
  "But let me say what seems to me to be best.
No one else will have a better thought than mine, which I
have had for a long time and still have, from the time when   100
you, Agamemnon, nurtured of Zeus, went to Achilles'
tent and, enraging him, you took the girl Briseïs,
not at all according to our advice. I explicitly
warned you against doing this very thing, but you
gave in to your proud spirit and dishonored a very   105
powerful man whom the gods have highly honored.
You went and you seized his prize, and you hold her still!
But let us even now consider how we might soothe him
and persuade Achilles with noble gifts and honeyed words."

  King Agamemnon then answered: "Old man, it is not   110
a false tale you have told of my blindness. I have been *blind*!
I don't deny it. A man is worth many people if Zeus
loves him in his heart, even as now he honors this man
while he destroys the army of the Achaeans.
                                          "But since I have
been *blind*, giving in to my vile persuasions, I would like to make   115
amends and to give boundless penalty tokens. Let me enumerate
to all of you the great things I'll give: seven unfired tripods,
ten talents of gold, twenty shining cauldrons, twelve powerful

---

92   *begin*: A formula ordinarily used when speaking with gods.

97   *on you*: Here is the social contract that underlies power: Agamemnon is a sceptered king, but he still must
     listen to others and, when others' counsel is better, follow that course. Because he violated this rule in deal-
     ing with Achilles, he now stands on the brink of ruin. This is his *atê*, his "blindness"—he could not foresee
     the ill consequences of a certain manner of behavior.

horses, winners all, who have taken prizes through their speed.
120 Nor will you ever lack for booty, nor lack in precious
gold when you have as many prizes as I have won
through my horses' swiftness of foot.
                              "I will give Achilles seven
women from LESBOS, skilled with their hands, whom he himself
once captured when he sacked that well-built city, women
125 of surpassing beauty that I chose from the spoil. These
I shall give him, along with the woman I took from him,
the daughter of Briseus. And I shall swear an oath: Never
did I enter her bed, nor mix with her in love,
as is the custom of men and women.
                              "All these things
130 shall be ready to his hand. And if the gods shall grant us
to sack the high city of Priam, then he can load his ship
with all the gold and bronze he wants at the division
of the spoils. And he can take twenty Trojan women,
those who are most beautiful, after Argive Helen.
135   "And if we return to Achaean Argos, the rich land,
may he be my son! I will honor him like Orestes,°
my darling, who is raised in the midst of abundance. I have
three daughters in my well-built hall, Chrysothemis and
Laodikê and Iphianassa.° Of these he may take as wife
140 whichever he wants—no bride-price necessary!—and lead her
to the house of Peleus. I will give her a dowry, too,
so much as no man ever gave: seven towns
densely populated, Kardamylê, Enopê, and grassy Hirê,
and holy Pherai, and Antheia rich in meadows,
145 and beautiful Aipeia and vine-girt Pedasos, all of them
close by the sea on the edge of sandy Pylos.°
The men who dwell within them are rich in sheep
and rich in cattle. They will shower him with many gifts,
as if he were a god. They will gladly obey his scepter-given
150 commands.

---

136   Orestes: Agamemnon's son Orestes is mentioned only here in the *Iliad*, but six times in the *Odyssey*.

139   *Iphianassa*: Agamemnon does not include the Electra famous from later tradition, who conspired with her brother Orestes to murder Agamemnon when he returned home from the war. "Iphianassa" is probably a variant of "Iphigeneia": Homer does not seem to know the famous story of the sacrifice of Iphigeneia at Aulis to make the winds blow fair that carried the ships to Troy.

146   ... *Pylos*: None of these towns is mentioned in the Pylian entry in the Catalog of Ships. They seem to be located around the MESSENIAN GULF with "Pylos" here designating the general territory controlled from the town of PYLOS, a sort of buffer area between the kingdoms of Nestor in the town of Pylos and Menelaos in the town of SPARTA.

"All this I will bring to pass, if only
he gives over his rage. Let him yield—Hades can never
be soothed or overcome, for which reason he is the most
hated of all the gods by men! So let him submit
to me, for I am more kingly and the older in age."

Gerenian Nestor then answered Agamemnon: "Son   155
of Atreus, covered in glory, king of men Agamemnon,
these gifts you offer Achilles, son of Peleus, can no man
despise. But come, let us send some chosen men
who may go as quickly as possible to the tent of Achilles,
son of Peleus. And those whom I choose, let them agree to go.   160
First of all, Phoinix,° beloved of Zeus—may he lead.
Then Big Ajax and the good Odysseus. As heralds, let Odios
and Eurybates follow along.° So bring water now
for our hands, and order all to keep silent so that we may pray
to Zeus, son of Kronos, if he will take pity."°   165

So spoke Nestor.
He had spoken words pleasing to all. Immediately the heralds
poured water over their hands. Youths filled bowls to the brim
with drink, which they served to all—but first a dollop
for the gods. When they had poured out an offering, they drank
as much as each man wished. Then they went from Agamemnon's hut,   170
the son of Atreus. The horseman Gerenian Nestor
looked at each man, especially Odysseus, and gave
strict orders to members of the embassy that they persuade
Achilles, the son of Peleus.

The two men° walked along
the shore of the turbulent sea, praying hard to the shaker   175

---

161 *Phoinix*: Achilles' aged tutor, about whom we learn a good deal in this book, but he is not earlier mentioned
     and scarcely again after Book 9.

163 *follow along*: Nestor does not select Talthybios, Agamemnon's herald, who took Briseïs, which might offend
     Achilles. Both Odios, "road man," and Eurybates, "far-traveler," have "speaking names." Odios
     appears only here, but Eurybates seems to be one of Odysseus' men (Book 2) and reappears in the
     Odyssey (Book 19).

165 *take pity*: In such formal prayers first comes purification of the hands; then an order that everyone keep
     silent so that no words of ill omen are spoken; then a pouring out of sacrificial wine, a libation, is made, or a
     sprinkling of barley; then the prayer itself (here for some reason suppressed).

175 *two men*: Suddenly Homer switches into the dual number (Greek has a dual form, in addition to the singular
     and plural), but he has just said that five men (or three, not counting the heralds) have been chosen for the
     embassy. Apparently in an earlier oral version only Ajax and Odysseus were on the embassy, but Homer
     has added Phoinix (and the heralds), who has a special role to play, without adjusting his diction.

of the earth, that they might persuade Achilles, the grandson
of Aiakos. They came to the huts and the swift ships
of the Myrmidons.° They found Achilles refreshing his spirit
in the bright and beautiful sound of the lyre, wonderfully made.
180 The bridge on it was silver, loot from the time when he burned
the town of Eëtion.° With it now he refreshed his spirit
as he sang of the famous deeds of men.° Patroklos sat
opposite him, all alone, silent, waiting until the grandson
of Aiakos should finish his singing.

                    The two men came up,
185 and Odysseus stood before Achilles, who, amazed,
leaped from his seat holding the lyre. Patroklos too
rose when he saw them. Achilles, the fast runner,
spoke, greeting the two men: "Welcome! Some sorry
need must bring you here. But you come as friends!—
190 of all the Achaeans you are most dear to me,
though I am very angry."

               So speaking, he led
them to his tent, and he invited them to sit on chairs
covered in purple cloths.° He spoke at once
to Patroklos, who stood nearby: "Son of Menoitios,
195 bring out the big bowl, mix in it stronger wine,
and give each man a cup. These men who have come
beneath my roof are most dear."°

                Patroklos obeyed
his comrade. He placed a chopping block in the glare

---

178 *Myrmidons*: We cannot get a clear picture of the Achaean shelters. The Greek word *klisia* means either
"tent," or "hut," and I translate it both ways. The *klisia* must be covered with cloths or skins, but sometimes,
as in the description of Achilles' *klisia* in Book 24, it is a very elaborate nearly permanent structure with a
heavy bolted gate. There must be a smoke-hole in the center for the hearth. Here the embassy simply walks
in without ceremony.

181 *Eëtion*: The king of Asiatic Thebes, where Chryseïs was captured.

182 *deeds of men*: Achilles is behaving like an *aoidos*, an "oral-singer," in celebrating the "deeds of men." But
otherwise in Homer *aoidoi* are always professionals, not amateurs. This is the only example in Homer of a
private singer.

193 *cloths*: Homeric heroes sit to eat, either on a stool or armless chair. Not until around 600 BC was the
custom of lying on a couch and dining from a central table (as in the Last Supper) imported from the Near
East. The purple color indicates that the clothes are of Phoenician origin and of the highest quality.

197 *most dear*: Ordinary wine, diluted with water, was apparently too heavy to be drunk straight, or the Greeks
simply had a taste for wine punch of which huge quantities were drunk at drinking parties (*symposia*),
to judge from pottery of the Classical Period. There are no servants in Achilles' hut, but Patroklos and
Automedon, the second and third in command, help out. Every man serves himself as equals in this most
elaborately described nonsacrificial meal in Homer.

of the fire. On it he laid the back of a sheep and a fat
goat and the backbone of a big porker, brimming   200
with fat. Automedon gripped the meat while Achilles
sliced it. He cut small pieces and threaded them on spits.
The son of Menoitios, a man like a god, stoked up
the fire. When the fire had burned, and the flame had abated,
Patroklos scattered the coals and placed the spits   205
upon them. He sprinkled delicious salt on the flesh,
supporting the spits by means of andirons. When the meat
was cooked, he stacked it on platters. Patroklos took
bread and set it out on a table in lovely baskets
while Achilles served the meal.   210

                  Achilles sat down
opposite godlike Odysseus, who sat against the wall.
He urged his companion Patroklos to make the gods
an offering. Patroklos cast pieces of meat into the fire.
Then they ate the succulent meal before them.

    When they had satisfied their desire for drink   215 🔊
and food, Ajax nodded to Phoinix. Odysseus noticed
and, filling his cup with wine, he toasted Achilles:
"Hail to you Achilles! There is no lack of the abundant feast,
either in the tent of Agamemnon, son of Atreus,
nor here either, where there is fine fare aplenty.°   220
But now this succulent feast is not our concern.
God-nurtured Achilles, we are terribly afraid … We see
complete disaster looming before us. We doubt
that we can save our well-benched ships. We fear
they will be destroyed if you do not don your mantle   225
of power. For the Trojans, intrepid in their hearts, have set
up camp outside the wall near the ships, along with
their allies of wide renown. Their campfires burn
all along the battleline. Nor do they think they will go on
holding back, but soon they will fall on our dark ships.   230
Zeus, the son of Kronos, sends lightning on their right.
Hector, exulting, rages like a madman, trusting
in Zeus. Nor does he care about men or gods. A mighty
insanity has taken hold of him. He prays for dawn.
He boasts he will cut the ensigns from our ships'   235
sterns and that he will set them afire, and destroy the Achaeans

---

220 *aplenty*: Odysseus, Ajax, and Phoenix have just eaten their fill in Agamemnon's hut!

FIGURE 9.1   Embassy to Achilles.   Achilles sits on a chair covered by a goat skin, his head wrapped in a cloak of mourning, his hand to his head in grief. He holds a gnarled staff. Opposite sits Odysseus, with his characteristic hat on his back, holding two javelins. Behind Odysseus stands the aged Phoenix with a staff similar to Achilles', and on the right Patroklos looks on, leaning on his own staff. Ajax does not appear. Athenian red-figure vase, c. 480 BC, by Kleophrades.

confused from the smoke that consumes the hulls. And I
greatly fear in my heart that the gods will bring this
to pass—that it will be our fate to die on the windy
plain of Troy, far from Argos rich in herds.   240
     "But come Achilles, we implore you to save the sons
of the Achaeans even at this late hour, cowering as they are
at the war-din of the Trojans. You'll be sorry if you don't,
nor will you find a remedy for the harm once done.
No, think now how you might ward off that evil day   245
for the Danaäns! Did not your father Peleus say to you,
on that day when he sent you from PHTHIA to Agamemnon,
'O my son, Athena and Hera will give you strength
if you restrain the heart rampant in your breast.
Moderation is best. Keep aloof from strife that only brings   250
evil. In this way the Argives will honor you the more,
both the young and the old.' Thus your father advised you.
Do not forget his words. Let it go—give up your bitter
anger. Agamemnon will reward you richly, if only you
cast aside your rage.   255
                    "Now hear me out!—I will tell
you what Agamemnon has for you in his tent:
seven unfired tripods, ten talents of gold,
twenty shining cauldrons, twelve powerful horses,
winners who have taken prizes through their speed.
Never will you lack for booty, nor want for precious   260
gold, when you have the prizes Agamemnon has won
through his horses' swiftness of foot.
                              "He will give you seven
women of Lesbos, women of surpassing beauty and skilled with
their hands, whom you yourself once captured when you
sacked that well-built city. These he shall give you, along   265
with the woman he took from you, the daughter of Briseus.
And Agamemnon shall swear an oath: Never did
he enter her bed, nor mix with her in love, as is
the custom among men and women.
                              "All these things
are immediately available. And if the gods shall grant that   270
we sack the high city of Priam, then you can load your ship
with all the gold and bronze you want at the division
of the spoils. And take twenty Trojan women, those
who are most beautiful, after Argive Helen.
     "And if we return to Achaean Argos, the rich land,   275
he will make you his son. He will honor you like Orestes,
his darling, whom he raises in the midst of abundance. He has

three daughters in his well-built hall, Chrysothemis
and Laodikê and Iphianassa. Of these you may take as wife
280 whichever you want—no bride-price necessary!—and lead her
to the house of Peleus. He will give you a dowry too,
so much as no man ever gave: seven towns
densely populated, Kardamylê, Enopê, and grassy Hirê,
and holy Pherai, and Antheia rich in meadows,
285 and beautiful Aipeia and vine-girt Pedasos, all of them
close by the sea on the edge of sandy Pylos.
The men who dwell within them are rich in sheep
and rich in cattle. They will shower you with many gifts
as if you were a god. They will gladly obey
290 your scepter-given commands. All this he will bring
to pass, if only you give over this rage of yours.
      "But if your hatred for the son of Atreus, and all
his gifts, is too great, at least take pity on the Achaeans
ravaged throughout, men who will honor you
295 as if you were a god. For now you might
attain great glory in their eyes. Now is the time
you might put to death Hector, who comes in close,
thinking only of his destructive rage. He thinks
there is no one of the Danaäns, whom the black ships
300 have carried here, who is equal to himself."

                              In answer
Achilles the fast runner spoke to him: "Wise Odysseus,
son of Laërtes, god-nourished, I must speak to you directly,
just as I see it, and how I think it will come to pass,
so that you might not sit there, and me here, wasting
305 our time in idle talk. I hate that man like
the gates of Hades' house who conceals one thing
in his heart, but says another. I will say to you
how matters seems to me.
                  "I don't think Agamemnon, the son
of Atreus, can persuade me, nor any other of the Danaäns.
310 For there is no thanks for endlessly fighting the enemy.
The same lot comes to him who holds back as to him
who fights eagerly. In like honor are the shirker
and the brave. Death is the same reward for the man
who does much and for him who does nothing. It is
315 of no advantage to me that I have suffered pains
in my heart, ever risking my life in these contendings.
Like a bird who brings tidbits to her chicks, whatever
she can find, but goes herself without, so have I spent

many sleepless nights and bloody days passed
fighting with men on account of their wives. I laid
waste twelve cities from my black ships, and eleven
by land, throughout the Troad. From these I captured
a huge quantity of fine booty. Always I would
give the spoil to Agamemnon, son of Atreus. And he,
hanging back by the ships, took it all, apportioning
a small amount, but keeping most for himself.
So he gave some prize to the chiefs and the big men—
they have their prizes. But from me alone of the Achaeans
he took my bedmate, dear to my heart. Well, let him
lie beside her and take his pleasure!
                "But why,
I ask, must Argives fight against the Trojans?
Why has the son of Atreus gathered an army
and brought them here? Was it not for the sake of
fair-haired Helen? I suppose of *all men* the sons of Atreus
alone love their wives? No, every good and sensible
man loves and cherishes his wife, even as I loved
that woman with all my heart, though she was a captive
of my spear. As matters stand, Agamemnon has taken
my prize out of my arms. Surely he has deceived me.
He will not persuade me. I know him too well.
He shall not persuade me! "So Odysseus,
I think he should take counsel how with you
and all the other captains he might ward off
the consuming fire. Why, he has accomplished so much
without me! He has built a wall, and he has dug a ditch
along it, wide and grand! He has fixed stakes within it!
Even so, he cannot stop the force of Hector, killer of men.
So long as I fought among the Achaeans, Hector
never roused the battle-cry away from the walls,
but ventured only as far as the Scaean Gates
and the oak tree. There once he awaited me alone,
and scarcely did he escape my attack.
                "But as it is,
because I will not war against shining Hector, tomorrow,
after sacrifice to Zeus and the other gods, and heaping high
my ships, you will see me at the crack of dawn launch
forth on the salt sea—that is if you even care—
sailing on the Hellespont teeming with fish and my men
eagerly rowing. And if the mighty Shaker of Earth
grants us a fair voyage, on the third day we'll arrive in the rich
plowland of Phthia. There I have much wealth that I left behind

when I came here. I will add to it much more,
gold and ruddy bronze and lovely women and gray iron—
loot that I gained by lot, though King Agamemnon,
the son of Atreus, has seized with violence the prize
that once he gave me. You tell him everything, openly
in order that the other Achaeans may be angry
if he hopes by deceit to rob any other of the Danaäns,
clothed as he is in shame. For never would he dare
to look me in the face, what a dog!
                              "No, I shall
give him no advice, nor shall I do anything on his behalf.
For he has deceived me, and done me harm. No, never
again will he trick me with words. I am through with that.
May he go in comfort straight to hell! Zeus,
I suppose, has taken away his wits. I despise
his gifts! He isn't worth a hair! Not if he gave me ten times
as much, or twenty times as much as he possesses—
even if he acquired still more. Not if he offered me
as much as Orchomenos holds, or Egyptian Thebes—
where the greatest wealth is stored in their houses—a city
of one hundred gates through each of which two hundred men
sally forth with their horses and cars.° Not if he gave me
as many things as there are sands by the sea or dust in the road—
not even then would Agamemnon persuade my heart before
he has paid the full price for the anguish that torments my heart!
    "As for Agamemnon's daughter, I would not
marry her, not if she rivaled Aphrodite the golden in beauty,
or equaled flashing-eyed Athena in craft. No, I will
not marry her! Let her choose some other Achaean,
one of the same class, one of a higher station than I.
For if the gods will save me, and I come home,
Peleus will find me a wife. There are many daughters
of the Achaeans throughout HELLAS and Phthia, daughters
of the chiefs who guard the towns. From these I shall choose
a wife and make her my own, if I wish. Many times
my proud heart urged me to marry a suitable helpmate,
to rejoice in the riches that old Peleus acquired.

381 ... *cars*: Orchomenos in northern Boeotia was just a village in Homer's day c. 800 BC, but in the Bronze
Age it was a great power, to judge by its ruins. Homer has heard something about the great capital of the
Egyptian New Kingdom, c. 1600–1150 BC, for some reason called Thebes in Greek (its Egyptian names
were quite dissimilar). What Achilles thinks are gates in walls are really pylons in the amazing temples
built there on both sides of the Nile—but hardly big enough for one hundred cars! Still today the ruins of
these temples are astounding. Egypt and the Near East was a dim place for Homer, about which he has only
distorted information.

"Not worth a life is all the wealth that they say
Ilion once possessed, that well-peopled city, in the time
of peace before the coming of the sons of the Achaeans.
No, nor the wealth that the stone threshold of Phoibos Apollo,   400
the archer, contains in rocky Pytho.° You can always
take cattle by rapine, and stout sheep, and you can acquire
tripods in the same way, and chestnut mares. But the life
of a man does not come again. It cannot be captured
or taken once it has passed the barrier of the teeth.   405
    "My mother Thetis, the goddess with silver feet,
says that a twofold fate carries me toward my
death. If I remain and fight to take the city
of the Trojans, then my homecoming is no more, but
my fame will be forever. If I return to my home   410
in the land of my fathers, there will be no glorious renown,
yet I will live long, and the doom of death will not
soon find me.
        "And I strongly advise you others also
to sail to your homes. You can no more hope for steep Ilion.
Zeus, whose voice is heard from afar, holds his   415
hands in protection over her, and her people are emboldened.
Go now and tell the chiefs of the Achaeans what
I have said. For that is the burden of old men, so that
they may concoct some other plan, a better one—
some way to save the ships and the host of the Achaeans   420
beside the hollow ships. The plan they have
devised will not work so long as I stand apart
in my anger.
        "But let Phoinix remain here and take his rest,
so that he may follow me to my beloved native land,
tomorrow, if he wants. But I will not force him to go."   425

    Thus Achilles spoke. They all fell into silence, numbed
by his words. For he had rejected them utterly. At last old man
Phoinix the horse-driver spoke, bursting into tears—because he feared
for the ships of the Achaeans: "If you are really thinking about
going home, excellent Achilles, nor are you at all willing   430
to help us ward off consuming fire from our swift ships
because a rage has settled on your heart—how can I, my dear child,
be left here without you, alone? It was to you that the horseman,
old man Peleus, sent me on that day when he sent you
forth from Phthia to Agamemnon, still a child, knowing nothing   435

---

401   *Pytho*: That is, in DELPHI, north of the GULF OF CORINTH.

of the horrors of war, nor of assemblies where men show
themselves to be excellent. For this reason he sent me along
to teach you everything—how to be a speaker of words and a doer
of deeds.° For this reason, my child, I would not want
440 to be left apart from you, not even if a god should
stand by me personally and promise to wipe away
old age and replace it with glowing youth, such as
I had when first I left Hellas° where the women are beautiful.
    "I fled a quarrel with my father Amyntor, son of Ormenos,
445 who grew angry because of the whore with the beautiful hair. My father
loved her, but he dishonored his bed-mate, my mother, who constantly
asked me, clasping my knees, to sleep with the woman
so that she might come to despise the old man. And I did that.
My father knew at once and called down many curses
450 on my head, and he called on the hateful Erinyes,° that never
should my dear grandson take a seat on his knees.
    "The gods fulfilled his curses, Zeus who lives beneath
the ground and the dread Persephonê.° So then I contemplated
how I might kill my father with the sharp sword. But one
455 of the deathless ones stopped my anger, reminding me of
what people would say, and of the insults of men—the Achaeans
would call me the murderer of my father! Then my heart
could no longer be stayed to remain at all in the halls
of my angry father. My fellows and relatives, surrounding me,
460 begged me to stay there in his halls, and they sacrificed
many good sheep and crooked-horned shuffling cattle,
and many swine rich with fat were stretched to be singed
over the flame of Hephaistos.° And much wine
was drunk from the jugs of the old man. For nine nights
465 they watched over me. Taking turns they held guard,
nor did their fires ever go out, one burning
beneath the portico of the well-fenced court, the other

---

439   *of deeds*: In the popular postHomeric tradition it was Cheiron, the one wise centaur, who taught Achilles all
these things. Many pictures survive of Cheiron educating the young Achilles (see Figure 11.3).

443   *Hellas*: A small territory in Thessaly under the political control of Amyntor, Phoinix's father. Peleus
controls nearby Phthia, though it unclear what is meant by "Phthia," whether it is a town or a territory.
Later "Hellas" came to designate all of Greece.

450   *Erinyes*: The Erinyes ("avengers") are underworld spirits who are the guardians of oaths and curses: the
"Furies." If an oath is violated, they persecute the person who violates it; when invoked in a curse, they
attack someone else, as here. They are associated with Fate because they also guarantee the natural order
of things. They punish such violations of the natural order as killing one's parents (or when a horse talks,
in *Il.* 19).

453   ... *Persephonê*: Hades and his wife.

463   *Hephaistos*: Apparently they sacrificed to the Erinyes to drive them away, but their intentions are unclear.

on the porch in front of the doors of my chamber.
But when the tenth dark night came on, I broke
the well-fitted doors of the chamber and easily leaped 470
over the wall around the court, avoiding the guards
and the slave women. I then fled afar through spacious Hellas.
  "I came to Phthia with its deep soil, the mother
of sheep, to Peleus the king. He happily received me,
and he loved me as a father loves his only son, 475
the heir to his many possessions. He made me rich
and he gave me to rule over many people. I lived
in the furthermost part of Phthia, presiding over
the Dolopians. I made you such as you are, like to the gods,
Achilles, loving you from my heart. And you would never go 480
to the feast with another, nor take meat in the halls before
I set you on my knees and fed you with a tasty morsel
cut for you, and then gave you wine. Often you
wet the shirt on my breast, blubbering out the wine
in your sorry helplessness. So I have suffered much 485
and labored hard, realizing that the gods would never
grant me an offspring. I made you my child, godlike Achilles,
so that you could protect me from shameful ruin.
                              "But Achilles,
now you should control your mighty spirit, not have a heart
without pity. Even the gods can be persuaded, whose worth 490
and honor and strength is greater. Men turn their anger
aside by beseeching with incense and gentle prayers, and pouring
out wine and the smell of sacrifice when one has crossed
the line and made a mistake. *Prayers* are the daughters
of great Zeus—lame, wrinkled, and with eyes askance. Prayers 495
make it their concern to follow after *Blindness*. But *Blindness*
is strong and fast-moving so that she outruns them all, and goes
before *Prayers* over all the earth, bringing harm to mankind.
But *Prayers* come afterward, trying to heal. Whoever
respects the daughters of Zeus when they come near, 500
Prayers will help him. They hear him when he asks for something.
But whoever denies and strongly refuses *Prayers*, they go
and they pray to Zeus the son of Kronos that *Blindness* may follow
him and cause him to fall and to pay the full price.°

---

504 *price*: A rare Homeric allegory. *Prayers* are the daughters of Zeus, that is, they are of divine origin, but they
     are old and slow. *Blindness* (*atê*) is much swifter, for example overtaking Agamemnon and causing him to
     take the girl Briseïs. But *Prayers* eventually come along to make things whole, for example the embassy's
     supplication. So Achilles should accept the *Prayers* and take what is offered. If not, then *Prayers* will see to it
     that *Blindness/Disaster* (*atê* means both) will overtake *him*.

505　　　"Achilles, you should see that honor attend these
　　　daughters of Zeus, who like to bend the minds of upright men.
　　　If the son of Atreus were not bearing gifts and naming others
　　　to come later, but remained furiously angry, I would not
　　　counsel you to cast aside your anger and come to the defense
510　of the Argives, even though they are in much need.
　　　But as it is he gives you many things right away
　　　and promises others later. He has sent forth the best
　　　men to beseech you, choosing them from throughout the army,
　　　who are those men dearest to you. Do not scorn them,
515　nor their coming here.
　　　　　　　　　　"Before, no one could blame you
　　　for being angry. And so we have heard of the famous deeds
　　　of warriors of a time long ago, when a ferocious anger would
　　　come upon them: They could still be won by gifts, turned aside
　　　by words. I have in mind a deed from the olden days, how it was,
520　not something recent. I will tell it to you who are all my friends.
　　　　　"The Kuretes and the Aetolians, steadfast in war, were fighting
　　　around KALYDON and slaughtering one another, the Aetolians
　　　defending lovely Kalydon, the Kuretes eager to destroy it
　　　by war.° For golden-throned Artemis had sent an
525　affliction against them, angry because Oeneus had
　　　failed to offer to her the first fruits of his burgeoning
　　　orchard.° While the other gods dined on great sacrifices, to the
　　　daughter of Zeus alone he did not offer sacrifice, either because
　　　he forgot or thought it not important.° *Blindness* struck him
530　deep in his heart. She became angry, the archer-goddess,
　　　begotten of Zeus, and sent forth a fierce wild boar
　　　with white tusks, who did much harm, wasting the orchard land
　　　of Oeneus. Many a tall tree did he tear up and throw
　　　to the ground, roots and all, and the blossoms of apples.
535　Meleager, the son of Oeneus, killed the boar after he had
　　　gathered hunters and hounds from many cities. The boar
　　　was not to be overcome by a few men. He was huge
　　　and he sent many men to an unhappy pyre.
　　　　　　　　　　　　　　　　　"But around
　　　the head and shaggy skin of the pig there arose a great clamor

---

524　　... *by war*: The name Kuretes means simply "young warriors." The tribe is known only from this story.
　　　　Their capital was at Pleuron about ten miles west of the town of Kalydon, which is in southwest mainland
　　　　Greece (see Map 2).

527　　*orchard*: Oeneus, "wine-man," was an early king of Kalydon. The famous Kalydonian Boar Hunt took place
　　　　during his reign, two or three generations before the Trojan War. According to the Catalog of Ships, all the
　　　　sons of Oeneus are now dead and Thoas leads the Aetolian contingent.

529　　*not important*: In ancient Greek religion intention counts for nothing, the act for everything.

FIGURE 9.2 **Kastor and Polydeukes.** The brothers of Helen (probably) attack the Kalydonian Boar. The fish beneath the ground-line indicates a lake or stream. Spartan black-figure wine-cup, c. 555 BC.

540 and shouting between the Kuretes and the great-hearted Aetolians.°
    So long as Meleager, dear to Ares, fought, so long it went badly
    for the Kuretes, nor were they able to remain outside the wall,
    although they were very many. But when anger came
    to Meleager, which also swells in the breasts of other
545 sensible men—anger against his own mother
    Althaia—then he stayed in bed with his beautiful wife
    Kleopatra of the beautiful ankles, the daughter of Marpessa.
    Marpessa's father was Euenos. Her husband was Idas,
    one of the strongest men on the earth at that time.
550 Idas even raised his bow against Phoibos Apollo because
    of Marpessa, the girl with the beautiful ankles.° Marpessa's
    father Euenos and her mother then called Marpessa
    'Alkyonê' because her mother suffering the fate
    of the sorrowing Halcyon bird, wept when Apollo,
555 who works from a long ways off, snatched away her daughter.°
        "Meleager lay by Kleopatra's side, nursing a bitter
    anger because of the curses of his enraged mother,
    who prayed ardently to the gods, grieving over her dead
    brother. Althaia pounded the rich earth, crying out to Hades
560 and to terrible Persephonê. She knelt down and wet the folds
    of her gown with tears, begging that they bring death to her son.
    The Erinys that walks in darkness, with the brittle heart,
    heard her from Erebos.° Soon there came the noise of the Kuretes
    at the gates and the thud of walls being battered. The Aetolian elders

---

540 *Aetolians*: According to later reports about the Kalydonian Boar Hunt, the huntress Atalanta, whom
     Homer does not mention, drew first blood, then Meleager killed the boar. When Meleager gave the skin
     as a trophy to Atalanta, a fight broke out between the Kalydonians and the neighboring Kuretes, who did
     not think a woman should have the skin. During the war Meleager killed his mother's brothers, who were
     Kuretes. In revenge she burned up a firebrand that contained Meleager's soul, and so he died. Homer may
     know this account, but he shapes his narrative to the dramatic needs of the *Iliad*.

551 *beautiful ankles*: According to later sources, when Idas carried off Marpessa, Apollo pursued them. Idas
     drew his bow against the god to protect her from the god's advances. Zeus forced Marpessa to choose; she
     chose Idas over Apollo, fearing that Apollo would be unfaithful. Idas and his brother Lynkeus were impor-
     tant in heroic myth: They journeyed on the Argo and were killed in a cattle raid by Helen's brothers.

555 *daughter*: "Alkyonê" is Greek for kingfisher, which in reality has no voice, but in myth sings a calming dirge
     for her dead mate (named Keux). Once Alkyonê was human, but in her grief for her dead husband was
     changed into a mourning kingfisher ("Halcyon Days" are those days when the bird sings its calming song).
     In this very obscure reference Homer implies that Apollo was somehow successful in possessing Marpessa,
     giving rise to her nickname "Alkyonê." Marpessa's mother suffered the same sorrow for her daughter as
     Alkyonê felt for her dead husband.

563 *Erebos*: The realm of darkness, the underworld. The Erinys (now singular) is the agent of Hades and
     Persephonê. Because the Erinys heard, Meleager's death is certain. A primitive social structure seems to
     underlie this story in which a mother's emotional obligation to her brothers is stronger than to her son.

begged Meleager. They sent their best priests of the gods,   565
who promised a great gift if Meleager would come out.
Where the fattest plain of lovely Kalydon lies, there
they urged him to pick a splendid district fifty acres big,
the half of it wine country, the other half to be clear plowland,
cut from the plain. The old man Oeneus, Meleager's father,   570
the horse-driver, begged him again and again—standing
on the threshold of his high-roofed chamber, shaking the joined
doors, supplicating his son. And his sisters and revered mother°
begged Meleager too. He only denied them the more.
    "Meleager's companions were most true and dear to him—   575
but even so, they could not persuade his heart
before the chamber was under attack. The Kuretes
were on the walls and the great city was going up in flames.
Only then did Kleopatra, Meleager's nicely belted wife,
beg him, wailing, describing to him all the horrible things   580
that happen to people when a city is taken: men murdered,
fire consuming the city, men leading away little children
and low-girdled women. His spirit was stirred when
he heard about these evil things. He got up to go.
Meleager put on his shining armor.   585
                        "And so he warded off
the evil day for the Aetolians, giving in to his spirit.
To Meleager thereafter they did not give the gifts,
many and dear, but still he warded off the evil.
Don't think like that! Don't let some spirit turn you
in that direction! It is a harder thing to do to ward off fire   590
once the ships are burning. But come—while there are still
gifts to be had. The Achaeans will honor you like a god.
If you enter without gifts the battle that destroys men,
you will not enjoy an equivalent honor, even if you win
the war."   595

    Achilles the fast runner answered him:
"Phoinix, dear fellow, old man nurtured of Zeus, you see I have
no need of this honor. I think that I am honored in the allotment
of Zeus, which will sustain me beside the beaked ships so long
as there is breath in my lungs and my legs still move.
    "I will tell you something else, and please take it to heart. Do not   600
confuse my spirit with your weeping and wailing as you do the pleasure
of the warrior son of Atreus. You should not love him so that you are

---

573 *revered mother*: Who has just cursed him to his certain death!

hated by me, who love you. It is a better thing that you trouble those
who trouble me. Be a captain like me. Share half of my honor.
605   This embassy will carry my message. You stay here on a soft bed.
At the break of dawn we will give thought, whether we will
go home or remain."

             As he spoke he silently signed to Patroklos
with his brows to charge him to spread a thick bed for Phoinix,
so that the others might quickly leave the hut. But Ajax,
610   the godlike son of Telamon, spoke: "Zeus-born, son of
Laërtes, resourceful Odysseus, let us leave. I don't think
we are going to accomplish our purpose. We must quickly
announce our message to the Danaäns, not a welcome one,
for I imagine that they anxiously await it. Achilles has let
615   the great heart in his breast go wild—cruel man!—and he cares
nothing for the love of his companions, nor how we honored
him beside the ships above all others—a pitiless man!
     "You know, if a brother is killed, or a child, a man
will take a penalty-payment for the dead. And the killer stays there
620   in his own land once he's paid that high price. The heart
and the proud spirit of the kinsman are restrained by receiving
the penalty-payment. But you!°—the gods have put a stubborn
and evil spirit in your breast on account of a single girl.
We offer you seven girls, and those by far the best, and other
625   things beside. Have a generous heart. Respect your hall!°
We have come from the mass of the Danaäns under your roof.
We want to be dearest and beloved above all the other Achaeans."°

        Answering him, Achilles the fast runner said:
"Zeus-born Ajax, son of Telamon, captain of the people,
630   everything you say seems to me to be spoken
in accord with my own mind. But my heart seethes
with anger whenever I think of that—how the son of Atreus
treated me with indignity among the Argives as if
I were some kind of man in flight, without status!
635   "But you return and give this message: I will not think
of bloody war before good Hector, the son of wise Priam,

---

622   *you*: Ajax now addressed Achilles directly.

625   *hall*: As guests in Achilles' house, the embassy is entitled to friendliness and respect.

627   *Achaeans*: In a society where behavior is controlled by honor, disputes must be resolved by preserving the
       honor of both parties. The aggrieved party should accept recompense. If he does not, he dishonors the
       other party and brings censure on himself. But in his anger Achilles rejects this whole system, making him
       a man alone.

comes to the tents and ships of the Myrmidons,
killing Argives, and he sets fire to the ships.
Around my hut and black ship I think that Hector
will be stopped, eager though he is for battle." 640

So he spoke. Each of them took up a two-handled
cup and poured out an offering, then they returned back
along the line of ships, Odysseus leading the group.

But Patroklos ordered his companions and female slaves
to spread a thick bed for Phoinix as soon as possible. 645
Obeying him, the female slaves spread the bed
as ordered—fleeces and a rug and a linen sheet.
There the old man lay down and awaited the bright dawn.
But Achilles slept in the innermost part of his well-built hut.
Beside him lay a woman whom he had taken from Lesbos, 650
Diomedê of the lovely cheeks, the daughter of Phorbas.
Patroklos slept on the other side. Beside him slept the nicely
belted Iphis, whom Achilles had given him when he took
Skyros, the steep city of Enueos.°

                The embassy arrived
at the huts of the sons of Atreus. The sons of the Achaeans 655
received them with golden cups, standing about on this
side and that, and they then questioned the embassy.
First Agamemnon, king of men, asked: "Tell me, Odysseus,
much-praised great glory of the Achaeans—either he is willing
to ward off the consuming fire from the ships, or he 660
has refused because anger still holds his proud spirit?"

Much-enduring good Odysseus then answered:
"O son of Atreus, most glorious king of men, Agamemnon,
that man is not willing to extinguish his anger, but is filled
with still more anger. He rejects you and your gifts. For you, 665
he advises that you consider how you will save the ships
and the army of the Achaeans. As for himself, he threatens
that when dawn appears he will drag his well-benched
curved ships into the sea. He also said that he would advise others
to sail home too, because there is no more hope that you 670

---

654 *Enueos*: Nothing otherwise is known of this raid on the island of SKYROS east of EUBOEA (Map 2), where
    according to later tradition Achilles was raised in the harem of the king, dressed as a girl until Odysseus
    unmasked and recruited him for the war.

can win the goal of steep Ilion. 'Zeus, whose voice is heard
from afar, holds his hand over her. Her people are filled
with courage.' So he spoke. These men who followed
me there—Ajax and the two heralds, prudent men—
675   can confirm the tale. Old man Phoinix has gone to sleep there,
as Achilles urged, so he can follow in the ships to his beloved
fatherland tomorrow, if he wants. He will not force him."

So spoke Odysseus and everybody fell into silence,
amazed at his words. For he had spoken very strongly in his address
680   to the gathering. For a long time the sons of the Achaeans were
silent in their grief, but at last Diomedes, good at the war cry,
spoke: "O son of Atreus, most glorious king of men, Agamemnon,
I wish you had never sought in supplication the son
of Peleus, offering him a thousand gifts. He was arrogant
685   before, but now you have led him to still more arrogance.
But we will let him be. Either he goes or he stays. He will come
back and fight when the spirit in his breast urges him
and a god rouses him.
                     "But come, let us act on what I say.
Go now to your rest once you have satisfied your hearts with
690   food and wine. There is strength and force in them. But when
beautiful Dawn appears with her fingers of rose,
quickly array your people and horses before the ships
and urge them on. And yourselves fight among the foremost!"

So he spoke, and all the captains assented,
695   inspired by the words of Diomedes, the tamer of horses.
Then after pouring a drink offering, each man went to his tent.
There they lay down and took the gift of sleep.

BOOK 10. *The Exploits of Dolon*°

The other captains of the Achaeans slept through the night
overcome by gentle sleep. But sweet sleep did not possess
the son of Atreus, Agamemnon, the shepherd of the people,
whose mind was occupied by many matters. As when
the husband of Hera of the lovely hair sends down   5
the lightning, making a mighty unspeakable rain,
or hail, or snow, when snow-flakes sprinkle the fields,
or even the wide mouth of bitter war, even so often
did Agamemnon groan from the depths of his breast,°
and his mind trembled within. Whenever he looked   10
toward the Trojan plain, he was amazed at the fires that
burned before the city of Troy, and at the sound of flutes
and pipes and the roar of men. But when he looked
toward the ships and the people of the Achaeans, he pulled
out hanks of hair by the roots from his head, praying   15
to Zeus on high, and his noble heart groaned deeply.

   This seemed to his mind to be the best counsel,
to go first of all to Nestor, the son of Neleus,
to see if he might contrive some blameless device
to ward off evil from all the Danaäns. So he straightened   20
up and put on a shirt over his breast, and beneath
his feet he bound beautiful sandals, and then he put
around him the brown-yellow skin of a lion, fiery
and huge, that reached to his feet. And he took up
his spear.   25

° *Dolon:* The authenticity of Book 10, called the Doloneia in ancient sources, was uniquely called into question even in
the ancient world. Many modern scholars, too, doubt its authenticity: Events in it are never mentioned in the rest of
the poem (nor are events in the critical Book 9); it contains unusual vocabulary (but the epic style always admits of
unusual words and the style of the book is the same as the rest of the *Iliad*); the behavior of Odysseus and Diomedes
is "unheroic" (yet it is hard to say what is "heroic" except the observed behavior of heroes). Certainly the Greek seems
different, and the handling of direct speech and standard topoi is different. However, it is hard to imagine a motive for
such a long interpolation, or see how an interpolator could have seamlessly inserted it into the narrative, or made it
part of the early text, as it certainly was. Dolon appears in Greek art from the seventh and sixth centuries BC (see also
Figure 10.2). Euripides wrote a play based on the Doloneia in the fifth century BC. On balance, we should consider
the Doloneia as part of the original *Iliad*, striking in its cut-throat descriptions of a night raid against the enemy.

9 *breast:* That is, as often as Zeus sends the lightning in a storm, so often did Agamemnon groan.

Thus in the same way did fear take hold
of Menelaos. Nor did sleep sit on his eyes. He feared
that something might happen to the Argives who on
his account had crossed the vast water to Troy,
eager for horrid war. First he covered his broad
30 shoulders with a dappled panther skin. Then he lifted up
and placed on his head a bronze helmet, and he took up in his
powerful hand a spear. Then Menelaos went to rouse up
his brother, who ruled mightily over all the Argives,
whom the people honored like a god. He found him putting on
35 his beautiful armor around his shoulders beside the stern
of his ship.

Agamemnon was glad to see him. Menelaos,
good at the war cry, spoke first: "Why, my brother,
are you arming? Have you got one of your companions to spy
on the Trojans? I fear that you will never find someone
40 willing to go alone and spy on the enemy through
the undying night. He will need to have a strong heart!"

Agamemnon answered him: "You and I need some shrewd
counsel, O god-nourished Menelaos, that will save and deliver
the Argives and the ships, because the mind of Zeus is turned.
45 He finds Hector's sacrifices more pleasing than our own.
For I have never seen, nor heard of one man, in his
audacity, doing so many horrible things in a single day
as this Hector, beloved of Zeus, has done to the sons
of the Achaeans—by himself alone, neither being a son
50 of a goddess nor of a god. He has accomplished things that
I think will be a sorrow to the Argives for a long time,
so many dire actions has he brought to the Achaeans.

"But go now! Run swiftly along the ships. Call Ajax
and Idomeneus. I will go to the good Nestor and urge
55 him to get up and go to the sacred company of the sentinels
and give them orders. They are most likely to obey Nestor.
His son is captain of the guard, along with Meriones,
companion to Idomeneus. We gave them the most authority."

Menelaos, good at the war cry, then answered Agamemnon:
60 "With what exactly do you charge and command me? Shall I
wait there with Ajax and Idomeneus until you come? Or do you
want me to check back here after I have given the command?"

The king of men Agamemnon then said: "Stay there,
or we might miss one another as we go. For there are many
paths through the camp. Call out as you go. Order   65
each man to wake up. Call him by his father's name.
Refer to his ancestry. Call him by his own name.
Honor them all. Don't be proud of heart!° Let us both
be busy—even so has Zeus laid upon us a heavy
pain at birth."   70

          So speaking, Agamemnon sent off his brother
with this strong command. Agamemnon went to find Nestor.
He found him beside his hut and his black ship,
on a soft bed. His fancy armor lay nearby,
his shield and two javelins and his gleaming helmet.
Nearby lay his flashing belt, which the old man put on   75
when he was about to go into man-killing battle,
leading forth his people, for he did not give in to
mournful old age.

          Nestor rose up on his elbow, lifting his head,
and he spoke to the son of Atreus, and questioned him:
 "Who is this man who goes through the ships and the camp,   80
alone through the dark night, when the other men are sleeping?
Are you looking for one of your mules, or one of your companions?
Tell me, and don't sneak up on me without speaking! What is it
that you need?"

          Then the king of men Agamemnon
answered: "Nestor, son of Neleus, great glory of the Achaeans,   85
you know me—I'm Agamemnon, the son of Atreus,
whom above all Zeus has plunged into everlasting pain,
as long as the breath remains in my breast and my knees
still move. I stalk about in this way because sweet sleep
has not settled on my eyes because I am worried   90
about the war and the sufferings of the Achaeans.
I am terrified for the Danaäns. My mind is not firm
but awfully distressed. My heart is jumping out of my breast!
My shining limbs are shaking.
                    "But maybe you can do something,
because sleep has not come to you, it seems ... Let us go   95

---

68   *heart*: Ordinarily one would use heralds to summon the troops, but the crisis demands direct intervention.

to the sentinels so we can find out if, overcome by exhaustion
and sleepiness, they have fallen into sleep and have forgotten
about the watch. The enemy soldiers sit nearby and we do
not know if maybe they will fight even in the night."

100   Then Gerenian Nestor, the horseman, answered:
"Son of Atreus, most glorious king of men Agamemnon,
I don't think that Zeus the counselor is about to fulfill
all he intends concerning Hector—all that he plans.
I think that Hector is about to suffer pains still
105   greater than our own. If only Achilles would turn
his heart away from bitter anger! But I will follow you.
Let us rouse up the others—the son of Tydeus, clever with
the spear, and Odysseus, and swift Ajax, and the bold
Meges, son of Phyleus. And somebody should also go
110   and summon godlike Ajax° and King Idomeneus,
For their ships are the furthest away, not nearby.
      "But I will reproach Menelaos, though he is
honored and dear, even at the risk of your anger.
Nor will I conceal my thought—he is asleep and has left
115   it to you to do all the work alone! I wish that he were
going among the captains, beseeching them.
We need to act!"

              Then the king of men Agamemnon
answered him: "Old man, you can reprove Menelaos
at some other time, and with my approval. He is often
120   a slacker and unwilling to pull his share of the load.
He should not give in to laziness or carelessness
of mind, but he should look to me and await my leadership.
But as it is, he was awake even before I was. He came
to *me*! I sent him forth to summon those very men
125   you asked about. But let us go. We will find them before
the gates, among the sentinels, where I told them to gather."

      Then Gerenian Nestor the horseman answered:
"So no one of the Argives is going to be resentful at anyone else,
or disobey him when someone urges on a man, or gives

---

110   ... *Ajax*: The "swift Ajax" is Little Ajax, son of Oïleus; Meges, the son of Phyleus, leader of the men from
       the island of Doulichion and the mainland Epeians, is a shadowy figure; "godlike Ajax" is Big Ajax, son of
       Telamon.

commands!"° So speaking he put on his shirt around his chest,   130
and on his shining feet he bound his beautiful sandals,
and around his body he buckled his purple cloak,
double, wide, whose nap sprouted thick upon it.
Nestor took up a strong spear fitted with a bronze tip,
and he went through the ships of the Achaeans, who   135
wear shirts of bronze.

               First then Gerenian Nestor
the horseman woke up Odysseus, the equal of Zeus in counsel,
by shouting. Immediately the voice rang through Odysseus'
head. Odysseus came out of the tent and spoke to them:
"Why do you wander alone throughout the ships' encampment   140
through the undying night? What is the great need?"

   Then Gerenian Nestor, the horseman, answered
him: "Zeus-begotten, son of Laërtes, most resilient
Odysseus, do not be angry. For such a sorrow has come
over the Achaeans. But follow us, so that we may   145
wake up another, somebody whom it suits to consider
the 'ifs' and 'whats' of war, and whether to flee or to fight."

   So Nestor spoke. Resourceful Odysseus went
to his tent and hoisted on his shoulders a shield with variegated
design, and he went after them. They went to Diomedes,   150
the son of Tydeus. They came upon him outside
his hut with his armor. His companions slept around
about with their shields beneath their heads. They had fixed
their spears in the ground with the spikes fitted to the butts.°
The bronze flashed afar as the lightning of father Zeus.   155

   But the fighter Diomedes slept. Beneath him was
spread the hide of an ox of the field. Beneath his head
a bright carpet stretched. Gerenian Nestor, the horseman,
stood beside him and woke him up, moving him with his heel.
He aroused Diomedes and reproached him to his face: 160
"Get up, you son of Tydeus! Are you going to sleep the whole
night through? Haven't you heard that the Trojans are

---

130   *commands*: Agamemnon now seems to accompany Nestor to wake up Odysseus and Diomedes, but Nestor
      does all the talking.

154   *butts*: The end opposite the spear point was sharpened so that the spear could be fixed in the ground.

sitting near our ships on the rising ground of the plain?
They are only a little ways off!"

               So he spoke. Diomedes
165 immediately rose up from sleep, and he spoke to him words
that went like arrows: "You are a real go-getter, old man.
You never leave off work. Aren't there younger sons of the Achaeans
who might rouse each of the chieftains, going everywhere
through the army? You are impossible, old man!"

                      Gerenian Nestor,
170 the horseman, answered him: "Well, my friend, what
you have said is altogether reasonable. I do have
blameless sons,° and there are people aplenty
who could go and call the others. But a great necessity
has befallen the Achaeans. Now the decision stands on
175 the razor's edge°—whether there will be sad destruction
for the Achaeans, or whether they might yet live.
But go now and rouse up swift Ajax and the son of Phyleus.
For you are younger—if you have pity on me!"

   So Nestor spoke. Diomedes put on the skin of a lion
180 around his shoulders, gleaming, huge, that reached to his feet.
He took up his spear. He went along, and the fighter
Diomedes roused up those soldiers from where they were,
and he brought them.

                When they had joined the gathering
of the sentinels, they found that the leaders of the watch
185 were not sleeping but sat wide awake, fully armed.
As when hounds keep painful watch over sheep in a fold,
and they hear the cry of the wild beast, powerful of heart,
who roams through the woods on the mountains, and there is
a cry over the animal from men and dogs and for the hounds
190 sleep disappears—even so from the lids of the sentinels did sweet
sleep perish as they kept watch through the menacing night.
Constantly they turned toward the plain, to see if they could hear
the Trojans coming on.

---

172 *sons*: Only two sons of Nestor are mentioned in the *Iliad*: Thrasymedes, who is with the watch, and
     Antilochos, who has temporarily dropped from the story.

175 *razor's edge*: The first appearance of what was to become a common metaphor for a crisis.

Old Man Nestor was gladdened
when he saw the sentinels, and he spoke encouraging words
that went like arrows: "Keep your watch just like this,   195
my children! Never let sleep take hold! Let us not
become objects for our enemies' rejoicing!"

                    So speaking
he hurried through the trench, and with him followed all the
captains of the Argives, as many as were at the council.
Meriones and the glorious son of Nestor went with them—   200
the captains had asked that they participate in the council.
Going through and out from the ditch, they sat down in a clean space,
where the area seemed clear of corpses—where mighty Hector
had turned back from killing the Argives when night came on.°

   There they sat down and spoke to one another.   205
Gerenian Nestor, the horseman, began to speak:
"My friends, is there not some man who would trust his own
adventurous spirit to go among the great-hearted Trojans?
He might capture some heedless straggler of the enemy,
or learn some rumor among the Trojans about what they intend,   210
whether to remain in place near our ships or to return
back to the city because they have overcome the Achaeans.
He might learn all these things, then return to us unscathed.
His fame would be great among all men beneath the heaven,
and there would be fine gifts too: All the captains in charge   215
of ships will give him a black ewe with a lamb on the teat—
there is hardly any possession so grand!—and he will
always be with us at banquets and drinking parties."

   So Nestor spoke, and everybody fell into silence.
Then Diomedes, good at the war cry, spoke: 220
"Nestor, my heart and my proud spirit urges me
to enter the army of the enemy Trojans camped nearby.
But if some other man wanted to follow along,
there would be more comfort and more daring.
When two go together, one sees before the other   225
where the advantage lies. If one observes something
alone, his wit is slight and his stratagems slim."

---

204   *came on*: No commentator, ancient or modern, has explained why the Achaean captains should go across the
      ditch into the no man's land between the Achaean camp and the Trojans in order to hold a council of war.

So spoke Diomedes. Many wished to follow him.
The two Ajaxes, the followers of Ares, wanted to go,
230 as did Meriones. Nestor's son wanted very much to go.
The son of Atreus, Menelaos famed for his spear,
wanted to go. The enduring Odysseus was eager
to enter the crowd of the Trojans, for the sprit in his breast
was ever-daring.

         The king of men Agamemnon spoke
235 now among them: "Diomedes, son of Tydeus, dear
to my heart, you shall choose whom you wish as your
comrade, the best of those who volunteer, for many are eager.
Do not out of respect for rank leave the better man
behind and take a lesser, thinking only of status and birth—
240 not even if it is royal!"

         So he spoke, for Agamemnon feared that
Diomedes would choose Menelaos. Diomedes, good at the war cry,
then said: "How could I forget godlike Odysseus,
whose heart and fine spirit are eager beyond all others
in the midst of trouble? And Pallas Athena loves him.
245 If this man follows me, we might return together
even out of blazing fire. He is smarter than others."

         Then much-enduring good Odysseus said to him:
"Son of Tydeus, neither praise nor condemn me.
You are speaking among the Argives who know all about
250 these things.° But let us go. The night is getting old, dawn
is near, the stars have advanced. Two parts of three of the night
are gone, but still a third remains."

         So speaking,
the two men put on their fearsome armor. Thrasymedes,
stubborn in the fight, gave Diomedes, the son of Tydeus,
255 a two-edged sword—for Diomedes had left his own by the ship—
and a shield. Diomedes put on his head a helmet
made of bull's hide, without plates or a crest,
which they call a "skull-cap," that guards the heads

---

250 *things*: Odysseus and Diomedes are paired in many postHomeric Trojan adventures, especially the theft
     from Troy of a magic protective idol of Athena, the *palladium*. Odysseus represents the thoughtful, clever
     man in the tradition and Diomedes the man of action, but so far in the poem we have learned little of Odys-
     seus. In Book 5 he is briefly successful on the battlefield; in Book 8 he flees and ignores Nestor's plea.

of hot youths. Meriones gave Odysseus a bow and a quiver
and a sword, and on the head of Odysseus he placed a cap   260
made of hide. The cap was stiffened by many thongs
within. Outside the white teeth of a wild boar
of gleaming tusks were thickly set, turned in opposite
directions in different rows, well and cunningly made.
Inside was fixed a lining of felt. This cap Autolykos   265
once stole out of Eleon when he had broken
into the sturdy house of Amyntor, son of Ormenos.
Autolykos gave it to Amphidamas of CYTHERA
to take to Skandeia, and Amphidamas gave it
to Molos as a guest-gift. Molos gave it to his son   270
Meriones to wear.° Now, set on Odysseus' head,
the cap protected it.

　　　　　When the two had put on
their terrible armor, they set off, leaving all
the chieftains there. For them Pallas Athena sent forth
on their right a heron, close to the road. They did   275
not see the heron with their eyes through the dark night
but they heard its cry. Odysseus rejoiced at the omen,
and he prayed to Athena:° "Hear me, O daughter of Zeus
who carries the goatskin fetish, who always stands
by my side in every labor, let me not escape   280
your attention as I rouse myself for action. Be now
a special friend to me, Athena! Grant that I return
with renown again to the ships after having accomplished
a great deed that will cause anguish to the Trojans."

　　After him Diomedes, good at the war cry,   285
prayed: "Hear me now, O daughter of Zeus, unwearied one!
Protect me as once you followed my father to Thebes,
the good Tydeus, when he went there as a messenger
for the Achaeans. He left the Achaeans with shirts of bronze
by the stream of Asopos while he bore a honeyed word to the   290
Kadmeians. And coming back he performed an astonishing

271　*to wear*: Autolykos was a clever thief, the maternal grandfather of Odysseus; Eleon is near Mycenae; Amyn-
　　tor is the father of Phoinix; Amphidamas is otherwise unknown; Skandeia is the port of Cythera, the large
　　island just south of the mainland toward Crete—Meriones was a Cretan prince. The distribution of guest-
　　gifts was important in the economy of Bronze Age and Iron Age Greece.

278　*Athena*: She does three things in the *Iliad*: (1) she instills strength in Achaean heroes; (2) she gives advice;
　　and (3) she sponsors craftsmanship. She is especially interested in three heroes—Achilles, Diomedes, and
　　Odysseus—and never in Agamemnon, the two Ajaxes, Nestor, Idomeneus, or any Trojan.

FIGURE 10.1 Mycenaean armor.   Little sense could be made of Homer's description of the boar's tusk helmet until in modern times actual specimens were found. Here is the only surviving example of a complete Mycenaean suit of armor, from a Mycenaean grave, c. 1400 BC, at Dendra in the Peloponnesus near Mycenae. The reconstructed boar's tusk helmet is of a type most popular around 1600 BC, but pieces of helmets are found from as late as Homer's own day c. 800 BC, so it was a traditional type of helmet in use for nearly a thousand years. The helmet Homer describes is an heirloom. This helmet has bronze cheek pieces. About thirty wild boars died to provide ivory for such a helmet, so that the helmet is a statement of the hunter's status in addition to offering real protection. The suit consists of fifteen pieces of bronze that encased the wearer from the neck, protected by a high collar, down to the knees. Leather thongs held the pieces together. Similar armor appears as an ideogram on Linear B tablets from Knossos, Pylos, and Tiryns. The chest-protector consists of two pieces joined by a hinge—one piece for the chest and one for the back. Shoulder-guards fit over the chest-protector to which plates are attached that protect the armpit when the arms are raised. Three pairs of curved plates hang from the waist to guard the lower part of the body. The beaten bronze sheets are backed with leather and fastened by thongs to permit some flexibility. Not shown here, the suit included shinguards and guards for the lower arms.

deed with your help, divine goddess, when you stood
beside him with a ready heart.° Even so do you now
willingly stand by my side and guard me. I will sacrifice
a cow in your honor, one year old, with broad brow,   295
that has never known the goad, which no man ever led
beneath the yoke. I shall kill it for you after bedecking
its horns with gold."

        So he prayed, and Pallas Athena
heard him. When both had prayed to the daughter of great
Zeus, they went like two lions through the dark night   300
amidst the rough slaughter, amidst the corpses
and amidst the armor and black blood.

        Likewise Hector
did not permit the noble Trojans to sleep, but he called
together all the captains, those who were the leaders
and rulers of the Trojans. He presented to them a cunning   305
plan: "Who will promise this deed and bring it to pass
for a great reward? I think he will be happy with his reward.
I will give a chariot and two long-necked horses, the best
to whoever will dare—a chance for abundant glory!—
to go in close to the swift ships of the Achaeans to see   310
if he can learn whether their ships are guarded as before,
or whether, overcome at our hands, the Achaeans discuss
among themselves whether to take flight, and so do not want
to guard all the night, beaten down by dread fatigue."

    So he spoke, and they all fell into silence. There was   315
a certain Trojan, Dolon° by name, son of Eumedes
—who was a good herald, rich in gold and bronze—
ugly to look at but fast of foot. Dolon was
an only son with five sisters. He spoke a word
to the Trojans and to Hector: "Hector, my heart   320
and spirit urge me to go close to the swift ships
to find out what is going on. But come, lift up your staff
and swear to me that you will give me the horses
and chariot decorated with bronze that carries Achilles,
the blameless son of Peleus—then I will not be a spy   325

---

293 *ready heart*: When fifty Theban nobles ambushed Tydeus returning from his mission, he killed all but one.

316 *Dolon*: "Sneaky," no doubt created for this story.

for you in vain, nor will I disappoint your hopes! I will go
straight into the camp until I come to the ship of Agamemnon
where the captains discuss their plans, whether to flee
or to fight."

So he spoke, and Hector took the scepter
330   in his hands and swore: "Let Zeus himself be my witness,
the loud-thundering husband of Hera, that no other man
of the Trojans shall mount behind Achilles' horses,
but I promise that you shall have pride in them forever."°

So Hector spoke and he swore a meaningless oath,
335   and so stirred up Dolon's heart. Dolon promptly put
his bent bow around his shoulders. For a cloak he wore
the skin of a gray wolf and on his head put a cap
of weasel skin. He took up a sharp spear and headed off
toward the ships from their camp. He would never
340   return from the enemy ships, bearing information for Hector.

When he had left the crowd of horses and men, Dolon
went eagerly along a path. Godlike Odysseus saw him
coming, and he spoke to Diomedes: "Look, Diomedes,
somebody is coming from their camp. I'm not sure whether it is
345   someone spying on our ships, or whether he is despoiling
some one or other of the dead. Let's let him run out ahead
a little onto the plain. Then we can ambush and quickly
take him. If he tries to outrun us by speed of foot,
turn him away from their camp and toward our ships.
350   Prod after him with your spear and keep him
from escaping to the city."

So speaking, they lay down
in the field of corpses on the side of the path. Dolon
ran past them in his folly. When he was as far away
as a mule plows in a single pass—for they are
355   preferable to oxen for plowing deep fallow land
with the jointed plow—they ran after him. He stood still
when he heard the noise, hoping in his heart that some
Trojan comrades were coming to turn him back
because Hector was commanding a retreat. But when

---

333   *in them forever*: There is something ludicrous in this ugly fellow named "Sneaky" wanting the horses of
Achilles, and the audience is meant to laugh.

they were a spear's cast away, or less, he saw   360
that they were the enemy.

            He moved his limbs swiftly
in flight. Quickly Diomedes and Odysseus set out
in pursuit. As when two sharp-fanged hounds, skilled
in the hunt, press hard upon a doe or a rabbit in the woods
and the animal runs screaming before them, even so did the son   365
of Tydeus and city-sacking Odysseus ever pursue Dolon,
cutting him off from the Trojan camp. But when, fleeing
toward the ships, Dolon was about to become mixed with
the Achaean sentinels, then Athena sent strength into the son
of Tydeus so that no other Achaean, who wear shirts of bronze,   370
might beat him and boast that *he* struck the blow and
that Diomedes had come in late. Mighty Diomedes
rushed on him with his spear. Diomedes hollered:
"Stop! Stop! or I will reach you with my spear, and I do
not think that you will long escape complete destruction   375
at my hands!"

           He spoke, then cast his spear and purposefully
missed the man. The point of the polished spear went
over Dolon's right shoulder and fixed in the ground.
Dolon stood still, terrified, stuttering. His teeth chattered
from a green fear.   380

           The two Greeks, breathing heavily,
came up and seized him by the hands. Pouring forth tears,
Dolon spoke: "Take me alive! I will post my own ransom!
I have bronze and old and well-worked iron at home.
My father would grant you boundless ransom
if he heard that I were alive at the ships of the Achaeans."   385

    Resourceful Odysseus answered him: "Take it easy—
don't think about death. But come, tell me and speak
the truth. Where are you going alone from the camp
through the ships during the dark night when all the others
are sleeping? Are you about to rob one of the dead?   390
Or did Hector send you out to spy on all of us, or did
your own heart urge you?"

           Then Dolon answered, his limbs
atremble beneath him: "With many blind hopes Hector
led my thoughts astray. He promised to give me the

FIGURE 10.2   The Capture of Dolon.   The Trojan stands in the center, wearing a wolf skin and a weasel cap, with his bow and arrow, just as Homer describes. He raises his hands in a gesture of surrender to Odysseus, who wears a cap inspired by Homer's description of the boar's tusk helmet. Odysseus carries a sword, as Homer describes, and Diomedes to the right carries a spear. Both Greeks are in "heroic nudity." Probably the comic exaggeration of the figures depends on a southern Italian so-called *phlyax* play, a burlesque dramatic form that developed in the Greek colonies of Italy in the fourth century BC. South Italian red-figure wine-mixing bowl, c. 380 BC.

single-hoofed horses of the brave son of Peleus   395
and his chariot decorated with bronze. He urged me
to go through the swift black night close to the enemy
to see if I could learn whether your ships were guarded
as before, or whether, overcome at our hands,
the Achaeans discuss among themselves whether   400
to take flight, and whether they no longer want
to guard through the night, beaten down by dread fatigue."

    The resourceful Odysseus smiled and said:
"Surely you have schemed on great gifts, even the horses
of Achilles, the wise grandson of Aiakos—but you know   405
it is hard for ordinary mortals to master them or drive them,
other than Achilles, whose mother is an immortal.
    "But come, tell me, and tell me truthfully:
Where have you left Hector, shepherd of the people,
to come here? Where is his battle gear? Where   410
are his horses? How are the watches of the other
Trojans arranged? Where are they sleeping? What counsel
do they take with one another, whether to remain here near
our ships or to retreat up to the city because they have
overcome the Achaeans?"   415

                        Dolon, the son of Eumedes,
then spoke: "I shall tell you the entire truth! Hector
with the other counselors are holding council beside
the tomb of Ilos° far from the melée. Concerning
the guards you ask about, warrior, no special guard
is posted over the army, nor guards it. Beside all the fires   420
of the Trojans, where the need is clear, everybody is awake
and urges one another to keep the guard. But our famous
allies are asleep. They have turned over the guard to the Trojans
because neither their children nor their wives are near."

    The resourceful Odysseus answered him: "Do they sleep   425
mixed in with the Trojans, or apart? Tell me so that I may know."

---

418 *Ilos*: Ilos, a descendant of Dardanos, was the founder of Troy and gave the city his name, Ilion. He is the
     father of Laomedon and the grandfather of Priam. His tomb, along with the oak of Zeus, is one of the land-
     marks on the Trojan plain.

Dolon, the son of Eumedes, then answered: "I shall tell you
these things truly. The Carians and the Paeonians with curved bows
camp near the sea, and the Leleges and the Kaukones and
430   the good Pelasgians. Toward Thymbrê fell the lot of the Lycians
and the lordly Mysians and the Phrygians who fight from chariots,
and the Maeonians, lords of chariots.° But why do you ask me
these things? If you are anxious to enter the throng of
the Trojans, here apart are the Thracians, who have just arrived,
435   camped on the outermost edge. Rhesos is their leader,
the son of Eïoneus. He has the most beautiful horses
I've ever seen, and the largest, whiter than snow, like
the winds in their running. His chariot is fitted with gold
and silver. He has come wearing armor golden
440   and huge, a wonder to see. It does not seem
like armor for a man, but for the immortal gods.
      "But will you bring me now to the swift-faring ships,
or tie me with cruel binding and leave me here
until you go and find out whether what I told you
445   is true or not?"

            The powerful Diomedes looked at him
from beneath his brows and said: "Don't bother with your talk
of escape, Dolon. You have given us good information,
for you have fallen into my hands. If we now turn you
free and let you go, later you will come to the swift ships
450   of the Achaeans either as a spy or to fight in the
hand-to-hand. But if you die subdued by my hands,
you will be no further trouble to the Argives."

            He spoke. Dolon was about to touch his chin
with his strong hand and beg for his life,° but Diomedes
455   jumped at him and with his sword struck him in the middle
of the neck. He cut through both the tendons. Even while
still speaking, Dolon's head tumbled into the dust. Then they
stripped the weasel-skin cap from his head and took
his wolf skin and back-bent bow and long spear.

---

432   *lords of chariots*: Thrymbrê seems to have been south on the Skamandros. The allies correspond to those in
      the middle distance in the Trojan Catalog of Book 2, except that Leleges and Kaukones have replaced the
      distant Halizones and Paphlagonians.

454   *beg for his life*: To touch the chin of an enemy was a suppliant's gesture, indicating complete submission to
      the enemy's will.

And the good Odysseus held up in his hand the spoil   460
to Athena the driver of spoil and spoke thus
in prayer: "Rejoice, goddess, with this offering.
We shall make a gift to you first of all the gods
who are on Olympos. Now send us against the horses
and the sleeping places of the Thracian warriors."   465

So he spoke and lifted the spoils on high and placed
them on a bush. He left a clear marker by gathering up reeds
and the luxuriant branches of the bush so that they would not
miss it, returning through the swift black night. Then they
went ahead through the armor and the dark blood,   470
and quickly they came to the camp of the Thracians.
They were asleep, exhausted by their labors. Beside them
their beautiful armor lay on the ground next to them,
arranged in three rows, all in good order. Beside each man
was a yoke of horses. Rhesos slept in the middle of the Thracians,   475
beside him his swift horses tied to the chariot-rail by means
of thongs.

Odysseus saw Rhesos first and pointed
him out to Diomedes: "This is the man, Diomedes,
and these are the horses that Dolon, whom we killed, told
us about. So let us begin. It makes no sense for you   480
to stand about idle with your weapons. You get the horses.
Or you can kill the men and I'll get the horses."

So he spoke, and flashing-eyed Athena breathed
strength into Diomedes so that he killed at every hand.
A sickening groan arose from the Thracians as they were struck   485
by the sword, and the ground ran red with blood. Just as
a lion coming on flocks unguarded by a shepherd,
either of goats or pigs, leaps upon them with evil
intent, so did the son of Tydeus go up and down
through the ranks of Thracians until he had killed twelve.   490
Whomever the son of Tydeus would strike with his sword,
the resourceful Odysseus would seize by the foot and pull
out of the way, thinking that in this fashion the horses with
fine manes would easily pass through and not be spooked by
walking over dead bodies. They were not used to this!   495

When the son of Tydeus came to King Rhesos,
he took away honey-sweet life from him, his thirteenth
victim, and Rhesos breathed raucously. Like to an

evil dream, the son of the son of Oeneus stood that night
over the head of Rhesos by the design of the goddess
Athena.

In the meanwhile the enduring Odysseus
undid the single-hoofed horses, bound them together
with the reins, and hitting them with his bow drove
them out of the herd. He had forgotten to take the shining whip
from out of the decorated car. He whistled to signal
Diomedes, but Diomedes hung around, trying to think
of what awful thing he could do. Should he take the chariot,
which was cannily made, wherein was the fancy war-gear
of King Rhesos? Should he drag it out by the pole,
or pick it up and carry it?° or should he just take the lives
of more Thracians?

While he was pondering these things,
Athena stood near him and spoke to the good Diomedes:
"Think now, O son of great-hearted Tydeus, of your return
to the hollow ships so that you are not chased there if
some other god rouses up the Trojans."

So she spoke.
Diomedes recognized the voice of the goddess as she spoke.
Quickly he mounted the horses.° Odysseus struck them
with his bow and they fled toward the swift ships of the Achaeans.

But no blind man's watch did Apollo of the silver bow
keep when he saw Athena attending the son of Tydeus.
Angry with her, he entered the thick throng of the Trojans.
He aroused a counselor of the Thracians, Hippokoön, a noble
cousin of Rhesos. When he jumped up from sleep he saw
the empty space where the horses had been tied, and the men
gasping for breath in gruesome murder. Then he cried out
and called the name of his companion Rhesos. An outcry
arose among the Trojans and an unspeakable clamor as they
gathered. They gazed in dread at the horrible deeds
that the Achaeans had done before going to their hollow ships.

510 *carry it*: Ancient chariots were made of light rods, a wicker floor, and detachable wheels, easily carried by
one man.

518 *horses*: The only reference in Homer (outside of similes) to riding horseback; the two warriors seem to have
left the chariot behind and in any event would not have had time to yoke it.

FIGURE 10.3   The killing of Rhesos.   Oddly, the adventure with Rhesos is never shown in Greek art until the fourth century BC. The scene on this pot, made in southern Italy, seems to be inspired by a scene from a tragedy included in the works of Euripides, the *Rhesos*. To the right, Odysseus, "heroically nude" and wearing a cloak and skull cap and brandishing his sword, seizes the prize horses. Diomedes stands at the left. At the top are three dead Thracians in contorted poses. South Italian red-figure jug by the Lycurgus Painter, c. 360 BC.

530　　When Odysseus and Diomedes came to the place where
　　they killed Hector's spy, then Odysseus pulled up the swift horses.
　　The son of Tydeus jumped to the ground and placed the bloody
　　spoils in the hands of Odysseus, then remounted. The horses,
　　touched by the lash, raced not unwillingly toward the hollow ships.
535　That is where they longed to be.°

　　　　　　　　　　Nestor was first
　　to hear their approach and he said: "My friends, leaders
　　and rulers of the Argives, shall I tell a lie, or shall
　　I tell the truth? My heart bids me speak truly. I hear
　　the sound of swift-footed horses. I hope that Odysseus
540　and the powerful Diomedes have driven single-hoofed
　　horses speedily from the Trojan camp. But I greatly fear
　　that the best of the Argives have suffered losses through
　　the battle din of the Trojans."

　　　　　　　　　　　　But he had not completed his word in full
　　when the men came up themselves. They jumped to the ground.
545　The Achaeans received their warriors with joy, clasping
　　their right hands and speaking to them honeyed words.

　　　　Gerenian Nestor, the horseman, was first to ask:
　　"Come now, tell me, Odysseus who are much praised,
　　great glory of the Achaeans, how you took these horses?
550　By entering the throng of the Trojans? Or did some god
　　meet you and give them to you? They are wondrously like
　　the rays of the sun. I am forever mingling with the Trojans,
　　and I do not wait beside the ships, although I am an aged
　　warrior, but I have never seen such horses, nor even imagined
555　them. I think that a god must have met you and given
　　them to you. For Zeus the cloud-gatherer loves
　　both of you, also flashing-eyed Athena, the daughter
　　of Zeus who carries the goatskin fetish."

　　　　　　　　　　In answer
　　to him the resourceful Odysseus said: "Nestor,
560　son of Neleus, great glory of the Achaeans, a god
　　might easily have given horses better than these, for gods
　　are much stronger. These horses you ask about

535　*longed to be*: Why the horses of Rhesos should want to be at the ships is completely unclear.

are recently arrived from Thrace. Diomedes killed
their master, also twelve of their comrades, the best
of men. We took a thirteenth man, a spy, close   565
to the ships. Hector and the other noble Trojans
sent him forth to be a spy on our camp."

                        So speaking
he drove the single-hoofed horses across the trench,
exulting. Together with him the other Achaeans
went joyfully. When they arrived at the well-built hut   570
of the son of Tydeus, they bound the horses with supple
thongs at the horse feeding-trough,° where the swift-footed
horses of Diomedes were stationed, eating honey-sweet wheat.
Odysseus hung up the bloody spoils of Dolon on the stern
of his ship until they could make ready a sacred offering   575
to Athena.

    As for themselves, they washed off the abundant
sweat from their shins and the back of their necks and thighs
by going into the sea. And when the abundant sweat
was washed from the skin, their hearts were refreshed.
They entered a polished bath and bathed.° When the two   580
of them had bathed and anointed their flesh with sleek oil,
they sat down to dinner. From the full wine bowl they drew
off an offering of honey-sweet wine and poured it to Athena.

---

572 *feeding-trough*: These horses are never heard of again.

580 *bathed*: No doubt in hot water to remove the sea salt, but a bathtub is a surprising amenity for an army in
     the field. The incident is something you would expect in the *Odyssey*.

BOOK 11. *The Glory of Agamemnon and the Wounding of the Captains*

Dawn arose from the bed of noble Tithonos° to bring
light to the deathless ones and to mortals. Zeus sent
Eris to the swift ships of the Achaeans, bitter Eris,
having in her hands a portent of war.° She took her stand
5   at the huge-hulled black ship of Odysseus, which held
a middle position in the line of ships so that a shout
was heard at either end, both to the huts of Ajax,
son of Telamon, and to the huts of Achilles. These men
had drawn up their ships at opposite ends of the row, trusting
10   in their valor and the strength of their hands. Taking
her stand there the goddess shouted a great and awesome
cry, the shrill cry of war, and she placed great strength
in the heart of every Achaean to fight and make war
unceasingly so that war seemed sweeter to them than
15   to return in their hollow ships to the land of their fathers.

The son of Atreus shouted too and urged
the Argives to buckle on their armor. He himself put on
his gleaming bronze. First he placed the shinguards
around his shins, beautiful and fitted with silver
20   ankle-pieces. Second, he placed a chest-protector around
his chest, the one Kinyras once gave to him as a guest-gift.
A rumor had reached CYPRUS° that Achaeans were about
to launch a naval expedition against Troy. Therefore
he gave Agamemnon the chest-protector to do pleasure

---

1   *Tithonos*: A child of Laomedon and half-brother to Priam. The goddess Dawn snatched him away to be her lover. According to postHomeric, he was father to Memnon, the last great hero killed by Achilles. Dawn obtained immortality for him but forgot to ask for eternal youth: Tithonos shriveled up with age and became a cicada. This dawn marks the fifth since Book 2 and the twenty-fifth since the beginning of the *Iliad*. This day will be the longest in the poem: The sun does not set until Book 18.

4   *portent of war*: Eris, "strife," is not really a goddess, more a personification. We cannot know what the portent was.

22   *Cyprus*: The only time that the island of Cyprus is mentioned in the *Iliad*. Kinyras was in later tradition the father of Myrrha and, by an incestuous union with her, the father of Adonis.

to him. There were on it ten bands of dark lapis-lazuli,   25
twelve of gold, and twenty of tin. Lapis-lazuli
snakes wound their way toward the neck, three
on each side, like the rainbows that the son of Kronos
has fixed in the clouds, a portent to mortal men.° He cast
a sword about his shoulders, whose golden studs   30
glimmered, and around the sword was a silver scabbard
fitted with golden chains. He took up his mighty
shield, that shelters a man on both sides, highly decorated,
beautiful. Round about it were ten circles of bronze,
and inside twenty white tin bosses, and one big one   35
in the center, of dark lapis lazuli. And thereon
Gorgo, horrid to look on, was set as a crown,
glaring terribly, and around her Terror and Rout.°
There was a silver strap. On it was worked
a snake of lapis-lazuli. It had three heads   40
growing from a single neck, turned in different
directions. He placed on his head a helmet with doubled
crest of horsehair divided into four parts,°
the crest nodding terrifyingly above. He took up
two sharp strong spears tipped with bronze,   45
bronze that shined far away into the heaven.

Athena and Hera thundered to show honor
to the chief of Mycenae, rich in gold.° Then every man
ordered his driver to hold his horse in good order
there at the ditch, while they themselves, arrayed   50
in their armor, advanced on foot. An unquenchable cry
went up before the dawn. Far sooner than the charioteers
the infantry arranged themselves along the trench, and after
a little space followed the charioteers.° Among them the son

---

29   *mortal men*: We cannot form a picture of the chest-protector because we do not know in what direction the
     "bands" are arranged, nor what is their pattern.

38   *Terror and Rout*: Probably the "circles of bronze" are concentric. Gorgo must appear beneath the central
     boss, but it is hard to reconcile "was set as a crown" with the twenty small bosses and the one large central
     boss; nor is it clear how Terror and Rout were represented.

43   *parts*: It is obscure how this helmet worked, but in any event the horsehair crest of a Homeric helmet was not
     stiff, as on later classical helmets, but a kind of plume that bobbed and terrified one's opponent.

48   *rich in gold*: In fact Mycenae was rich in gold during the Bronze Age, when this epithet must have begun, to
     judge by the spectacular archaeological finds there (for an example, see Figure 11.2). Agamemnon's entry
     into battle needs a divine accompaniment, but at the moment Zeus is on the side of the Trojans. Agamem-
     non must be satisfied with a rumble from the goddesses on Olympos.

54   *charioteers*: The Achaeans must be assembled on the outer side of the ditch, toward Troy, though it is not said
     how they crossed the ditch. The foot soldiers are at the front of the line, the charioteers follow behind them,
     then comes the ditch, then a space, then the Achaean wall.

FIGURE 11.1   Gorgo.   Shown as the winged Near Eastern "Mistress of Animals," Gorgo holds a goose in either hand. The scary face is depicted with large eyes, snaky hair (but not here), pig's tusks, and a lolling tongue. The Gorgon's stare turns away evil. Here Gorgo is shown with four wings and large, pendulous breasts. Painted red on white ware from Kameiros, Rhodes, c. 600 BC, excavated by Auguste Salzmann and Sir Alfred Biliotti, photo by Marie-Lan Nguyen.

of Kronos raised up an evil din, and from the heaven   55
he rained down dew dripping with blood. For he was about
to send the heads of many strong men down to Hades.

   The Trojans, for their part, on the other side on the rising
ground of the plain, assembled around great Hector
and blameless Polydamas° and Aeneas, honored by the Trojans   60
like a god, and the three sons of Antenor—Polybos and the good
Agenor and the young Akamas, like to the deathless ones.°

   Hector carried his perfectly round shield among
the foremost, even as a star full of menace appears out
of the clouds, shining, then sinks again behind the shadowy   65
clouds— so did Hector appear now among the foremost,
now among the hindmost, giving orders. All in bronze
he showed forth like the lightning of Zeus the father, who carries
the goatskin fetish.

                Even as reapers face one another
across a field of wheat or barley and drive a swathe   70
so that the handfuls fall thick and fast, even so the Trojans
and the Achaeans leaped on one another and killed, nor
did either side take thought of ruinous flight.° The battle
had equal heads.° Like wolves they raged. Eris, who
causes many groans, rejoiced at the sight. She alone   75
of all the gods was among the fighters. The other gods
were not with her, but took their ease at peace
in their halls, where for each was built a beautiful
house in the folds of Olympos. All the gods
heaped blame on the son of Kronos, he of the dark clouds,   80
because he wished to glorify the Trojans, but Zeus
certainly did not care at all what they thought.
He sat alone, turned aside from them, apart, exulting

---

60 *Polydamas:* Son of the Trojan elder Panthoös, he is an important figure who soon becomes Hector's
    strongest advisor.

62 *to the deathless ones:* Polybos is otherwise unknown, but Antenor is mentioned thirteen times in the *Iliad.*
    Akamas is in the Trojan catalog, leads troops in Book 12, and is killed in Book 16. Antenor is of Priam's
    generation; he loses seven sons in the war.

73 *ruinous flight:* The simile is slightly confused. Because each army cuts down the other, Homer must combine
    the notion of reaping with that of two opposing sides. He pictures two teams of reapers working at opposite
    ends of a field and moving toward each other to be like the Trojans and Achaeans moving toward each other.
    But at the same time the crop, which is cut down, must also represent the Trojans for the Achaeans and the
    Achaeans for the Trojans.

74 *equal heads:* That is, neither side had the advantage.

in his glory, looking down on the city of the Trojans
85 and the ships of the Achaeans, on the flashing of the bronze,
on the killers and the killed.

So long as it was morning and the
sacred day progressed, just so long the weapons from both
sides struck home and the warriors fell. But when the time
came that a wood cutter prepares his meal in the valleys
90 of a mountain, when he has worn out his arms with the cutting
of tall trees, and weariness comes over his soul, and desire for
sweet food takes hold of his heart, just then the Danaäns broke
the Trojan battalions through their valor, calling to their fellows
along the lines.

Among them Agamemnon rushed forward
95 first, and he took down a man named Bianora, the shepherd
of the people, and afterward he killed his comrade Oïleus,
the driver of horses.° Oïleus had leaped down from his car
and faced Agamemnon. As Oïleus rushed at him
Agamemnon struck him with his sharp spear on the forehead
100 and the helmet heavy with bronze did not stop the spear.
It went through helmet and through bone and splattered
the brains within.° Thus Agamemnon overcame
the furiously charging Oïleus.

And the king of men
Agamemnon left the bodies there, gleaming with their shining
105 breasts after he had stripped away their shirts. He went
on to kill Isos and Antiphos, two sons of Priam, one a bastard
and the other legitimate, both riding in a single car.
The bastard Isos was the driver and the most famous Antiphos
stood by his side. These two men Achilles once bound with
110 willow branches when he caught them as they herded their sheep
in the valleys of Ida, and he let them go after taking ransom.

The son of Atreus, wide-ruling Agamemnon, hit Isos
with his spear above the nipple on the chest, and he struck
Antiphos by the ear with his sword. He cast Antiphos from the car.

---

97   *... driver of horses*: Oïleus (also the name of Little Ajax's father) and Bianor are stock names like the names
of Agamemnon's many victims that follow. Of the about 340 Trojans and their allies named in the *Iliad*,
two-thirds have Greek names.

102   *within*: Though Agamemnon took two throwing spears when he armed (line 45), he now fights with a single
thrusting spear.

Working quickly Agamemnon stripped the beautiful armor   115
from the two men, whom he knew—he had seen them when
they were by the swift ships when Achilles, the fast runner,
had brought them from Ida. Even as a lion easily
crushes the speechless young of a swift deer,
coming into its lair, seizing them in its powerful   120
teeth and taking away their tender life— the mother,
even if she happens to be near, can do nothing.
On herself, too, comes a dread trembling and she runs
swiftly through the thick underbrush and through
the woods, moving fast, sweating, under attack by the powerful   125
beast—even so could no one of the Trojans ward off
destruction from Isos and Antiphos, but they were themselves
driven in flight before the Argives.°

                Then Agamemnon took Peisander
and Hippolochos, a hold-out in the fight, sons of wise
Antimachos, who more than the others opposed giving Helen   130
back to Menelaos because Antimachos hoped to receive
gold and more shining gifts from Alexandros—
Agamemnon took them down as they rode together
in a car, trying to gain control of their swift horses.
The shining reins had slipped from their hands and   135
the two horses were running wild. The son of Atreus
leaped upon them like a lion. They begged him from the car:
"Please, take us alive, son of Atreus! Take a worthy
ransom! There is much treasure in the house of Antimachos,
bronze and gold and well-worked iron that our father would   140
give you as boundless ransom if he learned that we were alive
at the ships of the Achaeans."

                So weeping, the two men addressed
Agamemnon with honeyed words. They heard
an unhoneyed reply: "If you are really the two sons of wise
Antimachos, who, when Menelaos came with godlike Odysseus   145
on an embassy, urged in public assembly that Menelaos
be killed on the spot and not permitted to return to the Achaeans—
then accept repayment for your father's vile behavior!"

---

128 … *Argives*: Isos and Antiphos are like the young of the deer crushed by the attacking lion, Agamemnon.
     It is unclear whether Homer ever saw a lion, though it is one of his favorite animals in similes; he may
     depend on earlier Near Eastern descriptions. Probably there were few lions in Greece in Homer's day.
     In Homer lions never roar, as they often do in life.

Agamemnon spoke and threw Peisander down from the car,
150 striking him in the chest with his spear. Peisander was hurled
backward onto the earth. Then Hippolochos jumped down
and Agamemnon killed him on the ground. He cut off his arms
and head and rolled him through the throng like a wooden mortar.°

Then he let them be. There, where most of the battalions
155 were being driven in rout, Agamemnon leaped in and with him went
others of the Achaeans with fancy shinguards. Foot soldiers
killed foot soldiers as they fled, compelled by necessity, and drivers
killed drivers.° Beneath them dust arose from the plain,
driven by the thundering feet of the horses. Everywhere
160 was havoc made with the bronze. And King Agamemnon,
killing as he went, followed after his troops, commanding
the Argives. As when consuming fire falls upon a wild
wood, and everywhere a whirling wind carries it
and the thickets crumble as they are assailed by the onrush
165 of the fire—just so tumbled the heads of the Trojans
under attack by the son of Atreus, Agamemnon,
as they fled. Many long-necked horses rattled
empty cars across the bridges of battle,° lacking their
drivers. Those drivers lay on the earth, more beloved
170 of buzzards than of their own wives.

Zeus had removed
Hector from the rain of weapons and the dust and the killing
of men and the blood and the din of war. But the son
of Atreus followed after, calling fiercely to the Danaäns.
Past the tomb of ancient Ilos, a descendant of Dardanos,
175 the Trojans rushed, over the middle of the plain beside
the fig tree, longing for the city. Screaming ever followed
the son of Atreus. His invincible hands were drenched in gore.
And when the Achaeans came to the Scaean Gates
and the oak tree, there the two sides took their stand
180 and awaited each other.

But some Trojans were still being driven
across the middle of the plain like cattle that a lion

---

153   *mortar*: Heads get cut off elsewhere, but only here are the arms cut off, too, and the body rolled like a
      column of wood!

158   *drivers*: We cannot be sure what Homer meant by this because, in general, fighting is never done from chari-
      ots. In individual encounters charioteers never kill charioteers in the *Iliad*.

168   *bridges of battle*: The word "bridges" is of uncertain meaning, but the phrase is formulaic for "battlefield."

has put to flight, coming on them in the dead of night.
The lion has scattered all of them, but on one
is fixed a terrible death. He breaks her neck,
first seizing her in his powerful teeth, then he gulps   185
down all the blood and guts—even so the son of Atreus,
King Agamemnon, pursued the Trojans, always killing
the ones who fell behind as they fled before him.

   Many fell from their cars on their faces
and on their backs beneath the hands of the son of Atreus.   190
All around and before him he raged with the spear. But when
he was about to come under the city and the steep wall,
then the father of men and gods came down from the sky
and took his seat on the peaks of Ida that has many
fountains. He held a thunderbolt in his hands.   195

   Zeus sent down Iris, who has golden wings,° to deliver
a message: "Go, hurry swift Iris, and give this message
to Hector: So long as he sees Agamemnon, the shepherd
of the people, raging among the foremost fighters and slaughtering
the ranks of men, just so long should he hold back from   200
the fighting. Urge others to fight the enemy in the ferocious
contendings. But when Agamemnon is wounded by a spear or arrow,
and he leaps up into his car, then will I give Hector the power
to kill and kill until he reaches the fine-benched ships,
and the sun sets and on comes the sacred darkness."°   205

   Zeus spoke, and quick Iris, swift as the wind, obeyed.
She went down from the peaks of Ida to holy Ilion.
There she found good Hector, the son of wise Priam,
standing among his horses and cars made of well-fitted
parts. Standing close, Iris, swift of feet, declared: 210
"O Hector, son of Priam, like to Zeus in your
intelligence, father Zeus has sent me down
to give you this message: So long as you see Agamemnon,
shepherd of the people, raging among the foremost fighters,

---

196   ... *wings*: The thunderbolt is Zeus's emblem; he is not about to use it. Only here (and once of Iris in Book 8)
      does a god have wings.

205   *sacred darkness*: Homer wants to present an *aristeia*, a "moment of greatness," of Agamemnon, but a hero's
      aristeia only excites the attention of the best fighter on the other side. Because this is Hector, Homer must
      remove Hector temporarily from the fighting in accord with Zeus's "inscrutable will." Hector is Achilles'
      opponent, not Agamemnon's.

215 slaughtering the ranks of men, just so long should
you hold back from the fighting. Urge others to fight
the enemy in the ferocious contendings. But when Agamemnon
is wounded by a spear or arrow, and he leaps up into
his car, then Zeus will instill in you the power
220 to kill and kill until you reach the fine-benched ships,
and the sun sets and the sacred darkness comes on."
She spoke and, having spoken, went off, Iris swift of foot.

Hector leaped down from the car in full armor,
and shaking his sharp spears he went everywhere throughout
225 the camp, urging on the fight, stirring up the dread
lust for war. And so were the Trojans roused to stand up
against the Achaeans, and the Argives on their side
strengthened their battalions. The battle lines were drawn.
They stood up against each other, and from them Agamemnon
230 rushed forth first. He wanted ever to fight in the forefront.

Tell me now, you Muses who live in houses
on Olympos, who first came against Agamemnon, either
of the Trojans themselves or of their famous allies?

Iphidamas, the son of Antenor, great and strong,
235 who was raised in fertile Thrace, the mother of flocks.
Kisseus, the father of his mother, Theano° of the beautiful
cheeks, raised him in his halls when he was a child.
But when he came to the measure of glorious youth
Kisseus tried to keep Iphidamas there in Thrace.
240 Kisseus gave Iphidamas his daughter. But after
Iphidamas married, he left the wedding chamber in pursuit
of glory over the Achaeans. Twelve ships with beaks
followed him. He left the well-balanced ships
at PERKOTÊ°and went on foot to Ilion.

It was Iphidamas
245 who opposed Agamemnon, the son of Atreus. When
they came near each other, the son of Atreus missed his mark.
Agamemnon's spear was turned aside, but Iphidamas
stabbed him on the belt beneath the chest-protector.

---

236 *Theano*: Theano is the priestess of Athena in Troy.
244 *Perkotê*: On the Dardanelles (Map 6).

Iphidamas put his weight into the thrust, trusting to his
strong hand, but he could not pierce the flashing belt.   250
The point struck silver and was turned aside like lead.
Taking the spear in his hand, wide-ruling Agamemnon
pulled Iphidamas toward him like a lion and wrenched
the spear from his hand. And then Agamemnon struck
him in the neck with his sword. Iphidamas' limbs went loose.   255

And there he fell and slept the sleep of bronze,°
a wretched youth, far from his wedded wife, bringing aid
to the people of Troy. His wife was a bride of whom
he had never known pleasure, though he gave much for her:
First, he gave a hundred cattle, then he promised   260
a thousand goats and sheep together, herded for him
in flocks past counting.

Agamemnon the son
of Atreus stripped off his armor and went off through
the throng, displaying the beautiful armor.° When Koön,
the oldest son of Antenor, preeminent among warriors,   265
saw Iphidamas killed, a powerful sorrow fell over his eyes
for his fallen brother. He stood to the side with his spear,
unnoticed by the good Agamemnon, and stabbed Agamemnon
on the forearm by the elbow. Straight through went the point
of his shining spear. Agamemnon, the king of men, shivered.   270
But he did not leave off from battle and war—he leaped on Koön
with his wind-nurtured spear. Koön was dragging Iphidamas
by the foot, his own brother, begotten by the same father,
and shouting to all the best fighters. But even as Koön dragged
the corpse of Iphidamas through the throng, Agamemnon   275
pierced him beneath his bossed shield with the smoothly
polished spear, tipped with bronze. Thus were Koön's
limbs loosened. Agamemnon cut off Koön's head.
And so two sons of Antenor went down to the house
of Hades, fulfilling their fate at the hands of the king,   280
the son of Atreus.

---

256 *bronze*: The sleep of death is unbreakable, like bronze.

264 *armor*: Stripping the body of the dead was important to the ritual of Homeric warfare, contributing to
     the *fame* (*kleos*) and the *glory* (*kudos*) of the victor and to the shame of the defeated. It was, however,
     very dangerous (as here with Agamemnon) because in kneeling to strip the corpse, one exposed oneself
     to attack.

Thus Agamemnon ranged among the ranks
of the warriors with his spear and sword and with great stones,°
for so long as the blood still ran from his wound. But when
the wound dried up, and the blood ceased to flow,
285 then sharp pains overcame the strength of the son of Atreus.
As when a sharp arrow strikes a woman in labor, sent by
the Eileithyiai,° the daughters of Hera who cause birth pangs,
who have bitter pains in their charge, even so
did sharp pains come over the mighty son of Atreus.

290 Agamemnon mounted into his car and told his driver
to return to the hollow ships, for his heart was in pain.
He gave forth a piercing cry to the Danaäns: "O my friends,
leaders and rulers of the Argives, you must now ward off
the awful din of battle from our seafaring ships!
295 Zeus the counselor does not allow that I fight all day
long against the Trojans!"

So he spoke. The driver lashed
the horses with beautiful manes toward the hollow ships.
Not unwilling, the two of them sped onwards, their breasts
covered with foam, their bellies beneath spattered
300 with dust as they bore the wounded king from the battle.

When Hector saw Agamemnon leaving the field of battle,
he called to the Trojans and the Lycians° in a booming voice:
"Trojans and Lycians and Dardanians who fight in close,
be men, my friends, and remember your furious valor!
305 Their best man has departed. Zeus, the son of Kronos,
has given me great glory, so now drive your single-hoofed
horses straight at the mighty Danaäns, that you might win
the glory that comes with victory!"

---

282 *great stones*: It is perfectly good form to throw stones at the enemy, but Agamemnon would have to put
down his thrusting spear in order to pick up stones. In any event Agamemnon's *aristeia* is over. He killed
eight named Trojans and numerous unnamed ones. His weapon has been four times the spear, three times
the sword, and once unspecified. In Homeric fighting the spear is primary; then, when the spear is
disabled, the sword is drawn for close-in work.

287 *Eileithyiai*: "The goddesses who come," the protectors of women in childbirth, sometimes singular
(Eileithyia), worshiped already in the Mycenaean Age. Eileithyia appears in the Mycenaean
Linear B tablets. Or the name is preGreek.

302 *Lycians*: Probably the Lycians who lived northeast of Troy, where Pandaros came from, who are called
"Trojans," not the Lycians from southwest Asia Minor, where Sarpedon and Glaukos were princes.

So speaking, he roused
up the strength and the spirit of each man. As when a hunter
urges his white-toothed dogs on a wild boar or lion,   310
so did Hector, son of Priam, urge on the great-hearted
Trojans. He was the image of murderous Ares. He himself,
proud of spirit, went among the foremost. He fell
into the war-fury like a blustery storm that leaps down
and stirs up the violet sea.   315

    Then who first and who last
did Hector kill, the son of Priam, when Zeus gave him glory?°
First he killed Asaios and Autnonoös and Opites and Dolops,
son of Klytos, and Opheltios and Agelaos and Aisymnos
and Oros and Hipponoös, sturdy in battle. These leaders
of the Danaäns he killed, and then many of the common people.   320
As when West Wind drives the clouds of the rapid South Wind,
striking them with a violent storm, and a huge wave
goes rolling along, and high up the foam is scattered
from the blast of the wide-wandering wind—even so thickly
rolled the heads of the people at Hector's hands.   325

    Then disaster would have followed and deeds impossible
to control, and now the Achaeans would have thrown themselves
in flight onto their ships, had Odysseus not called out to Diomedes,
the son of Tydeus: "Son of Tydeus what has happened to us?
Have we forgotten our furious valor? Come here, my good friend,   330
stand beside me. We will be drenched in shame if Hector
of the flashing helmet takes our ships."

    Powerful Diomedes
answered: "I stand with you and we shall endure! It will
give us little pleasure, though, because Zeus, who gathers
the clouds, wants to give strength to the Trojans and not to us."   335

    He spoke and threw Thymbraios from his car to the ground,
striking him with his spear beneath the left nipple, while Odysseus
took out Molion, the godlike attendant of Thymbraios.
Then they left them alone, having put them out of the war.
The two warriors Odysseus and Diomedes pushed through the throng,   340

---

316 *him glory*: Now follows an *aristeia* of Hector, but much compressed into a list of the names of aristocrats he
    kills and three short similes. Homer likes to balance one *aristeia*, in this instance that of Agamemnon, with
    another from the other side. The commoners that Hector kills are not entitled to names.

bringing disaster everywhere they went, as when two boars
with raging hearts fall on hunting hounds—just so
they killed the Trojans, turning on them, letting the Achaeans
gladly catch their breath in their flight before Hector.

345   Next they took down a chariot with two men in it,
the best of their people, the two sons of Merops of Perkotê°
—Merops was superior to all in seercraft and did
not wish his sons to go to the man-killing war. But they
would not listen, driven by the fate of black death.
350 Diomedes, the son of Tydeus, famous for his spear work,
deprived them of their breath and their breath-souls. He took
their wonderful armor.

                    Then Odysseus dispatched Hippodamos
and Hypeirochos.° The son of Kronos stretched out evenly the line
of battle for them as he looked down from MOUNT IDA.°
355 Both sides kept up the killing. The son of Tydeus
wounded with his spear Agastrophos, the son of Paion,
on the hip. His horses were not near because from his blindness
of heart Agastrophos had his attendant hold them apart
while he raged on foot amid the foremost fighters—until
360 he lost his life!

                    Hector quickly recognized Diomedes
and Odysseus across the ranks and he rushed upon them,
whooping, while the Trojan battalions followed.
When Diomedes, good at the war cry, saw Hector, he shivered.
Quickly he spoke to Odysseus who was nearby: "Mighty
365 Hector springs now to rain ruin on the two of us.
But come, let us make our stand here, and ward off
great evil by standing where we are."

                    Thus he spoke,
and poised his far-shadowing spear and threw it. He did not
miss the mark at which he aimed, but hit Hector

---

346   *sons of Merops of Perkotê*: Named in the Trojan Catalog as Amphios and Adrestos of Paisos, leaders of a
       Hellespontine contingent. Their names are similar to Amphiaraos and Adrastos, two famous leaders in the
       story of the Seven Against Thebes.

353   ... *Hypereichos*: These are stock figures with "speaking names": "Hippodamos" means "horse-tamer," an
       epithet of the Trojans generally; "Hypereichos" means "preeminent."

354   *Mount Ida*: The metaphor of stretching a line in order to convey intensity of conflict is common in the *Iliad*,
       but the precise image remains unclear.

in the head on the top of the helmet. Bronze was bent   370
on bronze and the spear did not penetrate Hector's beautiful skin.
The threefold helmet that Phoibos Apollo gave him,°
with tube affixed, stopped it. Hector swiftly
sprang away and mixed with the crowd. He stopped
and fell to his knees, supporting himself with his   375
powerful hand on the earth. Black night enclosed his eyes.

   While the son of Tydeus went rushing after his spear
through the foremost fighters, to find where it had sped
down to the earth, Hector meanwhile revived.
He leaped into his chariot and drove off into the throng.   380
And thus Hector avoided black fate. Rushing after him
with his spear, the powerful Diomedes cried: "And so
you escape death for the moment, you dog! The evil day
came close to you! Now for the moment Phoibos Apollo
has saved you.° You should pray to him as you go through the din   385
of missiles, but I shall kill you when I come upon you later,
when I can get some great god on my side. Now I will pursue
the others, to see if I can catch them."

                    So Diomedes spoke
and went on to strip the armor from Agastrophos, the son
of Paion, famous for his spear. But Alexandros,   390
the husband of Helen with the lovely hair, aimed
an arrow against the son of Tydeus, shepherd of the people.
He leaned against the block of stone on the tomb that men
had built for Ilos, a descendant of Dardanos, an elder
of the people in the olden days. Diomedes was taking off   395
the shining chest-protector from the chest of strong Agastrophos
and removing the shield from around his shoulders
and his weighty helmet when Paris drew back the center of
his bow and fired. The missile did not go in vain from his hand,
but struck the flat of Diomedes' right foot. The arrow   400
went straight through and was fixed in the earth.°

---

372   *gave him*: Apollo did not literally give Hector the helmet; the expression means that the helmet is of the
      finest manufacture. Perhaps the rather mysterious "tube" on the helmet is to hold the crest.

385   *has saved you*: In fact the gods have not been acting on the battlefield, in accord with Zeus's mandate.

401   *earth*: The only time that anyone in the *Iliad* is wounded in the foot. Nowhere does Homer say that Paris
      will one day shoot Achilles in the foot or heel and kill him, as in later tradition, but perhaps this detail is
      meant to make us think of that. In many respects Diomedes is a little Achilles, dominating the action while
      the great hero is in his tent.

Laughing sweetly, Paris leaped from his ambush
and boasted: "You are hit! Not in vain did my arrow fly!
How I wish I had hit you in the lower gut and taken your life!
405 Then would the Trojans be recovering from your onslaught,
who tremble before you like bleating goats before a lion!"

Not in the least afraid, the powerful Diomedes answered:
"You, bowman, always insolent, goldie locks, girlie-peeper—
I would like to take you on in the hand-to-hand, fully armed.
410 Then your bow and your thickly falling arrows would do you
no good. As it is you have scratched the bottom of my foot—
you boast for nothing! I don't care at all about it, it's as if a woman
or a mindless child struck me. The arrow of a man without strength
is blunt, a man of no consequence. Quite different is the cast
415 of my own weapon. Even if a man is just touched by it, the sharp
edge proves itself and quickly he lies dead! Then the cheeks
of his wife are rent with wailing. His children are without
a father. He reddens the earth with blood. Then he rots.
Birds rather than women gather around him!"

So Diomedes spoke.
420 Odysseus, famous for his spear, came close and stood
in front of Diomedes, who sat down. Odysseus drew out
the sharp arrow from his foot. A savage pain stabbed through
Diomedes' flesh. He clambered into his car and ordered his driver
to make for the hollow ships, for he was sore at heart.

425 Odysseus, famed for his spear, was now alone,
nor did any of the Argives remain with him.
Fear had taken hold of all. Perplexed, he spoke
to his own great heart: "Oh me, what will happen to me?
It would be a great evil if I fled, fearing the multitude.
430 But it would be still more shivery if I am taken alone.°
The son of Kronos has put to flight the other Danaäns.
But why do I deliberate on these things? I know that those
who withdraw from war are cowards. And he who is best
in the fight must of necessity hold his ground with power,
435 even if he is wounded, or if he wounds another."

---

430 *alone.* The monologue "Shall I stand and fight or withdraw?" is a type-scene of which there are numerous
examples. The hero always decides to stand and fight.

While Odysseus pondered these things in his heart and spirit
the ranks of the shield-bearing Trojans came upon him.
They surrounded him, to their own pain! Just as when hounds
and red-hot youths press on a wild boar from this side and that,
and the boar comes out of the deep woods wetting   440
his white teeth in his curving jaws, and they charge on him
from both sides, and the sound of gnashing teeth resounds
but they withstand his attack, though he is a terrible beast—
even so the Trojans pressed on both sides of Odysseus,
beloved of Zeus, who withstood them.   445

                              Odysseus struck first
Deïopites in the shoulder, coming at him from above
with his sharp spear. Then he killed Thoös and Ennomos.
Then he stabbed Chersidamas as he leaped down from his car,
reaching him from beneath the bossed shield. Odysseus dropped
him in the dust. Chersidamas gripped the earth with bent hand.   450

    Odysseus let them go. Then he wounded Charops,
son of Hippasos, with his spear, the brother of wealthy Sokos.
To defend Charops, Sokos moved in, a man like to a god.°
Sokos stood close to Odysseus and said: "O Odysseus,
much-praised, insatiate for clever devices and the labor of war,   455
today either you will boast that you have killed
the two sons of Hippasos and taken their armor, or struck
by my spear you will give up your life."

                              So speaking, Sokos
struck Odysseus' shield, balanced on every side.
The shining powerful spear went through the shield   460
and it forced its way through the highly decorated chest-protector.
It tore all the tender flesh from Odysseus' side,
but Athena did not allow the spear to mix with the guts
of the warrior,° and Odysseus knew that the spear did not hit
in a fatal spot.   465

    He drew back and spoke to Sokos:
"Ah wretch, surely a steep destruction has fallen upon you!
Yes, you have stopped me from fighting the Trojans, but I say

---

453   *like to a god*: Charops and Sokos ("strong") only appear in this episode.

464   *warrior*: If taken literally, Athena would be in violation of Zeus's proclamation that the gods not get
      involved. Probably what is meant is "had it not been for the will of God …"

that this day shall bring death and black fate upon you.
Killed by my spear you will give me a cause for boasting
470 and you will give a soul to Hades, famous for his horses."

    He spoke and Sokos turned to run, but Odysseus
speared him in the back as he turned, between the shoulder blades.
The spear went through his chest and Sokos fell with a thud.
Odysseus boasted over him: "O Sokos, son of wise Hippasos,
475 the horse-tamer, the end of death has been quick in coming
to you. You have not escaped it! Poor wretch, your father
and mother will never close your dead eyes, but the flesh-eating
birds will devour you, beating their wings thick and fast.
Whereas if I die, good Achaeans will give me burial."

480   So speaking, he pulled out the strong spear of wise Sokos
from his own flesh and from his own shield. When he pulled it out,
the blood came spurting forth, distressing Odysseus' heart.

    When the great-hearted Trojans saw the blood of Odysseus,
they called to one another throughout the throng. They banded
485 together to attack him in a crowd. But Odysseus drew back,
shouting to his comrades—three times he shouted, as much
as a man can shout. And three times Menelaos,
dear to Ares, heard him. Menelaos called to Ajax
standing nearby: "Ajax, sprung from Zeus,
490 son of Telamon, leader of the people, the voice
of enduring Odysseus comes to my ears like the voice
of a man near ruin. He stands alone, cut off
by the Trojans in the savage conflict. But let us go
through the throng. It is upon us to help him out.
495 I am afraid that, all alone, he might suffer more ills
from the Trojans—though he is from the best among us!—
and then a great longing will fall on the Danaäns." So
Menelaos spoke, then led the way, and Ajax
followed, a man like a god.

                    They found Odysseus,
500 dear to Zeus. The Trojans surrounded him like tawny
jackals in the mountains surround a wounded horned stag
that a man has hit with an arrow from his string.
The stag has escaped, fleeing on its swift feet so long
as the blood is warm and its legs move easily, but when
505 the swift arrow overcomes it, then the jackals, who eat
raw flesh, rend him in a shadowy wood in the mountains.

But look—a god has sent a ravening lion!
The jackals scatter while the lion enjoys a feast—
even so did the Trojans, many and brave, press
on the wise Odysseus, crafty in counsel, while   510
Odysseus darted forth with his spear to ward off
the day of doom.°

      Ajax then came close, carrying
his shield like a tower. As he stood beside Odysseus,
the Trojans took flight, running this way and that.
Menelaos led Odysseus out of the melée, holding his arm   515
until Menelaos' driver brought up the horses.° Then Ajax
leaped on the Trojans. He took down Doryklos, a bastard
son of Priam. He wounded Pandokos, and he wounded
Lysander and Pyrasos and Pylartes.° As when a swollen
river comes down from the mountains onto the plain   520
in winter, swollen by the rain of Zeus, and it carries along
with it many dry oaks, and many pines, and it casts
much mud and rubbish into the sea—even so shining
Ajax charged in tumult across the plain, killing
horses and men.   525

      Hector, not yet aware of these things,
fought on the left of the battle beside the Skamandros,
where the heads of men fell, and an unquenchable cry arose
around great Nestor and warlike Idomeneus.°
Hector skirmished among them, performing awful deeds
with his spear and his horsemanship° as he smashed detachments   530
of youth. Still, the good Achaeans would not have turned away
from their course if Alexandros, the husband of Helen with
the beautiful hair, had not put a stop to the rampaging Machaon,°
shepherd of the people, by hitting him in the right shoulder

---

512   *day of doom*: Odysseus is the wounded stag beset by jackals. Ajax is the lion who then disperses the jackals.

516   *horses*: Being an islander, Odysseus has no chariot of his own.

519   *... Pylartes*: Doryklos, only here, is one of Priam's many bastards; the names of both Pandokos, "all-receiver," and Lysander, "looser of men," are curiously appropriate to the death Lord; Pyrasos is also a town in Thessaly; Patroklos kills a Pylartes in Book 16.

528   *Idomeneus*: Not heard of since Book 8, and not again until Book 13, after which he is prominent. Idomeneus is older and hence appropriately in Nestor's company.

530   *horsemanship*: Seems to imply fighting from a chariot, but that would be highly unusual.

533   *Machaon*: He was the son of Asklepios, who became god of medicine, and brother of the Trojan-fighter Podaleirios. Like Podaleirios, Machaon was a physician as well as warrior.

535 with a three-barbed arrow. The Achaeans, who breathed power,
feared for Machaon, that the Trojans might take him in the turning
of the fight.

Immediately Idomeneus spoke to the good Nestor:
"O Nestor, son of Neleus, come, mount your chariot!
Save Machaon—guide your single-hoofed horses
540 to the ships as quickly as you can. A doctor is worth many
other men. He can cut out arrows and apply soothing ointments."

So he spoke, and Gerenian Nestor, the horseman,
obeyed. Immediately he mounted his chariot. Beside him
mounted Machaon, the son of Asklepios, the blameless
545 doctor. Nestor lashed the horses and not unwilling they sped
on to the hollow ships, where they longed to be.

Kebriones,° seeing that the Trojans were driven
in rout, stood beside Hector in his car and spoke to him
as follows: "Hector, here we contend with the Danaäns
550 at the edge of painful war while the other Trojans are routed
in confusion, both the horses and men. Ajax, the son
of Telamon, rages. I know him well. He always
carries a broad shield around his shoulders. But let us turn
our horses in that direction, where most of all the horsemen
555 and the foot soldiers, steeped in evil contention, kill one another,
and the unquenchable cry of war goes up."

So speaking
Kebriones lashed the horses with beautiful manes with his
sharp lash. Responding to the whip, they swiftly drove the fast car
through the Trojans and the Achaeans, running over the dead bodies
560 and shields so that the axle beneath the car was wholly splattered
with blood, and the railings which run around the chariot too,
from the blood thrown up by the horses' hooves and by the tires.

Hector was eager to enter and smash the throng
of warriors. He sent an evil din among the Danaäns, gave scant
565 rest to his weapons, and ranged among the ranks of the other
warriors with his spear and his sword and his great stones,
but he avoided battle with Ajax, son of Telamon.

---

547 *Kebriones:* Hector's charioteer, promoted to this role in Book 8 after the death of Archeptolemos.
Kebriones is a bastard son of Priam. Patroklos will kill him in Book 16 (see Figure 16.3).

                              Father Zeus,
sitting high on his throne, then put flight in the mind of Ajax.
Ajax stood in a daze. On his back he cast his shield
made of seven bulls' hides. He retreated, glancing   570
at the melée like a wild animal, turning constantly
to the side, retreating step by step. Even as dogs
and country men turn aside a yellow lion from a pen
containing cows, not allowing the savage lion
to take the fattest of the cows, staying up all night long—   575
and the lion, in love with flesh, accomplishes nothing
though he goes on, for a rain of missiles flies
to meet him and burning sticks cast by bold hands.
The lion quails before them, although he is eager,
and at dawn slinks away with a heavy heart—   580
even so Ajax withdrew before the Trojans
with a heavy heart, much unwilling. For he feared
for the ships of the Achaeans.

                    As when an ass goes past
a field of wheat, and he gets the better of the boys,
a sluggard over whose flanks the boys break many a cudgel,   585
but he ravishes the deep crop though they strike him
with their clubs—their power is puny, they barely get him out
and only after he's had his fill—even so did the proud
Trojans and their allies, assembled from afar, stab
the middle of Ajax's shield and ever press in on him.°   590

But strong Ajax remembered his furious valor,
and wheeling on them he now held back the battalions
of the horse-taming Trojans, now turned to flee,
preventing anyone from making a way to the swift ships.
He positioned himself midway between the Trojans and the   595
Achaeans, raging. Spears were thrown by bold Trojan hands.
Some of them fixed in his great shield as they rushed on,
and many of them, before they touched his white skin,
fell midway into the earth, eager to gorge on flesh.

Then Eurypylos, the excellent son of Euaimon,°   600
saw that Ajax was about to be overcome by a torrent of missiles.

---

590   ... on him: This is the fifteenth and last simile in this book. Similes enliven and give variety to the battle
       scenes but do not appear in the leisurely talk of Nestor and Patroklos coming up.

600   son of Euaimon: An Achaean fighter from Thessaly of some consequence, Eurypylos is involved in one of
       the earliest clashes in the Iliad when he kills the Trojan Hypsenor (Book 5). He is mentioned in Books 6, 7,
       8, and 10 as well.

He moved in close to him and threw his shining spear,
striking Apisaon, son of Phausios, the shepherd
of the people, in the liver, below the lungs. At once
605 his knees loosened. Eurypylos leaped on him
and began to strip the armor from his shoulders. Godlike
Alexandros saw him removing the armor of Apisaon,
and immediately he aimed his bow at Eurypylos. He hit him
in the right thigh with an arrow. The shaft of the arrow
610 was broken, the thigh grew heavy, but Eurypylos slipped
back into the mass of his comrades, avoiding death.

Eurypylos gave a piercing shout to the Danaäns:
"My friends, leaders and rulers of the Argives, turn around
and make a stand! Protect Ajax from the pitiless day,
615 overwhelmed by missiles. I don't think he will run
from hateful war! So take your stand now against
the enemy—defend great Ajax, the son of Telamon!"

So cried the wounded Eurypylos, and the Achaeans
stood close beside Ajax, leaning their shields against
620 their shoulders and raising high their spears. Ajax came toward
them and turned and stood and fought when he had come
to the crowd of his companions.

And so they fought like blazing fire.
The mares of Neleus, drenched in sweat, carried Nestor
from the battle along with Machaon, shepherd
625 of the people. Achilles, the fast runner, noticed them
while standing by the stern of his hollow-hulled ship,
watching the rough going and fearful rout. Directly he spoke
to Patroklos, his comrade, calling to him from beside the ship.
Patroklos heard and came forth from the tent, like to Ares—
630 and this was the beginning of evil for him.
The valiant son
of Menoitios answered Achilles first: "Why do you call,
Achilles? What do you need of me?"

Achilles, the fast runner, replied:
"Good son of Menoitios, most beloved to my heart, I think
that now the Achaeans will be standing about my knees
635 in prayer. An unbearable necessity has come upon them!°

---

635 *upon them*: These words seem to ignore the embassy of Book 9, as if the Achaeans had never attempted to
appease him, but for the story to move ahead Achilles needs to send Patroklos to Nestor's tent. At the same time
Homer wants to return our attention to Achilles and his plight. Here Achilles expresses anew his anger with the
Achaeans and how sorry they will be because he is not in the fight. This anger has never abated.

But go now, Patroklos, dear to Zeus, ask Nestor who is
the wounded man that he carries from the war. From here
he looks like Machaon, the son of Asklepios, but I did not see
the man's eyes. For the horses ran past me, quickly pressing on."

So he spoke. Patroklos obeyed his comrade. He ran along   640
the huts and ships of the Achaeans. When Nestor and Machaon
arrived at Nestor's hut, they got down from the car onto
the bounteous earth. Eurymedon, Nestor's aide,° undid
the old man's horses from the car. They dried the sweat
of their shirts in the breeze, standing by the shore of the sea.   645
Then they went into the hut and sat on chairs. Hekamedê
made a restorative drink for them. The old man had taken her
from TENEDOS when Achilles sacked it, the daughter of
great-hearted Arsinoös. The Achaeans chose her for him
because in giving counsel she was the best of all. First she   650
drew up a beautiful table with feet of lapis lazuli, highly
polished, and on it she placed a bronze bowl, and with it
an onion as relish for drink,° and pale honey, and a
meal of sacred barley, and a very beautiful cup that the
old man had brought from home, studded with rivets   655
of gold. It had four handles and around each two doves
were feeding, and two supports were beneath. Another
man could scarcely have lifted it from the table
when it was full, but old man Nestor raised it easily.
In it the woman, like to the goddesses, mixed a refreshing   660
drink of Pramnian wine,° and over it she grated goat's
cheese with a bronze grater. Then she sprinkled on
some white barley and urged them to drink, when she
had made ready the drink. The two men drank it and put
aside their parching thirst. Then Nestor and Machaon   665
delighted one another by telling tales.

                              Looking up
they saw Patroklos standing at the door, a man
like a god. When Nestor saw him the old man leaped up
from his shining chair. He took him by the hand and led

---

643   *aide*: In Book 8 he is called Nestor's charioteer. Agamemnon also has a charioteer named Eurymedon.

653   *for drink*: One of the very few time that vegetables are mentioned in the *Iliad*. The heroes are meat-eaters
      and avoid fish and vegetables.

661   *Pramnian wine*: No place known as Pramnos or the like has been identified, but Pramnian wine was
      evidently of good quality.

FIGURE 11.2 "The Cup of Nestor."   From the fourth shaft grave at Mycenae (sixteenth century BC), this amazing solid-gold cup, excavated and named by Heinrich Schliemann in 1876, does bear a remarkable resemblance to the cup described in Book 11 of the *Iliad*. It could be said to have "four handles" with "two supports beneath" and "two doves" feeding at the handles, except that the birds seem to be falcons.

In modern excavations on the island of Ischia in the Bay of Naples off the southern Italian coast, a modest clay pot was found with one of the two oldest known Greek inscriptions. It is from about 740 BC and may be a literary allusion. The first line is prose, and the second two lines are dactylic hexameter, the meter of Homer:

"I am the cup of Nestor.
Whoever drinks from this cup, at once that man
the desire of beautiful-crowned Aphrodite will seize."

The inscription seems to refer to the text of Homer, one of the strongest pieces of evidence in our effort to date Homer. Probably it is a "capping" or "one-upping" game. The first diner says, "I am the cup of Nestor," holding up the modest clay vessel, which is, of course, a joke. The next diner then introduces a curse formula that usually runs "Whoever steals this cup, he will ..." go blind, or the like (here the curse formula becomes "whoever drinks from this cup ..."). For the fulfillment of the curse, the third diner turns the tables by suggesting that he will enjoy a pleasant sexual experience ("the desire of beautiful Aphrodite will seize")! Whatever its exact meaning, somebody who knew how to write hexameters in the earliest days of Greek literacy inscribed this joke on the "Cup of Nestor." It was later placed in a child's grave and rediscovered in the mid-twentieth century.

him in and urged him to have a seat. Patroklos   670
from his side refused and said: "I won't sit, old man,
nourished of Zeus, nor can you persuade me. Revered
—to be feared!—is the man who sent me to find out who
is this man that you bring wounded from the battle. I see now
that it is Machaon, shepherd of the people. Now I must   675
return to Achilles and tell him what I've learned. I think
you know, old man, nourished of Zeus, what kind
of awesome man he is. He is quick to blame one in whom
there is no blame."

    Then Gerenian Nestor, the horseman,
answered him:° "Well, why does Achilles suddenly   680
have pity on the sons of the Achaeans, with all those wounded
by missiles? Does he not know the suffering spread
through the camp? For the captains are lying among
the ships, shot by arrows and cut by spears. The powerful
Diomedes, son of Tydeus, is wounded by an arrow. Odysseus,   685
famed with the spear, has a spear wound, and Agamemnon too.
Even Eurypylos has been hit in the thigh with an arrow.
This man Machaon is still one more that I have brought out
of the battle, struck by an arrow from the string. But Achilles,
though he is brave, does not care for the Danaäns or take pity   690
on them! Will he wait until the swift ships near the sea
are set aflame with devouring fire in spite of the Argives,
and we are killed all in a row?
                "My strength is not
what once it was when my limbs were supple. Would
that I were young and my strength were as when a quarrel   695
broke out with the Eleians and ourselves over some stolen cattle—
then I killed Itymon, the noble son of Hypeirochos, who
lived in ELIS,° when I was driving off booty seized
in reprisal. He was defending his cows and got hit among
the foremost by a spear thrown from my hand.   700
He fell, and the country folk around him fled in terror.
We took booty aplenty from the plain—fifty herds of cows,
as many flocks of sheep, as many herds of pigs, as many

---

680 *answered him*: Now follows the longest speech in the *Iliad* by the long-winded Nestor. Homer is somehow
     familiar with a tradition of song centered on PYLOS in the Peloponnesus, portions of which he places in
     Nestor's mouth.

698 *Elis*: The tribe of Eleians, famous from classical times, is mentioned only here in the *Iliad*, as is Itymon, son
     of Hypereichos. A few lines later the *Eleians* are called *Epeians*, a more general term to refer to inhabitants
     of the northwestern Peloponnesus in the heroic age.

herds of roving goats, and one hundred-fifty
705 tawny horses, all mares, and there were many with foals
at the teat. We drove them toward Neleian Pylos during
the night, toward the city.° Neleus rejoiced
in his heart when he learned that I had been successful
in going to war, though still a youth. Heralds
710 loudly proclaimed at the break of dawn that all
those should come to whom a debt was owed in good Elis.
The leaders of the Pylians all gathered together and distributed
the booty, for the Epeians owed a debt to many. We
in Pylos were few and oppressed, for mighty Herakles had
715 come in earlier years and killed all our bravest men.
The sons of handsome Neleus were twelve, but I
alone was left. All the others perished. Then the arrogant
Epeians, wearing shirts of bronze, did violence against us
and committed evil acts. So old man Neleus
720 took from them a herd of cattle and a large flock of sheep,
choosing three hundred and their herdsmen too. For they owed
him a huge debt in good Elis—four prize-winning horses
with their car had gone to the games to race for a tripod,
but Augeias,° the king of men, retained them. He sent back
725 the driver, sorrowing for his horses! Old man Neleus,
angry over words exchanged and acts committed,
took recompense beyond telling. Then he gave the rest
to the people to distribute, so no one should go
cheated of an equal share.
                    "So we were disposing of all
730 that was left, and around the city we set up sacrifices
to the gods. But on the third day the Epeians speedily
assembled, both themselves and their single-hoofed horses.
The Molionê° put on their battle gear, although they were still

---

707 *toward the city*: Elis is north of Pylos in the northwest Peloponnesus. Some have thought that another Pylos
     is meant because Nestor's Pylos, in the southwest Peloponnesus, is 100 miles away, hardly reachable in one
     night. But Homer is vague about the geography of the western Peloponnesus.

724 *Augeias*: Augeias was the father of Phyleus, the father of the Meges who leads a contingent from DOULICHION
     and Elis and fights side by side with Nestor. Homer shows no knowledge of Augeias' famous stables or the story
     of Herakles' cleansing of them.

733 *Molionê*: The Molionê, a dual form, are so called, oddly, by their mother's name (or maybe their mother's
     father), meaning the "two sons of Molos." They are also called the Aktorionê, the "two sons of Aktor."
     Aktor was the brother of Augeias, so the Aktorionê are the nephews of Augeias (the father of Menoitios,
     Patroklos' father, is also named Aktor). It is highly unusual to have figures who bear two patronymics (in
     fact, we soon learn, they are the sons of Poseidon!). In Homer they are twins, but all later writers describe
     them as Siamese twins. Herakles killed the Molionê, so here they must escape Nestor's attack. The sons of
     the Aktorionê/Molionê, Amphimachos and Thalpios, are now part of the Achaean force.

youths and did not yet know furious valor. There is a city
called Thryoëssa, on a steep hill, far away on the ALPHEIOS   735
in the farthest reaches of sandy Pylos. The Epeians set up
their camp around this city, eager to raze it to the ground.
But when they had scoured the plain, Athena came to us
as messenger, running down from Olympos during
the night, saying we should arm ourselves. She gathered   740
none but the ready fighters in Pylos, brave men eager
for the fight. Neleus did not permit me to put on my armor,
and he hid my horses, for he did not think I yet knew
enough of the doings of war. Even so I stood out among
the horsemen, although I went on foot, because Athena   745
had so ordered the fight.
              "There is a certain river,
the Minyeïos,° that goes into the sea near Arenê, where we
horsemen of the Pylians waited until the bright dawn.
The throngs of foot soldiers followed behind. Then we
speedily came, fully armed, at noon, to the sacred flow   750
of the Alpheios. There we sacrificed beautiful victims
to mighty Zeus, to Alpheios a bull, to Poseidon a bull,
but to flashing-eyed Athena a cow from the herd. We took
our meal through the camp, assembled in bands. Then we
lay down and slept, each man in his armor, on the shores   755
of the river. The great-souled Epeians were arranged
around the city, eager to raze it utterly.
                        "But before that
happened, a great deed of Ares occurred. When the sun
appeared shining over the earth, we attacked, after
praying to Zeus and Athena. When the strife of the Pylians   760
and the Epeians began, I was the first to kill a man and to
take his single-hoofed horses. It was the spearman Moulios,
a son-in-law of Augeias. He had married Augeias' oldest
daughter, the blond Agamedes, who knew everything
about the drugs nourished in the broad earth.° I hit him   765
with the bronze spear as he came on, and he fell in the dust.
I seized his car and took my stand in the midst of the vanguard.
    "The great-hearted Epeians ran this way and that
when they saw Moulios fall, a leader of the charioteers

---

747 *Minyeïos*: Location unknown.

765 *in the broad earth*: "Agamedê" means "very intelligent." In Homer only women are specialists in drugs and
     potions.

770 who excelled in the fight. And then I leaped upon them like
a black storm. I seized fifty cars and two men from each one
bit the earth with his teeth, overcome by my spear. Now I would
have killed the two Molionê, the sons of Aktor, except
that their father Poseidon, the wide-ruling shaker of the earth,
775 hid them in a thick mist and saved them from early death.
      "Then Zeus gave great power to the Pylians. For so long
did we follow them across the vast plain, killing as we went
and collecting their beautiful armor, until we drove
our horses toward Bouprasion,° rich in wheat, and the rock
780 of Olenia and to where is the hill called Alesios.
From there Athena turned the people back. There I killed
my last man and left him. Then the Achaeans° turned
their swift horses from Bouprasion toward Pylos, and all
gave glory to Zeus among the gods and to Nestor among men.
785   "In those days I was with men, if ever there were men!
But Achilles should know we have need of his valor, else
he will certainly have much to weep about when
everybody is dead. Remember what Menoitios told
you on that day when he sent you forth to Agamemnon
790 from PHTHIA—Odysseus and I were there in the halls
at the time and we heard what he said. We came to the well-built
house of Peleus as we were gathering the people
throughout Achaea with its rich soil. That's when
we found the warrior Menoitios° in the house and you,
795 Patroklos, and with you, Achilles. Old man Peleus, the driver
of horses, was burning the fat thigh pieces of a bull
to Zeus who delights in the thunder in the enclosure of the court.
He held a golden cup, pouring out an offering
of flaming wine over the glowing flesh of sacrifice.
800 You and Achilles were busy with the flesh of the bull
when we stood in the doorway. Achilles, amazed,
jumped up and led us in, taking us by the hand
and urging us to sit down. He gave us excellent
entertainment, as is the custom in greeting strangers.

---

779 *Bouprasion*: Both a territory and a town located somewhere in northwest Elis.

782 *Achaeans*: He means the "Pylians."

794 *Menoitios*: Conveniently for the story, Menoitios, the father of Patroklos, is now living at Phthia, but his former home is never clear. Later sources gave it as LOCRIS (in eastern mainland Greece) or even that he was a brother of Peleus.

"When we had partaken of food and drink, I began   805
to speak, urging you, Patroklos, to follow along.
You were quite eager, and Peleus and Menoitios laid
on you many commands. Peleus, the old man,
commanded Achilles, his child, to always be the best,
to be better than all others. To you Menoitios   810
the son of Aktor commanded: 'My child, in birth
Achilles is higher than you, but you are the older.
In strength he is superior, but you must tell him
the truth, explain all things and give him guideposts.
He will be persuaded to his benefit.' So commanded the   815
old man—you have forgotten!
               "Even now you can say so
to wise Achilles, in hopes he will be persuaded. Who knows
if, with the help of some spirit, you might rouse his heart
with your persuasive speech? Advice from a comrade
is always good. If Achilles is avoiding some oracle in his heart,   820
and his revered mother has reported something to him from Zeus,
then he can send you forth, and with you the people
of the Myrmidons may follow. Then you may become a light
to the Danaäns. And let him give you his beautiful armor
to wear into the war, so the Trojans may mistake you for him   825
and withdraw from the battle. The warlike sons of the Achaeans
can get their breath. They are much worn down. It is hard
to catch your breath during war. Easily might you,
who are not tired, drive back men exhausted by battle
towards the city, away from the ships and huts."   830

    So Nestor spoke, and he stirred the spirit
in the breast of Patroklos, who broke and ran along the ships
towards the hut of Achilles, grandson of Aiakos.
But when Patroklos, as he ran along, got to the ships
of godlike Odysseus, to the very center place of assembly   835
where they gave out the rules,° and where there were
altars built to the gods—there he ran into Eurypylos,
the Zeus-begotten son of Euaimon, wounded in the thigh
with an arrow and limping from the battle. Sweat ran like rain
from his shoulders and head, and from his vicious wound   840
black blood was gushing. But his mind was steady.

---

836 ... *rules*: Odysseus' ships were parked in the center of the line. The assembly was at the center of the line.

FIGURE 11.3   Achilles and Cheiron.   In spite of Phoenix's claims in Book 9 to have educated Achilles, in the usual version referred to by Eurypylos Cheiron the Centaur taught him. Cheiron was the one learned and civilized Centaur in a wild race of savages. Cheiron taught Achilles the arts of a gentleman: to play the lyre and recite poetry, to hunt, and to heal. Here in this Roman fresco from Herculaneum in Italy, Cheiron, bearded and wearing an ivy wreath, holds a plectrum and shows the young Achilles how to play on the lyre. The Romans loved these mythical tales and painted them on their walls as decoration, usually set in a painted frame. This fresco was preserved when Herculaneum was destroyed by the eruption of Mount Vesuvius in AD 79.

When Patroklos saw Eurypylos, the bold son of Menoitios
took pity and, wailing, he spoke to him words that went like arrows:
"Ah, wretched leaders and rulers of the Danaäns, it seems
you were destined to glut the swift dogs of Troy with your white fat,   845
far from your friends and the land of your fathers. But come,
tell me this, Eurypylos, nourished of Zeus and a fighting man:
Will the Achaeans still hold back the giant Hector, or will they perish,
overcome by his spear?"

           The wounded Eurypylos answered:
"No longer, Patroklos nourished of Zeus, will there be   850
a defense for the Achaeans, but they will die among
the black ships. All those who once were the best fighters
now lie among the ships wounded by arrow or spear
at the hands of the Trojans, whose strength grows ever stronger.
But save me!—carry me to my black ship. Cut out the arrow   855
from my thigh. Cleanse the dark blood with warm water
and put soothing ointments on it, as they say that you learned
from Achilles, whom Cheiron, the most learned of the
Centaurs, instructed. As for the physicians Podaleirios
and Machaon—Machaon, I've heard, lies wounded among the ships,   860
needing a physician himself, and Podaleirios on the plain
holds out against the Trojans in the sharp contendings."

           The bold son of Menoitios then answered: "How has
all this come to pass? What are we going to do, Eurypylos,
fighting man? I will go to wise Achilles to tell him what Gerenian   865
Nestor, the guardian of the Achaeans, has advised. But even so
I will give you a hand, because you are in distress."

           Patroklos spoke and, grasping Eurypylos beneath the chest,
brought him to his tent. When his aide saw him, he spread out
some cow hides. There, stretching him out, Patroklos cut the sharp   870
piercing arrow from his thigh, and he washed the dark blood
from him with warm water. On it he placed a bitter
painkilling root, rubbing it in his hand, removing every pain.
The wound closed and the blood ceased to flow.

BOOK 12. *The Attack on the Wall*

And so Patroklos, the bold son of Menoitios tended
to the wounded Eurypylos. The Argives and the Trojans
fought on in crowds. The Danaäns had dug a great ditch
and built a wide wall behind it to protect their swift ships
5   and abundant booty. But it would not hold—because they did
not offer glorious sacrifice to the gods! Because it was built
against the will of the deathless gods, it did not last long.
While Hector was alive and Achilles was enraged and the city
of King Priam remained intact, for so long the great wall
10   of the Achaeans stayed in place. But when the bravest of the Trojan
captains had died, and of the Argives many perished, though many
survived, and when the city of Priam was destroyed in the tenth year
and the Argives had gone back to the land of their fathers in their ships,
then Poseidon and Apollo contrived to sweep away the wall,
15   rousing the strength of all the rivers that flow forth from Ida
to the sea—Rhesos and Heptaporos and Karesis and Rhodios
and Granikos and the shining AISEPOS and SKAMANDROS and SIMOEIS°—
along which many shields of ox-hide and many helmets had fallen
in the dust, and the race of men who were half gods. Of all
20   these rivers, Phoibos Apollo turned the mouths together,
and for nine days they poured against the wall. Zeus rained
constantly, so that the wall would quickly disappear into the sea.
The shaker of earth, holding his trident in his hands,° led the way.
He swept away on the waves all the foundations of beams and stone
25   that the Achaeans had laid with such trouble. He made smooth the shore
along the powerful flow of the Hellespont. He covered the great
beach with sand, sweeping away the wall. He returned the rivers
to flow in their channels, where previously they made the beautiful water
to flow. So were Poseidon and Apollo to arrange things after the war.

---

17   *Simoeis*: Rhesos and Heptaporos and Karesos and Rhodios and Granikos are mentioned only here in the
Iliad. The first four rivers are unidentified; the Granikos and Aisepos flowed well to the east of the Troad.
Only the Skamandros and Simoeis actually flow across the Trojan plain (Map 3).

23   *in his hands*: The only place in the *Iliad* where Poseidon has his characteristic emblem, the trident, with
which he is always depicted in the visual arts (see Figure 13.1).

But for now war and the din of war blazed around   30
the well-built wall, and the beams of the towers rang
as they were struck. The Argives, overwhelmed by the whip
of Zeus, were penned-in beside their hollow ships. They were held
in check, terrified by Hector, the mighty master of rout.
He raged as before, like a whirlwind.   35

               Even as when
a wild boar or lion turns on dogs and hunters, exulting in his
strength, and the dogs stand before the boar arrayed like a wall,
and the hunters rain spears from their hands—but his mighty
boar-heart does not take fright nor flee, though his bravery
presages his death. Often he wheels around, testing the ranks   40
of men, and wherever he charges, the ranks of men give way—
even so Hector went through the throng and encouraged
his companions to cross through the ditch. His swift horses
would not dare it, but loudly neighing they stood on the steep
lip, in awe of the wide ditch. It was impossible to leap across,   45
impossible to drive across. On both sides all along the ditch
were overhanging banks, and at the top were fixed sharp stakes
that the sons of the Achaeans set up, thick and large,
as a defense against enemy attack. There a horse drawing
a well-wheeled car might not easily go, but the Trojans   50
preferred to see if they could do it on foot.

               Then Poulydamas°
spoke to bold Hector, standing beside him: "Hector and you
other leaders of the Trojans and allies, it would be folly
to try to cross the ditch with our swift horses. It is too hard
to get across! There are sharp stakes fixed in it, and close by is the wall   55
of the Achaeans. It is impossible for drivers to go down in the ditch
and fight. It is narrow, and I think we will be cut to pieces.
If Zeus, who makes thunder high in the sky, would utterly
destroy in his anger our enemy and give aid to us Trojans,
then I wish this would happen right now, and that the Achaeans   60
should perish without a name, far from Argos. But if they turn
on us and we are driven back from the ships and become tangled
in the ditch they have dug, then I think that not even a messenger
will return to the city once the Achaeans have rallied.

---

52 *Poulydamas*: A son of the Trojan elder Panthoös. He is a warrior and advisor to Hector who seems to have
   survived the war.

65   "But come, please, let all be persuaded by what I say.
      Let the drivers hold back the horses at the ditch while we in a group,
      fully armed, follow Hector. The Achaeans will not hold up once
      the bonds of destruction are fitted upon them!"

                                     So spoke Poulydamas.
      His prudent advice pleased Hector. Immediately Hector leaped
70   from his car in full armor to the ground. The other Trojans did not
      hesitate, gathered in their chariots, but everyone jumped down
      when they saw the good Hector come forth. Each man ordered his
      driver to hold his horses in good order there at the edge of the ditch.
      Then the men divided and arranged themselves in five companies,°
75   and followed their leaders. Some went with Hector and
      the blameless Poulydamas, the most numerous and the best fighters.
      They were eager to break the wall and to get at the hollow ships.
      Kebriones° followed them as a third man, for Hector
      had left a lesser man with the chariot. Of the second company
80   Paris was chief, along with Alkathoös° and Agenor. Helenos
      and Deïphobos, like a god, led the third company, two sons
      of Priam, and the fighting man Asios°—Asios the son of Hyrtakos,
      whom his horses bore from ARISBÊ, from the river Selleïs.
      Aeneas led the forth company, the valiant son of Anchises,
85   and with him went two sons of Antenor, Archelochos
      and Akamas,° skilled in every kind of fighting. Sarpedon
      led the glorious allies, and as comrades he chose
      Glaukos and the martial Asteropaios,° for they seemed
      to be by far the best of the others, after himself—
90   for Sarpedon was the best of them all.

---

74 *five companies*: This might be taken to imply that there were five gates in the Achaean wall, but nowhere is
    that stated. In fact, Homer soon forgets about the division of the Trojan army into five companies.

78 *Kebriones*: A bastard son of Priam, now Hector's charioteer.

80 *Alkathoös*: He appears only here and Book 13, where he is killed and called a son-in-law of Anchises.

82 *... Asios*: Helenos is said in Book 6 to be "far the best of the bird-prophets," but nowhere else are his mantic
    powers mentioned. However, he has an important role to play in the next book. Deïphobos, mentioned here
    for the first time, was a full brother to Hector and in later tradition the husband of Helen after Paris was
    killed; Athena will take on his appearance to lure Hector to his death, and he is said in the *Odyssey* to have
    accompanied Helen when she walked around the Trojan Horse mimicking the voice of the wives of the men
    within. Idomeneus kills Asios in Book 13. Arisbê is in on the south shore of the Hellespont.

86 *... Akamas*: Archelochos and Akamas are associated with Aeneas in the Catalog of Ships; Akamas has not
    been seen since Book 5, where he ignominiously faced Diomedes. Aeneas is not heard of again in this book.

88 *... Asteropaios*: Sarpedon and Glaukos, cousins from Lycia, are second only to Hector in their fighting prow-
    ess. Patroklos kills Sarpedon in Book 16. Asteropaios, first mentioned here, a leader of the Paeonians not
    listed in the Catalog of Trojans, reappears in Books 17 and in 21, where Achilles kills him.

When they had closed
up their well-made shields of ox-hide, they eagerly made
straight for the Danaäns. They did not think they would
be restrained, only that they would fall upon the black ships.
And so the other famous Trojans and allies obeyed
the counsel of blameless Poulydamas. But Asios, the son of   95
Hyrtakos, commander of men, did not want to leave his horses
and his charioteer. Together with them he went toward
the swift ships—the fool! He would not avoid evil fate
and return to windy Ilion, rejoicing in his horses and car.
Before that, his ill-omened fate enfolded him, from the spear   100
of Idomeneus, the son of noble Deucalion.

Asios made for
the left flank of the ships, where the Achaeans went with
their horses and cars when they fled the field. There he drove
his horses and car, nor did he find the gates closed
and the long bar drawn, but Achaean men held them open   105
in case any of their companions wished to be saved, fleeing
from the war to their ships. There, setting his mind, Asios
drove his horses, and his men followed, shouting shrilly.
They thought the Achaeans could not hold them off, but that
they could plunder among the black ships—fools! For they found   110
at the gates two fine fighting men, proud sons of the Lapith
spearmen°— Polypoites, the strong son of Peirithoös, and Leonteus,
like to Ares, the curse of men. The two of them were standing
in front of the high gates like high-crowned oaks in the mountains
that withstand the wind and the rain every day, firmly   115
fixed by their deep-thrusting roots—even so these two men,
trusting to their own hands and their own power, awaited
great Asios as he came on, nor did they flee.

Thus the Trojans
came on straight against the well-built wall, holding high
their shields of dried bulls' hides and launching great shouts: Asios 120
and Iamenos and Orestes and Adamas, son of Asios, and Thoön
and Oinomaos.° Within the walls the Lapiths had for awhile

111–112 *Lapith spearmen*: Although the tribe of Lapiths is famous because of their fight with the Centaurs, they
        are never mentioned except here and later in this book. Polypoites and Leonteus are listed in the Cata-
        log of Ships as coming from "northern Thessaly." Nestor refers to Peirithoös, the father of Polypoites, in
        his account in Book 1 of the battle with the Centaurs.

122   ... *Oinomaos*: All the names of these nonentities are Greek (except possibly Iamenos). Iamenos and
      Orestes die just below, and the rest are killed in Book 13.

urged the Achaeans, who wear fancy shinguards, to defend
the ships. But when they saw the Trojans rushing on
125 the wall while the Danaäns fled with a cry, the two Lapiths
rushed forth from the gates to fight in front. Like wild pigs
in the mountains who withstand the noisy assault of men
and dogs, then, rushing slantwise, they shatter the trees
about them, cutting them at their roots, and there arises
130 a clatter of tusks until someone throws a missile and kills them—
even so clattered the shining bronze on their chests as they
were struck, turned toward the enemy.° For they fought with
power, trusting in the troops above them and in their own strength.
And those above, defending the tents and the swift-sailing ships,
135 threw stones from their well-built towers. The stones fell to the earth
like snowflakes that a strong wind, driving the shadowy clouds,
pours down in thick showers over the bountiful earth.
Thus weapons fell from the hands of both Achaeans and Trojans.
Their helmets rang harshly, and their bossed shields, as they were
140 struck with huge stones.

          Then Asios, son of Hyrtakos, groaned
and slapped both his thighs, and filled by great anger he blurted:
"Father Zeus, you are proved to be a great lover of lies! I did
not think Achaean warriors could withstand our power,
our invincible hands. Like wasps with nimble waists
145 or bees who have made their nests on a rugged path
and do not leave their hollow home, but stay to fight
off hunters° on behalf of their children, even so they will
not back away from their gates, though there are but two
of them, before either they kill or are killed."° So he spoke,
150 but Zeus was not persuaded by his speech. His spirit wanted
to give Hector glory.

          The other Trojans fought around other
gates. It would be hard for me to tell of all these things
as if I were a god. Everywhere before the stone wall
arose a wondrous blazing fire.° The Argives, being in deep

---

132 *enemy*: The point of comparison is between the *sound* of the boars' tusks with the *sound* of the Trojan armor
being struck, not between the boars' aggression and the Trojan attack.

147 *hunters*: Those looking for the bees' honey.

149 *killed*: That is, the wasps and the Lapiths are alike in their tenacity. Similes are unusual in speeches, and one
that takes up over half the speech is unparalleled.

154 *fire*: Many commentators have complained that the wall is not really made of stone. Fire, later, is used only
on the wooden gates.

distress, had no choice but to defend their ships. The gods   155
were troubled, all those who were helpers to the Danaäns.

   But the Lapiths clashed in war and contention.° The mighty
Polypoites, son of Peirithoös, pushed his spear through the helmet
of Damasos with cheek pieces of bronze. The bronze helmet could not
withstand that mighty blow—the bronze tip broke through the bone   160
and splattered the brains inside. Polypoites overcame Damasos
as he raged. And then Polypoites killed Pylon and Ormenos.
Then the Lapith Leonteus, of the line of Ares, struck Hippomachos,
the son of Antimachos, with his spear—Hippomachos, hitting
him on the belt. Pulling the sharp sword from his scabbard,   165
he next leaped on Antiphates in the crowd and cut him down
in the hand-to-hand. Antiphates fell on his back, stretched out
on the ground. The Lapith next brought down to the nourishing
earth Menon and Iamenos and Orestes, one after another.

   While Leonteus was stripping off their flashing armor, most   170
of the youths, the best fighters who followed Poulydamas and Hector,
who wanted most to break the wall and set fire to the ships,
stood on the edge of the ditch, hesitating. A bird had come on them
as they were about to cross—a high-flying eagle, skirting
the army toward the left.° He held in his talons a huge blood-red   175
snake, alive and gasping, but the serpent, not avoiding combat,
writhed backward and struck at the eagle's breast beside the neck.
Stung with pain, the eagle dropped the snake and it fell in the midst
of the crowd. The eagle cried and flew off in the blasts of the wind.
The Trojans shivered when they saw the snake lying there   180
writhing in the midst of them, a portent of Zeus who carries
the goatskin fetish.

        Then Poulydamas spoke to brave Hector,
standing at his side: "Hector, you always rebuke me in the assembly
when I have useful things to say, because a man of the people
should not speak against you, neither in the assembly nor   185
in the war, but he should always acknowledge your power.°
But now I will say what seems to me best: Let us not fight

---

157   *contention*: This is the *aristeia* of the Lapith fighters from Thessaly, their moment of glory. We do not hear of
      them again until the funeral games for Patroklos in Book 23.

175   *on the left*: The unlucky direction (as in English *sinister* means originally "on the left hand").

186   *power*: Poulydamas is of the highest birth, but he calls himself a "man of the people" out of deference to
      Hector's authority.

FIGURE 12.1   Trojan and Greek warriors fighting.   One warrior grabs the other by the hair as he flees. The tree on the left may be the "oak of Zeus" where Sarpedon recovered (Book 5). Frieze on the tomb of a Lycian prince, the Heroön of Goelbasi-Trysa in Lycia, Turkey, c. 380 BC.

against the Danaäns over their ships! For I think that this
will come to pass, if this bird has come as a true omen
to the men eager to cross the ditch—a high-flying   190
eagle skirting the army toward the left, holding a huge
blood-red snake in its talons, still alive, and he then
let it fall before he reached his nest—he did not finish
his course, to deliver the snake to his little babies.
Likewise, if we break the gates and the wall of the Achaeans   195
with our great strength, and the Achaeans pull back, we will not
return in good order from their ships, nor on the same paths.
But we will leave behind many Trojans whom the Achaeans
will overcome with their bronze, defending the ships. That is
the way a prophet would interpret this omen, one who   200
knows portents well, one whom the soldiers believe."

   Hector of the flashing helmet looked at Poulydamas
from beneath his brows and said: "Poulydamas, what you say
is not pleasing to me! You know how to devise better words
than these! If in truth you speak in earnest, then the gods have   205
taken your wits. You urge me to forget the counsels of Zeus,
who delights in the thunder! He himself promised me and bowed
his head to it.° But you urge that I believe in long-winged birds!
I pay no attention to them. I do not care whether they go
to the right, toward the dawn and the sun, or whether they go the left,   210
toward the shadowy darkness.° But let us be obedient to the counsel
of great Zeus, who rules over all mortals and the deathless ones.
One omen is best: to defend the land of one's fathers.
Why are you afraid of war and contention? If the rest
of us will be killed at the ships of the Argives, there is   215
no fear that *you* will perish too—for your heart
seems not resolute in the fight, not warlike. But if
you hold aloof from these contendings, or if you persuade
somebody else to turn aside, just then you will die, struck
by my spear!"   220

      So speaking, Hector led the way forward.
The others followed with a tremendous shout.° And Zeus

---

208   *head to it*: Hector refers to the message that Iris delivered in Book 11, saying that Hector would reach the
      ships and be victorious until nightfall.

211   *darkness*: The soothsayer faces north when looking for bird signs in the sky: The sun rises on his right and
      sets on his left.

221   *tremendous shout*: Somehow the Trojans have gotten across the ditch, which caused them so much trouble
      before.

who delights in the thunderbolt roused from the mountains of Ida
a blast of wind that carried dust straight against the ships.
He enchanted the minds of the Achaeans, gave glory to the Trojans
225 and to Hector. Trusting to the portents° and to their own strength,
they attempted to smash the great wall of the Achaeans. They tore
down the tops of the fortifications. They dragged down the battlements
and pried out the supporting beams that the Achaeans had placed
in the earth to be buttresses for the wall.° They tried to drag out
230 the beams, in hopes of smashing the wall of the Achaeans.

But the Danaäns did not even now withdraw from the path,
but closing up the battlements with the hides of bulls they threw rocks
down from there onto the Trojans coming under the wall. The two
Ajaxes ranged everywhere along the wall, stirring up the men,
235 encouraging the might of the Achaeans. To some they spoke
honeyed words, but to others, when they saw them pulling
back from the fight, they reproached with harsh words:
"Friends of the Argives! Those of you who are superior
in the fight, those who are of middling quality, and those
240 who are lesser—for in war not all men are equal—now
there is work for everyone, I think you know that! So don't
turn back to the ships now that you have been encouraged.
Throw yourselves forward and urge each other on in hopes
that Zeus of the lightning bolt may grant us to push back
245 this assault and drive the Trojans toward their city."

Thus the two Ajaxes stirred the Achaeans with their shouting.
As snowflakes fall thickly on a winter's day, when Zeus
the counselor is stirred to let snow fall, showing forth to men
his arrows and, lulling the winds, he pours forth constantly
250 until he covers the peaks of the high mountains and the high
headlands and fields overgrown with lotus and the rich
plowlands of men, and the snow is poured over the harbors
and the shores of the gray sea though the pelting wave
keeps off the snow, but all things beside are wrapped
255 in snow from above when the storm of Zeus drives it on—
even so the stones fell thickly on either side, some on

225 *portents*: Presumably the ambiguous portent of the eagle and the snake.

229 *for the wall*: We cannot form a clear picture of how the Achaean wall was constructed. The word translated
      "tops" in "tops of the fortifications" is in fact of unknown meaning. Ordinarily in ancient warfare siege lad-
      ders would be placed against a defensive wall, but the Trojans do not use them.

the Trojans and some from the Trojans onto the Achaeans as they
cast at one another. And a clanging din arose over the entire wall.

Nonetheless the Trojans and noble Hector would never
have broken the gates of the wall and the long bolt if Zeus   260
the counselor had not stirred his son Sarpedon against
the Argives, like a lion against cattle with curled horns.
Sarpedon held his shield before him, perfectly round,
beautiful, worked in bronze that a smith had hammered out.
The bronze-smith had sewn ox-hides stitched within   265
with thick stiches of gold that ran continuously around the inside.
Holding the shield before him, Sarpedon brandished two spears
and went like a lion raised in the mountains, who for long
has been without meat, and his proud spirit urges him to attack
the flocks, to go against a sturdy household. Even if he finds   270
herdsmen there with dogs and spears guarding the flocks,
he is not inclined to flee the fold without a fight, but leaps
into the flock and seizes one—or like a foremost champion
he is struck by a spear from a swift hand. Just so his spirit
urged godlike Sarpedon to leap onto the wall and to smash   275
the battlements.

He exclaimed loudly to Glaukos, the son
of Hippolochos: "Glaukos, why are we honored above all
with the best seats, best cuts of meat, and with fat cups
in Lycia? And why do all regard us as gods and we dwell
in large districts along the banks of the XANTHOS,° a fine tract   280
of orchard and wheat-bearing plowland? Therefore we must now
take our stand among the foremost of the Lycians and face
this blazing battle so that many of the heavy–armed Lycians
might say: 'Not without fame do these men rule Lycia,
our chieftains. They eat fat sheep and drink choice wine,   285
sweet as honey, true—but their valor is unmatched,
and they fight among the foremost Lycians.' Yes,
my friend, if escaped from battle it were possible for the two
of us never to grow old and never to die, I would not myself
fight among the foremost, nor would I send you into the fight   290
where men win glory. But as it is, the fates of death
stand over us, ten thousand of them—no man can flee or escape

---

280 *Xanthos*: The greatest of the rivers of Lycia (Map 6), whose valley forms the heart of the country. Consider-
able ruins survive from the classical city, including a tomb from which Figures 12.1 and 12.2 are taken.

from them—so let us go forward and give glory to another,
or to ourselves."

            So Sarpedon spoke. Glaukos did not turn aside
295 or disobey. The two of them went straight on, leading
the large contingent of Lycians. Seeing them, the son of Peteos,
Menestheus,° shivered. For they brought devastation to his part
of the wall. Menestheus looked along the wall of the Achaeans,
hoping to see any of the captains who might ward off destruction
300 from him and his companions. He saw the two Ajaxes
standing there, ever lustful for war, and Teucer, who had just come
from his tent nearby. But it was impossible to make himself heard,
so great was the clamor, the din from the shields being struck
and the helmets with horsehair plumes. The clanging of the
305 closed gates reached the sky. The Trojans stood without and attempted
with great violence to force the gates and to burst inside.

    Quickly, Menestheus sent the herald Thoötes° to Ajax:
"Go, good Thoötes, run and call Ajax, rather, call both Ajaxes—
that would be best, for hideous destruction will soon
310 befall us. The captains of the Lycians lean heavily upon us,
they who earlier raged in furious battle. But if labor
and quarrel have arisen for the Ajaxes where they are—
at least beg Telamonian Ajax to come alone, and may Teucer,°
the great bowman, follow with him."

                So he spoke, and the herald
315 Thoötes, hearing him, obeyed, and set off running by the wall
of the Achaeans who wear shirts of bronze. Arriving, he stood
near the two Ajaxes, and promptly said: "You two Ajaxes,
leaders of the Achaeans who wear shirts of bronze: Menestheus,
the beloved son of god-nourished Peteos, urges you
320 to come at once so that if only for a brief time you may face
this labor of war—both of you! That would be far the best case,
else steep destruction will likely befall us. The captains
of the Lycians weigh heavily upon us, they who earlier raged
in furious battle. But if labor and quarrel has arisen
325 for you here, let at least Telamonian Ajax come alone,
and may Teucer, the great bowman, follow with him."

---

297 *Menestheus*: The leader of the Athenian contingent, seen here for the first time since Agamemnon
reproached him in Book 4. His performance is typically ineffectual.

307 *Thoötes*: "Swifty," a "speaking name."

So he spoke, nor did Telamonian Ajax decline.
But immediately he spoke to Little Ajax, the son of Oïleus,
words that flew like arrows: "Ajax, son of Oïleus, the two
of you— you and strong Lykomedes°—stay here and urge   330
the Danaäns to fight to the utmost. But I will go away
with Thoötes and face up to the war. I will come back
here quickly, once we have achieved a good defense."

So speaking, Telamonian Ajax went off and with him
went Teucer,° his brother from the same father, and with them   335
Pandion, who carried Teucer's bent bow. When going along
the inside of the wall they came to the part defended by great-souled
Menestheus—they came to men hard pressed!—the powerful
leaders and rulers of the Lycians were astride the battlements
like a dark whirlwind. Thus they clashed together in battle   340
and the din of war arose.

              Ajax, the son of Telamon,
was first to kill his man, Epikles, a great-hearted
companion of Sarpedon, hitting him with a sharp rock
that lay, huge, on top of the wall near the battlement.
No man could lift it easily with both hands, no matter   345
how young, such as men are today. But he raised
it high, threw it and smashed the helmet with four ridges.
Thus Big Ajax crushed all the bones of Epikles' head,
who fell like a diver from the high wall, and his breath-soul
left his bones.   350

              And Teucer hit Glaukos, the son
of Hippolochos, with an arrow from the high wall as Glaukos
rushed on Teucer. He saw where Glaukos' arm
was exposed, and he put Glaukos out of the fight.

Glaukos covertly leaped back from the wall so that no one
of the Achaeans might notice he was hit and so boast over him.   355
Distress settled over Sarpedon immediately when he saw
that Glaukos was missing.° All the same he did not forget
the battle, for he stabbed Alkmaon, son of Thestor,

---

330 *Lykomedes*: A Boeotian, son of Kreon, one of the seven captains who went on guard-duty outside the
      Achaean wall.

335 *Teucer*: In Book 8 Teucer was wounded by Hector and taken back to his tent, but no reference is made to
      this earlier injury.

357 *was missing*: Glaukos survives the *Iliad*, but in postHomeric tradition Ajax or Agamemnon finally kills him.
      The kings of Lycia traced their descent from Glaukos.

FIGURE 12.2   Combat between a Trojan and a Greek.   They are dressed as hoplites. The warrior on the left spears the other fighter in the chest. Frieze on the tomb of a Lycian prince, the Heroön of Goelbasi-Trysa, Lycia, Turkey, c. 380 BC.

hitting him with his spear. He then pulled it out, pulling
Alkmaon with it. He fell on his face and his armor,   360
inlaid with bronze, rang around him. Then Sarpedon seized
the battlement in his strong hands and pulled. The whole
length of it gave way. The wall above was exposed—
he had made a path for many. But Ajax and Teucer
acted together against him. Teucer hit Sarpedon with an arrow   365
on the shining strap of the protective shield that guarded
his chest. But Zeus warded death from his son, so he was not
overcome on the sterns of the ships. Ajax leaped on him
and stabbed at his shield, but the spear did not go through.
Ajax pushed him back as Sarpedon rushed on.   370
Ajax withdrew a little from the battlement, but he did not
wholly withdraw, for his spirit hoped to win glory.

   Wheeling around, Sarpedon called out to the godlike
Lycians: "O Lycians, why have you backed away from
your furious valor? It is hard for me alone, though I am strong,   375
to break down the wall and make a path to the ships.
But let us attack together. The job is better done when many
people do the work."

                  So he spoke. The Lycians, fearing
the reproach of their king, pushed harder around their advisor
and captain. The Argives from their side strengthened the battalions   380
inside the wall—the task before them was great. The powerful Lycians
were unable to break the wall and make a path to the ships, but the
Danaän spearmen could not drive the Lycians from the wall
when once they closed on it. Even as when two men argue
about boundary-stones in a field held in common, having measuring   385
sticks in their hands and in a narrow space disagree about the equal
division, even so little did the battlements keep them apart.°
And above them they struck the ox-hide shields of one another,
well-rounded, like fluttering targets. The relentless bronze wounded
many in the flesh, both when they exposed their backs, turning around   390
while they fought, and sometimes getting hit straight through their shields.

   Everywhere the walls and the battlements were splattered
with the blood of men fighting on either side, blood from Trojans

---

387   *apart*: Two men are arguing over a small amount of common ground; they are no further apart than the
        breadth of the battlements.

and Achaeans alike. But the Trojans could not make the Achaeans
395 flee. The Achaeans held their ground, as a woman, an honest weaver
for hire, holds the balance to make equal the wool
and the weight in the scale so that she might earn a paltry
reward for her children—even so the battle and war was
stretched equally, until Zeus gave the glory of victory to Hector,
400 son of Priam—the first to leap within the wall of the Achaeans.

He roared a piercing shout, calling to the Trojans:
"Rise up, you horse-taming Trojans! Smash the wall of the
Argives. Cast glorious destroying fire into their ships!"
Thus Hector bellowed, urging them on.° All the Trojans heard.
405 They charged the wall straight-on in a massed formation.
They climbed to the top of the wall carrying their sharp
spears while Hector picked up and carried a stone found
near the gate, thick at the bottom but sharp at the top, so large
that two men, the best of the people, could not easily
410 have muscled it from the ground onto a cart such as men
are today. But Hector swung it up easily all by himself.
Zeus, the son of clever Kronos, made it light
for him. As when a shepherd readily lifts the fleece
of a ram all by himself, taking it in one hand
415 with little trouble doing so, even so Hector raised the stone
and carried it straight against the doors that closed
the tightly fitted and powerful gates—double gates,
and high, and two crossbars coming from opposite directions
held them, and a single bolt fastened them.°

                                        Hector went up close
420 to the gates, and taking a firm stand he threw the stone
at the middle of the gates, spreading apart his feet so that
his throw would have maximum power. He broke
both pivots° away and the stone fell inside of its own weight.

---

404   *them on*: It is logical that Hector attacks the portion of the wall abandoned by Big Ajax and Teucer when
they went to help Menestheus, but in Book 13 Hector is fighting "where he first went over the wall, near
the ships of Ajax and Protesilaos." We are not sure which Ajax is meant, however, or where are the ships of
Protesilaos (the first man to die at Troy). Probably the center of the camp fits best, where the ships of Little
Ajax were anchored, but the narrative is not clear.

419   *fastened them*: Hector carries his two spears in one hand and with the other he picks up the rock, which he
then uses as a kind of battering ram.

423   *pivots*: Ancient doors did not have hinges as we think of them but were attached by pegs at the inside top
and the inside bottom that rotated in holes in the threshold and the lintel. Hector does not burst open the
gates but smashes them from their seating in the masonry.

The gates on either side groaned. The bars did not hold.
The doors were smashed apart on this side and that   425
under the onrush of the stone. Glorious Hector leaped
inside, his face aglow like the sudden night. He shone
with the terrible bronze that he wore around his flesh,
and he held two spears. No one who met him could have
held him back once he leaped within, unless he were a god.   430
His eyes burned like fire. He whirled around in the crowd.
He called out to the Trojans to come over the wall
and they obeyed his urging. Some came over the wall,
others poured in through the strong gates. The Danaäns were
driven in rout through the hollow ships. An endless tumult arose.   435

BOOK 13. *The Battle at the Ships*

When Zeus had brought the Trojans and Hector to the ships,
    he left them there to endure their pain and endless sorrow.
But he averted his shining eyes, looking far away
to the land of the horse-riding Thracians and that of the Mysians
5 who fight in close, and of the noble Mare-milkers who live
from milk, and of the Abioi, the most just of men.° For he did
not expect in his heart any of the deathless ones to come
to the aid of the Trojans or the Danaäns.

                         But Poseidon, the king,
the shaker of the earth, was not blind to developments
10 He sat on the top of the highest peak of SAMOTHRACE,
marveling at the war and the skirmishes. From there all IDA
was clear, and he could see the city of Priam and the ships
of the Achaeans.° There he came out of the sea, because
he took pity on the Achaeans, beset by the Trojans. And he was
15 very angry with Zeus. He came straight down from the rugged
mountain, moving resolutely on his immortal feet; the high
mountains and the woods shook beneath Poseidon as he went.
Three times he strode out, and on the fourth pace he reached
his goal of Aigai,° where his famous house of gold
20 and stone was built for him in the depths of the water,
deathless forever. When he got there he readied the two
bronze-hooved horses with flowing golden manes, swift of flight,
beneath the chariot. Then he himself wrapped gold
about his flesh. He gripped the whip, nicely made
25 of gold, then mounted his car and set out to drive
over the waves. Dolphins leaped beneath him from

---

6 *... of men*: Zeus is looking north, across the PROPONTIS first to Thrace, then beyond to the Mysians (in
    modern Bulgaria), somehow related to the Mysians who lived in Anatolia east of Troy (Map 6); then to the
    Mare-milkers, no doubt across the Danube in Scythia, where Herodotus describes tribes that live on milk;
    and finally to the Abioi, a mythical pacific tribe beyond the Mare-milkers.

13 *Achaeans*: The island of IMBROS intervenes between TROY and SAMOTHRACE (Maps 1, 6), but Samothrace's
    highest mountain peak is visible over Imbros. This detail, hardly traditional, seems to prove that Homer had
    visited the site of Troy.

19 *Aigai*: Probably a headland on the coast of ASIA MINOR opposite the southeast corner of Lesbos.

hidden places—they knew their king! The sea parted
joyfully before him. The horses sped swiftly on,
and the bronze axle beneath was not dampened
The prancing horses brought him to the ships of the Achaeans.   30

There is a broad cave in the depths of the deep water,
midway between Tenedos and rugged Imbros, where Poseidon,
the shaker of the earth, stationed his horses, uncoupling
them from his car and setting before them food to eat.
Around their feet he placed golden hobbles, unbreakable,   35
never to be loosened, that they might remain there until their king
returned. Then he went off to the camp of the Achaeans.

The Trojans, ever eager for battle, gathered like flames
or storm clouds. They followed Hector, son of Priam, shouting loudly
and crying out. They believed they would take the ships of the Achaeans,   40
killing all their best men. But Poseidon, the holder and shaker
of the earth, roused-up the Argives, coming from the deep sea
in the likeness of Kalchas—with his shape and untiring voice.

He spoke first to the two Ajaxes, both already
eager to fight: "You two Ajaxes,° you are the ones to save   45
the army of the Achaeans, remembering your valor and giving
no thought to icy rout! I do not fear the mighty hands of the Trojans
in some other part of the fight, but here where they have climbed
the high wall in a mass—the Achaeans who wear fancy shinguards
will hold them! But right here I am terribly worried that some   50
calamity will happen—here where that mad-dog Hector,
like a flame, is in the lead—he who *says* he is a son of Zeus.
So I trust that some god puts it into your hearts to make
a strong stand here and move others to do the same.
The two of you can push Hector back from the swift-sailing   55
ships, despite his eagerness, even if the Olympian himself
drives him on!"

Then the holder of the earth, the shaker
of the earth, struck the two Ajaxes with his rod and filled
them with powerful strength. He made their limbs light,

---

45   *two Ajaxes*: In Book 12 Telamonian Ajax went to the Achaean right wing along with Teucer to fight against Sarpe-
     don, allowing Hector to break through the center. Oïlean Ajax stayed in the center, to which Telamonian Ajax
     has now somehow returned. But the "two Ajaxes" that Poseidon addresses could mean "Ajax and his brother
     Teucer"; probably in preHomeric epic "the two Ajaxes" did mean that, and sometimes in Homer the phrase has
     its old meaning.

FIGURE 13.1 **Poseidon in his chariot.** The god of the sea rides across the waves in a scene inspired by Homer's description. He holds his trident in his left hand and points in the direction he wants to go. The chariot is drawn by four horses with dolphin tails. Roman mosaic, AD second century, from a Roman villa in Sousse, Tunisia.

their feet and their hands fast and strong. Then, like a hawk   60
swift of wing who hovering over a steep high rock
speeds forth to fly, then pursues over the plain
another bird, even so Poseidon, shaker of the earth,
darted away from them.

        Of the two men swift Ajax,
the son of Oïleus, first recognized who it was, and at once   65
he spoke to the other Ajax, the son of Telamon:
"Ajax, some one of the gods who live on Olympos, taking on
the appearance of the prophet Kalchas, urges us to fight
beside the ships—for I don't think that was Kalchas,
the bird-prophet! I easily recognized him as a god by the trail   70
he left when he went away. For it is easy to know a god.
And now the spirit in my breast is more eager to make war
and to fight. My feet below and my hands above are bristling,
eager to go!"

        Telamonian Ajax answered him:
"Yes, my own invincible hands are eager now   75
to grip the spear, my strength is up and both my feet
stir beneath me. Even alone I am impatient to take on
Hector, son of Priam, who rages without end."

        So they spoke to one another words such as these,
rejoicing in the fury of battle that a god put into their   80
hearts. Meanwhile the earth-shaker roused up the Achaeans
who were in the rear beside the swift ships, refreshing their
spirits. For their limbs had been weakened by the arduous labor,
and grief came to their hearts as they saw the Trojans
coming over the great wall in a mass. As the two Ajaxes looked,   85
tears poured forth from beneath their brows, for they did
not think they could escape the Trojan evil. But the earth-shaker,
hastening among them, urged them to form into strong battalions.

        First he went to Teucer and to Leïtos, bidding them on,
then to the warrior Peneleos, and to Thoas and Deïpyros   90
and Meriones and Antilochos, masters of the war cry.° Urging
them on, he spoke words that went like arrows: "For shame,

---

91 *masters of the war cry*: Poseidon exhorts troops in the center and on the Achaean left. Teucer is with the two
    Ajaxes now. Leïtos fights with the Locrians. Peneleos, prominent only in this battle, fights along with the
    Boeotians. The unknown Deïpyros is killed later in the book. Meriones leads the Cretans. Antilochos, the
    son of Nestor, is with the Pylians.

FIGURE 13.2 Poseidon as Kalchas.   In the likness of the prophet, Poseidon holds his trident between the two Ajaxes, Oïlean Ajax and Telamonian Ajax, encouraging them to fight. Telamonian Ajax holds a hoplite shield emblazoned with a ram and behind him to the right is his brother, the bowman Teucer, and another warrior. A fifth warrior stands at the far left. Athenian black-figure wine-cup by Amasis, c. 540 BC.

Argives! Mere boys! I was persuaded that in your fighting
you would save our ships—but if you hold back from savage war,
I believe the day has come when the Trojans will overwhelm you.   95
Yes, I foresee this great disaster before my own eyes, a dread thing
that I thought would never come to pass, that the Trojans could
break through to our ships. Before they were like panicked deer,
wandering through the woods, prey to jackals and leopards
and wolves—wandering in vain, as if impotent, and there is   100
no fight in them. Before the Trojans were not willing to face
the massed might and the hands of the Achaeans, not even
for a little while. Now they fight beside the hollow ships far from
their city because of the baseness of our leaders and the slackness
of the army, who fighting against Hector are unwilling to defend   105
the swift-sailing ships. Instead, you are killed in the midst
of them!
   "But if in truth the warrior Agamemnon,
son of Atreus, the wide-ruling king, is the cause of it all because
he dishonored the son of Peleus, the fast runner, still we must not
go soft in the war. Let us quickly get over this! The hearts   110
of good men can be cured. It is not right that you give over your
furious valor, all you who are the best in the army. I would
not quarrel with a man who slacked off in the war because of
cowardice. But you, you kindle anger in my heart. The fact is
you quickly foster a greater evil by your slackness. Everyone   115
of you must bear shame and reproach in your hearts, for a great
fight has arisen. The mighty Hector, good at the war cry,
makes war at the ships. He has broken the gates and the long bar!"

   Thus did the earth-holder rouse up the Achaeans with his
exhortations. The powerful battalions rallied around the two Ajaxes,   120
so mighty that even Ares would not have made light of them if he
took them on, nor Athena who drives on the army. Those
who were selected for bravery withstood the Trojans and Hector,
meeting spear against spear, shield against overlapping shield,
buckler against buckler, helmet against helmet, man   125
against man. The horsehair crests with their shining plates
touched together as the men nodded their heads,
standing in thick array against one another. Their spears
were arranged in tiers, brandished in their bold hands.
Their intention was evident: They were eager to fight!°   130

---

130 *to fight:* Sometimes this passage is taken anachronistically to refer to a hoplite formation, but the men are
    simply densely grouped together to stop the Trojan attack.

The Trojans struck forward in a mass, with Hector
in the lead, vehemently pressing ahead, like a rolling stone
from a cliff that a river, swollen by winter rain,
has dislodged from the brow of a hill when it has broken
135   the foundations of the ruthless stone with its immense flood.
The stone leaps high, flying through the air and crashes
in the forest below and runs on constantly, without cease,
until it comes to the flat plain and the stone rolls no more,
though it is eager to do so—even so had Hector
140   threatened to go through the tents and ships of the Achaeans
all the way to the sea, killing as he went.

                                    But when Hector came
to the tightly packed battalions, he was stopped as he moved
close in. The sons of the Achaeans, standing against him
and stabbing with their swords and spears whose points
145   were curved on both sides, drove him back from them.
Reeling, Hector gave ground. He gave a piercing cry, shouting
to his cohort: "Trojans and Lycians and Dardanians who fight
in close—hold your ground! The Achaeans won't stop me for long,
though they've arranged themselves like a wall. Just watch them give
150   ground before my spear if, as I believe, the best of the gods
drives me on, the loud-thundering husband of Hera."
So speaking, he roused up the strength and spirit of each man.

Then Deïphobos,° a son of Priam, with high heart strode
among them, holding in front his shield, well balanced
155   on every side. Moving lightly on his feet he strode
forward under his shield's protection. Meriones° aimed
at him with his shining spear. Meriones cast—
he did not miss the shield of bull's hide, but he hit it,
well balanced on every side. Yet Meriones did not drive
160   the shaft through. The long spear was broken in the socket.
Deïphobos held his shield of bull's hide in front of him,
fearing the spear of war-minded Meriones, who faded
back into the throng of his companions. Meriones was angered
for his shattered spear, also for the loss of victory.

---

153   *Deïphobos*: Helen's lover after Paris is killed (in the action after the *Iliad*). He is a prominent warrior in
this book but appears only twice later in the *Iliad*: once in Book 22 when Athena takes on his form and in
Book 24.

156   *Meriones*: The second in command of the Cretan contingent, a good fighter and a subordinate of Idomeneus,
one of the men whom Poseidon, in the form of Kalkhas, has just exhorted.

He set off to the tents and the ships of the Achaeans   165
to get a long spear left in his hut, while the others went on
fighting as an inextinguishable roar arose.

                                        First Teucer,
the spear-fighter,° the son of Telamon, killed a man,
Imbrios, the son of Mentor, who had many horses.
He lived in Pedaios before he came against the sons   170
of the Achaeans. He had as wife a bastard daughter
of Priam, Medesikastê.° But when the ships
of the Danaäns came, curved at both ends, he returned
to Ilion. He was foremost among the Trojans and lived
in the house of Priam, who honored him as if he were one   175
of his own children.

                        Teucer, the son of Telamon,
pierced Imbrios beneath the ear with his sharp spear,
then he yanked it out.° Imbrios fell like an ash tree
on the top of a mountain, seen from afar on every side,
that is cut down by the bronze and brings its tender leafage   180
to the ground—even so Imbrios fell, and around him
his armor worked in bronze clanged.

                                Teucer leaped forth
eagerly and began to strip the armor, and Hector
cast at him with his bright spear as Teucer came on.
But Teucer, fixing Hector with his eye, dodged the bronze   185
spear by a hair, and it hit Amphimachos instead,
the son of Kteatos, the son of Aktor.° It smashed him
in the chest as Amphimachos rushed into the fight.
Amphimachos fell with a thud and his armor clanged
about him. Hector rushed forward to rip off the helmet fitted   190
to the temples of great-hearted Amphimachos, but Ajax lunged

---

168 *spear-fighter*: In fact he fights principally with the bow; see Figure 13.2.

172 ... *Medesikastê*: Imbrios is named after the island of IMBROS, just off the Troad. The location of Pedaios is
     unknown. Medisikastê is the only illegitimate daughter of Priam mentioned in the *Iliad*.

178 *yanked it out*: Odd, because in Book 12 Teucer was armed with his usual bow and carries it again in
     Book 15. Perhaps Homer has for the moment confused Teucer with Oïlean Ajax, unsure what he meant
     by "the two Ajaxes."

187 *son of Aktor*: Kteatos is also said to be a son of Poseidon, and, just below, Poseidon is angry because of the
     death of his grandson, Amphimachos, one of four leaders of the Epeians (from Elis in the northwestern
     Peloponnesus), according to the Catalog of Ships.

with his spear toward Hector as he came on. Yet Hector's
flesh was unassailable, for he was covered by a coat of bronze.
Ajax struck the boss on Hector's shield° and he pushed
195 Hector back with his mighty strength, moving Hector
away from the two corpses, which the Achaeans then drew off.

Stichios° and the good Menestheus, leaders of the Athenians,
dragged Amphimachos back into the midst of the Achaeans
while the two Ajaxes, mindful of their zealous valor,
200 carried off Imbrios. As when two lions snatch away a goat
from sharp-toothed hounds and carry it through the thick brush,
holding it high above the ground in their jaws—even so
the two Ajaxes carried off Imbrios, holding him on high.
Ajax, the son of Oïleus, angry because of Amphimachos,
205 cut off Imbrios' head from his tender neck and,
twirling the head, threw it like a ball through the crowd.

Now Poseidon grew angry in his heart when he saw
his grandson Amphimachos fallen in the dread contendings.
He set out among the huts and ships of the Achaeans
210 to stir up the Danaäns, to cause woe to the Trojans. He met
Idomeneus, famed for his work with the spear, as he came
away from a comrade who had recently withdrawn from the war,
stabbed with sharp bronze in the back of the knee.° His companions
carried him. Idomeneus, having given instruction to the doctors,
215 went off toward his tent, though he still wanted to fight.

The earth-shaker, the lord, came up Idomeneus, taking
on the appearance in his voice of Andraimon's son, Thoas,°
who ruled over the Aitolians in all Pleuron and steep KALYDON
and was honored like a god by the people. He said: "Idomeneus,
220 counselor of the Cretans, where now are the threats with which
the sons of the Achaeans threatened all the Trojans?"

Idomeneus, the captain of the Cretans, said in reply:
"O Thoas, no man is at fault as far as I can tell.

---

194   *on Hector's shield*: The boss does not appear on Mycenaean armor but characterized armor between the
      eleventh and eighth centuries BC. The boss consisted of a flat circular bronze disk with a central protrusion.

197   *Stichios*: "he who orders men in ranks" is merely a name. Hector kills him in Book 15.

213   *of the knee*: Homer does not name the wounded man. It is not clear why Idomeneus, last seen in Book 11, is
      not now in the fight, but he will quickly remedy this failing by a great *aristeia*, or moment of glory. Idome-
      neus is gray at the temples and the second oldest fighter, after Nestor.

217   *Thoas*: One of the men whom Poseidon earlier exhorted.

We all know how to fight. It is not through cowardly
fear, nor giving in to misgivings that anyone holds back   225
from the evil war—it must be the pleasure of the son
of Kronos, supreme in power, that the Achaeans are destroyed
without a name, here far from Argos. But Thoas, you were
staunch in the fight before and always urged others on
whenever you saw someone holding back, so don't   230
stop now! Call out to every man!"

       Then the earth-shaker
Poseidon answered him: "Idomeneus, may that man never
return from Troy who willingly holds back from the fight,
but may his flesh become a plaything for dogs.
Quickly now, put on your armor and let us go back out.   235
It is right that we hurry on together, if there is any chance
we can do some good, even though there are only the two
of us. Working together, even indifferent fighters can show
prowess. But we two know how to fight even against the best!"°

 So speaking, Poseidon, though a god, entered again   240
into the contendings of men. When Idomeneus came to his
well-built hut, he put on his beautiful armor and took up
two spears.° He went like the lightning that the son of
Kronos takes in his hands and brandishes from shining
Olympos, showing a sign to men, and brightly flashes   245
the rays of it. Thus his bronze flashed around his chest
as he ran.

   Meriones, a good and brave companion,
came on Idomeneus while he was still nearby his hut,
as Meriones was going to get a bronze spear. Powerful
Idomeneus spoke to him: "Meriones, son of Molos,   250
swift of foot, most beloved of my companions, why have
you withdrawn from the war and the contendings? Have you
been wounded by chance? Has the point of an arrow torn
your flesh, or have you come to give me some message?
I am not happy myself to sit in my hut, but long to fight!"   255

---

239 *against the best*: That is, two are always better than one: Even two poor fighters can accomplish something
   when working together, so how much more should the two of *us* accomplish, who are superior fighters.
   Though Poseidon/Thoas nonetheless goes off by himself, Meriones will soon join Idomeneus.

243 *two spears*: The *aristeia* is always preceded by an arming scene, here reduced to this single sentence.

The prudent Meriones answered: "Idomeneus,
counselor to the Cretans who wear shirts of bronze, I have come
to get another spear, hoping you have one left in your tent.
For I broke the one I started with when I hit the shield
260 of the boastful Deïphobos."

And Idomeneus, captain of the Cretans,
answered: "If you want a spear, whether one or twenty,
you will find plenty standing in my hut against the bright walls
of the vestibule—Trojan spears that I took from men I killed.
You should know that I don't fight standing apart from the enemy!
265 So I have many spears and shields with bosses and helmets
and breastplates that shine brightly."

The prudent Meriones
answered him: "Yes, well I have a lot of Trojan armor
in my *own* hut and beside my black ship, but it is quite
a distance to get them. Neither am I a stranger to valor—
270 I don't think! I too take a stand in the forefront
of the battle where men win glory when the strife of war
is stirred up. Perhaps my skill at fighting is unknown to some
other of the Achaeans who wear shirts of bronze, but I think
you know it very well."

Idomeneus, captain of the Cretans,
275 answered Meriones: "I know what sort of man you are
when it comes to bravery. Why do you need to say
these things? For if all the best men were gathered beside
the ships in preparation for an ambush, where the courage of men
is made clearest, then it is obvious who is the coward and who
280 the brave. The coward's skin blanches in fear, turning
every color, nor does the spirit in his breast rest without fear.
He fidgets and shifts his weight from one leg to the other,
and his heart beats hugely in his breast as he contemplates
his doom. And his teeth chatter. But the color
285 of the brave man does not change, nor does he fear
much when he goes into an ambush of warriors, but he longs
to mix as soon as possible in the dread contendings. Not even
there would one complain about your courage or the strength
of your hands. If you were hit with an arrow in the fight or pierced
290 by a spear, the shaft would not fall in your neck from behind,
nor in your back, but it would strike either your chest or groin
as you pressed with desire in the craved encounter of the foremost

fighters.° But come, let us not discuss these things like children,
standing here, or some other warrior may become
exceedingly angry. Go into my hut and get a strong spear."   295

So he spoke, and Meriones, like to swift Ares,
quickly took a bronze spear from the hut and followed
after Idomeneus, craving combat. Even as Ares,
the destroyer of men, goes to war, and with him follows
Rout, his son, just as powerful and fearless, who puts   300
to flight even the warrior who is enduring of heart—the two gods
arm themselves and go forth from Thrace to the Ephyroi or
the great-hearted Phlegyes where they do not listen to the prayers
of both sides, but give glory to one side or the other°—
even so Meriones and Idomeneus, the leaders of men,   305
went to the war, armed in flame-like bronze.

Meriones spoke first to Idomeneus, saying: "Son
of Deukalion,° where do you want to enter the fray? On the right
of the army, in the middle, or on the left? In no other part
than the left do I think that the long-haired Achaeans so come   310
up short in the fight."°

Idomeneus the leader of the Cretans
answered him: "In the middle of the ships there are others
to put up a defense—the two Ajaxes and Teucer, who is best
of the Achaeans in archery and also good in the hand-to-hand.
These men will give Hector, the son of Priam, his fill   315
of war, though he is zealous and even though he is strong.
Hector will find it heavy going, though he is keen to fight,
to overcome their might and their invincible hands and set fire
to the ships, unless the son of Kronos himself throws a burning

---

293   ... foremost fighters: Among whom the spear seeks its victim like a man seeks a woman. This whole passage
       is permeated with playful sexual innuendo.

304   or the other: Ares is traditionally said to come from Thrace, a place of wild barbarism. The Phlegyes ("burn-
       ing ones") are, however, usually thought to be a tribe from Thessaly: Phlegyas was a son of Ares and the
       father of Koronis, the mother of the healing god Asklepios. Phlegyas was also the father of Ixion, the great
       sinner, who begot the Centaurs. The mysterious Ephyra, presumably the hometown of the Ephyroi, is often
       equated with Corinth (as in Glaukos' story of Bellerophon), making altogether obscure Homer's reference
       to these two warring tribes from Thrace.

308   Deukalion: A son of Minos and father of Idomeneus. Deukalion has the same name as Prometheus' son, the
       first man, located in north or central Greece.

311   in the fight: "left," "middle," and "right" are always from the Achaean perspective, even when the Trojans are
       talking.

320 brand into the fast ships! Great Telamonian Ajax would not
yield to a man who was mortal and eats the wheat of Demeter,°
a man who can be broken by the bronze and by great stones.
Not even to Achilles, the breaker of men, would Ajax yield,
at least in the hand-to-hand. But in swiftness of foot no one
325 yields to Achilles. So let the two of us head for the left of the army
so that we may quickly see whether we will give glory
to another, or another to us."

　　　　　　　　So he spoke. Meriones,
the equal of swift Ares, led the way until they came to the part
of the army where Idomeneus urged them to go.
330 When the Trojans saw Idomeneus, in valor like a flame, and his
subordinate with their fancy armor, they all made at him, calling
to one another through the mass of fighters.

　　　　　　　　　　　　By the sterns
of the ships the strife of men clashing together arose.
As when gusts are driven by shrill winds on the day when dust
335 lies thickest on the roads and the winds raise up a great fog
of dust in confusion—even so they clashed together
in war. All in the throng were eager to kill one another
with their sharp bronze. The battle that destroys men
bristled with long spears that they held for slashing flesh.
340 The blaze from the bronze of the gleaming helmets and the newly
cleaned breastplates and from the glaring shields blinded
them as they came at one another in confusion. He would be
a cold man at heart who would rejoice when he saw such labor
and did not grieve!

　　　　　　Thus the two mighty sons of Kronos,
345 Zeus and Poseidon of differing minds, fashioned terrible
sorrow for mortal warriors. For Zeus wished victory
for the Trojans and Hector, giving glory to Achilles, the fast runner.
He did not want to destroy the Achaeans completely
before the walls of Troy, but he wanted to give glory to
350 Thetis and her son, strong of spirit. Poseidon, on the other hand,
coming secretly from the gray sea, drove the Argives on.
For he hated that they were being beaten by the Trojans,
and was therefore angry at Zeus. They came from the same stock
and they had a single ancestry, but Zeus was the older

---

321 *Demeter*: The goddess who makes grain of any kind grow.

and knew much more. Thus Poseidon avoided giving aid   355
openly, but secretly he roused the Argives, going through
the army in the semblance of a man. And so they stretched
the cord of powerful strife and equal war over the two sides,
unbreakable and not to be undone, which loosed
the knees of many.°   360

       Then Idomeneus, though his hair was
half-gray, shouted to the Danaäns, then leaped amid the Trojans,
putting them to flight. He killed Othryoneus from Kabesos,
a guest in Troy, recently arrived following the rumor of war.
He sought in marriage the most beautiful of Priam's daughters,
without giving gifts, though he promised a great deed: to push back   365
the unyielding sons of the Achaeans from Troy. The old man
Priam promised, nodding his head in agreement, that he would
give Cassandra in marriage. So Othryoneus fought, trusting in this
promise. But Idomeneus aimed with his bright spear. He threw
and hit Othryoneus as he strutted vainly along. The breastplate   370
he wore was of no use, for the spear was fixed full in the middle
of his stomach. He fell with a thud.°

       Idomeneus said
in boast: "Othryoneus, I commend you above all men
if you can accomplish all that you promised Priam
of the line of Dardanos! For he promised you his daughter.
Well, we too can make the same promise, and bring it to pass!   375
We can give you the most beautiful of the daughters of the son
of Atreus, bringing her here from Argos to be married,
if only you come with us to sack the well-peopled city of Ilion.
So come along now, we can make a deal about that marriage
here beside the sea-faring ships, because we are not   380
hard to deal with in accepting gifts to arrange a match."

    So speaking, the warrior Idomeneus was dragging
Othryoneus by the foot through the mighty contendings

---

360 *of many*: That is, the two gods made the Trojans and Achaeans fight a fierce but indecisive battle. This recur-
ring image is taken from a tug-of-war.

372 *with a thud*: The name of Othryoneus is based on a word for "mountain" (*othrys*). Kabesos is variously
located. Homer ignores the prophetic powers of Cassandra. In the Classical Period, a bride's dowry
was more common than the giving of bridal gifts by the groom, probably because the rising population
made it harder to marry off girls. Agamemnon offers Achilles one of his daughters "without gifts"
in Book 9. Othryoneus seems to be strutting about without a shield, overconfident in his fighting skill,
a boastful fool.

when Asios° came in support of him, afoot in front of his horses
385 that the charioteer drove so that they breathed heavily on
the shoulders of Asios. He desired above all to spear Idomeneus,
but Idomeneus anticipated the throw and hit Asios in the throat
beneath the chin, driving the bronze straight through.
Asios fell as when an oak falls, or a poplar, or a tall pine
390 that carpenters in the mountains cut with newly edged axes
to make a ship's timbers. Asios lay stretched out before the horses
and the chariot, gurgling and clutching at the bloody dust.

    The driver lost all of whatever wit he had before.
He did not dare to turn his horses back to escape
395 the hands of the enemy. Antilochos, stalwart in the fight,
ran the charioteer through,° hitting him in the gut
with his spear. The breastplate that he wore was of no use,
for the spear fixed in the middle of his belly. Gasping,
the charioteer fell from the well-built car, and Antilochos,°
400 the son of great-hearted Nestor, drove the horses away from
the Trojans into the midst of the Achaeans who wear fancy
shinguards.

        But Deïphobos, standing near, came at Idomeneus
in deep grief for Asios, and cast at him with his shining spear.
Idomeneus, eyes locked-in on him, avoided the bronze spear.
405 He took cover behind his shield, well balanced on all sides,
adorned with bulls' hides and bright bronze and fitted
with two rods.° Idomeneus crouched behind it when the bronze
spear flew his way. The shield rang harshly as the spear
grazed its edge.

        But not in vain did Deïphobos cast
410 the spear from his strong hand! It struck Hypsenor,
son of Hippasos, shepherd of the people, right in the liver
beneath his belly and at once it loosed his knees. Deïphobos

---

384 *Asios*: One of the leaders of the Trojan advance (Book 12). His name means "the man of Asia," which appar-
ently means "the good land" in an Anatolian language. Asios disobeyed Poulydamas' earlier advice that the
Trojans leave their chariots behind the ditch; he now pays the price. We last saw him in Book 12, where he
calls Zeus a liar. His son Adamas will soon fall too, killed by Meriones.

396 *charioteer through*: The charioteer is not named, unless his name is Heniochos (= "charioteer"). The killing
of a charioteer is a common exploit for a minor warrior like Antilochos.

399 *Antilochos*: Like Meriones, Antilochos was one of the Achaeans earlier encouraged by Poseidon.

407 *two rods*: Probably crossed on the inside to give the shield its shape.

exulted over him savagely, shouting aloud: "Ho! Not unavenged
lies Asios, for I think that he will rejoice in his heart, although
he goes to the house of Hades, the powerful warden,   415
for I have given him an escort!"

                So Deïphobos spoke, giving the Argives
great pain at his boasting, and especially he stirred the spirit
of Antilochos, lover of war. Though saddened, he did not neglect
his companion, but rushing up he stood over Hypsenor
and covered him with his shield. Then two trusty comrades—   420
Mekisteus, son of Echios, and the good Alastor—bore Hypsenor,
groaning deeply,° to the hollow ships.

                Idomeneus did not
lessen his furious power. He was constantly keen
either to seal some one of the Trojans in black night,
or himself to fall, fending off destruction from the Achaeans.   425
Then the dear son of Aisyetes, of the line of Zeus,
the warrior Alkathoös—he had married the eldest daughter
of Anchises, Hippodameia, whom her father and revered
mother loved from their heart, she who surpassed
all her agemates in beauty and cleverness, and for this   430
reason the best man in broad Troy had married her—
this Alkathoös Poseidon destroyed at the hands of Idomeneus.
For he cast a spell over Alkathoös' shining eyes and bound
his glorious limbs so that he was not able to flee
nor avoid the spear when the warrior Idomeneus   435
speared him right in the middle of the chest. Alkathoös
stood there fixed like a gravestone or a high leafy tree
as Idomeneus broke the shirt of bronze that enveloped him,
which had fended off destruction from his flesh. The breastplate
rang with a grating sound as it split with the spear in it.   440
Alkathoös fell with a thud, the spear fixed in his heart,
the butt of the spear quivering as his breath labored on.
Then strong Ares stayed its fury.°

                Idomeneus exulted
over him savagely, shouting aloud: "Deïphobos, is it

---

422 *groaning deeply*: Though he is dead! The slip is a clear sign of oral composition.

443 *... its fury*: Mekisteus ("giant") and Alastor are just names. In Book 2 the "tomb of old Aisyetes" is a Trojan land-
     mark. Alkathoös, son-in-law of Anchises (father of Aeneas), led a Trojan column in Book 12. Hippodameia is a
     common name in Greek legend. Ares is a personification of war; the spear is imagined to have its own vitality.

445 enough that I have killed three for one?° —since you boast
in this fashion! Hey, strange guy, now you yourself must
stand against me that you might know of what sort is the son
of Zeus who has come to this place. First Zeus fathered Minos
to watch over Crete, and Minos fathered the blameless
450 Deukalion as son, and Deukalion fathered me as king over
many men in broad Crete.° And now the ships have carried
me here to be a torment to your father and to the other Trojans."

So Idomeneus spoke. Deïphobos considered two courses—
whether he should give ground and take one of the great-hearted
455 Trojans as his comrade-in-arms, or whether he should attack
Idomeneus by himself. As he pondered, it seemed to Deïphobos
to be the better course to go find Aeneas.

He found him
standing at the edge of the crowd, angry at the good
Priam because Priam seemed not to respect him at all,
460 though Aeneas was brave among warriors.° Standing
nearby, Deïphobos spoke words that went like arrows:
"Aeneas, counselor to the Trojans, you should come quickly
to bring aid to your sister's husband, if care and grief for your kin
will move you. Come now, let us honor Alkathoös. He was your
465 sister's husband and raised you up in his halls when you were
just a youngster. But Idomeneus, famed for his spear, has killed him."

So he spoke, arousing strong feeling in Aeneas' heart.
And so Aeneas pursued Idomeneus, greatly athirst for making war.
Flight was not the stuff of Idomeneus, as if he were
470 a spoiled child—he made his stand like a boar in the mountains
who trusts in his strength, who awaits the noisy rabble

---

445 *for one*: The three killed are Othryoneus, Asios, and Alkathoös, in exchange for Hypsenor. Asios' nameless driver, killed by Antilochos, is ignored.

451 *broad Crete*: Minos is somehow related to Minoan power in Crete (c. 3000–1400 BC); his name might mean simply "king" (the first pharaoh in Egypt was *Min*). "Idomeneus" is derived from the Cretan "Mount Ida," one of the central mountains in Crete (not the Mount Ida behind the Troad). Idomeneus is of course not the "son of Zeus," but his descendant.

460 *among warriors*: Aeneas, leader of a Trojan column in Book 12, has not appeared since then. Aeneas was a member of the Trojan royal house. Homer does not explain the cause of his disagreement with Priam, but a warrior's withdrawal from the fight, then return, is a dominant theme in epic, including the story of Achilles. Aeneas was produced by Anchises' sexual union with Aphrodite; oddly, Anchises never appears in the *Iliad*, perhaps in agreement with the tradition that he was punished for sleeping with Aphrodite. Aeneas is the ancestor of the Roman people in Vergil's epic the *Aeneid* (29-19 BC) and one of the greatest Trojan fighters.

of men as they come upon him in a lonely place. His back
bristles and his two eyes burn like fire as he sharpens
his tusks, eager to ward off dogs and their men—
just so Idomeneus, famed for his spear, did not give ground   475
as Aeneas came at him, bearing aid to Deïphobos.

Idomeneus called to his comrades, looking to Askalaphos,
Aphareus, and Deïpyros, Meriones, and Antilochos, all masters
of the war cry.° Urging them on, he spoke words that went
like arrows: "Come here, my friends! Help me, for I am alone!   480
I greatly fear Aeneas as he comes on, swift of foot. He is about
to attack me, he who lusts to kill men in the fight. He has
the flower of youth, the fullness of power. If we were of the same
age with our mood such as it is, then quickly he would win
the victory, or would I!"   485

So he spoke, and they all with a single
spirit took their stand in close order, leaning their shields against
their shoulders. And from the other side Aeneas called to his
companions, looking to Deïphobos and Paris and the good
Agenor, who with himself were the leaders of the Trojans.
The army followed after them, as sheep follow the ram   490
to water from the place of feeding and the shepherd rejoices
in his heart—even so the heart of Aeneas rejoiced
in his breast when he saw the throng of the army following
after him.

Both sides charged on one another in the hand-to-hand
with their long spears, and the bronze rang awfully around   495
their chests as they aimed at one another in the melée. But above
all the rest, Aeneas and Idomeneus, the equals of Ares,
slashed at the flesh of the others with their pitiless bronze.

Aeneas cast first at Idomeneus, but Idomeneus saw it
coming and avoided the bronze spear. Aeneas' spear was fixed   500
quivering in the earth, having gone in vain from his powerful hand.
And then Idomeneus struck Oinomaos° in the middle of the stomach,

---

479 *war cry*: Askalaphos ("owl") is a son of Ares and leader of the Achaean forces from ORCHOMENOS in
Boeotia. Along with Aphareus and Deïpyros, he becomes cannon fodder for the upcoming battle, where
these men are killed in the order in which they are listed here.

502 *Oinomaos*: A follower of Asios, he has the same name as the king of Pisa who lost a chariot race and his life
to Pelops, son of Tantalos, after which Pelops married Oinomaos' daughter, another Hippodameia. Homer
never mentions this story.

breaking the metal of his breastplate. The bronze let his guts
ooze out through the spear hole. Oinomaos fell in the dust
505   and clutched the dirt with his palm. Idomeneus drew forth
his long-shadowed spear from the corpse, but he was not able
to lift the armor from Oinomaos' shoulders, for he was oppressed
by missiles. The joints of his feet were no longer steady under him
so that he could rush forth after a cast, or avoid an enemy's.
510   Therefore while in close fighting he could ward off danger,
his feet were not so nimble that he could flee in terror from the battle.

　　　Deïphobos threw at Idomeneus as he retreated step
by step, for he nourished a lasting hatred for Idomeneus,
but this time he missed again and instead hit Askalaphos,
515   the son of Enyalios,° with his spear. The powerful
spear went through his shoulder, and falling in the dust
Askalaphos gripped the dirt with his palm. Loud-voiced
powerful Ares did not yet know that his son had fallen
in the furious contendings, but he sat on the top of Olympos
520   beneath the golden clouds, constrained by the will of Zeus,
where the other deathless gods also sat, shut out of the war.

　　　Then they clashed over Askalaphos in the hand-to-hand.
Deïphobos tore off Askalaphos' shining helmet,
but Meriones, like to swift Ares, leaped on Deïphobos
525   and wounded him in the arm with his spear, and the crested helmet
fell to the ground with a clatter. Meriones leaped again,
like a vulture, and pulled out the powerful spear from Deïphobos'
upper arm, then withdrew into the crowd of his companions.

　　　But Polites,° Deïphobos' brother, stretched out his arms
530   around his waist and led Deïphobos from the savage war
until they came to the swift horses standing in wait at the rear
of the battle with their driver and fancy car. Then the car
carried Deïphobos toward the city. He groaned heavily,
worn out, and blood flowed from his freshly wounded arm.

535   　　　The others fought on amid an undying din. Then
Aeneas leaped on Aphareus, son of Kaletor, who was

---

515   *Enyalios*: Enyalios/Ares does not learn of his son's death until Book 15. Ironically, Ares' son is killed by the
　　　Trojans, whom Ares sponsors.

529   *Polites*: The first appearance of Polites, "townsman," except for Book 2, where Iris takes on his form. He
　　　appears again in Books 15 and 24.

turned toward him, slicing Aphareus in the throat
with his sharp spear. Aphareus' head snapped back,
his shield and helmet knocked to one side as Death
that kills the spirit poured over him. Antilochos,   540
watching carefully, now leaped and slashed Thoön as
he turned his back, completely severing the vein that runs
straight along the back until it reaches the neck.° He severed
it completely, and Thoön fell on his back in the dust,
stretching out his hands to his dear companions. Antilochos   545
rushed up and, believing himself safe, began to take the armor
from Thoön's shoulders. The Trojans surrounded Antilochos
and thrust from every side at his broad shining shield,
but they were not able to penetrate it and graze the tender
flesh of Antilochos with their pitiless bronze. Poseidon,   550
the earth-shaker, protected the son of Nestor even in the midst
of many missiles.° For Antilochos never shirked the enemy,
but ranged among them. Nor was his spear ever at rest,
for he always brandished it. Likewise, his zeal was ever
to strike someone as he rushed upon men in the hand-to-hand.   555

   Thus engaged amidst the throng, Antilochos did not escape
the notice of Adamas, the son of Asios, who, rushing up close,
smashed the middle of his shield with his sharp bronze.
But dark-haired Poseidon, unwilling to give Adamas
Antilochos' life, sapped the strength from his spear. Part of   560
it remained, like a fire-hardened stake, stuck in Antilochos' shield,
and the other half lay on the ground. Adamas himself
shrank back into the crowd of his companions, avoiding death.

   But Meriones followed after Adamas as he pulled back.
He hit him with his spear halfway between his sexual organs   565
and his navel, gruesome, the most savage kind of wound
mortals can suffer. And there the spear fixed. Adamas
followed where the spear led him as Meriones pulled it,
writhing like a bull that herdsmen in the mountains drive all
unwilling, bound by cords—even so Adamas, when hit,   570
writhed a little while, but not for long, until the warrior

---

543 *the neck:* There is no such vein. Probably Homer means the spinal cord. Thoön ("swifty") is a common
     heroic name.

552 *many missiles:* Antilochos is the great-grandson of Poseidon: Poseidon fathered Neleus; Neleus fathered
     Nestor; and Nestor fathered Antilochos. In fact Poseidon was worshiped in Nestor's town of Pylos in the
     southwestern Peloponnesus, as proven by Linear B tablets (from c. 1200 BC) found there.

Meriones came up close and pulled the spear from his flesh.
Darkness enfolded his eyes.

Then Helenos hit Deïpyros
on the temple in the hand-to-hand with a great Thracian sword
575 and tore away his helmet.° Dashed from his head, it fell
to the ground, and one of the Achaeans picked it up as it rolled
among the feet of the fighters. Black night enfolded Deïpyros' eyes.

Then grief took hold of Menelaos, the son of Atreus,
good at the war cry. He went forth to threaten Helenos
580 the prince, the warrior, brandishing his sharp spear. Helenos
drew back his bow string. Thus they let fly at the same time,
the one with his sharp spear, the other with an arrow from the string.
Helenos, the son of Priam, hit Menelaos on the breast
with his arrow, on the metal of his breastplate, and the bitter
585 arrow flew off from it. As when from a flat winnowing-fan
in a grand threshing floor the dark-skinned beans or chick-peas
leap before a shrill wind or the strength of the winnower,
even so the bitter arrow glanced aside and flew far from
the breastplate of glorious Menelaos.

Then the son of Atreus,
590 Menelaos, good at the war cry, threw his spear and hit
Helenos on the hand that held his polished bow, driving
the bronze spear straight through his hand and into
the bow. Helenos withdrew back into the crowd
of his companions, avoiding death, his hand hanging useless
595 by his side, the ash spear trailing behind him. Great-hearted Agenor°
pulled the spear from his hand and bound it with a twisted strip
of sheep's wool, a sling that his aide, shepherd of the people,
carried with him.

And then Peisander° made straight for glorious
Menelaos, but a cruel fate led him to his death, to be killed
600 by you, Menelaos, in the dread contendings. For when

---

575   *... his helmet*: Helenos, Hector's brother, shares command of a division with Deïphobos, also Hector's brother.
Deïpyros was one of the Achaeans earlier encouraged by Poseidon. The wild Thracians were famous for their
weaponry. Helenos cuts the strap that holds the helmet to Deïpyros' head, causing the helmet to fly off.

595   *Agenor*: Agenor is the leader of the second Trojan column, now helping the leader of the third column.

598   *Peisander*: "persuader of men," the same name as a man earlier killed by Agamemnon (Book 11). Peisander,
aptly named, is the son of the man whom Paris bribed to persuade the Trojans to kill the Greek captains
during their peaceful embassy to Troy at the beginning of the war.

they came close to one another, the son of Atreus
missed and his spear was turned aside. Peisander hit
the shield of glorious Menelaos, but he was unable to drive
the bronze straight through, for the broad shield stopped it
and the spear was broken in the socket. Still, Peisander rejoiced   605
in his heart and hoped for victory.

                    But the son of Atreus
pulled out his silver-studded sword and leaped on Peisander.
Peisander pulled out a long ax from beneath his shield,
of beautiful bronze, well polished and hafted to an olive
handle. And they set upon one another. Peisander   610
hit the plate of the high-crested helmet—he struck
on the topmost part beneath the plume. But Menelaos hit him
on the forehead above the base of the nose as Peisander
came against him. The bones broke and his two eyes, all bloody,
fell in the dust at his feet. Peisander doubled up and fell.   615

   Menelaos put his foot on Peisander's chest and stripped
off the armor. Boasting, he said: "Even so shall the haughty
Trojans, ever thirsting for the dread din of battle, leave
the ships of the Danaäns with their fast horses! You have no lack
of iniquity and villainy by which you have outraged me—   620
filthy dogs! Nor have you shown any fear in your hearts
for the harsh anger of loud-thundering Zeus, the god of hospitality,
who one day will destroy your high city. You wantonly took
my wedded wife and much treasure because you found her amusing.
Now, again, you want to light devastating fire on the seafaring   625
ships and to kill the Achaean warriors. But Father Zeus, truly
they say you are superior to others in wisdom, both to men
and the gods. From you all these things come. Being such,
you show favor to the malevolent Trojans, whose strength is always
reckless, nor can they ever be gorged with the awesome din   630
of war. Of all things there is enough, of sleep and lovemaking
and sweet song and blameless dance. Of all these things
would a man rather have his fill than of war. But the Trojans
are insatiate for battle!"

           So speaking, blameless Menelaos took
off the bloody armor from around Peisander's flesh and gave it   635
to his companions. Then he ran forward and engaged with the fighters
at the forefront. There Harpalion, the son of King Pylaimenes,
who followed his dear father to fight at Troy but never returned
to the land of his fathers—Harpalion leaped at Menelaos.

640 He came in close and thrust with his spear at the middle
of the shield of the son of Atreus, but he was unable to drive
the bronze through it. Harpalion shrank back into the crowd
of his companions, avoiding death, looking warily all around
in case someone should wound his flesh with their bronze.
645 Meriones fired a bronze arrow at Harpalion as he pulled back,
hitting him in the left buttock. The arrow pierced straight through
to the bladder beneath the bone. Sitting down where he had stood,
Harpalion breathed out his life in the arms of his companions,
like a worm stretched out upon the earth, the black blood running
650 from him to wet the ground. The great-hearted Paphlagonians
tended him. They sat him in a car and drove him toward
sacred Ilion, grieving, and with them went his father, pouring
down tears. But there would be no revenge for his dead son.°

Harpalion's death greatly angered Paris, for among
655 the many Paphlagonians Harpalion had been his host.
Angry for his sake, Paris fired a bronze arrow.
There was a certain Euchenor, the son of the prophet
Polyidos, rich and well born, dwelling in Corinth,
who knowing well his dread fate went, still, on his ship.
660 Often his old father, the noble Polyidos, had told him
that either he would perish of disease in his halls, or he would
be killed by the Trojans amid the ships of the Achaeans.
Thus he avoided the heavy fine of the Achaeans° and terrible
disease, so that he might not suffer a woeful heart. Paris
665 hit him beneath the jaw, under the ear. Swiftly
his spirit left his limbs and black darkness took him.

Thus the armies fought like blazing fire. Hector,
dear to Zeus, was not aware that on the left flank
his army was being slaughtered by the Argives. Soon
670 the Achaeans would have gained glory—of such power
was the earth-holder, the earth-shaker, who drove on the Argives
and helped them with his own strength. But Hector pressed on
where first he had leaped within the gate and the wall, breaking

---

653 *... his dead son*: Much of the pathos of the *Iliad* depends on the death of sons: "In peace sons bury fathers,
but in war fathers bury sons" (Herodotus 1.87.4). Other father/son pairings are Asios/Adamas and Nestor/
Antilochos. Harpalion's father, Pylaimenes, is king of the Paphlagonians (see Map 6): Menelaos killed
Pylaimenes in Book 5. The use of a chariot is notable because only Asios brought his chariot over the ditch.
Homer sometimes forgets such details. Harpalion is dead, the only time in the *Iliad* that a dead man is
transported from the battle by car.

663 *fine of the Achaeans*: If he refused to go to the war.

the thick ranks of the Danaän shield-men, where the ships of Ajax
and Protesilaos were drawn up on the shore of the gray sea,   675
where the wall was built the lowest and where most of the men
and the horses were raging in battle.° There the Boeotians
and the Ionians with trailing shirts, and the Locrians
and the Phthians and the glorious Epeians had big trouble keeping
the fiery Hector away from the ships as he rushed onward,   680
unable to push him back from their positions—even the picked
men of the Athenians, among whom was Menestheus, the son
of Peteos, and Pheidas and Stichios and brave Bias, while
the Epeians were led by Meges, son of Phyleus, and Amphion
and Drakios.   685

　　　In the forefront of the Phthians were Medon,
a bulwark in the battle, and the fast Podarkes. Medon was
a bastard son of godlike Oïleus and brother of Ajax, but
he lived in Phylakê, far away from the land of his fathers,
because he had killed the brother of his stepmother Eriopis,
whom Oïleus had as wife.° As for Podarkes, he was the son   690

677　… in battle: By "Ajax" Homer usually means Telamonian Ajax, but here he must mean Oïlean Ajax. Homer is not always consistent in his ordering of the ships, but the following seems to be the general pattern, except in the Catalog of Ships, where the order differs considerably. Some ships are pulled further inland than others, and the line is organized from west to east, with the troops facing south (see Map 3). The wings of the battle are from the point of view of someone standing behind the line near the edge of the sea and facing the backs of the troops:

the sea

Right (west)				Center			Left (east)	
	Boeotians		Protesilaos/Podarkes		Diomedes	Nestor	Menelaos	Teucer
Achilles		Menestheus	Meges	Oïl. Ajax	Odysseus	Agamemnon	Idomeneus	Tel. Ajax

In Book 10 the ships of Meges (Doulichion) and Oïlean Ajax (Locris) are near the ships of Odysseus (Ithaca), while those of Idomeneus (Crete) and Telamonian Ajax (Salamis) are a good ways off. In Book 11 Odysseus' ships are at the center of the line and those of Telamonian Ajax at the left edge, but here Menestheus (Athens), Meges (Doulichion, Elis), and both of the Ajaxes are stationed together. The confusion may result from Homer's persistent confusion between "the two Ajaxes" meaning, on the one hand, Oïlean Ajax and Telamonian Ajax and, on the other, Telamonian Ajax and his brother Teucer.

690　… had as wife: Several names in this catalog of fighters appear only to be killed. The Ionians, never mentioned again, are the same as the Athenians, who colonized Asia Minor in the "Ionian migration" of the eighth to sixth centuries BC. Oïlean Ajax—soon prominent in the fighting—is a leader of the men from Locris northwest of Boeotia, in classical times divided into three areas. The Phthians, also not mentioned elsewhere, are from Achilles' homeland of Phthia, but are otherwise called Myrmidons, Achaeans, or Hellenes. Here the Phthians are ruled by Podarkes, "fast runner," an epithet of Achilles, and Medon. Medon's name means simply "ruler." In the Catalog of Ships, Medon takes over for Philoktetes, bitten by a serpent on the island of Lemnos and abandoned, but here Homer reinvents Medon to replace (along with Podarkes) Protesilaos, the first Achaean to die at Troy. He brings Medon to Phylakê (where Protesilaos ruled) through the common device of exile because he had killed a relative. The location of Phylakê is unknown, but it is someplace in Phthia. Aeneas kills Medon in Book 15. The Epeians are from Elis in the northwestern Peloponnesus, now led by Meges from Doulichion, an island just northwest of Elis that the Epeians seem to have occupied. The Athenians Stichios and Menestheus rescued the Epeian Amphimachos earlier in this book.

of Iphiklos, the son of Phylakos.° These men, dressed in armor,
fought in the forefront of the great-hearted Phthians and defended
the ships along with the Boeotians.

                          Ajax, the swift son
of Oïleus, would never leave the side of Ajax, son of
695 Telamon, not even for a moment. For even as in fallow
land two oxen, dark as wine, strain with a single heart
to pull the jointed plow, and around the roots of their horns
sweat gushes in streams, and the polished yoke
alone holds them apart as they labor through the furrow
700 until the plow cuts to the turning-point at the end of the field—
just so the two Ajaxes, standing together, remained close
by one another. Many fine troops followed the son of Telamon
as companions. One would take up his tower shield whenever
sweaty fatigue came over Ajax's limbs.

                         But the Locrians
705 did not follow the great-hearted son of Oïleus, for their hearts
were not made for fighting in the hand-to-hand. They did not have
helmets of bronze with thick plumes of horsehair, nor did
they have rounded shields, nor spears of ash, but trusting
to their bows and well-twisted slings of sheep's wool they had
710 followed Ajax to Ilion. With these weapons, after their arrival,
they fired thick and fast and with them tried to break the ranks
of the Trojans.

                 So some men fought in the front in their fancy
armor against the Trojans and Hector dressed in bronze,
while others behind kept firing from cover. The Trojans,
715 oppressed by arrows, forgot their lust for battle.

     The Trojans would have withdrawn sadly from the ships
and huts to windy Ilion if Poulydamas had not stood beside
Hector and said, scolding: "Hector, you don't like giving heed to
persuasive words! Because the god has given to you as to no other
720 the works of war, you think that you surpass all others
in counsel as well. But there is no way that you alone will be able

---

691   ... *Phylakos*: Podarkes, "swift-foot," is named for Iphiklos, son of Phylakos, a famous fast runner who impris-
oned the seer Melampous at Phylakē in Thessaly when he came to rustle Iphiklos' cattle as a bride-price for
his brother Bias. Bias wanted to marry the Pylian princess Pero. Melampous was freed when he unraveled the
mystery of Iphiklos' impotence, who went on to father Podarkes and then Protesilaos. The story of Melamp-
ous' exploits in Phylakē is told twice in the *Odyssey* and must have been well known.

to do all things. To one the god has given the deeds of war,
to another the dance, to another the lyre and song.
And in the breast of another, Zeus, whose voice carries far,
has placed a fine mind for discernment, from which many men benefit.   725
Zeus has saved many, which he himself knows best.
    "But I will say what seems to be right: A circle of war
burns all around you. Some of the great-hearted Trojans,
now that they have passed over the wall, stand idle in their armor.
Some fight, but they are outnumbered and scattered among the ships.   730
So be wise! Fall back and summon the best fighters. Then
we will shape the best counsel, whether to fall among the ships
with many benches, if a god is willing to give us victory.
Or we might pull back from the ships without suffering harm.
But I fear that the Achaeans will pay back yesterday's debt.   735
For there is a man among their ships lusting for combat,
who I think will no longer keep himself apart from the war."°

    So spoke Poulydamas, and his good counsel was pleasing
to Hector. At once he leaped from his car to the ground
in full armor. He spoke to Poulydamas words that went   740
like arrows: "Poulydamas, you hold back all the best fighters here,
and I will go there and face the fight. I will return quickly again,
once I have given my orders."

                    So he spoke, and he set forth
like a snowy mountain.° He flew, screaming, through the Trojans
and their allies. They hurried, one and all, toward the hospitable   745
Poulydamas, son of Panthoös, when they heard the voice of Hector.
Hector ranged through the forefighters in search of Deïphobos
and the powerful prince Helenos, and Adamas, son of Asios,
and Asios, son of Hyrtakos, expecting he might find them sound.
But he did not find them unharmed or untouched by destruction.   750
Some lay motionless at the sterns of the ships, destroyed
at the hands of the Argives, and some were within the wall,°
hit by arrows or wounded by spears.

                    But Hector
did find one comrade on the left of the tearful battle,
the good Alexandros, husband of Helen whose hair   755

---

737   *from the war*: That is, Achilles.

744   *snowy mountain*: Because (1) he is huge and (2) his armor gleams like sun reflected from the snow.

752   *within the wall*: That is, of Troy, not the Achaeans' defensive wall.

is beautiful. Paris had incited his companions to fight.
Standing near, Hector spoke words of shame: "Evil Paris
pretty boy, girl-crazy, con-man! Where is our Deïphobos
and the powerful prince Helenos? Where Adamas, son of Asios,
760 and Asios, the son of Hyrtakos? Where is Othryoneus? Now
all of steep Ilion is utterly ruined. Your own destruction is next!"

Godlike Alexandros then said to him: "Hector, you have
in mind to blame one who is not blameworthy. At other times,
yes, I may have withdrawn from the war, but my mother bore
765 me not as a coward. From the time that you stirred up battle
for your comrades beside the ships, we have remained
steadfast here and mixed, deadly, with the Danaäns
without cease. As for the companions you ask about, they
are mostly dead. Only Deïphobos and the powerful prince Helenos
770 have departed, both wounded in the arm by the long spears.
But the son of Kronos has warded off death. Now lead
where your heart and spirit leads you. We will follow along
eagerly, and I don't think we will fall short in valor, but fight
as we are able. No man can fight beyond his strength,
775 no matter how keen."

So speaking, the warrior Paris turned
his brother's mind. They set off to where the din of battle
was greatest, around Kebriones and blameless Poulydamas.
And Phalkes and Orthaios and godlike Polyphetes. And Palmys
and Askanios and Morys, son of Hippotion, who had
780 come to relieve their companions from Askania, with its deep soil,
just the morning before—and now Zeus roused them to fight.°

They went like a blast of savage wind that rushes down
upon the earth, accompanied by the thunder of father Zeus,
and with a wondrous howl mixes with the salt sea,
785 and in its track are many bubbling waves of the turbulent sea,
arched, specked with white, some in the front, some following—
even so the Trojans, packed tightly together, some in the front,
some following, all glittering with bronze, followed their leaders.

---

781 ... to fight: The action now returns to the center where Poulydamas and Hector's brother and charioteer,
Kebriones, followed Hector's earlier orders to assemble warriors to fight. The supernumeraries Phalkes,
Morys, and Hippotion all die in Book 14, along with a Periphetes (here Polyphetes). The death of Hippotion
seems a slip, because here he is mentioned simply as the father of Morys. Askania is someplace in PHRYGIA,
but they must have arrived earlier than the day before because Askanios is mentioned in the Catalog of Ships.

Hector, son of Priam, was in the lead, like man-destroying
Ares. He held his shield before him, equal on all sides,   790
made of thick ox-hide with added bronze. His shining helmet
shimmered around his temples. Everywhere on this side
and that he strode forward and made trial of the battalions,
to see if they would give way as he advanced under cover of his shield.
But he could confound no hearts in the breasts of the Achaeans.   795

Ajax was the first to call him out, not mincing words:
"Hey, tough fellow, come closer! Do you really believe
you can make the Argives fearful? We are in no way ignorant
of battle—only by the evil stroke of Zeus were we Achaeans
beaten down. Doubtless you have great hopes to destroy   800
our ships, but we have hands and the will to defend them.
It's much more likely that your own well-peopled city will fall
and be laid waste by our hands. And I think the time
is near when you will flee and pray to father Zeus and the other
deathless ones that your horses with fine coats be swifter   805
than falcons—those horses that carry you through the dust
over the plain to the city!"

                    Even as he spoke a bird
flew across his right hand, a high-flying eagle. The army
of the Achaeans cried aloud, cheered by the omen.° But glorious
Hector answered thus: "Ajax, you are a rash speaker,   810
a bully—so you say! As I would like to be the son
of Zeus who carries the goatskin fetish, and my mother
be the revered Hera, and as I would like to be honored as Athena
and Apollo—so may this day bear a great evil for all the Argives!
And you too shall die. Stick around and my long spear   815
will feast on your lily-white skin. Yes, and you will glut
the dogs and birds of the Trojans with your fat and your flesh
when you fall amid the ships of the Achaeans!"

                    So Hector spoke
and led the way forward. The Trojans followed after him
with a wondrous din, and the people behind shouted assent.   820
And the Argives shouted from the other side, their valor
not misplaced. And so they withstood the best of the Trojans
as they came rushing on. And the clamor of both sides
traveled to the upper air and the eye-rays of Zeus.

---

809   *omen:* Bird omens always come true in the *Iliad.*

BOOK 14. *Zeus Deceived*

Nestor, although he was drinking his wine, still heard
the cry of battle,° and he spoke words that went
like arrows to the son of Asklepios: "Think, good Machaon,
how these things will be. The hotheaded youths
5 beside the ships shout louder still. But you—you
sit here now drinking the flaming wine until Hekamedê
with the lovely hair heats up a warm bath to wash
away your bloody gore, while I must go to a
lookout site to see what's what out there."

                                  So speaking,
10 Nestor took up the gleaming bronze shield of his son
horse-taming Thrasymedes that lay in the hut.°
For the son had taken his father's shield. Nestor took up
a mighty spear, tipped with sharp bronze, and he stood
outside his hut, where he beheld a work of shame—Achaeans
15 driven back in rout and the high-hearted Trojans pursuing
them … and the wall of the Achaeans utterly knocked down!

As when the great sea heaves with a soundless swell,
trying vainly to foresee the nimble paths of the shrill winds,
its waves rolling aimlessly this way or that until a decisive wind

---

2 *cry of battle*: By a convention of epic storytelling, Homer presents simultaneous scenes as happening
sequentially. Thus Nestor in his tent, here drinking with Machaon and served by Hekamedê, goes back to
Book 12 *before* the intercession of Poseidon, when the Greeks are in disorder and the Trojans are advancing.
The cry that Nestor hears is the same one at the end of Book 12 (line 437: "An endless tumult arose").
This is why Nestor is still drinking in Book 14, which he began in Book 12. Here is an outline of earlier and
upcoming events, with the simultaneous events indented and italicized:
> breaking down of the rampart (end of Book 12)
> > *arrival of Poseidon (beginning of Book 13)*
> battle leading to Hector's duel with Ajax (end of Book 13)
> > *council of the captains (beginning of Book 14)*
> > *deception of Zeus and aftermath (middle of Book 14)*
> Hector's duel with Ajax (end of Book 14)

11 *in the hut*: Thrasymedes, the son of Nestor, lent his shield to Diomedes the night before during the Doloneia
(Book 10), because Diomedes forgot to bring his own shield. Then Thrasymedes was obliged to borrow his
father's shield. In the meanwhile, Diomedes must have returned the borrowed shield. Such cross-references
to small details suggest that the Doloneia was part of the original poem. Thrasymedes has not yet appeared
in the fighting.

comes down from Zeus°—even so the old man pondered,   20
his mind divided this way and that, whether he should go forth
into the crowd of the Danaäns with their swift horses,
or whether he should go find Agamemnon, shepherd of the people.
Thus he pondered, and then it seemed the better course to go
after the son of Atreus. But the others went on fighting and killing   25
one another. The unyielding bronze clanged about their bodies
as they stabbed at one another with their swords and their
two-edged spears.

       Nestor met up with the god-nourished captains
as they went up from the ships, all those who were wounded
by Trojan bronze—Diomedes and Odysseus and Agamemnon,   30
the son of Atreus.° The ships were drawn up a good distance
from the battle on the shore of the gray sea. They had drawn up
the first ships and beached them toward the plain, and they built
the wall near their sterns. But the beach was not wide enough
to hold all the ships. The army was crowded, so they drew them   35
up in rows in a curve around the entire shore of the deep bay
between the two headlands.

       The captains, leaning on their spears,
were traveling in a body to see what was going on in the war
and the battle. What they saw pained their hearts. Old man Nestor
met them and he startled the hearts in their breasts. Lifting up   40
his voice, King Agamemnon spoke to him: "O Nestor,
son of Neleus, great glory of the Achaeans, why have
you left the man-destroying war and come here? I am afraid
that mighty Hector has made good his word when he threatened,
speaking among the Trojans,° that he would not return to Ilion   45
from the ships before he had burned them with fire and killed
all our men. So he said, and now that is coming to pass.
Surely, I fear, the other Achaeans who wear fancy shinguards
are storing up anger in their hearts, just like Achilles,
and do not want to fight at the sterns of the ships."   50

---

20 *down from Zeus*: The image is of a turbulent sea that takes no particular direction, "vainly foreseeing the nimble paths of the shrill winds," until a strong wind gives the sea a firm direction. Even so Nestor at first cannot make up his mind, then he does.

31 *son of Atreus*: All three were wounded in Book 11.

45 *the Trojans*: How would Agamemnon know what Hector said to the Trojans? By convention, if the audience knows, then the characters in the story know too.

Then Gerenian Nestor, the horseman, answered him:
"Yes, these things have happened, nor could Zeus himself,
who thunders from on high, make them otherwise. For the wall
has been broken down in which we placed our trust, that it would be
55 an unbreakable defense for ourselves and our ships. The enemy
is at our swift ships and conducting a pitiless campaign.
Nor could you tell any more, though you looked closely,
from what side the Achaeans are driven in rout, so mixed up
do they die, and the war cries reach the sky. Let us say how these
60 things will be, if any scheme will do any good. But I do not
suggest that *we* ourselves enter the war—in no way may
a wounded man ever do battle!"

                    The king of men, Agamemnon,
then answered him: "Nestor, because they are fighting
at the sterns of the ships, and the wall is breached, nor is
65 the ditch at which the Danaäns worked so hard of any use,
though they hoped it would be an unbreakable defense of the ships
and the men. It seems sure that almighty Zeus has decided
to let the Achaeans perish here, far from Argos, without
a name. I knew it when he willingly helped the Danaäns,
70 but I know now that he gives honor to the Trojans as if they were
the blessed gods, and he has bound-up all of our might.
      "But come now, you should be persuaded to do what I say:
Let us drag all the ships that are in the first row down to the sea,
and let us draw them all into the bright sea and moor them
75 in the deep water with anchor stones until the immortal night
comes, if the Trojans at that point will hold back from war.
Then we can launch *all* the ships, for I see nothing shameful
in fleeing destruction, not even though it is night. It is better
that one flee destruction and escape than to be taken!"

80   But resourceful Odysseus, glaring from beneath his brows,
said: "Son of Atreus, what words have escaped from the fence
of your teeth! Accursed man, would that you commanded
some other inglorious army and did not rule us,
to whom Zeus has given from our youth up to old age
85 to wind into a ball the yarn of grievous war, until we perish
every man.° Do you really mean to flee the city
of the Trojans with its broad streets on account of which

---

86 *every man*: The rather obscure image evokes the thread that constitutes one's fate, now wound into a ball.

we have suffered terrible wounds and losses? Just be quiet,
so that no other of the Achaeans hears these words, which no man
should ever allow to pass through his mouth—any man   90
who knows in his heart to speak what is right, who is a
sceptered king whom so many people obey as obey you,
the king of the Argives. As you blather, I despise altogether
your thought, the things you have said—asking us, when the war
and the cry of war is all around us, to launch the ships   95
with fine benches into the sea! Thus what the Trojans prayed for
may come to pass: to put us to rout. Already they are winning,
about to bring sheer destruction upon us. For the Achaeans
won't stay in the fight once the ships are launched, but they too
will look to flee, pulling back from the fight. Then your counsel   100
will prove our destruction. Some shepherd of the people you are!"

    The king of men, Agamemnon, answered: "O Odysseus,
you have moved my heart with your harsh reproach.
It's now certain I won't urge the sons of the Achaeans *against*
their will to drag down the ships with fine benches into the sea.   105
I wish that someone, young or old, could come up with a better
plan—that would be most welcome ..."

                   Then Diomedes, good
at the war cry, said: "That man stands near you. You shall
not seek him for long, if you are willing to be persuaded
and are not indignant and angry, every one of you, because I am   110
the youngest among you in years. But I can boast a fine father,
Tydeus, whom the heaped-up earth covers in Thebes.°
For to Portheus three excellent sons were born, who lived
in Pleuron and in steep KALYDON—Agrios and Melas
and third was the horseman Oineus, the father of my father.   115
Oineus was the utmost in valor among them. He remained
in Kalydon, but my father Tydeus wandered to ARGOS
and settled there,° for it was the will of Zeus and the other gods.
Tydeus married one of the daughters of Adrastos,° and he lived

---

112   *in Thebes*: Tydeus was one of the Seven Against Thebes. Homer omits, however, the unflattering story of
      Tydeus' eating the brains of Melanippos, one of the defenders of Thebes, as Tydeus lay dying. Discovering
      him in the act, Athena refused to give Tydeus the immortality she had planned. The story was told in the
      lost epic the *Thebaïd*, attributed (perhaps rightly) to Homer himself.

118   *settled there*: After Tydeus killed one of his relatives in Kalydon, or several of them. His "wandering" is
      really a forced exile. Tydeus and Meleager (Book 9) have the same father, Oineus.

119   *Adrastos*: Leader of the disastrous expedition of the Seven Against Thebes.

120 in a house rich in substance. He had an abundance
     of wheat-bearing fields and many orchards around him,
     and many herds too. He surpassed all the Achaeans in his use
     of the spear. You probably have heard these things, whether or not
     I speak the truth. Therefore you ought not say that I am of low birth
125 and cowardly and fail to honor the council that I give you,
     if it is well spoken.
                         "So come! Let us go up to the war,
     though wounded, because it is what we must do. Let us hold back,
     however, from the fight, away from the missiles, so that
     we don't pile wound on wound. But we will spur on the others
130 and send them forth to battle, those who before have indulged
     in resentment and have stood aloof and do not fight."

     So Diomedes spoke, and they listened to him and agreed. They set off
     and Agamemnon, the king of men, led them. The famous earth-shaker
     kept no blind watch, but he went among them in the likeness
135 of an old man. He took hold of the right hand of Agamemnon,
     the son of Atreus, and he spoke to him words that went
     like arrows: "Son of Atreus, surely now the resentful heart
     of Achilles is happy to see the death and rout of the Achaeans,
     for he has no understanding, not even a little. Well,
140 may he come to ruin soon, and a god bring him down!
     But the blessed gods are still not angry with *you*. Even yet
     the leaders and rulers of the Trojans may make the broad
     plain dusty with their flight, and you yourself will see them
     driven in rout toward the city, away from our ships and our tents."

145 So speaking, Poseidon shouted loudly as he sped over
     the plain. As loud as nine or ten thousand men shout in the battle
     when they join in the strife of Ares, even so loud did the lord,
     the shaker of the earth, shout from his breast. In the heart
     of every Achaean he cast great strength, to make war
150 and to fight without cease.

◀ϗ   Now Hera, whose throne is golden,
     saw Poseidon as she stood on a peak of Olympos. Right away
     she recognized Poseidon busying himself with the battle
     in which men win glory—her own brother and her husband's
     brother—and she rejoiced in her heart. Then she saw Zeus sitting
155 on the topmost peak of Ida with its many fountains, and he
     seemed hateful to her in her heart. Then cow-eyed revered
     Hera pondered how she might charm the mind of the bearer
     of the goatskin fetish. In her heart this seemed the best plan:

to go to Ida after making herself alluring, to see
if Zeus might desire to embrace her flesh and lie   160
by her side in love so that she might pour out harmless
gentle sleep over his eyes and quell his wily mind.

She entered her chamber, which her son Hephaistos had
made for her. He had fitted thick doors into the doorposts with
a secret bolt that no other god could open. She went inside   165
and closed the shining doors. First of all she cleansed
her lovely skin with ambrosia° and washed away
every defilement. She anointed herself with a rich oil,
ambrosial, sweet, with a lovely fragrance. If this
were shaken in the house of Zeus with its bronze threshold,   170
the scent would reach to the earth and the wide heaven alike.
With this she anointed her beautiful skin. She combed
her hair and with her hands plaited her bright tresses,
beautiful and ambrosial, that fell from her imperishable head.
She put about her an ambrosial robe that Athena had scraped   175
into a finished product,° and placed on it many beautiful
embroideries. This she pinned around her breast with golden
pins. She bound a belt fitted with a hundred tassels
about her waist. In her pierced ears she placed earrings
with three drops shaped like mulberries. A great grace   180
shone from them. Then the bright goddess covered her head
with a kerchief over all—sparkling, brand-new, white
like the sun. She bound beautiful sandals beneath her shining feet.

When she had decked out her body with every adornment,
she went forth from the chamber and called Aphrodite apart   185
from the other gods, and she spoke to her these words:
"Will you obey me, my child, and do what I am about to request?
Or will you refuse me because you hold anger in your heart
because I give aid to the Danaäns and you to the Trojans?"

Then Aphrodite, the daughter of Zeus, answered her: 190
"Hera, august goddess, daughter of great Kronos, say
what you are thinking. My heart urges me to accomplish it,
if I can accomplish it and in fact it can be done."

---

167   *ambrosia*: "immortal," the food of the gods as *nectar* is their drink. Ambrosia prevents death and decay and
      is used to embalm the dead. The immortals also use ambrosia to cleanse their skin, as mortals use olive oil.
      This amusing scene parodies the arming of a warrior as he prepares to go out on an *aristeia*.

176   *finished product*: The cloth was scraped either to make it smooth or to form a nap on its surface.

The revered Hera answered her, with crafty thought:
195 "Give me now love and desire, by which you overcome
all the deathless ones and mortal men too. For I am about
to visit the limits of the much-nourishing earth, and Ocean,
the origin of the gods, and mother Tethys, who nourished
and reared me in their home. They received me from Rhea when
200 far-thundering Zeus shoved Kronos down beneath the earth
and the murmuring sea.° I am going to pay them a visit, and I hope
to resolve their quarreling without respite. For a long time
they have held aloof from the marriage bed and from lovemaking,
because anger has invaded their hearts. If by my words I might
205 persuade the hearts of these two, and bring them back
to be joined in lovemaking, then I might forever be cherished
and thus be honored by them."

                    Aphrodite, who loves laughter,
then answered her: "It is not right that I deny you, for you sleep
in the arms of Zeus, the greatest of us all." So speaking,
210 she unfastened from her breasts an ornate decorated strap
in which all kinds of spells° were fashioned. In it
were lovemaking, and desire, and the murmuring of sweet
nothings that steal the wits of even the wise. Aphrodite
placed it in Hera's hands and spoke and addressed her:
215 "There, place this embroidered strap against your breasts.
In it are all things fashioned. And I do not think
that you will return without accomplishing the goal
that you have in mind."

                    So she spoke, and the revered Hera,
with eyes like a cow, smiled, and then smiling she placed
220 the gift against her breasts. Aphrodite, the daughter of Zeus,
went to her house while Hera darted down and left
the peak of OLYMPOS. Hera stepped on Pieria and lovely
Emathia, and sped to the topmost peaks of the snowy
mountains of the Thracian horsemen. Her feet did not touch

---

201 *murmuring sea*: Homer refers to a different cosmogony from that familiar in Hesiod's *Theogony*, where first
     came Chaos; then Earth; then the offspring of Earth and Ocean, the Titans; then the Olympians, who
     under Zeus's leadership overthrew the Titans under Kronos' leadership, a victory to which Hera refers.
     Evidently Homer has heard the Mesopotamian story wherein the first gods were Apsu (Ocean, the fresh
     water) and Tiamat (Tethys, the salt water) so that all the world descends from these primordial waters. It is
     not clear why Rhea, Hera's mother and Kronos' consort, gave her to Ocean and Tethys to be raised.

211 *kinds of spells*: There has been much speculation about the nature of this amulet. It is not a belt, but perhaps
     a strap that went over one shoulder, between the breasts, and under the other arm, to judge from artistic
     representations of nude, Near Eastern fertility goddesses.

the ground. Then from ATHOS she stepped onto the swelling   225
sea and came to LEMNOS, the city of the godlike
Thoas.° There she met Sleep, the brother of Death.

She took him by the hand and addressed him: "Sleep,
lord of all the gods and all men, if ever you hearkened
to my word, obey me now, and I will owe you thanks   230
for all my days. Put the shining eyes of Zeus
to sleep beneath his brows right after I lie with him
in love. I will give you the gift of a beautiful imperishable
throne made of gold. Hephaistos, my own son, the god
with crippled feet, will fashion it with skill, and he will place   235
a footstool under it for your feet. You will be able
to rest your shining feet upon it at the banquet."

Sweet Sleep then answered her: "Hera, august goddess,
daughter of great Kronos, another of the gods that last
forever I might easily put to sleep, even the streams of the river   240
Ocean who is the origin of them all. But I would
not come near the son of Kronos, nor lull him to sleep,
unless he himself urged me. For I remember another time
one of your commands pricked me on—that day
when Herakles, that mighty son of Zeus, sailed   245
from Ilion after he sacked the city of the Trojans. For I put
to sleep the mind of Zeus who carries the goatskin fetish,
pouring sweetly my potion about him while you devised
evil in your heart. You raised up the blasts of savage
winds over the sea, and then you carried Herakles   250
to the well-peopled island of KOS, far from his loved ones.
When Zeus woke up he was more than angry and tossed the gods
all around his house—but it was me he sought above all.
And he would have thrown me from the sky into the sea,
to be seen no more, if Night, the tamer of gods   255
and men, had not saved me. I came to her in flight,
and he left off a little, though he was angry. For he feared
that he might do something displeasing to swift Night.°

---

227   … *godlike Thoas*: Pieria is a district of southern MACEDONIA, north of Mt. Olympos. Emathia, "sandy," is the
        coast of Macedonia. THRACE is here rather west of where it is usually located. The peak of Mt. Athos reaches
        to over 6,600 feet (since medieval times the site of famous monasteries). The grandson of Thoas ("swifty"),
        Euneos ("good with ships"), traded with the Achaeans in wine, metals, hides, Phoenician handiwork, and
        slaves (Book 23). Euneos was the son of Jason, the Argonaut, and Hypsipylē, the daughter of Thoas.

258   *swift Night*: Sleep refers to Herakles' earlier sack of Troy, already mentioned in Book 5. Hera was the implacable
        persecutor of Herakles, presumably because he was fathered by Zeus on a mortal woman. Sleep never says why the
        island of Kos, off the southwest coast of Asia Minor, was a dangerous place, or what happened to Herakles there.

And now, again, you urge me to do something else
260　that is impossible!"

　　　　　　　The revered Hera with cow eyes then answered
him: "Sleep, why do you ponder these matters in your heart?
Do you think that far-thundering Zeus will help the Trojans
just as he became angry on account of his own son
Herakles? Come—I will give you one of the youthful
265　Graces to marry and to be called your wife."

　　　　　　　　　　　　So she spoke.
Sleep was glad for her words and answered: "Come now,
swear to me by the inviolable water of Styx. With one hand
lay hold of the bountiful earth and with the other the shining
sea, so that one and all they may be witnesses between
270　the two of us—I mean the gods who are below with Kronos—
that truly you will give me one of the younger Graces—
Pasithea, whom I myself have longed for all my days."°

　　So he spoke, and white-armed Hera did not refuse.
She swore just as he asked, and she called on all the gods
275　below in Tartaros, who are called the Titans.° When she had sworn
and completed the oath, the two of them left the cities
of LEMNOS and IMBROS and, clothed in a mist, sped swiftly
on their way. They came to IDA, the mother of wild animals,
with its many fountains, then to Lekton, where they left
280　the sea. The two of them went over the dry land
and the tops of the trees shook beneath their feet. There Sleep
waited out of sight of Zeus, hidden in a high fir tree,
the highest on Ida, which reached through the mists into the sky.
There he perched, in the form of a shrill-voiced mountain bird
285　which the gods call Chalkis, but men call Kymindis,° hidden
by the dense needles of fir trees.

272　*all my days*: An oath sworn by the underworld river Styx ("hateful") cannot be broken. The "gods below"
　　with Kronos are the Titans, imprisoned there after their war with the Olympians, a story told in Hesiod's
　　Theogony. The Graces (*Charites*), usually three in number, were the embodiment of feminine charm.
　　Pasithea means "all-divine."

275　*the Titans*: This is the only time that Homer mentions the Titans by name. Tartaros, a word of unknown
　　meaning, is the deepest part of the underworld.

285　*Kymindis*: The Kymindis was a kind of large owl. Gods seem to have a more elevated speech than men, but
　　otherwise in myth Chalkis was the mortal woman after whom the famous city of CHALCIS on the island of
　　Euboea was named.

FIGURE 14.1 **The wedding of Zeus and Hera.** The scene is depicted on a metope (a square sculpture on a frieze) from the gigantic temple to Hera (the so-called temple E) at Selinus, at the southwestern tip of Sicily. Selinus ("parsley") was the westernmost of the Greek cities in Sicily and destroyed by the Carthaginians in 409 BC. A half-naked Zeus, sitting on a rock, clasps the wrist of Hera. One of her breasts is exposed as Hera removes her head covering in a traditional gesture of sexual submission. c. 540 BC

Hera quickly advanced
to Gargaros, the highest peak of lofty Ida. Zeus
the cloud-gatherer saw her. He saw her and lust overran
his wise heart, just as when first they lay together
290 in love, going to the couch without the knowledge
of their parents.

He stood before her and spoke, addressing her:
"Hera, with what desire have you come here from Olympos?
Your horses are not at hand, nor your chariot for you to mount."

With crafty mind the revered Hera answered:
295 "I have come to visit the limits of the much-nourishing earth,
and Ocean, the origin of the gods, and mother Tethys,
who nourished and reared me in their home. I am going
to pay them a visit, and I hope to resolve this endless
quarreling of theirs. For a long time they have held aloof
300 from the marriage bed and from lovemaking, because anger has
taken their hearts. My horses stand at the foot of Ida
with its many fountains. They will carry me over the solid
land and the watery sea. But now it is on your
account that I have come down here from Olympos, so that
305 you will not become angry with me afterwards, if I go
without saying anything to the house of deep-flowing Ocean."

Zeus the cloud-gatherer then answered her: "Hera,
you can always go there later, but for now let the two
of us take delight, going to bed and making love.
310 For never yet has the desire for goddess or mortal woman
so poured itself about me and overmastered my heart
in my breast—no, not when I lusted after the wife of Ixion,
who bore Peirithoös, a counselor equal to the gods.
Nor when I desired Danaë of the delicate ankles,
315 the daughter of Akrisios who bore Perseus, preeminent above
all men. Nor when I longed for the far-famed daughter
of Phoinix, who bore Minos and godlike Rhadamanthys. Not even
when I fell in love with Semelê, nor Alkmenê in Thebes,
who gave birth to strong-minded Herakles as her son. And Semelê
320 bore Dionysos, a joy to mortals. Nor when I loved queen Demeter,
who has beautiful tresses. Not even when I loved famous Leto—

nor even yourself! as now I long for you and sweetest desire
possesses me."°

        The revered Hera answered him with crafty
words: "Most dread son of Kronos, what words you've spoken!
If you want to make love on the peaks of Ida, where everything   325
is out in open, how would it be if some one of the gods,
whose race is forever, should peep at us as we sleep and then
go tell all the gods? Then I could not rise up from the bed
and go to your house—it would be too shameful! But if you want
and it is your desire, there is always your chamber, which your dear   330
son Hephaistos made for you, and fitted with strong doors
to the door-posts. Let us go and lie down there, since the couch
is your pleasure."

        The cloud-gatherer Zeus then answered her:
"Hera, have no fear that the gods or men will see! I will wrap
a cloud about us, a golden cloud. Not even Helios° could see   335
through it, he whose sight is the keenest for seeing things."

He spoke and the son of Kronos clasped his wife in his arms.
Beneath them the shining earth made the luxuriant grass
to grow, and lotus covered with dew, and crocus, and thick
and tender hyacinth that bore them up from the ground.   340
The two lay there and were covered in a cloud—beautiful, golden!—
from which fell drops of dew. And so the father slept peacefully
on the peak of Gargaros, overcome by sleep and love.
Thus he held his wife in his arms.

---

323   ... *possesses me*: This hilarious scene is predicated on the *hieros gamos*, "sacred marriage," when sexual inter-
       course took place between someone impersonating the storm-god and someone impersonating the mother-
       goddess, a fertility ritual prominent in the temples of the Near East and, probably, in Corinth and on the
       island of Cythera south of the Peloponnesus (where Aphrodite, the "Cytherean," was said to have been born).
       But Homer has changed this catalog of women into a delightful parody sure to amuse his all-male
       audience: a husband trying to seduce his wife by listing all the women by whom he has betrayed her! Ixion
       was himself a notorious rapist who lusted after Hera, then ejaculated his semen into a cloud that took her
       shape and so begot the Centaurs, who raped the women at Peirithoös' wedding. Zeus came to Ixion's wife as
       a stallion and begot Peirithoös ("very swift"); later Peirithoös tried to rape Persephone but was entrapped in
       the lower world. Zeus came to Danaë as a shower of gold that fell into her prison chamber. The daughter of
       Phoinix is Europa, whom Zeus carried to Crete from Phoenicia in the form of a bull and there possessed her.
       Her son Minos became king of CRETE and his brother Rhadamanthys a judge in the underworld. Zeus ap-
       peared to Semelê while pregnant in the form that he appeared to Hera—a thunderbolt!—and burned her to a
       crisp; Dionysos was brought to term by being sewn into Zeus's thigh. Zeus appeared to Alkmenê disguised as
       her husband, but her husband impregnated her on the same night so that she gave birth to one son fathered by
       Zeus, Herakles, and another son fathered by her husband. Zeus begot Persephonê with Demeter. Hera drove
       Leto all over the earth before she gave birth to Apollo and Artemis on the Aegean island of DELOS.

335   *Helios*: Ordinarily the sun-god Helios sees all things.

But sweet Sleep set out on a run
345 to the ships of the Achaeans, bearing the news to the earth-holder,
the shaker of the earth. Standing close he spoke words
that went like arrows: "Poseidon! Go now with enthusiasm
to the aid of the Danaäns and grant them glory, though it is
for a short time only—only so long as Zeus is asleep. For I have poured
350 a soft slumber over him. Hera has deceived him into lying
in his bed in love."

So speaking, Sleep went off to the glorious
tribes of men, and pressed Poseidon still more
to come to the aid of the Danaäns. Quickly Poseidon
leaped among the foremost fighters and cried aloud:° "Argives,
355 are we again to yield victory to Hector, the son of Priam?
Should we let him capture our ships and win all the glory?
He boasts that he will do it because Achilles still stays out of the fight
beside the hollow ships, churning anger in his heart. But we
will not miss that man so much if the rest of us get better
360 organized, turning to help one another. Come all,
do what I say. Let us dress ourselves in the shields that are
the best in the camp and the largest. Let us conceal our heads
in gleaming helmets! Let us take in our hands spears that
are longest, and go forth! I will lead the way. I do not think
365 that Hector, the son of Priam, will long withstand our attack,
though he is eager. And whichever man is tough in the fight—
if he has a small shield on his shoulder, let him give it to a lesser
man and take up a bigger shield."

So he spoke, and all heard him
well and obeyed. The captains themselves, although wounded,
370 placed themselves in order—Tydeus and Odysseus and Agamemnon,
the son of Atreus. Going through the army, they swapped
their gear of war. A good man donned good armor
and gave lesser armor to a lesser man. When they arranged
the pitiless bronze about their bodies, they set out.
375 Poseidon shaker of the earth led them, holding in his strong
hand a dreaded long-edged sword, quick lightning, against
which no one would advance in battle, held back by fear.

On the other side, glorious Hector again deployed
the Trojans. Then dark-haired Poseidon and glorious

---

354 *cried aloud*: It is not clear what form Poseidon is taking, but his vigor ill suits the appearance of "an old
man" (line 135), his earlier form.

Hector stretched the cords of the dread strife of war, the one   380
bearing aid to the Trojans, and the other to the Argives.
The sea rushed up against the tents and the ships of the Argives
as the two sides clashed with a mighty din.° Not so loudly
does the wave of the sea roar against the dry land,
driven from the deep by the blast of the terrible North Wind,   385
nor so loud is the bellow of blazing fire in the woods
of the mountains when it leaps to burn the forest, nor so loud
does the wind shriek around the high-leafed oaks when raging
most in its anger, as then were the terrifying screams
of the Trojans and Achaeans when they set upon one another,   390
shrieking taunts.

    First of all glorious Hector fired at Ajax
with his spear when Ajax turned full toward him. Nor did he miss,
but he hit him where the two straps were stretched across his chest,
one strap of his shield, the other of his silver-studded sword.
They protected his tender flesh. Hector was angry because   395
his swift weapon had flown from his hand in vain, and he backed
off into the crowd of his companions, avoiding fate.

    But as he pulled back, great Telamonian Ajax hit him with
a rock—there were many propping the fast ships, rolling under
the feet of the men as they fought. Lifting up one of them, Ajax   400
hit Hector on the chest above the shield rim, near his neck.
Hector whirled like a top from the blow, spinning round
and round. As when an oak falls uprooted by the blow of father Zeus
and the terrible stench of sulfur arises from it—the man
who sees it up close loses all his courage, for the thunderbolt   405
of great Zeus is mighty—even so the powerful Hector
fell at once to the ground in the dust. His spear fell from
his hand. He was covered on top by his shield and helmet,
and around him rang his armor, decorated with bronze.

    Shouting loudly, the sons of the Achaeans ran up, hoping   410
to drag Hector off, and they cast their spears in a thick rain.
But no one was able to wound the shepherd of the people
by thrusting or throwing, for the best of the Trojans stood up
to guard him: Poulydamas and Aeneas and good Agenor
and Sarpedon, leader of the Lycians, and the blameless   415

---

383 *mighty din*: The uproar of the two sides clashing returns us to the exact moment in Book 13
    (lines 823–824) when Ajax's duel with Hector was interrupted; there the two sides also roared. Now at last
    Ajax and Hector meet. The curious episode of the captains' exchange of armor is a kind of arming scene,
    which always precedes an *aristeia*, but here it involves the whole army.

FIGURE 14.2 The duel between Hector and Ajax.   Hector falls to his knees as Ajax stabs him with his spear—unlike in Homer's text, in which Ajax hits him with a stone. To the right of the illustration, Aeneas comes to the rescue. Ajax wears a linen breastplate and bronze plumed helmet and shinguards. Hector wears a plumed helmet and shinguards but is otherwise "heroically nude." Hector's shield has an unusual design, perhaps a basket on its side filled with flowers. The figures are labeled in Corinthian script. Corinthian black-figure wine-jug, c. 570.

Glaukos.° The others saw what had happened to Hector,
and they held their round shields about him, and his comrades
lifted him up and carried him away from the labor of war
until they reached his swift horses that stood at the rear of
the battle and the war, waiting along with his charioteer,   420
fancily decked out. They carried him to the city, groaning
deeply. When they came to the ford of the swift-flowing river,
whirling Xanthos° whom deathless Zeus had begotten,
they lifted him from the chariot and placed him on the ground
and poured water over him. He came to and looked around.   425
Kneeling, he vomited black blood. Then he sank back
to the ground again and black night covered his eyes.
Ajax' blow had stifled his spirit.

                    When the Argives saw
Hector leaving the field, they rushed more aggressively
against the Trojans, mindful of the savage war.   430
Then swift Oïlean Ajax immediately wounded Satnios,
son of Enops, leaping on him with his sharp spear. A blameless
naiad nymph conceived Satnios as Enops tended his herds
beside the banks of the Satnioeis.° The famous son of Oïleus
drew up close and stabbed him between the ribs and his hip.   435
Satnios fell backwards as around him Trojans and Danaäns
contended in vicious struggle.

                    Poulydamas, son of Panthoös, wielder
of the spear, came to the defense. He hit Prothoënor, the son
of Areïlykos, in the right shoulder, driving the strong spear
through his shoulder. Prothoënor fell in the dust   440
and gripped the earth with his palm. Poulydamas stood over him,
shouting a gruesome boast: "I think that once again
the spear of the great-hearted son of Panthoös has sped
truly from his powerful hand! One of the Argives

---

416   ... *blameless Glaukos*: These are the Trojan fighters active in Book 13, except for the Lycians, last seen in
        Book 12. Glaukos, shot by Teucer in Book 12, still suffers from his wound in Book 16. Probably Homer
        forgot about Glaukos' earlier wound, or we are to suppose that Glaukos is fighting wounded.

423   *Xanthos*: The first mention of the ford of the Xanthos (another name for the Skamandros). Homer is casual
        about the topography of the Trojan plain; nowhere before is it stated that the Trojans must cross the
        Xanthos to reach the line of battle. Zeus may be called the "father of Xanthos" in the sense that the rain
        feeds it, but Ocean is the father of all rivers.

434   *Satnioeis*: Satnios is named after the river. His father's name means "brilliant" (Enops). The naiad
        ("flowing") nymphs ("young girls") were a type of water spirit who presided over freshwater fountains,
        wells, springs, and streams.

445 has got it stuck in his flesh, and I think that leaning
on it as support he will go into the house of Hades!"

So he spoke, and pain came to the Argives. Especially
he stirred the martial spirit of Ajax, son of Telamon, who stood
nearby where Prothoënor fell. Swiftly Ajax threw
450 his shining spear as Poulydamas backed off. Poulydamas
himself leaped to the side, avoiding black death.
But Big Ajax hit Archelochos, the son of Antenor,
for the gods had willed his death. Ajax struck him
where the head joins the neck, on the topmost joint
455 of the spine, and he sheered off both the sinews. His head
and mouth and nose reached the ground far quicker, as he fell,
than his legs and knees.

Ajax then called aloud
to blameless Poulydamas: "Tell me Poulydamas, say the truth,
whether this man was not worthy to be struck down in exchange
460 for Prothoënor? He does not seem to me to be of low birth,
nor descended from men of low birth, but the brother of horse-taming
Antenor, or his son. For he seems to be just like him in build."

So Ajax spoke, knowing full well the truth, as pain took hold
of the spirits of the Trojans. Then Akamas, standing over his brother
465 Archelochos, stabbed Promachos from Boeotia with his spear.
Promachos was trying to drag Archelochos' body away
by the feet. Akamas boasted gruesomely, shouting aloud:
"You Argives who rage with bow and never cease your threats,
the labor of war and woe will not be on us alone,
470 for you too shall die in the same way. Consider how your
Promachos sleeps, beaten down by my spear. Revenge
for my brother Archelochos was not long in coming.
Thus a man prays that a kinsman be left in his halls
as a warder-off of ruin."

So Akamas spoke, and pain came to the Argives
475 as he boasted. Especially he stirred up the heart of martial Peneleös,
who rushed on Akamas. But Akamas did not await the charge
of Peneleös the king. Instead Peneleös stabbed Ilioneus, son of Phorbas,
rich in herds, whom Hermes loved above all the Trojans
and gave him wealth. To Hermes his mother bore Ilioneus,
480 an only child. Peneleös stabbed him beneath the brow,
right through the roots of his eye, popping out the eyeball.
The spear went straight through the eye and came out through

the bone at the back of his head. Ilioneus thumped down,
spreading out both hands. Then Peneleös drew his sharp sword,
driving straight at the middle of Ilioneus' neck. He struck off 485
his head. It hit the ground, still wearing its helmet, the strong spear
still stuck in his eye.

Holding the head up like the head of a poppy,
Peneleös showed it to the Trojans, crying out in boast:
"Hey you Trojans, tell the dear father and mother
of the good Ilioneus to wail in their halls! Neither 490
will the wife of Promachos, son of Alegenor, rejoice
at her dear husband's return, when we youths of the Achaeans
go back home from Troy in our ships." So he spoke,
and a trembling took hold of the limbs of all the Trojans,
each man looking around to see how he might escape dread 495
destruction.

Tell me now, you Muses who have houses on
Olympos, who first carried off the bloody warrior's spoils
when once the famous shaker of the earth had turned the battle?

Telamonian Ajax first stabbed Hyrtios, son of Gyrtios,
leader of the strong-hearted Mysians. Then Antilochos stripped 500
away the armor of Phalkes and Mermeros, and Meriones killed
Moros and Hippotion, and Teucer cut down Prothoön and Periphetes.
Then Menelaos, the son of Atreus, killed Hyperenor,
shepherd of the people, hitting him between the ribs and the thigh,
and the bronze let forth the guts as it sliced through his entrails. 505
His breath-soul sped on its way through the open wound
and darkness shuttered his eyes.° But Ajax, the swift son
of Oïleus, killed the most men. There was none other like him
to follow with speed of foot through the riot of men,
once Zeus had turned the Trojans in rout to flight.° 510

---

507 *his eyes*: The names of the warriors killed are mostly invented just for this gruesome scene.

510 *to flight*: Of course Zeus is on the side of the Trojans, but he turned them to flight in the sense that the will
of Zeus determines everything that happens.

BOOK 15. *Counterattack*

But when in flight the Trojans had crossed through the stakes
and the ditch, and many were overcome at the hands of the
Danaäns, then they were stopped and halted beside their cars,
pale white from fear—terrified. And Zeus awoke on the peaks
5 of Ida beside Hera of the golden throne. He sprang up, stood,
and saw the Trojans and the Achaeans contending, and the Trojans
being routed—the Argives were driving them out from the rear,
and among them was Poseidon the king. Zeus saw Hector
lying on the plain, and around him sat his companions. Hector
10 was gasping for breath, distraught in mind, vomiting blood,
for it was not the weakest of the Achaeans who had struck him!

Seeing Hector, the father of men and gods felt pity,
and looking out from beneath his brows he said this
to Hera: "Well Hera—impossible to deal with!—your evil
15 trickery has put Hector out of the battle. And you have driven
the Trojans in rout. I think that again you should be the first
to profit from your troublesome scheming—to be whipped for it!
Or do you not remember when I hung you up on high,
fastening two anvils to your feet, and around your wrists
20 I threw an unbreakable golden bond? And you hung in the air
and clouds. Then throughout high Olympos the gods were plenty
angry, but they could not come near and set you free.
Whomever I caught, I laid my hands upon him and threw him
from the threshold until he fell to the earth, all strength gone!
25 Even so, endless pain did not release my heart for godlike
Herakles, whom you, in league with blasts of North Wind,
sent across the barren sea, devising evil as you carried him
to well-peopled Kos. I saved him then and brought him again
to horse-pasturing Argos, after he had suffered many pains.
30 Let me remind you of these things so you might give up your
deceptions and see whether your lovemaking and the couch
are really of any use to you. You tricked me into it, coming
forth from among the gods!"

So he spoke, and cow-eyed revered Hera
shivered. Addressing him, she spoke words that went like arrows:
"May Earth be my witness, and the broad Sky above, and the water   35
of Styx that flows, which is the greatest and most solemn oath
among the blessed gods—and by your own holy head I swear,
and by the couch of the two of us by which I would truly never
forswear myself: Not by my will does Poseidon, the earth-shaker,
work harm to the Trojans and Hector, nor give aid to the Achaeans.   40
It is his own heart that urges and drives Poseidon. He has taken
pity on the Achaeans, seeing them worn down beside the ships.
But I would counsel even him to walk in the path where you,
O lord of the dark cloud, do lead."

So she spoke, and the father
of men and gods smiled, and in answer he spoke words   45
that went like arrows: "Well then, O cow-eyed revered Hera,
if you wish to sit among the deathless ones with thoughts
like mine, then I think that Poseidon would quickly reorder
his mind to follow your heart and mine, even if he doesn't like it.
But if you speak truly and frankly, go among the tribes   50
of the gods and summon Iris to come here, also Apollo famed
for his bow—so that Iris might go among the army of the
Achaeans, who wear shirts of bronze, and tell Poseidon the king
to stop interfering in the war and to get to his own house.
"As for Apollo, let him rouse up Hector to the fight. Let him   55
restore Hector's strength and make him forget the pain that tears
at his lungs. Let him again drive back the Achaeans when he has stirred
panic in them so that in flight they fall among the many benched
ships of Achilles, son of Peleus. Then he shall send out
his companion Patroklos. Shining Hector will kill him   60
with his spear before Ilion, after Patroklos has killed many other
young men, including my own son the godlike Sarpedon. Angered
because of Patroklos, godlike Achilles will then kill Hector.
After that I will cause a constant and steady retreat from the ships
until the Achaeans take high Ilion, through the plans of Athena.   65
Before that I will not give up my anger nor allow another of the
deathless ones to come to the aid of the Danaäns, before the desire
of the son of Peleus be fulfilled that I promised at the first,
and nodded my head to it, on that day when the goddess Thetis
took hold of my knees and begged me to give honor to Achilles,   70
the sacker of cities."°

---

71 *sacker of cities*: From time to time Homer give a précis and foretelling of the action to remind his listeners
    (and himself) of what the story is and where it is going.

So he spoke, and the goddess white-armed Hera
did not disobey. She went from the peaks of Ida to high Olympos.
As when the mind of a man who has traveled over far lands
darts about, and he forms a thought in his clever heart—
75 "Would that I were here, or there!"—and he conceives many wishes,
even so quickly the revered Hera sped on in her eagerness.
She arrived at steep Olympos and came to the deathless gods
gathered in the house of Zeus.

When they saw her, they all leaped up
and greeted her with cups of welcome. She passed over the others,
80 but took a cup from Themis who has beautiful cheeks.° For she came
running to her first, and spoke words that went like arrows:
"Hera, why have you come? You seem so distraught! It looks
as though the son of Kronos has frightened you, who are
his bedmate."

Then the goddess white-armed Hera
85 answered: "Please, Themis, do not ask me about these
things. You know yourself how he has a rough and aloof
manner. But do begin the feast in the house of the gods
and you will hear among all the deathless ones
what evil deed Zeus has done. I don't think most of you
90 will be glad, if perhaps someone is still feasting
with a light heart!"

So speaking, the revered Hera
took a seat. And the gods *were* angry in the house of Zeus.
Hera laughed with her lips, but her forehead above her dark
brows was cold. With indignation she spoke to all: "Fools!
95 We who are stupidly angry with Zeus! We should go up
close to him and stop him either by word or by force.
But he, sitting apart, doesn't care a bit—not a damn.
For he believes that he is the best of all in strength and power.
Therefore, just take whatever evil he sends to each
100 of you! For now I think that he has made great pain for Ares.
Ares' son, the dearest of men, has perished in battle—
Askalaphos, whom mighty Ares says is his own."

So she spoke, but Ares struck his lusty thighs
with the flat of his hands, and wailing he said: "Well,

---

80 *beautiful cheeks:* Themis, "law" or "order," presides over feasts. In fact *themis* can mean "feast." She has
friendly relations with Hera.

do not blame me, O dwellers on Olympos, if I go to the ships   105
of the Achaeans to avenge the death of my son! I don't
care if it is my fate to be struck by the bolt of Zeus
and to lie together with the dead amid the blood and the dust!"

    So he spoke, and he ordered Terror and Rout to yoke
his horses as he himself put on his shining armor. And then   110
a greater and more terrible rage would have been raised
between Zeus and the deathless ones, if Athena had not rushed
through the front doorway in fear for the gods, leaving the chair
where she sat. She took the helmet from his head and the shield
from his shoulders and the bronze spear from his powerful hand   115
and set it down. And then Athena rebuked the furious Ares:
"Madman, crazed fool—are you out of your mind! Have you ears
for hearing? Your wits are gone. You have no sense of shame.
Do you not hear what the goddess white-armed Hera is saying?
She who has just now come from Olympian Zeus? Or do you want   120
yourself to come back to Olympos *by force* after indulging
your pain, in spite of your grief, and for the rest of us sow
the seeds of terrible torment? Surely Zeus will leave the proud
Trojans and the Achaeans alone and cause havoc among us
on Olympos. He will seize each of us in turn, those who are at fault   125
and those who are not. So set aside your anger for your own son.
Before this time many greater in strength and might of hand
have perished, and more will yet perish. It is hard to preserve
the descent and offspring of all men!"

                            So speaking, Athena
made furious Ares sit in his chair. Then Hera summoned   130
Apollo to come outside the hall, also Iris the messenger
of the gods, and she spoke to them words that went like arrows:
"Zeus orders the two of you to come as quickly as possible.
And when you come and look upon the face of Zeus, then do
whatever he orders and commands."   135

                        After she had spoken
the revered Hera went back and took her seat in her chair,
but the two gods flew off in a rush. They came to Ida,
the mother of wild beasts with its many fountains. They found
the far-thundering son of Kronos sitting on the peak of Gargaros.
A fragrant cloud surrounded him. They came and stood   140
before Zeus who gathers the clouds. Seeing them, his heart
was not angry, because they had swiftly obeyed the words
of his dear wife.

He first addressed Iris with words
that went like arrows: "Go quickly, swift Iris, to Poseidon
145 the king and tell him all these things, and be sure you speak
truthfully. Command him to cease from battle and the war!
Let him go among the tribes of gods or into the shining sea.
If he will not obey my words, but pays them no attention,
let him consider in his heart and spirit that, no matter
150 if he is strong, he will not withstand my coming. I would
remind him that I am much greater in strength, and older
than he is. He seems to think it is nothing to say that he is my equal—
I, whom all the others dread!"

So he spoke, and swift Iris,
with feet like the wind, obeyed. She went down from the
155 mountains of Ida to sacred Ilion. As when snow or icy hail
flies from the clouds, driven by a blast from North Wind,
born in the clear air, even so swiftly did swift Iris
eagerly fly off.

Standing near, she spoke to the famous
shaker of the earth: "I have come here bearing a certain message,
160 O enfolder of the earth, O dark-haired one. Zeus has ordered
that you cease from the battle and the war and go into
the tribes of gods or into the bright sea. If you are not
persuaded by his words, but find them of no consequence,
he threatens to come here and take you on in person.
165 And he warns you to avoid his hands because he says that he
is much greater in strength, and older too. Your heart
thinks it is nothing to say that you are his equal—he whom
all others dread!"

Greatly angered, the famous shaker of the earth
said: "Well then, though he is strong, he has spoken
170 quite ill-chosen words. So he thinks that he will hold me back
against my will—I who am equal to him in honor?
For we are three brothers whom Rhea bore, fathered
by Kronos—Zeus and I and, third, Hades who rules
over those under the earth. The whole world is divided
175 into three parts, and each of us has his share of honor.
When the lots were shaken, I took the gray sea to dwell in
forever, and Hades took the misty darkness, and Zeus
took the broad heaven in the air and the clouds. But the earth
and high Olympos is common to us all, for which reason
180 I will not accede to the will of Zeus. Though he is powerful,

may he remain in peace in his own third domain! May he not try
to frighten me with the might of his hands as though I were
some miserable coward! It would be better if he threatened his
daughters or his sons with his blustering words, those whom
he himself begot, who will necessarily pay attention to whatever   185
is on his mind."

       Then swift Iris, with feet like the wind,
answered him: "So, O holder of the earth, O dark-haired one,
do you want me to carry to Zeus this harsh and uncompromising
word? Or can you in any way be turned? For the hearts of the good
can be turned. You know how the Erinyes always follow the elder."°   190

   Poseidon, the shaker of the earth, then said: "Iris, goddess,
you have spoken well and in accordance with what is right.
This is good, when the messenger has a righteous heart.
Still, this comes as dread grief to my heart and spirit,
when one is willing to upbraid with angry words   195
another who is of like portion and provided with an equal
allotment. All the same, I will give in for now, though I am
justly angry. And I will tell you something else, and in my anger
I will make this threat: If in spite of me, and Athena who forages
for booty, and Hera, and Hermes, and Hephaistos the king,   200
Zeus will spare steep Ilion, and be unwilling to destroy the city,
and shall not give great strength to the Argives—well, he must
know that there will be imperishable anger between the two of us!"

   So speaking, the shaker of the earth left the army of the Achaeans.
He went to the sea and plunged in, and the Achaean warriors   205
missed him sorely.

       Then Zeus, who gathers the clouds,
spoke to Apollo:° "Go now, dear Phoibos, to Hector,
armed in bronze. Already the holder of the earth, the shaker
of the earth, has gone into the bright sea, evading our
dangerous anger. Else the other gods would have learned   210
of our quarrel, those who are beneath the earth in the company
of Kronos.° This was a much better outcome both for me and for him,

---

190   *the elder*: The Erinyes, avenging spirits of the underworld (the "furies"), punish breaches of respect within
      the family, here the disrespect of the younger son toward the elder.

207   *to Apollo*: Apollo is appropriate for this task because he is on the side of the Trojans and he is a healing god.

211–212   *in the company of Kronos*: The Titans.

that, although angry, he has yielded to my hands. Otherwise
there would have been a clammy outcome! But take the tasseled
215   goatskin fetish in your hands and shake it over the Achaean
fighters. Put them to flight! May glorious Hector be your care,
O you who strike from a long way off. For a little while
excite his power so that the Achaeans flee to their ships
and to the HELLESPONT. From that point on I will contrive both word
220   and deed to see that the Achaeans have respite from the battle."

So he spoke, and Apollo obeyed his father. He went down
from the mountains of Ida like a swift hawk, the speediest
of winged creatures, the killer of pigeons. He found
the son of wise Priam, the good Hector, sitting up—
225   he was no longer lying down, for he had recently begun
to recover his strength. He recognized his companions around him.
His gasping and sweating had stopped, for the will of Zeus,
who carries the goatskin fetish, had revived him. Standing
nearby, Apollo, who works from afar, spoke to him: "Hector,
230   son of Priam, why do you sit apart from the others
in a faint? Is something amiss?"

Hector, whose helmet
flashes, his strength spent, said: "Which god are you,
most powerful one, who speaks to me face to face?
Do you not know that at the sterns of the Achaean ships,
235   as I wreaked havoc on his companions—that Ajax, good
at the war cry, hit me in the chest with a stone and put a stop
to my furious valor? Surely, I thought on this day that I had
died and gone to the house of Hades, that I had breathed
forth my life."

Apollo te far-shooter, the king,
240   answered him: "Have courage! So mighty a helper has
the son of Kronos sent forth from Ida to stand by your side
and to aid you: I am Phoibos Apollo who carries a golden
sword—I who have saved you before, both you yourself
and the steep city. But come now, order your many charioteers
245   to drive their swift horses against the hollow ships. I will go
before and smooth the way clear for the horses, and I will turn
around the Achaean fighting men."

So speaking, he breathed
great power into the shepherd of the people. Even as when
a horse confined to his stall, well fed at the grain crib,

FIGURE 15.1   The arming of Hector.   Hector arms for battle in the presence of Priam and Hekabê. Hector has already donned his shinguards and now pulls a breastplate around his middle over a shirt. His mother, represented as a young woman, holds out his helmet with her right hand and with her left holds his spear. Hector's shield, decorated with the head of a satyr, leans against Hekabê's leg. The aged Priam, with balding head, supports himself with a knobby staff and instructs his son. The characters' names are inscribed. Athenian red-figure water-jug, c. 510 BC.

250 breaks his bonds and runs galloping over the plain, exulting,
he who is accustomed to bathe in the fair-flowing river,
holding his head high, and around his shoulders his mane flows
and in his splendor he trusts his nimble knees to carry him
to the haunts and pastures of mares°—even so Hector moved
255 his feet and his knees, urging on his horses when he heard
the voice of the god. Or as when dogs and hunters pursue a horned
stag or wild goat, but he is saved by a sheer rock or a shadowy
thicket, for it was not fated that they catch him—and then at their
shouting a bearded lion shows himself in the way and quickly
260 he turns back the hunters, although they are avid—even so,
the Danaäns for awhile followed on in a crowd, thrusting with their
swords and their two-edged spears. But when they saw Hector
going up and down the battalions of men, they took fright,
and the spirits of the men sank to their feet.

                                 Then Thoas,
265 the son of Andraimon, spoke to the Achaeans.° He was
by far the best of the Aitolians in the use of the spear, good also
in the hand-to-hand. In the assembly few of the Achaeans
surpassed him when the young men contested in words.
With good intent, he spoke to them and said: "Well then,
270 I see a great wonder with my eyes! Hector has again stood up,
avoiding death. Truly, every man's spirit hoped that he had died
at the hands of Ajax, son of Telamon. But some god has
saved and delivered Hector, he who has loosed the knees
of many Danaäns, as I think that he will again.
275 For not without Zeus of the loud thunder does he stand up
as an eager champion. But come, let us all be persuaded
by what I say. Let us bid the multitude to return
to the ships, but ourselves—as many as claim to be best
in the army—let us stand our ground, in case we can hold
280 him off, can push Hector back with our extended spears.
I think that, though zealous, he will fear in his heart to enter
the throng of the Danaäns!"

        So Thoas spoke, and they readily
hearkened and obeyed. Those who were in the company of Ajax

---

254 *of mares*: The same simile appears in Book 6 (lines 500–506), of Paris returning from Helen's boudoir to
the plain to fight. There are about 180 similes in Homer; 8 of them are repeats (7 in the *Iliad*). Similes often
precede battle scenes, as does this one.

265 *to the Achaeans*: Thoas is a respected older fighter of the second rank. In Book 13 Poseidon took his form to
exhort Idomeneus. He does not figure in the upcoming battle, but in Book 4 we saw his superior work with
the javelin.

and King Idomeneus and Teucer and Meriones, the equal to Ares,
marshaled the fight against Hector and the Trojans, calling   285
to the chieftains. But behind them the multitude slunk back
to their ships. The Trojans pressed forward in a mass, Hector
in the lead, taking long strides. Before him went Phoibos
Apollo, his shoulders wrapped in a cloud, holding
the dreaded goatskin fetish with its shaggy fringe—awesome,   290
gleaming bright, which the smith Hephaistos had given
to Zeus to put warriors to rout.

               Holding the fetish in his hands,
Apollo led the Trojans. But the Argives held their ground,
massed together. And the shrill war-cry rose from both sides
as the arrows flew from the bow strings. Many spears   295
were cast by daring hands, and many of them were
fixed in the ground before they could eagerly gorge
themselves on their share of white flesh, while others
were fixed in the skin of young men. So long as Phoibos
Apollo held the goatskin fetish firmly in his hands,   300
for so long did the missiles find their mark on both sides,
and the people fell. But when Apollo looked the Danaäns
with their fast horses full in the face and shook the fetish,
and he himself screamed aloud, then he bewitched
the spirit in their breasts and they forgot their furious valor.   305

   As when two wild animals drive a herd of cattle or a large
flock of sheep in confusion in the dead of black night when they
suddenly come upon them, and there is no herdsman nearby,
even so the Achaeans fled, their strength completely gone.
Thus Apollo sent panic among them, and contrived glory   310
for the Trojans and for Hector.

             Then man killed man and the fight
was scattered. Hector killed Arkesilaos and Stichios, the one
a leader of the Boeotians who wear shirts of bronze, the other
a trusted companion of great-hearted Menestheus. Aeneas
put down Medon and Iasos. The first, Medon, was a bastard   315
son of godlike Oïleus, the brother of Little Ajax.
He lived in Phylakê, far from the land of his fathers,
after he killed a relative of his stepmother, Eriopis,
the wife of Oïleus. But Iasos was a captain of the Athenians,
a son of Sphelos, who was a son of Boukolos. And then   320
Poulydamas killed Mekisteus, and Polites took down Echios
in the forefront of the fight, and good Agenor killed Klonios.

Paris hit Deïochos from behind at the base of his shoulder
as he fled from among the forefront fighters—he drove the bronze
325   straight through.°

> While Trojans stripped the armor from these men,
the Achaeans flung themselves into the ditch and the sharp stakes,
fleeing here and there, forced to take refuge behind the wall.
Hector called to the Trojans in a loud voice to attack
the ships and to let the gory armor go: "Whosoever I see
330   standing apart from the ships on the other side of the ditch,
I will kill on the spot, nor will his relatives, male and female,
burn him on the pyre when he is dead, but the dogs will devour
him before our city!"

> So speaking, Hector drove his horses
ever forward, whipping them with a downward sweep of his arm.
335   He called to the Trojans along the ranks, and they all raised
a shout along with him—a marvelous din—as they guided
the horses that drew their cars. And before them Phoibos
Apollo easily tore down the banks of the steep ditch
with his feet, collapsing them into the middle of the ditch,
340   and he built a causeway as a bridge, as long and wide as a spear cast
that a man throws when he tests his strength. The Trojans poured
over it, rank after rank, and before them went Apollo, holding
the precious goatskin fetish. He had torn down the wall
of the Achaeans with ease.

> As when some child near the sea
345   scatters sand when he has made a plaything in his childishness,
then in frolic he tears it all down with his feet and his hands—
even so easily did you, O far-darting Phoibos Apollo,
raze the long labor and toil of the Argives and drive them in rout.

And so the Achaeans were halted beside their ships,
350   calling to one another and to all the gods and raising
their hands in prayer, every one of them. Nestor from Gerenia,
especially, the guardian of the Achaeans, raised his hands
in prayer to the starry sky: "O father Zeus, if ever anyone

---

325   *... straight through*: Many of these victims were introduced in Book 13. Arkesilaos and Klonios were among
the Boeotian leaders in the Catalog of Ships; two of their relatives died in Book 14. The Athenian Stichios
was a follower of Menestheus in Book 13. Medon, "ruler," a captain of the Phthians, also appears in Book 13.
Iasos, a common name, is otherwise unknown. Deïochos is obscure, but later his descendants were said to
have colonized the island of Samos from Athens. In Book 13 Mekisteus is not a comrade of Echios, but his son
(13.421–422)!

in Argos, rich in wheat, burned in homage to you the fat
thigh bones of a bull or a sheep, and prayed that he might   355
return home, and you promised that he would and nodded
your head—remember these things now and keep from us,
O Olympian, this pitiless day of doom. Don't allow
the Achaeans to be conquered by the Trojans."

So Nestor spoke in prayer, and Zeus the counselor   360
thundered mightily, hearing the prayers of the old man,
the son of Neleus. But the Trojans, when they heard the thunder
of Zeus who carries the goatskin fetish, rushed even more
on the Argives, setting their minds to the battle. As when a great
wave of the sea with its broad ways pours over the sides of a ship   365
when the power of the wind drives it on, which most of all
causes the waves to swell—even so the Trojans came over
the wall with a great cry, and driving their horses they fought
at the sterns of the ships in the hand-to-hand against
the two-edged spears. The Trojans fought from their cars,   370
the Achaeans went up high onto the decks of their black ships
and fought with long pikes that lay at hand for them
for fighting at sea—jointed together, fitted at the tip
with bronze.

While the Achaeans and the Trojans fought at
the wall beside the swift ships, Patroklos was sitting in the tent   375
of the hospitable Eurypylos,° and Patroklos entertained him with talk.
And on Eurypylos' bitter wound he spread ointments as a remedy
for black pain. But when he saw the Trojans rushing at the wall,
when a cry arose from the Danaäns in their panic, then he groaned
and slapped both his thighs with the flat of his hands, and wailing   380
he said: "Eurypylos, I can no longer stay here with you,
although your need is great. For a great struggle has arisen.
Let your aide attend you while I hurry to Achilles so that I can urge
him to fight. Who knows if with a little luck I can excite his spirit
by talking. The advice of a companion is good."   385

So speaking,
he hastened on. In the meanwhile, the Achaeans stoutly
withstood the attacking Trojans, but they were not able
to push them back from the ships though the Trojans were fewer
in number. Nor were the mighty Trojans able to break through
the battalions of the Danaäns and to engage with them among   390

---

376   ... *Eurypylos*: We last saw Patroklos at the end of Book 11, when he operated on Eurypylos' thigh.

the tents and the ships. But as a carpenter's line makes a ship's
timber straight in the hands of a clever workman who is skilled
in all manner of craft through the counsels of Athena, even so
was their battle and war stretched equally.°

And so they fought on.
395 Some skirmished around some ships, others around other ships.
But Hector made straight for Ajax. The two of them contended
around a single ship. Hector was unable to drive Ajax back
and set fire to the ship, nor was Ajax able to push
back Hector, for a god drove him on. Then the glorious Ajax
400 hit Kaletor, the son of Klytios,° in the chest with his spear
as he carried fire to the ship. Kaletor thudded to the ground
and the torch fell from his hand.

When Hector saw his cousin
fallen in the dust before the black ship, he called out
in a loud voice to the Trojans and Lycians: "Trojans
405 and Lycians and Dardanians who fight in close, don't pull back
from the fight in this narrow spot, but come to the aid
of the son of Klytios so that the Achaeans do not take his armor,
now that he has fallen amid the gathering of the ships."

So speaking, Hector threw his shining spear at Ajax,
410 but he missed him and hit instead Lykophron, the son of Mastor,
an aide to Ajax from CYTHERA.° Lykophron lived with Ajax
because he had killed a man in holy Cythera. Hector hit him
in the head above the ear with his sharp bronze as Lykophron.
stood close by Ajax. Lykophron fell back to the ground in the dust
415 at the stern of the ship, and his limbs were loosened.

Ajax shivered,
and he spoke to his brother: "O Teucer, a trusted companion
of ours has been killed, the son of Mastor from Cythera, whom we
honored in our halls like our own parents, while he lived there.
Great-hearted Hector has killed him. Where now are your arrows

---

394   *stretched equally*: That is, the line of battle is straight, with neither side penetrating the other. The carpenter's line
     is a string infused with a pigment; when twanged, it leaves a mark on the wood, like a modern chalk line.

400   *Klytios*: Klytios was a son of Laomedon, so his son Kaletor, "caller" (apt name for a herald), would be
     Hector's cousin.

411   *Cythera*: This island, off Cape Malea on the southernmost tip of the Peloponnesus (Maps 1, 2), is not in the
     Catalog of Ships, and it is not clear who ruled there; nor is it clear who Lykophron (= "with the mind of a
     wolf") killed there or why he fled to Ajax on the island of Salamis off the coast of Athens. But Phoinix,
     Patroklos, and Medon, too, were exiled for murder, a standard epic theme.

FIGURE 15.2 Ajax defends the ships.   A bearded Ajax, clad in helmet, breastplate, and shin-guards, attacks Hector (?), who backs off before the prow of a ship. Hector holds a curiously shaped shield. Between them a dying beardless Achaean falls to the ground, a folded leg and one hand touching the earth. Etruscan two-handled water jug, c. 480 BC.

420 that bring a swift death, and the bow that Phoibos Apollo
gave you?"

So Ajax spoke, and his brother Teucer heard him.
Teucer ran up and stood beside Ajax with his back-bent
bow in his hands and the quiver that held his arrows.
Quickly Teucer rained his arrows on the Trojans. And he hit
425 Kleitos,° the glorious son of Peisenor, the noble companion
of Poulydamas, son of Panthoös, as he held the reins in his hands,
busy with his horses. Kleitos was driving them to where the bulk
of the battalions were being driven in rout, giving pleasure
to Hector and the Trojans. But swiftly there came to him an evil
430 that none could prevent, however much someone desired it.
The arrow, filled with groaning, hit him in the back of the neck.
He fell from the car and the horses started in all directions,
rattling the empty chariot. Prince Poulydamas saw him at once
and was first to go calm the horses. These he gave to Astynoös,°
435 son of Protiaon, and, watching him, he told him to hold the horses
nearby. He himself returned to the melée amid the foremost fighters.

Then Teucer drew another arrow on Hector, armored
in bronze, and he would have put a stop to his battle
at the ships of the Achaeans if he had hit him in the flush
440 of his power and taken his life. But Zeus's clever mind,
which watched over Hector, was aware of what happened,
and he took away the glory from Teucer, son of Telamon.
Zeus broke the well-twisted string° of the blameless bow
as Teucer drew it. The arrow, heavy from the bronze,
445 was turned aside, and the bow fell from his hand.

Teucer shivered and he addressed his brother: "Hear
brother, some god is intent on cutting short our counsels of war!
See how he has cast the bow from my hand! And he broke
the string, which I twisted and bound fast this very morning
450 so that it would speed the arrows flying thick and fast
from it."

Great Telamonian Ajax then answered him:
"Alright then, let the bow go and the many arrows that lie

---

425 *Kleitos*: Apparently invented just for this scene.

434 *Astynoös*: Another Trojan with this name dies in Book 5. Protiaon is unknown.

443 *string*: The bow string would be made of twisted ox sinew. Homer has no word for a "chance" event. All events are willed by a god, even if there is an obvious human cause.

about, for some god has made them useless in malice
toward the Danaäns. Take up your long spear, instead,
and a shield on your shoulder and fight the Trojans, and urge   455
on the others. Let us prevent them from taking the ships with their
fine benches without a struggle, even if they defeat us!
Let us turn our thoughts to war!"

                So he spoke, and he placed
the bow in his tent, and he hoisted a shield made of four layers
of ox-hide around his shoulders, and on his powerful head   460
he put on his well-made helmet with a crest of horse hair,
and the plume waved terribly down from above. He took up
a strong spear tipped with the sharp bronze. Then he set out,
running quickly up to Ajax and standing beside him.°

  When Hector saw that the arrows of Teucer were useless,   465
he called out to the Trojans and the Lycians in a loud voice:
"Trojans and Lycians and Dardanians who fight in close,
be men, my friends! Keep in mind your furious valor
amidst the hollow ships! I've just seen how Zeus
has brought to nothing the arrows of a captain. It is easy   470
to recognize the power of Zeus, and those to whom
he grants superlative glory and those he makes small
and will not help, as even now he makes small the strength
of the Argives. But he increases ours. So go in mass to fight
at the ships! If any of you is hit by an arrow or spear,   475
and meets his death and fate—then die! It is not a bad thing
to die defending the land of your fathers. Then your wife
is safe, and your children whom you leave behind, and your house
and your lots of land are untouched, if only the Achaeans
go back home to the land of their fathers in their ships."   480

  So speaking, Hector roused the strength and the spirit
of each man. But Ajax on the other side also called to his companions:
"Shame, Argives! Now it is sure that either we will die
or be saved by pushing back the danger to the ships. Do you think
that if Hector with his flashing helmet takes the ships   485
you will get back home on foot? Do you not hear Hector
in his fury urging on his men to burn all our ships?
I don't think he is inviting them to come to a dance, but to fight!
For us there is no better plan and counsel than this—that we
fight in close combat with our hands—our power against theirs.   490

---

464 *beside him*: But Teucer in his armor achieves nothing, and he drops from the narrative hereafter.

It is better once and for all to live or die than for long to be
squeezed out like this, drop by drop, in the dread contendings
among the ships, at the hands of men who are less than us."

So speaking, Ajax roused the strength and spirit of each man.
495　Then Hector killed Schedios, son of Perimedes, a captain
of the Phocians, and Ajax killed Laomedon, a leader
of the foot soldiers, the glorious son of Antenor. Poulydamas
killed Otos from Kyllenê, a companion of Meges, the son
of Phyleus, the great-hearted leader of the Epeians.° Meges saw
500　what had happened, and he leaped toward Poulydamas, but Poulydamas
swerved away and Meges missed—Apollo was not going to allow
the son of Panthoös to be killed among the frontline fighters!
Instead Meges stabbed Kroismos in the chest with his spear.
Kroismos fell to the ground with a thud.

　　　　　　　　　　　　　　Then Meges went
505　to strip the armor from his shoulders, but in the meanwhile
Dolops, the son of Lampos, well-skilled in the use of the spear,
rushed on him. Lampos, son of Laomedon, fathered
Dolops, his bravest son, learned in furious valor.
Dolops stabbed the middle of Meges' shield, hitting him
510　from close in. But the thick breastplate that Meges wore,
fitted with plates, saved him. Phyleus had brought it from Ephyrê,
from the river Selleïs.° A guest-friend of Phyleus had given
it to him, Euphetes the king of men, to carry to war—a defense
against the enemy. This breastplate now warded off death
515　from the flesh of Phyleus' son. Meges then struck with his sharp
spear the topmost plate of Dolops' helmet of bronze with its
horsehair plume. He cut off the horsehair plume and the whole
thing fell to the dirt and dust, shining with its new scarlet dye.

Meges held his ground and fought with Dolops, still hoping
520　for victory. In the meanwhile the martial Menelaos came to the aid

---

499　... the Epeians: Hector kills another Phocian leader named Schedios in Book 17, but his father is Iphitos.
　　　Of the eleven sons of Antenor mentioned in the Iliad—here Laomedon, who has the same name as that of
　　　Priam's father—nine are killed. Otos is unknown. Kyllenê is the mainland port of ELIS opposite the island
　　　of DOULICHION, where Otos' friend Meges is ruler (this is not the famous Mount Kyllenê in ARCADIA in
　　　the PELOPONNESUS). The Epeians are the inhabitants of Elis.
512　... river Selleïs: Kroismos is a unique name. Dolops is a cousin of Hector because Priam, Lampos, and
　　　Klytios are all sons of Laomedon. Klytios lost a son earlier in this book (line 400). One Ephyrê was in
　　　THESSALY (Book 13), another was CORINTH (Book 5), but this Ephyrê must be in Elis, Phyleus' place of
　　　origin before he migrated to the island of DOULICHION, explaining why Otos of Kyllenê in Elis was one of
　　　his officers. This river Selleïs must be in Elis, too. The breastplate appears to be an heirloom, like the boars'
　　　tusk helmet in the Doloneia (Book 10).

of Meges. He stood on one side with his spear, unnoticed
by Dolops, and he threw and hit Dolops in the shoulder from behind.
The spear in its fury went through Dolops' chest, speeding eagerly
onward, and Dolops fell on his face.

Then Menelaos and Meges   525
were eager to strip the bronze armor from Dolops' shoulder.
But Hector called to his kinsmen, one and all, and first
of all he reproached the powerful Melanippos, son of Hiketaon.
Up to this time Melanippos had herded his cattle, who shuffled
as they walked, in PERKOTÊ° while the enemy was still far away.
But when the curved ships of the Danaäns came, he came back   530
to Troy. He was outstanding among the Trojans, and he lived in the house
of Priam, who honored him as if he were his own child.

Hector remonstrated with Melanippos, saying: "Melanippos,
why do you slack off now? Is your heart not moved by the death
of your cousin? Do you not see how they are stripping Dolops'   535
armor? Follow me! We can no longer fight the Argives from afar—
either we kill them or they utterly destroy steep Ilion and kill
everyone in the city."

So speaking, he led the way, and Melanippos
followed him, a man like a god. But Telamonian Ajax likewise
stirred on the Argives: "Comrades, be men! Take shame   540
into your hearts, and feel shame each for the other in these fierce
contendings. When men feel shame, more are saved than perish.
But for men who flee, there is neither glory nor help."°

So he spoke.
But the Trojans themselves were still eager to attack the enemy.
Just so they took to heart Hector's words, and they fenced in the ships   545
with a hedge of bronze. For Zeus, too, urged on the Trojans.

But Menelaos, good at the war cry, stirred up Antilochos:°
"Antilochos, no young Achaean runs faster than you, nor is so courageous

---

529 *Perkotê*: On the Hellespont; see Map 3. Melanippos, too, is Hector's cousin, apparently invented for
     this scene.

543 *... nor help*: An explicit statement of the basis for action in a "shame culture," where one's worth is
     dependent on others' valuation; as opposed to a "guilt culture," where valuation comes from one's inner
     sense of worth.

547 *Antilochos*: Antilochos is a son of Nestor. He saved Menelaos' life in Book 5 and is important in the
     narrative later on.

in the fight. I wish you would leap forward and cut down one
550   of the Trojans!"

          So he spoke and hurried back again, rallying the others.
Then Antilochos leaped forward among the foremost fighters.
Looking about him, he cast with his shining spear.
The Trojans withdrew as he threw, but his weapon did not fly
in vain—he hit the high-hearted Melanippos, son of Hiketaon,
555   as he came into the battle, in the chest next to the nipple.
Melanippos fell with a thud, and darkness covered his eyes.

     Antilochos rushed up, like a dog that rushes on a wounded
fawn that a hunter has hit as the fawn leaped from his lair,
and he loosed limbs—even so, O Melanippos, did Antilochos,
560   stubborn in the fight, leap on you to take your armor.

     But the good Hector saw what was going on, and he ran to face
Antilochos in the midst of the battle. Antilochos did not await him,
though he was a seasoned warrior, but he fled in terror, like a wild
animal that has done something vile—one that has killed a hound
565   or a cowherd working his cattle, and then flees before a throng
of men can be gathered. Even so fled the son of Nestor,
and Hector and other Trojans poured on him with wondrous war
whoops, their arrows filled with groans. Antilochos stopped running
and turned around when he came to the tribe of his companions.

570   The Trojans rushed on the ships like flesh-eating lions,
fulfilling the commands of Zeus, who constantly inspired
great strength among them, while he bewitched the spirit
of the Argives, depriving them of glory as he urged on the Trojans.
For his heart was set on giving glory to Hector, son of Priam,
575   that his own eyes might see him cast wondrous unwearied fire
into the curved ships, thus fulfilling to the utmost
Thetis' immoderate prayer. Zeus the counselor had waited
for this—to see with his own eyes the glare of a burning
ship. From that time onwards he was going to order
580   a retreat of the Trojans from the ships and grant glory
to the Danaäns.

          With this plan in mind, he was rousing Hector,
the son of Priam, at the hollow ships, though Hector
was furious enough by himself. He raged like Ares,
wielder of the spear, or a dangerous fire on the mountains
585   in the thickest part of a deep wood. He foamed at the mouth,

and his two eyes shone beneath his bushy brows, and his helmet
shook terribly around his temples as Hector fought. Zeus
himself was his defender from on high—Zeus honored him
and gave him glory, peerless as he was among the many
warriors. But he would not last long! Already Pallas Athena   590
hastened-on the fateful day at the hands of Achilles,
the mighty son of Peleus. Hector wanted to break
the ranks of men, trying them in war wherever he saw
the largest grouping and the finest armor. But he was not
able to accomplish his keen desire. The Danaäns   595
held their ground. They arranged themselves like a wall,
like a crag, steep and high, close to the gray sea that withstands
the sudden paths of the shrill winds and the swollen waves
that break foaming against it—even so the Danaäns
held their ground against the Trojans steadfastly,   600
and they did not run away.

            But Hector, lit-up like fire,
leaped among them. He fell upon them from all sides,
as when beneath the clouds a furious wave falls
on a swift ship, driven by the wind, and she is hidden
by the foam, and the ghastly blast of the wind breaks   605
against the sail, and the sailors, terrified, tremble in their hearts,
for only by a little have they escaped death—even so
were the hearts of the Achaeans torn within their breasts as Hector
fell upon them, like a vicious lion attacking a herd of cattle
that graze in the meadow of a great marsh, an enormous   610
number of them. And the herdsman as yet has little experience
in fighting off a wild beast from the carcass of a cow
with curly horns that has been killed. He walks along now
with the foremost cattle, now with the hindmost, but the lion
attacks in the middle and devours a cow as the rest run away   615
in terror—even so, divinely guided, did the Achaeans,
one and all, run away under the attack by Hector
and his father Zeus.

            Still, Hector killed only one Achaean:
Periphetes from Mycenae, the dear son of Kopreus. It was
the custom of Kopreus to relay messages between the king,   620
Eurystheus, and mighty Herakles. Kopreus, a baser man, fathered
a son far better in every kind of excellence, both in fleetness
of foot and in the battle, and in intelligence he was one of the best
in Mycenae. It was Periphetes who then yielded the glory of victory
to Hector, for as he turned back he tripped on the rim   625

of his shield that, reaching to his feet, he carried as a defense
against javelins.° He stumbled on its rim and fell backward, and
his helmet rang terribly around his temples as he fell. Hector saw
that happen, and he ran up beside Periphetes and stabbed his spear
630 into his breast and killed him close by his companions, who were
unable to do a thing for their comrade. Though they were in sorrow,
they were themselves wholly afraid of brash, intrepid Hector.

Now the Trojans were in the midst of the ships, but the outermost
ships that were first drawn up confined them. The Argives rushed
635 at the Trojans, but gave way and of necessity pulled back from
the outermost ships. They made their stand in a crowd among the huts,
nor were they scattered throughout the camp. Shame held them—
and fear. They called to one another without cease.

Gerenian Nestor,
the guardian of the Achaeans, sought to rouse each man in the name
640 of his parents, beseeching them: "O my friends, be men and place
in your hearts shame before other men, and remember,
every one of you, your children, your wives, your possessions
and your parents, whether they are alive or dead. In their name
I earnestly beg you, even though they are not present here—
645 make your stand! Do not turn away in panic!"

So speaking,
he encouraged the strength and the heart of every man. Athena
pushed away from their eyes the bedeviling cloud of mist. A great light
appeared to them from both sides—from the side of their ships
and from that of the terrifying war. And they all saw Hector,
650 good at the war cry, and his companions, both they who stood
at the back and did not fight, and they who contended
beside the swift ships.

But it no longer pleased the heart
of great-hearted Ajax to stand where the other sons
of the Achaeans stood in the rear and did not fight.

---

627   ... *against javelins:* Kopreus, "dungman" or simply "farmer," was a son of Pelops and the herald of
Eurystheus, Herakles' cousin who held tyrannical power over the great hero. Eurystheus communicated
his commands to Herakles through Kopreus because he was frightened to deal with Herakles in person.
Periphetes, the only "Mycenaean" in Homer, is otherwise unknown and no doubt invented for this scene.
The shield he trips over could be an early Mycenaean tower shield (see Figure 4.1). Hector's oxhide shield
(Book 6) is similar, because its rim taps his neck and ankles as he walks, and of course Big Ajax carries such
a shield. Periphetes seems to wear no breastplate, in accord with early Mycenaean custom.

And so he trod up and down the half-decks of the ships,°   655
taking long strides, and he wielded a great pike for sea-fighting
in his hands, a pike joined with glue and pegs, thirty-two
feet in length.° As when a man, highly skilled in riding tricks,
harnesses together four horses selected from many,
and he races from the plain toward the great city along a public   660
highway as many men and women gaze at him,
as ever with sure step he leaps from one horse to another
and they fly along—even so Ajax ranged over the decks
of the swift ships, taking long strides, and his voice went up
to the sky. Shouting terribly, he commanded the Danaäns   665
to defend the ships and the huts.

Hector did not wait
among the crowd of the thickly mailed Trojans, but as a tawny
eagle leaps on a flock of winged birds feeding along a river's bank,
of geese or cranes or long-necked swans—even so Hector
went straight toward a dark-prowed ship, rushing right at it.   670
Zeus pushed him on from behind with his great hand,
and Hector roused his army along with him. Again the piercing
battle blazed beside the ships. You might think that unwearied
and fresh they went against one another in war, so furiously
did they fight. These were their thoughts as they fought: 675
The Achaeans believed that they would not escape from the peril,
but that they would perish, and the heart of every Trojan hoped
to set fire to the ships and to kill all the Achaean warriors.
These were their thoughts as they stood against one another.

Hector then seized the stern of a sea-faring ship—   680
beautiful, fast on the salt sea, that had carried Protesilaos° to Troy,
but did not bear him back to the land of his fathers. Around his ship
the Achaeans and Trojans fought one another in the hand-to-hand.
No longer did they await the whizzing bow-shots of arrows
and javelins, but standing close to one another, all of one mind,   685
they fought with keen battle-axes and hatchets, great swords
and two-edged spears. Many beautiful swords fastened
with dark thongs at the hilt fell to the ground,
some from their hands, others from the shoulders of the men
as they fought there. The black earth ran with blood.   690

---

655   *of the ships*: Homeric ships had two half-decks, one at the prow and one at the stern; the steersman worked
      from the stern's half-deck. The center was open with benches for the rowers, and a large beam across the
      center gave the hull strength and supported the mast when it was raised (see Figure 2.2).

658   *in length*: Perhaps epic exaggeration, but the Macedonians in classical times used spears as long as 22 feet.

681   *Protesilaos*: The first man to die at Troy.

Hector had seized the stern of a ship, and he did not let go
but held onto the carved stern-post° as he commanded the Trojans:
"Bring fire! Together in a mass raise the war cry! Now Zeus
has given us a day as repayment for all— let us take
695 the ships that came here against the will of the gods
and brought us so much pain through the cowardice of the elders
who held me back and restrained the people when I wanted
to fight at the sterns of the ships.° But if loud-thundering Zeus
baffled our wits then, now he himself urges us on and gives
700 the command."

     So he spoke, and they rushed still harder
at the Argives. Ajax could take it no longer. Oppressed
by missiles he backed off a little, thinking he would die there
on the seven-foot bench—he abandoned the half-deck of
the well-balanced ship.° There he took his stand, watching,
705 and he ever warded off the Trojans who carried fire from the ships,
Shouting ever terribly, he commanded the Danaäns: "My friends,
Danaän warriors, followers of Ares—be men, be men
my friends! Remember your furious valor! Or do we think
that there are other helpers at our backs, or a stronger wall
710 that will ward off destruction from our men? There is no city nearby
fenced with walls by which we can defend ourselves—no,
we have no other people who will turn the tide of battle.
We are sitting in the plain of the thickly mailed Trojans, far
from our native land, with nothing as support save the sea.
715 Therefore the light of deliverance is in our hands,
not in wavering in the fight!"

     So Ajax spoke and kept driving
furiously with his sharp spear. He awaited the man who
would bring blazing fire to the hollow ships, doing the
pleasure of Hector's bidding. Ajax waited, hoping to pierce
720 Hector with his long spear. And he did kill twelve
Trojan warriors in the hand-to-hand before the ships.

---

692   *stern-post*: Evidently a kind of curved horn fixed to the stern, to judge from pictures on pottery.

698   *of the ships*: Hector's tendency to self-delusion is clear here: In fact the gods *did* will the Achaean expedi-
       tion, because Paris had violated *xenia*, protected by Zeus, by taking Helen; and the Trojan elders did not
       through cowardice prevent Hector and his men from fighting, but through fear of Achilles' prowess.

704   *well-balanced ship*: The "seven-foot bench" is the wide cross beam in the center of the ship that gave the ship
       stability and supported the mast. Ajax seems to retreat from the half-deck at the stern to the central bench,
       though the description is not clear.

BOOK 16. *The Glory of Patroklos*

As they fought around the well-benched ships, Patroklos
came up to Achilles the shepherd of the people.° Tears
poured down his cheeks, like the dark water of a spring
that pours its black waters over a high cliff. When Achilles
saw him, godlike Achilles the fast runner felt pity   5
and he spoke words that flew like arrows: "Why do you weep,
Patroklos? You are like a little girl, a babe who runs
to her mother and begs to be picked up, clutching her gown,
holding the mother back from her work. Crying
she stares upward, begging to be lifted—you are like   10
that little girl, pouring forth your tender tears.
Do you have something to say to the Myrmidons, or to me
myself? Or have you heard some private news from PHTHIA?
Surely your father Menoitios, the son of Aktor,
is still alive, they say, and Peleus too, the son   15
of Aiakos, among the Myrmidons. Certainly
we would grieve to hear that either had died!
Or are you sad because of the Argives, who die beside
the hollow ships on account of their own arrogant action?
Say it, don't hide it, so that we both may know."   20

   You groaned deeply then, Patroklos the horseman,
and said: "O Achilles, son of Peleus, by far the best of
the Achaeans, do not be angry! For so great an anguish has
come to the Achaeans. Those who before were best in the
contendings, all of them now lie wounded among the ships,   25
pierced by missiles. The great Diomedes, son of Tydeus,
is wounded. Odysseus too, famed for his work with the
spear. And Eurypylos is shot with an arrow in the thigh.
The doctors, learned in drugs, are working to heal them.

---

2 *shepherd of the people*: In Book 11 Achilles sent Patroklos to ask about the wounded Machaon, but his errand
  was interrupted when he met Nestor (he never gets to Machaon), who asks him to try to persuade Achilles to
  return to the fight, or at least to allow Patroklos to fight in Achilles' place. This will give the Achaeans a break.
  Patroklos starts back to Achilles' hut but stops on the way to help the wounded Eurypylos. He does not leave
  Eurypylos' hut until Book 15. Now at the opening of Book 16, he finally returns to Achilles.

30   "But you, Achilles, are impossible! I hope that no such
        anger ever lays hold on me such as you nourish—a rashness
        that only destroys! How shall anyone yet to be born
        ever have benefit of you if you will not ward off from the Argives
        a terrible fate? You are pitiless. I don't think that Peleus
35   the horseman was your father, or Thetis your mother.
        The gray sea bore you and the steep cliffs! For your mind
        is unbending.
                    "But if in your mind you are avoiding some
        oracle, and your revered mother has told you something she heard
        from Zeus, at least quickly send *me* forth, and with me
40   the host of the Myrmidons, so that I might be a light
        of salvation for the Danaäns. Let me wear your armor—
        perhaps if I look like you, the Trojans will pull back from
        the war and the sons of the Achaeans can catch their breath,
        worn out as they are. For the breathing space in battle is brief.
45   Easily, I think, we who are fresh may drive back
        toward the city men worn out by the battle cry, away
        from the ships and the huts."

                            So he spoke in supplication.
        The fool! For in truth he prayed for his own dark death
        and fate.

                    Deeply moved, Achilles the fast runner, said:
50   "Patroklos, who are like a god, what words you have spoken!
        I take no heed of any oracle that I know of, nor has
        my revered mother said anything to me that she learned
        from Zeus. But this terrible grief lies on my heart
        and soul—when a man aims to steal from his equal
55   and take from him his prize, because he is greater in power.
        This is a horrendous grief to me. I have suffered
        pain in my heart! The girl that the sons of the Achaeans
        chose for me as prize, whom I myself captured
        when I sacked a well-walled city—this very girl
60   King Agamemnon, the son of Atreus, has taken from my
        hands, as if I were some mere wanderer without rights!
            "All the same, we will let that pass. It is something
        that happened. It was never my intention to nurse an unending
        anger in my heart. I thought I would hold onto my anger
65   only until the war cry and battle should reach my own ships …
            "But go ahead—you can dress in my glorious armor
        and lead the war-loving Myrmidons to battle. If in truth the dark

cloud of the Trojans has powerfully shrouded the ships,
and only the shore of the sea supports the others,
and the Argives have a scant dab of land still left,   70
and the whole city of the Trojans has come without fear
against them—for the Trojans do not see the face of my helmet
glinting before them. Or they would soon fill the channels
with the bodies of the dead as they flee—if only Agamemnon
were well disposed toward me!   75
      "As it is, the Trojans have
surrounded the camp with battle. For the spear in the hands
of Diomedes, son of Tydeus, does not rage to ward off
destruction ... Nor have I yet heard the voice of the son
of Atreus, as he bellows from his loathed maw. No,
it is the voice of man-killing Hector that breaks about me   80
as he urges on the Trojans, who with their din possess
the whole of the plain, overwhelming the Achaeans in battle!
 "But even so, Patroklos ... go, fall upon them with power.
Ward off destruction from the ships, so that they do not burn
the ships with blazing fire and take away our homecoming.   85
Only listen! Let me place in your mind the sum of my counsel,
that you might win for me great honor and glory
among all the Danaäns, who then will return that most
beautiful woman along with wonderful gifts.°
 "Once you have driven the Trojans from the ships,   90
come back. If the loud-thundering husband of Hera grants
you success, do not desire to fight without me against
the war-loving Trojans. You will make my honor less.
And do not exult in war and the contendings, in killing the Trojans.
Do not lead on to Ilion! I fear that one of the Olympians,   95
who never die, may enter the fight. For Apollo,
who works from afar, loves them very much. Come back,
then, once you have shown a light of salvation
among the ships. Let the others fight on the plain.
 "How I wish that father Zeus and Athena and Apollo   100
would allow not *one* of the Trojans to escape, of all
there are, and not one man of the Argives either,
but that just the two of us might escape death, that alone
we might loose the sacred veil of the city!" And so
the two spoke to one another in this fashion.   105

---

89 *wonderful gifts*: Critics have complained that in Book 9 the Achaeans made this very offer to Achilles. But
although Achilles then rejected Agamemnon's attempt to buy him off, he remains angry and anxious to
receive restitution.

But Ajax no longer held his ground, overcome
by missiles. The mind of Zeus and the mighty Trojans wore him
down with their constant firing. His shining helmet
rang incessantly around his temples as it was struck,
110 hit constantly on the handsome cheek pieces. His left shoulder
grew weary from holding the gleaming shield, but still
the Trojans could not drive it back upon him with their steady
fusillade. Ever tormented by heavy breathing, sweat poured
everywhere from his limbs in abundance, nor could Ajax
115 get a chance to catch his breath. Everywhere evil
piled on evil.

Tell me now, Muses who live
on Olympos, how fire first fell on the ships of the Achaeans!

Hector closed in on Ajax and with his great sword
struck his spear of ash just behind the socket.
120 He cut it clean away so that Ajax, son of Telamon,
now wielded a useless shaft. The spear's bronze point
spun away and clanged on the ground. Ajax saw
in his daring heart the doing of gods and he shivered,
seeing how Zeus, who thunders on high, had brought
125 to nothing Ajax' counsels of war, and how
he willed a Trojan victory.

Ajax withdrew
from the hail of arrows as the Trojans cast consuming
fire into the ship. Quickly an unquenchable flame
engulfed it. Thus fire took hold of the ship's stern,
130 but Achilles, striking both his thighs, addressed Patroklos:
"Rise up now Patroklos, master of horses. I see the rush
of consuming fire in the fleet. May they not take the ships
and prevent our escape! Quick, put on my armor. I will
assemble our companions."

So Achilles spoke. Patroklos put on
135 the gleaming bronze. First he bound the beautiful shinguards
to his calves, fitted with silver fasteners. Second,
he placed around his chest the breastplate of the swift-footed
grandson of Aiakos,° handsomely made, decorated with stars.

---

138 *grandson of Aiakos*: Achilles.

FIGURE 16.1 Patroklos and Achilles. The younger, beardless Achilles wraps a bandage around the arm of his older, bearded friend. Achilles is in full armor, but without shinguards. Patroklos, who looks away in pain and squats on a shield decorated with a tripod (?), carries a quiver and bow on his back. He wears a felt cap. An arrow lies parallel to his calf. There is no such scene in the *Iliad*, but the painting was inspired by the intimacy of the two men and modeled on the scene where Patroklos binds the wounds of Eurypylos. Athenian red-figure wine-cup (*kylix*) by Sosias found in Vulci, Italy, c. 500 BC.

Around his shoulders he slung the sword of bronze with silver
140 studs, then he took up the large and powerful shield,
and on his mighty head he set the helmet, well made,
with a crest of horsehair. Its plume nodded terribly
from on high. He took two strong spears that perfectly
fitted his grasp, but he did not take the spear of the grandson
145 of Aiakos—heavy, great, powerful! No other Achaean
could wield this spear. Achilles, son of Peleus, alone
could wield it. Cheiron from the peak of Pelion had given
it to his father to be used for the killing of heroes.

Achilles ordered Automedon,° the breaker of ranks,
150 quickly to yoke the horses. Patroklos honored him
most after Achilles, trusting him to await his call
in the midst of battle. Automedon led the swift horses
Xanthos and Balios, who ran like the breath of the wind,
beneath the yoke. The Harpy Podargê had born them
155 to Zephyr, West Wind, as she grazed in the meadow beside
the stream of Ocean.° In the traces he placed the fine horse
Pedasos, whom Achilles had captured when he sacked the city
of Eëtion, a mortal stallion following deathless horses.°

But Achilles went through the huts and urged all
160 the Myrmidons to arm. And they ran out like flesh-eating wolves
in whose hearts is an unspeakable rage—wolves who have killed
a horned stag in the mountains and who dine upon him,
and their cheeks are red with blood, and in a pack they course
to the black waters of a dark spring. With their thin tongues
165 they lap the surface of the water, all the while vomiting
blood and gore, and their hearts in their breasts are unflinching,
and their bellies are gorged—even so did the leaders
and rulers of the Myrmidons swarm forth around Patroklos,
the companion of the grandson of Aiakos the fast runner.
170 And among them stood warlike Achilles, urging on the horses
and the men in their armor.

---

149   *Automedon*: First mentioned in Book 9, he is third in command among the Myrmidons. He serves as
Patroklos' driver, as Patroklos was Achilles' driver.

156   *... of Ocean*: Xanthos is "red" and Balios is "patches." Podargê is either "white-foot" or "swift-foot." The
Harpies, "snatchers," were personified storm winds, perhaps originally spirits of Death, but here Podargê
takes on the form of a horse. It was widely believed in antiquity that the wind could impregnate mares in
sexual heat. With both parents being winds, Achilles' horses were the fastest at Troy.

158   *deathless horses*: Pedasos was taken in the same raid on which Achilles captured Chryseïs.

Fifty fast ships did Achilles,
beloved of Zeus, lead to Troy, and in each fifty
men rowed, his companions. He appointed five men
whom he trusted as leaders, to give commands, but he
himself ruled all, great in his power. Menesthios°   175
of the flashing corselet led one band, son of the
heaven-fed river Spercheios. The daughter of Peleus,
lovely Polydora,° bore him to untiring Spercheios, bedding
down with the god, but in name Menesthios was the son
of Boros, the son of Perieres, who wedded Polydora in a public   180
rite after Boros gave wedding gifts beyond counting.

Warlike Eudoros led the second band. His mother
was unmarried, Polymelê the daughter of Phylas fair
in the dance. The powerful killer of Argos fell in love
with her when he saw her among the singers on the dance floor   185
of Artemis of the golden arrows and the echoing chase.
Hermes the Deliverer promptly went to her upper chamber
and slept with her in secret, and she gave him the noble son
Eudoros, superior in running and war. When the goddess
of childbirth Eileithyia had brought him forth into the light   190
and he saw the rays of the sun, Echekles, strong
and powerful, the son of Aktor, led Polymelê to his house,
after giving countless wedding gifts. The old man Phylas
raised Eudoros, nursing him and cherishing him as if
he were his own son.°   195

Peisander led the third band,
the warlike son of Maimalos. He stood out among
all the Myrmidons for his spear-fighting, second only
to Patroklos, the companion of the son of Peleus, in his fighting
skills. Phoinix, the old horseman, led the fourth band,
and the fifth was commanded by Alkimedon, son of Laerkes.   200

When Achilles had organized them all in companies with
their leaders, he lay upon them a powerful command: "Myrmidons,
do not forget the threats that you made against the Trojans
as you waited beside the fast ships, all during the time of my anger.
And then you criticized me, saying, 'Cruel son of Peleus,   205

---

175 *Menesthios*: In the following catalog of Myrmidon leaders, the names seem to be made up—they do not
reappear in the narrative—except for old man Phoinix, Achilles' tutor (Book 9, also 17).

178 *Polydora*: Hence Achilles' half-sister (by another woman, not Thetis).

195 *his own son*: Because Polymelê abandoned Eudoros when she married Echekles.

surely your mother suckled you on bile, pitiless one,
who hold your unwilling companions back beside the ships.
Let us sail home in our seafaring ships, because an evil anger
has fallen on his heart.' Often you would gather together
210 and make such criticism. But now the great work of war,
which before you so desired, is set before you. So let every
man go to the fight against the Trojans with a brave heart."

So speaking he roused up the strength and the spirit
in each man. They closed up their ranks when they heard
215 their king. As when a man builds a wall of close-set stones
for a high-roofed house that will resist the blasts of the winds,
even so they set side by side their helmets and their bossed
shields. Shield leaned against shield, helmet against helmet,
man against man! The horse-hair crests attached to the bright
220 shield-plates touched each other as the men nodded their heads,
so close to one another did they stand. In front of all, two men
put on their armor, Patroklos and Automedon, being
of a single mind—to fight in the forefront of the Myrmidons.

But Achilles went off to his hut, and he opened the lid
225 of a chest—beautiful, ornate—that silver-footed Thetis
had placed in his ship to carry with him, after filling it with shirts
and cloaks that keep away the wind, and woolen rugs.
He kept a well-made cup there, nor did any other man
drink from it the flaming wine, nor did he pour from it
230 an offering to any other god than father Zeus.
Achilles took it from the chest. He first purified it
with sulfur, then he washed it in beautiful streams of water.
Then he washed his hands and poured out the flaming wine.

Standing in the middle of the court, he prayed to Zeus.°
235 He poured out wine looking to the sky, and Zeus
who delights in the thunder was aware of him: "Zeus
the king, lord of Dodona, Pelasgian, you who live
far away, ruler of wintery Dodona—around you
live the Selloi, your diviners, who sleep on the ground
240 with unwashed feet.° Surely in earlier times

---

234   ... to Zeus: Achilles' hut is imagined to have an open courtyard with an altar to Zeus Herkeios, "Zeus of the
        Courtyard," the guardian of the house to whom the hero prays. Such altars were typical of Greek houses
        throughout antiquity.
240   unwashed feet: Achilles prays to the Zeus of DODONA, far west from PHTHIA across the PINDUS range
        in a remote mountainous part of EPIRUS, where there was an ancient shrine to Zeus. Dodona is 12 miles
        southwest of the modern city of Yaninna. Homer derives Peleus' family from here. The Pelasgians were

you heard my word when I prayed, and you honored me:
You punished the army of the Achaeans. So fulfill for me
now my desire. I myself remain now amidst the gathering
of the ships, but I send forth my companion with my many
Myrmidons to fight. O Zeus who thunders from afar,   245
grant him glory! Make brave his heart in his breast, so that
even Hector will know whether my companion knows
how to fight alone, or whether his hands rage invincibly
only when I have entered the toil of Ares.
                                          "But when he has driven
the battle and war cry away from the ships, may he then   250
return unscathed to the swift ships, with all his armor
and his companions who fight in close."

                              So he spoke in prayer,
and Zeus the counselor heard him. The father gave him one half
his wish, but the other he refused: He granted that Patroklos
push back the war and the battle from the ships, but he denied   255
that he return safe from the battle.

                              Once he had poured out
a drink-offering and prayed to Zeus the father, Achilles
went back into his hut, and he put the cup back into the chest.
He came forth and stood outside his hut. For he desired
in his heart to behold the dread contendings of Trojan   260
and Achaean.

                    They who were arrayed with great-hearted
Patroklos rushed out in high spirits against the Trojans. At once
they poured forth like wasps on the roadside that boys habitually
torment, always teasing them in their houses on the road, the foolish
young children, and the wasps make a common evil for many.   265
And if some wayfaring man stirs up the wasps by accident,
they all fly out in the bravery of their hearts to defend
their children—with a heart and spirit like this the Myrmidons
poured from the ships, and an unquenchable cry arose.

---

a prehistoric tribe who did not speak Greek, attesting to the shrine's antiquity. The unwashed feet of the Selloi
and their practice of sleeping on the ground are probably ritual taboos. At first Zeus was thought to indwell the
sacred oak itself, which had the power of speech, then the Selloi were the interpreters of the sounds made by the
wind in the tree. In classical times the Selloi were replaced by women. Some read "Helloi" instead of "Selloi,"
and Aristotle said that the *Hellenes* originated from here before migrating to Hellas near Phthia. Dodona was
also the home of the tribe of the Graikoi, from whom the Romans, just across the Adriatic Sea, took the name
"Greeks" to refer to the inhabitants of the southern Balkan peninsula—the name we use today.

270   Patroklos gave a loud shout, calling out to his companions:
"Myrmidons, companions of Achilles, the son of Peleus!
Be men, my friends! Remember your furious valor that
we might show honor to the son of Peleus, who is by far
the best of the Argives—himself and his followers who fight
275 in close—so that the son of Atreus, wide-ruling Agamemnon,
may know his blindness, who showed no honor to the best
of the Achaeans!"

     So speaking, he roused up the strength
and the spirit of each man, and they fell upon the Trojans in a mass.
Around them the ships rang terribly from the shouting
280 of the Achaeans. When the Trojans saw the powerful son
of Menoitios, himself and his aide° shining in their armor,
the heart in every man was stirred, and the battalions were shaken,
thinking that among the ships the swift-footed son of Peleus
had cast aside his anger and chosen to work as a team.
285 Each Trojan looked to where he might flee total destruction.

     Patroklos threw his shining spear straight into the midst
of them, where men thronged the closest, beside the stern
of the ship of great-hearted Protesilaos. He hit Pyraichmes,
who led the chariot-fighting Paeonians from Amydon,
290 from the wide-flowing AXIOS RIVER.° He hit him in the
right shoulder. Pyraichmes fell on his back in the dust, groaning,
and his companion Paeonians were driven in rout. Patroklos
drove them all in rout when he killed their leader,
who was the best in the fight. He drove them from the ships.
295 He extinguished the blazing fire. The ship was left
there half-burned as the Trojans fled with a wondrous roar
as the Danaäns poured forth from the hollow ships. An
unquenchable cry ensued. Just as when Zeus who gathers
the lightning moves a thick cloud from the highest peak
300 of a great mountain, and all the mountain toplands and the high
headlands and the valleys are revealed as the infinite air breaks out
from heaven, so the Danaäns drove back the destructive fire
from the ships and gained a brief breathing space. But there was
no end to the war.° For the Trojans did not yet run headlong

---

281   *his aide*: Automedon.

290   *Axios River*: Pyraichmes means "fire-spear," appropriate to the action. The location of Amydon on the
     Axios river in northern Macedonia (Map 1, 2) is unknown.

304   *... to the war*: As the sudden light breaks through the clouds during a storm, so did the Achaeans suddenly
     gain the advantage over the Trojans, but the storm is not yet over.

from the black ships before the war-loving Achaeans—they still   305
held their ground and backed off from the ships only when
hard pressed.

    Then among the captains man killed man
as the fighting was scattered. First Patroklos, the powerful
son of Menoitios, hit the thigh of Areïlykos with his sharp
spear just as Areïlykos turned around, and he drove the bronze   310
straight through. The spear broke the bone, and Areïlykos fell
on his face on the earth.

    Then war-loving Menelaos stabbed Thoas
where his chest was exposed by his shield. He loosed his limbs.
Meges, the son of Phyleus, watched the Trojan Amphiklos
as he rushed at him, but Meges was quicker and hit him on top   315
of his leg, where a man's muscle is thickest. The tendons were
cut by the point of the spear and darkness fell over his eyes.

    Then of the sons of Nestor, one, Antilochos,
stabbed Atymnios with his sharp spear and he drove
the bronze spear through his side. Atymnios fell forward.   320
But Maris, his brother, standing nearby, rushed on Antilochos
with his spear, enraged because of his brother, and he took a stand
in front of the dead body. But godlike Thrasymedes, another
son of Nestor, was too quick for him, and before
his enemy could thrust he stabbed at Maris. He did not miss   325
but hit him in the shoulder. The point of the spear sliced off
the base of the arm from its muscles and completely broke
the bone. Maris fell to the ground with a thud and darkness
closed over his eyes. Thus the two brothers, conquered
by two brothers, went to Erebos, the noble companions   330
of Sarpedon—the spearman sons of Amisodaros, the man
who raised up the raging Chimaira, an evil to men.°

    Ajax the son of Oïleus leaped on Kleoboulos and took him
alive as he tripped in the melée, but then he loosed
his strength by hitting him in the neck with his hilted sword.   335

---

332   *... to men*: A Greek also has the name Areïlykos in Book 14. Thoas is a common name, also borne by a
     Greek in Books 13 and 17. This is the only time that two brothers, the sons of Nestor—Antilochos and
     Thrasymedes—kill two other brothers, the sons of Amisodaros, Amphiklos and Atymnios. Erebos,
     "darkness," is the daughter of Night, and refers to the subterranean gloom where the dead dwell. Nothing
     else is known about Amisodaros' rearing of the Chimaira, the three-bodied fire-breathing monster that
     lived in Lycia, killed by Bellerophon (Figure 6.1).

The whole sword was warmed by his blood, and the
powerful fate of dark death covered Kleoboulos' eyes.

Boeotian Peneleös and the Trojan Lykon ran right up
on one another, for with their spears they had missed—
340 the two men cast their spears in vain! So then they ran against
one another with their swords. Lykon smashed down on the plate
of Peneleös' helmet with its plume of horsehair, but the sword
was shattered at the hilt. Peneleös slashed Lykon on the neck,
beneath the ear, and the whole blade went in so that only
345 skin held on his head. The head hung to one side as Lykon's
limbs were loosened.

Then the Cretan captain Meriones
overtook Akamas with swift strides and hit him in the right
shoulder as he was mounting his car. Akamas fell from the car,
and a mist came over his eyes. Meriones' companion
350 Idomeneus stabbed Erymas in the mouth with his pitiless
bronze.° The bronze spear went straight through
and came out beneath his brain, splitting the white bones.
Erymas' teeth came flying out and both his eyes
filled with blood. He gaped, spewing blood through his mouth
355 and nostrils, and the black cloud of death came down over him.

And so each of these men, the leaders of the Danaäns,
killed his man. As ravening wolves assail sheep or kids,
selecting them from a flock who are scattered over a mountain
through the carelessness of a shepherd, and seeing the flock
360 the wolves quickly snatch them up, for the flock knows no valor—
even so the Danaäns assailed the Trojans, who thought only
of shrieking flight, forgetful of their zealous valor.

And Big Ajax wished to throw his spear at Hector,
clothed in bronze, but Hector, through his knowledge of war,
365 hid his broad shoulders beneath his shield of bull's hide,
watching the whizzing of arrows and hearing the thud of spears.
Truly, he knew that the tide of victory was turning,
but he nonetheless held his ground and sought to save
his trusting comrades. As when from Olympos a cloud
370 comes into the heavens after clear weather when Zeus

---

351   ... *pitiless bronze*: Kleoboulos is otherwise unknown. In Book 14 Peneleos, from Boeotia, missed Akamas,
the son of Antenor, but beheaded another Trojan. Here the Cretan archer Meriones kills Akamas, and
Peneleos beheads the unknown Lykon. Another Erymas dies later in this book!

spreads out a squall, even so did the cry of the rout
come from the ships,° nor did Trojans cross the ditch
again in good order. Hector's swift horses bore him away
in full armor, but he left his Trojan troops behind,
for the ditch held them back against their will.° In the trench   375
they had dug, many swift horses who drew chariots
broke the poles behind their yokes and abandoned the cars
of their riders.

      Patroklos followed close in, calling
violently to the Danaäns, urging on evil to the Trojans
who filled all the ways with cries of rout, for their ranks   380
were broken. On high a storm of dust spread up to beneath
the clouds, and the single-hoofed horses strained to go back
to the city, away from the ships and the tents. Patroklos,
wherever he saw the Trojans most huddled together
in rout, there he went, screaming. And the men kept falling   385
from their cars—headlong beneath the axles, and their chariots
fell over, rattling. Straight over the ditch leaped his swift horses,
immortal, that the gods had given to Peleus as a glorious gift.
Flying ever onwards, his heart urged him to go up against Hector.
He wanted to strike him down, but Hector's swift horses   390
carried him safely away.

      As when a storm weighs down
the whole black earth on the harvest day, when Zeus
pours down the rattling rain because he rages against men
who by violence give false judgments in the assembly,
driving out justice without regard for the vengeance   395
of the gods, and all the rivers rise in flood, and the torrents
gouge ravines into many hillsides, and down to the dark sea
the rivers rush with a mighty roar headlong from the mountains
and they ruin the fields of men—even so mighty
was the crash of the Trojan mares as they raced away.   400

  When Patroklos had cut off the foremost battalions, he hemmed them in
by turning back toward the ships. Nor would he allow them to enter
the city, though they desired to, but in the space between the

---

372 *from the ships*: The cloud starts on Zeus's mountain top, then moves off it as Zeus builds the storm, just as
    the Trojans are moved off from the ships.

375 *their will*: Evidently Hector escapes across the causeway that Apollo cleared earlier, while the other Trojans
    are caught in the ditch.

ships and the river and high wall of the city he rushed
405 upon them, killing as he went, taking revenge for many.

First of all he struck Pronoös with his bright spear
on his chest where the flesh was exposed, next to his shield,
and he loosed his limbs. Pronoös fell with a thud. Next
he rushed on Thestor, son of Enops, as he cowered
410 in his highly polished car, his wits distraught with terror,
and the reins had slipped from his hands. Patroklos came up
close and hit him with his spear in the right jaw. The spear
went through the teeth and with the spear Patroklos
dragged Thestor over the chariot rail, as when a man
415 sitting on a projecting cliff hauls in a sacred fish°
out of the sea to the land with a line and a gleaming
bronze hook—even so he dragged him, gaping,
with his shining spear. He released him face down.
Thestor's breath-soul left him as he tumbled down.

420 Then Patroklos hit Erylaos with a rock as Erylaos
rushed on him. He hit him full on the head.° The head
split in two inside the heavy helmet. Erylaos fell prone
on the earth, and death that dissolves the breath-soul was poured
all around him. Then one after another he brought down
425 to the nourishing earth Erymas and Amphoteros and Epaltes
and Tlepolemos, son of Damastor, and Echios and Pyris
and Ipheus and Euippos and Polymelos, son of Argeas.°

When Sarpedon saw his companions, who wore their
shirts unbelted, fallen at the hands of Patroklos, the son
430 of Menoitios, he called aloud, scolding the godlike Lycians:
"Shame, O Lycians! Where are you running to?
Now sharpen up! I will myself take on this man so that I
might know who is wielding this power here and doing
so many evils to the Trojans.° For he has loosed the knees
435 of many fine men."

---

415 *sacred fish*: No one has ever explained what Homer means by "sacred fish."

421 *on the head*: Patroklos must now be on the ground to pick up a rock: Homer takes it for granted that his audience understands how Patroklos mounts and dismounts his chariot as the need arises.

427 *... Argeas*: All these victims' names are Greek. Most are unknown. Erymas is reused from earlier in the book, and Echios, "snake," from Book 15. Epaltes means "owl."

434 *to the Trojans*: Sarpedon knows only that the man is not Achilles, not that this is Patroklos. Homer makes surprisingly little use of the dramatic device of Patroklos being mistaken for Achilles because he wears Achilles' armor.

He spoke and leaped from his chariot
in full armor. Patroklos from the other side saw him jump
from the car, and just as vultures with bent claws and curved
beaks fight on the top of a high peak, scolding terribly,
even so did they rush on one another, shrieking. The son
of wily Kronos took pity when he saw them, and he spoke   440
to Hera, his sister and wife: "Woe, woe, that Sarpedon,
the dearest of men to me, is fated to die at the hands
of Patroklos, son of Menoitios!° My heart is divided
in two ways as I consider whether to snatch him alive
myself from the tearful battle and place him in the rich   445
land of Lycia, or whether I should kill him
at the hands of the son of Menoitios."

           Then the cow-eyed
revered Hera answered: "Most dread son of Kronos,
what words you have spoken! You want to relieve from
painful death a mortal man long ago doomed by fate? Do it!   450
But all the other gods will disapprove. And I will tell you
something else, and you best give it careful consideration:
If you send forth Sarpedon still alive to his own home,
consider then whether another of the gods will wish
also to send his own dear son out of the ferocious   455
contendings. For there are many offspring of the deathless
ones fighting around the great city of Priam,° and you
will instill a dread anger among them. But if he
is so dear to you, and your heart grieves for him—
well, let him be killed at the hands of Patroklos, son of   460
Menoitios. But when his breath-soul and life have left him,
then send Death and sweet Sleep to carry him off until
they come to the land of broad Lycia, where his brothers
and relatives will bury him in a tomb and set up a marker.
For that is the reward of mortals."   465

           So she spoke, and the father
of men and gods did not disobey. He poured out a bloody
rain to the earth in honor of his dear son, whom Patroklos
was about to kill in deep-soiled Troy, far from the land
of his fathers.

---

443 *son of Menoitios*: The Lycian leader Sarpedon is second only to Hector in prowess. Fate is stronger even
     than Zeus, whose power is thus limited.

457 *city of Priam*: Actually, not very many. The sons of the gods who fight at Troy are: Sarpedon (Zeus) and
     Aeneas (Aphrodite) on the Trojan side, and Achilles (Thetis), Eudoros (Hermes), and Askalaphos and
     Ialmenos (Ares) on the Achaean side.

When the two men had come close
470 to one another, Patroklos cast at famous Thrasydemos,
the gallant aide to Prince Sarpedon. He hit him
in his lower belly and loosed his limbs. Then Sarpedon,
throwing at Patroklos next, missed Patroklos with
his bright spear, but he killed the trace-horse Pedasos,
475 hitting the horse with his spear in the right shoulder.
Pedasos whinnied aloud and breathed out his life
as he fell down in the dust and his spirit flew from him.
The other two horses reared in opposite directions. The yoke
creaked and the reins were tangled as the trace horse
480 died in the dust. But for this Automedon, famed for his spear,
found a solution. Drawing his stout sword from beside
his thigh, he leaped down and cut away the trace horse,
and he succeeded in doing so. The other two horses straightened
and strained at the reins.

Then the two fighters again
485 came together in strife that consumes the soul. Sarpedon
missed his shot with his bright spear. The point
of the spear went over Patroklos' left shoulder and did not
hit him, and Patroklos then rushed on with the bronze.
His missile did not leave his hand in vain. He got Sarpedon
490 there where the lungs shut-in around the throbbing heart.
Sarpedon fell, as when some oak falls or a poplar
or a tall pine that carpenters cut in the mountains with
their sharpened axes to be a beam for a ship—even so
before his horses and his car he lay stretched out, groaning
495 and grasping at the bloody dust.

Just as a lion goes
into a herd and kills a tawny great-hearted bull
among the cows that shuffle as they walk, and the bull
perishes moaning in the jaws of the lion, even so the leader
of the shield-bearing Lycians raged as he lay dying at the hands
500 of Patroklos, and he called out to his dear companion:
"Dear Glaukos, a warrior among men, now you must be
the spearman and the bold fighter. Now let evil war be your desire,
and you must be swift! First go up and down the ranks
and urge the leaders of the Lycians to fight for Sarpedon,
505 then yourself fight for me with the bronze. If the Achaeans
take my armor now that I have fallen in the gathering
of the ships, I will on every day in time to come be a shame

and a reproach to you. Hold your ground with power
and urge on all the people."

                So speaking, the end that is death
covered his eyes and nostrils. Patroklos set his foot   510
on Sarpedon's chest and drew the spear out of the flesh.
Sarpedon's lungs came with it. At one moment he drew out
the point of the spear and with it came the breath-soul.
The Myrmidons held Sarpedon's snorting horses who longed
to flee, no longer connected to the chariot of their master.°   515

   But dread grief came on Glaukos when he heard the voice
of Sarpedon. His heart was sore because he had been unable
to defend him. With his hand Glaukos took his own arm
and pressed it. The wound that Teucer had dealt him with his arrow
when Glaukos rushed on the high wall, defending his companions,   520
tormented him.°

           In prayer, Glaukos called out to Apollo who works
from afar: "Hear me, O king, who may be in the rich land
of Lycia or in Troy! But you are everywhere able to hear
a man in trouble, even as now trouble has come to me.
For I have a terrible wound. My arm on both sides   525
is wracked with sharp pains, nor can I stop the flow
of blood, and my shoulder is heavy from the wound.
I cannot hold a spear firmly so that I can go and fight against
the enemy. A man has perished, Sarpedon, by far our best—
the son of Zeus, who cannot defend even his own son!   530
But do you, O king, heal this terrible wound. Make the pain
go away. Give me strength so that I may call aloud to urge on
the Lycians to make war, and myself fight around the body
of him who has died."

           So he spoke in prayer, and Phoibos
Apollo heard him. At once he stopped the pain in the grievous   535
wound. He dried up the blood, and he placed strength
in his spirit. Glaukos recognized what had happened
and rejoiced that the great god had quickly heard his prayer.
First he urged on the leaders of the Lycians to fight
around Sarpedon, going up and down the troops.   540

---

515   *their master*: In fact the horses are still attached to the chariot—a slip.

521   *his companions*: Teucer wounded Glaukos in Book 12.

Then he went into the ranks of the Trojans, taking long strides,
to Poulydamas, the son of Panthoös, and good Antenor,
and he went after Aeneas and Hector clothed in bronze.

Standing near Hector, he spoke words that went like arrows:
545 "Hector, certainly now you have forgotten the allies who on
your account waste away their lives far from their loved ones
and the land of their fathers. But you are not willing to defend them!
Sarpedon, the leader of the shield-bearing Lycians, lies dead—
he who guarded Lycia by his judgments and strength.
550 Brazen Ares has killed him beneath the spear of Patroklos.°
My friends, take your stand beside him. Feel anger in your hearts!
Don't let the Myrmidons take away his armor and treat his body
with contempt, angry because of all the Danaäns who have died,
all those whom we killed with our spears beside the swift ships."

555 So he spoke, and deep grief seized the Trojans—unbearable,
not to be endured. For Sarpedon was a bulwark of the city
although he came from afar. Many men followed him,
but he himself was best in the fight. Then the Trojans
went straight for the Danaäns in a vengeful rage. Hector
560 led the way, aflame because of Sarpedon.

                                        But Patroklos of the shaggy
heart,° the son of Menoitios, urged on the Achaeans.
First he addressed the two Ajaxes, already anxious to fight:
"Ajaxes, now is the time! Let it be your desire to put up
a defense for us, acting as you always did in the midst
565 of warriors, or braver still. A man lies dead who first leaped
within the wall of the Achaeans—Sarpedon. Let us see
if we can take his corpse and mutilate it and then strip the armor
from his shoulders, and with the pitiless bronze perhaps kill
some of his companions who come to defend the corpse."

570 So Patroklos spoke, and the Ajaxes themselves were
eager to put up a defense. When the fighters on either side
had bolstered their battalions—the Trojans and Lycians
and the Myrmidons and Achaeans—they gathered around
the dead man to fight, shouting terribly. Greatly resounded
575 the arms of the men. Zeus stretched all-destroying night

---

550 *Patroklos*: So ends the motif, little developed, of Patroklos deceiving the Trojans by wearing Achilles' armor.

561 *shaggy heart*: Apparently Homeric heroes have a strong heart in a hairy chest!

over the dread contendings so that a ruinous labor
of battle might rage around his own son.

At first the Trojans
drove back the Achaeans with twinkling eyes. A man
was hit, in no way the worst among the Myrmidons—
the good Epeigeus, the son of great-hearted Agakles.   580
He ruled in Boudeion, well populated, in olden times.
But then he killed a noble relative and fled to Peleus
and to Thetis with feet of silver. They sent him to follow
along with Achilles, breaker of men, to Ilion
with its fine horses in order to fight the Trojans.°   585

   Hector got Epeigeus when he was taking hold of the corpse,
hitting him on the head with a stone. The whole head split
in two within its heavy helmet, and he fell on his face
over the corpse, and over him poured out death that rends
the spirit.   590

         Pain overcame Patroklos when his companion
was killed. He headed straight through the forefighters
like a swift falcon that puts to flight crows and starlings—
like that, O Patroklos, master of horses, did you rush
straight at the Lycians and Trojans, and your heart was filled
with anger on account of your companion.   595

                    Patroklos smashed
Sthenelaos, the dear son of Ithaimenes,° in the neck with a rock
and it broke away the tendons. Glorious Hector
and the foremost Trojans gave ground beneath the assault.
As far as the flight of a long javelin that a man makes
when he tests himself in a contest and also in war   600
under pressure of the murderous enemy—even so far
did the Trojans pull back and the Achaeans advance.

   Glaukos, leader of the shield-bearing Lycians, first turned
around and killed great-hearted Bathykles, the dear son of Chalkon,
who lived in Hellas, outstanding among the Myrmidons for his   605

---

585   *to fight the Trojans*: Epeigeus, perhaps "hastener," and Agakles, "very famous," are invented for this scene.
      The place Boudeion is unknown but is probably in Phthia. The motif of exile because of murdering a
      relative is common in epic.

596   *Ithaimenes*: Both Sthenelaos, "strength of the people," and Ithaimenes, perhaps "of sure courage," are unknown.

riches and prosperity.° Glaukos stabbed him in the middle
of the chest with his spear, turning around suddenly when
Bathykles was about to overtake him in pursuit. Bathykles
hit the ground with a thud.

A heavy grief took hold
610 of the Achaeans when that good man fell, but the Trojans
were happy. They moved up and surrounded Bathykles in a crowd.
The Achaeans did not forget their courage, but carried
their power straight against the Trojans. Meriones took a Trojan,
Laogonos, heavy with armor, the brave son of Onetor,
615 a priest of Idaean Zeus° whom the people honored
like a god. Meriones hit him beneath the jaw under the ear
and swiftly his breath-soul left his limbs, and hateful
darkness took him.

Aeneas threw his bronze spear at Meriones,
for he hoped to get him as he advanced under cover of his shield.
620 But Meriones saw it coming and avoided the bronze spear,
stooping forward. The long spear was fixed in the ground
behind him, and the butt of the spear quivered. Then Ares
at length put a stop to the spear's fury.° Aeneas grew angry
and said: "Meriones, although you dance nimbly, my spear
625 would have put a quick end to your dancing forever, if I'd hit you!"

Meriones, famed for his spear, then answered him:
"Aeneas, it's a hard thing for you, although you are strong,
to stifle the strength of every man who defends himself
and comes against you. For you are mortal too. If I
630 should hit you a direct blow with my sharp spear, though
you're strong and depend on the strength of your hands,
soon you would give up your glory to me, and your breath-soul
to Hades, famed for his horses."

So he spoke, but the brave
Patroklos reproached him: "Meriones, why do you,

---

606   *and prosperity*: Bathykles, "of deep fame," and Chalkon, "man of bronze," are just names, although Chalkon
      has a name from Glaukos' own family. Hellas, a region in southern Thessaly (Maps 1, 2), is close to or
      includes Phthia, Achilles' territory.

615   *Idaean Zeus*: Laogonos, "child of the people," and Onetor, "beneficiary," are handy names used elsewhere.
      Zeus had cults on both Trojan Mount Ida and on the Mount Ida in central Crete.

623   *spear's fury*: The spear is like a living thing that has fury and courage, to which Ares, the force of war, puts a
      stop; that is, the spear stopped quivering.

a good man, start this kind of talk? Surely, I do not think   635
that insulting words will drive back the Trojans from the corpse!
Before that the earth will hold many. The outcome of the war
is in your hands. Words are for the council—there is no need
to multiply words, but to fight!"

              So Patroklos spoke
and led the way, and Meriones, a man like a god, followed   640
after him. As a clamor of woodcutters arises in the valleys
of a mountain, and the sound is heard from far off,
even such a clamor arose from the earth with its broad roads,
a clanging of bronze and of hide and of well-made shields
as they thrust at on another with sword and two-edged spears.   645

    No longer could even a clever man have seen good Sarpedon,
because he was wrapped in missiles and blood and dust
from his head all the way to the bottom of his feet. They crowded
around the corpse as when flies swarm in a farmstead
around the full milk pails in the season of spring when   650
milk drenches the vessels—even so they crowded
around Sarpedon's corpse. Nor did Zeus ever turn his shining
eyes away from the savage contendings, but he gazed steadily
at the men and pondered much in his heart about the killing
of Patroklos. He wondered whether there in the savage fight   655
over godlike Sarpedon glorious Hector should kill Patroklos
with the bronze and strip away the armor from his shoulders,
or whether he should increase the labor of war for still more men.
As he thus pondered, this seemed to him to be the better course—
that the valiant aide to Achilles, the son of Peleus, should   660
again drive the Trojans and the heavily armed Hector
toward the city, and take the lives of many.

              In Hector first
of all he implanted the coward's spirit: Mounting his chariot,
Hector turned in flight, and he called to the other Trojans
to flee. For he recognized a turning of the sacred scales   665
of Zeus. The brave Lycians did not wait then but they
fled, all of them, when they saw their leader pierced
in the heart, lying in the assembly of the dead with many
fallen on top of him, for the son of Kronos strained taut
the cords of war.   670

      From the shoulders of Sarpedon they stripped
the armor—bronze, shining!—and they carried it to the hollow

ships. The brave son of Menoitios gave it to his companions
to carry. And then Zeus who gathers the clouds spoke to Apollo:
"Come now, dear Phoibos, cleanse Sarpedon of the dark blood
675 when you have removed him from the shower of arrows, and carry
him far away and bathe him in the streams of the river. Anoint him
with ambrosia, and put around him immortal clothing. Send him
to be borne by swift conveyers, the twins Sleep and Death,
who will quickly place him in the rich land of broad Lycia,
680 where his brothers and relatives will bury him in a tomb and set up
a grave stone. For that is the reward for mortals."

So he spoke,
and Apollo obeyed his father. He went down from the mountains
of Ida to the dread din of battle, and immediately he raised up
Sarpedon from the storm of arrows. He carried him far away
685 and washed him in the streams of the river. He anointed him with
ambrosia and put around him immortal clothing. Then he sent him
to be borne by swift conveyers, the twins Sleep and Death,
who quickly set him down in the rich land of broad Lycia.

But Patroklos with a call to his horses and to Automedon
690 went after the Trojans and the Lycians—he was blind, blind,
the fool! If he had obeyed the word of the son of Peleus,
he would have avoided the dire fate of black death. But the intent
of Zeus is always stronger that that of men. He drives even
brave men to rout and easily takes away victory when he
695 himself rouses men to fight. And it was Zeus who then put
spirit into the breast of Patroklos! Who first, who last
did you kill, O Patroklos, when the gods called you to death?
Adrastos first and Autnoös and Echeklos and Perimos, son of
Megas, and Epistor and Melanippos, and then Elasos and Mylios
700 and Pylartes°—you killed all these men, and all the rest,
every last one, thought only of flight.

Then the sons
of the Achaeans would have taken high-gated Troy at the hands
of Patroklos, for he raged around them and in front of them with his spear,
if Phoibos Apollo did not take his stand on the well-built wall,
705 aiming destructive thoughts against Patroklos and helping the Trojans.
Three times Patroklos leaped on the corner of the high wall,
three times did Apollo push him back, thrusting against his
shining shield with his deathless hands. But when Patroklos leaped

---

700 *Pylartes*: The names of these cannon-fodder Trojan characters are all Greek.

FIGURE 16.2 Death of Sarpedon. Sleep and Death prepare to carry away the dead Sarpedon in the presence of Hermes. Two unknown warriors, Leodamas and Hippolytos, look on from either side; the names are inscribed. Sleep, to the left, and Death, to the right, are winged, but otherwise fully armed mature warriors. The naked Sarpedon, stripped of his armor, is pierced by three wounds—one to his throat, one to his belly, and one on his thigh. The messenger-god Hermes, in charge of all transportation, wears a traveler's cap with broad brim and carries his wand, the caduceus. His feet are winged. One of the most celebrated of ancient paintings, the Euphronios wine-mixing bowl was a possession of the Metropolitan Museum in New York City between 1972 and 2008, when it was repatriated to Italy. It is now in the Villa Giulia in Rome. Athenian red-figure wine-mixing bowl signed by Euxitheos (potter) and Euphronios (painter), c. 515 BC, found in Cerveteri, Italy.

on them for the fourth time, like a god, Apollo spoke words
710 with a terrible cry that went like arrows: "Pull back, god-nourished
Patroklos! It is not fated that the city of the high-minded
Trojans perish beneath your spear—nor by that of Achilles,
who is much better than you!" So he spoke, and Patroklos retreated,
avoiding the anger of Apollo who shoots from a great distance.

715   Hector pulled up his single-hoofed horses at the Scaean Gates.
He debated whether he should fight, driving again into the melée,
or whether he should call out to the people to shut themselves
behind the walls. While he was so pondering, Phoibos Apollo
stood beside him in the form of a man, young and strong—
720 Asios, the uncle of horse-taming Hector, the brother
of Hekabê, the son of Dymas, who lived in PHRYGIA
on the banks of the SANGARIOS RIVER.

                              Taking his likeness,
Apollo, the son of Zeus, said: "Hector, why do you cease fighting?
Gather yourself! I wish that I were as much stronger than you
725 as I am weaker. Then you would regret pulling back from the war.
But come, send your strong-hooved horses against Patroklos.
Maybe you can take him and Apollo will give you glory."

     So speaking, he went again, a god, into the labor of men.
Glorious Hector ordered wise Kebriones to lash his horses
730 into the battle. But Apollo went away into the crowd.
He sent evil tumult into the Argives and gave glory
to the Trojans and to Hector. Hector let the other Danaäns go
and did not try to kill them, but he drove his strong-hooved
horses against Patroklos, who from his side leaped
735 to the ground from his car, holding his spear in his left hand.
With his other hand he picked up a rock—shining, jagged—
his hand covered it completely. He planted his feet firmly
and threw it. He did not back off from his enemy, nor did he hurl
in vain, but he hit Hector's charioteer Kebriones, bastard son
740 of the famous Priam, right on the forehead with the sharp stone
as Kebriones held the reins of the horses. The stone smashed
both his brows together, and the bone did not withstand the blow.
His eyes fell to the ground in the dust right there before his feet.
Like a diver he sailed from the well-made car, and his breath-soul
745 left his bones.

     Mocking him, O horseman Patroklos,
you said: "Ha, hey, here is a nimble man! How lightly he dives!

If he should ride on the fishy sea, he would satisfy many by
diving for oysters, leaping from the ship even in a storm—
considering how he now dives onto the plain from his car!
Well now, there are plenty of divers among the Trojans."   750

So speaking, he made for the warrior Kebriones, swooping
on him like a lion that in laying waste a farmstead has taken
a blow on its chest, and his own bravery brings him to ruin—
even so, O Patroklos, did you leap eagerly on Kebriones.

And against him Hector leaped to the ground from his car.   755
The two of them grappled like lions who fight on the peaks
of a mountain over a dead deer, both hungry, both with high heart—
even so the two masters of the war-cry fought over Kebriones.
Patroklos, the son of Menoitios, and glorious Hector
tried to slash each other's flesh with the pitiless bronze.   760
Hector took hold of the head of the corpse and would not let go.
Patroklos pulled at the foot, and other Trojans and Danaäns
joined the dread contending.

　　　　　　　As East Wind and South Wind
strive with one another to shake a deep wood in the valley
of a mountain—a wood of oak and ash and smooth-barked   765
dogwood that dash their long branches against one another
with a wondrous sound amid a crashing of broken branches—
even so the Trojans and Achaeans leaped upon one another
and cut each other to pieces. Nor did either side think of ruinous
flight. Many sharp spears were fixed around Kebriones   770
and arrows flew from many bowstrings, and many large stones
smashed against the shields of the men as they fought around Kebriones,
where he lay great in his greatness, in the whirl of the dust, forgetful
of his horsemanship.

　　　　　　　Now for as long as Helios straddled mid-heaven,
for so long missiles hit men on both sides, and the people fell.   775
But when Helios turned to the time for the unyoking of oxen,
then the Achaeans were stronger than what was fated to be.°
Out from the range of arrows they carried the warrior Kebriones,
out of the battle-din of the Trojans, and they stripped the armor
from his shoulders. And then Patroklos, intending evil, fell on   780

777　*fated to be:* This is the only time in Homer that something happens "beyond what is fated," emphasizing the
　　extraordinary nature of Patroklos' achievements.

FIGURE 16.3 Kebriones.   Hector's charioteer mounts his chariot before being killed by
Patroklos. Hector, holding a spear and wearing a robe, and an armed companion stand to the left of
the chariot; Glaukos, holding a spear and wearing a similar robe, and an armed companion stand to
the right. Kebriones is in the chariot. The figures are labeled. It is a four-horse chariot, which never
appears in Homer, unless the outside horses are trace-horses. Athenian black-figure wine-jug,
c. 575–550 BC.

the Trojans. Three times he rushed on them, the equal to swift Ares,
screaming terribly, and three times he killed nine men. But when
for the fourth time he charged, like a god, then, O Patroklos,
came the end of your life. For Phoibos met you in the dread
conflict, an awesome power.   785

     Patroklos did not see Phoibos
as he came through the melée: Hidden in a thick cloud Apollo
met him. Apollo stood behind him and struck him on the back
between his broad shoulders with the flat of his hand, and his eyes
went spinning. Phoibos Apollo then knocked the helmet
from Patroklos' head, and it rolled ringing beneath the feet   790
of the horses—the helmet with its fitted crest and plumes,
all befouled with blood and dust! It was not allowed before
that this helmet with horse-hair plume be befouled with dust,
for it protected the head of a godlike man and his handsome
forehead—Achilles! But then Zeus gave it to Hector   795
to wear on his head. And now destruction was coming on Hector.

And the long-shadowed spear that Patroklos held in his hands
was wholly broken—heavy, large, strong, with a bronze tip.
From his shoulders the tasseled shield with its shield-strap fell
to the ground. And Apollo, the son of Zeus, the king, loosed   800
the breastplate.

     Now blindness seized Patroklos' mind,
his shining limbs were loosed beneath him, and he stood
in a daze. Then Euphorbos, the son of Panthoös, a Dardanian,
cast at him with his sharp spear from close range and hit him
in the middle of the back between the shoulders—Euphorbos   805
who surpassed all his agemates in throwing the spear and
in horsemanship and in swiftness of foot. He had
already thrown twenty men from their cars, coming
recently with his chariot to learn the art of war. He first cast
his spear at you, O horseman Patroklos, but he did not kill you.°   810

Euphorbos pulled his ashen spear from Patroklos' flesh
then ran back to mix-in with the crowd. He did not come again

---

810 ...*not kill you*: Patroklos' death is strange. Probably in an early form of the story the armor was magical,
   invulnerable, and so could only be removed by a god. The scene is perhaps modeled on the death of Achilles
   told in some other epic. Euphorbos, of whom we have never heard, is a stand-in for Paris, who killed
   Achilles at the Scaean Gates in alliance with Apollo. Like Paris, he is a noble herdsman, good at the games,
   handsome, and an enemy of Menelaos, who kills him in Book 17.

at Patroklos, now naked in the fight. Patroklos, overcome
by the blow of the god and by the spear, withdrew back into
815 the throng of his companions, avoiding death. When Hector
saw great-hearted Patroklos withdraw, wounded by the sharp bronze,
he came close to him through the ranks, and he stabbed him with his spear
in the lower part of the belly. He drove through the bronze.
Patroklos fell with a thudding sound, greatly paining the Achaeans.

820   As when a lion conquers an untiring boar in fight, struggling with
high hearts over a small spring on the peaks of a mountain
that they both want to drink from—the boar pants hard but the lion
overcomes him with his strength—even so did Hector, son of Priam,
take away the life of the brave son of Menoitios, who had
825 killed many, standing near him and striking him with his spear.

    Boasting, Hector spoke words that went like arrows:
"Patroklos, you said that you would sack our city and take away
the day of freedom from our Trojan women, and drive them
in your ships to the land of your fathers—fool! In front of them
830 the swift horses of Hector stride out to fight. And I myself
am preeminent among the war-loving Trojans, I who can keep them
from the day of slavery. But you—vultures will devour you now, dog!
Achilles for all his excellence did you no good. He no doubt
gave you much advice as you went forth and he remained behind.
835 'Don't return to the hollow ships, Patroklos, master of horsemen,
before you have torn the bloody breastplate from around the chest
of man-killing Hector!' Thus, I imagine, he spoke to you,
and he persuaded you in your folly."

                    Patroklos, the horseman,
you spoke back to Hector, all strength gone: "You make a great
840 boast now, O Hector. Zeus the son of Kronos has given you victory,
and Apollo, who easily overcame me—for they took my armor
from my shoulders. But if twenty men such as you had faced me,
all would have perished here, conquered by my spear.
But ruinous fate and the son of Leto has killed me,
845 and of men, Euphorbos. You are only the third in my killing.
    "But I will tell you something, and you best lay it to heart:
Your own life is not long, but death already stands close beside you,
and powerful fate, that you be killed at the hands of Achilles,
the blameless grandson of Aiakos."°

---

849 *of Aiakos*: Dying men are thought to have prophetic powers.

So he spoke, and then death
covered him, and his breath-soul fled to the house of Hades,   850
lamenting its fate, leaving behind manliness and youth.

Even though he was dead, glorious Hector spoke to him:
"Patroklos, why do you prophesy for me my sheer destruction?
Who knows whether Achilles, the son of Thetis with pretty hair,
might first be hit by *my* spear and lose *his* life?"   855

So speaking he put his heel on the corpse and pulled out his bronze
from the wound, and he pushed Patroklos backwards from the spear.
At once he went after Automedon with his spear, the godlike
aide of Achilles the fast runner, for Hector wanted to strike him.
But the swift immortal horses, which the gods had given   860
to Peleus as splendid gifts, bore Automedon away.

BOOK 17. *The Fight Over the Corpse*
of Patroklos

It did not escape the notice of war-loving Menelaos, the son
of Atreus, that Patroklos had been killed in battle by the Trojans.
He strode through the vanguard troops armed in shining bronze.
He stood over the corpse like a mother stands over her calf,
5 whimpering, the first one she has given birth to—even so
light-haired Menelaos stood over Patroklos. He held
before him his spear and shield, equal on all sides,
eager to kill whoever should come against him.

Nor was Euphorbos, the son of Panthoös, unaware
10 that the blameless Patroklos had fallen, so he strode up close
and accosted war-loving Menelaos: "O Menelaos, son
of Atreus, god-nourished leader of the people—step back!
Leave the corpse! Let the bloody armor go! For before me
not one of the Trojans or her famous allies struck the good Patroklos
15 with his spear in the dread contendings. So let me gain
a noble reputation among the Trojans—and I'll now
cast at you and take away your life, sweet as honey!"

Growling deeply, light-haired Menelaos spoke:
"Father Zeus, it is no good thing to make a proud boast!
20 But the strength of a leopard is not so great, nor a lion,
nor a wild destroying boar whose spirit in its breast
exults in its power more than any creature, as is the spirit
of the sons of Panthoös who hold fine ashen spears!
Nor did the might of horse-taming Hyperenor have much
25 profit of *his* youth, when he scorned me and awaited
my coming, and said I was the worst fighter among the Danaäns.°
I don't think that he went home on his own feet to bring joy
to his beloved wife and caring parents! Even so, I think,
will I loose your own strength, if you stand against me.
30 So back off, I urge you, into the crowd! Don't stand against me,

---

26 *the Danaäns:* In Book 14 Menelaos killed Hyperenor, apparently the brother of Euphorbos and Poulydamas,
all sons of the powerful Trojan noble Panthoös. Menelaos had the reputation of being a lackluster fighter.

or you will suffer some evil. Even a fool is smart once
the deed is done!"

So he spoke, but Euphorbos did not
heed him. He said in reply: "Now, god-nourished Menelaos,
you will pay the price. You killed my brother and now
you boast. You made his wife a widow in her newly   35
built bridal chamber, and you fashioned unspeakable sorrow
and pain for his parents. Surely I will end their grief,
their sorrow, when I bring home your head and armor and place
them in the hands of Panthoös and the queenly Phrontis.
But the struggle will not be untried or unsought for long,   40
either for victory or flight!"

So speaking, he stabbed
at Menelaos' shield, balanced on every side, but the bronze
did not break through. The point of the spear was bent
in the powerful shield. Then, swiftly, Menelaos, the son of Atreus,
rushed on Euphorbos with his spear, praying to father Zeus.   45
As Euphorbos faded back, Menelaos hit him at the base of the throat
and he put his weight in it, trusting to his powerful thrust.
The spear point went straight through the tender neck
and Euphorbos fell with a thud. His armor clanged about him.
His hair was drenched in blood—hair like the Graces'—   50
and his locks pinched together with gold and silver, like
the waist of a wasp.° As a man nourishes a blooming olive
in a lonesome place where an abundance of water wells up—
a beautiful tree, luxuriant, and the blasts of all the winds
make it quiver, and it teems with white blossoms, but suddenly   55
a wind comes up in a destructive tempest and tears
it from its trench and lays it low on the earth—
even so Menelaos, the son of Atreus, stripped off
the armor of Euphorbos after he killed him: Euphorbos,
who carried a fine ashen spear, the son of Panthoös.   60

As when a lion reared in the mountains, trusting
in its power, seizes the best of the cows from a herd while
it grazes, and first he seizes her neck in his strong teeth
and breaks it, then gulps down the blood and the guts
in his rage, and all around him the dogs and herdsmen wail   65

---

52   *waist of a wasp*: Spirals of gold, apparently for binding braids of hair, are found in graves from
     c. 1000–800 BC, and Homer could be referring to them here.

loud from a distance, but they do not want to get too close,
for giddy fear has taken hold of them—even so,
no heart in any Trojan breast dared to come against
the mighty Menelaos.

Then the son of Atreus would
70 easily have carried away the famous armor of the son
of Panthoös, but Phoibos Apollo would not allow it.
Apollo aroused Hector, the equal to swift Ares, in the likeness
of Mentes, a leader of the Ciconians.° He spoke and addressed
him with words that went like arrows: "Hector, you are
75 running now after what you can never attain, the horses
of the war-loving grandson of Aiakos. They are hard for mortal
men to control or to hold fast—except for Achilles, the child
of an immortal mother. In the meanwhile the warrior Menelaos,
the son of Atreus, bestrides Patroklos after killing Euphorbos,
80 son of Panthoös, the best of the Trojans, and he has put an end
to his bravery."

So speaking Apollo, a god, went back
into the work of men. But a dread grief covered Hector's dark
spirit. He glanced then along the ranks, and immediately he saw
Menelaos stripping away the glorious armor from Euphorbos
85 lying on the ground. The blood poured from the open wound.
Hector went through the forefighters, armed in his flaming
bronze, shouting aloud like the unquenchable flame of Hephaistos.

The son of Atreus heard his shrill cry. Groaning,
he spoke to his own abundant spirit: "Well, if I let
90 go of the beautiful armor,° and Patroklos, who died
for the sake of my own honor, I fear that many of the Danaäns
may be angry with me, if somebody should see. But if
from shame I fight against Hector and the Trojans,
being alone, I fear that they will surround me—there
95 are so many! Hector of the flashing helmet is leading
all the Trojans here!
    "But why is my heart having
this conversation? When a man wants against the gods'
will to fight another man, a man whom the god honors,
great pain comes quickly rolling down upon him.

---

73   *Ciconians*: A Thracian tribe (Map 6). Odysseus' first stop on his way home from Troy is in the land of the
     Ciconians, where he and his men raid the land.

90   *armor*: The armor of Euphorbos, because Hector has the armor of Patroklos.

FIGURE 17.1 **Hector and Menelaos fight over Euphorbos.** Hector is on the right, Menelaos on the left, while Euphorbos lies dead between them. The warriors, labeled, are armed as classical hoplites. Hector's shield is emblazoned with a crow. Two apotropaic eyes ("turning away evil") are suspended from a central decorative device. Hector does not actually fight Menelaos over Euphorbos in the *Iliad*, but he tries to. The philosopher Pythagoras (c. 570–c. 495 BC), who taught metempsychosis, claimed to be a reincarnation of Euphorbos. He said that he recognized Euphorbos' shield as his own, hung in the temple to Hera at Argos where Menelaos had taken it. An early representation of an Iliadic scene on a plate made in Rhodes around 610 BC.

100 Therefore no man of the Danaäns will be angry with me
who sees me back off from Hector, for he fights with the
support of the gods. But if I might somewhere find Ajax, good
at the war cry, the two of us may return, having
relish for the war, even if the gods are against us.
105 Then perhaps we can drag out the body of Patroklos and
deliver it to Achilles, the son of Peleus. Of evil outcomes,
that would be best."

         While he thus meditated in his heart
and mind, the ranks of the Trojans came on with Hector
in the lead. Menelaos pulled back and left the corpse,
110 turning constantly around like a long-whiskered lion
that dogs and men chase from a farm with swords
and shouts, and the lion's brave heart is congealed in his breast
as he goes unwilling from the fold—even so light-haired
Menelaos pulled back from Patroklos.°

         He stopped and turned
115 around when he reached the throng of his companions, looking
around for Big Ajax, the great, the son of Telamon. He saw
him quickly on the far left of the battle, arousing his companions
and urging them to fight. For Phoibos Apollo had cast a strange
fear into the Achaeans.

         Menelaos ran to meet him,
120 and soon stood by his side and said: "Ajax,° come quick,
my friend, so that we might retrieve the dead Patroklos,
and maybe we can carry his body to Achilles, his naked corpse.
But Hector of the flashing helm has his armor."

         So he spoke,
and he wakened the warlike spirit in Ajax, who strode
125 through the front fighters together with light-haired Menelaos.

    Now Hector, when he had stripped off Patroklos' glorious
armor, tried to pull him away so that he could cut off the head
from his shoulders with the sharp bronze and drag away the corpse
and give it to the dogs of Troy. But Ajax came near,
130 carrying his shield like a tower. Then Hector gave ground,

---

114   *Patroklos*: We hear no more about the body of Euphorbos, presumably recovered by the Trojans along with
his armor.

120   *Ajax*: Last seen in Book 16 fighting over the body of Sarpedon.

back into the crowd of his companions, and he leaped into
his chariot. He gave the beautiful armor to the Trojans to carry
to the city, to be a great glory for him.

                    Meanwhile Ajax
covered the son of Menoitios with his broad shield. He stood
there like a lion around his cubs, one that the huntsmen   135
have met in the forest while he leads his young, and he exults
in his power as he draws down the skin over his brows so as
to cover his eyes—even so Ajax bestrode the warrior Patroklos.
The war-loving Menelaos, son of Atreus, took his stand
on the other side of the corpse, nursing great sorrow in his breast.   140

    Glaukos, the son of Hippolochos, leader of the Lycians,
with an angry glance from beneath his brows, spoke to Hector
hard words: "Hector, nice to look at, in battle you are
exceedingly lacking! Your fine reputation is worthless. You are
a coward! So have a thought for how you will save your country   145
and its capital alone with only those born in Ilion
at your side. Of the Lycians no one will go forth to fight
the Danaäns on behalf of the city when there is no thanks
for fighting against the enemy constantly, without respite.
    "For how is it that you would save a worse man in the   150
press of battle—scoundrel!—when you left Sarpedon, your
guest-friend and companion, to be the prey and spoil of the Argives,
one who was a help to the city and to yourself while he was alive?
As it is, you have not had the courage to defend him from the dogs.
If any Lycian will obey us, we will head home, and utter destruction   155
for Troy will be certain. I wish that the Trojans were fearless
and undaunted such as men are who fight and contend against
the enemy for their fatherland—then right away we would drag
Patroklos into Ilion. If we could get his dead body into the great city
of King Priam and snatch him from the battle, the Argives would   160
quickly give up the beautiful armor of Sarpedon, and we could bring
Sarpedon's body back to Ilion.° For Patroklos was aide to Achilles,
the best of the Argives by the ships, and his followers are fighters
in the hand-to-hand. But you did not have the courage
to take your stand before great-hearted Ajax and to look   165
him in the eye in the contest of foes, nor to fight him—
he is a better man than you are!"

---

162   *into Ilion:* Glaukos does not know that Sarpedon's body has been taken to Lycia by Sleep and Death.

                              Peering at him from beneath
his brows, Hector of the flashing helmet said: "Glaukos,
why do you talk with such arrogance, considering what kind
170 of man you are? Yes, I thought that you were superior
in understanding to all those who dwell in Lycia with its rich soil.
But now I despise your intelligence, in light of your words,
who say I would not stand up to huge Ajax! I do not shudder
at the battle nor the thundering of horses, but always the mind
175 of Zeus who carries the goatskin fetish is stronger,
who puts to flight even brave men and easily deprives
them of victory—it is thus when Zeus rouses men to fight.
But come now, my friend, stand beside me and watch what I do,
whether I will be proven a coward all day long, as you say,
180 or whether I will put a stop to the valor of any of the Danaäns
who is eager to mount a defense over the dead body of Patroklos."

      So speaking, he shouted aloud to his armies: "Trojans and Lycians
and Dardanians who fight in close—be men, my friends!
Turn your thoughts to the dread contendings while I put on
185 the beautiful armor of blameless Achilles, which I took
from powerful Patroklos after I killed him."

                              Having thus spoken,
Hector of the flashing helmet went off from the dire war.
At a run, he quickly arrived to his companions who were nearby,
hurrying after them on swift feet. They were carrying the glorious
190 armor of the son of Peleus to the city. Standing aside
from the fearful fighting, he exchanged armor. He gave
his own armor to the war-loving Trojans to carry to sacred Ilion,
but dressed himself in the immortal armor of Achilles,
the son of Peleus, which the heavenly gods had given to his
195 father Peleus, and he gave the armor to his son when he grew old.
But the son was not to grow old in this armor of the father.

      When cloud-gathering Zeus saw from afar Hector
putting on the armor of the godlike son of Peleus,
he shook his head and addressed his own heart: "Ah wretch,
200 death is not in your thoughts, but it is close. You put on
the immortal arms of a very great man, of whom all others
are in terror. You have killed his companion who was gentle
and strong, and you removed the armor from his head and shoulders
not in accordance with what is right. But for now I will instill
205 a great power in you, in recompense for this fact—that never

will Andromachê receive from you, as you return from battle,
the glorious arms of the son of Peleus."

Zeus spoke,
and the son of Kronos nodded with his dark-blue brows.°
Zeus fitted the armor to Hector's flesh, and Ares entered
into him, the terrifying Enyalios, and he filled Hector's limbs   210
with strength and power. Hector went his way, shouting loudly,
into the company of his renowned allies, and he appeared
in front of all, shining in the armor of the son of Peleus.
He urged the Trojans on, man by man, addressing them
as he went up and down the ranks: Mesthles and Glaukos° and Medon   215
and Thersilochos and Asteropaios and Deisenor and Hippothoös
and Phorkys and Chromios and the bird-prophet Ennomos.°

   He urged them on, speaking words that went like arrows:
"Hear me, you ten thousand tribes of allies who live hereabouts!
Not because I sought or needed a huge number of you did I   220
gather each man of you here from your cities, but so that you might
with a ready heart save the wives and little children of the Trojans
from the war-loving Achaeans. With this in mind I waste
the substance of the people with gifts and food so that I might
increase the strength of every one of you—and now is the time   225
that you turn against the enemy and either perish or be saved!
Such is the sweet-talk of war. Whoever succeeds in pulling
Patroklos, although he is dead, into the midst of the horse-taming
Trojans, and makes Ajax to back off, him I will give half the spoils
and take half for myself. Thus he will win as much glory as I."   230

---

208   *dark-blue brows*: Probably based on the Near Eastern practice of inlaying statues of the gods with dark-blue
      lapis lazuli.
215   *Glaukos*: This is the last time we see Glaukos in the *Iliad*, but he has played an important role so far: He is
      introduced as a comrade of Sarpedon in the Catalog of Ships (Book 2); he encounters Diomedes (Book 6)
      and kills a Greek (Book 7); he leads a charge in the company of Sarpedon, listens to Sarpedon's disquisition
      on honor, and is wounded by Teucer (Book 12), but is present at the rescue of Hector (Book 14); the dying
      Sarpedon begs Glaukos to defend his armor; he is healed by Apollo, rebukes Hector, and kills a Greek
      (Book 16). According to later tradition, Ajax finally kills Glaukos in the fight over the body of Achilles.
217   *... Ennomos*: Mesthles the Maeonian appears only in the Trojan Catalog (Book 2); later in this book Ajax
      will kill Hippothoös the Pelasgian and Phorkys the Phrygian; Ennomos the bird-prophet did not foresee
      his own upcoming death in the river, at Achilles' hands, according to the Trojan Catalog (but in fact Achil-
      les does not kill him in the river: Book 21); Asteropaios the Paeonian arrived just 10 days before, so does
      not appear in the Trojan Catalog, but Sarpedon chooses him, along with Glaukos, as the bravest Lycian
      fighter after himself (Book 12)—Asteropaios dies after wounding Achilles (Book 21); Chromios may be
      the same as Chromis the Mysian, an associate of Ennomos according to the Trojan Catalog; Achilles will
      kill Thersilochos in the river (Book 21); Medon and Deisenor are unknown.

So Hector spoke, and they went straight for the Danaäns,
putting all their weight into it, holding their spears high.
They hoped very much to snatch the corpse away
from Ajax, son of Telamon—the fools! Truly, Ajax
235 took the lives of many in the fight over Patroklos!

Ajax spoke to Menelaos, good at the war cry: "My friend,
god-nourished Menelaos, I don't think that the two of us
are going to get out of this war by ourselves alone.
I am not so much afraid for the corpse of Patroklos, who will soon
240 glut the dogs and birds of the Trojans, as I fear for my own life
that is in danger, and for yours, because the cloud of war
covers everything, including Hector, and sheer destruction
is plain for us to see. But come, call the chiefs of the Danaäns,
in the hopes that someone will heed." So he spoke,
245 and Menelaos, good at the war cry, did not disobey.

Menelaos let out a piercing shout and called to the Danaäns:
"My friends, leaders and rulers of the Argives, those of you
who drink at the king's expense with Agamemnon and Menelaos
as hosts, the sons of Atreus, and give commands to your own
250 people—from Zeus comes your honor and your glory!—it is hard
for me to spy out each of you leaders because so great
burns the strife of war. But let every one of you go forth
by himself and have shame in his heart that Patroklos
becomes a flesh-toy for the dogs of Troy!"

                                    So he spoke,
255 and swift Ajax, the son of Oïleus, heard Menelaos clearly.
He came first on a run to meet him in the battle, and after him
Idomeneus and the comrade of Idomeneus, Meriones, the equal
to man-killing Enyalios. Of the others who came, who could name
them from his own intelligence?—so many there were who aroused
260 the battle of the Achaeans.

                            Then the Trojans pressed forward
in a mass with Hector in the lead. As when at the mouth
of a river swollen with rain a great wave of the sea roars
against the stream, and round about the cliffs of the shore
echo as the salt sea belches beyond—so great was the shouting
265 of the Trojans.

                    But the Achaeans took their stand around
the son of Menoitios, and with a single mind fenced

with their shields of bronze. And the son of Kronos
poured a great mist over their shining helmets, for he had
no hatred for the son of Menoitios in earlier times,
while he was alive and aide to the grandson of Aiakos.   270
Zeus deplored that Patroklos might become the booty for the dogs
of the Trojan enemy, and so he roused the Achaeans to defend him.

At first the Trojans drove back the bright-eyed Achaeans,
who left the corpse and shrank back, but not a single man
did the high-hearted Trojans kill with their spears, although   275
eager to do so, as the Trojans tried to drag off the corpse.
Flagging, the Achaeans held off only a short while from their task
before Ajax quickly rallied them, superior in his bearing
and in the deeds of war to all other Danaäns, after the blameless
son of Peleus. Ajax went straight through the forefighters   280
like a wild boar in his strength who easily scatters dogs
and lusty youths, wheeling on them in a clearing of the woods—
even so the illustrious Ajax, son of noble Telamon,
easily scattered the battalions once he had got among
the Trojans, those who had gathered around Patroklos,   285
longing to carry the body to their city and so gain glory.

Then Hippothoös,° the glorious son of Pelasgian Lethos,
got a strap around the tendons of both ankles and dragged
Patroklos through the ferocious contendings, bringing pleasure to Hector
and the Trojans. But swiftly did an evil come on him that no one   290
could prevent, though desiring it. For the son of Telamon darted
through the crowd and struck Hippothoös up close through the helmet
with its bronze cheek pieces. The helmet with its crest of horsehair
was split around the point of the spear, smashed by the great spear
from Ajax's powerful hand. And the bloody brains ran out   295
along the socket from the wound. Hippothoös' strength
was loosened, and out of his hands he dropped to the ground
the foot of great-hearted Patroklos. Hippothoös fell there
on his face beside the body of Patroklos, far from Larisa
with its deep soil, nor did he pay back to his beloved parents   300
the cost of his upbringing. Brief was the span of his life,
fallen beneath the spear of great-hearted Ajax.

Then Hector
threw his shining spear at Ajax, but Ajax, watching him steadily,

---

287 *Hippothoös*: The leader of the Pelasgians in the Trojan Catalog, mentioned earlier in this book in the list of
     Trojan leaders, along with Phorkys.

avoided the bronze spear by a hair. Instead Hector struck
305 great-hearted Schedios, the son of Iphitos,° by far the best
of the Phocians, who dwelled in a house in famous Panopeus,°
ruling over many men. He hit him beneath the middle of his
collar bone. The point of the bronze spear went straight through
and came out beneath the base of his shoulder. He fell with a thud.
310 His armor rattled about him.

                         Then Ajax hit Phorkys,
the warlike son of Phainops, full in the middle of the belly
as Phorkys strode over Hippothoös, and he broke the curved plate
of his breast protector, and his guts oozed out through the bronze.
He fell in the dust and clutched the earth in his palms.
315 Shining Hector and his vanguard retreated, and the Argives
shouted aloud and pulled out the bodies of Phorkys and
Hippothoös and undid the armor from around their shoulders.

Then the Achaeans would again have driven back the Trojans
to Ilion, vanquished in their cowardice, and the Argives would have won
320 glory through their strength and power beyond what was fated,
but Apollo himself roused up Aeneas. He took on the likeness
of Periphas the herald, son of Epytos,° grown old in the house
of Aeneas' aged father Anchises while heralding,
and being well disposed to Aeneas. In Periphas' likeness,
325 Apollo, the son of Zeus, said: "Aeneas, how could you ever
protect steep Ilion in defiance of a god? Surely I have
seen other men, dependent on their strength and their power
and their bravery, hold their realm in spite of scanty resources.
But Zeus *wants* a victory for us more by far than for the Danaäns—
330 yet you are held by unbounded fear! You do not fight!"

So he spoke, and Aeneas realized when he looked on his face
that it was Apollo who shoots from a long way off, and he shouted
over to Hector: "Hector, and you other captains and leaders
of the Trojans, this would be a shame, to be driven back
335 to Ilion by the war-loving Achaeans, vanquished by our cowardice.

---

305 ... *Iphitos*: Hector kills a Phocian named Schedios in Book 15, but there he is the son of Perimedes—
Homer has a mental lapse. Iphitos was an Argonaut, according to later tradition.

306 *Panopeus*: A town near Delphi, listed without comment in the Catalog of Ships. In the *Odyssey*, Panopeus is
said to be the place where the giant Tityos attempted to rape Leto, a crime for which he was punished in the
underworld (*Odyssey* Book 11).

322 *Epytos*: Heralds usually have "speaking names," so Periphas means "speaker" and his father, and no doubt
predecessor, Epytos means "caller."

But one of the gods has just stood by my side and said
that Zeus the Most High Counselor is our helper in the fight.
So let's go straight at the Danaäns. Let them not drag the dead
Patroklos at their ease to the ships!"

            So he spoke,
and leaping in front of the forefighters he took his stand.   340
Then the Trojans whirled around and stood against the Achaeans.

   Aeneas stabbed Leokritos° with his spear, son of Arisbas,
the brave companion of Lykomedes.° War-loving Lykomedes
took pity on Leokritos when he fell, and he moved in close
and gored Apisaon, son of Hippasos, shepherd of the people,   345
with his shining spear, in the liver beneath the stomach. Immediately
he loosed his knees—Apisaon who came from PAEONIA
with its rich soil and after Asteropaios° was best in the fight.

   The warring Asteropaios took pity on Apisaon when he fell
and he rushed forward, anxious to take on the Danaäns.   350
But he could do nothing, for the Achaeans with their shields were
fenced in on all sides around Patroklos, and they held their spears
in front of them. Ajax ranged back and forth before them all,
stirring them up, and he enjoined them not to retreat
from the corpse, nor for any single man to fight in front   355
of the Achaeans as one preeminent above the others,
but to stand in front of the corpse and fight in the hand-to-hand.

   So mighty Ajax ordered them, and the ground was wet
with dark blood, and the dead fell thick and fast of both
the Trojans and their mighty allies, and of the Danaäns.   360
For they did not fight without the shedding of blood, although
far fewer of the Achaeans were dying, because they were
accustomed always to push off fell destruction from one another
in the midst of the melée.

        And so they fought like blazing fire,
nor would you say that there was a sun or a moon, for they   365
were shrouded in the darkness of battle, all the chieftains who stood

---

342 *Leokritos:* The name of one of Penelope's suitors!

343 *Lykomedes:* One of the lesser Greek leaders, mentioned in the groups of captains (Book 7, 19) and once in
     the company of Little Ajax (Book 12).

348 *Asteropaios:* Mentioned in the catalog of Trojan fighters earlier in this book, he had arrived at Troy only 10
     days before this battle.

around the corpse of Patroklos. But the other Trojans and Achaeans
who wear fine shinguards fought more freely in the open air.
Above them the piercing rays of the sun were spread,
370 and no cloud appeared over all the earth or the mountains.
They took some ease at fighting, avoiding the groan-bearing
weapons of one another by standing far apart from each other. But those
in the middle suffered agonies because of the darkness and the war.
They wore each other to pieces with the pitiless bronze, all those
375 who were captains.

        Now two men—fine men—Thrasymedes
and Antilochos° had not yet heard that the blameless Patroklos
was dead, but thought he was still alive and fighting in the forefront
against the Trojans. The two men, guarding against the death
and flight of their companions, were fighting apart, because Nestor
380 had ordered them to do so when he was rallying them to battle
from the black ships.°

        And so the great strife of their skirmishes
raged the whole day through. The knees and legs and feet
beneath each man were wet with the sweat of war-work,
eyes and hands too, as the two sides fought over the good aide
385 of the grandson of Aiakos, the fast runner. As when a man
gives to his people the hide of a great bull, drenched
with fat to stretch, and when they have taken it they stand
around in a circle and stretch it out, and right away
the moisture evaporates but the fat sinks in as many pull
390 on the hide, and the whole hide is stretched to the utmost°—
even so the Trojans on one side and the Achaeans
on the other dragged the corpse now here, now there.

    The Trojans greatly desired to pull the corpse
to Ilion, but the Achaeans wanted to drag it to the hollow ships.
395 Around Patroklos a savage turmoil of battle arose.
Not Ares, the savior of the people, nor Athena, would have made
light of it, seeing the battle—not even if their anger
was very great, so mighty a labor of men and horses
did Zeus on that day stretch out over Patroklos.

---

376 *Thrasymedes and Antilochos*: The two brothers, sons of Nestor, have been fighting together since Book 16. Antilochos is important further on in this book, but according to tradition died later in the war. Thrasymedes survived the war and you could see his tomb near Pylos.

381 *black ships*: Homer has not recorded these instructions of Nestor.

390 *to the utmost*: Nothing is known of this process.

The good Achilles did not yet know anything about   400
the death of Patroklos, for they fought very far from
the swift ships under the wall of the Trojans. Never did he imagine
in his heart that Patroklos was dead, but thought that he would
return, still alive, once he had reached the gates. Not at all
did he think that Patroklos would take the city without him—   405
nor with him, because often he had heard this from his mother,
listening to her in private when she brought to him information
about great Zeus's intent. But his mother did not say
a word about this great calamity, that his companion, by far
the most dear, would perish.   410

                        So they pressed on continually
around the corpse, holding their sharp spears as they killed
one another. Thus would one of the Achaeans, who wear shirts
of bronze, say: "My friends, there will be no fame if we retreat
back to the hollow ships, but may the black earth open
up right here—for us all! That is a far better outcome   415
than if we are going to let this man go to the horse-taming
Trojans, to carry it to their city and to win all the glory!"
And in similar manner one of the great-hearted Trojans
would say: "My friends, if it is our fate to fall—
all of us—before this corpse, still let no one   420
step back from the fight!" Thus one would speak and arouse
the might of each. And so they fought, and an iron shout
rose up to the brazen sky through the turbulent air.

The horses of the grandson of Aiakos wept, standing
apart from battle, when once they realized that Patroklos,   425
their charioteer, lay in the dust, killed by man-killing Hector.
In truth Automedon, the son of brave Diores, often
would use the quick lash to drive them on, and often
spoke to them with honeyed words, and often with threats,
but the two horses did not want to go back to the ships   430
along the broad HELLESPONT, nor did they want
to go out among the Achaeans. As a pillar waits forever,
standing on the tomb of a dead man or woman,
even so they waited, immovable beside the beautiful car,
bowing their heads to the earth. Hot tears ran   435
to the ground from beneath their eyelids, weeping from
sorrow for their charioteer.° Their rich manes were befouled

---

437   *charioteer*: Patroklos was the horses' *regular* charioteer, but Automedon has fulfilled this function for
      Patroklos.

as they streamed on both sides from beneath the yoke-pad
next to the yoke.°

　　　　　　　When the son of Kronos saw them weeping,
440　he took pity, and shaking his head he spoke to his own heart:
"You poor beasts, why did we ever give you to King Peleus,
a mortal, when you are ageless and deathless! So that
you might share the sufferings among wretched men?
For there is nothing more miserable in all the world than a man,
445　who breathes and slithers along the earth. But Hector,
the son of Priam, will not mount you in the fancy car.
I won't allow it! Isn't it enough that he has the armor
and is going around boasting—in vain! I shall put strength
in your knees and in your hearts so that you might save Automedon
450　from the war and carry him to the hollow ships. For still
I will grant glory to the Trojans, to go on killing until
they reach the ships with their fine benches, and the sun
goes down, and holy darkness comes on."

　　　　　　　　　　　　So speaking,
Zeus breathed a noble power into the horses. And the two horses
455　shook the dust from their manes to the ground and quickly carried
the swift chariot into the melée of the Trojans and the Achaeans.
Behind them Automedon fought, although sad for his comrade
Patroklos, swooping down with his horses like an eagle after swans.
With a light touch he fled from the Trojan melée, then just as lightly
460　he charged, pressing hard through the crowd. But he killed no men
as he hastened to pursue them, for it was not possible, being alone
in the sacred car,° for Automedon to overwhelm someone
with his spear and at the same time hold onto the swift horses.

　　　　　At last a companion saw him—Alkimedon,° the son
465　of Larkes, the son of Haimon. He stood behind the chariot
and spoke to Automedon: "Automedon, what god has put
a profitless counsel in your breast and taken away your intelligence?
You fight against the Trojans at the forefront of the throng, alone!
But your companion is dead, and Hector himself has taken

439　*yoke*: Apparently there was some kind of protective pad between the yoke and horse's neck, which here
　　　imprisons the horses' manes. Soiling one's hair is a standard display of grief.

462　*sacred car*: Perhaps because it is drawn by two divine horses.

464　*Alkimedon*: He led a contingent of Myrmidons to battle in Book 16. Later, he is in charge of Achilles' horses
　　　(Book 19), helps Achilles serve a meal, and unyokes the horses of the suppliant Priam before Achilles' hut
　　　(Book 24).

his armor and wears it on his shoulders, the armor of the grandson   470
of Aiakos. And he glories therein!"

        Automedon, the son of Diores,
then answered: "Alkimedon, what other man of the Achaeans
is of similar worth to guide and tame these immortal horses
except Patroklos, the equal to the gods in counsel while
he was alive? But now death and fate have intervened. But you   475
should take the whip and the shining reins while I dismount
from the car, so that I can fight."

        So he spoke, and Alkimedon
leaped into the car, swift in the battle, and quickly he grasped
in his hands the whip and the reins while Automedon
jumped down. Glorious Hector saw them and immediately   480
he spoke to Aeneas, standing nearby: "Aeneas,
counselor to the Trojans who wear shirts of bronze, I see
the two horses of the grandson of Aiakos, the fast runner,
coming into the battle, with weakling charioteers. I would like
to take these horses, if your heart is willing, because I don't think   485
those two will dare to stand against us in battle if we rush
upon them."

        So he spoke, and Aeneas, the good son of Anchises,
did not disobey. The two men went straight ahead, their
shoulders wrapped in the shields of bull's hide—dry, tough!—
and with plates of bronze affixed to the shields. With them   490
went both Chromios and godlike Aretos,° both hoping in their hearts
to kill Automedon and Alkimedon and take the long-necked
horses—the fools! For they were not to return from Automedon
without the shedding of blood.

        Automedon prayed to father Zeus
and his dark heart within him was filled with strength and power.   495
Right away he turned to Alkimedon, his trusty companion,
and he said: "Alkimedon, hold the horses close to me
so that they breathe on my back. I don't think that Hector,
the son of Priam, will give up his fury before he mounts
behind the horses of Achilles, with their lovely manes, and kills   500

---

491   ... *Aretos*: Chromios (perhaps "thunderer") is a common name: five different persons in the *Iliad* bear
       this name. He is listed in the catalog of Trojan captains early in this book. Aretos ("longed for") is also the
       name of a son of Nestor. He is introduced here for the first time, only to be killed.

the two of us and puts the ranks of the Argives to flight,
or he is himself killed."

So speaking, Automedon called
to the two Ajaxes and to Menelaos: "Ajaxes, both of you,
leaders of the Argives, and Menelaos—turn over the corpse
505   to those who are bravest to stand firm about it and ward off
the ranks of men. Come, defend us who are living
from the pitiless day of doom, for Hector and Aeneas,
the best of the Trojans, are pressing hard in the tearful war.
But all this lies on the knees of the gods. I will cast my spear,
510   then the rest is up to Zeus."

Thus Automedon spoke and brandished
his long-shadowing spear. He threw it, and he struck Aretos
in the center of his shield, well balanced on every side.
But the shield did not stay the spear. It went straight through,
and Automedon drove it through the belt into Aretos' lower belly.
515   As when a lusty man with a sharp ax strikes behind the horns
of an ox of the field and cuts entirely through the tendon,
and the ox leaps forward and falls—even so Aretos leaped
forward, then fell on his back. The sharp spear, quivering
in his guts, put an end to life.

Hector now threw
520   at Automedon with his shining spear, but Automedon saw
the bronze spear coming and avoided it as he stooped forward,
and the butt of the long spear quivered, fixed in the ground
behind him. Finally, strong Ares stopped its fury.

Hector and Automedon would have rushed each other
525   with swords, except that the Ajaxes in their fury separated them
when they came through the crowd, answering Automedon's cry.
Then Hector and Aeneas and godlike Chromios backed
away in fear, leaving Aretos lying there, stricken to death.
Automedon, the equal to swift Ares, looted the armor of Aretos
530   and bragging said: "Well, I have eased just a little
my sorrow for the dead Patroklos, the son of Menoitios,
although I have killed a far lesser man."

So saying he took up
the bloody armor and placed it in his car and himself

mounted the car, his feet and hands, too, covered in blood,
like a lion who has just eaten a bull.° 535

Then again dread conflict
was stretched over Patroklos—terrible, tearful!—and Athena
stirred up the fight, coming down from the sky. For far-seeing
Zeus had sent her to urge on the Danaäns. His mind
was turned. Even as Zeus stretches out a dark-shimmering
rainbow from the heavens as a portent to men, either of war, 540
or a freezing storm that puts an end to the work of men
on the earth and distresses the flocks, even so Athena
cloaked in a dark-shimmering cloud went down into the tribe
of the Achaeans, where she roused up each man.

Stirring the son
of Atreus first of all, she spoke to powerful Menelaos,° 545
for he was close by. She took on the appearance of Phoinix
in form and untiring voice: "To you, Menelaos, it will be
shame and reproach if the swift dogs rend the loyal companion
of noble Achilles under the wall of the Trojans. So hold
your ground, and urge everybody on!" 550

Then Menelaos,
good at the war cry, answered her: "Phoinix, you dear man,
old-timer from long ago—if Athena would only give me
strength and protect me from the onrush of arrows, I'd be
proud to stand by Patroklos' side and make a defense.
For his death has very much touched me to the heart. 555
Yet Hector has the dread fury of fire in him. He is not going
to give up killing with the bronze. It is Zeus who gives him glory."

So he spoke and flashing-eyed Athena rejoiced because,
of all the gods, Menelaos prayed to her first, and she put
strength into his shoulders and into his knees and injected 560
in his breast the brashness of a fly: No matter how many times
a man brushes it away from his skin, it persists in biting,

---

535   ... *eaten a bull*: Automedon and the horses now disappear until Book 19, when Automedon prepares them
      for Achilles' *aristeia*. One might wonder why Automedon does not tell Achilles about Patroklos' death, but
      this task is left to Antilochos.
545   *Menelaos*: The two Ajaxes have gone off to help Automedon, leaving Menelaos as the principal defender of
      Patroklos' body.

so sweet to it is the blood of a man. With such boldness she filled
his dark spirit.

                    Thus he stood over Patroklos and thrust
565 with his shining spear, and he took down Podes, the son
of Eëtion,° rich and noble. Hector honored Podes most
of all the people because he was a companion and a beloved
comrade at the feast. Light-haired Menelaos hit him on the belt
as he started to run away, and he drove the bronze straight through.
570 Podes fell with a thud. Then Menelaos, son of Atreus,
dragged the corpse out from under the Trojans into the midst
of his companions.

                  Next Apollo, standing beside Hector,
urged him on in the likeness of Phainops, son of Asios,° who of
all his guest-friends was dearest to him. He lived in ABYDOS.
575 In his likeness Apollo, the far-shooter, spoke to Hector:
"Hector, who of the Achaeans will ever be afraid of you now?
now that you tremble before Menelaos, who before was a weakling?
Now he is going off with a corpse snatched all by himself
from under the Trojans. And he has killed a noble companion
580 of yours among the vanguard—that Podes, the son of Eëtion."

    So Apollo spoke, and a black cloud of pain overcame Hector.
He went through the forefighters armed in all his glimmering bronze.
And then the son of Kronos took his tasseled goatskin fetish—
it flashed!—and he covered Ida in clouds and he lightened
585 and thundered mightily, and he shook the fetish, giving victory
to the Trojans and putting the Achaeans to rout.

                   First of all Peneleos°
the Boeotian started the rout. Always facing the enemy, a spear
hit him in the shoulder, just on the surface, a glancing blow,
but the spear point of Poulydamas° still pierced to the bone—
590 for Poulydamas threw it up close.

---

566 *son of Eëtion*: Presumably this Podes is not the son of the Eëtion who was king of Thebes, the father of
Andromachê, whose seven sons Achilles killed (Book 6). There is a third Eëtion too, of Imbros, who
ransomed a son of Priam (Book 21).

573 *son of Asios*: Another Phainops is mentioned earlier in the book and still a third in Book 5.

587 *Peneleos*: Listed in the Catalog of Ships as one of the five leaders of the Boeotians. He was prominent in the
attack inspired by Poseidon (Book 14) and in that led by Patroklos (Book 16).

589 *Poulydamas*: Last mentioned with Glaukos in Book 16, he will have a big scene with Hector in the next
book.

Then Hector in a tight fight
stabbed Leïtos, the son of Alektryon,° on the hand at the wrist
and put him out of the fight. Leïtos looked around, then pulled back
in fear because he no longer thought that he could hold a spear
in his hands to fight against the Trojans. Then as Hector
leaped after Leïtos, Idomeneus hit Hector in the breastplate   595
that covered his chest, beside the nipple—but the long spear was broken
in the socket.° All the Trojans shouted aloud! Then Hector
threw at Idomeneus, the son of Deukalion, as he stood in his car,
and he missed him only by a little, but hit Koiranos,
the comrade and charioteer of Meriones, who had followed   600
Meriones from well-built LYKTOS.° Idomeneus had first come
on foot from the ships with curved prows. He would have given
a great victory to the Trojans if Koiranos had not quickly brought up
the swift-footed horses, for Koiranos came as a light of deliverance
to Idomeneus, warding off the pitiless day. But he himself   605
gave up his life at the hands of Hector, killer of men.
Hector hit him beneath the jaw and the ear, and the base
of the spear smashed out his teeth and cut his tongue in two.
Koiranos pitched from the car and the reins poured to the ground.

Meriones stooped and took the reins from the earth   610
into his own hands, then yelled to Idomeneus:° "Use the whip!
Get to the swift ships. I think that you know very well
that victory no longer belongs to the Achaeans." So he spoke,
and Idomeneus drove the horses with beautiful manes back
to the hollow ships, for fear had fallen upon his spirit.   615

Nor did it escape the notice of great-hearted Ajax
and Menelaos that Zeus had now given to the Trojans the victory
that turns the tide of battle. Great Telamonian Ajax
then spoke out: "Even a fool could tell that father Zeus
himself is behind the Trojan advance! No matter who throws   620
them—whether coward or brave—their missiles strike home.

---

591   ... *Alektryon*: Leïtos, perhaps "booty man," is in the Catalog of Ships along with Peneleos. Leïtos killed a
      Trojan in Book 6 and is mentioned when Poseidon exhorts the troops in Book 13. The name of his father
      Alektryon appears in the Linear B tablets.

597   *in the socket*: Homer does not mention that Hector is now wearing armor made by Hephaistos, which, pre-
      sumably, is invulnerable.

601   *Lyktos*: A city in central Crete mentioned in the Catalog of Ships.

611   ... *Idomeneus*: Idomeneus has come to the battle on foot without a chariot as support, but in the battle
      Koiranos, the charioteer of Meriones, drives up to help him. Meriones has earlier left the chariot in order to
      fight on the ground.

Zeus guides theirs, as ours fall uselessly to the ground. But come,
let us ourselves devise the best plan, so that we can both
drag away our dead man and ourselves return home as a joy
625 to our companions, who are pained when they look this way and think
that the power and irresistible hands of man-killing Hector cannot
be stayed, that he will again fall on the black ships. But there must
be some comrade who can quickly go tell the son of Peleus—
because I do not think that he has learned the sad news—that his dear
630 companion has been killed. But I can't see such an Achaean,
for they are all wrapped in darkness, they and their horses.
Father Zeus, please save the sons of the Achaeans from this darkness!
Let there be light, let our eyes see! Let us be destroyed in the light,
if that is your pleasure!"

So Ajax spoke and the father pitied him
635 as he wept. He quickly scattered the mist and then pushed aside
the darkness. And the sun shone, and the battle was plain
for all to see.

Then Ajax spoke to Menelaos, good
at the war cry: "Look now, god-nourished Menelaos: If you
can see Antilochos still alive, the son of great-hearted
640 Nestor, tell him to go quickly to war-loving Achilles to tell him
that his companion, the most dear to him, has been killed."

So he spoke, and Menelaos, good at the war cry, did not disobey.
He went off like a lion from an outbuilding who grows tired
from the harassment of dogs and men, who staying up all night
645 do not allow him to snatch the fattest of the herd. But the lion,
lusting for flesh, goes straight on, yet it does no good.
The javelins fly thick at him from bold hands, and blazing
firebrands too, which cause him to quail although he is eager.
At dawn the lion goes off with a sad heart—even so
650 Menelaos, good at the war cry, went off from Patroklos,
much unwilling. For he very much feared that the Achaeans,
giving into rout, would leave the body of Patroklos as a prey
to the enemy.

Menelaos instructed Meriones and the two Ajaxes:
"You two Ajaxes, and Meriones, commanders of the Argives,
655 don't forget the kindliness of sad Patroklos. To all
he was like honey when he was alive. Now death and fate
have overtaken him."

Having thus spoken, light-haired Menelaos
went off, looking around like an eagle, which they say has the keenest
sight of all the birds beneath heaven. Even when he is on high
he sees the swift-footed hare lying down beneath a thick bush,   660
and he leaps upon him and grabs him and in a moment takes
his life—even so, O god-nourished Menelaos, did your bright eyes
scan everywhere across the tribes of your many companions, looking
for the son of Nestor, if he was still alive.°

He soon saw Antilochos
on the left of the battle line, urging on his companions and exhorting   665
them to fight. Coming up near him, light-haired Menelaos said:
"God-nourished Antilochos, come here so that you might learn
bad news, that I wish had never happened. I think that,
by looking around, you already know that some god is bringing
defeat to the Danaäns. The Trojans are winning! The best   670
of the Achaeans is dead, Patroklos, and a great sadness is felt
among the Danaäns. But you—run fast to the ships of the Achaeans
and tell Achilles in hopes that he might quickly bring
the naked corpse safe to his ship. Hector of the flashing
helmet has taken the armor."   675

So Menelaos spoke, and Antilochos
was horrified when he heard. For a long time he was speechless,
his eyes filled with tears, his full voice checked. Nonetheless,
he did not hesitate to fulfill Menelaos' command.
He ran off, first giving his armor to a blameless companion,
Laodokos,° who wheeled his single-hoofed horses nearby.   680

The swift feet of Antilochos bore him out of the battle.
Pouring tears, he brought that dismal news to Achilles,
son of Peleus. And you, O god-nourished Menelaos, did not
want to come to the aid of your much-worn companions whom
Antilochos had just abandoned. But a great longing for Antilochos   685
fell over the men of Pylos. Instead, you sent the good
Thrasymedes° to them, while you yourself went to stand
over the body of the warrior Patroklos.

---

664   ... *still alive*: Homer addresses Menelaos directly seven times in the poem, always when he is about to
      perform some admirable service or otherwise evoke our sympathy.
680   *Laodokos*: Never heard of again.
687   *Thrasymedes*: The brother of Antilochos.

Menelaos ran up and stopped
beside the two Ajaxes, then right away he said: "I have sent
690 that man over there to the swift ships, to Achilles the fast runner.
But I don't think that Achilles will come out now, though he is very
angry with godlike Hector. I don't think he will fight
against the Trojans naked! Let us ourselves think of the best plan—
how we might rescue the body and ourselves flee death and fate
695 in the battle din of the Trojans."

Great Telamonian Ajax then
answered him: "You have spoken aright, O renowned Menelaos.
Look, you and Meriones get under him and raise the corpse
up quickly and get it out of the fighting. In the meanwhile, we will fight
the Trojans and godlike Hector, one in heart as we are in name,
700 men who have before stood firm in battle, standing each
by the other's side."

So he spoke. Then Meriones and Menelaos
took the corpse in their arms and raised it high off the ground.
The Trojan fighters cried out loudly when they saw the Achaeans
raising up the corpse. They charged straight ahead like dogs
705 that leap on a wounded boar in the presence of young hunters:
For awhile they pursue him, longing to rip him apart,
but when the boar wheels around, trusting in his strength,
the hunters run off and fade into fear, one here, one there—
even so the Trojans followed in a crowd for awhile,
710 stabbing with their swords and their two-edged spears. But when
the two Ajaxes wheeled around and stood against them,
then their color would change and not one dared to dart
forth and fight for the corpse.

Thus Menelaos and Meriones
hastened to carry the corpse out of the war to the hollow ships.
715 But a conflict like savage fire was stretched against them,
fire that rushes on a city of men in sudden attack
and sets it afire, and houses fall in the mighty radiance,
and the power of the winds sets it to roar—even so
the unceasing din of horses and spear-bearing men
720 came against them as they went. As mules put forth
all their strength to drag a beam, or a great ship's timber,
from the mountain down a rugged path, and within them their
hearts are worn by work and sweat, even so the Achaeans
hastened to rescue the corpse. Behind them the two Ajaxes
725 held the Trojans in check—like a ridge holds back water,

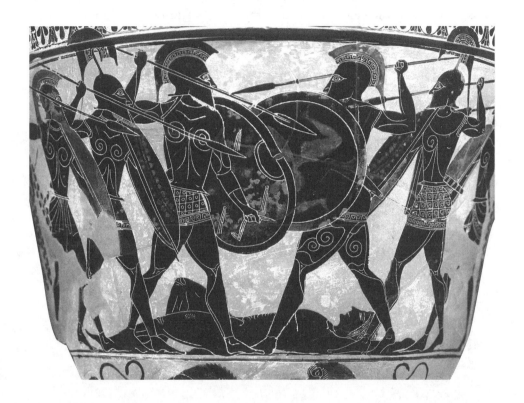

FIGURE 17.2 Fight over Patroklos. Big Ajax, on the left, holds a "Boeotian" shield, either an artistic adaptation of the ancient Mycenaean figure-of-eight shield or an actual shield shape (but no such shield has been found). His opponent is presumably Hector, holding a shield with a "triskelis" blazon, a design showing three running legs. Other unnamed Trojans and Greeks fight. Patroklos' corpse lies in the center. Black-figure wine-drinking bowl in the style of Exekias, c. 530 BC, from Pharsalos, Greece.

a wooded ridge that lies by chance across a plain, containing
the dread streams of the powerful rivers, and at once
it turns their flow back over the plain, but never does
the might of the flood break through—even so the two Ajaxes
730 held back the Trojans.

But the Trojans continually followed after,
and especially two among them, Aeneas, the son of Anchises,
and glorious Hector. As a cloud of starlings flies or crows,
shrieking doom when they see a hawk that brings death
to little birds coming at them, even so were the Achaean youth
735 shrieking doom, forgetful of valor as they fled before Aeneas
and Hector. Many beautiful arms fell around and about
the ditch as the Danaäns fled. And there was no end of war.

BOOK 18. *The Shield of Achilles*

And so they fought like blazing fire, and Antilochos,
a fast runner, came as a messenger to Achilles. He found him
in front of his ships with pointed bows and sterns.
Achilles feared in his heart that what had actually happened
would come to pass.   5

          Sorely troubled, Achilles spoke
to his own great spirit: "But why are the Achaeans with their
long hair again gathering in confusion around the ships,
driven in rout from the plain? I only hope that the gods
have not made terrible suffering for me, as once my mother
predicted. She said that while I was yet alive the best   10
of the Myrmidons would leave the light of the sun at the hands
of the Trojans. I fear that the strong son of Menoitios is dead—
the fool! I told him to come back to the ships when he had pushed
consuming fire away from the ships. And not to take on Hector!"

    While he pondered thus in his heart and spirit, the son   15
of brave Nestor came up close. Pouring down hot tears,
Antilochos spoke the sad message: "O son of Peleus, lover
of war, you are about to hear a sad tale, which ought never
to have happened. Patroklos is struck down, and they war
around his naked corpse. And Hector of the flashing helmet   20
has taken his armor."

          So he spoke, and a dark cloud
of pain covered Achilles. With both his hands he took up
the grimy dust and poured it over his head, wrecking
his pretty face, and black ashes° fell on his scented shirt.
He lay outstretched in the dirt, great in his greatness,   25
and with his hands he tore at his hair and disfigured it.
The slave girls that Achilles and Patroklos had taken as booty
cried aloud in anguish of heart, and they ran outside
to the battle-hardened Achilles, and all of them struck their breasts

---

24 *black ashes*: From the hearth fire.

30 with their hands, and the limbs of each were loosened beneath them.
Opposite them Antilochos wailed, pouring down tears.
Antilochos held Achilles' hands as Achilles moaned
in his noble heart, and Antilochos feared that he would cut
his throat with a knife.°

As Achilles groaned terribly,
35 his revered mother heard him, sitting in the depths
of the sea beside her aged father. She then let out
a shrill cry, and the goddesses gathered around her,
all the daughters of Nereus who were in the deep sea:
Glaukê and Thaleia and Kymodokê were there, and Nesaiê
40 and Speio and Thoê and cow-eyed Heliê and Kymothoê
and Aktaiê and Limnoreia and Melitê and Iaira and Amphithoê
and Agavê and Doto and Proto and Pherousa and Dynamenê
and Dexamenê and Amphinomê and Kallianeira and Doris
and Panopê and the very famous Galatea and Nemertes and Apseudes
45 and Kallianassa. And there Klymenê came and Ianeira and Ianassa
and Maira and Oreithyia and Amatheia with the lovely hair,
and other Nereids who were in the deep sea.°

The bright cave
was filled with them and they all beat their breasts, and Thetis
led in the wailing: "Listen, my sister Nereids, so that all of you
50 may know and hear the sorrow that is in my heart. I am wretched.
I am miserable in having borne the best of men. After I gave birth
to a son blameless and strong, the finest of warriors—he shot up
like a sapling, and I nourished him like a tree in a rich
orchard plot. Then I sent him forth in the beaked ships
55 to fight at Troy. But I shall never receive him again

---

34 *a knife*: At this point Antilochos drops from the scene.

47 *in the deep sea*: Such lists of sea-deities are common in early oral poetry, and many of these same names
appear in Hesiod's *Theogony*. Homer's catalog contains thirty-three names (but he adds that there were
other Nereids): *Glauke* "blue" is an epithet of the sea; *Thaleia* "blooming" is the name of one of the Muses
and one of the Graces; *Kymodokê* is "calmer of the sea"; *Nesaiê* "island girl"; *Speio*, "cave" in the sea; *Thoê*
"swift" (as of waves); *Heliê* "of the salt sea"; *Kymothoê* "swift wave"; *Aktaiê* "of the shore"; *Limnoreia*, perhaps
"harbor protector"; *Melitê* "sweet as honey"; *Iaira* "swift"; *Amphithoê* "very swift"; *Agavê* "wondrous"; *Doto*
"giver"; *Proto*, perhaps "provider"; *Pherousa*, perhaps "she who carries ships along"; *Dynamenê* "enabler";
Dexamenê, perhaps "protector"; *Amphinomê* "rich in pasture land"; *Kallianeira* "handsome"; *Doris* "giver";
Panopê "all-seeing"; *Galatea* "milk-white," referring to the foam of the sea; *Nemertes* "infallible" and *Ap-
seudes* "truthful" are qualities of Nereus, the old man of the sea, a prophet; *Kallianassa* "beautiful queen";
Klymenê "famous"; *Ianeira* and *Ianassa* both mean "strong"; *Maira* "sparkler"; *Oreithyia* "mountain-rushing,"
perhaps of the wind rushing from a mountain down to the sea; *Amatheia* "sandy."

coming home to the house of Peleus.° While he lives and sees
the light of the sun, he has sorrow, and I am not able to go
to him and help … I will go all the same, so that I might see my dear
son and hear what sorrow has come to him while he stayed
apart from the war."   60

          So speaking, she left the cave. The Nereids
went with her, pouring down tears, and around them the waves
of the sea broke. When they came to Troy with its rich soil,
they stepped out onto the beach, one after another, to where
the ships of the Myrmidons were packed in close around swift Achilles.

     Standing beside him as he groaned deeply, and crying shrilly,   65
Thetis took hold of the head of her son. In pitying tones
she spoke words that went like arrows: "Why do you weep, my son?
What sorrow has come to you? Tell me, don't hide it!
Zeus has fulfilled your wish, what you earlier prayed for
and raised your hands to—that the sons of the Achaeans be huddled   70
at the sterns of the ships, longing for you, and that they should suffer
disastrous things."

          Then Achilles the fast runner spoke, groaning deeply:
"My mother, yes, the Olympian has fulfilled my wish. But what   ◀))
pleasure is this to me when my dear companion has died—
Patroklos, whom I honored above all my other companions,   75
like myself. I have done him in. Hector killed him and has taken
my beautiful armor, huge in size, a wonder to behold.
The gods gave it as a glorious gift to Peleus on that day
when they placed you in bed with a mortal man. I wish that you
had stayed where you were, with your deathless friends of the sea,   80
and that Peleus had taken a mortal wife!
                    "But as it is—
now you too will have ten thousand pains in your heart because
of your dead son, whom you will never receive at home again.
But my heart no longer wants to live and remain among men—
unless Hector first, stabbed by my spear, gives up *his* life   85
in revenge for making Patroklos the son of Menoitios his spoil!"

     Then Thetis answered him, pouring down tears: "Then
you are doomed to a quick death, my son, if you do what you say.
For your death will follow soon after the death of Hector."

---

56 *house of Peleus*: According to the story current later, Thetis abandoned Peleus shortly after Achilles' birth,
     but here Thetis speaks as if she and Peleus were still married.

FIGURE 18.1 Thetis consoles Achilles. Thetis has pulled a cloak over her head in a sign of mourning. Achilles, lying on a couch before which stands a table filled with food, holds his hand to his forehead in a sign of grief for the death of his friend Patroklos. In this representation Thetis has already brought Achilles new armor from Hephaistos, which hangs on the wall. The shield is decorated with the face of a lion. Shinguards hang nearby. To the right of the couch is old man Phoinix and to the left Odysseus—unlike in Homer's description—and Nereids (?) stand on either side. The names of all figures (except the Nereids) are written out. Black-figure Corinthian wine jug, c. 620 BC.

Greatly moved, Achilles the fast runner said: "Then may I die   90
soon! For I was of no use in warding off death from my companion.
He has perished far from the land of his fathers, and he needed me
to ward off ruin from him. So, seeing that I am never going
home to the land of my fathers, and when Patroklos was alive
I was no light of deliverance to him, nor to his other comrades,   95
the many who perished at the hands of the good Hector—
but here I sit beside the ships, a useless burden on the land,
I who in war am such as none other of the Achaeans who wear
shirts of bronze, though in the conference others are better.

"I wish that strife would perish from among gods and humans,   100
and anger that drives a man mad, though he is wise.
Much sweeter is anger than honey. It drips down into the hearts
of men and it swells there like smoke ... even so the king of men,
Agamemnon, angered me. But let all that go, though it makes
us sad. We must overcome the spirit in our own breasts.   105
We have to! And now I will go out to find the killer of the man
I loved—Hector."

As for my own fate, I will accept it, because
Zeus and the other deathless gods wish to bring it about.
Not even mighty Herakles, who was the dearest of all
to Zeus the king, the son of Kronos, escaped fate, but fate   110
overcame Herakles and the terrible anger of Hera. Even so—
if a like fate is really fashioned for me—I will be brought low
when I am dead ... But for now I will seize noble fame!
I will set many of the women of Troy, and of the deep-bosomed
Dardanians, to wail as they wipe away with both hands the thick tears   115
from their tender cheeks! May they see that for a long time
I have held back from the war. So don't try to keep me from going
to war, though you love me. You will not persuade me."

Then silver-footed Thetis, the goddess, answered him:
"Yes my child, as you have said, in truth it's not a bad thing to ward   120
off sheer destruction from your friends when they are hard pressed.
But your beautiful armor is held by the Trojans—bronze, glimmering.
Hector of the sparkling helmet has it. He wears it on his shoulders,
exulting. But I do not think he will glory in your armor
long—for his death is very near. But do not enter into   125
the turmoil of war before your own eyes see me coming
here again. In the morning I will return as the sun comes up,
bringing beautiful armor from Hephaistos the king."

So she spoke and turned away from her son. And, turning,
130 she spoke to her sisters: "Go down now into the broad bosom
of the waters to visit the old man of the sea, in the house of our father.
Tell him everything. I am off to high Olympos, to the house of Hephaistos,
the famous craftsman, to see if he is willing to give my son glorious,
shining armor."

So she spoke, and the Nereids plunged immediately
135 beneath the surge of the sea. Thetis, whose feet are silvery,
went off to Olympos so that she might bring glorious armor
to her son. While her feet bore her to Olympos, the Achaeans fled
with a fearful shouting, driven by man-killer Hector as they
came to the ships and to the Hellespont. Nor were the Achaeans
140 with their fine shinguards able to drag away the body
of Achilles' aide from the flying weapons.° For they were again
overtaken by the Trojans and their horses, with Hector, son
of Priam, in fighting glory like a flame. Three times brilliant Hector
seized the corpse from behind by the feet, anxious to drag it off,
145 as he called mightily to the Trojans. Three times did the two Ajaxes,
putting on the mantle of furious valor, hurl him back from the corpse.
But Hector, trusting always in his valor, would again charge at them
in the tumult of battle, then he would stand and howl aloud. And in no
way did he retreat, even a little. Just as when shepherds in the fields
150 cannot drive away a tawny lion from a carcass when the lion is hungry,
even so the two Ajaxes could not frighten away the armored
Hector, son of Priam, from the corpse.

And Hector would have dragged
off the corpse and won undying renown if the swift-footed Iris,
sent from Olympos, had not come running to the son of Peleus
155 as a messenger: He should arm himself! She came unbeknownst
to all the other gods: Hera sent her forth. Standing near,
Iris spoke these words that went like arrows: "Rise up,
son of Peleus, most fear-inspiring of all men. Defend Patroklos!
On his account have the dread contendings arisen before the ships.
160 Men kill men! The one side wants to defend the dead body,
the other side—the Trojans—wants to take it to windy Ilion,
and above all brilliant Hector wants to drag it off. He wants
to cut off his head from the tender neck and to fix it onto a stake.
So get up! Don't lie around! Be enraged that Patroklos

---

141 *flying weapons*: The last time we looked (17.713ff.), Meriones and Menelaos were carrying off Patroklos'
body, but this effort seems to have failed.

become a plaything for the dogs of Troy. Shame on you   165
if his body is mutilated!"

               The godlike Achilles, swift of foot,
then answered: "Iris, goddess, who of the gods sent you here
as a messenger?"

              The swift-footed quick Iris answered him:
"Hera sent me, the illustrious wife of Zeus. The high-throned son
of Kronos knows nothing about it, nor do the other gods   170
who dwell on snowy Olympos."

                Achilles, the fast runner, then
answered her: "But how am I to go into the melée? They have
my armor! My mother forbade me to prepare for the fight before
I see her coming with my own eyes. She vowed to bring beautiful
armor from Hephaistos. I know of no other man whose glorious armor   175
I might wear, except for the shield of Ajax, son of Telamon.
But I think he is mixed in with the forefighters who rage
with their spears around the dead Patroklos."

                  Then Iris,
swift as the wind, said: "We know well that the Trojans have
your armor. Nonetheless, go to the trench as you are and show   180
yourself to the Trojans—perhaps you will put a fright into them
and they will pull back from the war, and the warlike sons of the
Achaeans will catch their breath. For the Achaeans are worn out.
It is hard to catch your breath in the midst of war."

                So speaking,
Iris went off, swift of foot. Achilles, dear to Zeus, stood up.   185
Around his strong shoulders Athena threw the tasseled
goatskin fetish, and around his head the goddess made
a golden cloud—now a blazing flame burned from the man!

  As when smoke goes up from a city and reaches the heavens
from afar, from an island that the enemy has surrounded—all day   190
long the besieged have fought a savage battle from the city, but when
the sun goes down, beacon fires burst forth close by one another,
and high above shines the glare, visible to all who live nearby,
so that the dwellers around may come in their ships and avert
destruction—even such a brilliance went from the head of Achilles,   195
to the heavens.

He went from the wall to the trench and took his stand
there. He did not mingle with the Achaeans. He respected his mother's
firm command. Standing there, he shouted, and Pallas Athena
added her own voice from afar. He created an unspeakable
200 confusion in the Trojans. As when the trumpet sounds its clear voice
in the midst of a murderous enemy who have invested a city,°
even so clear was the voice of the grandson of Aiakos.

When the Trojans heard the brazen voice of the grandson
of Aiakos, the spirit was crushed in the heart of each man. All at once
205 the horses with lovely manes turned their cars backwards—
they foresaw evil things. The charioteers were struck with terror
when they saw the unstinting fire burning above the head
of the great-hearted son of Peleus. The flashing-eyed goddess
Athena made the fire burn. Godlike Achilles shouted
210 three times over the trench—three times the Trojans
and their far-famed allies were stunned. Twelve of their best
men died right there! tangled in their cars and fallen
on their spears, as the Achaeans happily pulled out
Patroklos from the rain of arrows. They placed him on a bier.
215 His beloved comrades stood about it and wept.

In their midst
Achilles the fast runner followed, pouring down hot tears
when he saw his beloved comrade lying on the bier, mangled
by the sharp bronze. He had sent Patroklos forth with his horses
and chariot into the war, but he did not receive him returning.

220 The revered Hera with the cow eyes sent the tireless
sun to the shores of Ocean, although he did not want to go.
But the sun went down, and the godlike Achaeans eased
from the bitter strife and the evil war. The Trojans,
on their side, pulled back from the dread contendings
225 and set loose the swift horses from their cars. They gathered
into an assembly° before having any thought of dinner.
They kept to their feet. During the assembly none dared
take a seat, for fear held all—Achilles had appeared, after
shunning engagement in battle for so long a time.°

---

201 *a city*: It is not clear whether the trumpet has sounded to signal an attack or to rally the defenders.

226 *assembly*: The last Trojan assembly was in Book 8 after they had pushed the Greeks back behind the ditch.
Then they approved, without dissent, Hector's suggestion that the Trojans camp that night on the plain.

229 *so long a time*: In fact Achilles has been absent from the fighting for only three days.

Poulydamas,° the son of Panthoös, was first to speak   230
his sage advice, for he alone saw both first and last things.
He was Hector's companion, born on the same night, but that
one was best with words, while the other ranked first by far
with the spear. Poulydamas spoke, making a civil address:
"Consider both sides of the matter. I for my part urge you   235
to go to the city right now, not to wait for the bright dawn
on the plain beside the ships. We are far from the wall!
So long as Achilles raged at the good Agamemnon, the Achaeans
were easier to war against. I was glad when we slept
beside the swift curved ships, hoping we would take them.   240
But as it is, I fear terribly the swift-footed son of Peleus. His spirit
is so violent that he will not be willing to stay on the plain.
There, in the middle, the Trojans and Achaeans are accustomed
to do their fighting, but Achilles will fight near the city
and for its women.   245
          "But let us go to the city—trust me!
This is the way it will be. Now the deathless night holds back
the fast running son of Peleus. If he comes across us still here
in the morning, when he comes in full armor, one will notice!
With joy every man will arrive at sacred Ilion then—that is,
he who escapes!—and the dogs and birds will consume many   250
Trojans. I don't want to think a bit more about it.
          "But if all will follow my words, though distressing, at night
we shall have our army in a good gathering place. The walls
and high gates, the well-polished doors fitted inside and bolted,
will protect the city. In the morning, at the coming of dawn   255
we will stand on the wall in our full armor. The worse
it will be for him who wants to come from the ships
and fight against us around the walls! For he will go back
to the ships, when his high-necked horses are tired prancing
back and forth before the city. But no matter how great   260
his anger, that anger will not let him carry the attack
within the city, and he shall not lay it waste. Before that
the swift dogs will devour him!"

          Hector of the flashing helmet
looked angrily at Poulydamas from beneath his brows: "Poulydamas,
you no longer speak to my liking. You advise us to go back   265
to the city, to be confined in the city. Haven't you had your fill
of being penned up in the city? In the old days mortal men

---

230 *Poulydamas*: Last seen in Book 17 fighting alongside Hector and wounding the Boeotian Peneleos.

used to tell stories about the city of Priam and its abundant
gold and bronze. Now the beautiful treasures have disappeared
270 from our houses. Many things have been sold off to PHRYGIA and lovely
MAEONIA,° ever since great Zeus grew angry with us. But now
that the son of Kronos has given to us the winning of glory at the ships
and to pen in the Achaeans by the sea, don't—you fool!—
be voicing such thoughts before the people! You will not persuade
275 any of the Trojans. I won't allow it!
                                    "But come, just as I say.
Let us all be persuaded. Now take your meal throughout the army
by companies, and put up a watch. Let every man stay awake.
As for those Trojans who are overmuch concerned about
their possessions, let them gather them together and give all
280 to the people to enjoy in common. Better that the Trojans
profit from it than the Achaeans!
                                    "But early in the morning,
at the coming of dawn, in full armor we will arouse steep war
at the hollow ships. If it is true that the godlike Achilles
has stood up at the ships, the worse for *him* if that's
285 what he wants! *I* shall not flee from savage war but face
to face I will hold my ground, to see if he wins a great victory,
or I. Enyalios is common to all, and he kills whom he wants."

       So Hector spoke to the gathering, and the Trojans shouted
assent—the fools! Pallas Athena had taken away their wits.
290 They all gave praise to Hector, though he advised them
badly, but no one praised Poulydamas, whose advice was good.
The army took their meal and bedded down.

                                        But the Achaeans
stayed up all night lamenting Patroklos, and the son of Peleus
began the sad wailing, placing his man-killing hands on the chest
295 of his companion, moaning deeply, like a whiskery lion
from whom a stag-hunter has snatched its brood in the thick
wood, and the lion, coming back to his lair, is desolate
and tracks the hunter through valley after valley in hopes
of finding him, for an extreme anger has come over the lion—
300 even so, groaning deeply, Achilles addressed the Myrmidons:
"I spoke a vain word on the day when I encouraged the warrior
Menoitios in my halls. I said that when I had sacked Ilion,

---

271 *Phrygia … Maeonia*: Inland territories to the east and southeast of Troy (Map 6).

I would bring back to OPOEIS° his glorious son, with a rich
share of the spoil. But Zeus does not allow all the designs
of men. Both of us are fated to redden with blood the selfsame   305
soil here in Troy, because I doubt that the aged horseman
Peleus will receive me in his halls when I have returned,
nor will my mother Thetis. Here the earth will hold me.

"But as things stand, because I will go under the earth
after you, O Patroklos, I will not bury you, big-hearted man,   310
before I bring here the arms and the head of Hector,
your killer. And I will cut the throats of twelve glorious sons
of the Trojans in front of your pyre, in my anger at your killing.
Until then, you will lie beside the beaked ships, just as you are,
and the Trojan and Dardanian women, with full breasts,   315
will bewail you night and day, pouring forth tears—all those
whom the two of us captured by the force of our long spears
when we ravaged the rich cities of mortal men."

                    So speaking,
the godlike Achilles called to his companions to put a large
tripod in the fire so that they could wash away the bloody gore   320
from Patroklos as soon as possible. They set on the blazing fire
a tripod for filling the bath, and they poured water in it.
They took some wood and added it beneath the tripod.
The fire licked around the belly of the tripod, and the water warmed.
When the water had boiled in the bright bronze, they washed   325
the body and anointed it with soothing oils. They filled
his wounds with ointment that was nine years old. They lay him
on a bed and covered him over with a soft linen cloth,
from his head to his feet, and on top of that they placed a white robe.
Then all night long the Myrmidons, in the company of Achilles   330
the fast runner, bewailed and lamented Patroklos.

                    In the meanwhile
Zeus spoke to Hera, his sister and wife: "You've got your way,
then, O revered Hera with eyes like a cow. You've roused
Achilles, the fast runner. Truly, the Achaeans with their long hair
are your own children!"   335

                Then said the revered Hera,
whose eyes were like a cow's: "Most dread son of Kronos,
what words you have said! Why, even a man will achieve

---

303 *Opoeis:* The chief city of Locris, northeast of Boeotia, mentioned in the Catalog of Ships, the birthplace of
    Patroklos (Map 2).

what he can for another man, one that is mortal and does
not know all that I know. How could I—who say I am
340 the best of the goddesses, both because of my birth
and because I am called the bedmate of one who rules
over all the other deathless ones—you!—How could I *not*
in my anger against the Trojans contrive evil for them?"

Thus they spoke to one another. But Thetis with the silver feet
345 came to the house of Hephaistos—deathless, decked with stars,
outstanding among the dwellings of the immortals, made of bronze.
Hephaistos himself had made it, though he had a lame foot.
She came on him when he was sweating around the fires,
going back and forth in haste. He was making twenty tripods
350 to stand around the wall of his well-built hall. He cleverly
placed golden wheels beneath the foot of each of them
so that they could run all by themselves into the assemblies
of the gods, then go back to his house, a marvel to behold.
He had, however, not yet finished. He was still affixing
355 the handles, like ears, cunningly fashioned. These he was fitting,
and forging the rivets.

While he was working on this project
with his clever skill, the silver-footed goddess Thetis came up
close to him. The beautiful Charis,° wearing a gleaming
head-covering, came forward and saw her. The famous god
360 with his two strong arms had married Charis, and she took
Thetis by the hand and spoke her name: "Why, O Thetis
of the long robe, have you come to our house, an honored guest
and a welcome one? Before you were not used to visit.
But come here, so that I may set before you some good food."

365 So speaking, the goddess guided her on. Charis made Thetis
sit on a chair with silver rivets—beautiful, highly-wrought,
and there was a footstool for her feet. She called to Hephaistos,
the cunning craftsman, and said: "Hephaistos, come here!
Thetis needs you."

Then the famous god with two strong arms
370 answered: "Well then, an august and welcome goddess
has come here, who saved me when pain came to me.
I had fallen far, through the will of my bitch mother!

---

358 *Charis*: "Grace." In Hesiod, Hephaistos is married to another of the Graces. Perhaps his marriage and divorce to the adulterous Aphrodite, reported in the *Odyssey*, took place earlier than this marriage.

She wanted to hide me because of my bum leg.°
Then I would have suffered pains in my heart if Eurynomê°
and Thetis had not received me in their bosom—Eurynomê,   375
the daughter of back-flowing Ocean. I spent nine years making
many lovely things—brooches, and golden spirals for the hair,
and rosette earrings, and necklaces—in their hollow cave.
And around about me flowed the stream of Ocean, murmuring
with foam, an unspeakable flood. Nor did any other of the gods   380
or mortal men know, but Thetis and Eurynomê knew—
they saved me! And now she has come to my house. So I think
I need to make full payment to Thetis with the beautiful tresses
for saving my life. But Charis, you place before her now some good
things to eat while I put aside my bellows and all my tools."   385

　　He spoke and arose from the huge puffing anvil, limping.
But beneath him his thin legs moved nimbly. He placed the bellows
away from the fire, and all the tools with which he worked
in a silver chest. He washed off his face and his two arms
and his strong neck and his hairy chest with a sponge, and he put on   390
a shirt. He took up a stout staff and walked to the door, hobbling.
Then handmaidens made of gold moved swiftly to support their master,
looking like living girls. There is a mind within them and the power
of speech and strength and they know clever handiwork,
a gift of the deathless gods. They bustled about their master.   395
He limped over to where Thetis was and then sat on a shining chair.

　　He took her hands in his and addressed her by name:
"Why, Thetis, who wears a long gown, have you come here to our house,
august as you are, and welcome? Before you were not accustomed
to visit us. Tell me what you are wanting. My spirit urges me   400
to accomplish it, if I can, and it can be done."

　　　　　　　　　　　　Thetis answered him,
pouring down tears: "Hephaistos, is there any other goddess
on Olympos who has suffered so many awful pains as Zeus,
the son of Kronos, has heaped upon me before all others?
Of all the daughters of the sea he subjected me alone   405
to a mortal—Peleus, the son of Aiakos. I had to put up with

373　*bum leg*: In Book 1 Hephaistos tells how Zeus threw him from heaven when he went to help Hera, and he
　　was received by the Sintians on the island of Lesbos; the fall must explain his lameness. In this version,
　　Hera threw him from heaven because she was disgusted by his lameness, the only time in Homer that the
　　same myth is told twice, with different details.

374　*Eurynomê*: According to Hesiod, a daughter of Ocean and mother of the Graces, hence Hephaistos' mother-
　　in-law.

lying with a mortal, although I was unwilling.° Now he stays
in his palace fitted out with horrid old age, but other causes
for grief are now mine. Peleus gave me a son to bear
410 and to raise up, the finest of warriors. He shot up
like a sapling. When I had raised him like a plant in a rich
orchard, I sent him forth on the beaked ships to Ilion,
to fight against the Trojans. I will never receive him again
coming home to the house of Peleus. And while he lives
415 and sees the light of the sun, if he is in pain, I am unable
to go to him and to be of help. A girl whom the sons of the
Achaeans chose out for him as his prize—King Agamemnon
took her from his hands. Achilles wastes away grieving for her.
In the meanwhile, the Trojans have hemmed the Achaeans in
420 at the sterns of the ships and will not let them come out. The elders
of the Argives begged Achilles to return and offered him many gifts,
but he refused to help them ward off ruin. Instead he dressed
Patroklos in his own armor and sent him out to the war,
and he sent many troops along with him. They fought all day
425 around the Scaean Gates, and on that same day Patroklos
would have taken the city, had not Apollo killed him after he had
wounded many fighting in the forefront—and so gave Hector the glory.

◀�))   "For this reason I have come now to your knees,
to see if you are willing to give my son, doomed to die soon,
430 a shield and a helmet and beautiful shinguards fitted with ankle
chains, and a breastplate.° For trusty Patroklos lost his armor
when he was killed by the Trojans. And now my Achilles
lies on the ground, troubled at heart."

                              The famous god with two
strong arms answered her: "Courage! Don't be undone
435 by any of this. As I wish that I could protect Achilles from
a miserable death, when dread fate comes on, I assure you that beautiful
armor will be his, such that in the aftertime men will be astonished seeing it."

     So speaking, he left her there and went to the bellows.
He turned them toward the fire and ordered them to get to work.°

---

407 *unwilling*: Thetis seems to refer to the story that Zeus had lusted after her, but when a prophecy revealed
that her child would be greater than the father, Zeus forced her to marry a mortal. Of course Achilles was
greater than Peleus.

431 *breastplate*: For some reason Thetis forgets to request a sword, but the spear was the main weapon, which
Achilles already has because Patroklos was not warrior enough to carry it.

439 *work*: The bellows are intelligent robots, like the "handmaidens made of gold" and the tripods (metal bowls
supported by three legs).

FIGURE 18.2 Peleus wrestles Thetis.   Thetis is dressed in an elaborate gown, probably linen, and an elegant cloak. She tugs at her hair-covering while turning into various shapes to escape Peleus' attentions, here symbolized by the lion that bites Peleus on the arm. The young beardless Peleus wears only a shirt and a sword. It is not clear what the building on the right symbolizes. According to the story, Peleus hung on in spite of the transformations until Thetis relented and agreed to marry him. Athenian red-figure wine-cup, c. 490 BC, from Vulci, Etruria.

440 The bellows, twenty in number, blew from all angles on the crucibles,
sending forth a generous blast of every kind of force on hand
for the busy smith as he time and again employed their blasts
to help in whatever way he might wish—thus Hephaistos got on
with his work.

        He put the stubborn bronze and tin and precious
445 gold and silver on the fire. Then he placed a great anvil
on the anvil block. He took a massive hammer in one hand,
and in the other he took the tongs. First he made a great
and powerful shield, decorating it cleverly in every part,
and around it he set a glittering threefold rim, and a silver
450 shield-strap. The shield was of five layers, and on it he made
many fancy devices with his cunning skill.° On it he made
the earth and the sky and the sea and the unwearied sun
and the full moon and all the constellations with which the sky
is crowned—the Pleiades and the Hyades and mighty Orion
455 and the Bear, which men also call the Wagon, which always
goes around in the same place, watching Orion. The Bear alone
has no part in the baths of Ocean.°

        He made on it two
cities of mortal men—beautiful! In the one there was a wedding
going on, and a feast. By the light of burning torches the men
460 led brides from their chambers through the city and the bridal song
rose loudly. Young men whirled in the dance, and among them
flutes and lyres gave forth song. Women stood each
at the doorway and marveled. People were crowded into the assembly
area. A dispute had arisen there. Two men were quarreling
465 over the blood-price for a man who had been killed. The one
said that he would pay for all, declaring recompense to the people.
The other refused to accept anything. Each wanted to win

---

451 *cunning skill*: We cannot really reconstruct how this magical, living shield was decorated, but in the usual
view the heavenly bodies are in the center with the various scenes occupying successive bands, moving
outwards toward the rim. The innermost band is divided between the city at peace and the city at war; the
second band is divided into the three seasons of the farmer (plowing, reaping, harvest); the third band has
the cattle attacked by lions and the sheep; the fourth band is given to the dance; finally, the river Ocean sur-
rounds the whole. The five "layers" may consist of progressively larger circles moving out from the center, as
in a target, but it is not clear what is meant by a "threefold rim."

457 ... *Ocean*: These constellations still bear the same names. The meaning of *Pleiades* is unknown, but a later
form *Peleiades* means "doves"; they are the seven daughters of the Titan Atlas, for some reason changed into
stars by Zeus. The five *Hyades* were also daughters of Atlas, by a different mother; when their brother Hyas
("rain"?) died, Zeus changed the mourning sisters into stars. *Orion* was the great hunter, still pursuing the
Bear (the Big Dipper) in the sky. Orion was killed for some sexual offense against Artemis, then turned into a
constellation. Of course the Big Dipper never sets in Ocean, that is, it never disappears beneath the horizon.

the judgment by turning the matter over to someone who knew the facts.
The people applauded both parties, showing favor now to this side,
now that. The heralds held the people back, while the elders   470
sat on polished stone seats in the sacred circle,° holding
in their hands the scepters of the heralds, whose voices resound
through the air. With these they then rose up and gave judgments
in turn. In the center lay two talents of gold that they would give
to the elder who gave the soundest judgment.°   475

                              But around
a second city two forces of armed men sat in siege,
resplendent in their gear. They were of two minds—either
to lay the city waste, or to divide in two all the property
that the lovely city contained.° The townspeople would not
go along with the plan, but instead put on their armor in secret,   480
to meet the enemy in ambush. Their dear wives
and their children guarded the wall, standing upon it,
and also the old men. But the rest marched out. Ares
and Pallas Athena led them, all set in gold, and they wore
golden clothes—beautiful and majestic were they   485
in their armor, as is appropriate to gods! They stood out
amid the rest because the people were somewhat smaller.

   When the townspeople came to the place of ambush—
a riverbed where there was a watering place for all their herds—
there they sat down, clothed in flaming bronze. They sent out   490
two scouts, apart from the army, to wait until they saw
the sheep and the cattle with curly horns. These came soon,
and two herdsman followed them, playing on their panpipes.
They did not suspect the ambush. Then when the townsmen

---

471 *sacred circle*: Sacred because Zeus presides over judicial proceedings.

475 *... soundest judgment*: It is uncertain exactly what are the rules of the legal proceeding that Homer is de-
      scribing. One man has killed another and he offers to pay a blood-price, but the relative of the dead man
      will not accept it. If he does not accept it, then blood vendetta will follow. Judgments are not made by kings,
      but by a body of elders who voice their views in turn in a public assembly. On the shield of Achilles Homer
      describes the society of his own day in the late Iron Age, as contrasted with his fictitious construction of a
      "heroic age" in the narrative. The elders will decide if the offended party *must* accept payment, and if so how
      much. Whoever speaks "straightest" in this matter apparently will receive the two talents of gold. In Book
      23, two talents of gold are fourth prize in a chariot race, after an unused cauldron and before a two-handled
      jar. Still, it is a very large sum.

479 *... contained*: The besiegers have made an offer to the townspeople: either be destroyed or give up half of all
      their property without a fight, and the attackers will go away. The image of two forces attacking the city may
      be based on artistic representations from Homer's time that show city walls under attack from both sides:
      Examples of such a scene survive on a Phoenician metal plate from the eighth century BC.

495 saw them coming, they ran out and quickly cut off the herds
of cattle and fine flocks of white sheep, and then killed
the herdsmen.° The besiegers, when they heard the noise
among the cattle, being seated in assembly,° immediately
mounted their chariots drawn by high-stepping horses and set out.
500 They came upon the townspeople quickly. They put the battle
line in place and fought beside the banks of the river, striking
each other with bronze spears. In their midst Eris and Tumult
mixed in, and deadly Fate,° who grasped one wounded man
still alive, another without any wounds, and she dragged
505 another, dead, by the feet through the melée. Her cloak
around her shoulders was red with the blood of men.
Like living mortals, they mixed in the contendings and fought,
and each hauled off the dead of the other.

And on the shield

Hephaistos worked soft rich fallow-land—broad, three-times
510 plowed.° Many plowmen in the field were whirling
their yokes around and driving this way and that.
When after turning they came to the end of the field,
a man would come up to them and place in their hands
a cup of honey-sweet wine. They turned around
515 in the furrows, anxious to reach the other end of the deep
fallow-land.° The field grew black behind, just as if
it had been plowed, although it was made of gold.°
Thus was fashioned the astounding marvel of his work!

Then Hephaistos set in a royal estate, where laborers
520 were holding sharp sickles in their hands. Some dropped handfuls
to the ground thick and fast along the furrow, others the sheaf-binders
were binding with twisted ropes. Three sheaf-binders stood
nearby, and behind them boys gathered together handfuls.
They carried the sheaves in their arms, and busily gave

---

497 *herdsmen*: You would think that the *besiegers* would be attacking flocks near the city, not the townspeople; Homer may have misunderstood some picture showing a town besieged and the capture of cattle.

498 *assembly*: No doubt to discuss what course of action to take.

503 *Fate*: The only time that Fate acts like this in Homer.

510 *three-times plowed*: For good luck.

516 *fallow-land*: The description is not clear, but the general situation is that the plowmen are going back and forth over a fallow field, and at the turning at one end of the field a boy comes up to them with refreshment.

517 *of gold*: Homer seems to be thinking of dark inlay in a precious metal, such as we find on the dagger blades in Mycenaean graves (Figure 4.1). *Niello* is a black mixture of copper, silver, and lead sulfides used as an inlay on engraved metal, known to the Mycenaeans but not used in Greece after the Bronze Age.

them to the binders. Among them the boss-man stood in silence,   525
setting his staff on the furrow, joyful at heart. Apart, under an
oak tree, heralds prepared a feast. They were dressing an ox
they had killed at sacrifice, while the women sprinkled
the flesh with white barley as a meal for the reapers.°

   Then Hephaistos placed a vineyard bursting with large   530
grapes—beautiful, golden! The grapes were black, and set up
on silver vine poles throughout. And around the vineyard
he put a dark-blue trench, and around that he fashioned a fence
of tin. A single path led up to it on which the vine-workers
came and went when they harvested the grapes. Young girls   535
and youths carried the honey-sweet fruit in woven baskets
with glee. In the middle of them a boy made pleasant
music with his clear-toned lyre. He sang the Linos-song° sweetly
with his fine voice, and his companions all together stamped
their feet and followed on with skipping feet in the midst   540
of dance and joyful shoutings.

                And Hephaistos inlay a herd
of straight-horned cattle, made of gold and tin. With lowing
they set out from the farmyard to the pasture beside the burbling
river, beside the waving reeds. The herdsmen who followed
along with the cattle were golden, four of them, and nine dogs   545
swift of foot followed along. But two terrible lions
held down a lowing bull among the foremost of the cattle,
and dragged him off as he bellowed. The dogs and young men ran
after him. But the two lions had broken open the hide
of the great bull and were eating the guts and the black blood   550
while the herdsmen tried vainly to scare them off, urging on
their swift dogs. But the dogs shrank back from ripping the lions,
standing nearby and barking, avoiding the beasts.

                   And the far-famed god
with strong arms made a pasture in a beautiful clearing—large in size,
filled with white sheep, and corrals and roofed huts and pens.   555
And the far-famed god with the two strong arms made a dancing
floor like that which Daidalos once made in broad KNOSSOS

---

529 *meal for the reapers*: Likewise in the *Odyssey* the swineherd Eumaios prepares a meal of pork by sprinkling it
     with barley (Book 14).

538 *Linos-song*: Linos was a mythical musician, said to be the first mortal gifted with song by the gods. He was
     killed by a jealous Apollo and mourned by his mother Ourania, one of the Muses. The "Linos-song" was
     some kind of lament, but not much is known about it.

FIGURE 18.3   Hephaistos prepares arms for Achilles.   The smithy-god, bearded and wearing a felt cap, sits in an elaborately draped hall on a platform holding a cloth with which he is polishing the finished shield. A servant holds it up for inspection. The surface of the back of the shield is so bright that it reflects the figure of Thetis, sitting in a chair with a footstool just as Homer describes. Behind Thetis stands Charis, Hephaistos' wife. Another servant works on the helmet in the lower left. Between him and Thetis are the breastplate and the shinguards (the surface of the fresco is damaged here). From Pompeii, c. AD 60.

for Ariadnê with the lovely hair. There youths danced
with young girls worth many cattle, holding their hands
each on the wrist of another.° Of these, the young girls wore fine   560
linen and the youths wore shirts wonderfully woven, faintly
glistening with oil. The girls had beautiful chaplets, the boys
had golden daggers hanging from silver chest straps.
They moved around with skillful movements, light on their feet,
as when a potter sits by his wheel fitted in his hands   565
and makes trial to see if it will go. And then they would run
in rows towards one another. A large crowd stood around
the lovely dance, taking joy. Two tumblers whirled through
their middle as leaders in the dance.

                And Hephaistos set
the great power of the river Ocean around the outermost rim   570
of the strongly made shield. When he had finished the great
and powerful shield, he then made a breastplate brighter than
the blaze of fire. And he made a helmet fitted to Achilles'
temples—beautiful, richly worked! On it he set a plume
of gold, and he made shinguards of pliant tin.   575

                   When the far-famed
god of two strong arms was done, he took the armor and placed
it before the mother of Achilles. Like a falcon she sprang down
from snowy Olympos, carrying the flashing armor from Hephaistos.

---

560 *of another*: The Cretans were famous dancers. Daidalos has a "speaking name," meaning "decorator."
     He built the labyrinth that contained the Minotaur. The dancing boys and girls may refer to the myth
     that the Minotaur required a periodic sacrifice of boys and girls. A *daidaleon* is referred to in the Linear B
     texts from Knossos, evidently a shrine. Dancing circles have been identified in Minoan ruins,
     c. 1400 BC. *Ariadnê* means "the most holy one" and in origin was probably one of the names of the
     Cretan mother goddess.

BOOK 19. *Agamemnon's Apology*

Dawn with her robe of saffron rose from the streams
of Ocean to bring light to the deathless ones and to mortals.
And Thetis came to the ships bearing the gifts of the god.
She found her son lying down, clinging to Patroklos,
5   wailing shrilly. Around him his companions wept.

The goddess stood beside him and she took
his hand and she called his name: "My son, we must let
this man lie, though we grieve much, seeing he has been killed
beyond mending by the will of the gods. Now you must take
10 this exquisite sturdy armor, such as no man ever wore
on his shoulders."

So speaking the goddess set down the armor
in front of Achilles—it rang in its terrible splendor. Dread took
hold of all the Myrmidons, and not one dared to look,
as they shrank back in fear. But when Achilles saw the armor,
15 anger gripped him even more strongly, and his eyes blazed
forth beneath his lids as if they were flames. He exulted,
holding the glorious gifts of the god in his hands.

But when he had taken delight in his heart, looking
at the exquisitely wrought objects, right away he addressed
20 his mother with words that went like arrows: "My mother,
the arms that the god has given are just as the works
of the deathless ones should be, and nothing that a mortal man
could fashion. Now I will arm myself. But I am so afraid that
flies will come down into the wounds of the brave son of Menoitios,
25 rent by the bronze, and beget maggots, and defile the corpse,
for the life in him is gone, and all his flesh will rot."

Silver-footed Thetis, the goddess, answered him:
"My child, don't let these things be a trouble to you in your heart.
I shall surely ward off from him the savage tribes of flies,
30 who devour men killed in battle. Even if he should lie there
for a whole year, his flesh will remain always fresh, or even
better than it now is. But you call the fighting men of the Achaeans

FIGURE 19.1 Achilles receives the arms from Thetis.   Thetis hands her son, in "heroic nudity" and carrying a spear, a wreath of victory. With her other hand, she give him a "Boeotian" shield. Behind her a Nereid named Lomaia ("bather"?), not named by Homer, carries a breastplate and what seems a jug for oil. Behind her an unnamed Nereid carries the plumed helmet and the shinguards. To the left, an armed Odysseus keeps guard (not in Homer). The figures are labeled. Detail of an Attic black-figure hydria, c. 550 BC.

to an assembly and give up your anger at Agamemnon,
shepherd of the people. Then arm yourself quickly for the war,
35 and resume your valor."

       So speaking, Thetis instilled
in Achilles unvanquished courage, and on Patroklos she let seep
through his nostrils ambrosia and a red nectar so that his flesh
would remain incorruptible.° Then the godlike Achilles strode along
the shore of the sea, roaring a terrible cry, and so roused the fighting
40 men of the Achaeans. And those who remained in the gathering
of the ships—the pilots and the steersmen and those who provided
food beside the ships—these men too came to the assembly,
because Achilles had returned, he who had too long absented himself
from the grievous war. Two followers of Ares came limping along,
45 the stalwart son of Tydeus, Diomedes, and godlike Odysseus,
leaning on their spears. For painful wounds still afflicted them.
They went and they sat down in front of the assembly. Last of all
came wounded Agamemnon, the king of men. For Koön,
the son of Antenor, had cut him in the savage contendings
50 with his bronze-tipped spear.°

       When all the Achaeans were
gathered together, Achilles the fast runner stood up and spoke
before them: "Son of Atreus, was this, then, the better course
for you and me—that we two raged in spirit-devouring strife
on account of a *girl*? I wish that amid the ships Artemis
55 had killed her with an arrow on that day when I took her from
the loot after I sacked Lyrnessos!° Then so many of the Achaeans
would not have bitten the vast earth with their teeth
at the hands of the enemy because of my ferocious anger.
This is better for Hector and for the Trojans. I suspect
60 that the Achaeans will long remember the disharmony
between us.
     "But let us leave all these things as past and done,
though we are full of grief. Of necessity we must tame
the spirit in our breasts. So here and now I renounce my anger.

---

38 *incorruptible*: Homer seems to refer to some kind of embalming. In Egyptian embalming, the brains were
     removed through the nostrils and various preservative resins poured in, but no such technique is known
     from Greece.

50 *spear*: Diomedes, Odysseus, and Agamemnon were all wounded in Book 11, but on the day after this day
     they are well enough to participate in the funeral games of Patroklos (Book 23).

56 *Lyrnessos*: The account of its sacking is in Book 2.

There is no need for constant, unending anger. Come, let us
rouse the Achaeans who wear their hair long to battle, so that   65
I may go against the Trojans and put them to the test, to see
if they still are willing to spend the night beside the ships.
But I think that many of them will be happy to bend their knees
in rest—whoever escapes from our savage war and my spear!"

    Thus he spoke, and the Achaeans with their fancy shinguards   70
rejoiced that the great-hearted son of Peleus had given up his anger.
The king of men Agamemnon spoke to them from his seat,°
not standing up in their midst: "My dear friends, fighting men,
Danaäns, the followers of Ares—it is a good thing to listen to a man
who is standing up, and it is not proper to interrupt him. That is   75
hard even for a man skilled at speaking. And in the middle of an
uproar of men, how can one hear or speak? That man is hampered,
though he speaks with clear voice.° Now I will explain to the son of
Peleus how things stand, and you other Argives pay attention,
and mark my words, each one of you. Often the Achaeans   80
have spoken, and were ever happy to revile me. But I am
not at fault. Zeus and Fate and Erinys who walks in darkness° are.
It was they who in the assembly infected me with a wild blindness,
on that day when I myself took away the prize of Achilles.
But what could I do? The gods are responsible for everything!   85
Blindness is the oldest daughter of Zeus, who blinds everyone—
ruinous Blindness!° Her walk is gentle, but she does not get close
to the ground—she walks across the heads of men, doing them harm.
She ensnares now this one, now that.
                            "Even Zeus was subject
to Blindness, and they say that he is the best of men and gods.   90
Hera, who is but a female, deceived him with tricks on that day
when Alkmenê was about to give birth to powerful Herakles
in Thebes with its fine battlements. Zeus spoke, invoking
all the many gods: 'Hear me, all you gods and goddesses,
so that I might speak what the spirit in my breast urges me to.   95

---

72 *seat*: Because he is wounded.

78 *clear voice*: Achilles had the advantage of standing up when he spoke, but Agamemnon will do the best he
can from his sitting position.

82 *in darkness*: Ordinarily in Homer Erinys, mentioned on a Linear B tablet, is the goddess who executes
curses, punishes oath breakers, and takes revenge for misdeeds against parents, but here she seems to be the
force who sees that the decrees of Fate are carried out.

87 *Blindness*: We earlier saw Blindness (*atê*) in Phoenix's parable of Blindness and Prayers in Book 9. *Atê*, the
"blindness" that prevents one from seeing the consequences of one's actions, is an important concept in
early Greek thought.

On this day Eileithyia, the producer of birth-pangs, will bring forth
into the light a man who will rule over all those who dwell nearby,
of the race of men who have my blood.' And crafty revered Hera
replied: 'You are lying. You will never bring this word to pass.
100 Come, then, O Olympian, and swear a strong oath to me,
that he who on this day shall fall between a woman's feet°
will rule over all those who dwell nearby, a man who is of the race
of men who have your blood.' So she spoke, and Zeus
did not see the trick, but he swore a great oath, for he succumbed
105 to great Blindness. Hera jumped up and left the peak
of Olympos, and swiftly she came to Achaean Argos, where,
she knew, was the strong wife of Sthenelos, son of Perseus,
pregnant with a dear child and in her seventh month.
Hera brought the child out into the light, though it was premature,
110 and she held up the birth of Alkmenê's child—she held back the Eileithyia
goddesses. Hera, making a pronouncement, spoke to Zeus,
the son of Kronos: 'Zeus, father, lord of the white lightning—
listen to me now. A man of good birth has been born
who will rule over the Argives: Eurystheus the son of Sthenelos,
115 the son of Perseus. Your own line!° It is not unseemly
that he shall rule over the Argives.' So she spoke, and a sharp pain
struck him in the depths of his heart. At once he seized Blindness
by the head with her bright tresses, angry in his heart, and he
swore a mighty oath, that never again would Blindness come
120 again to Olympos and the starry heaven, she who blinds everyone.
So speaking he whirled her in his hand and flung her from the starry
heavens, and quickly she fell to the tilled fields of men. He groaned
constantly at the thought of her, whenever he saw his own son
engaged in an unseemly task because of the contests that Eurystheus
125 imposed on him.
          "Even so did I, when great Hector of the flashing helmet
was destroying the Argives at the sterns of the ships, constantly
think of Blindness by whom at first I was blinded. But because
I was blinded and Zeus took away my wits, I am willing
to make amends and to give a boundless recompense. So rouse up
130 battle and rouse up your other people! I am willing to give you
all the gifts that Odysseus described yesterday° when he came

---

101 *feet*: Evidently in Archaic Greece women gave birth in a standing position.

115 *own line*: Zeus's pronouncement comes true because both Herakles and Eurystheus are of Zeus's blood line,
although only Herakles was Zeus's son. Zeus was the father of Perseus, who was the father of both Elek-
tryon, Alkmenê's father, and of Sthenelos, father of Eurystheus.

131 *yesterday*: Actually it was the day before yesterday.

to your hut. If you want, wait awhile, though you are eager for the war,
and I will have my aides take the gifts from my ship and bring them
here so that you might see that I am giving you gifts that will satisfy
your heart."

135

Achilles the fast runner answered him in this way:
"Son of Atreus, most glorious king of men, Agamemnon, you can give
the gifts if you want, as is fitting, or you can keep them—
it is up to you. But for now let us think as soon as possible of battle.
We should not spend time wasting words, nor make delay.
For our great work is still undone—as each man again sees Achilles
among the foremost, destroying the battalions of the Trojans
with his spear of bronze! So let each one of you take thought
of this as he fights his man."

140

But the resourceful Odysseus
answered him: "Godlike Achilles, though you are valiant,
please don't be urging the sons of the Achaeans to go against Ilion
with an empty stomach, to fight the Trojans. For the din of battle
will not be for a short time once the battalions of men come together
and the gods breathe might into each side. Bid the Achaeans
beside the swift ships first to take their share of food and wine.
Therein is strength and courage. For a man without food
cannot fight against the enemy until the sun goes down.
He may want in his heart to fight, but unawares his limbs
grow heavy— thirst and hunger come over him, and his knees
grow tired as he moves along. But the man who has had his fill
of wine and food can fight against the enemy all day long,
and his heart in his breast is filled with courage, and his limbs
do not grow tired before everyone has withdrawn from the war.
So come, dismiss the men and ask them to prepare the meal.
"In the meanwhile, Agamemnon will bring out the gifts into
the middle of the assembly so that each of the Achaeans can see them
with his own eyes, and you may be warmed by looking upon them.
And let Agamemnon swear an oath, standing up among the Argives,
that never did he go into her bed or have intercourse with Briseïs
as is the custom, O king, of men and women. And Achilles, let your heart
be open to appeasement. Thus let Agamemnon makes amends
to you by a rich banquet in his hut so that you are in no way lacking
in justice. And, son of Atreus, you must be more just in your future
dealings with men. There is no blame for a king to appease a man
fully when a king has started the trouble."

145

150

155

160

165

The king of men

170 Agamemnon answered Odysseus: "I am glad to hear your opinion,
O son of Laërtes. You have set the matter forth appropriately
and told the tale. I am willing to swear this oath. My heart
bids me to do it, and I shall not forswear myself before
the gods. But let Achilles remain here, though he is anxious
175 to go to war. All you others remain together until the gifts
arrive from my hut and we have a chance to swear the oaths
of faith with a sacrifice. But to you yourself do I make
this command and give this order: Pick young men,
the best of all the Achaeans, to bring the gifts from my ship,
180 all those that we promised to Achilles the other day,
and you bring the women too. And let Talthybios quickly
make ready a boar in the broad camp of the Achaeans
to sacrifice to Zeus and to Helios the sun."

Achilles

the fast runner answered him in this way: "Son of Atreus,
185 most glorious king of men, Agamemnon, be busy with these
matters at some other time, when there is some pause
in the war and the fury in my heart is not so great. As it is,
the men lie all mangled up whom Hector the son of Priam
killed when Zeus was giving him glory. And you two
190 are urging us to eat! I would rather urge the sons of the Achaeans
to fight hungry, with an empty stomach, until the sun goes down,
then make ready a big meal once we have taken revenge
for that shame. Down my throat, at least, neither drink nor food
shall pass, for my companion lies dead in my tent, torn
195 by the sharp bronze, his feet turned toward the door,° and around him
his companions mourn. Other matters are of no moment
to me, but only death and blood and the agonized groans
of men!"

Then the resourceful Odysseus answered him:
"O Achilles, son of Peleus, by far the strongest of the Achaeans,
200 you are greater than I, and stronger with the spear by not just a little.
But I am much superior to you in counsel because I am born
first and I know more things. So please allow your heart
to pay attention to my words. Men quickly have their surfeit

---

195   *toward the door*: So the ghost knows the way out of the house.

of war wherein the bronze strews the most straw on the ground,
but the harvest is sparse when Zeus inclines his scales—he 205
who dispenses for men what happens in war.° But fasting
is no way for the Achaeans to mourn a corpse. As it is,
too many fall one after another day after day—when is
one to find respite from the labor of war? We should bury
the man who has died, steeling our spirits and weeping 210
for just one day. But for all those who are left alive
from this hateful war, they should have a mind for drink
and food, that they might fight against the enemy without cease
with the unwearied bronze about their skin. Then not one of you
may hold back, awaiting some other summons. *This* is the summons! 215
It will go ill for anyone hanging around the ships! Setting out
in a horde, let us stir up dread war with the horse-taming Trojans!"

Odysseus spoke, and then he made the sons of bold Nestor
follow him—also Meges the son of Phyleus and Thoas and Meriones
and Lykomedes, the son of Kreon, and Melanippos.° They made 220
their way to the hut of Agamemnon, son of Atreus. In a moment
the word was spoken and the deed was done. They carried
seven tripods from the tent, which he had promised, twenty gleaming
cauldrons and twelve horses. They quickly led forth the women,
seven of them wise in handiwork, and the eighth was Briseïs 225
of the beautiful cheeks. Odysseus measured out ten talents
of gold and led the way, and with him many youths of the Achaeans
carried the gifts. Then they placed them in the middle of the gathering place,
and Agamemnon stood up. Talthybios, in his voice like to a god,
stood beside him, the shepherd of the people, holding the boar 230
in his hands. The son of Atreus drew out the knife that always
hung next to the great scabbard of his sword, and cutting away
the hairs from the boar,° he raised his hands and prayed.
All the Argives sat in silence, by themselves, listening
to the king, as was appropriate. 235

---

206 *in war:* The point of these lines has been much discussed. Apparently, the meaning is that many die, as men
are cut down like the stalks of wheat at the harvest, but the harvest is sparse, that is, there is little profit
from the labor. It all depends on the will of Zeus.

220 *Melanippos:* "Nestor's sons" are Antilochos and Thrasymedes, who often fight together. Meges from
DOULICHION and Thoas from AETOLIA are mentioned in the Catalog of Ships and appear with the Cretan
Meriones in Hector's *aristeia* (Book 15). Meges is listed among important leaders in Book 10 and wears
notable armor in Book 15; Poseidon takes on the form of Thoas when he speaks to Idomeneus (Book 13).
Lykomedes avenges a friend in Book 17. No Greek named Melanippos is found elsewhere, but three men of
this name (presumably all different) are killed on the Trojan side (Books 8, 15, 16).

233 *from the boar:* The hairs are cut off from the head as a first offering and usually thrown in the fire, but be-
cause there is no fire at an oath-sacrifice, they are distributed to the chiefs (as in Book 3).

FIGURE 19.2   Achilles and Briseïs.   Achilles stands armed with a spear, sword, helmet, shinguards, and breastplate. Briseïs is dressed in an elegant gown and smells a flower. Two sides of an Athenan red-figure water jug by Oltos, c. 510 BC.

Agamemnon spoke in prayer, looking up
to the heavens: "Be first witness, O Zeus, highest and best
of the gods, and Earth and Helios the sun and the Erinyes
who under the earth take vengeance on those men
who swear false oaths—that never did I lay hands on the girl
Briseïs, either to make love to her, or for any other reason,   240
but she remained untouched in my hut. And if any of this oath
is false, then may the gods give me full many afflictions, as many
as they reserve for whoever has transgressed against them
in his swearing."

Agamemnon spoke, and then cut the throat
of the boar with the pitiless bronze. Talthybios whirled and threw   245
the boar into the mighty depths of the gray sea to be food for fishes.
But Achilles stood up and spoke to the war-loving Argives:
"O father Zeus, truly, great is the Blindness that you set upon men.
Otherwise the son of Atreus never would have aroused anger
in my heart, nor ruthlessly led the girl away against my will—   250
but, I suppose, Zeus wished many of the Achaeans to die.
Go now to your meal, so that, after, we may join in battle."

So he spoke, and he quickly dissolved the assembly.
They scattered, each man to his own ship, while the great-hearted
Myrmidons busied themselves with the gifts, bearing them to the ship   255
of godlike Achilles. And they placed them in his hut and made the women
sit down and then the noble aides drove the horses into the herd.

Then Briseïs, like golden Aphrodite, when she saw Patroklos
torn by the sharp bronze, threw herself about him and shrieked
aloud, and with her hands she tore at her breasts and her tender skin   260
and her beautiful face. With a wail she spoke, a girl like the goddesses:
"O Patroklos, most dear to my sad heart, I left you alive
when I went from the tent, but now when I return, I find you dead,
a leader of the people. So to me evil ever follows evil.
I saw my husband, to whom my father and revered mother gave me,   265
torn by the sharp bronze before our city, and my three brothers,
whom my mother bore, beloved—all of them met their day
of doom. But you would not let me weep, when swift Achilles
killed my husband and sacked the city of godlike Mynes,° but you
said you would make me the wedded wife of godlike Achilles,   270
and that he would carry me to Phthia in his ships, and make me

---

269 *Mynes*: The king of Lyrnessos, assumed by later commentators to be Briseïs' husband, but nothing in
     Homer suggests this.

a marriage feast among the Myrmidons. So, dead, I bewail you
without end, for you were always kind to me."

                            So Briseïs spoke,
wailing, and the women too mourned, ostensibly for Patroklos,
275 but each one really bemoaned her own sorrows. Around Achilles
the elders of the Achaeans were gathered, begging him to eat.
In his sorrow he refused: "I beseech you, if I can persuade
any of my dear companions, do not urge me to satisfy
my heart with food or drink, for a dread pain has fallen
280 upon me. I will hold out until the sun goes down.
I will endure even as I am."

                            So speaking, Achilles sent
the other chieftains from him, but the two sons of Atreus
remained, and godlike Odysseus and Nestor and old-time
Phoinix, the driver of horses, seeking to comfort him
285 in his terrible sorrow. But his heart would not be comforted
before he had entered the mouth of bloody war.

    Thinking about the matter, Achilles breathed a deep sigh
and said: "Yes Patroklos, in the old days you were accustomed
to prepare a hasty pleasant meal in my tent, poor fellow, most
290 beloved of my companions, when the Achaeans scrambled to carry
tearful war against the horse-taming Trojans. But now you
lie mangled, and my heart will have nothing of drink and food,
though they are at hand, from desire for you. I could suffer
nothing more awful, not if I should learn of the death
295 of my own father, who now in Phthia sheds tender tears
for lack of a son like me, while I make war against the Trojans
in a foreign country because of the detested Helen—not though
it were for my own son who is reared for me in Skyros,
if in fact godlike Neoptolemos still lives.° Before, the heart
300 in my breast hoped that I alone would perish far from Argos,
the nurturer of horses, here in Troy, and that you would return
to Phthia so that you could take my son in your swift black
ship from Skyros and show him all my things, my possessions—
my slaves, and my great house with the high roof. For by now

---

299   *still lives*: The only mention of Achilles' son in the poem. Later tradition reported how Odysseus went to
       Skyros after Achilles' death and took Neoptolemos back to Troy, where he gave him his father's armor.
       During the sack of Troy, Neoptolemos killed Priam on the altar of Zeus. Achilles had fathered Neoptolemos
       on one of the daughters of the local king when as a young man he was hidden in the women's quarters dressed
       as a girl. Thetis placed Achilles there, fearing he might one day go to Troy and die on the windy plain.

I think that Peleus is dead and gone, or if he still lives,   305
that he is now sorely pressed by hateful old age, and by ever
waiting to hear bitter tidings of me—when he shall hear
that I am dead!"

        So, moaning, he spoke, and the old men
groaned with him, each remembering what he had left in his own
house. As they grieved, the son of Kronos took pity on seeing them,   310
and quickly he spoke to Athena words that went like arrows:
"My child, surely you have altogether abandoned your man!
Is there no longer a care in your heart for Achilles? There
he sits in front of his ships with upright horns, bewailing
his dear companion. The others have gone to their meal,   315
but he will not eat, he fasts. But go and drip nectar
and lovely ambrosia into his breast so that the pangs
of hunger do not come to him."

        So speaking he urged
on Athena, who was already alarmed. She darted down
to Achilles from heaven, through the sky like a long-winged   320
falcon with shrill voice. While the Achaeans speedily armed
themselves throughout the camp, she poured nectar and lovely
ambrosia into Achilles' breast so that the painful pangs
of hunger did not seep into his limbs.

                                She herself went then
to the well-built house of her powerful father, while the   325
Achaeans burst forth from the swift ships. As when thick
chill snowflakes fly down from Zeus beneath the blast
of North Wind, engendered in the bright air, even so the splendid
shining helmets issued forth from the ships, and the bossed
shields and the breastplates with massive pieces of metal,   330
and the spears made of ash wood. Their gleam reached the sky.
All the earth around laughed from the flashing bronze.
A din went up from the beneath the feet of the men.

    In their midst, godlike Achilles armed himself for battle.
There was a gnashing of teeth, and his two eyes showed like   335
the gleam of a fire. Into his heart an unbearable pain descended.
And raging against the Trojans, he put on the gifts
that the god Hephaistos had labored so to make. First,
he strapped on the shinguards around his legs—beautiful,
fitted with silver ankle straps. Second, he placed   340

the breastplate around his chest. Around his shoulder
he set the silver studded sword of bronze. Then he took up
his great sturdy shield, and its sheen gleamed like
the moon. As when the flash of a burning fire appears
345 to sailors over the sea, a fire that blazes high on the mountains
in the corral of a lonely farm—but much unwilling the storm
winds carry the sailors over the fishy deep far from
their friends—even so the gleaming of the shield of Achilles,
beautiful, skillfully made, reached the heaven. He lifted
350 the strong helmet and placed it on his head and it shone
like a star with its crest of horsehair. And around it waved
the golden plumes that Hephaistos set thick around the crest.

Then godlike Achilles made a test of his armor, to see
that it fitted him well, that his glorious limbs were free to move
355 within it. Achilles felt as though he wore wings, and the armor
lifted him, the shepherd of the people. He drew forth his
father's spear from the spear case—heavy, huge, strong.
None other of the Achaeans could brandish it, but Achilles
alone knew how to wield it—the Pelian spear of ash
360 that Cheiron had given his father from the peak of Pelion
to be the death of warriors.

Automedon and Alkimos busied
themselves with yoking the horses.° Around them they placed
the beautiful harness-straps. They put bits in the horses' jaws
and drew the reins back toward the jointed car. Automedon
365 grasped in his hand the bright well-fitted lash and he
leaped onto the car. Achilles mounted behind him,
adorned for the fight, shining in his armor like bright
Hyperion.° He cried aloud a terrible cry to the horses
of his father: "Xanthos and Balios, far-famed offspring
370 of Podargê!° Think how better to save your driver
and bring him back into the throng of the Danaäns when

---

362 *yoking the horses:* Alkimos is a shortened form of Alkimedon. The two men and the horses figure together in a scene in Book 17.

368 *Hyperion:* The sun, a Titan.

370 *Podargê:* A Harpy. Achilles' horses Xanthos ("red") and Balios ("patches") were begotten by the West Wind (Zephyros) on Podargê ("swift-foot"), according to Book 16. Two of Hector's horses also have the names Xanthos and Podargos (Book 8).

FIGURE 19.3 Achilles' horses. The great hero prepares his team of divine horses for battle. Here they are named Chaitos (probably short for Pyrsochaitos, "red-haired") and Eutheias ("straight-ahead") instead of Xanthos and Balios. With his right hand Achilles (labeled) adjusts the harness and with his left holds the horse's mane. He is "heroically nude" from the waist down, but wears a breastplate and shinguards. To the far right Automedon (?) seems to attach a trace horse. Between Achilles and Chaitos are the words "Nearchos painted me." Fragment of an Athenian white-ground vase, c. 560 BC.

we have had enough of war. You must not leave your
driver there, dead, as you did Patroklos!"

Then beneath the yoke
nimble Xanthos, swift of foot, spoke to him, as suddenly
375 Xanthos bowed his head, and all his mane streamed from beneath
the yoke-pad next to the yoke and touched the ground.
The white-armed goddess Hera gave him a voice:
"Yes, for *this* time we will save you, mighty Achilles, but near
is the day of doom. We will not be the cause, but a great
380 god and powerful Fate will be. It was not through our slowness
or laxity that the Trojans stripped the armor from the shoulders
of Patroklos, but the best of the gods, whom Leto of the fair
tresses bore, killed him among the vanguard and gave glory
to Hector.° As far as we are concerned, we might run as fast
385 as the West Wind, which men say is the swiftest of all the winds.
But you yourself are fated to die by the strength
of a god and a man."°

When Xanthos had so spoken, the Erinyes°
stopped his voice. Then, groaning deeply, Achilles the fast runner
said: "Xanthos, why do you foretell my death? There is no need.
390 I know well, of myself, that it is my fate to perish here, far from
my beloved father and my mother. Nonetheless I will not cease
until I have give the Trojans their fill of war." He spoke,
and with a cry drove his single-hoofed horses into the forefront.

---

384 ... *to Hector*: This is the first time that Achilles has heard of Apollo's role in the death of Patroklos. Achilles
had warned Patroklos of the danger of Apollo in Book 16.

387 *of god and a man*: In Book 22 Hector reveals that the god and man who will kill Achilles are Apollo and
Paris.

388 *Erinyes*: This is the only time in Homer that the Erinyes function as guardians of the natural order.
Probably Homer is thinking of their more usual function as the punishers of those who violated the rights
of the gods (as in the breaking of oaths) and the rights of older family members (as in Books 9, 15, and 21),
extended here to cover maintaining the normal rules of behavior.

BOOK 20. *The Duel Between Achilles and Aeneas*

A nd so around you, O son of Peleus, insatiate of battle,
the Achaeans armed themselves beside the beaked ships,
and over against them the Trojans did the same on the rising
ground of the plain. Zeus ordered Themis to call to assembly
the gods from the top of Olympos with its many ridges.   5
She went all around and ordered the gods to come
to the house of Zeus. There was no river that did not come,
except Ocean, nor any nymph of those who dwell in the beautiful
woods and the springs of the rivers and the grassy meadows.
Coming to the house of the cloud-gatherer Zeus, they sat down   10
within the polished colonnades that Hephaistos had made for his father
Zeus with his matchless skill.

                  And so they were gathered
within the house of Zeus, nor did the shaker of the earth
fail to listen to the goddess, but he came to the assembly
from the sea. He sat down in the middle and he questioned   15
the purpose of Zeus: "Why, O lord of the white lightning,
have you called the gods to assembly? Do you have some
thoughts about the Trojans and the Achaeans? For now
is the time their battle is beginning."

                  Answering him, Zeus who
gathers the clouds said: "You know, O shaker of the earth,   20
the purpose in my heart for which I have called you together.
These men are a concern of mine, even though they are about
to die. Well, I will remain here sitting in a fold of Olympos,
from where I will look down with pleasure. But you others go forth
until you come amid the Trojans and the Achaeans, and bear   25
aid to this side or that, however you are inclined. For if
Achilles will fight alone against the Trojans, they will not
withstand the son of Peleus, the fast runner, even for
a little. Even before they trembled in looking upon him,
but now that he is enraged because of his friend's death, I fear   30
that he might smash the wall beyond what is fated to be."

FIGURE 20.1   Achilles.   The beardless youthful warrior is labeled ACHILLEUS. Dressed in a diaphanous shirt beneath a breastplate decorated with a Gorgon's head, he stands looking off pensively to his left. In his left hand he holds a long spear over his shoulder, his right hand propped on his hip. A cloak is draped over his left arm and a sword in a scabbard hangs from a strap that crosses his chest and rests at his side. He has no helmet, shield, or shinguards. On the other side (not visible) a female, probably Briseïs, holds the vessels for a drink-offering. Athenian red-figure water jar by the Achilles Painter, c. 450 BC.

So spoke the son of Kronos, and he roused up war that is not
to be turned aside. And the gods went each their way into the war,
being divided in their minds. Hera went to the gathering of the ships,
and Pallas Athena and Poseidon, who embraces the earth,   35
and the helper Hermes who surpasses all in the cleverness
of his mind. Together with them Hephaistos went, exulting
in his power, halting, though beneath him his slender legs moved
quickly. But Ares, whose helmet flashed, went to the Trojans,
and with him Phoibos, whose locks are unshorn, and Artemis,   40
who pours forth arrows, and Leto and the river Xanthos,
and laughter-loving Aphrodite.

      So long as the gods were apart
from the mortal men, the Achaeans triumphed mightily because
Achilles had come forth, he who had kept apart from
the contendings for such a long time. An awesome trembling   45
came to the limbs of the Trojans in their terror when they saw
the son of Peleus, the fast runner, blazing in his armor,
the likeness of man-destroying Ares. But when the Olympians
came into the crowd of men, up stood mighty Eris,
the rouser of the people, and Athena shouted aloud. Standing   50
now beside the ditch outside the wall, now on the loud-sounding
shore, she would give her brash cry. On the other side, Ares
cried like a dark whirlwind, summoning the Trojans
with shrill tones from the topmost citadel, now speeding toward
Pleasant Hill° that rises beside the Simoeis.   55

       Thus the blessed
gods urged on the two sides to clash in battle, and among
them made deadly war break forth. The father of men
and gods thundered terribly from on high, but from below
Poseidon caused the huge earth and the steep peaks of the mountains
to quake. All the foothills of Ida with its many fountains   60
were shaken, and all her peaks, likewise Troy and the ships
of the Achaeans. Hades, the king of the dead, was terrified
from below, and in fear he leaped from his throne and cried out,
fearing that Poseidon the shaker of the earth might cleave
the earth above his head and his house be opened to mortals   65
and to the deathless ones—a dreadful moldy place

---

55 *Pleasant Hill*: In the Greek, *Kallikolonē*, mentioned only once again later in this book when the proTrojan
  gods assemble there.

that the very gods do loathe. So great a din arose from
the strife of the gods as they came together! For against
King Poseidon stood Phoibos Apollo, with his winged shafts,
70 and the goddess flashing-eyed Athena stood against Enyalios.
Against Hera stood the clanging huntress of the golden arrows,
the archer Artemis, sister of the god who strikes from a long way
off. And against Leto stood the strong helper Hermes, and against
Hephaistos stood the great deep-eddying river that the gods
75 call Xanthos, but men say Skamandros.

                         And so gods went forth
against gods,° but Achilles wanted above all to meet Hector,
the son of Priam, in the melée, for his spirit urged him more
than anything to glut Ares with Hector's blood, that warrior
with the toughest shield of hide. But Apollo, rouser of the people,
80 made Aeneas to go forth against the son of Peleus, and he instilled
in him great power. Apollo made his voice like that of Lykaon,°
the son of Priam, and in his likeness Apollo, the son
of Zeus, spoke to him: "Aeneas, counselor of the Trojans,
where are the threats that you made to the captains of the Trojans
85 over wine, that you would war in the hand-to-hand against Achilles,
the son of Peleus?"

               Aeneas said in reply: "Son of Priam,
why are you asking me to fight against the bold-hearted
son of Peleus though I do not want to? I will not stand now
for the first time against Achilles the fast runner. Once before now
90 he drove me forth from Ida when he came against our cattle,
and he destroyed LYRNESSOS and Pedasos. But Zeus saved me—
he roused up my strength and made my knees nimble.
Otherwise I would have been overcome at the hands of Achilles
and Athena, who went before him and set a light over him
95 and urged him to kill the Leleges° and Trojans with his brazen
sword. And so no man should fight against Achilles,
for there is always one of the gods at his side who shields him
from ruin. And his spear flies straight by itself, and does not

---

76 *against gods*: After so long a build-up, nothing comes of this war of the gods until the next book.

81 *Lykaon*: Mentioned so far only in Book 3, but killed in a famous scene in the next book.

95 *Pedasos ... Leleges*: Most commentators place the Leleges someplace in southwest Asia Minor. Pedasos was
their principal city, which Achilles sacked on one of his forays. But others place the people and their city
somewhere in the southern Troad.

slacken before it has pierced the flesh of a man. But if
a god should put the war on an equal footing, Achilles   100
would not easily conquer me, not even if he boasts to be made
wholly of bronze."

      Apollo the son of King Zeus
then answered Aeneas: "But come, warrior, you too
pray to the gods that are forever. They say that you
were borne of Aphrodite, the daughter of Zeus, whereas Achilles   105
is from a lesser god. Your mother is a daughter of Zeus,
whereas his mother is a child of the old man of the sea.
So bear against him your stubborn bronze, and do not let him
turn you back with contemptuous speech and with threats."

  So speaking, Apollo breathed great power into the shepherd   110
of the people. Aeneas strode through the forefighters arrayed
in flaming bronze. Nor did the son of Anchises escape
the notice of white-armed Hera as he went through the storm
of men to find the son of Peleus. She gathered the gods
together and spoke among them: "Consider in your breast,   115
the two of you, Poseidon and Athena, how these things will be.
Here Aeneas has gone forth arrayed in flaming bronze
to find the son of Peleus, and it is Phoibos Apollo who has set
him on. But come, let us turn him back at once, or else
let one of us stand at Achilles' side and give him great strength   120
and not allow the heart in his breast to fail, so that he might know
that the best of the deathless ones love him, and that those who
earlier warded off war and battle from the Trojans are as empty
as the wind. We have all come down from Olympos to participate
in this battle so that Achilles not suffer any hurt from the Trojans   125
on this day. Later he will suffer whatever Fate has spun
with her thread at the time that his mother bore him. If Achilles
does not learn this fact from the voice of the gods, he shall take fear
when some god comes against him in the war. It is hard when the gods
appear in their true forms!"   130

      Then Poseidon, the shaker of the earth,
answered her: "Hera, don't be angry beyond reason. There's no need.
I would not wish that we set the other gods against each other,
for we are much better than that. But let us move away from that
path, let us take our seats on a place of outlook, and leave the war
to men. But if Ares or Phoibos Apollo get in the fight,   135
or hold Achilles in check and do not permit him to make war,
then we will enter the strife of war at once. I think that

they will then quickly separate themselves from the battle
and go back to Olympos, to the gathering of the other gods,
140   overwhelmed through the power of our hands!"

So speaking,
the dark-haired god led the way to the wall heaped high
for the godlike Herakles, which the Trojans and Pallas Athena
made so that he might flee there and escape from the sea-monster,
when the monster drove him from the seashore to the plain.°
145   There Poseidon and the other gods sat down, and they put an
impenetrable cloud about their shoulders. But the proTrojan gods
sat down opposite them on the brow of Pleasant Hill—around you,
O archer Phoibos, and you, Ares the sacker of cities. So they sat
on either side, devising plans. Both sides hesitated to begin the grievous
150   war, although Zeus, who sits on high, had urged them to.

◀»   Now the whole plain was filled and flashed with the bronze
of men and horses, and the earth resounded beneath their feet
as they rushed at one another. Two warriors, by far the best,
came into the space between the two armies, eager to fight—Aeneas
155   the son of Anchises, and godlike Achilles. Aeneas first stalked forth
in a threatening manner, his heavy helmet nodding above him.
He held his great shield before his breast, and he brandished
his bronze spear. From the other side the son of Peleus leaped
like a lion, a ravening lion that an entire press of men gathered
160   together long to kill—at first the lion ignores them as he goes
on his way, but when one of the youths, swift in the battle,
hits him with the cast of a spear, then he pulls himself together
with gaping mouth. Foam gathers around his teeth and in his heart
his bold spirit groans, and he lashes his tail against his ribs
165   and flanks on both his sides as he rouses himself to fight,
and with glaring eyes he rushes on in his fury, either to kill
one of the men in the foremost throng or to die himself—

---

144   *to the plain*: Poseidon sent a sea monster against Troy as punishment when Laomedon refused to pay him
and Apollo (who sent a plague) for building the walls of Troy. Laomedon exposed his daughter Hesionê as
a sacrifice to the sea monster, but Herakles, returning from an expedition against the Amazons along with
Telamon the father of Ajax, promised to save her on one condition: that Laomedon give him the horses that
he received from Zeus as compensation for Zeus's kidnapping of Ganymede. Herakles killed the monster,
but Laomedon refused to give up the horses. In revenge Herakles later attacked Troy and killed Laomedon
and all Laomedon's sons except the youngest, named Podarkes. Podarkes was renamed *Priam* ("ransomed
one") when Herakles allowed Hesionê to ransom one of her brothers with her veil of chastity (that is, she
submitted sexually to Herakles). Herakles then gave Hesionê to Telamon, to whom she bore a son, the
famous archer Teucer, the half-brother of Big Ajax.

even so Achilles roused up his strength and his brave heart
to go against great-hearted Aeneas.

When they had come near
to one another, godlike Achilles, the fast runner, first spoke: 170
"Aeneas, why have you come so far from the crowd? Does your
heart drive you on to fight against me in the hopes of winning
Priam's rule over the horse-taming Trojans? But if you kill me,
not even then will Priam place the power in your hands.
For he has sons, he is of sound mind and not thoughtless.   175
Or have the Trojans cut out for you a territory superior to all,
a beautiful tract of orchard and a plowland, so that you might have
it if you kill me? I think that you will find that hard to do!
Yes, I recall that on another day I drove you in flight with my spear—
or do you not remember when you were alone with your cattle   180
and I drove you headlong down from the peaks of Ida with
swift steps? You did not look back one time in your flight.
From there you fled to Lyrnessos, but I sacked it with the aid
of Athena and Zeus the father, and I took the women captive.
I took away their day of freedom. But you yourself Zeus   185
and the other gods saved. I don't think that Zeus will save
you today, as you may think in your heart! You best go back
into the crowd and not to stand against me, before you suffer
great misfortune. Even a fool recognizes a deed when it is done!"

    Aeneas answered him and said: "Son of Peleus, don't think   190
that you can frighten me with words as if I were a child,
for I know well myself how to speak words that are mocking and evil.
We know the lineage of one another, we know one another's parents.
We have heard the tales told in olden times by mortal men.
But you have never seen my parents with your own eyes,   195
nor have I seen yours. They say that you are the offspring of blameless
Peleus and that your mother was Thetis of the lovely hair,
a daughter of the sea. But I am proud to be the son of great-hearted
Anchises, and my mother is Aphrodite. Of these one pair
or the other will today bewail their son! For not, I think,   200
with childish words will the two of us depart from one another
and return from the battle. But if you need to hear this again so that
you might remember my lineage—well, many men know it!°

---

203 *men know it*: See note to Book 2, line 819, for the stemma of the Trojan House.

"Zeus the cloud-gatherer first begot Dardanos, and Dardanos
205 founded Dardania, for not yet was holy Ilion built
in the plain to be a city of mortal men. Still they lived
on the slopes of Ida with its many fountains. Dardanos
begot a son, King Erichthonios,° the richest of mortal men.
He had three-thousand horses that fed in the marshland, mares
210 who delighted in their tender foals. North Wind loved them
as they grazed, and taking on the appearance of a dark-maned horse
he covered them. They became pregnant and bore twelve foals.
When the foals bounded over the earth, the giver of grain, they
would run over the topmost of the ripened wheat without breaking it,
215 and when they bounded over the broad back of the sea, they
would course over the topmost breakers of the gray sea.
    "Erichthonios begot Tros, king over the Trojans. Three blameless
sons were begotten of Tros—Ilos and Assarakos and godlike Ganymede,
the most beautiful of mortal men. The gods brought Ganymede up on high
220 to be cupbearer to Zeus on account of his beauty, that he might dwell
with the deathless ones. Then Ilos begot the blameless Laomedon
as a son. Laomedon begot Tithonos and Priam and Lampos and Klytios
and Hiketaon, the child of Ares. Assarakos begot Kapys, who begot
Anchises as a son, and Anchises was my father, as Priam was
225 the father of the good Hector.
                            "Such is my genealogy, the blood from which
I am sprung. But it is Zeus who increases the valor of men
or diminishes it, as he wishes. For he is the strongest of all.
But come, let us not long speak of these things as if we were children
standing in the midst of furious war. There are plenty of revilings
230 to make on both sides, so many that a ship of a hundred benches
could not bear the weight. The tongues of men are glib,
and there are strong pronouncements of all kinds we could make,
and the range of words is large on this side and that. Whatever word
you speak, you will hear the same. So what is the point
235 for us two to bandy in strife and to wrangle at each other
as if we were women, angry in soul-consuming quarrel,
who go to the middle of the street only to fuss with one another,
saying many things that are true and many that are not?
Anger leads people on to speak in this way. You will not turn me

---

208 *Erichthonios*: "peculiarly of the earth," curiously also the name of a primordial king of Athens, a
coincidence never explained.

FIGURE 20.2   Zeus and Ganymede.   Zeus, naked except for a cloak wrapped over his arms, his scepter at his side, seizes the handsome naked boy by the arm and shoulder. Ganymede holds a cock in his left hand, a typical gift in pederastic relationships. He looks down modestly. Zeus's thunderbolt rests against the frame of the picture to the left. Athenian red-figure wine cup by the Penthesilea Painter, fifth century BC.

240 away from battle with your words, I who am eager to fight
in the hand-to-hand with the bronze. Come, let us quickly get
a taste of each other with our bronze-tipped spears!"

So he spoke,
and he drove his powerful spear into the dread and terrible shield,
and loud it rang around the point of the spear. But the son
245 of Peleus held the shield away from him with his strong hand,
gripped with fear. He thought the far-shadowing spear of great-hearted
Aeneas would easily penetrate the shield—fool! who did
not recognize in his breast and his spirit that it is not easy for men
to master or to make yield the glorious gifts of the gods.

250   The mighty spear of warlike Aeneas did not then break
the shield. The gold held it back, the gift of the god,
but it did penetrate two layers, yet there were three more still,
for the lame-footed god had fashioned five layers, two of bronze,
two of tin on the inside, and one of gold, which stopped
255 the spear of ash.°

Now Achilles threw his spear that made a
long shadow. It hit on the well-balanced shield of Aeneas beneath
the outermost rim where the bronze ran thinnest, and the bull's hide
was thinnest. The ashen spear of the son of Peleus drove
straight through, and the shield rang loudly from the blow.
260 Aeneas cringed and held the shield away from him
in fear. The spear shot over his back and in its fury
was fixed in the ground. But it tore apart two circles of
the protecting shield. Escaping the long spear, Aeneas stood up
and an immense pain spread over his eyes in terror
265 that the spear was fixed in the ground so nearby.

Achilles drew
his sharp sword and in a fury attacked, crying a terrible cry.
But Aeneas took up a rock in his hand—a mighty deed!—
that not two men could carry today, such as men are now.
But he brandished it easily all by himself. Then Aeneas
270 would have struck Achilles as he rushed upon him,

---

255 *spear of ash*: Many commentators, beginning in the ancient world, have noted how improbable is such a
shield, with two outer layers of bronze, two inner layers of tin, and a layer of gold sandwiched between.
Homer seems to follow the model of a leather-layered shield, but this one, according to Hephaistos' manu-
facture in Book 18, is made up of three precious metals.

either on the helmet or on the shield that had warded off
grievous destruction from Achilles, and the son of Peleus
would have taken away Aeneas' life too with his sword, fighting
in close combat, except that Poseidon, the shaker of the earth,
right away saw what was happening.   275

                      Poseidon spoke at once
to the deathless gods: "Well, I am pained for great-hearted
Aeneas who quickly, overcome by the son of Peleus, will go
down to the house of Hades because he trusted the words
of Apollo who shoots from afar—the fool! Nor will Apollo
ward off grievous destruction from Aeneas. But why should   280
this man, who is without blame, suffer vain evils because
of grievances that belong to others?° Does he not always give gifts
that are pleasing to the gods who dwell in broad heaven?
But come, let us lead him out of death so that the son of Kronos
does not become angry if Achilles should kill him. For it is fated   285
that Aeneas escape and that the race of Dardanos not be
without seed, seen no more—Dardanos, whom the son
of Kronos loved more than all his children who were begotten
from mortal women. For the son of Kronos has come to hate
the race of Priam. The mighty Aeneas will be king among   290
the Trojans, and his sons' sons who come in later times."°

    Then the revered Hera with the cow eyes answered him:
"Earth-shaker, you yourself take counsel in your own heart
whether you will save Aeneas or whether you will permit Achilles,
the son of Peleus, to kill him, though Aeneas is brave.   295
But we two—Pallas Athena and I—have sworn many oaths
to all the deathless ones never to ward off that evil day
from the Trojans, when all of Troy burns in the destroying fire
and the warlike sons of the Achaeans do the burning."

    When Poseidon, shaker of the earth, had heard these things,   300
he set off to the battle and the press of spears, and he came to where
Aeneas and glorious Achilles were. He shed a mist over the eyes

---

282   *to others*: Poseidon refers to the insult that Laomedon gave to Poseidon and Apollo by not paying
       them for building the walls of Troy; Aeneas is not descended from Laomedon and should bear no
       responsibility.

291   *later times*: This remark is usually taken to refer to a dynasty of the descendants of Aeneas ruling in the
       Troad. The same prediction is made in the *Hymn to Aphrodite* (which Homer may himself have composed),
       but there is no other evidence. This passage is the basis for the legend of Aeneas told in Vergil's Roman epic,
       the *Aeneid* (c. 19 BC).

of Achilles and drew out the ashen spear, clad in bronze,
from the shield of great-hearted Aeneas, and he placed it before
305 the feet of Achilles. Then he lifted up Aeneas and swung him on high
from the earth. Aeneas sprang above the many ranks of warriors,
and the many chariots, rushed by the hand of the god, and he came
to the outermost edge of the furious war where the Kaukones°
were armed for the battle.

                    Then Poseidon the earth shaker
310 came close to Aeneas and he spoke words that went like arrows:
"Aeneas, who of the gods urges you to fight like a crazed man
against the high-hearted son of Peleus, who is stronger
than you and dearer to the deathless ones? Just draw back,
whenever you come near to him, so that you do not go beyond
315 fate into the house of Hades. When Achilles has met his death
and fate, then take courage and fight among the foremost. No other
of the Achaeans can kill you then."

                    So speaking, Poseidon left him there,
after he had told him everything. Then quickly Poseidon dispersed
the marvelous mist from the eyes of Achilles. Achilles stared hard
320 with his eyes, and groaning he spoke to his big-hearted spirit:
"Well, I see this great marvel with my eyes. My spear lies here
on the ground, but I do not see the man at whom I hurled it,
desiring to kill him. Surely this Aeneas too is beloved
by the deathless gods, though I thought his boasting was idle,
325 vain. Let him go! He will not have the heart to try me again
who has now fled gladly from death.° But come, I will call
the war-loving Danaäns. I will go against the other Trojans
and make trial of them."

                    Achilles spoke, and leaped along the ranks,
giving commands to every man: "No longer, now, let any man
330 stand apart from the Trojans, you good Achaeans. But may every
man go against his man—let every man be avid for battle.
It is hard for me, although I am strong, to pursue so many men
and to fight against all. Not even Ares, though he is an immortal god,
nor Athena, could control the jaws of such a conflict. But let

---

308 *Kaukones*: In Book 10 Dolon mentions the Kaukones, evidently a tribe that lived somewhere in Asia Minor,
      allies of the Trojans.

326 *from death*: In fact Aeneas is not mentioned again in the *Iliad*.

this be known: However much I accomplish with my power,   335
be assured I will never slacken, not a bit. I will go straight
through their line. I don't think that any Trojan will be glad,
whoever comes close to my spear!"

                  So Achilles spoke, urging them on.
And glorious Hector called out to his Trojans. He said he would
go up against Achilles: "You Trojans of high spirit, do not fear   340
the son of Peleus! I too could fight against the immortals
with words, but with a spear it is hard, for they are much stronger.°
Nor will Achilles bring to fulfillment all his words, but a part
he will accomplish, and a part will he leave incomplete. I will go
against him even if his hands are like fire—yes, if his hands   345
are like fire, and his strength like the shining steel!"

                 So Hector spoke,
urging on his men. Thus the Trojans faced their enemy.
They raised their spears on high, and the fury of both sides
clashed in confusion, and the war cry rose up. And then Phoibos
Apollo, standing at his side, spoke to Hector: "Hector,   350
do not go forth as a champion against Achilles, but wait
for him in the crowd amid the din of battle, so that he does
not hit you with a cast of his spear or cut you down
with his sword, coming in close." So Apollo spoke, and Hector
again withdrew into the crowd of men, seized with fear   355
because he had heard the voice of a god speaking to him.

   But Achilles leaped amid the Trojans, crying fearsomely,
his heart clothed in might. First of all he took down Iphition
the noble son of Otrynteus, the leader of many people, whom
a Naiad nymph bore to city-sacking Otrynteus beneath snowy   360
TMOLOS in the rich land of Hydê. Awesome Achilles hit him
with his spear, full in the head, as he came straight on, eager.
His skull was split in half, and he fell with a thud.

   Then dreaded Achilles boasted over him: "You lie there,
most dread of men, you son of Otrynteus. Here is your   365
death, though you were born beside LAKE GYGAIA,
where the territory of your father is, on the banks of Hyllos

---

342 *much stronger*: That is, talk is cheap, deeds are another matter.

and the whirling HERMOS."° So he spoke, boasting, and darkness
covered Iphition's eyes. The chariots of the Achaeans
370 tore him to pieces with their metal tires in the forefront
of the fray.

Then on top of Iphition he pierced the temples
of Demoleon,° the son of Antenor, a noble defender in the battle,
right through the bronze cheek pieces of his helmet. Nor did
the bronze helmet stay the spear, but through it the spear
375 point sped and smashed the bone, and the brains within
were spattered all over. Thus Achilles killed him in his fury.
Then he hit Hippodamas in the middle of his back
with his spear as Hippodamas leaped down from his car
and ran before him. As Hippodamas breathed out his spirit,
380 he bellowed like a bull bellows when he is dragged by
young men around the altar of the lord of Helikê.° In such
sacrifices the shaker of the earth delights. Even so Hippodamas
bellowed as his noble spirit left his bones.

Then Achilles
went after godlike Polydoros with his spear, a son of Priam.
385 His father would not allow him to fight because he was the youngest
of his children and dearest to him, and in fleetness of foot he
surpassed all. But now in his folly, showing off his fleetness of foot,
he was rushing through the foremost fighters until he lost his life.
Fearsome Achilles, the fast runner, hit him in the middle
390 of the back with a cast of his spear as he rushed past,
hit him where the clasps of his belt were fastened and the pieces
of the breastplate overlapped.° The point of the spear went
straight on its way beside the navel, and he fell to his knees
with a groan, and a cloud of darkness enveloped him. But as
395 Polydoros collapsed, he clutched his guts tightly with his hands.

When Hector saw his brother Polydoros bent down
to the earth and holding his guts, a mist sank down over his eyes.

---

368 *whirling Hermos*: Iphition is one of the Meiones, mentioned in the Trojan Catalog. Its leaders are associated
with Mt. Tmolos and Lake Gygaia. The location of Hydê is unknown, but it may be the same as SARDIS
beneath Mt. Tmolos. The Hyllos is a tributary of the Hermos River.

372 *Demoleon*: Not heard of elsewhere.

381 *Helikê*: Hippodamas appears only here. Helikê was on the coast of Achaea in the northwestern Peloponne-
sus, where there was a temple to Poseidon. The bull is a typical sacrifice to Poseidon.

392 *was fitted*: The belt was made of or decorated with metal and was put on above the breastplate to hold it in
place, but its fasteners are mentioned only here.

He no longer endured to range apart, but he turned
against Achilles, brandishing his sharp spear like a fire.
Achilles, when he saw him, sprang up and, boasting, spoke: 400
"The man is near who above all has stung me to the heart, the one
who killed my honored companion. We'll no longer shrink
from one another along the bridges of war!" He spoke,
and looking angrily from beneath his brows he addressed
the good Hector: "Come close, so that you may the sooner   405
come to the means of your destruction!"

                           Hector, whose helmet
flashed, was not afraid, and he said: "Son of Peleus, do not hope
to frighten me with words as if I were a child, for I myself
know well myself how to speak mocking stinging words.
I know that you are brave, and that I am much weaker than you.   410
But these things lie on the laps of the gods, whether I
will take away your life by a cast of my spear, though I am weaker,
for my weapon has been keen enough until now."

                           He spoke,
and brandishing his spear he cast it, but Athena with a breath—
breathing full lightly—turned it back from glorious Achilles.   415
The spear went back to good Hector and fell before his feet.
Achilles leaped on Hector with a fury, anxious to kill him,
crying terribly, when Apollo snatched up Hector full easily,
as a god can do, and Apollo concealed Hector in a thick mist.

   Three times the good Achilles, the fast runner, leaped on Hector   420
with his spear of bronze, and three times he struck the thick mist.
But when he rushed onward a fourth time, like a spirit, then with
an awesome shout Achilles spoke words that went like arrows:
"You have escaped death for now, you dog! But your evil day
comes close enough. Phoibos Apollo has saved you, to whom   425
you ought to offer a prayer when you go into the hurtling
of spears. But surely I will make an end of you when next
we meet, if any god is a helper to me too. For now
I will go after others, to see whom I can find."

   So speaking, he hit Dryops in the middle of the neck   430
with his spear, and Dryops fell down before his feet. Achilles
let him go, and he knocked bold and tall Demouchos the son
of Philetor from the fight, hitting him on the knee with one cast
of his spear. Then Achilles sliced him with his great sword
and took away his life.   435

And then he set on Laogonos and Dardanos,
the sons of Bias. He forced them from their chariot to the ground,
hitting the one with his spear, the other with his sword
in the hand-to-hand. Then Tros, the son of Alastor—he came
to him and grasped his knees in the hope that Achilles
440 would take him captive and let him go alive, not kill him,
taking pity on one of a similar age. The fool! He did
not know there was to be no persuading, for Achilles
was in no way a man soft of heart or gentle of mind,
but excessively ferocious. Tros tried to seize Achilles' knees
445 with his hands, longing to make a prayer, but Achilles
cut him in the liver with his sword, and the liver slipped out.
The black blood coming from him filled Tros's breast.
Tros lost consciousness as darkness covered his eyes.

Then Achilles came close to Moulios. He cut him on his ear
450 with his spear—the bronze went straight through the other ear.
Then he hit Echeklos the son of Agenor full on the head with his
hilted sword, and the whole blade grew warm with the blood.
Down over the eyes of Echeklos came dark death
and powerful fate.

Then Achilles pierced Deukalion through the arm
455 with his bronze spear where the sinews of the elbow come together.
Deukalion awaited him, his arm dangling heavily down.
He saw death before him. Achilles hit Deukalion on the neck
with his sword, whirling the head afar, still wearing its helmet,
and the marrow spurted forth from the spine,° and the body
460 lay stretched out on the ground.

Then Achilles went after the blameless
son of Peires, Rhigmus, who came from THRACE with its rich soil.
He hit him with his spear. The bronze fixed in his belly
and he fell from his car. He stabbed his aide Areithoös
in the middle of the back with his sharp spear, and thrust him
465 from the chariot as he was turning his horses around, and they
ran wild.°

---

459 *from the spine*: This is quite impossible.

466 *ran wild*: Achilles' victims are mostly named only to be killed. *Dryops* and *Demouchos* appear only here, as
do *Dardanos* and *Tros*, although they bear names famous from Trojan history. *Laogonos*, son of Bias, ap-
pears only here (though Meriones kills a man of the same name, but son of Onetor, in book 16). Patroklos
also killed a *Moulios* and an *Echeklos* (Book 16). *Deukalion* is found only here (another Deukalion was
father to Idomeneus, Book 13). *Rhigmos* and *Areïthoös* appear only here.

As a wondrous-blazing fire rushes through
the deep folds of a dry mountain, and the deep forest burns,
and the winds whirl on the flame, driving it every which way,
even so Achilles raged everywhere with his spear, like a god,
following hard on those he killed. And the dark earth ran   470
with blood, as when a man yokes bulls with broad brows
to trample down the white wheat in a well-built threshing
floor, and quickly the grain is trodden out beneath the feet
of the bellowing bulls—even so beneath Achilles, with his
great soul, the single-hoofed horses trampled alike on the bodies   475
and the shields, and all the axle beneath was totally
drenched in blood, and the rails at the front and sides
of the car too, splattered by drops driven by the horses' hooves
and the tires.° But Achilles, the son of Peleus, pressed on
to win glory, and his invincible hands were splashed with gore.   480

---

479 *and the tires*: Nothing has been said about Achilles mounting his chariot to pursue the Trojans, but omission of such details are normal.

BOOK 21. *The Fight with the River and the Battle of the Gods*

And when they came to the ford of the easy flowing river,
the whirling Xanthos, the child of deathless Zeus, there
Achilles cut them in half, and the one troop he drove
to the plain toward the city where the Achaeans had fled
5 in rout only the day before, when brave Hector was raging.
Some fled away in rout there, and Hera spread out
a deep mist as they went, to hinder them. And the other half
Achilles penned up in the deep-flowing river with its silvery
eddies. Those fell in the water with a great racket,
10 and the descending steep streams resounded, and the high banks
boomed all around. They thrashed every which way in uproar,
whirled about in the eddies, as when beneath the surge
of a fire locusts take wing to flee to a river as the
relentless fire sears them with its sudden oncoming,
15 and they shrink down beneath the water—even so before
Achilles' onslaught the sounding stream of the deep-eddying
Xanthos was filled with a confusion of horses and men.

    Then Zeus-begotten Achilles left his spear there on the bank,
leaning against a tamarisk bush, and like a wraith he leaped in,
20 having only his sword. He had stored wicked deeds in his heart,
and turning now here, now there, he stabbed and he struck,
and a horrible groaning rose as the Trojans were cut down
by the sword, and the water ran red with blood. As when fish
flee before a voracious dolphin and fill the crannies of a harbor
25 with good anchorage in their terror, for the dolphin greedily
devours every one he can catch, even so the Trojans
cowered in the streams of the dread river beneath
the steep banks.

    When Achilles' arms grew tired
from killing, he chose twelve youths from the river, alive,
30 as blood-price for the dead Patroklos, son of Menoitios.
He hauled them forth, dazed like fawns, and he bound
their hands behind them with well-cut thongs that they

themselves wore around their stoutly woven shirts. He gave
them to his companions to drag away to the hollow ships.°
Then he leaped back in again, eager to kill.   35

   He came upon Lykaon, a son of Dardanian Priam,
trying to flee from the river—Lykaon, whom he had once
taken on a night raid, quite to Lykaon's surprise, catching
him in his father's orchard. Lykaon was cutting young
shoots of wild fig with the sharp bronze to serve as the rims   40
of a chariot. Achilles came on him like an unexpected evil,
and then he sold him into well-built LEMNOS, taking him
there in his ships. The son of Jason gave Achilles
a price for him.° From there a guest-friend paid a high sum
for him, Eëtion of Imbros. And Eëtion sent Lykaon   45
to shining ARISBÊ, from where he escaped and returned
to his father's house.° Escaped from Lemnos, he enjoyed himself
with his friends for eleven days. But on the twelfth day a god
cast him again into the hands of Achilles, who would send him
to the house of Hades, where he had no desire to go.   50

   When godlike Achilles, the fast runner, saw Lykaon
naked without helmet or shield, nor did he have a spear because
he had thrown these things to the ground as his sweat oppressed him
when he fled from the river, and weariness overcame his knees
beneath him—then, Achilles spoke to his own large-hearted spirit: 55
"Well now, I think I see a great wonder with my eyes!
Truly the great-hearted Trojans that I have killed will rise up again
beneath the murky darkness! Look, this man has come back
after fleeing his day of doom, although he was sold into holy Lemnos.
The deep of the gray sea that holds back many against their   60
will has not held him. But now he will taste the point
of my spear so that I may see whether in like manner he will
come back from *there* too, or whether the life-giving earth,
which holds down even strong men, will hold him down too."

   Thus Achilles pondered as he took his stand. But Lykaon   65
came close to him, bewildered, eager to grasp his knees,

---

34   *to the hollow ships*: This is the only time in the *Iliad* that prisoners are taken. Probably the "well-cut thongs"
     are belts that the men wore.

44   *price for him*: According to Book 23, Euneos, son of Jason and Hypsipylê, gave as payment for Lykaon a valu-
     able mixing-bowl of Phoenician manufacture.

47   *father's house*: Eëtion has the same name as the father of Hector's wife, Andromachê. Living in Arisbê on the
     Hellespont (Map 3), this Eëtion was evidently a guest-friend of the house of Priam.

for Lykaon wanted very much in his heart to escape
evil fate and black death. The good Achilles raised his long
spear high, ready to stab him, but Lykaon ran beneath
70 it, and stooping down he took hold of Achilles' knees.
The spear went over his back and was fixed in the ground,
though eager to be glutted with a man's flesh.

                                                    But Lykaon
with one hand beseeched Achilles, holding Achilles' knees,
while with the other he grasped the sharp spear and would not let go.
75 Speaking words that went like arrows he addressed Achilles:
"I beg of you, O Achilles, respect me and take pity! In your eyes,
O Zeus-nurtured one, I am already a holy suppliant,
for at your table I first tasted of the grain of Demeter on that
day when you captured me in the well-ordered orchard,
80 and you sold me far away, taking me from my father and my
friends, into the sacred island of Lemnos. And I brought you
the value of a hundred oxen. But now I have bought my freedom
by paying three times as much.° This is the twelfth morning
since I have come back to Ilion, and I have suffered very much.
85   "And now deadly fate has again placed me in your hands.
Surely I am hated by Father Zeus, who has again given me
to you. My mother bore me to a short life, Laothoê,
the daughter of aging Altes—Altes who is king over
the war-loving Leleges, who hold steep Pedasos on the Satnioeis
90 river. Priam had Altes' daughter as a wife, and many other
women too. The two of us were born from Laothoê, and you
will butcher us both! For you killed godlike Polydoros
among the soldiers who fight in the forefront when you hit him
with your sharp spear. But right here, now, an evil will come
95 on me too, for I do not think I will escape your hands. A spirit
has brought me close to you. But I will tell you something,
and you lay it to heart: Do not kill me! I do not come
from the same belly as Hector, who killed your friend,
kind and strong!"

        So spoke the bold son of Priam,
100 begging Achilles with words, but the voice Lykaon
heard was unlike honey: "Fool! Don't promise *me*
your ransom or hope to persuade me. Before Patroklos

---

83   *as much*: Apparently Lykaon had to pay Eëtion back the price of his freedom even though Eëtion was a
      guest-friend in the house of Priam. And a fancy Phoenician bowl must be worth a hundred oxen!

met his day of destiny, I was more inclined to have
mercy on the Trojans, and many whom I took captive
I sold for ransom overseas. But now of all the Trojans   105
no one whom the god has placed in my hands before Ilion
will escape death—and above all not the sons of Priam!
So, my friend, you die too. Why are you sad? Patroklos
died, he who was much better than you. Don't you see
how I am more handsome than you, and taller? I come   110
from a good father, and my mother was a goddess.
But dread fate and death hang on me too, whether it will be
at dawn, at dusk, or at noon, when someone will give
my spirit to Ares by a cast of the spear or an arrow
flying from the string."   115

        So he spoke, then he loosed the knees
and the strong heart of the man. Lykaon let go of Achilles'
spear and he crouched and spread his arms wide, both of them.
Achilles drew his sharp sword and cut him on the collarbone
beside the neck, and then he buried the double-edged sword
in his neck. Lykaon fell flat on the earth, and he lay there stretched   120
out as the black blood flowed from him and wet the ground.

   Achilles picked him up by the foot and threw him in the river
to be carried away, and he went on boasting, speaking
words that went like arrows: "Lie there now with the fishes,
who will gladly lick the blood from your wound without a care for you.   125
Nor will your mother get to weep over you and lay you out
on your bed, but Skamandros will bear you spinning to the broad
breast of the sea. Many a fish, as it leaps amid the waves,
will dart up beneath the black ruffling of the water to eat
your white fat, rash Lykaon.   130
           "So die Trojans! while I come
to the city of sacred Ilion—you in flight and I plundering
the rear! The broad-flowing river with its silver swirls will be
of no use to you, to whom you sacrificed many bulls and cast
single-hoofed horses alive into its eddies. In this way you will
perish by an evil fate until all of you pay the price for the death   135
of Patroklos and the sorrow of the Achaeans whom you killed
at the swift ships when I was away!"

        So he spoke, and the river Xanthos grew
more angry in his heart, and he pondered in his spirit how he should
put a stop to Achilles and ward off destruction. from the Trojans.

140　　　In the meanwhile the son of Peleus with his long-shadowing
spear leaped on Asteropaios, eager to kill him, the son of Pelegon
whom the broad-flowing Axɪos begot on Periboia, the eldest
daughter of Akessamenos—the deep-eddying Axios had
intercourse with Periboia. Well, Achilles rushed on Asteropaios
145　as he stepped out of the river, awaiting Achilles. Asteropaios
had two spears, and Xanthos had placed courage in his breast,
angry because of all the young men killed in the battle,
whom Achilles had cut in pieces along the bank,
without pity.

　　　　　When the two warriors had advanced
150　in close against each other, then first of all Achilles
the fast runner addressed Asteropaios: "Who are you
among men, and where do you come from, you who dare
to stand against me? You are the children of wretched men
who stand against my power!"

　　　　　The fine son of Pelegon
155　answered Achilles: "O great-hearted son of Peleus, why do you
ask about my lineage? I am from Paeonia, with its
rich soil, far away, leading the Paeonians with their long
spears. This is now the eleventh dawn since I have come
to Troy. As for my lineage, I am a descendant of the Axios,
160　the most beautiful water of those that go on the earth,
who begot Pelegon famous for his spear. They say that
I am his son. Now let us fight, most glorious Achilles!"

　　　So he spoke in a threatening manner. The good Achilles,
the son of Peleus, then raised high his ashen spear, but the warrior
165　Asteropaios hurled with both spears at once, for he was ambidextrous.
The one spear struck Achilles' shield, but did not break through,
for the gold layer, a gift of the god, held it.° But with the other
he grazed the right forearm of Achilles, and the black blood
flowed.° Then the spear went beyond and stuck in the earth,
170　longing to be glutted on flesh.

　　　　　Then Achilles let loose
his straight-flying spear of ash at Asteropaios, eager to kill.
But he missed him and hit the high bank, and the ashen spear

167　*held it*: Now the gold layer seems to be on the top!

169　*black blood flowed*: This is the only time that Achilles in wounded in the *Iliad*.

was fixed half its length in the bank. Then the son of Peleus drew
his sharp sword from his thigh and leaped furiously on
Asteropaios, who tried but could not withdraw Achilles'   175
spear from the river bank with his powerful hand. Three
times he made it quiver as he eagerly tried to pull it out,
three times he gave up the effort. For a fourth time he tried
to bend and break the ashen spear of the grandson of Aiakos,
but before that Achilles moved in close and took his life   180
with his sword. He stuck him in the stomach beside the navel
and out poured all his guts to the ground. Darkness covered the eyes
of Asteropaios as he struggled to breathe.

                       Achilles leaped
on his breast and stripped him of his armor° and, boasting, said:
"Lie there then. It is a hard thing to fight against the children   185
of the mighty son of Kronos, even for one begotten of a river.
You say that you are begotten of the race of the wide-flowing river,
but I claim to be of the line of great Zeus! A man begot me
who was king over the plentiful Myrmidons—Peleus, the son
of Aiakos. And Aiakos was a son of Zeus. Even as Zeus   190
is stronger than rivers that gurgle their way to the sea,
so stronger is the seed of Zeus than the seed of a river.
And look, there is a river right beside you, a great river,
if it can do you any good. You ought not to go up against
Zeus the son of Kronos. Even King ACHELOÖS° does not think   195
he is equal to him, nor is the great power of deep-flowing
Ocean, from whom all the rivers flow and every sea and all
the fountains and the deep wells. Even he fears the lightning
of great Zeus and the ferocious thunder that he smashes
down from heaven."   200

              So he spoke, and out of the bank
he pulled his bronze spear, and he left Asteropaios there
lying on the sand after he had taken away his life, and the dark
water lapped around him. The eels and the fishes finished
off Asteropaios, tearing away the fat from his kidneys,
plucking it away as Achilles went his way among the Paeonians,   205
masters of the chariot, who fled along the bands of the swirling

---

184   *his armor*: In Book 23 Achilles will offer the breastplate and sword of Asteropaios as prizes in the funeral
      games for Patroklos.

195   *Acheloös*: The longest river in Greece, in northwest Greece (another Acheloös river, in Lydia, is mentioned
      in Book 24).

river, because they saw their best man killed in the savage
contendings at the hands and sword of the son of Peleus

    Then he killed Thersilochos and Mydon and Astypylos
210 and Mnesos and Thrasios and Ainios and Ophelestes—
and swift Achilles would have killed a lot more except that
the deep-swirling river spoke to him in anger, taking on the form
of a man and speaking from the whirling depths: "O Achilles,
you are strong beyond all other men, and you do evil things
215 beyond all men. For the gods themselves are always
on your side. If the son of Kronos has given it to you
to destroy all the men of Troy, at least drive them
out of my stream and do your dirty work on the plain.
For my lovely streams are filled with dead bodies,
220 and I can no longer run my waters into the bright sea
because it is crammed with corpses that you ruthlessly kill.
So leave off! Astonishment holds me, O leader of the people!"

    Achilles the fast runner then answered him: "So it will be,
O Skamandros, nurtured of Zeus, just as you command.
225 But I shall not give over killing the Trojans before I have driven
them into the city and made trial of Hector in the hand-to-hand.
Either he will destroy me, or I him."

                So speaking, Achilles
leaped on the Trojans like a power from the spirit world.
And then the deep-swirling river spoke to Apollo: "You
230 of the silver bow, son of Zeus—Why have you not kept
the commandments of the son of Kronos, who strictly ordered
you to stand by the Trojans and to defend them until the late-setting
sun comes forth and casts the deep-soiled earth into shadow?"

    Xanthos spoke and Achilles, famed for his spear, sprang
235 from the bank and leaped into the middle of the river.
But Skamandros rushed upon him with a swelling flood,
and he roused all his streams, stirring them up, and he swept along
the many bodies of the dead that lay thick within his bed,
whom Achilles had killed. These he cast forth onto the dry land,
240 bellowing like a bull, but the living he saved beneath
his beautiful streams, hiding them in the enormous deep eddies.

    A sudden tumultuous wave stood up around Achilles,
and the stream fell over his shield and drove him backward.
He could not stand. He grabbed onto an elm tree with his hands—

shapely, tall—but it fell uprooted and carried away the whole   245
bank with it. The elm stretched over the beautiful streams
with its thick branches, damming the river, falling entirely
into the river. In fear Achilles tried to leap out of the eddy
and to run with his powerful feet over the plain, but the great god
did not let up. He rushed on him with his dark-crested wave   250
so that he might hold back powerful Achilles from his labor,
and ward off destruction from the Trojans. But the son of Peleus
sprang backward as far as a cast spear, like a swooping black eagle,
a hunter who is both the strongest and the swiftest of birds.
Like him, Achilles darted back and on his breast   255
the bronze rang terribly. Swerving, he ran beneath the flood,
but the river flowed just behind him with a great roar.

   As when a man draws off dark water from a spring
to flow beside his plants and garden plots, holding a mattock
in his hands as he clears away obstructions in the channel,   260
and as the water flows all the pebbles beneath are pushed
along and the water murmurs as it glides swiftly down a
slope and outstrips even the man who guides it—even so
the wave of the stream overtook Achilles although he was fleet
of foot: For gods are stronger than men!   265

                    For as long
as the good Achilles, the fast runner, tried to make a stand
against the river and to learn if all the gods who hold the broad sky
were putting him to flight, for so long the great wave of the
Zeus-nourished river would strike his shoulders from above,
and he sprang up high with his feet, agonized in spirit.   270
The river ran at his knees with a vicious current, and it
snatched away the ground from his feet.

                    The son of Peleus
groaned and looked into the broad heaven: "Father Zeus, why does
not any one of the gods undertake to save me, pitiful as I am now?
If I escape, I should not mind dying later! I do not blame   275
any other of the heavenly gods so much as my mother,
who tricked me with lying words, saying that I would perish
from the fast missiles of Apollo beneath the wall of the heavily armed
Trojans. I wish that Hector had killed me there, the best man
they have. Then a brave man would have been my killer,   280
and a brave man he would have killed. But am I now
destined to die a miserable death, trapped in the great river

like a swine-herder boy swept away as he tries to cross
a water course in the winter?"

So he spoke, and very quickly
285 Poseidon and Athena went to him and stood close by,
taking on the appearance of men. Holding his hand
in their hands, they made pledges of trust with words.
Among them Poseidon, the shaker of the earth, began to speak:
"Son of Peleus, don't tremble so, nor be so afraid.
290 We two are your helpers from the gods, and Zeus has given
his approval to Pallas Athena and me. It is not your destiny
to die by the river. The river shall soon let up. You will know
it yourself! But we shall give you some good advice,
if you will listen: Do not let your hands rest from the wicked
295 war before you have penned up the Trojan army
behind the famous walls of Ilion—those who get away!
Then get back to the ships, once you have taken Hector's life.
We grant that you gain victory."

When the two had spoken,
they went off to the deathless ones. Achilles went towardx
300 the plain, for the bidding of the gods had much roused him.
But now the plain was entirely filled with water. A great deal
of fine armor and the corpses of young men killed in battle floated
there. His knees flashed on high as he rushed straight at the flood,
and the broad-flowing river could not stop him, for Athena
305 placed great power in him. Yet Skamandros did not give up
his own power, but raged still more at the son of Peleus.

Raising himself on high, Xanthos formed the wave
of his flood into a crest, and he called with a shout to SIMOEIS:
"Dear brother, let us work together to put a stop to this man's might,
310 or he will quickly sack the great city of King Priam, and the Trojans
will be unable to stop him and the din of battle. So come quickly
to my aid—fill your streams with the waters of springs!
Arouse all your torrents, and raise a great wave, and stir
a huge roar of tree trunks and stones so that we might stop
315 this savage man who vies with the gods, and who now prevails.
I don't think that his strength will do him any good, nor his
good looks, nor his fancy armor that will soon lie at the bottom
of a slime-covered lake. For I will cover his body with sand and pour
on a ton of gravel, and the Achaeans will not know where to gather
320 his bones, with so great a quantity of mud will I enshroud him!

FIGURE 21.1   The Skamandros River.   Two shepherds herd their sheep on a hill above the Skamandros River in the Troad. Homer seems to have had personal knowledge of the Troad and the river's steep banks. Photo taken May 1, 1915.

This will be his tomb, so there will be no need of a burial mound when
the Achaeans celebrate his funeral."

                            Xanthos spoke and rushed
in tumult on Achilles, raging from on high, seething with foam
and blood and corpses. The dark wave of the god-nourished river
rose up high in the air and was about to overwhelm the son
of Peleus when Hera called aloud, in terror for Achilles
that the great deep-eddying river might sweep him away.
At once she spoke to Hephaistos, her beloved brother:
"Get up, my little club-footed boy! It was against you, I suppose,
that the swirling Xanthos was matched in battle! So help us
right now. Make clear your mighty flame. I will go
and arouse from the sea a ferocious blast of West Wind
and the rapid South Wind that will burn the Trojan bodies
and armor, driving on an evil flame. And you must
burn the trees along the banks of the Xanthos—surround
the river with fire! Don't let Xanthos turn you aside
with sweet talk and threats. Don't give up your fury until I call
to you with a shout. Then stop your tireless fire."

    So she spoke, and Hephaistos prepared his wondrous fire.
First the fire was kindled on the plain. He burned the many corpses
whom Achilles had killed that lay thick upon it. All the plain
was dried up and the bright water was halted. As when at harvest
time North Wind speedily dries up an orchard that has recently
been watered, and glad is he who tills it, even so Hephaistos
dried the entire plain and also burned up the corpses.
Then he turned his gleaming fire against the river. The elms
were burned and the willows and the tamarisks and the lotus were
burned, and the reeds and the marsh-grass that grew in abundance
along the beautiful streams of the river. The eels and the fishes
were tormented in the eddies. In the beautiful streams they tumbled
this way and that, ruined by the blast of clever Hephaistos.

    The might of the river was burned too, and Xanthos
spoke, addressing the god: "Hephaistos, no one of the gods
is able to resist you, blazing with fire, nor can I
fight against you. Let go of strife! As for the Trojans,
may the good Achilles drive them forth from their city.
What is strife to me? Why should I concern myself
with bringing aid?"

So Xanthos spoke, burning with fire,
and his beautiful streams bubbled up. As a cauldron boils
within when a furious fire is lit beneath it, and the 360
cauldron melts the lard of a fat hog that bubbles
in every part, and dried wood is set on the fire,
so burned the river's beautiful streams with fire and its
waters boiled. Nor did Xanthos wish to flow onward—
he was stayed: The blast from the might of wise Hephaistos 365
had worn him down.

          Then, pleading to Hera, Xanthos spoke words
that went like arrows: "Hera, why has your son attacked
my stream so as to torment it above all the other allies of Troy?
Surely I am not so much to blame as the other defenders
of the Trojans. I will step back if you so command, 370
but let him step back too. I will swear this oath:
not ever to ward off the day of evil from the Trojans,
not even when all of Troy burns with raging fire
and the warlike sons of the Achaeans are burning it!"

  When the goddess, the white-armed Hera, heard this, 375
she called at once to Hephaistos, her dear son: "O Hephaistos,
my glorious son—stop! It is not right that you jostle
an immortal god for the sake of mortals."

                So she spoke,
and Hephaistos extinguished his wondrous fire, and backward
rolled the wave along the beautiful streams. When the might 380
of Xanthos had been overcome, the two gods ceased the struggle.
Hera stopped them, although she was angry.

            But on the other gods
fell a grave and heavy strife, and the spirit in their breasts
moved in different directions. They clashed together
with an enormous clamor and the wide earth rang out, and all 385
around the sky rang as from a trumpet.° Zeus heard it, sitting
on Olympos. His own heart laughed, rejoicing, when he saw
the gods coming together in strife.° Then none dared stand apart.

---

386 *from a trumpet*: Homer knows about war trumpets, but they are never used in battle.

388 *in strife*: Why Zeus should have laughed at the war of the gods has been much debated, but evidently it is
    because of the comic scenes that follow: As Zeus laughed, so are we the audience supposed to laugh at the
    ridiculous antics of these gods acting so absurdly.

Ares, the piercer of shields, began, and first he
390 leaped on Athena, holding his spear of bronze, and
he gave this insulting speech: "Why, O fly of a dog,
do you again set on the gods to fight in your reckless
daring, as your proud spirit impels you? Have you
forgotten the time when you set on Diomedes
395 the son of Tydeus to wound me, and you yourself took
the spear, in the sight of all, and drove it straight into me,
and you rent my handsome flesh? Therefore you will
now, I think, pay the full price for what you have done!"

So speaking, Ares stabbed at the tasseled goatskin fetish,
400 the awesome thing that not even the thunderbolt of Zeus can
subdue. The blood-stained Ares stabbed at it with his long spear,
but Athena gave ground and took up in her thick hand
a stone that lay on the plain—black, jagged, and huge,
which men of former times had placed to be a marker for a field.
405 Athena cast it and struck the bold Ares in the neck and loosed
his limbs. He fell down over two acres! His hair mixed with
the dust, and his armor clanged.

Pallas Athena laughed,°
and boasting over him she spoke words that went like arrows:
"Fool! Not even yet have you learned how much better I am
410 than you—that you should match your strength against mine!
Thus will you satisfy to the full the Erinyes of your mother,°
who in her anger devised evil against you because you abandoned
the Achaeans and brought aid to the proud Trojans."

So speaking
Athena turned her bright eyes away. Aphrodite, the daughter of Zeus,
415 took Ares by the hand and led him away as he groaned mightily.°
Scarcely could he gather his spirit.

When the goddess Hera,
whose arms are white, saw Aphrodite, at once she spoke

---

408 *laughed*: This second mock battle of the gods (the first is in Book 5) puzzled ancient commentators and
inspired allegorical interpretations, but it provides comic relief between the scene of Achilles' fight with
Skamandros and Achilles' killing of Hector.

411 *of your mother*: In Book 5 Athena says that Ares has broken his promise to her and Hera that he would help
the Greeks against Troy. The Erinyes take vengeance for broken oaths.

415 *groaned mightily*: In a famous story in the *Odyssey*, Ares and Aphrodite are lovers. No doubt the Judgment
of Paris, referred to obliquely in Book 24, lies behind the enmity between Aphrodite and Hera and Athena.

to Athena words that went like arrows: "Well look at this!
O child of Zeus who carries the goatskin fetish, unwearied
one—there she goes again! This fly of a dog is leading   420
man-destroying Ares out of the tearful war, beyond the melée.
Well, after her!" So Hera spoke, and Athena went off
in pursuit, glad at heart. Rushing upon Aphrodite she struck
her on the chest with her thick hand. Aphrodite's knees
were loosened right there, and her heart too.   425

                                        So the two of them,
Ares and Aphrodite, lay on the bountiful earth, and Athena,
boasting, spoke words that went like arrows: "So be it to all
who are helpers of the Trojans when they fight against
the heavily armed Argives. Yes, they are bold and reckless,
just like Aphrodite who came to the aid of Ares—   430
going up against my power! Then we would long ago have
ceased from this war, after sacking the well-built city
of Ilion."

    So she spoke, and the goddess Hera, whose arms
are white, smiled. But the kingly earth-shaker Poseidon
spoke to Apollo: "Phoibos, why do the two of us stand apart   435
from the battle? I don't think it's right, for the others have begun.
It would be shameful if we were to go back to Olympos to the house
of Zeus, with its bronze threshold, without a fight. So begin!
You are the younger in age. It would not be appropriate
for me to begin, because I was born first and I know more.   440
    "And you have a stupid heart, fool! Do you not remember
all the ills that we alone of all the gods suffered at Ilion
when we served the proud Laomedon for a year for a fixed wage
on Zeus's command? Laomedon was the boss and laid on
the orders. Well, I built a wall for the Trojans all around the city—   445
broad and very beautiful—so that the city could never be taken.
And you herded the sleek cattle who have a shuffling walk
in the folds of wooded Ida, with its many ridges.° But when
the glad seasons brought an end to the term of our hire, then the awful
Laomedon defrauded us of the entire sum. He sent us away   450
with a threat. He threatened to bind our feet and hands
above and sell us off into islands that are far away.

---

448   *many ridges:* In Book 7 Poseidon says that they *both* built the walls, but here Apollo's service was as a herds-
man. No reason is given why Zeus ordered that Poseidon and Apollo should perform this service.

He made as if he would cut off the ears of both of us
with the bronze! So we went off with anger in our hearts,
455 furious that he did not pay us our fee, which he promised
but then did not give. You are showing favor to this man's people,
nor do you try along with the rest of us to see that the proud
Trojans perish in deserved ruin, along with their children
and their chaste wives."

Then King Apollo, who shoots
460 from a long way off, spoke: "Earth-shaker, you would not
think me to be of sound mind if I should fight against you
for the sake of wretched mortals, who like the leaves of the trees
now are filled with flaming life, eating the fruit of the field
before they dwindle away and perish. However, let us quit
465 the battle as soon as possible. Let the mortals battle by themselves."

So speaking, Apollo turned his back. He was ashamed to mix
in war against his own father's brother. But his sister upbraided him,
Artemis of the wild wood, the mistress of the wild animals,
as she spoke a reproachful word: "So you are fleeing,
470 you who work from afar, turning over the whole victory
to Poseidon, giving him the glory for nothing. You fool!
Why do you have your bow, now worthless as the wind?
Let me no longer hear you in the halls of your father boasting,
as you have done earlier among the deathless gods, that you
475 would fight against Poseidon in the hand-to-hand."

So Artemis
spoke, and Apollo, who works from a long way off, said nothing,
but the respected wife of Zeus grew angry and upbraided
the archer queen with reproachful words: "What? You want
to stand against me, you fearsome *bitch*? I am hard to oppose
480 in power, although you carry the bow. Zeus made you
a lion against women, and he gave you the power to kill
whomever of them you wish.° But it is better to be cutting
down beasts and wild deer on the mountains than to fight
with those who are stronger than you. If you want to learn
485 about war, so that you might know how much stronger I am than you,
inasmuch as you *want* to match your strength against mine—"
but then Hera caught both of Artemis' hands by the wrist

---

482 *you wish*: When a woman died in ancient Greece from "natural causes," she was said to fall before the
arrows of Artemis.

FIGURE 21.2   Apollo and Artemis.   Apollo was the *aoidos*, the "singer," among the gods. Here young and beardless and holding a lotus staff, he greets his sister Artemis, who carries a bow and is accompanied by a deer, her usual attributes. In classical times the triad Leto, Apollo, and Artemis made up a holy family, although in origin they were unrelated. Athenian red-figure wine-cup by the Brygos painter, c. 470 BC.

with her left hand, and with her right she removed the bow
and quiver from her shoulders. With them, smiling, she beat
490 Artemis around the ears as she struggled this way and that,
and the swift arrows fell from her quiver. Weeping, the goddess
fled from Hera like a dove that takes refuge in a hollow rock,
a cleft, when a falcon attacks—for it was not Aphrodite's
destiny to be taken. Even so she fled, weeping, and she left
495 her bow and arrow there.

                    Then Hermes, the killer of Argos,
the messenger, spoke to Leto: "Leto, I will not fight
with you. It is a rough matter to exchange blows with the wives
of Zeus who gathers the clouds. Just say it—speak right out
and tell the deathless gods that you beat me with your mighty
500 strength ..."

        So Hermes spoke, and Leto gathered up the curved
bow and the arrows that fell scattered in the swirl of dust.
She took the bow and arrows and went after her daughter. But Artemis
had gone back to Olympos. There that maiden came to the house of Zeus
with its bronze threshold. Weeping she sat down on the knees
505 of her father. The fragrant robe trembled around her. Her father,
the son of Kronos, clasped Artemis and asked, laughing sweetly:
"Who, of the dwellers in heaven, my dear child, has treated
you ill, to no purpose, as if you were doing some wicked thing
in full view?"

        Artemis answered him, the fair-crowned huntress
510 of the echoing chase: "It was your wife who beat me up,
O father—Hera who has white arms, from whom strife
and quarreling have fallen upon the immortals!"

                      So they said these
things to one another. But Phoibos Apollo went into holy Ilion.
He was concerned about the wall of the well-built city, in case
515 the Danaäns, tempting fate, should knock it down that very day.
The other gods, who live forever, went back to Olympos,
some angry, others exulting greatly. There they sat down beside
the father, lord of the dark cloud.

              But Achilles was still killing
the Trojans and their single-hoofed horses. As when smoke
520 rises up and enters broad heaven from a burning city, and
the anger of the gods drives it on, causing pain to all

and inflicting woes on many, even so did Achilles cause pain
to the Trojans and inflict woes upon them.

                       Old man Priam stood
on the heaven-built wall and from there watched the monstrous
Achilles. The Trojans were being driven in headlong rout   525
before him. There was no help! With a groan he descended
from the wall and then he called out to his glorious gatekeepers
along the wall: "Hold open the gates wide so that the army
can come into the city, chased in rout. For Achilles is here,
and he is driving them on. Now there will be ghastly destruction.   530
But when our troops have found respite, gathered tightly behind
the walls, then shut the closely fitted doors again. For I am afraid
that this ravaging destroying man will leap inside the wall!"
So he spoke, and they undid the gates and thrust back the bars.
Then the gates, thrown wide open, offered the light of deliverance.   535

   And Apollo leaped forth so that he could stave off ruin
from the Trojans as they fled straight for the city and the high wall,
burning with thirst and covered with dust from the plain.
Achilles stayed on them ferociously with his spear, for a wild
madness had seized his heart and he longed to capture glory.   540
Then the sons of the Achaeans would have taken high-gated
Troy, if Phoibos Apollo had not roused up the good
Agenor, son of Antenor, blameless and strong. He filled
his heart with courage and himself stood by his side
so that he could ward off the heavy hands of death.   545
Apollo leaned against the oak, hidden in a thick mist.

   When Agenor saw Achilles, the sacker of cities,
he stopped, and many were his dark thoughts as he held
his ground. Moved deeply, he spoke to his own great-hearted
spirit: "What should I do now? If I flee before mighty Achilles,   550
there where the others are driven in rout, he will take me
anyway, and he will butcher me in my cowardice. But if I let
these men be driven before Achilles the son of Peleus,
I can flee on my feet away from the wall to the Ileïon plain°
until I arrive at the valleys of Ida where I can hide in the   555
thickets. When the sun sets I can wash myself in the river,
ridding myself of the sweat, and then return to Ilion.

---

554 *Ileïon plain*: Referred to only here. Apparently the plain "of Ilos" is meant, the early king of Troy whose
     tomb is mentioned in Book 10.

But why does my spirit ponder these things? Let him not
see me as I turn away from the city toward the plain
560 and overtake me, coming after me on his swift feet.
Then there will be no way to avoid death and the fates,
for he is more powerful than all other men.
                                        "And if I go
to meet him in front of the city? Well, that man's flesh
too can be torn by the sharp bronze. There is but one life
565 in him! Men say that he is mortal ... It is Zeus, the son of Kronos,
who gives him glory!"

        So speaking, Agenor pulled himself
together and awaited Achilles, his brave heart now stirred up
to fight—to do battle. Even as a leopard goes forth
from a deep thicket in full view of a hunter and he is not afraid,
570 he does not flee when he hears the baying of the hounds.
And even if the hunter gets in first and stabs the leopard
or hits him with an arrow, even pierced through with the spear
he does not give up his attack before the leopard grapples
with the hunter or is killed—even so the good Agenor,
575 son of brave Antenor, was not going to flee before
he put Achilles to the test.

        He held his shield before him,
well balanced on every side, and he aimed with his spear, and he
cried aloud: "I suppose you hope in your heart, O excellent
Achilles, on this day to sack the city of the brave Trojans—fool!
580 Many are the pains that shall be borne on her account. There are
many brave men within her, ready to defend Ilion under the eyes
of our dear parents and wives and children. You will meet
your doom here, although you are a bold fighter and dreaded in war!"

        He spoke and cast his sharp spear from his heavy hand,
585 and he hit Achilles on the shin beneath the knee. He did not miss!
The shinguard of newly wrought tin clanged terribly and back
leaped the bronze from the man it had struck. But it did not
penetrate, for the gift of the god stayed it.

                                        Then the son
of Peleus rushed on godlike Agenor, but Apollo did not
590 allow him to win glory. He snatched Agenor away
and hid him in a thick mist. He sent him out of the war
to go his way in peace. Then by craft he kept the son

of Peleus away from the Trojan army. Taking on the exact
likeness of Agenor, Apollo who works from afar stood before
Achilles' feet, and Achilles rushed on him in pursuit.   595
While Achilles pursued Apollo over the wheat-bearing plain,
turning him toward the deep-eddying river of the Skamandros,
Apollo running just a little ahead, for Apollo beguiled Achilles
with this trick, making him think he could at any time overtake him.

Meanwhile the other Trojans, fleeing in rout, came in a glad   600
crowd toward the city, and the city was filled with the throng
of them. Nor did they dare any longer to await one another
outside the city and the wall, and to learn who had fled
and who had been killed in the fight. With haste they poured
into the city—whoever was saved by the swiftness of his feet.   605

BOOK 22. *The Killing of Hector*

So throughout the city, huddled like fawns, they cooled off
their sweat and they drank and quenched their thirst, leaning against
the beautiful battlements. But then the Achaeans came close
to the wall, propping their shields on their shoulders,° and
5 a dreadful fate bound Hector to remain where he was, there
in front of Ilion and the Scaean Gates.

                  And then Phoibos
Apollo spoke to Achilles the son of Peleus: "Why, O son
of Peleus, do you pursue me on your swift feet when you are
but a mortal and I a deathless god? Haven't you yet recognized
10 that I am a god? And still you rage incessantly. Are you indifferent
to all the trouble you went through, routing the Trojans,
and now they are safe inside the city while you are stuck out here!
You will never kill me—I am immortal!"

                  With a flash of deep
anger the fast runner Achilles said: "You have fooled me,
15 you most destructive of gods, you who shoot from afar!
You have turned me away from the wall. Otherwise, many Trojans
would have bitten the earth with their teeth before they got
into Troy. As it is you have robbed me of great glory,
while you have saved them easily. You had no fear that
20 I would take revenge for your actions in the future, for truly
I *would* take revenge upon you if it were in my power!"
So speaking, Achilles went off toward the city with grand ambition,
running like a race horse, a prize-winner who pulls a chariot,
who easily runs full-out over the plain—even so Achilles
25 swiftly moved his feet and his knees.

                  Then old man Priam
first saw him as he sped all-gleaming over the plain, like the star
that appears at harvest time, when its rays shine in the midst

---

4 *shoulders*: Apparently holding out their shields horizontally and propping one end on their shoulders, to
create a protection against missiles thrown from the walls.

of many stars in the murk of the night, the star called the dog
of Orion.° It is most brilliant, but a sign of evil, bringing
much fever to wretched mortals—just so, the bronze shone   30
around Achilles' chest as he ran. The old man groaned,
and he beat his head with his hands, raising them up high,
and moaning mightily he called out, begging, to his dear son,
who stood motionless before the gates, eager to do battle with
Achilles. The old man spoke pitiful words, stretching out his arms: 35
"Hector, do not wait for this man, my dear son, alone
without others, or you may quickly meet your doom,
killed by this son of Peleus! He is much more powerful—
a cruel man! I wish that the gods loved him just as I do!
Then the dogs and vultures would quickly devour him as he lay   40
unburied, and this terrible sorrow would leave my breast.
For he has taken away many of my noble sons,
killing them or selling them off to islands that lie far away.
And now I do not see two of my sons Lykaon and Polydoros—
whom Laothoê, princess among women bore me—gathered   45
into the city of the Trojans. But if they are still alive and in the
Achaean camp, then we will ransom them for bronze and gold.
We have it! For the famous old man Altes gave away much wealth
at the wedding of his daughter. If they are dead and in the house
of Hades, there will be agony in my heart and in that of their mother,   50
she who bore them. But there will be less suffering to others
if you do not also die, Hector, overcome by Achilles!
    "So come inside the wall, my son, so that you might save
the Trojan men and women, and so that you do not give
abundant glory to the son of Peleus, and you yourself lose your life.   55
Take pity on me, who yet can feel! O how wretched
I am, how ill-fated I am—I whom the father, the son
of Kronos, will destroy in a pitiful fate at the threshold
of old age, I who have seen many evils—the death of my sons,
my daughters hauled away, treasure-chambers looted,   60
little children thrown to the earth in the horrid war, my sons'
wives taken away at the hands of the deadly Achaeans.
And now, *now* the savage dogs will rip me to pieces at the doors
of my own house after someone has taken the life from my limbs
with a blow, or a cast from some sharp bronze. And my   65

---

29   *of Orion*: Sirius, the brightest of the fixed stars, called the dog-star. It appears at the same time as the rising
of the sun in July, and henceforth until mid-September it brings excessive heat in Greece and Asia Minor.
These are the "dog days," when the dog-star is in the ascendant. Throughout antiquity the rising of the dog-
star was considered to bring disease and pestilence.

own dogs, those that I raised in my halls at my own table—
after drinking my blood in the madness of their hearts, they will
then lie down in the forecourt!
                              "Certainly, all looks good when
a young man dies in war, slashed by the sharp bronze, and there he lies—
70 everything is lovely that shows, though he is dead. But when dogs
put to shame a gray head and a gray beard and the shameful parts°
of a dead old man—this is the most pitiful thing for wretched mortals."

    So spoke the old man and with his hands he plucked
the gray hairs from his head. Still, he did not persuade Hector.
75 Then his mother Hekabê, standing beside Priam, wailed and shed tears,
exposing her chest, and with one hand she held her breasts
and poured forth tears, speaking words that went like arrows:
"Hector, my child, honor these breasts! Take pity on me!
If ever I gave you suck to ease your pain—remember these,
80 my son, and ward off that savage man from within the wall.
Do not stand forth to face him, stubborn boy! If he kills you,
I shall never bewail you on your bier, my dear child, whom I bore
from my own body. Nor will your wife, with her rich dowry,
but far away, beside the ships, the swift dogs will devour you!"

85   Thus importuning, they spoke to their son, begging him.
But they could not persuade Hector. He awaited Achilles
as he came ever closer in his might. As a serpent in the mountains
waits in his hole for a man to come along after eating
noxious herbs,° and a terrible rage has gone into him,
90 and he glares ferociously as he coils about in his hole,
even so Hector in his voracious might did not retreat
but leaned his shining shield against the projecting wall.

    Grieving, Hector spoke to his great-hearted spirit:
"Oh no! If I go through the gate and behind the walls, Poulydamas
95 will be the first to criticize me. For he encouraged me to lead
the Trojans to the city during this deadly night, when godlike Achilles
rose up.° But I wouldn't listen. It would have been a lot better if I had!
And now, after I have destroyed many through my own stupidity,

---

71 *shameful parts*: In general Homeric decorum prevents all reference to the genitals, except here and in
    Book 2 when Odysseus threatens to expose Thersites' private parts. Also, decorum prevents any reference to
    excretion or urination.

89 *noxious herbs*: Evidently snakes were thought to acquire their poison through the food they ate.

97 *rose up*: Poulydamas urged retreat behind the city wall in Book 18, advice rejected by Hector.

I am ashamed before the Trojans and the Trojan women with
their fine robes. I fear that someone, some lower-class type, will say,   100
'Hector, trusting in his own strength, has destroyed the army!'
They will say that. It would be much better for me to meet
Achilles in the hand-to-hand, then return home after killing
him, or myself perish in glory for the land of my fathers.

   "Or what if I set my bossed shield aside and my powerful   105
helmet, and lean my spear against the wall and myself go up
to the relentless Achilles and promise that we will give up Helen
and with her all the treasure that Alexandros took to Troy
in the hollow ships for the sons of Atreus to take away—
the beginning of this dread conflict ... And in addition, what if   110
we were to divest ourselves of half of all the things that the city
contains? I will take from the Trojans an oath sworn by the elders
on behalf of the Trojan people that they will not conceal *anything*,
but will divide in half all the wealth that our lovely city holds within ...°
   "But why am I having this conversation with myself?   115
I must not go to him! He will not pity me nor have any regard.
He will kill me right there, all unarmed, as if I were a woman,
once I have taken off my armor. There is no way, as if from
an oak or a rock, I may exchange pleasantries with him,
such as when a young girl chats with a youth—a young girl!   120
a youth!° Better to fight this out, and the sooner the better.
Then we will know to which man Zeus the Olympian gives glory."

   So he pondered as he waited. But Achilles was already
upon him, like Enyalios, warrior of the waving helmet, brandishing
over his right shoulder his terrifying spear of Pelian ash.   125
Around him the bronze flashed like the flames of a blazing fire
or the rays of the sun as it rises.

                    A trembling came over Hector
when he saw Achilles, and he did not dare to stay there
any longer, but he left the gates behind him and ran in fear.
The son of Peleus rushed after him, trusting in his powerful feet.   130
As a falcon in the mountains, the fastest of all birds swoops down
on a trembling dove who flees before him, but he darts in right

---

114   *within*: This same proposal was made by the besieged city on the Shield of Achilles in Book 18.

121   *a youth*: Hector seems to fix on the pastoral scene of peaceful flirtation by repeating these words. In spite of
    speculation ancient and modern, no one has been able to explain what is meant by "from an oak or a rock,"
    a figure of speech that occurs only here in the *Iliad*. In any event, Hector realizes that he will be unable to
    chat in a friendly way with Achilles.

on top of her, crying shrilly, close, for his falcon spirit urges him on
to devour the dove—even so Achilles in his fury sped straight on.

135   Hector fled in terror beneath the wall of the Trojans,
swiftly plying his limbs. He ran beneath the place of watching,°
past the wind-tossed fig—always out from under the walls,
along the wagon track. He ran to the two fair-flowing
fountains where the two springs of the eddying Skamandros rise.
140 One flows with warm water, and around it much smoke rises
as if from a blazing fire. The other flows cold even in the summer,
like hail, or cold snow or ice formed from water.
There, close to the springs are broad-flowing washing-tanks—
beautiful stone tubs—where the lovely Trojan women
145 and their daughters used to wash their shining clothes in the old
days of peace, before the coming of the sons of the Achaeans.°

They ran past that place, one fleeing, the other close behind.
A man of worth fled in front, and behind him a man far greater
in strength swiftly pursued. It was not for a sacrificial beast
150 or for a bull's hide, which are prizes in a foot-race, that they competed,
but they ran for the very life of Hector, tamer of horses.
As when single-hoofed prize-winning horses turn swiftly around
the turning-posts, a great prize is at stake, a tripod or a woman
in games celebrated for a dead man—even so three times
155 they ran around city of Priam on their fast feet.°

And all the gods looked on. The father of men and gods
was first to speak: "Look now, I see with my own eye an esteemed
man pursued around the wall. My heart goes out to Hector,
who has burned the thigh-bones of many oxen on the crests of Ida
160 with its many ridges,° and at other times made sacrifice in the upper
parts of the city. And now godlike Achilles is chasing Hector
around the city of Priam on his quick feet. But come, contemplate
and decide, my fellow gods, whether we will save Hector
from death, or whether we will deliver him to destruction at the hands
165 of Achilles, the son of Peleus, although he is a fine man."

---

136   *place of watching*: Not clear where this would be, but the fig is near the city walls (Book 6).

146   *of the Achaeans*: No such springs have ever been found in the vicinity of Troy, but Homer wants to empha-
size the contrast between the days of peace and the time of war.

155   *fast feet*: In fact you cannot run around Troy, located on a headland that projects into the plain.

160   *many ridges*: In Book 8 Zeus has a precinct on Gargaros, a peak of Ida.

Flashing-eyed Athena then answered him: "O father
of the white lightning, gatherer of the dark clouds, what words
you have spoken! Again you want to pull back from evil death
a mortal man who has long ago been doomed by fate?
Well, go ahead and try it. But none of the other gods will agree."   170

Zeus the cloud-gatherer then said in reply: "Ease up,
Tritogeneia, my dear daughter, I am not so set on what
I have been saying! I want you to be pleased—do whatever
is your pleasure. Don't hold back!"

                                        So speaking, he urged on Athena,
who was clearly anxious. She went dashing from the peaks   175
of Olympos while swift Achilles was unrelenting in pursuit of Hector.
As when a dog has rousted the fawn of a deer from its lair and chases
it through valleys and woods, and although the fawn evades it
for a while, hiding in a thicket, still the hound tracks him
down, running ever on until he finds him—even so Hector   180
could not escape the son of Peleus, the fast runner.

As often as Hector rushed toward the Dardanian Gates°
to gain shelter beneath the well-built walls, in hopes
that the Trojans could defend him with missiles from above,
just so often Achilles would anticipate his movements and move   185
in front and turn him back, toward the plain, while he himself
sped on beside the city's walls. As in a dream where you
cannot snare someone fleeing from you—the one cannot evade
and the other cannot capture—even so Achilles could not
overtake Hector with his fleetness, nor could Hector get away.   190

How could Hector then have escaped from the fates
of death were it not that Apollo came close to him
for the last time, to rouse his strength and quicken his knees?
Godlike Achilles nodded with his head to his followers—
he did not want anyone shooting deadly arrows or javelins   195
at Hector so that someone else might gain the glory
with a cast and he lose out.

                                When Achilles and Hector
came for a fourth time to the springs, then the father lifted
the golden scales. He placed in the pans two fates of bitter death,

---

182 *Dardanian Gates*: It is not certain whether these are same as the Scaean Gates or different.

200 the one for Achilles, the other for Hector, tamer of horses.
Zeus took the scales by the balance and held it up.
Down plunged the fateful day for Hector. He went toward
the house of Hades, and Phoibos Apollo deserted him.

Flashing-eyed Athena then came up to the son of Peleus.
205 She stood near him and spoke words that went like arrows:
"Now I hope that the two of us, O glorious Achilles, beloved
of Zeus, will be able to carry off to the ships great glory
for the Achaeans, once we have killed war-crazed Hector
in the hand-to-hand. Now he can no longer escape us,
210 not even if Apollo, who works from a long way off,
should suffer a great deal, thrashing around before father Zeus
who carries the goatskin fetish! Take your stand now—
catch your breath, while I will go and persuade that man
over there to fight in the hand-to-hand."

So spoke Athena,
215 and Achilles obeyed, glad in his heart, and he stood leaning
on the ashen spear with barbs of bronze. Athena left him
and went up to the majestic Hector in the likeness of Deïphobos°
both in shape and familiar voice. Standing next to him
she spoke words that went like arrows: "My dear brother,
220 surely Achilles is doing you awful harm, pursuing you
with his swift feet around the city of Troy. But come,
let us take our stand, and staying here let us repel his attack."

And big Hector, whose helmet flashed, said to her:
"Deïphobos, of all the brothers whom Hekabê and Priam bore,
225 you were in the past always to me the most beloved!
And now I think that I will honor you still more in my heart,
because you have dared to come out from the wall on my account
when you saw me, while the others remained within."

Then the goddess flashing-eyed Athena said to him:
230 "My dear brother, truly my father and my revered mother,
and our comrades around me, begged me in turn—pleaded mightily—
that I stay. For they all tremble before Achilles. But my head
was troubled with bitter grief. Now let us charge straight at him

---

217 *Deïphobos:* Hector's brother, first mentioned in Book 12. He has a strong presence in Book 13, where he
is wounded by Meriones, Idomeneus' aide. According to postHomeric tradition, Deïphobos took up with
Helen after Paris' death (probably implied in *Odyssey* Book 4).

and fight, and let there be no sparing our use of the spears,
so that we might learn whether he will kill us and carry away   235
the bloody armor to the hollow ships, or whether you will kill
him with your spear."

              So speaking and with such cunning
Athena led him on. When they came near Achilles, as each
advanced against the other, Hector, whose helmet flashed,
spoke first, saying to Achilles: "I will flee from you   240
no more, O son of Peleus, as before I ran three times
around the great and shining city of Priam, when I did
not dare to await you as you came on. But now
my heart urges me to take my stand against you,
to see if I will kill you or you kill me. And let us take   245
the gods to witness—they will be the best witnesses
and guardians of our covenant! For I will do nothing unseemly
to you, if Zeus grant me to outlast you and I take your life.
After I have taken the famous armor of Achilles, I will give back
your dead body to the Achaeans. And you do the same ..."   250

   Then Achilles, the fast runner, glaring angrily from beneath
his brows, said: "Hector, you are mad! Don't talk to me of covenants!
As there are no trusted oaths between lions and men, nor do
wolves have a friendly heart toward lambs but always they
think evil toward one another—even so there is no way   255
that you and I can be friends. Nor will there be oaths
between us before one or the other shall fall and glut
Ares with blood, the warrior with a tough hide shield.
So think now of all your fancy valor. Now you must be
a spearman and a bold fighter. There is no more escape.   260
Pallas Athena will kill you by my spear. Now you
will pay full price for the sorrow of my companions
whom you killed, raging with your spear!"

                  Thus Achilles spoke,
and brandishing his long-shadowing spear he cast. But the bold
Hector saw it coming and ducked, crouching in anticipation.   265
So the bronze spear flew over him and stuck fixed in the earth.
But up leaped Pallas Athena and gave it back to Achilles,
unseen by Hector, shepherd of the people.

                Then Hector spoke
to the blameless son of Peleus: "You missed! Nor have you
learned from Zeus—O Achilles like to the gods!—of my fate,   270

though surely you thought so. But you have been glib of tongue
and a thug with words so that you frightened me out of my power.
You made me forget my valor. But you shall not spear me
in the back as I flee. Drive your spear straight through my breast
275 as I charge upon you, if any god grants it! Or avoid *my* spear of bronze—
may you take it entirely in your flesh ... This war would be lighter
for the Trojans, if you were dead, for you are our greatest evil!"

    Hector spoke, and brandishing his long-shadowing
spear he cast it, and it hit in the middle of the shield of the son
280 of Peleus—he did not miss. But the spear glanced far away
from the shield. Hector raged that his missile had flown in vain
from his hand, then he stood abashed, for he did not have another
ashen spear. He called aloud for Deïphobos of the white shield,
requesting another long spear. But Deïphobos was nowhere near.

285   Hector then knew in his heart, and he spoke: "I understand.
The gods have called me to my death. I thought that Deïphobos
the warrior was nearby, but he is behind the walls. Athena has
deceived me. Now wretched death is near, not far away. I cannot
avoid it. In the olden times Zeus was more friendly to me,
290 and the son of Zeus, Apollo who shoots from a long ways off.
He who in times before stood by me with a steady heart.
But now my doom has come upon me. Let me not die without
a struggle, without fame, but having done something great,
something for those in later times to remember."°

                           So speaking
295 Hector drew his sharp sword, large and powerful, which hung
at his side, and pulling himself together he swooped like a
high-flying eagle that goes over the plain and through
the dark clouds to seize a tender sheep or a cowering hare—
even so Hector swooped, brandishing his sharp sword.
300 Achilles rushed to meet him. He filled his heart with wild
strength, and he protected his chest by holding the sturdy
finely crafted shield before him. As he ran he tossed the crest
of his shining four-plated helmet. All around it waved
the beautiful plumes of gold that Hephaistos set thick as the crest.

---

294 *to remember*: Divine forces are behind it all: Athena, Zeus, Apollo, Fate. But the fame that will last forever
    depends on the warrior's personal effort.

As the evening star, the most beautiful star in the sky,   305
goes forth among all the other stars in the gloom of night,
just so the sharp spear that Achilles balanced in his right hand
gleamed as he looked at the fair flesh of majestic Hector,
looking to find the place that was most open to a thrust.
Now, bronze armor covered up all the rest of Hector's flesh,   310
the beautiful armor that he had plundered from the body
of Patroklos when he killed him. But there was an opening
where the collarbone joined the neck with the shoulders,
the gullet where the destruction of life comes most quickly.
Achilles drove in his spear right there as he rushed on Hector,   315
and the point of the spear went straight through the tender neck.
But the bronze-heavy ash did not cut the windpipe, so that
Hector was able to speak and make answer to his enemy.

Thus Hector fell in the dust. And then Achilles gloated
over him: "Hector, you probably thought that you could despoil   320
Patroklos and stay safe. You had no thought of me, who remained
a long way off—you fool! Far from Patroklos a far greater helper
was left behind at the ships—me! I, who have just killed you!
Dogs and birds will eat you now, in an unseemly manner. But the
Achaeans will bury Patroklos."   325

Hector, whose helmet flashed, spoke
as his strength drained away: "I beg you by your life and your knees°
and your parents—do not give me to be devoured by the dogs
beside the ships ... My father and mother will give you bronze
and a lot of gold as gifts if you give back my body to be taken home,
so that the Trojans and the wives of the Trojans can give me my due   330
of fire when I am dead."

Achilles, the fast runner, said to him,
looking with anger from beneath his brows: "Don't beg me,
you dog, by my knees or by my parents. As much as I wish
that my anger and my spirit would drive me on to cut up your flesh
and eat it raw for the things you have done, just as much   335
I know that no one will save the dogs from your skull—
not though your parents should come here and offer ten times
as much, or twenty times, and promise still more. Not if Dardanian
Priam should promise to weigh out your body in gold. Not even so
will your revered mother place you on a bier to bewail   340
her dear son. But dogs and birds will devour you completely!"

FIGURE 22.1 Achilles kills Hector. The figures are labeled. The illustration does not follow Homer's account very well. Both men are in "heroic nudity." A beardless Achilles attacks from the left, wearing shinguards, a helmet, and carrying a hoplite shield, sword, and spear. The bearded Hector is similarly armed (but without shinguards). He has already been wounded in the left thigh and in the chest and is about to go down. Blood flows from the wounds. Athena (half-visible) stands behind Achilles wearing the goatskin fetish as a cape. Athenian red-figure wine-mixing bowl by the Berlin Painter, c. 490–460 BC. Found at Cerveteri, Lazio, Italy.

Then, dying, Hector whose helmet flashed answered:
"I know you too well. I knew this would be—that I could not persuade
you. The heart in your breast is of iron. Only think of this —
that I will become the anger of the gods on that day when Paris   345
and Phoibos Apollo kill you at the Scaean Gates,° though you
are great ..."

        Thus Hector spoke. Then death covered him over, and his
breath-soul flew out of his limbs and went to the house of Hades,
bewailing her fate,° leaving behind manliness and youth.
Godlike Achilles addressed him, though he was dead: 350
"Die then! I will meet my own fate whenever Zeus and
the other deathless gods want to bring it about."

                So Achilles spoke
and he pulled his bronze spear from the corpse. He laid it aside
and stripped Patroklos' bloody armor from Hector's shoulders.
The other sons of the Achaeans ran up to admire the physique   355
and the wonderful handsomeness of Hector. And they all dipped
in their weapons, those who went near. And so one would say,
turning to his neighbor: "Yes, Hector seems more gentle to the
touch now than when he burned the ships with deadly fire!"

    Thus someone would speak and plunge his weapon in the corpse,   360
standing nearby. When the good Achilles, the fast runner,
had finished stripping the corpse, he stood up among the Achaeans
and spoke words that went like arrows: "My dear leaders
and rulers of the Argives—because the gods have given it to us
to overcome this man who has done more harm than all the other   365
Trojans combined, let us stand in our might in front of the city,
fully armed, to find out what are the Trojans' intentions—
whether they will leave their high city now that their man is dead,
or whether they are eager to remain even though Hector is gone.
    "But why does my heart have this conversation with itself?   370
Patroklos still lies dead at the ships, unwept and unburied.
I will never forget him, not so long as I am among the living
and my limbs still function. Even if in the house of Hades
men forget their dead, even there I will not forget my dear

---

346 *Scaean Gates*: Hector foretells the death of Achilles as Patroklos had foretold the death of Hector: Achilles
     will die by an arrow fired by Paris, guided by Apollo, according to the usual account.

349 *her fate*: "breath-soul" is feminine in Greek.

375 companion. Anyway, let the Achaean youth sing our song
of victory and return to the hollow ships. We will bring
Hector there. We have won great glory. We have killed
the gallant Hector, to whom the Trojans prayed throughout
their city as if he were a god."

So he spoke, contemplating how he
380 would treat Hector shamefully. He pierced the tendons of both feet
from behind, from the heel to the ankle, and made fast ox-hide
thongs, which he tied to the back of his chariot. He let Hector's head
drag on the ground. Then he mounted his chariot and loaded
the famous armor. He snapped the whip and drove away,
385 and his two horses gladly sped onward. The dust rose up
from Hector's head as he was dragged, and his dark hair
spread out on either side, and all in the dust lay the head that
before was so charming. But now Zeus had given him to the enemy
to be treated shamefully in the land of his fathers. And all of
390 his hair was befouled by the dust.

His mother tore at her own hair,
and she flung her shining headscarf far away—Hekabê wailed
aloud when she saw her son. His father Priam piteously bewailed
him too, and the people fell into a howling and shrieking throughout
the city. It was as if all of Ilion with its beetling brows burned utterly
395 with fire.

The people could scarcely hold back the old man,
torn by grief, who wanted to go outside the Dardanian gates.
He prayed to everyone, rolling around in the filth, and he called
each man by name: "Hold off my friends, though you are distressed,
and let me go alone outside the city, to the ships of the Achaeans.
400 I will beseech this wicked man, this doer of evil, if perhaps
he will take shame before his fellows and have pity for my old age.
He has a father like me too—Peleus, who begot him and raised him
to be a curse to the Trojans. He has made sorrow for me above all
other men, so many are my sons that he killed in their prime.
405   "But of all those I do not rue any so much, though I am rent
with sorrow, as for this one—Hector. Grief for him
will carry me into the house of Hades. How I wish that he had
died in my arms! Then we'd have had our fill of lamentation—
his mother who bore him to her sorrow, and I myself."

410   So Priam spoke, weeping, and the citizens cried too.
Among the Trojan women Hekabê led the loud lament:

"My child, how wretched I am! How will I live in my bitter
anguish with you dead? You who night and day were
my boast throughout the city—a help to all the Trojan men
and the Trojan women in the town. They greeted you as a god.   415
You were a great glory to them while you were alive.
Now death and fate has come upon you."

                       So she spoke, wailing.
But Hector's wife Andromachê had not yet heard, for no truthful
messenger had come to her to announce that her husband
remained outside the gates. She was weaving in a corner   420
of her high room, weaving a double cloth, purple in color.
Andromachê was weaving-in a design of multicolored flowers.
She called out through the house to her handmaids with lovely hair
to set a great tripod on a fire so there would be a hot bath for Hector
when he came home from the battle—poor woman! She did   425
not yet know that flashing-eyed Athena had killed him at the hands
of Achilles, far from any warm bath.

                    Then Andromachê heard
the shrieking and shouting from the wall. Her limbs spun around
and the weaving comb fell from her hand to the earth.
She spoke to her handmaids with the lovely hair: "Come here,   430
the two of you—follow me so that we can see what has happened.
I heard the voice of my husband's mother, and from my breast
my heart leaps into my mouth, and beneath me my knees are numb.
Some evil is close by for the children of Priam. Would such word
be far from my ear, but I fear terribly that stalwart Achilles   435
has cut off Hector alone from the city and pursues him
over the plain, that he has put an end to the reckless manhood
that possessed him. For Hector would never remain in the mass
of men, but always ran ahead, yielding to no one in his power."

   So speaking Andromachê rushed out of the hall like a mad woman,   440
with throbbing heart. Her handmaids went with her, and when
they came to the wall and the crowd of men, she stood gazing
over the wall, and she saw Hector dragged before the city.
The swift horses dragged him without pity toward the hollow ships
of the Achaeans.   445

          Dark night covered her eyes. Andromachê fell backward
and gasped out her breath-soul. She threw the shining bonds
far from her head —the frontlet and the cap, and the woven band

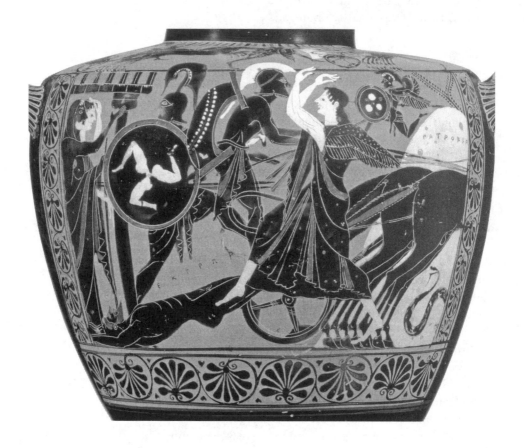

FIGURE 22.2   Achilles drags Hector.   Achilles (labeled) has already tied Hector to his car. As he steps up behind his charioteer, he looks behind at Priam and Andromachê lamenting from the wall. His shield bears a triskelis ("three-legged") design. Iris appears (she is white) to ask him not to treat Hector in this fashion (see Book 23). Behind the horses is the tomb of Patroklos. His breath-soul (*psychê*), shown as a miniature winged armed warrior, hovers above the tomb. Patroklos' name is inscribed on the tomb. Notice the serpent at the base: The beneficent spirits of the dead were thought to live as friendly snakes in tombs ("good spirit," *agathos daimon*). Athenian black-figure wine-mixing bowl, c. 510 BC.

and the headscarf° that golden Aphrodite had given her on that day
when Hector, whose helmet flashed, led her from the house of Eëtion
after Hector had given countless bridal gifts. Around about her 450
came Hector's sisters and the wives of Hector's brothers
and they bore her up, distraught unto death, in their midst.

When Andromachê caught her breath and her spirit was
gathered in her breast, she spoke to the Trojan women with
a deep moan: "Hector, I am wretched. We were born to a single fate, 455
the two of us—you in the house of Priam in Troy, I in THEBES
beneath Plakos covered in woods, in the house of Eëtion that
nourished me when I was little, an unlucky father to a
cruel-fated child. I wish I had never been born! But now you go
beneath the depths of earth to the house of Hades. You have 460
left me in dreadful sorrow, a widow in my halls. And our child
is still a mere babe, that you fathered and I bore—we who
are doomed to a wretched fate! You will be of no use to him,
Hector, now that you are dead. Nor he to you. If he escapes
the tearful war of the Achaeans, still there will be nothing 465
but labor and sorrow ahead for him. Others will take
his fields. The day of orphanhood cuts off a child completely
from those his own age. He bows down his head, his cheeks
are covered with tears. He goes in need to the companions
of his father, plucking one by the cloak, another by the shirt—, 470
and of them who are touched by pity one holds out his cup
for a moment. The child wets his lips, but he does not wet
the roof of his mouth.° And one whose father and mother
still live pushes him from the feast, striking him with his hands
and reproving him with insulting words: 'Get away from here! 475
You have no father to dine with us!' Then in tears the boy
comes back to his widowed mother ...
   "O Astyanax! Before
he ate only marrow and the rich fat of sheep, sitting on his
father's knees. And when sleep came on him and he left off
his childish play, he would sleep on his couch in the arms 480
of his nurse, in a soft bed, his heart filled with happy thoughts.
But now he will suffer much sorrow because he has lost his dear father—
Astyanax, whom the Trojans call by that name because you alone

---

448 *frontlet ... headscarf*: The first three items are named only here in Homer and it is not clear what they are,
but the fourth word means "headscarf" (*krêdemnon*). The "headscarf" was the symbol of Andromachê's
married state, now brought to nothing.

473 *of his mouth*: That is, he receives only crumbs, but never enough to satisfy his hunger.

save their gates and their high walls.° Now by the beaked ships,
485 far from your parents, wriggling maggots will eat you after
the dogs have had their fill, as you lie naked … All the while
that finely woven and lovely garments made by the hands of women
lie in your halls. But I will burn all these things in the blazing fire.
They are no longer of use to you. You shall not lie in them.
490 I'll do it as an honor to you from the men and women of Troy."
So she spoke through her tears, and all the women lamented too.

---

484 *their high walls*: The name Astyanax means "king of the city," that is, its defender.

BOOK 23. *The Funeral of Patroklos*

Thus the Trojans lamented throughout the city. And when
the Achaeans came to the ships and the Hellespont, some
of them scattered to their own ships, but Achilles would not
allow the Myrmidons to scatter. He spoke to his war-loving
companions: "My Myrmidons, with your swift chariots,   5
my faithful companions—let us not unharness our single-hoofed
horses from the cars, but with horses and chariots let us draw
near Patroklos and bewail him. For such rite is due the dead.
And when we've had our fill of unbridled lamentation,
then let us unhitch all our cars and eat a meal, all of us."   10

So he spoke, and all together they raised their sorrowful wail,
and Achilles was their leader. Three times they drove their horses
with fine manes around the dead body, keening. Among them
Thetis stirred the desire for weeping. The sands were moistened,
the armor of the men was wet with their tears. They grieved   15
for their mighty deviser of rout.

Among them the son
of Peleus began the sad lament, placing his man-destroying
hands on the chest of his companion. "Greetings, Patroklos,
even in the house of Hades. I am bringing to fulfillment
all that I promised earlier—that I would bring Hector here and   20
give him to the dogs to eat raw, and that I would cut the throats
of twelve glorious sons of the Trojans on your funeral pyre,
in my anger at your death."

He spoke and thought about how
he could treat the valiant Hector in a cruel way, stretching him
out on his face in front of the bier of the son of Menoitios.   25
As for the Myrmidons, all of them doffed their armor
of shining bronze and unhitched their horses. They sat down
beside the ship of Achilles the fast runner as he prepared
for them a fitting funeral feast. Many sleek bulls bellowed
around the iron knife as their throats were cut, and many sheep   30
and bleating goats. And many swine with white tusks,
dripping with fat, were stretched over the flame of Hephaistos

to singe away the hair. There was so much blood streaming
around the corpse that you could easily dip in a cup!

35   But first the chiefs of the Achaeans took their chief,
the swift-footed son of Peleus, to the good Agamemnon.
They had considerable trouble persuading him to go, so distraught
was Achilles on account of his companion. When they came up
to the tent of Agamemnon, they immediately sent out the clear-voiced
40   heralds to set a great tripod on the fire, in hopes that they
might persuade the son of Peleus to wash off the bloody gore.

But he absolutely refused, and swore a great oath: "No,
by Zeus, who is the highest and best of the gods—it is not right
that cleansing water be used on my head before I have placed
45   Patroklos on the pyre and built a mound for him, and cut
my hair. Never again will such a pain come to my heart
for as long as I will live.

                    "But for now let us yield to
the hated banquet. In the morning, King Agamemnon,
rouse your men to gather wood to prepare everything required
50   for a dead man when he is about to go into the murky gloom.
Let the untiring fire consume him quickly and remove him
from our sight. Then the people can return to their tasks."

So he spoke, and they heard him and obeyed. Eagerly each
man prepared his meal and they ate, nor did anyone lack a thing
55   in the equal feast. When they had put the desire for drink and food
from themselves, each man went to his tent to lie down.
But the son of Peleus lay on the shore of the much-resounding
sea in the midst of the many Myrmidons, groaning deeply
in an open space where the waves dashed against the shore.

60   When gentle sleep came upon him, pouring all around him
and loosing all cares from his spirit—for his glorious limbs were tired
from harrying Hector as far as windy Ilion—then there came
to him the breath-soul of wretched Patroklos, exactly like him
in size and beautiful eyes and voice, and he wore his usual clothing.°

65   He stood over Achilles' head and spoke thus to him:
"You sleep! Have you forgotten about me, Achilles? You were never

---

64 *clothing*: This is the only time in Homer that the vision of a ghost is described.

thoughtless of me in life, only in death. Bury me as soon as possible
so that I may pass inside the gates of Hades. The breath-souls
keep me far away, the phantoms of men whose labor is finished,
and they will not let me join them beyond the river, but vainly   70
I wander through the house of Hades with its wide gates.
    "And give me your hand, I beg you, for no more shall I come
back from the house of Hades when once you have given me
my fill of fire. No more, alive, will we talk things over,
sitting apart from our companions, for a hateful fate   75
has opened its maw for me, the fate that was my lot from birth.
And it is your fate too, O Achilles, who are like the gods,
to be killed beneath the wall of the wealthy Trojans. And I
will tell you something else, and I urge you to listen well:
Do not bury my bones separate from yours, O Achilles,   80
but let them be together, even as we were raised in your house.
Menoitios brought me, while still a little fellow, out of OPOEIS
to your country on account of a dreadful homicide,
on the day when I killed the son of Amphidamas.° I was foolish,
I did not want to kill him but I became angry over a game of dice.   85
The horseman Peleus then took me into his house and reared me
very kindly, and he made me your aide. Therefore, let a single
chest contain our bones, the one of gold with two handles that
your mother gave you."

        Achilles the fast runner answered him:
"Why, dear fellow, have you come here to give me orders   90
about these matters? You know that I will accomplish these things.
I will do as you ask. But come, stand near me ... let us throw
our arms about one another and for a little while take our fill
of sad lament."

        So speaking. Achilles reached out his hands,
but he could not clasp Patroklos. The breath-soul went beneath   95
the earth like smoke, gibbering faintly. Startled, Achilles stood up
and clapped his hands together, and he spoke a wailing word:
"Look, even in the house of Hades the breath-soul and the
phantom are something, although there is no mind there.
For all night long the breath-soul of miserable Patroklos   100

---

84   ... *Amphidamas*: Opoeis was the principal town of Locris, a territory south of Phthia. Hesiod sang at the fu-
     neral games of an Amphidamas, but there seems to be no connection with this Amphidamas. Exile because
     of homicide is common in the Homeric poems, occurring about seven times, but it is odd that Patroklos
     killed someone when he was just "a little fellow."

stood over me, wailing and weeping, and he gave me orders
about each thing, and was wondrously like himself." So Achilles
spoke, and in all his Myrmidon cohort he roused a feeling of sorrow.

Dawn with its fingers of rose appeared to them as they wept
105 around the wretched corpse. And then King Agamemnon
sent forth mules and men from all sides out of the huts
to gather wood. A noble man, Meriones, the aide of brave
Idomeneus, oversaw the proceedings. They took up wood-cutting
axes in their hands and well-woven ropes and went forth.

110 The mules went before them. They went upwards, downwards,
sideways, and at a slant, and when they came to the mountain
valley of Ida with its many springs, the men set out at once
to fell the tallest oaks with their long-edged bronze—
and the trees fell with a great roar. Then they split the trunks
115 in half and bound the logs to the mules. The mules
tore up the earth with their feet as they dragged the logs
to the plain through the thick underbrush. All the wood-cutters
carried logs, for thus did Meriones command them, the aide
of brave Idomeneus. They cast them down on the shore
120 one by one where Achilles planned to heap up a great mound
for Patroklos, and for himself. And when on all sides
they had put down the huge amount of wood, they sat down
and waited in a group.

Achilles at once ordered the war-loving
Myrmidons to arm themselves with their bronze and each
125 one to yoke the horses to his car. They got up and put on
their armor, and the fighting men and the charioteers
mounted their cars. The men in their chariots went in front,
and behind followed a cloud of foot soldiers, countless in number.
His comrades carried Patroklos in their midst. They clothed
130 his entire body with snippets they cut from their hair.°
Behind them Achilles held Patroklos' head in grief,
for he was sending his dear companion to the house of Hades.

When they came to the place that Achilles had designated,
they set down the corpse and quickly heaped up the huge supply
135 of wood. Then good Achilles, the fast runner, had another idea.

---

130 *from their hair*: They seem to be cutting off snippets of their hair as they walk along in the procession.

He stood apart from the fire and cut a lock of his golden hair,
which he grew as a rich growth, a dedication to the Spercheios° river.

Groaning, he spoke, looking over the wine-dark sea:
"Spercheios, it was in vain that my father Peleus promised you
that when I returned to the land of my fathers I would cut   140
this lock of hair for you and make a sacrifice, and on the same spot
sacrifice fifty uncastrated rams, there, at the springs
where your precinct and your fragrant altar are. So promised
the old man, but you did not fulfill that wish for Peleus.
Because I shall never return to the land of my fathers I want   145
to give this lock to the warrior Patroklos to carry with Peleus."
So speaking, he placed the lock in the hands of his dear
companion, and this roused in all the Myrmidons a great
desire to weep.

And then the light of the sun would have gone
down as they wept, if Achilles had not gone up to Agamemnon   150
and said: "O son of Atreus, it is correct that the people of Achaea
should have their fill of lamenting. But because they have special
regard for your words, please now disperse them from the pyre
and urge them to make their meal ready. We will take care of all that
is required to grieve for the dead. Only let the captains remain here."   155

When the king of men Agamemnon heard this, he at once
scattered the army through the well-balanced ships, but those
who were dearest to the dead man remained and heaped up
the wood. They made a pyre a hundred feet square. Hearts aching,
they placed the dead man on the top of the pyre. They skinned   160
and dressed-out many strong sheep in front of the pyre,
and sleek cattle with a shuffling walk. Great-hearted Achilles
collected the fat from all of them and covered the dead body
with the fat from head to foot. Then he flung the skinned
bodies on top. He placed two-handled carrying jars filled   165
with honey and oil against the bier. Swiftly he threw
four horses with long necks upon the pyre, groaning deeply.
Achilles the chieftain had nine dogs that fed beneath
his table. He cut the throats of two of these and cast
them on the pyre. He then killed twelve noble sons   170
of the great-hearted Trojans, slashing them with bronze,

---

137 *Spercheios*: The main river in Phthia, Achilles' homeland. In Book 16 the Spercheios is said to be the father
     of Menestheus by a daughter of Peleus named Polydorê. Menestheus was one of the five Myrmidon captains
     Patroklos led in his assault on Troy.

FIGURE 23.1   Achilles kills the Trojan captives.   On this large vase, of which this illustration is a detail, various events from the funeral of Patroklos are illustrated. Here Achilles prepares to cut the throat of a beardless Trojan youth. Achilles stands in "heroic nudity," but wears a cloak, in front of the pyre. A label across the bottom reads "tomb of Patroklos." Achilles grips the Trojan victim by the hair, the man's hands tied behind his back. Behind Achilles, to the far left, is the next Trojan in line, wearing a Phrygian cap. On top of the pyre and in front of it is stacked Patroklos' armor that Achilles has taken from Hector, once his own armor: two breastplates (for some reason), a helmet, a shield, and two shinguards. To the right, a fully clothed Agamemnon, holding a scepter, pours out a libation from a *phialê*, a kind of offering dish. A jug of wine or honey stands beside the pyre at Agamemnon's feet as in Homer's description. South Italian red-figure wine-mixing bowl, c. 340–320 BC, from Canosa.

for he was determined to do despicable things. He tossed
the iron might of fire on the pyre, giving it free range.

He groaned then, and called his companion by name:
"Greetings, O Patroklos, even in the house of Hades. For I am   175
bringing to completion all the things that I promised earlier.
Twelve sons of the great-hearted Trojans—the fire will devour them
along with you! But I will not give up Hector the son of Priam
to be devoured by fire, rather by dogs!"

So he spoke, threatening,
but the dogs did not molest the corpse of Hector. Aphrodite,   180
the daughter of Zeus, kept the dogs from Hector day
and night, and she anointed his body with a rose-scented
oil, ambrosial, so that when Achilles dragged him by his chariot
Hector's skin would not be torn. And Phoibos Apollo
cast a dark cloud around the corpse, drawing it from the heaven   185
to the plain. And he covered the place where Hector's body lay
so that the power of the sun might not too soon shrivel the flesh
around Hector's ligaments and limbs.

But the pyre of the dead
Patroklos would not burn. Then Achilles swift of foot
had another thought. He stood apart from the pyre and prayed   190
to the two winds, North Wind and West Wind, and he
promised beautiful sacrificial offerings. He prayed heartily,
pouring out liquor from a golden cup, that they come
so that the corpses might burn as fast as possible and the
wood might quickly be kindled. Iris swiftly heard his prayers   195
and went off as a messenger to the winds.

The winds were feasting
at banquet all together in the house of the tempestuous West Wind.
Iris stopped running and stood on the stone threshold. As soon
as their eyes saw her, the winds leaped up, and each called
her to himself. But she would not sit down and she said: 200
"I cannot sit. I must go back to the streams of Ocean, to the land
of the Ethiopians, where they are making great sacrifices
to the deathless ones, so that I too may partake of the sacred feast.
But Achilles prays that North Wind and noisy West Wind
come, and he promises beautiful sacrificial offerings   205
so that you might rouse the fire to burn where Patroklos lies,
whom all the Achaeans bemoan."

So speaking, Iris went off,
and the two winds arose with a wondrous ruckus, driving
the clouds in rout before them. Quickly they came to the sea,
210 and they blew upon it, and a wave swelled-up beneath
their strident blast. The two winds came to Troy with its rich soil,
and they fell on the pyre, and the fire cried out a loud
and wondrous cry. All night long the winds beat together
on the flames of the fire, blowing shrilly. And all night
215 long swift Achilles, taking a two-handled cup, poured wine
from a golden bowl to the ground, and the ground grew wet
as he mourned for the breath-soul of wretched Patroklos.
As a father weeps over the bones of his newly wed son
as he burns them, the son who in death brought sore pain
220 to his parents, even so Achilles wept, scrambling around the pyre,
groaning deeply.

At the hour when the morning star goes forth
announcing new light over the earth, and after it Dawn comes
in her robe of saffron and spreads over the sea, the flames
of the pyre grew faint, and then ceased. The winds went
225 back again, returning to their home over the Thracian sea,
which surged and roared with swollen flood.

Then the son
of Peleus withdrew from the pyre to one side and he lay down,
exhausted, and sweet sleep came over him. But those who
were with the son of Atreus gathered in a crowd and their noise
230 and uproar as they came by woke him up.
Achilles sat up straight and spoke to them, saying:
"Son of Atreus and you other captains of the Achaeans,
first extinguish all the fire with flaming wine, wherever
the fire is still strong. Then let us gather together the bones
235 of Patroklos, son of Menoitios. It will be easy to tell them from others
because they lie in the middle of the pyre, whereas the other corpses
were burned at the edge, where you'll find mixed bones of horse
and man. Then let us place the bones in a golden dish
wrapped in double layers of fat until the time when I myself
240 will be bidden to the house of Hades. I do not ask you to labor
to build a large tumulus, only one that is appropriate.
You Achaeans can build it high and wide later, you who
will remain behind, after me, in the ships with many benches."

So he spoke, and they obeyed the swift-footed son of Peleus.
245 First they extinguished the fire with flaming wine, as far as

the flame had reached, and the ash had settled deep. Weeping
for their gentle comrade, they gathered up the white bones
into a golden dish and wrapped them in a double layer of fat.
Then they placed them in the hut, covering the bones with
a linen cloth. Then they drew the circle of the mound and set up   250
a base of stones around the circumference of the pyre. They piled
on a mound of earth. After piling up the grave, they went away.

But Achilles called his people together and had them sit down
where they were, in a broad assembly, and he brought prizes out
of his ships—cauldrons and tripods and horses and mules   255
and many head of cattle, and women with slender waists,
and gray iron. For the horse race he set up as a glorious prize
a woman, blameless, good at craft, as well as an eared tripod
of twenty-two measures, as first prize.° As second prize
he put up a mare six years old, not yet knowing the bit,   260
and pregnant with a mule. For third prize he set up a brand-new
cauldron, beautiful, that held four measures, still white°
like the first pot. For the fourth prize he set up two talents
of gold,° and for the fifth prize he set up a two-handled dish,
untouched by fire.°   265

He stood up tall and spoke a word
to the Argives: "Son of Atreus, and you other Achaeans
with fancy shinguards, these prizes are set out in the assembly,
waiting for the horse race. If we Achaeans were holding games
for any other person, then truly I would myself take first prize
and carry it off to my hut. You know how my own horses   270
surpass all others in excellence—they are deathless. Poseidon
gave them to my father Peleus, and Peleus gave them to me.
But I and my single-hoofed horses will stay out of it.

---

259   *as first prize*: The measure is unknown, but this is a large vessel. The rest of this book is taken up with the
        games at the funeral of Patroklos. Achilles never gives an explanation of why these games honor his friend,
        and the origin of funeral games is not clear. Some think that all athletic contests come from such games,
        which in origin had a very different purpose from just sport, perhaps a form of human sacrifice, here repre-
        sented in the fifth event, the fight in armor.

262   *white*: Because the metal vessel has never been placed on the fire.

264   *of gold*: In the Classical Period a talent ("scales," "balance") was a very large sum of money, but it seems to
        be less in Homer, perhaps the value of an ox. As a unit of value it is applied only to gold, but we are not sure
        that there was any standardization in Homer's day, the eighth century BC.

265   *untouched by fire*: The two-handled dish is a *phialê* (see Figure 23.1), used in classical times for pouring drink-
        offerings to the gods but here used to hold Patroklos' bones until they can be mixed with Achilles' and placed in a
        proper box.

Such a valiant charioteer they have lost, and gentle too,
275 who often would pour oil on their manes after he had washed them
in bright water. They stand and mourn for him. Their manes
rest on the ground as the two horses stand there in grief.
But you others get ready throughout the army, whoever
of the Achaeans trusts his horses and his jointed chariot."

280   So spoke the son of Peleus. Then his fast drivers assembled.
Up sprang first of all Eumelos, a king of men, the dear son
of Admetos, a good horseman.° Next up came the powerful
Diomedes, the son of Tydeus, and he led beneath the yoke
the horses of Tros that he had taken from Aeneas, although Aeneas
285 himself Apollo snatched away. Next rose yellow-haired Menelaos,
the son of Atreus, Zeus-begotten, and he led his swift horses
beneath the yoke—Aithê, a mare of Agamemnon, and his own
horse Podargos. Anchises' son Echepolos had given the mare
to Agamemnon as a gift so that he would not have to follow him
290 to windy Ilion but could stay home and take his pleasure there.
For Zeus had given him great wealth, and he dwelled in roomy
SICYON. Menelaos led her beneath the yoke, and she took
great pleasure in the race.°

                    Fourth, Antilochos prepared his horses
with lovely manes—the brilliant son of Nestor, the king high
295 of heart, the son of Neleus.° Pylos-bred were the horses that
drew the car of Antilochos. His father Nestor came near him
and spoke words to him for his advantage, a wise man speaking
to one who already knew: "Antilochos, Zeus and Poseidon
love you, though you are young. And they taught you all
300 kinds of horsemanship. So there is not much to teach. You know
how to wheel round the turning-posts, but your horses are the
slowest in the race, so I think you are going to have a lot of trouble

---

282 *good horseman*: Eumelos was a son of Admetos and Alkestis. According to Book 2, Eumelos led eleven ships
      to Troy from Thessaly, and had the fastest horses at Troy, reared by Apollo himself.

293 *in the race*: Diomedes' capture of the horses of Tros is described in Book 5, and they are mentioned again in
      Book 8. Menelaos' horses are "fiery" (Aithê) and "fleetfoot" (Podargos). Anchises, the father of Echepolos,
      is not the same as the Trojan Anchises, father of Aeneas.

295 *son of Neleus*: Antilochos, the son of Nestor, is a descendant of Poseidon, god of horses. He appeared in ear-
      lier episodes with Menelaos (Books 5, 15, 17), his rival here in the chariot race. In later tradition Memnon,
      a warrior from the East, a son of Dawn, killed Antilochos after the action described in the *Iliad*. Achilles
      then killed Memnon.

with that. The horses of the other racers are faster, but they do
not know how to come up with more clever plans than you!

"So come, my dear son, lay up in your heart all kinds   305
of cunning so that the prizes do not escape you. A wood-cutter
is greater because of his cunning than because of his strength.
A helmsman too, as he guides his ship straight over the wine-dark
sea, buffeted by winds. So by cunning a charioteer comes
out ahead of the others. He who just trusts to his horse   310
and his car—well, the car goes all over the place and the
horses might wander up the track if he doesn't keep control
of them. But he who cunningly drives lesser horses—
he always keeps an eye on the turning-post. He cuts it close,
and he knows to keep a tight grip on his horses by using the   315
ox-hide reins. He keeps them under control as he watches
the man in the lead.

           "Now here's a clear sign, and bear this in mind.
There stands a dried stump about three feet above the ground,
either it's oak or pine, but the rain doesn't bother it. Two white stones
are fixed in the ground on either side of this stump at the point   320
where the two laps of the course meet, and there is smooth running
for the horses on either side.° Either it's the monument for someone
who died long ago, or maybe it's the turning-point made for
a race in the days of the men of old. Anyway, the good Achilles,
the fast runner, has set it up as the turning-post.   325

                           "Press hard upon it!
Drive your horses and your car very near it. Then lean
to the left of the horses in your well-plaited chariot,° and give
the whip to the horse on the right and call him out by name,
and let your hands give him rein. Let the left-hand horse come
near to the turning-post so that the hub of the well-made wheel   330
almost scratches its surface. But be careful to avoid the stones
so that you do not harm your horses and smash your car!
That would bring joy to the others, but disgrace to you.

"So, my son, you must be smart and on your guard.
If at the turning-post you pass the others as you go, there is no one   335
who can catch you, nor pass you even with a burst of speed,

---

322 *on either side*: Presumably the point is that the "smooth running" makes it easier to risk going close to the
post when making the turn, but Homer's description is unclear. The "two laps" are evidently the outward-
bound course and the inward-bound course.

327. *well-plaited chariot*: The breastwork and floor of chariots were made of woven ox hide.

not even if he drove Arion in pursuit, the swift horse of Adrastos
who was of a divine stock, or the horses of Laomedon, who
were raised here as a fine breed."°

So spoke Nestor, the son of Neleus,
340 then sat back down in his place, now that he had touched on
strategies to consider. Meriones stood up as the fifth
competitor.° He prepared his horses with fine manes.

The contestants mounted their chariots. They cast in their lots.
Achilles shook the helmet and out leaped the lot of Antilochos,
345 the son of Nestor. After him came the lot of noble Eumelos.
Then came Menelaos, famous with the spear, the son
of Atreus. Then came the lot of Meriones. Last was the lot
of the son of Tydeus, Diomedes, the best of them all.°

They took their places in a row. Achilles showed
350 them the far turning-post out on the smooth plain.
As umpire he set up godlike Phoinix, his father's follower,
so that he could monitor the race and report the truth about it.
All as one the drivers raised their whips above their horses.
They struck them with the thongs and called out urgent words.
355 The horses sped swiftly over the plain, far from the ships,
and beneath their breasts the dust arose and hovered like a
cloud, or a whirlwind, and their manes streamed on the blast
of the wind.

Now the chariots coursed over the bountiful earth,
now they bounded up in the air. The drivers stood up straight
360 in their cars, and the heart of each was throbbing as they strove
for victory. Each man called to his horses as they flew, covered
in dust, over the plain. And when the swift horses were
completing the last stretch of the race, back to the gray sea,

---

339 *fine breed*: Arion is first mentioned here, the swift horse of Adrastos, king of Argos in the story of the Seven
Against Thebes, a war to which Homer has often referred. Later tradition reported that Poseidon was Ari-
on's father, usually taking on the form of a stallion to cover Demeter, who had taken on the form of a mare.
The horses of Laomedon were those given by Zeus to Laomedon in compensation for having abducted the
beautiful Ganymede to be cupbearer to the gods (Book 5).

342 *competitor*: Meriones is the Cretan archer, companion to Idomeneus, as Patroklos was to Achilles. He is
first mentioned in the Catalog of Ships. He gives Odysseus a bow, quiver, sword, and the boars' tusk helmet
in the Doloneia (Book 10). He has a big scene with Idomeneus in Book 13.

348 *them all*: The lots determine the chariots' position, from inside to outside.

then the worth of each became clear. After making the turn
the horses ran full out. Then quickly the fast mares of Eumelos,   365
the son of Admetos, the grandson of Pheres, shot out in front.
Right after came the stallions of Diomedes from the breed of Tros,
and they were not far behind, but very close, as if about
to mount right up on Eumelos' car. From their breath Eumelos'
back and his broad shoulders grew hot, for they leaned   370
their heads right over him as they flew along.

And now
the horses of Diomedes would have overtaken Eumelos,
or left the issue in doubt, had not Phoibos Apollo grown angry
with the son of Tydeus and knocked from his hands the shining whip.
Then tears of anger ran from Diomedes' eyes, because he saw   375
Eumelos' mares running still faster while his own horses held back
because they no longer felt the lash. But Athena was aware
of Apollo's efforts to harm the son of Tydeus, and swiftly
she sped after the shepherd of the people, and she gave back
the whip to Diomedes and breathed power into his horses.   380
Then in anger she went after Eumelos, the son of Admetos,
and she broke the yoke of his horses. The mares ran off
the track as the yoke-pole crashed to the earth. Eumelos
was thrown from the car beside a wheel and the skin
was stripped from his elbows, his mouth, and his nose.   385
His forehead above his eyebrows was black-and-blue.
Both eyes were filled with tears, and the flow of Eumelos'
voice was stopped.

Diomedes, the son of Tydeus veered his
single-hoofed horses to the side and went on, darting out
in front of all the rest, for Athena filled his horses with strength   390
and shed glory upon him. Behind came light-haired Menelaos,
the son of Atreus.

Antilochos called to the horses of his father:
"Let's go, the two of you! Give it everything you've got!
I don't say go after the horses of the son of the fighter
Tydeus—Athena has given them speed and shed glory   395
on Diomedes!—but go speedily after the horses of the son
of Atreus. Don't be left behind! It will be shameful for you
to be beaten by Aithê, a mare! You are the best, why be
outstripped? I say this, and it will surely come to pass: Nestor,
the shepherd of the people, will no longer take care of you!   400
In fact he will put an end to you at once with the sharp bronze

if we take a worse prize because you won't make an effort!
So get back in the race, go as fast as you can, for I have
a plan—to slip past Menelaos where the track is narrowest—
405 and I won't miss it!"

So Antilochos spoke, and his horses were moved by
their master's plan and ran on stronger for a short while.
But right away Antilochos, stalwart in the fight, saw a narrow
spot in the hollow road. There was a gully in the earth
where water, swollen by the winter run-off, had broken away
410 the road and hollowed out the whole place. Menelaos
made for where two chariots could not run next to each other,
but Antilochos turned his single-hoofed horses aside and drove on
outside the track, and pursued him, a little to the side.

The son of Atreus was afraid, and he shouted to Antilochos:
415 "Antilochos, you're driving like a nut case! Rein in your horses!
This is the narrowest part of the track. Soon it will be wide
enough to pass. You're going to wreck us both if you hit my car!"

So he spoke, but Antilochos drove still harder, laying on
the lash as if he had heard nothing. As far as the range
420 of a discus that a young man throws hard from the shoulder,
testing his youth—even so far the two ran side by side.
Then the mares of the son of Atreus fell back. Menelaos
himself, of his own will, held back from urging them on,
fearing that the single-hoofed horses would crash together
425 on the track and the well-plaited cars turn over, hurling
them into the dust in his lust for victory.°

Upbraiding Antilochos,
light-haired Menelaos said: "Antilochos, you are the most hurtful
man around! You know where you can go! We Achaeans
wrongly thought you were smart, but you will get no prize
430 without an oath!"°

So Menelaos spoke, and he called out
to his horses and spoke to them: "Don't hold back now!

---

426 *for victory*: How Antilochos overtakes Menelaos is not obvious. It appears as if Antilochos is about to draw
level with Menelaos at the point where the road narrows. Here Menelaos drives along what is left of the
road while Antilochos veers off the road to ride on the far side of the gully. At some point he needs to rejoin
the track, but when he does so the track is still too narrow for two chariots. Menelaos gives way to avoid a
collision, a tactic that Menelaos views as being unfair and against the rules.

430 *an oath*: He will have to swear that he has not won the victory in an underhanded fashion.

Don't dog it! Pick up the pace now! Their hooves and legs will tire
sooner than yours—they are not young!"

                    So he called,
and his horses were roused to hear the clamor of their master
and ran faster still. Quickly they came close to the car   435
of Antilochos.

           The Argives were sitting in the gathering place
and looking for the horses as they flew over the plain,
covered with dust. Idomeneus, the captain of the Cretans,
was first to see the horses, for he sat outside the assembly
area, in a place of outlook, the highest of all.° He heard the   440
shouting of a man urging on his horses, though he was
far off. He recognized him as he got a clearer view and could
see the front of a horse—the one that was all bay except
for a white mark on its forehead, round like the moon.

    Idomeneus stood up and spoke to the Argives: "My friends,   445
leaders and rulers of the Argives! Do I alone see the horses
or do you too? It looks to me like there is a different car
in the front now, and I see a different charioteer in the lead.
It looks like Eumelos' mares took some damage out there
on the plain, because they were first on the outbound leg.   450
I'm sure I saw Eumelos sweeping past the first turning post,
but now I can't see him anywhere, and my eyes have scanned
everywhere over the Trojan plain.° I wonder if Eumelos
dropped the reins, or didn't make it round the turning-post?
Could he have failed to make the turn? He must have fallen out of   455
his car and smashed it up, and then his horses turned aside
when terror overcame them. But stand up—look! I can't see
very well, but the leader seems to be an Aetolian, ruler of the
Argives, the son of horse-taming Tydeus—mighty Diomedes!"°

    Swift Ajax, the son of Oïleus, then said to Idomeneus,   460
trying to put him to shame: "Idomeneus, why have you always

---

440   *of outlook*: No doubt Idomeneus was eager to know how his companion and aide Meriones was doing.

453   *Trojan plain*: Apparently Idomeneus could see the horses clearly until they got to the post but not what
happened after the turn.

459   *mighty Diomedes*: Diomedes' father Tydeus was from Aetolia in southwest mainland Greece, but Diomedes
ruled in Argos in the northeast Peloponnesus.

had such a big mouth?° Why, those high-stepping mares are far away,
racing over the open plain! You are not such a youngster among
the Argives. Your eyesight is no longer so keen, yet you
465 are always going on. You shouldn't be such a loud mouth.
There are others here who are better than you. I tell you,
the mares are in the lead like they were before—Eumelos
is there just like before, holding the reins!"

Then the captain
of the Cretans took offense and answered Little Ajax:
470 "O Ajax, best in quarreling—a stupid counselor! Why,
you are worse than all Argives, in everything. Mind in a bog!
Come, then, let us wager a tripod or a cauldron. Let's put up
Agamemnon, the son of Atreus, as judge of which
horses come in first. You'll learn and you'll pay!"

475   So Idomeneus spoke, but swift Oïlean Ajax rose up
in anger and spoke furious words, and the quarrel between
the two of them would have gone further if Achilles himself
had not stood up and smoothed things out: "That's enough
angry words between you, Ajax and Idomeneus! There is
480 no need, though it is understandable that you should be angry
at each another for acting in this fashion. But sit down now in the
place of assembly and watch these chariots race. They'll soon
be here at the finish, one driving on to victory. Then we'll all
know who is second and who is first."

So he spoke,
485 and just then Diomedes came in— nearer now as he
drove his horses on with the lash, bringing it down
from the shoulder. His horses leaped high in the air as swiftly
they completed the course. Grains of dust constantly struck
the charioteer and his chariot inlaid with gold and tin
490 as the swift-footed horses ran on. And there was little sign
of wheel tracks behind the first car in the light dust.

The two horses sped on until Diomedes came to a halt
in the middle of the place of assembly. Great quantities of sweat
gushed to the ground from the necks and the chests of the horses.
495 Then Diomedes jumped from his gleaming car to the ground.

---

462   *big mouth*: The rude speech of Oïlean Ajax to the older Idomeneus is in keeping with his coarse character.

FIGURE 23.2 **The funeral games of Patroklos.** Greeks perch on bleachers to watch the chariot race. Some of the spectators are standing, some sitting, some gesticulating as the four-horse chariot approaches. The nearest horse is white, the next two bays with black faces, and the fourth is black. Inscriptions in front of the horses say "Sophilos painted me" and "The funeral games of Patroklos." On the other side of the bleachers is written Achilles. Fragment of an Athenian black-figure wine-mixing bowl, c. 570 BC.

He leaned the lash against the yoke. The powerful Sthenelos°
did not hesitate, but he hurried to take the prize, and Sthenelos
gave the girl and the eared tripod to his comrades to take away.
Then Sthenelos himself unharnessed the horses.

500   Next Antilochos, of the stock of Neleus, drove in
his horses, for by a trick, not by speed, had he come in
before Menelaos. Then Menelaos drove in his swift horses
very close, just behind. As far as a horse stands from the wheel
on a car that, straining, the horse draws over the plain—
505 the outermost hairs of the horse's tail touch the tire
because the tire is running just behind it and there is not much
space between the horse and the tire as he runs across
the wide plain—by so little space was Menelaos behind
the blameless Antilochos. At first he was as far behind
510 as you can throw a discus, but Menelaos was quickly overtaking
Antilochos. The great strength of Aithê, the beautiful-maned mare
of Agamemnon, became ever greater. Had the track been longer
for both, surely Menelaos would have passed Antilochos
and left no doubt about it.

                      Meriones, the brave aide to Idomeneus,
515 came in a spear's throw behind Menelaos. His beautiful-maned
horses were the slowest, and he the least skilled to drive
a chariot in a race. Last of all came Eumelos, the son
of Admetos, dragging his beautiful chariot° and driving
his horses before him.

                      When the good Achilles, the fast runner,
520 saw Eumelos, he took pity. Standing up among the Argives, he spoke
words that went like arrows: "In last place comes the best man,
driving his single-hoofed horses. Come, let's give him a prize
that is suitable, a prize for the second place. But Diomedes, the son of
Tydeus, gets the first prize."

                      So Achilles spoke, and everybody shouted
525 assent to his proposal. And now Achilles would have given the mare
to Eumelos, as the Achaeans agreed, except that Antilochos the son
of great-hearted Nestor stood up and replied to Achilles with an appeal
to justice: "O Achilles, I will be very angry with you if you do what

---

496   *Sthenelos*: Diomedes' close companion.

518   *dragging his beautiful chariot*: Because it had earlier crashed.

you say! You are about to take away the prize thinking that his chariot
and his swift horses came to harm, and the man himself, though he was
a good man. He should have prayed to the immortals! Then he would
not have come in last in the race. If you pity him and he is dear
to your heart, well, there is plenty of gold in your tent, and bronze,
and flocks. You have slave girls and single-hoofed horses. Take
something from this store, something even better, and give it to him
later. Or give it now, so that the Achaeans will praise you. But I
will not give up the mare! Let any man who wants to do battle with me
in the hand-to-hand step up!"

So Antilochos spoke, and good Achilles,
the fast runner, smiled,° taking joy in Antilochos, because he was
his dear companion. And answering him he spoke words that went
like arrows: "Antilochos, if you are asking me to give Eumelos some
other prize from my store, this I will do too. I will give him the breastplate
that I took from Asteropaios.° It is bronze with a circle of shining tin
inlaid within. It's worth a lot."

So he spoke, and he ordered his dear
companion Automedon to bring the shield from the tent. Automedon
went and got it and placed the shield in Eumelos' hands, and Eumelos
was glad to receive it.

Then Menelaos stood up, grieving in his heart,
extremely angry with Antilochos. The herald placed the scepter
in his hand and ordered that the Argives be silent. He spoke
to them, a man like a god: "Antilochos, in earlier times you were
a decent fellow, but look what you have done now! You have made
a mockery of my skill. You have harmed my horses, thrusting your own,
which were inferior, out in front. But come, you leaders and rulers
of the Argives, let us decide this impartially between the two of us,
with no favor to either side, so that someone of the Achaeans
who wear shirts of bronze might not at a later time say, 'O Menelaos
beat Antilochos with his lies, and then went off with the mare, even
though Menelaos' horses were much worse, but he himself was stronger
in valor and in strength.' I will myself give the judgment, and I don't

530

535

540

545

550

555

---

539 *smiled*: Perhaps Achilles smiled because Antilochos repeats the same threats that Achilles himself made
when Agamemnon took away *his* prize. This is the only time in the poem that Achilles smiles, in keeping
with the general air of Achilles' good cheer during the funeral games, especially in his generosity in giving
gifts to all participants.

543 *Asteropaios*: In Book 21 Achilles killed the ambidextrous Asteropaios, grandson of the river Axios in
MACEDONIA, and took his armor.

560 think there will be any complaint from the Danaäns. For it will be a
straight judgment. Antilochos, nurtured of Zeus, come here, as is right,
and stand in front of your horses and your car, and hold your slender
whip in your hand by which you were earlier driving your horses,
and taking hold of your horses swear by the earth-holder, the shaker
565 of the earth,° that you did not willfully entangle my car by trickery.”

    Then the sensible Antilochos said to him: “Hold on now,
Menelaos! I’m a lot younger than you, King Menelaos. You are older
and a better man. I think you know how young men sometimes go out
of bounds—their minds are hasty and their understanding slight.
570 So let your heart be patient. I will myself give you the mare that
I have won. If you want something else from my store, something
of more value—why, you may have it. I would rather give you
something right now, Zeus-nurtured one, than be forever cast out
of your heart, and be guilty in the eyes of the gods.”°

                                            He spoke and Antilochos,
575 the son of great-hearted Nestor, brought up the mare and placed
it in the hands of Menelaos. His heart was warmed as the dew
around the wheat of the ripening crop when the fields are bristling—
in this way, O Menelaos, was the heart in your breast warmed.

    And Menelaos spoke words that went like arrows:
580 “Antilochos, I hereby give up all my anger, for in the past you
were no flighty fellow, nor witless, but just now your youth
has got the better of you. Next time don’t try to outtalk your betters!
No other of the Achaeans would have persuaded me so quickly,
but you have suffered a lot and gone through a lot of pain
585 on my account, you and your good father and your brother.° So I
listen to your prayers, and I will give you the mare—though it is mine!—
so that these men, too, may know that my heart is neither haughty
nor unfeeling.”

    He spoke, and Menelaos gave the mare to Noëmon
a companion of Antilochos, to take away. Then he took the shining
590 cauldron, and Meriones took the two talents of gold as fourth

---

565 *shaker of the earth*: Poseidon is not only the god of horses, but Antilochos’ ancestor.

574 *of the gods*: If Antilochos swore that he did not gain an advantage through a trick, he would perjure himself
and be guilty in the eyes of the gods. Cleverly, he avoids taking the oath while not admitting that he cheated.

585 *your brother*: Antilochos’ brother is Thrasymedes. Menelaos and Antilochos are often together in the poem:
In Book 5 Antilochos comes to the aid of Menelaos against Aeneas; in Book 15 Menelaos and Antilochos
fight side by side; in Book 17 Menelaos asks Antilochos to carry news of Patroklos’ death to Achilles.

prize, his place in the race. The fifth prize went unclaimed,
the two-handled dish.° Achilles gave it to Nestor, carrying it
through the assembly of the Argives, and standing near him he said:
"Take this now, old man, may it be a treasure for you,
a memorial of this funeral. You won't see Patroklos more   595
among the Argives. I give you this prize, though you have not won it.
You will not contend in the boxing match, nor will you wrestle.
You will not enter the lists in the javelin throw, nor will you run
in the race, for wretched old age weighs you down."

So speaking, he placed the dish in Nestor's hands,   600
and Nestor took it gladly. Nestor spoke to Achilles words
that went like arrows: "All you have said is right, my child.
My limbs are no longer strong, dear friend, nor my feet.
And my arms do not dart out lightly from both shoulders.
I wish I had the strength I had when I was young, as in the time   605
when the Epeians were burying Amarynkeus at Buprasion,
and his children gave out prizes in the king's honor.° Then
there was no man like me, whether he was an Epeian, or from
Pylos, or of the great-hearted Aetolians. I beat Klytomedes,
the son of Enops, in the boxing match, and Ankaios from Pleuron,   610
who stood up as my opponent in the wrestling match. I beat Iphiklos
in the footrace, though he was a good man, and I outthrew Phyleus
and Polydoros with the spear. Only in the chariot race did the twin
sons of Aktor outdo me, forging ahead through their superior number,°
throwing their horses out front in their zeal for victory.   615
The best prizes were reserved for that contest. Twins they were.
The one drove the horses with a sure hand—drove with a sure hand!—
while the other worked the whip.° So I was great—once.
Now let the young face such trials. I must give way to old age,
but then I was the best of warriors. So you go ahead,   620
honor the burial of your friend with contests. As for this gift,
I accept it with pleasure. My heart rejoices that you always

---

592 *dish*: The last prize is left over because Eumelos received an extra one from Achilles' tent.

607 *king's honor*: Amarynkeus is the father of one Diores, mentioned in the Catalog of Ships as a prominent
     Epeian fighter (Map 4); Diores is killed in Book 4. Bouprasion is a town, or region, in Elis.

614 *superior number*: It is not clear what Homer means by this.

618 *the whip*: The importance of the funeral games of Amarynkeus is reflected in the appearance of contestants
     from Aetolia, across the Corinthian Gulf from Elis, and from Pylos, south of Elis. Klytomedes appears only
     here, but there is an Enops in Books 14 and 16. Pleuron is in Aetolia, and later authors say that Ankaios and
     Iphiklos took part in the Kalydonian Boar Hunt (Kalydon is in Aetolia). In the *Iliad* Ankaios is the father
     of Agapenor, an Arcadian (Book 2). Iphiklos has a namesake as the Thessalian father of Podarkes (Book
     2, 11); the Thessalian Iphiklos was a fast runner too. Phyleus is a son of the famous Augeias, who (Book 2)
     migrated to Doulichion after a quarrel with his father; Phyleus is the father of Meges, who commands

remember me as your friend and that you do not forget me or the
honor that I rightly receive among the Achaeans. May the gods pay
625 you back richly for these things."

                    So he spoke, and the son
of Peleus went his way through the thick throng of the Achaeans
after he had heard this tale of praise from the son of Neleus.

    Then he set out the prizes for the perilous boxing contest.
He brought out a hardy mule and tied it in the gathering place,
630 six years old and unbroken, the age at which it is hardest
to break the animal. For the defeated he placed a two-handled cup.

    He stood up and spoke to the Argives: "Son of Atreus, and
you other Achaeans with fancy shinguards, we encourage two men
to compete for these prizes—two men who are the best, to put up
635 their hands and to box. To whomever Apollo gives the strength
to endure, and all the Achaeans will know it,° let him take this hardy
mule with him to his hut. And he who is beaten, he may carry away
this cup with two handles."

                    So he spoke, and at once Epeios,
the son of Panopeus,° stood up, a man big and strong, an experienced
640 pugilist. He took hold of the hardy mule and said: "May he
who wants to carry off the two-handled cup come forth. I don't
think that another of the Achaeans will win the boxing match
and take this mule —I say that I am the best! Is it not enough
that I fall short in battle? Well, there is no way to be skilled
645 in all things. I'll tell you something, and this will come to pass:
I will utterly smash his skin and break his bones! I think that
my opponent's relatives should wait here in a crowd—wait
to carry him out when he is overcome by my fists!"

---

the Trojan contingent from Doulichion. Polydoros is unknown (but the name of one of Priam's sons). In a
reminiscence in Book 11 Nestor describes the Aktorionê, the twin "sons of Aktor," as being his opponents
in a battle. In Hesiod and later authors, the Aktorionê are Siamese twins, but it is not clear that Homer
thought of them in this way (though that could explain why the two Aktorionê raced against the lone
Nestor). They are also called the Molionê after their mother Molionê and were said really to be the sons of
Poseidon, Aktor only being their mortal father.

636 *know it*: Apollo is the patron of boxers. There were no rounds in ancient boxing. The match went on until
the spectators declared it over because one man could not continue.

639 *son of Panopeus*: First mentioned here in the *Iliad*, Epeios is said in the *Odyssey* to be the builder of the Trojan
Horse. Panopeus is a grandson of Aiakos, the father of Peleus, so Epeios is a distant cousin of Achilles.

So he spoke,
and they all fell into silence. Euryalos alone stood up, a man
like a god, the son of King Mekisteus, the son of Talaos,   650
who once came to Thebes for the burial of Oedipus, when he
had fallen. There Mekisteus defeated all the sons of Kadmos.°

The son of Tydeus, Diomedes, famous for his work
with the spear, busied himself around Euryalos, encouraging
him with words and fervently wishing him victory. First he put   655
a loincloth around him, and then he gave him the well-cut thongs
of a field ox.° The two men, Epeios and Euryalos, after they
had put on their belts, stepped into the middle of the gathering
place. They raised their powerful hands and fell upon one another,
the fists of both dishing out heavy blows. The grinding of their   660
teeth was terrible and the sweat flowed everywhere from
their limbs. The good Epeios rushed on Euryalos as he looked
for an opening, and Epeios struck him with an uppercut to the jaw
that put Euryalos down—his bright limbs sank beneath him.
As when a fish jumps up through the current driven in the   665
weed-choked shallows by the North Wind, and then the black
water covers him, even so Euryalos struggled up after he was
decked. And then great-hearted Epeios took him in his arms
and set him upright , and Euryalos' dear companions gathered
around. They guided him, dragging his feet, through the place   670
of gathering, as he spit up clotted blood and let his battered head
loll to one side. They dragged him, dazed out of his mind,
and made him sit down in their midst before some went to get
the two-handled cup.

Then the son of Peleus set forth other prizes
before the Danaäns for the third contest, the brawling wrestling   675
match. For the winner he set up a large tripod to be set on the fire,
the tripod that the Achaeans valued among themselves as being
worth twelve oxen. For the loser he put out in their midst a woman,
excellent in handicrafts, of the value of four oxen. Then he stood
and spoke a word among the Argives: "Come up now, you two   680
who will give your all in this contest."

---

652 *sons of Kadmos*: Euryalos is mentioned in the Catalog of Ships as the third leader of the Argives, after Dio-
      medes and Sthenelos. He is related to Diomedes by blood and marriage. Mekisteus' defeat of the Kadmeians
      is like the victory of Diomedes' father Tydeus over the Kadmeians in a series of athletic contests (Book 4).
      Here Oedipus died at Thebes, where he continued to rule after his wife's suicide (unlike in the famous Athe-
      nian tradition preserved in the Oedipus plays of Sophocles, where he died in Athens as a blind old man).

657 *field ox*: Boxing at this time was not done in the nude, as in the Classical Period. The thongs are wrapped
      around the hands to make a kind of glove.

So he spoke, and big
Telamonian Ajax got up, and then up stood Odysseus of many
devices, a knower of tricks. They put belts around their waists
and went into the middle of the gathering place. They grasped
685　each other with their strong arms, as rafters that meet and cross
each other that a famous carpenter has fitted to a high house to ward
off the power of the winds. Their backs creaked with the force of their
bold arms as they firmly gripped one another. Their sweat flowed
down in streams, and many ridges red with blood sprang up along
690　their ribs and shoulders. They strove ever for victory, to win
the well-wrought tripod.

But Odysseus was not able to trip Ajax
and throw him to the ground, nor could Ajax trip him, for the strength
of mighty Odysseus held steady. But when they were about to tire
out the Achaeans, who wear fancy shinguards, then big Telamonian
695　Ajax spoke to Odysseus: "Son of Laërtes, nurtured of Zeus,
resourceful Odysseus—throw me, or I will throw you!
The outcome is up to Zeus!"

So speaking, Ajax lifted him.
But Odysseus did not forget his tricks. He hit the hollow
of Ajax's knee from behind and loosed his limbs. Down
700　he fell backwards as Odysseus fell on his chest. The people
watched what was happening and were astonished.°

The good long-enduring Odysseus tried to raise Ajax—
he moved him a little from the ground, but he could not lift him.
He hooked his knee behind Ajax's leg, and then both fell
705　on the ground, clinging to one another, and both were befouled
by the dust.

And for a third time they would have sprung
up again and wrestled, but Achilles himself stood up and held
them back: "Do not go on struggling, and do not wear each
other out more. A draw! Victory goes to you both! Take equal
710　prizes and go your way,° so that other Achaeans may compete
in the contests."

So he spoke, and they heard him and obeyed.
Wiping off the dust, Odysseus and Ajax put on their shirts.

701　*astonished*: Because they expected Ajax to win.

710　*go your way*: But it is not evident how they would divide the prizes!

The son of Peleus quickly put out other prizes for the footrace—
a silver wine-mixing bowl, very nicely made. In beauty
it was the finest on earth, and it held six measures. The Sidonians, 715
highly skilled in handcrafts, had expertly made it, and the
Phoenicians brought it over the misty sea and landed it in
harbor, and gave it as a gift to Thoas. Jason's son Euneos
gave it to the warrior Patroklos as a ransom for Lykaon,
son of Priam.° This bowl Achilles set up as a prize 720
in honor of his comrade Patroklos, for the runner who was
fastest afoot. As second prize he put up a large bull,
rich with fat. As last prize he put up a half-talent of gold.

    Then Achilles stood and spoke a word to the Argives:
"Up you go, you two who will have at it in this footrace." 725
He spoke, and right away Oïlean Ajax got up, and resourceful
Odysseus got up too. Then Antilochos, the son of Nestor,
for he was faster afoot than all his young peers. They took
their places in a row. Achilles showed them the goal.
A course was marked out from the turning-post. 730

    Oïlean Ajax quickly stormed ahead and behind
came the good Odysseus, very close, as close as the shed
rod is to the breast of a woman when she deftly draws it in
her hands, pulling the spool out past the warp as she holds
the rod near her breast°—even so close behind did Odysseus 735
run. He put his feet down in Ajax's footprints before
the dust settled there, and his breath poured down
on the head of Oïlean Ajax, so close behind was he as they
charged swiftly ahead. And all the Achaeans shouted,
hollering to encourage him as Odysseus drove on for victory— 740
just so they called out to him as he raced along. And as

---

720   *son of Priam*: The Sidonians were the Semitic seafaring inhabitants of Sidon on the coast of modern Leba-
non, but at sea, and as international traders, Homer calls them *Phoenicians*. Phoenicians only appear here
in the *Iliad*, but the Sidonians were mentioned before in Book 6 as the makers of the embroidered garments
that Paris brought from Sidon on his journey home to Troy after abducting Helen. Hekabê placed one of
these robes on the knees of Athena. Just such decorated silver and bronze bowls of Phoenician manufac-
ture from the ninth and eighth centuries BC have been found in excavations. Thoas was king of Lemnos,
father of Hypsipylê, who married Jason and produced Euneos. Homer does not explain the purpose of the
Phoenicians' gift of the bowl to Thoas (to allow trade?). In Book 21 Lykaon says he was sold for the "value
of one hundred oxen"; because Euneos is here said to have given a Phoenician bowl for him, the value of the
bowl is apparently one hundred oxen.

735   *to her breast*: The ancient loom was vertical and consisted of vertical strands attached to a horizontal pole
at the top and to loom weights at the bottom, usually small pieces of pierced pottery, to weigh down the
strings and keep them straight. A woman would stand before the loom and draw a rod toward her breasts
(the shed rod).

they neared the last part of the course, then right away
Odysseus prayed in his heart to Athena with the flashing
eyes: "Hear me, goddess! Come be a good helper to my feet!"

745   So he spoke in prayer, and Pallas Athena heard him.
She made his limbs light, and his feet and hands too.
Just when he was about to dart home and win first prize,
Ajax slipped as he ran—Athena did it! He fell in excrement
from the loud-bellowing bulls that Achilles the fast runner had
750 killed in honor of Patroklos. His mouth and nostrils were filled
with the dung from the bulls while the much-enduring Odysseus
took up the bowl. He came in first! And glorious Ajax
got the ox.

Oïlean Ajax stood there holding the horn
of the ox of the field in his hands, spewing out filth, and he said
755 to the Argives: "Oh man, some goddess tripped my feet,
the one who always stands beside Odysseus—like a mother—
and helps him out."

So he spoke, and they all laughed merrily
at him. Then Antilochos came in and got the last prize.
Smiling, he spoke to the Argives: "I know I only tell you what
760 you already understand, my friends, that still to this day
the deathless ones pay honor to men who are a little older
than we. Oïlean Ajax is a little older than I, and Odysseus
is of an earlier generation still, of men from another time.
People say he is of a green old age. Yet it is hard for any other
765 Achaean to go up against him in a footrace—except of course
Achilles!"

So he spoke, giving glory to the swift-footed
son of Peleus. And Achilles answered him: "Antilochos,
your praise will not go unrewarded. I will add to your prize
a half talent of gold."

So speaking, he placed the gold in his hands
770 and Antilochos gladly received it. Then the son of Peleus set up
a far-shadowing spear in the place of assembly, and to it he added

---

separating the alternate vertical strands of the weaving (the warp) to make a kind of tunnel between the two
sets of threads. Through this opening she would pass a horizontal strand (the weft) by means of a shuttle at-
tached to a spool. As close as the rod is to the woman's breast, so close was Odysseus to Oïlean Ajax!

a shield and helmet, the arms of Sarpedon that Patroklos had stripped.°
Then he stood up and he spoke thus to the Argives: "We invite
two men—the best there are—to compete for these prizes.
They should clothe themselves in their armor and take up   775
the flesh-cutting bronze and make trial of one another
in front of the crowd. Whoever of the two will first reach
the tender flesh, and touch the inward parts through the armor
and draw dark blood,° to him I shall give this handsome Thracian
sword with silver rivets, which I took from Asteropaios.   780
May the two of them take away these arms to have them
in common,° and we will set up a good banquet in our huts."

   So he spoke, and then big Telamonian Ajax got up,
and powerful Diomedes, the son of Tydeus rose too. They armed
themselves on either side of the crowd, then the two came into   785
the middle, eager to fight, staring at one another with terrible glances.
Amazement held all the Achaeans. And then they came up close
to one another. Three times they glared at each other, and three times
they clashed together. Then Ajax son of Telamon struck
the shield balanced on every side, but he did not penetrate   790
to Diomedes' skin, for the breastplate behind prevented it.

   Then Diomedes the son of Tydeus jabbed at Ajax's neck
with the point of his shining spear. But the Achaeans, in fear
for big Ajax's life, ordered them to stop the fight and divide
the prizes equally. Achilles, the great warrior, gave the great   795
sword to Diomedes, son of Tydeus, along with its scabbard
and its finely fashioned strap.

                        Now the son of Peleus
put up a mass of rough-cast iron that the mighty Eëtion
used to hurl. But the good Achilles, the fast runner, had
killed him, and he carried it here in his ships along with   800
all the other loot.° Achilles stood up among the Argives
and he said: "Stand up, you who want to compete in a contest
for this prize. Though his rich fields are very remote, the winner
of this iron will not use it up before five full years. Nor for lack

---

772   *stripped*: In Book 16.

779   *dark blood*: These troublesome lines seem to refer to real wounding and for that reason have puzzled com-
      mentators. Perhaps Homer is using language inherited from actual blood sport.

782   *in common*: How this is possible is not obvious.

801   *other loot*: Eëtion was the father of Andromachê; Achilles sacked his town of Thebes on a local raid
      (Book 6). In Thebes he captured Chryseïs (Book 1), his lyre (Book 9), and his horse Pedasos (Book 16).

805 of iron will his shepherd or plowman need to go into the city,
but this will supply him."°

So he spoke, and then Polypoites
rose up, a bastion in the fight, and the mighty strength
of godlike Leonteus,° and Telamonian Ajax, and the good Epeios.
They stood in a row, and the good Epeios picked up the iron
810 shot, then whirled and threw it. All the Achaeans laughed!
Then Leonteus, of the line of Ares, threw it. Third,
big Telamonian Ajax hurled it from his powerful hand
and it landed past the marks of all. But then Polypoites,
a bastion in battle, picked up the iron, and put it as far as
815 a cow herder throws his staff when he hurls it spinning
over a herd of cows.° It went far outside the gathering.
Everyone shouted. The companions of strong Polypoites
stood up and carried the prize to the swift ships of their captain.

Then for the archers Achilles set up dark iron as a prize—
820 ten double axes and ten single axes. He set up the mast
of a ship with dark prows far out on the sand, and he tied
a timorous dove from it, tying its foot with a thin cord,
and he urged the archers to shoot at it. "Whoever shall hit
this fearful dove, he will take all the double axes to his house.
825 And if he misses the bird but hits the cord, that shot
will be worth less, and he will take home the single axes."°

So Achilles spoke, and up rose powerful King Teucer,
and Meriones° the brave aide to Idomeneus. They shook the lots
in a bronze helmet, and Teucer then drew first place. And at once
830 he fired an arrow with power—but he forgot to promise to King
Apollo the glorious sacrifice of new-born sheep, and so he
missed the bird. Apollo begrudged him the shot, but he hit
the cord beside the bird's foot where the bird was tied to the pole.

---

806   *supply him:* Homer is living in an age when it was logical to go to the city for iron farm implements, yet they
      could be fashioned in a home, either by a wandering smith or by a local artisan.

808   *Leonteus:* Polypoites and Leonteus are leaders of the Lapiths (in Thessaly, Book 2) last seen fighting
      together at the gates of the Achaean wall (Book 12).

816   *of cows:* Perhaps used like a South American *bola,* a stone with a cord attached used to catch cattle.

826   *the axes:* In these confused terms of the match—who gets first prize if the cord is hit?—Achilles seems to
      foresee what actually happens.

828   *Meriones:* Meriones and Teucer, the half-brother of Telamonian Ajax, are the only two men to actually fight
      with the bow in the *Iliad,* although in the *Odyssey* (Book 8) Odysseus claims to have been the best bowman
      at Troy, after Philoktetes.

The bitter arrow went straight through the cord, and the dove flew
to the heavens while the cord hung loose toward the ground.   835
All the Achaeans shouted aloud.

                          But Meriones speedily grabbed
the bow from Teucer's hand—he had long held an arrow
while Teucer took his shot. At once he vowed to Apollo,
who works from a long way off, to offer a glorious sacrifice
from his new-born lambs. He saw the timid dove high   840
beneath the clouds. There, as she circled around, he hit
her in the middle beneath the wing. The shaft went through,
then fell to the earth in front of Meriones' foot. But the bird
settled on the mast from the ship with its dark prows
and bent down its neck, and her thick plumage drooped.   845
Swiftly the spirit flew from her limbs, and she fell far from
the mast. The people gazed on her and were astonished.
So Meriones took up all ten double axes, while Teucer carried
off the single axes to the hollow ships.

                               Then the son of Peleus
brought in a long-shadowed spear and a cauldron, brand-new,   850
embossed with flowers, worth an ox, and he set the prizes down
in the place of gathering.

                          The javelin-throwers got up—the son
of Atreus, wide-ruling Agamemnon, and Meriones, the aide
to Idomeneus. The good Achilles, the fast runner, spoke to them:
"Son of Atreus, we all know how much you surpass everyone   855
both in strength and in throwing the javelin. So why don't you take
this cauldron to the hollow ships, and we will give the warrior
Meriones the spear, if you think that is right. I recommend it."

   So Achilles spoke, and the king of men Agamemnon did not disagree.
Agamemnon gave Meriones the bronze spear, and to Talthybios   860
the herald he handed the exorbitantly beautiful cauldron.

BOOK 24. *The Ransom of Hector*

The gathering broke up, and the people scattered, each man
   going to his own ship. While the others took thought
of the pleasure of a meal and sweet sleep, Achilles wept,
thinking constantly of his dear companion. Sleep,
5 who conquers all, did not come to him, but he tossed
to this side and that, longing for the manliness and great strength
of Patroklos. He thought of all they had done together,
the pains they had suffered, the wars of men and the fierce
waves of the sea. Remembering these things he poured
10 down hot tears, lying now on this side, now on his back,
now face down. Then standing up straight he wandered
distraught along the shore of the salt sea. He always
saw the dawn, rising over the sea and the land.

     Then he would yoke his swift horses beneath his chariot
15 and bind Hector to drag him behind his car. Three times
he would drag him around the tomb of the dead son
of Menoitios, then he would rest in his hut. He let Hector lie
stretched out there, his face in the dust. But Apollo kept all outrage
away from Hector's flesh, taking pity on him even though
20 he was dead. Apollo held the golden goatskin fetish around
him° so that Achilles could not rip up Hector's body as he
dragged him around. Thus in his fury Achilles abused
the magnificent Hector.

            But the blessed gods took pity when
they saw what was happening. They urged the far-seeing
25 Hermes, killer of Argos, to steal away the corpse.
The plan was pleasing to all the other gods, but not
to Hera, nor Poseidon, nor the flashing-eyed daughter Athena,
for they held on to their hatred for sacred Troy even as
at first, and for Priam and his people too, because of the blind
30 foolishness of Alexandros, who insulted them when they came

---

21 *goatskin fetish*: The goatskin fetish (*aegis*) is variously the property of Zeus, Apollo, and Athena. It is an
    object that inspires terror but also is protective, as here.

to his courtyard, giving preference to her who furthered his
horrid lust.°

But when the twelfth dawn had afterwards come,
then Phoibos Apollo spoke to the deathless ones: "You gods are
cruel, workers of harm! Has Hector never burned for you the thighs
of bulls and goats without blemish?° Now you cannot bring   35
yourselves to save him (though he is a corpse), for his wife
to look upon and his mother and his child and his father Priam
and the Trojan people, who would burn him with fire and
offer the correct funeral rites. No, you gods want to help out
the baneful Achilles, whose mind is ever against   40
the ways of custom, and always the purpose in his breast
cannot be bent, so he acts like a savage lion who trusting
in his great strength and his noble spirit preys upon
the sheep of men so that he can take a meal. Even so
Achilles has ruined all pity, and there is no respect in him,   45
which can be very hurtful to men—or help them out!°
One may at some time lose someone even more dear
than this, a brother from the same womb, or even a son,
but when the person is bewailed and lamentation is made,
then he makes an end of it. For the Fates° have given an   50
enduring soul to men. But this man, now that he has taken
away the life from noble Hector—he binds him to his chariot
and drags him around the mound of his dear companion!
He shall have neither honor nor profit from this. He should
beware that we do not become angry with him, though Achilles   55
is a good man. But in his fury he outrages the dumb clay!"

White-armed Hera answered him in anger: "This may
even be as you say, O lord of the silver bow, but are we really
going to grant equal honor to Achilles and to Hector? Why,
Hector is mortal, he sucked at a woman's breast! But Achilles   60
is born of the goddess Thetis whom I myself nourished and reared

---

32 *horrid lust*: Oddly, this is the only time that the Judgment of Paris is referred to in the *Iliad*—if in fact it is
    referred to. According to the later story, the goddess Eris (Strife) tossed in an apple at the wedding of Peleus
    and Thetis, saying it was for the most beautiful goddess: Athena, Hera, or Aphrodite. Paris served as judge
    and chose Aphrodite, for which Helen was the prize. What this has to do with Poseidon is not clear; his
    enmity toward Troy was explained in Book 21 as coming from Laomedon's failure to pay him and Apollo for
    building the walls of Troy.

35 *without blemish*: An animal that was in any way disfigured was not an acceptable sacrifice.

46 *help them out*: How having respect for others can be hurtful to men is not apparent.

50 *Fates*: The Fates appear only here as a group in the *Iliad*.

FIGURE 24.1 **The Judgment of Paris.** On the right a youthful Paris sits on a stone in a rural location. The sheep near his feet indicates that he is a shepherd. He holds a lyre with a tortoise-shell sounding box because he is accustomed to the beauty of song. In front of him stand from left to right: Hera dressed in a demure robe; Athena, wearing the goatskin fetish as a snake-fringed collar; and a buxom Aphrodite, holding a scepter and the "apple of discord" that Paris has awarded to her. Athenian red-figure water jar, c. 450 BC.

and gave to a man to be his wife—to Peleus, dear to the heart
of the immortals. And all you gods attended the wedding!
You yourself dined there, holding your little lyre, a friend
of wicked men, ever untrustworthy!"° 65

            Zeus the cloud-gatherer
said in reply: "Hera, don't be so utterly angry against the gods.
There will never be an equal honor given these two men,
but Hector was dearest to the gods of the mortals who live in Ilion.
At least he was to me—he never failed of acceptable gifts.
Never did my altar lack in the equal feast, or in the drink-offering, 70
or in the smoke of sacrifice. We always got our prize of honor.
But as for stealing the valiant Hector without Achilles knowing,
let's forget about that. For his mother comes constantly to his side,
both night and day. But would some one of the gods please call
Thetis to come to my side so that I can say to her something 75
important—? that she arrange for Achilles to take gifts from Priam,
and let Hector go."

       So Zeus spoke, and Iris, swift as a storm,
rushed to give the message. Between SAMOTHRACE and wooded
IMBROS she plunged into the dark sea, and the waters resounded.
She sank to the bottom like a lead weight, a weight attached 80
to the horn of an ox of the field that goes bringing death
to the ravenous fishes.° She found Thetis in a hollow cave.
Other goddesses of the sea sat around her, all in a group.
Thetis was complaining in the midst of them about the fate
of her excellent son who to her sorrow was about to die 85
in fertile Troy, far from the land of his fathers.

    Standing beside her, Iris swift of foot said: "Get up,
Thetis! Zeus, knowing things that never perish, summons you!"

    Then silver-footed Thetis said in reply: "What does that
great god want of me? I am reluctant to socialize with the deathless 90
ones, for I suffer anguish in my heart. But I will go. Whatever
Zeus says will not be in vain."

---

65 *ever untrustworthy*: The wedding of Peleus and Thetis was celebrated in later Greek storytelling as the most
     glorious wedding ever. Hera's kind words about Thetis here disagree, however, with Hera's bitter suspicions
     in Book 1. According to the story popular later, Zeus took an interest in Thetis but then learned of a
     prophecy that Thetis' child would be greater than the father. Zeus therefore quelled his interest, and Hera
     condemned Thetis to unite with a mortal man. Of course Achilles was greater than Peleus.

82 *ravenous fishes*: The lead weight has been explained as being wrapped around the line above a hook made of
     horn (or it is an artificial lure?) to protect it from the fish's bite; or, the lead weight may simply be a sinker.

So speaking, the divine goddess
put on a dark veil—there was no cloth more black.° And thus
she set off. At first swift Iris, whose feet were like the wind,
95 went ahead, and the waves of the sea parted before them.
When they had come out on the shore, they sped toward heaven.
They came to the far-thundering son of Kronos. All the other
blessed gods who last forever were seated around him
in a knot. Thetis took her seat next to father Zeus—
100 Athena yielded her place, and Hera placed a beautiful
golden cup in her hands and cheered her with words.
Thetis took a drink and handed back the cup.

The father
of men and gods was first to speak among them: "You have
come to Olympos, goddess Thetis, though you are pained
105 at heart, having always in your breast an unforgettable sorrow.
I know it myself. But I will tell you why I have summoned
you here. For nine days there has been a quarrel among the
deathless ones about the corpse of Hector, and concerning Achilles
the sacker of cities. They are urging that Hermes, the far-seeing
110 slayer of Argos, should steal the body. But right now I want to accord
glory to Achilles,° and at the same time preserve your respect
and friendship for the future. So go quickly to the camp
and give this order to your son: Say that the gods grow angry,
and that I above all the deathless ones am filled with wrath
115 because in the madness of his heart he holds Hector
beside the hollow ships and will not give him up. Perhaps
from respect for me he will let Hector go! But I will send forth
Iris to great-hearted Priam to say that he should go to the ships
of the Achaeans to ransom his son, bearing gifts that will warm
120 the heart of Achilles."

So he spoke, and the goddess Thetis
of the silver feet obeyed. She went rushing from the peaks
of Olympos, and she arrived at the hut of her son. There
she found him groaning ceaselessly. His beloved companions
hurried all around him to prepare their morning meal.
125 Achilles had killed a large and shaggy ram for them in the hut.

---

93   *more black*: In mourning for the impending death of Achilles; the only time in Homer that black is used as
the color of mourning.

111   *to Achilles*: Apparently in the form of the treasure that will be offered for Hector's corpse.

Thetis sat down next to Achilles, his revered mother,
and stroked him with her hand. She spoke, calling his name:
"My child, for how long will you eat out your heart with sorrow
and mourning, and have no thought for food or sleep?
Also, it would be good if you lay with a woman, for you shall not   130
live long, as death and overwhelming fate stand near
you now. So listen to me, for I am a messenger from Zeus.
He says that the gods grow angry, and he especially
of the deathless ones is filled with wrath, because in the
madness of your heart you hold Hector beside the beaked ships   135
and will not let him go. But come, release him, taking
ransom for the corpse."

        Achilles the fast runner said in reply:
"Let it be so. Whoever brings ransom may carry away
the corpse, if that is what the Olympian himself really wants."

        Thus in the gathering of the ships, mother and son   140
spoke to one another many words that went like arrows.
And then the son of Kronos sent Iris to holy Ilion: "Go then,
swift Iris! Leave the seat of Olympos and announce to great-hearted
Priam in Ilion that he should go to the ships of the Achaeans
to ransom his son, bearing gifts that will warm the heart   145
of Achilles. Let him go alone, none other of the Trojan men
may go with him. An elderly herald may go along, someone
who can drive the mules and the wagon with its excellent wheels,
to carry the corpse back to the city—that man whom gallant
Achilles killed. May death not be his concern, nor terror.   150
We will send Hermes the killer of Argos as guide to lead him
to Achilles. When he gets inside the hut of Achilles,
Achilles will not kill him and he will not allow any
other to kill him. For Achilles is not mad, nor negligent,
nor evil, but with every kindness he will respect a suppliant."   155

        So Zeus spoke, and storm-footed Iris hurried
to carry his message. She came to the house of Priam, and
found therein all clamor and wailing. Priam's sons were seated
around their father within the court, all of their clothes
wet with their tears. The old man sat in the middle of them,   160
close-wrapped in his cloak. Priam had rubbed excrement in his
hair and around his neck, rolling around in it and smearing it
around with his own hands.° His daughters and his sons' wives

---

163 *his own hands*: As a sign of mourning, but nothing is said later about Priam's defiled condition.

wailed throughout the house, remembering all those fine
165 and noble men who now lay in Hades' house, killed at the hands
of the Argives.

The messenger of Zeus stood next to Priam,
speaking softly while trembling took hold of his limbs:
"Take courage in your heart, O Priam, son of Dardanos,
and have no fear. I come here not to foretell any evil, but only
170 with kind intent. I am a messenger from Zeus, who though
he is far away from you has compassion and takes pity.
Olympian Zeus has ordered that you go to the ships of the Achaeans
and ransom your son, bearing gifts that will warm the heart of Achilles.
You must go alone, no other of the Trojan men can go with you.
175 Only an elderly herald may go along—one who can drive
the mules and the wagon with its excellent wheels and then carry
the corpse back to the city—that man whom gallant Achilles killed.
Neither death nor terror should concern you, for he will send
Hermes the killer of Argos as a guide to lead you to Achilles.
180 When Hermes gets you inside the hut of Achilles,
Achilles will not kill you and he will not allow any other
to kill you. For Achilles is not mad, nor negligent, nor evil,
but with every kindness he will respect a suppliant."

So speaking Iris swift of foot went off, and Priam
185 ordered his sons to prepare a mule cart with excellent wheels,
and to attach a wicker box to it.° He himself went down
into his fragrant treasure-chamber, vaulted, made of cedar,
that contained many precious things.

Then he called to his wife
Hekabê and he said to her: "My darling, a messenger
190 has come from Zeus on Olympos. She said that I should go
to the ships of the Achaeans to ransom our son, bearing gifts
that will warm the heart of Achilles. But come, I want to
know—what do you think? For the desire in my heart urges
me to do this now—to go to the ships inside the broad
195 camp of the Achaeans."

So he spoke, but Hekabê uttered a shrill
cry and answered: "Woe to me! Where has the wisdom gone

---

186 *wicker box to it*: Apparently a device made of wicker for holding cargo, tied to the top of the wagon, but the
word appears only here.

for which in earlier days you were famous in foreign lands
and among those over whom you rule? How can you consider
going alone to the ships of the Achaeans—to meet the eyes
of the man who killed so many of your noble sons?   200
Your heart is iron! That bloodthirsty and faithless man
will disrespect you—if he sees you with his own eyes
and gets you in his grip, he will have no pity on you!
No, let us make our lament far away from him, sitting
here in our chamber. Such a destiny did mighty Fate spin   205
for Hector at his birth, when I bore my child—to glut
the swift-footed dogs, far from his parents, in the house
of a violent man. If only I could fasten my teeth into the middle
of his liver and eat it! Payback for my son, whom he killed
not while he was acting the coward, but while Hector   210
stood forth on behalf of all Trojans and the deep-bosomed
Trojan women. He did not think of flight or escape° then!"

    Old man Priam, like a god, answered her: "Don't hold me
back, woman, when I want to go! Do not be a bird of ill-omen
in my own halls. You will not persuade me. If some other of the men   215
upon the earth ordered me to do this, one of the prophets who foretell
things by looking at the smoke of offerings, or one of the holy men—
then we would say that it was a false thing and would stay at home
all the more. But as it is, I have myself heard it from the goddess.
I saw her face to face. I will go and that is all there is to it.   220
If it is my fate to die at the ships of the Achaeans who
wear shirts of bronze, I am willing. Let Achilles kill me
right away, once I have held my son close and have put
from me the desire for lament."

                He spoke and opened
the beautiful lids of the chests. From them he took twelve   225
very beautiful robes and twelve woolen cloaks of a single fold
and as many coverlets, and as many white cloths
of linen, and as many shirts on top of these. He took up
and weighed out ten talents of gold, and two shining tripods,
four wash-basins, and a very beautiful cup that the Thracians   230
gave to him when he went there on embassy—a great treasure.
The old man did not spare even this in his halls, because
in his heart he desired only to ransom his dear son.

---

212 *flight or escape*: He did, however, run three times around the walls of Troy!

Then he drove all the Trojans out of the portico, reviling them
as they went: "Get out you of here, you wretches, you bringers
of shame! Don't you have wailing enough in your own homes?
Why should you have to come here and attend my grief? Do you
make light of the fact that Zeus, the son of Kronos, has given me
this agony—that my best son is killed? But you yourselves will learn
soon enough. You will be easier for the Achaeans to kill now
that he is dead. As for me, may I go down into the house of Hades
before these eyes behold the city laid waste and sacked."

So he spoke and with his staff he cleared the room of them.
They scurried forth from the old man as he drove them along.
Then he called aloud to his sons, upbraiding them—Helenos
and Paris and noble Agathon and Pammon and Antiphonos
and Polites good at the war cry and Deïphobos and Hippothoös
and the noble Agauos.° To these nine the old man shouted orders:
"Get out of here, you wicked children! Disasters all! I wish
that you all had died beside the swift ships instead of Hector!
Wretched me—I never had any luck. I begot many *fine* sons
in broad Troy, but I don't think that a single one is still alive—
not godlike Mestor nor Troilos, who delighted in horses,
nor Hector, who was like a god among men. He did not
seem to be the child of a mortal man, but of a god. Ares killed
them all. Yet shameless things are left— liars and acrobats!
Great at beating out the dance! Thieves of your own
people's sheep and kids!° Would you *please* prepare
a wagon for me as soon as possible, and put all these goods
in it, so that we may get on the road?"

So Priam spoke, and in fear
of their father's rebuke the sons brought out the mule wagon
with excellent wheels—lovely, recently made—and they bound
the wicker box on top. They took the mule yoke down from a peg,
made of an evergreen wood with a knob on it, fitted with guides
for the reins. Then they brought out the yoke-binding, fourteen feet
in length, and the yoke. They fitted the yoke properly onto the front
end of the polished pole. Then they put the ring over the peg and
tied the yoke-binding three times on each side of the knob.

---

248   ... *noble Agauos*: In addition to well-known names (Helenos, Paris, Polites, Deïphobos) are other sons
only mentioned here and probably invented for the occasion (Agathon, Pammon, Antiphonos, Agauos).
A doublet of Hippothoös is mentioned as a leader of the Pelasgians (Book 2), later killed (Book 17).

258   *sheep and kids*: As delicacies in the party feast, to which Priam says his sons are given. It was no disgrace to
steal flocks from abroad, but it was immoral to steal from your own people.

They bound the yoke-binding fast to the knob in a succession
of turns, then tucked the end under the hook.°   270

                              Then they
brought forth the boundless ransom for Hector's head from
the treasure chamber and heaped it on the highly polished wagon.
They yoked the mules with powerful single hooves that
work in harness, which once the Mysians had given
to Priam as a splendid gift. They led horses beneath the yoke   275
that the old man had himself nourished in the polished stall.
Thus were wagon and chariot yoked for both Priam
and his herald in the high-roofed palace, despite the deep
foreboding in their hearts.

                      Hekabê came up to Priam
and his herald, stricken in heart. She had honeyed wine   280
in a golden cup in her right hand, so that she could pour
out a drink-offering before they went. She stood in front
of the horses and spoke: "Take this. Pour out a drink-offering
to father Zeus, and pray that you may come again from
these evil men, because your heart bids you to go to the ships.   285
But I am against it. So pray to the lord of the dark cloud,
the son of Kronos who has a shrine on Ida, who sees
whatever happens in Troy, and ask him to send his bird,
his swift messenger that is the dearest of birds to him,
whose strength is greatest, to appear on your right hand.°   290
So seeing the omen with your own eyes, you can trust that
it is safe to go to the ships of the Danaäns with their fast horses.
If far-seeing Zeus will not give you this sign, then I would not
urge you on, or bid you to go the ships of the Argives,
even though you want very badly to do so."   295

---

270 *under the hook*: A good example of Homer's ability to do with language what he wants: In the space of a few
     lines he uses six words that never appear again in Greek literature and one word that is used just once
     600 years later! The meaning of these terms for the wagon assembly is by no means clear, and it is hard to
     understand Homer's description, but it may work like this: The wagon has four wheels and a detachable
     body. It has a single shaft to which a yoke for two mules is bound by means of an unexpectedly long cord
     (the "yoke-binding"). The yoke has the approximate shape of an "M." The yoke has a central "knob" on it,
     and there are hooks on top on either side to guide the reins back from the animal's head, over the yoke,
     to the driver. A peg goes through the pole into the yoke to hold the yoke and pole together, and a "ring"
     attached to the yoke is slipped over (or through?) the peg to hold it. Then for greater strength the yoke-
     binder is wrapped around the pole and yoke. First it is wrapped around the pole on either side of the "knob"
     on the yoke, then around the "knob" on the yoke by a succession of turns. Then the end of the yoke-binding
     is tucked under a "hook" (?) fastened to the pole. But all this is very obscure.

290 *right hand*: And thus a good omen.

Then godlike Priam
answered her: "O woman, I won't deny you your request.
It is a good thing to raise up your hands to Zeus, in hopes
that he take pity."

Thus he spoke and then the old man told
a female slave in attendance to pour out pure water
300   over his hands. The slave came near, carrying in her hands
a basin for hand washing, and a vase. When he had washed
his hands, he took the cup from his wife. Then he prayed,
standing near the middle of the court. He poured out the wine
while looking up to heaven, and he said these words:
305   "Father Zeus who rules from Ida, most glorious and
greatest—grant that I come as a friend to Achilles,
and that he take pity on me. Send me your bird, your swift
messenger that is dearest to you of all birds and whose
strength is the greatest—on my right hand so that seeing
310   with my own eyes I may trust the sign and safely go
to the ships of the Danaäns with their swift horses."

So he spoke in prayer, and Zeus the counselor heard him.
At once he sent an eagle, the best omen among birds, a swamp eagle,
a hunter that men also call the dappled eagle. As wide as is
315   the door of a high roofed treasure-chamber of a man of wealth,
a door well fitted and keyed, even so far did his wings
reach on either side. He appeared to them on the right hand,
swooping over the city. Everyone who saw it rejoiced,
and the heart in every man was cheered.

Quickly the old man
320   mounted his chariot and drove outside the gate and the echoing
portico. In front the mules drew the wagon with four wheels,
and wise Idaios° was the driver. Behind followed the old man,
who with his whip drove the horses swiftly through the city.
Priam's kin followed, loudly as if he were going to his death.
325   But when they had gone down from the city and arrived
on the plain, the kinsfolk went back then to Ilion, his sons
and his daughters' husbands.

Far-seeing Zeus saw them
as they came out onto the plain, and seeing the old man

---

322   *Idaios*: The Trojan herald has appeared earlier in Books 3 and 7.

he took pity. At once he spoke to Hermes, his dear son:
"Hermes, because you enjoy accompanying men, and you   330
listen to whomever you want°—go now and lead Priam
to the hollow ships of the Achaeans in such a way that no one
of the other Danaäns sees him or is aware of his presence,
until you get to the hut of the son of Peleus."

So he spoke
and the messenger, the killer of Argos, did not disobey.   335
he bound his beautiful sandals beneath his feet—immortal,
golden—that bore him over the watery deep and the endless
dry land like the blast of the wind. He took up his wand
by which he charms the eyes of men, of those whom he chooses,
and then he rouses others from their sleep. Holding this wand   340
in his hand, the powerful killer of Argos flew off.
Quickly he came to the land of Troy and the Hellespont.
He went in the likeness of a young prince just beginning
to grow a beard, a man in whom youth is at its most charming.
When they had driven beyond the great tomb of Ilos,°   345
they stopped the mules and the horses so that they could drink
from the river. Already darkness settled on the earth.°

Then the herald saw Hermes close at hand, he saw him
and he spoke to Priam: "Think about this, O son of Dardanos—
we had better be careful! I see a man, I think he will quickly   350
cut us to pieces! Let us get out of here, in the chariot, or take hold
of his knees and beg for our lives, in hopes that he takes pity!"

So he spoke, and the old man's mind was distracted,
and he was terribly afraid. The hair on his bent limbs stood on end
and he stood in a daze. But Hermes the helper came near him   355
and took hold of old man Priam's hand, and Hermes questioned
him: "Where, father, do you drive your horses and mules
through the immortal night when other men are asleep? Do you
not fear the Achaeans, who breathe fury, who are hostile and
aggressive and very nearby? If one of them should see you bearing   360
so many treasures through the swift dark night, what would
you do then? You are not young yourself, and your companion is

---

331 *you want*: A polite way of saying that Hermes should be open to Zeus's suggestion that he accompany
     Priam.

345 *tomb of Ilos*: Mentioned as a landmark in Books 10 and 11.

347 *on the earth*: It is the evening of the thirty-eighth day of the poem.

an old man, too old to defend you against somebody who would attack
you for no good reason. But I will do you no harm, and I will defend
you against anyone else. You are like my own father."

The old man Priam, like a god, then answered Hermes:
"All these things, my dear son, are just as you say. Surely,
some god has stretched forth his hand over me, who has sent
a wayfarer such as you to meet me. You are a bringer of good
fortune, one wonderful in form and beauty. And you are wise
in your heart. You come from blessed parents."

The messenger,
the killer of Argos, then answered him: "You have spoken all
these things in accord with what is right. But come now, tell me
this and tell me truly—are you sending these many rich treasures
to some foreign people so that they may remain safe for you,
or are you all abandoning holy Ilion in fear? For so great a warrior
has perished—your son, the best, who never held back from
warring against the Achaeans."

Then old man Priam, like a god,
answered him: "Who are you, most excellent man, and who
are your parents? For you have said fitting things about
the fate of my luckless son."

The messenger, the killer of Argos,
then said: "You make trial of me, old man, asking about the brave
Hector! For I often saw him with my own eyes in the battle
where men win glory. After driving the Argives to the ships,
he would kill many, raging with his sharp bronze.
We stood there marveling. For Achilles, angry at the son
of Atreus, would not let us fight. I am Achilles' aide.
We came in the same well-made ship. I am one of the
Myrmidons. My father is Polyktor. He is rich, but an old
man now, like you. He had six sons, and I was the seventh.
We cast the lot and it fell to me to come here. Now I have
come to the plain from the ships, for at dawn the bright-eyed
Achaeans will launch their battle around the city. They do not
like sitting around, and the chieftains of the Achaeans are not able
to hold them back in their longing to go to war."

Then the old man Priam, like a god, answered him:
"If you are aide to Achilles son of Peleus, come, tell me
the whole truth. Is my son still beside the ships? or has Achilles

already cut him to pieces, limb from limb, and fed him
to his dogs?"   400

        Then the messenger, the killer of Argos,
said to him: "Old man, the gods and the birds have not yet
eaten him, but he still lies beside the ship of Achilles, amid
the huts, as he was at first. He has lain there for twelve days,
but his flesh has not rotted, nor have the worms eaten him,   405
which devour men killed in battle. Achilles ruthlessly drags
him around the tomb of his beloved friend when daylight appears,
but he does not mutilate the body. You yourself would marvel
if you were to come and see how he lies there as fresh as dew.
The blood is washed from him, and there is no stain anywhere.   410
All the wounds are closed, wherever he was hit, for many
drove their bronze into his flesh. Thus do the blessed gods
care for your son, although he is dead, for he was dear
to their hearts."

        So he spoke, and the old man rejoiced,
and he answered him in this way: "O my child, in truth   415
it is a good thing to give the gods the gifts that are their due,
for not ever did my son—if he even existed!°—forget in his halls
the gods who live in Olympos. So they have remembered him,
although he is caught in the fate of death. But come, take this
beautiful goblet from me, and guard me. Guide me with the   420
blessings of the gods until I come to the hut of the son of Peleus."

        The messenger, the killer of Argos, then said: "You would
try me, old man—I who am younger than you. But you shall
not persuade me. You ask that I take gifts from you behind
Achilles' back, but I fear him and I respect him in my heart.   425
If he should think that I defrauded him, in the future something
bad could happen to me. But as your guide I would go even
to famous Argos,° attending you kindly either in a swift ship
or on foot. Nor would any man scorn me as a guide and attack us."

        Thus Hermes the helper spoke. Then he leaped upon the chariot 430
and swiftly he took hold of the whip and took the reins in
his hands. He breathed great strength into the horses and the mules.
But when they came to the wall surrounding the ships, and the ditch

---

417 *even existed*: A formulaic phrase expressing regret at how drastically things have changed.

428 *Argos*: He means "Pelasgian Argos," in Thessaly, not the Argos in the Peloponnesus.

where the guards were just now busy with their meal,
435 the messenger, the killer of Argos, poured out sleep on them all,
and quickly he opened the gates and shoved back the bolts.
Then he drove in Priam and his glorious gifts in the wagon.

◀))   They came to the high hut of the son of Peleus, which
the Myrmidons had made for their king, hewing logs of fir,
440 and they roofed it over with a shaggy thatch gathered from
the meadow. And around the hut they built a great court
of heavy beams for their king. The door had a single bolt made
of fir, which three Achaeans would slam shut, and three men
would draw it back— but Achilles slammed it shut all by himself.
445 Hermes the helper opened the door for the old man and brought
in the glorious gifts for the son of Peleus, the fast runner.

Hermes stepped off the car onto the ground and said:
"Old man, I who have come to you am an immortal god:
Hermes. My father sent me to be your guide. But now I will
450 go back. I will not come into Achilles' sight. It would be
offensive for mortals to entertain an immortal god in this way,
face to face. But you go in and seize the knees of the son
of Peleus, and beseech him by his father, and his mother with
the lovely hair, and his child, so that you might stir his spirit."

455   So speaking, Hermes went off toward high Olympos.
Priam leaped from the chariot to the ground. He left Idaios
there to hold the horses and the mules. Then the old man
went straight toward the house where Achilles dear to Zeus
was accustomed to sit. He found him there, and his companions,
460 who sat apart. Only two, the warriors Automedon and Alkimos°
of the breed of Ares, busily waited on him. Achilles
had just finished his meal, eating and drinking. The table
still stood by his side. The aides did not notice great Priam
as he came in. Standing nearby, he took Achilles' knees
465 in his hands, and Priam kissed the terrible man-killing
hands that had taken so many of his sons. As when a painful
madness takes hold of a man and he kills someone
in his homeland, then comes to another people, to the house
of a rich man, and wonder takes hold of those who see him,—
470 even so Achilles was amazed when he saw godlike Priam.
And the others were amazed too and glanced at one another.

---

460 *Automedon and Alkimos:* These two aides, who have replaced Patroklos in the role of server, also appeared
together in Book 19.

FIGURE 24.2   Achilles and Priam.   The old man, leaning on his staff, approaches from the left. Behind him slaves carry the ransom. Achilles lies on his inlaid couch, holding a knife with which he has been cutting up the meat served on the table in front of the dining couch; strips of meat hang down over the side of the table, and he holds a strip in his left hand. He has not yet noticed Priam's presence, and he turns over his shoulder to call out to a slave boy to pour wine from a jug he holds. His shield (with Gorgon's head), helmet, shinguards, and sword hang from the wall. Beneath the couch lies Hector, his body pierced by many wounds. This is the most commonly represented scene from the *Iliad* in all of Greek art. Athenian red-figure drinking cup. c. 480 BC.

Making supplication, Priam spoke to Achilles:
"Remember your own father, O Achilles like to the gods!
He is old as I am, on the wretched threshold of old age.
475 Probably those who live around him are wearing him down,
and there is no one to ward off ruin and disaster.
But at least he rejoices in his heart when he hears that you
are alive, and he hopes every day that he will see his dear
son returning from Troy. But I have received an evil fate,
480 because I fathered many sons who were the best in broad
Troy, but of them I do not think that any remain.
I had fifty sons when the sons of the Achaeans came, nineteen
from one woman, the others from women in the palace.°
Though they were many, the fury of Ares has driven
485 most of them to their knees. And he who was left
to me, who by himself protected the city and those within it—
you have just killed him as he struggled to defend his homeland—
Hector! On his account I have come to the ships of the Achaeans
to ransom him from you. I bring boundless ransom.
490 So respect the gods, Achilles, and take pity on me,
remembering your own father. For I am far more to be pitied
than he—I who did what no man on earth has ever dared
to do—to stretch the hands of my son's killer to my mouth."

So Priam spoke, and he stirred in Achilles a great urge
495 to weep for his own father. Taking Priam by the hand
he gently pushed the old man away. And so the two men
thought of those who had died. Priam wept copiously for Hector
the killer of men, as he groveled before the feet of Achilles.
And Achilles cried for his own father and now, again, for Patroklos.
500 Their wailing filled the hut.

But when valiant Achilles
had his fill of wailing, and the desire for it had departed
from his heart and limbs, immediately he rose from his seat.
He raised up the old man with his hand, taking pity on his white
head and his white beard, and he spoke words that went like arrows:
505 "Yes, you wretched man, truly you have suffered many evils
in your heart. How did you dare to come alone to the ships
of the Achaeans beneath the eyes of the man who killed your many
fine sons? Your heart must be iron! But come, sit on a chair.

---

483 *palace:* Of Priam's fifty sons, twenty-two are mentioned by name in the *Iliad.* Two died before the poem
begins, eleven die during the course of the poem, and the remaining nine are named earlier in this book.

We will let our sufferings lie quiet in our hearts, though burdened
by them. There is nothing to be gained from cold lament.   510
    "For so have the gods spun the thread for wretched
mortals— to live in pain, while they are without care.
Two jars of gifts that he gives are set into the floor of Zeus,
one of evils, the other of good things. To whomever
Zeus who delights in the thunder gives a mixed portion,   515
that man receives now evil, now good. But to the man
to whom he gives only pain, he has made him to be roughly
treated, and ravening hunger drives him over the shining
earth. He walks dishonored by gods and by men.
    "So the gods gave to Peleus wonderful gifts   520
from birth. He exceeded all men in wealth and riches,
and he ruled over the Myrmidons, and the gods gave him
a goddess for a wife, although he is mortal. But to him
the god also gave evil, because in his halls there is no
offspring who will one day rule. He fathered a single child,   525
doomed to an early death. And I will not tend him
when he grows old, for I sit here in Troy very far
from my homeland, bringing misery to you and your children.
    "And yet, old man, we hear that in earlier times
you were rich—all the territory between LESBOS out to sea,   530
the seat of Makar,° and inland to PHRYGIA, and to the boundless
HELLESPONT. They say that you, old man, surpassed in wealth
and in the number of your sons all those that lived in these lands.
But from the time that the dwellers in heaven brought you
this curse, there is always fighting around your city, and the   535
killing of men. Bear up! Don't be complaining forever in your heart.
It's no use to bemoan your son, for he will never live again,
no matter what you do."

            Then the old man godlike
Priam answered him: "Please don't ask me to sit on a chair,
O Achilles, fostered by Zeus, so long as Hector lies among   540
the ships without the proper care due to the dead. But release
him quickly so that I may see him with my own eyes. Take
the abundant ransom that I have brought you. May you enjoy
these things, and may you come to the land of your fathers,
for from the first you have let me remain alive and behold   545
the light of the sun."

---

531 *Makar*: A legendary colonist of Lesbos, also called Makaria after him.

Then looking angrily from beneath his brows
Achilles the fast runner spoke: "Don't rile me, old man!
I fully intend to let you have Hector. My mother came to me
as a messenger from Zeus, she who bore me, the daughter
550 of the Old Man of the Sea. And I know full well in my heart,
O Priam, nor does it escape me, that some god has led
you to the swift ships of the Achaeans. For no mortal would
dare come to the camp, no, not even one very young. And he
would not escape the notice of the guards, nor would he easily
555 open the bolts of our gates. Therefore, do not stir more of wrath
in me, or perhaps I will *not* spare you within the huts, old man—
even though you are a suppliant—and so transgress the commands
of Zeus."

Thus Achilles spoke, and the old man
was afraid, and did what he said. Then the son of Peleus sprang
560 forth from the house like a lion, and he was not alone, for with him
followed two of his aides, the warriors Automedon and Alkimos,
whom he honored above all his companions after the dead
Patroklos. They unharnessed the horses and the mules
from the yoke, and they led in the herald, the crier of the old man,
565 and they set him on a chair. They took down from the well-polished
car the boundless ransom for Hector's head. They left two cloaks
and a finely woven shirt so that Achilles could wrap the corpse
and free him to be taken home. Then Achilles summoned
two slave girls to wash the body and anoint it, moving the corpse
570 to the side so that Priam could not see his son and in his grief
be unable to restrain his anger if he saw him, and Achilles'
own heart be then roused to anger so that he killed Priam
against the strict command of Zeus.

When the slave girls
had washed the body and anointed it with olive oil, they put
575 a beautiful cloak and a shirt around him. Achilles himself
raised Hector up and placed him on a bier. Together with
his aides, Achilles then lifted him into the polished wagon.

And then Achilles groaned and called out to his companion
by name: "Don't be angry, Patroklos, if you learn, though you are
580 in the house of Hades, that I have given up the valiant Hector
to his dear father. He brought a proper ransom, and I will
give you as many as is fitting of the things he brought."

So he spoke, and then glorious Achilles went back into his hut.
He sat on the inlaid chair on the opposite wall from which
he had arisen, and he spoke to Priam: "Your son is given back,   585
old man, just as you requested. He lies on a bier. At dawn
you will see him when you take him from here. Now let us
think of food.
       "For even Niobê with the lovely hair
thought of food. Twelve were her children who perished
in her halls, six daughters and six lusty sons. Apollo killed   590
the boys with his silver bow, for he was angry at Niobê,
and Artemis, who rejoices in arrows, killed the girls.
For Niobê had matched herself with their mother, Leto
with the lovely cheeks. Niobê said that Leto had borne
two children, but she herself had given birth to many. And so   595
Apollo and Artemis, though they were only two, killed all
of Niobê's children. For nine days they lay in their gore, and
there was no one to bury them, because the son of Kronos had turned
the people into stones. But on the tenth day the heavenly gods
buried them, and Niobê bethought herself of food, for she was   600
wasting away with her weeping.

       "Now somewhere amid
the rocks, in the lonely mountains, on Sipylos, where they say
the beds of goddesses are, the divine nymphs who dance
around the Acheloös river—there, although she is a stone,
she broods over her agonies sent by the gods.°   605
               "So come,
good old man, let us also think of food. Then you can bewail
your dear son, when you have carried him to Ilion. He will
cost you many tears."

       So Achilles spoke. Then he
sprang up and slaughtered a white sheep. His companions
flayed it and prepared it in accordance with custom.   610
They cut it up and skillfully threaded the pieces on spits.
They roasted them carefully, then drew them all off.

---

605   *of the gods*: The origins of the story must come from a rock image carved on Mount Sipylos, in LYDIA, northeast
     of SMYRNA, the water on its face likened to the tears of Niobê (a daughter of Tantalos). Such an image has been
     discovered: It is a Hittite carving of a mother goddess, probably Cybele, c. 1300 BC. The famous river Acheloös is
     in AETOLIA in southeast mainland Greece, but evidently there was another river of this name in Lydia.

Automedon took up bread and set it around the table
in beautiful baskets, while Achilles shared out the meat.
615 Then they put out their hands to take the good things set out
before them.

      When they had put aside the desire for drink
and food, then Priam the son of Dardanos wondered at Achilles—
how tall he was and of what bearing. For he was like the gods
to look on. And Achilles wondered at Priam, the son of
620 Dardanos, beholding his fine face and hearing his words.

   When they had had their fill looking at each other,
then the old man Priam, like a god, spoke first. "Let me now
to bed as soon as possible, O Zeus-nourished one, so that
we might lie down and be renewed in sweet sleep. For sleep
625 has not yet fallen upon my eyes beneath their lids from
the time that my son lost his life at your hands. Always,
I have been crying and nursing my ten thousand pains,
rolling through excrement in the closed spaces of the court.
But now I have tasted food and let flaming wine pass down
630 my throat. Before, I ate nothing."

      He spoke, and Achilles ordered
his companions and his slave girls to set up a bed in the portico
and to spread out beautiful purple blankets, and on top to place
coverlets, and to place on top of all woolen cloaks for clothing.
The girls went outside the hut holding torches in their hands,
635 and in haste they quickly spread two beds.

          Achilles, the fast runner,
now spoke mockingly° to Priam: "You sleep outside, dear
old man, in case some counselor of the Achaeans comes in.
They are always sitting down and taking counsel, as is only right.
But if someone should see you through the swift black night,
640 he might at once tell Agamemnon shepherd of the people
and then there would be delay in ransoming the corpse.
   "But come now, and tell me truly, how many days
will you need to bury valiant Hector properly? For so long
I will myself hold back from the fight and I will restrain the others."
645 The old man Priam, like a god, then answered him: "If you really
want me to accomplish the burial of valiant Hector, then you

---

636   *mockingly:* Perhaps because Achilles suspects that Priam will use sleeping outside under the portico as an
      opportunity to return to Troy, as in fact he does.

should do this, and it would please me greatly, O Achilles.
You know how we are pent-up in the city. It is far to bring wood
from the mountains, and the Trojans are very afraid. But we
would mourn his body for nine days in the halls, and on the tenth
we would bury him and the people would feast. On the eleventh day
we will make a tumulus for him. On the twelfth day we will fight
again, if we must."

        Then brave Achilles, the fast runner,
said to him: "It will be as you say, old man Priam. I will suspend
the war for as long as you say."

        So speaking he took hold
of the old man's right hand by the wrist,° so that he would not be
afraid. Then they lay down to sleep in the forecourt of the house,
the herald and Priam, with hearts of wisdom in their breasts.
But Achilles slept in the innermost part of his well-built hut,
and beside him lay Briseïs of the beautiful cheeks.

    The other gods and men, the masters of chariots,
slept all the night long, overcome by gentle sleep. But sleep
did not come over Hermes the helper as he pondered in his mind
how he would guide King Priam forth from the ships unseen
by the holy keepers of the gates.° Hermes stood over
Priam's head and spoke: "O old man, you must have
no thought of anything evil, if you still sleep in the midst
of the enemy simply because Achilles has spared you.
So you have ransomed your son, and you gave a high price.
But your remaining sons would pay three times as much
to have you back alive if Agamemnon, the son of Atreus,
should know that you are here, and all the Achaeans knew it too."

    So he spoke and then the old man was seized by fear.
He roused his herald. Hermes yoked the horses and the mules
for them, and swiftly Hermes drove them through the camp—
no one recognized them! But when they came to the ford
of the fair-flowing river, of the whirling Xanthos that deathless
Zeus had fathered, Hermes went off to high Olympos.
Saffron-robed dawn was spreading out over all the earth as they
drove the horses to the city, and the mules carried the corpse.

650

655

660

665

670

675

680

---

656 *by the wrist.* A gesture of reassurance

665 *holy keepers of the gate:* "holy" because of the seriousness of their role.

Nor did any other man or fine-belted woman recognize them,
except Kassandra, like golden Aphrodite, who had gone up to
Pergamos and saw her dear father standing in the car, and
the herald, the city-crier.°

           Seeing Hector lying in the bier drawn by
685 mules, she cried out shrilly and called throughout the entire city:
"Trojan men and women, come and see Hector, if you ever rejoiced
when he returned alive from the battle, a great joy to the city
and to all the people!"

          So she spoke, and no man or woman
stayed in the city. An unbearable sorrow came over all, and they
690 gathered around Priam at the gates as he brought in the corpse.
First of all Hector's dear wife and his revered mother threw
themselves on the light-running wagon and tore their hair,
holding Hector's head, while the throng stood around and wept.
And they would have spent all day until the sun went down
695 weeping and wailing for Hector in front of the gate, if the old
man had not stood up in the car and spoken to the people:
"Make a way for the mules to pass through! Later you can have
your fill of lament, when I have brought him to the house."
So he spoke, and they stood aside and allowed the wagon
700 to come through. When they came to his famous house, they placed
Hector on a corded bed, and beside them they set singers, leaders
of the lament, who began the song of mourning. They chanted it,
and the women made lament.

          Among them white-armed Andromachê
led the dirge for Hector, the killer of men, holding his head
705 in her hands: "O my husband, you have perished at a young age,
and left me a widow in our halls. Our child is still an infant,
whom we bore, you and I, doomed to a wretched fate. But I don't think
he will arrive at manhood—before that this city shall be utterly
destroyed. For you who watched over the city have perished—
710 you, who guarded it and kept safe its noble wives and little
children. Soon they will be carried away in the hollow ships,
and I among them. You, my child, will follow along with me
to a place where you will perform degrading tasks, working

---

684   ... *the city-crier*: Pergamos is the highest point of the city. Kassandra is mentioned only once before, in
      Book 13, where one Othryoneus is said to want to marry her, the most beautiful of Priam's daughters.
      Homer says nothing specific about Kassandra's prophetic powers, an important part of the later tradition,
      although her role as the crier of sad news may imply such powers.

for some ungentle master—or one of the Achaeans in his anger
will take you by the arm and throw you from the walls   715
to a savage death—someone whose brother Hector killed,
or his father, or his son.° For full many of the Achaeans have bitten
the vast earth with their teeth at the hands of Hector. Your father
was not gentle in the bitter war. And so the people wail for him
throughout the city, and you have made grief and unspeakable   720
sorrow for your parents, Hector. Savage pain is left for me
above all. You did not reach out your hands as you lay dying
on a bed, nor did you say to me some words full of meaning
that I might remember while weeping for you day and night."

   So she spoke, wailing, and the other women wailed too.   725
Among them Hekabê began her sobbing complaint: "Hector,
much the dearest to my heart of all my children ... while
you were alive you were dear to the gods. And they still
care for you, although you are snared in the fate of death.
Achilles, the fast runner, sold others of my sons whom   730
he captured beyond the untiring sea, to Samothrace and Imbros
and misty Lemnos. When he took your breath-soul with
his long-edged bronze, he used often to drag you around the tomb
of his companion Patroklos, whom you killed. But he could not
raise him up. Now you are as fresh as new-morning dew and lie   735
out in my halls like one freshly killed—like one whom Apollo
of the silver bow has come upon and killed with his gentle arrows."

   So she spoke, weeping, and she roused endless wailing.
Then Helen, third among the women, began her lament:
"Hector, much the dearest to my heart of all my brothers-in-law,   740
for my husband is godlike Alexandros who brought me to Troy—
would that I had perished before! It is already the twentieth
year since I went forth from there and abandoned the land
of my fathers. But I never heard an evil or unkind word
from you. And if some other of my brothers-in-law, or sisters-in-law,   745
or brother's wives with elegant dresses would reprove me
in my halls, or your mother—but your father was always
as gentle as if he had been my own father—you would restrain
them with your speech, and hold them back through your good
nature and your gentle words. And so I lament you, and I lament   750
my luckless self, with grief in my heart. For no longer

---

717   ... his son: According to later tradition, Andromachê becomes the captive and concubine of Neoptolemos,
      the son of Achilles. Astyanax, the son of Hector and Andromachê, is thrown from the towers.

is there anyone in Troy so gentle to me and such a friend.
Everyone abhors me!"

So she spoke, weeping, and the huge
throng moaned. And now old man Priam spoke to the people:
755 "Bring wood to the city, my Trojans. Have no fear of a cunning
ambush. When Achilles sent me off from the black ships,
he promised he would do us no harm until the twelfth day
has come."

So he spoke, and they yoked oxen and mules
to wagons, and quickly they gathered in front of the city.
760 For nine days they gathered a boundless supply of wood.
But when the tenth Dawn, who sends light for mortals, arose,
they carried out the brave Hector, pouring down tears.
They placed him on top of the pyre, and they cast in fire.
As soon as Dawn with her fingers of rose appeared, the people
765 gathered around the pyre of glorious Hector. When they
were gathered and assembled in a group, they first extinguished
the fire with flaming wine—all of it, as deep as the vast strength
of the fire had penetrated. Thereafter his brothers and companions
gathered the white bones in sorrow. Hot tears ran down their
770 cheeks. They took the bones and placed them in a golden chest,
covering them with delicate purple cloths. Then they placed
the chest in a hollow grave, and over the grave stacked great
thick stones. Quickly they built up a barrow, and all around it
they placed watchmen, in case the Achaeans with their fancy
775 shinguards should set on them before the end of the truce.
After they heaped up the barrow, they went back to the city.
Gathered together, they dined on a splendid meal
in the house of Zeus-nourished Priam, the king. In this way
they held the funeral for Hector tamer of horses.

Bibliography

EDITIONS (TEXTS IN HOMERIC GREEK)

Demetrius Chalcondyles, *editio princeps*, Florence, 1488

W. Leaf, *Iliad* (London, 1886–1888; 2d ed. 1900–1902)

D. B. Monro and T. W. Allen, *Homeri Opera* (5 volumes, 2d ed., Oxford, 1912)

H. van Thiel, *Homeri Ilias* (Hildesheim, 1996)

M. L. West, *Homeri Ilias*, 2 volumes (Munich/Leipzig, 1998–2000)

SELECTED ENGLISH TRANSLATIONS

Lang, W. Leaf, E. Myers, *The Iliad* (London, 1883)

S. Butler, *The Iliad* (London, 1898)

A. T. Murray, *Homer: Iliad*, 2 volumes (London, 1924); revised by William F. Wyatt (Cambridge, MA, 1999)

R. Lattimore, *The Iliad* (Chicago, 1951)

R. Fitzgerald, *The Iliad* (New York, 1974)

R. Fagles, *The Iliad* (New York, 1990)

S. Lombardo, *Iliad* (Indianapolis, 1997)

GENERAL WORKS ON HOMER

F. A. Wolf, *Prolegomena ad Homerum* (Halle, 1795; English translation, Princeton, NJ, 1985)

A. J. B. Wace and F. H. Stubbings, *A Companion to Homer* (London, 1962)

G. S. Kirk, *The Songs of Homer* (Cambridge, UK, 1962)

A. Heubeck, *Die homerische Frage* (Darmstadt, 1974)

I. Morris and B. B. Powell, *A New Companion to Homer* (Leiden, 1997)

J. Latacz, *Troy and Homer: Towards a Solution of an Old Mystery* (Oxford, 2004)

R. Fowler (ed.), *The Cambridge Companion to Homer* (Cambridge, UK, 2004).

B. B. Powell, *Homer* (2d ed., Malden/Oxford, 2007)

M. Finkelberg, *The Homer Encyclopedia* (Malden/Oxford, 2011)

INFLUENTIAL READINGS AND INTERPRETATIONS

U. von Wilamowitz-Möllendorff, *Die Ilias und Homer* (Berlin, 1916)

E. Auerbach, *Mimesis: The Representation of Reality in Western Literature* (Princeton, NJ, 1953; orig. publ. in German, Bern, 1946), Chapter 1

J. T. Kakridis, *Homeric Researches* (London, 1949)

J. Griffin, *Homer on Life and Death* (Oxford, 1980)

S. Schein, *The Mortal Hero: An Introduction to Homer's* Iliad (Berkeley, 1984)

M. W. Edwards, *Homer, Poet of the Iliad* (Baltimore, 1987)

COMMENTARIES

G. S. Kirk (gen. ed.), *The Iliad: A Commentary* (6 vols., Cambridge, 1985–1993)

J. Latacz (gen. ed.), *Homers Ilias. Gesamtkommentar. Auf der Grundlage der Ausgabe von Ameis-Hentze-Cauer* (1868–1913) (6 volumes published so far of an estimated 15, Munich/Leipzig, 2002–)

TEXT AND TRANSMISSION

T. W. Allen, *Homer: The Origins and Transmission* (Oxford, 1924)

J. A. Davison, "The Transmission of the Text," in A. J. B. Wace and F. H. Stubbings, *A Companion to Homer* (London, 1962), pp.215–233

M. L. West, *Studies in the Text and Transmission of the Iliad* (Munich, 2001)

HOMER AND ORAL TRADITION

A. B. Lord, *The Singer of Tales* (1960; 2d edition, Cambridge, MA, 2000)

M. Parry (intro. by A. Parry), *The Making of Homeric Verse* (Oxford, 1971)

G. S. Kirk, *Homer and the Oral Tradition* (Cambridge, UK, 1976)

E. Bakker, *Poetry in Speech: Orality and Homeric Discourse* (Ithaca, NY, 1997)

J. M. Foley, *Homer's Traditional Art* (University Park, PA, 1999)

B. B. Powell, *Writing and the Origins of Greek Literature* (Cambridge, UK, 2003)

DATING THE HOMERIC POEMS

R. Janko, *Homer, Hesiod and the Hymns* (Cambridge, UK, 1982)

B. B. Powell, *Homer and the Origin of the Greek Alphabet* (Cambridge, UK, 1991)

HOMER AND THE NEAR EAST

M. L. West, *The East Face of Helicon* (Oxford, 1997)

B. Louden, *The Iliad: Structure, Myth, and Meaning* (Baltimore, 2006)

Credits

23   Ancient Art and Architecture
        Collection Ltd.

24   Photograph courtesy of Barry B. Powell

25   Photograph courtesy of Barry B. Powell

1.1   Museo Archeologico Nazionale, Naples,
        Italy; from Pompeii, House of Apollo;
        Scala / Art Resource, NY

1.2   Museo Archeologico Nazionale, Naples,
        Italy; from Pompeii, House of the
        Tragic Poet; Samuel Magal © Sites &
        Photos / Alamy

2.1   Bibliotheque Nationale, Paris; Erich
        Lessing / Art Resource, NY

2.2   National Maritime Museum, Haifa, Israel;
        Erich Lessing / Art Resource, NY

2.3   British Museum; Zev Radovan © www.
        BibleLandPictures.com/Alamy

3.1   Museo Archeologico Nazionale,
        Tarquinia, Italy; Scala / Art Resource,
        NY

3.2   Musée du Louvre, Paris, France;
        Réunion des Musées Nationaux /
        Art Resource, NY

4.1   National Archaeological Museum, Athens;
        Vanni / Art Resource, NY

4.2   British Museum, London; Erich Lessing /
        Art Resource, NY

5.1   Museo Archeologico, Naples, Italy; Scala /
        Art Resource, NY

5.2   Museo Archeologico, Florence; Scala / Art
        Resource, NY

5.3   Museo Archeologico Nazionale, Naples;
        Scala / Art Resource, NY

6.1   National Archaeological Museum, Athens
        2179

6.2   Museo Nazionale Archeologico, Palazzo
        Jatta in Ruvo di Puglia (Bari)

7.1   Musée du Louvre, Paris; © RMN-Grand
        Palais / Art Resource, NY

8.1   Musée du Louvre, Paris; Bridgeman Art
        Library, London / SuperStock

8.2   Kunsthistorisches Museum, Vienna, Austria;
        Erich Lessing / Art Resource, NY

9.1   Staatliche Antikensammlungen , Munidh
        8770

9.2   Musée du Louvre; © RMN-Grand Palais /
        Art Resource, NY

10.1   Archaeological Museum, Nauplia, Greece;
        Gianni Dagli Orti / The Art Archive
        at Art Resource, NY

10.2   © The Trustees of the British Museum

10.3   Museo Nazionale Archaeologico, Naples

11.1   © The Trustees of the British Museum

11.2   The Art Gallery Collection / Alamy

11.3   Museo Archeologico Nazionale, Naples,
        Italy; Scala / Art Resource, NY

12.1   Kunsthistorisches Museum, Vienna, Austria;
        Erich Lessing / Art Resource, NY

12.2   Kunsthistorisches Museum, Vienna, Austria;
        Erich Lessing / Art Resource, NY

13.1   Bardo Museum, Tunis; World History
        Archive / Alamy

13.2   Norbert Schimmel Collection, New York

14.1   Museo Archeologico, Palermo, Sicily;
        Scala / Art Resource, NY

14.2   Vatican Museums 125, Rome

15.1   Staatliche Antikensammlungen, Munich
        2307

15.2   Staatliche Antikensammlungen, Munich
        3171

16.1   Antikensammlung, Staatliche Museen,
        Berlin F2278

16.2   Museo Nazionale di Villa Giulia, Rome;
        Scala/Ministero per i Beni e le Attività
        culturali / Art Resource, NY

16.3   © The Trustees of the British Museum

17.1   © The Trustees of the British Museum

Pronunciation Glossary/Index

I have included names that appear in the text together with a pronunciation guide, except for names where the pronunciation is obvious. I give the meaning of the names, where this is clear; many of the names in Homer are "speaking names," that is, they reveal the role of the character in the narrative and, in many cases, appear to be made up for the occasion. The meaning of many other names is opaque or unknown. I give the number of the Book in which the name appears, together with the page numbers, or *passim* for common names such as "Achilles" or "Agamemnon."

A

Abantes (a-**ban**-tēz), Homer's name for the Euboeans (*Il.* 2, 4) 77, 78, 123

Abioi (**a**-bi-oi), "devoid of violence," a nomadic Scythian tribe (*Il.* 13) 302

Achaeans (a-**kē**-ans), a division of the Greek people, Homer's word for the Greeks at Troy (*Il.* 1–24) *passim*

Acheloös (ak-e-**lō**-us), a river in Sipylos south of Troy (*Il.* 21, 24) 483, 563

Achilles, the greatest warrior at Troy (*Il.* 1–24) *passim*

Admetos (ad-**mē**-tos), "invincible," king of Pherai in Thessaly, son of Pheres, husband of Alkestis, father of Eumelos, who led the contingent from Pherai (*Il.* 2, 24) 84, 524, 527, 532

Adrasteia (a-dras-**tē**-a), the easternmost city of the Troad, which overlooked the southwestern shore of the Propontis (*Il.* 2) 89

Adrastos, (1) leader of the Seven Against Thebes, father-in-law of Tydeus, ruler of Sikyon (*Il.* 2) 78, 333; (2) a Trojan killed by Diomedes (*Il.* 2, 11) 89, 268; (3) a Trojan defeated by Menelaos, killed by Agamemnon, (*Il.* 6) 159; (4) a Trojan killed by Patroklos (*Il.* 16) 392

Aegina (e-**jī**-na), island in the Saronic Gulf in the Aegean Sea, belonging to the domain of Diomedes (*Il.* 2) 78, 89

Aeneas (ē-**nē**-as), son of Aphrodite and Anchises, greatest Trojan fighter after Hector, descended from Tros, ancestor of the Roman people (*Il.* 1, 2 ,5 , 6, 8, 9, 11–15, 17, 18, 21, 24) *passim*

Aeneid (ē-**nē**-id), poem by Vergil on founding of Rome, late first century BC, 20, 137, 318, 471

Aeschylus (**ē**-ski-lus, **es**-ki-lus) (525–456 BC), Athenian playwright, 21, 39

Aethiopians, "burnt-faced," a people who dwell in a never-never land in the extreme south, where Poseidon and Zeus sometimes visit (*Il.* 1) 55

Aetolia (e-**tō**-li-a), district north of the Corinthian Gulf, where were the cites of Pleuron and Kalydon (*Il.* 2, 4, 5, 9, 20, 24, 25) 76, 82, 121, 126, 150, 155, 228, 230, 231, 453, 529, 535, 563

Aetolians, from southwest mainland Greece, came in forty ships under Thoas (*Il.* 2, 5, 9, 23) 82, 155, 228, 230, 231, 535

Agamedê (a-ga-**mē**-dē), "very intelligent," oldest daughter of Augeias, wife of one Moulios killed by the young Nestor in the war between the Epeians and the Pylians (*Il.* 11) 281

Agamemnon (a-ga-**mem**-non), son of Atreus, brother of Menelaos, leader of Greek forces at Troy (*Il.* 1–14, 17–20, 24) *passim*

Agapenor (a-ga-**pē**-nor), "loving manliness," leader of the Arcadians (*Il.* 2, 24) 80, 535

Agelaos (a-ge-**lā**-os), (1) Trojan killed by Diomedes (*Il.* 8) 202; (2) Achaean killed by Hector (*Il.* 11) 267

Agenor (a-**jē**-nor), Trojan leader, son of Theano and Antenor, he makes first kill on the Trojan side (*Il.* 4, 11, 12, 13) 123, 211, 259, 288

Agrios (**ag**-ri-os), brother Melos and Oineus, hence uncle of Tydeus and Meleager, great uncle of Diomedes (*Il.* 14) 333

Aiakos (ē-a-kos), son of Zeus, father of Peleus, king of Aegina, judge in the underworld (*Il.* 21) 483

Aigai (ē-jē), where Poseidon had his palace, probably in Achaea in the northwestern Peloponnesus (*Il.* 1, 8, 13) 54, 199, 302

Aegeus (ē-jūs), father of Theseus, a king of Athens (*Il.* 1) 49

Aigialos (ē-**jē**-a-los), "seashore," (1) the northern coast of the Peloponnesus between Sicyon and Elis, part of Agamemnon's realm, the same as the later Achaea (*Il.* 2) 79; (2) a city of the Paphlagonians on the Black Sea (*Il.* 2) 80

Aisepos (ē-se-pos), (1) a Trojan, bastard son of Priam, killed with his twin brother Pedasos (*Il.* 6) 158; (2) a river in the Troad (*Il.* 2, 4, 12) 89, 110, 286

Aisyetes (**ēs**-ye-tēz), (1) Trojan hero whose tomb was a landmark on the Trojan plain (*Il.* 2) 88; (2) Trojan, father of Alkathoös (*Il.* 13) 317

Aithikes (ē-thi-kes), a Thessalian tribe (*Il.* 2) 85

Aithon (ē-thon), one of Hector's horses (*Il.* 8) 198

Aithra (ē–thra), daughter of Pittheus, king of Troezen, handmaiden to Helen, mother of Theseus, who had sex with Poseidon and her husband on the same night; she became Helen's slave when Helen was abducted from Athens by the Dioskouroi (*Il.* 3) 96

Ajax, (1) son of Telamon, "Big Ajax," half-brother to Teucer, ruler of Salamis; (2) son of Oïleus, "Little Ajax," ruler of the Locrians (*Il.* 1–18, 20, 23) *passim*

Akamas (**a**-ka-mas), (1) Trojan, son of Agenor, leader of the Dardanians with Aeneas (*Il.* 2, 11, 12, 14, 16) 89, 259, 288, 346, 382; (2) leader of the Thracian allies from across the Hellespont (*Il.* 2, 5, 6) 90, 142, 158

Akrisios (a-**kris**-i-us), father of Danaë, killed accidentally by Perseus (*Il.* 14) 380

Aktorionê (ak-tor-i-**ō**-nē), (1) a dual form, the "twin sons of Aktor," also called the Molionê, really the sons of Poseidon (*Il.* 11, 23) 280, 536; (2) their sons, leaders of the Epeians (*Il.* 2) 80

Alalkomenian, an obscure epithet of Athena, perhaps meaning "defender" (*Il.* 4, 6) 108, 157

Alastor, (1) a Trojan, father of Tros (*Il.* 20) 476; (2) a Lycian killed by Odysseus (*Il.* 5) 149; (3) a Pylian, one of Nestor's men (*Il.* 4, 8, 13) 117, 204, 317

Alexander the Great (356–323 BC) 1, 6, 21, 38

Alexandria, city in Egypt founded by Alexander the Great 6–8, 18, 10, 18

Alexandrian scholars, 8

Alexandros, "fighter-off of men," another name for Paris (which see); the son of Priam who brought Helen to Troy, named 44 times as Alexandros, 11 times as Paris (*Il.* 3–8, 11, 13, 22, 24) *passim*

Alkathoös, a prominent Trojan, son of Aisyetes, killed by Idomeneus 39; (*Il.* 12, 13) 288, 317, 318

Alkestis (al-**kes**-tis), "most beautiful of the daughters of Pelias," wife of Admetos, mother of Eumelos (a leader of the Thessalian contingent) (*Il.* 2) 84

Alkmaon (alk-**mā**-on), an Achaean, son of Thestor, killed by Sarpedon (*Il.*12) 297, 299

Alkmenê (alk-**mēn**-ē), daughter of Elektryon, wife of Amphitryon, mother of Herakles (*Il.* 14, 19) 340–341, 449–450

Alpheios, the largest river in the Peloponnesus and the god of this river (*Il.* 11) 281

Altes (**al**-tēz), king of the Leleges, lived in Pedasos near Mount Ida (*Il.* 21, 22) 480, 499

Althaia (al-**thē**-a), daughter of Thestios, wife of king Oineus of Kalydon, mother of Meleager (*Il.* 9) 230

Alybê (**al**-i-bē), a place that is the origin of the Halizones (*Il.* 2) 90

Amazons, a race of warrior women, descendants of Ares (*Il.* 3, 6, 20) 99, 164, 466

Amphidamas (am-fi-**dā**-mas), (1) from Cythera, one of the previous owners of the boar's tusk helmet loaned to Odysseus for his night raid (*Il.* 10) 243; (2) father of the playmate killed by Patroklos (*Il.* 23) 517

Amphimachos (am-**fim**-a-kos), (1) one of the four leaders of the Epeians (*Il.* 2, 11, 13) 90, 280, 309, 310, 325; (2) a leader of Trojan allies, the Carians (*Il.* 2) 91

Amphion (am-**fī**-on), a leader of the Epeians (*Il.* 13) 325

Amphitryon (am-**fit**-ri-on), descendant of Perseus, husband of Alkmenê (*Il.* 5) 140

Amyklai (a-**mē**-klē), a town south of Sparta, included within the realm of Menelaos (*Il.* 2) 79

Analysis, an approach to Homer that wishes to divide his texts into constituent parts that once had an independent existence, 3, 9

Analyst, a scholar who wishes to identify the small parts of which Homer's poems are made, a follower of F. A. Wolf, 9, 10, 13

Anatolia, "sunrise," the westernmost protrusion of Asia, modern Turkey, synonymous with Asia Minor, 20 (*Il.* 5, 6, 13) 143, 165, 302, 316

Anchialos, "close-to-the-sea," an Achaean killed by Hector (*Il.* 5) 146

Anchises (an-**kī**-sēz), (1) prince of Troy, lover of Aphrodite, father of Aeneas, 34; (*Il.* 2, 5, 12, 13, 17, 20, 23) 89, 134–136, 142, 288, 317, 318, 410, 415, 424, 465–468, 524; (2) an Achaean from Sicyon, father of Echepolos (*Il.* 23) 524

Andromachê (an-**drom**-a-kē), wife of Hector, mother of Astyanax, taken captive by Neoptolemos at end of the Trojan War (*Il.* 6, 8, 17, 21–24) 27, 32, 158, 171–175, 198, 407, 418, 479, 511–513, 541, 566, 567

Ankaios (an-**kē**-os) (1) an Arcadian hero in the generation before the Trojan War, father of Agapenor (*Il.* 2) 80; (2) an Aetolian from Pleuron beaten by Nestor in the funeral games of Amarynkeus (*Il.* 23) 535

Anteia (an-**tē**-a), daughter of king of Lycia, wife of Proitos, fell in love with Bellerophon (*Il.* 6) 163–164

Antenor (an-**tē**-nor), a Trojan elder (*Il.* 2–7, 11–12, 14–16, 19–21) *passim*

Anthedon (an-**thē**-don), a harbor town in Boeotia (*Il.* 2) 76

Antilochos (an-**til**-o-kos), son of Nestor of Pylos (*Il.* 4, 13, 16, 18, 23) 117, 122, 145, 146, 159, 214, 305, 316–319, 321, 324, 365, 366, 381, 412, 417, 421, 425, 426, 453, 524, 526, 527–529, 532, 533, 524, 539, 540

Antron, a coastal town in Thessaly, in the kingdom of Protesilaos (*Il.* 2) 83

Anu (**a**-nū), Mesopotamian sky god, 139

aoidos (a-**oi**-dos, pl. *aoidoi*), Greek word for such oral poets as Homer and Hesiod (contrast with "rhapsode") 11, 33, 36, 218, 493

Apaisos, a town in the Troad overlooking the Hellespont (*Il.* 2) 89

Aphareus (a-far-ūs), an Achaean, one of the seven men appointed by Nestor to the night watch (*Il.* 9, 13) 214, 319, 321

Aphrodite, Greek goddess of sexual attraction, related to Inanna/Astartê/Ishtar, equated with Roman Venus (*Il.* 2–6, 9, 11, 13–14, 16, 18–24) *passim*

Apisaon (a-pi-**sā**-on), a Trojan killed by Eurypylos (*Il.* 11, 17) 276, 411

Apollo, the second god to appear in the *Iliad* after Zeus, defender of Troy, son of Zeus and Leto, brother of Artemis, an archer god whose arrows are those of disease, protector and punisher of archers, connected with prophecy and perhaps healing (*Il.* 1–2, 4–24) *passim*

Apsu, Mesopotamian god of the primordial waters, 37, 336

Arcadia (ar-**kād**-i-a), mountainous region in the central Peloponnesus (*Il.* 2, 5, 7, 15, 23) 79, 80, 145, 181, 364, 535

Archelochos, a Trojan, leader of the Dardanian contingent, killed by Big Ajax (*Il.* 2, 12, 14) 89, 288, 346

Areïthoös (ar-e-**ith**-o-os), "swift in battle," the "mace-man," a warrior of Nestor's youth (*Il.* 7, 11) 177, 181, 476

Ares (**ār**-ēz), Greek god of war, 34; (*Il.* 1–24) *passim*

Argeïphontes (ar-jē-i-**fon**-tēz), "Argos-killer," epithet of Hermes (*Il.* 2) 65

Argissa, a town in northeastern Thessaly, part of the Lapith contingent (*Il.* 2) 85

Argives, one of Homer's names for the Greeks used indifferently with Achaeans and Danaäns, *passim*

Argos, city in the Argive plain in the northeastern Peloponnesus (*Il.* 1–4, 6–9, 12–17, 19, 21, 23–24) *passim*

Ariadnê (ar-i-**ad**-nē), "very holy one," Cretan princess, daughter of Minos and Pasiphaë who helped Theseus defeat the Minotaur (*Il.* 6, 18) 162, 445

Arisbê, a town on the Hellespont on the bands of the Selleïs River (*Il.* 2, 6, 12, 21) 90, 158, 288, 479

aristeia, "moment of greatness," when a warrior kills many in splendid display, 34, 263, 266, 267, 291, 310, 311, 335, 343, 417, 453

Aristophanes of Byzantium (c. 257–180 BC), Homeric scholar in Alexandria, 6

Aristotle (384–322 BC), Greek philosopher, 7, 21, 31

Arkesilaos, one of the five commanders of the Boeotians, killed by Hector at the battle of the ships (*Il.* 2, 15) 76, 357, 358

Arnê, a town in Boeotia (*Il.* 2, 5, 7) 76, 128, 177

Artemis, virgin daughter of Zeus and Leto, sister of Apollo, goddess of hunting and dancing, 33, 35; (*Il.* 3, 5–6, 9, 14, 16, 18–21, 24) 104, 128, 142, 166, 174, 228, 341, 377, 440, 448, 463, 464, 492–494, 563

Asinê (a-**sē**-nē), a town on the Argive plain controlled by Diomedes (*Il.* 2) 78

Asios, (1) a Trojan, brother of Hekabê, from Phrygia (*Il.* 16) 394; (2) a Trojan, leader of allies from Arisbê on the Hellespont (*Il.* 12, 13) 288–290, 316–319, 321, 324, 327, 328

Askalaphos (as-kal-**ā**-fos), "owl," a son of Ares and one of the leaders of the Orchomenos contingent, killed by Deïphobos (*Il.* 2, 9, 13, 15, 16) 77, 214, 319, 320, 350, 385

Askania, a region in northwest Asia Minor fielding a contingent of Phrygians (*Il.* 2, 13) 91, 328

Asklepios, father of the physicians Machaon and Podaleirios, in Homer not a god (*Il.* 2, 4, 11, 13, 14) 85, 115, 273, 274, 277, 313, 330

Asopos (ā-**sō**-pos), the largest river in Boeotia (*Il.* 4, 10) 120, 243

Aspledon (as-**plē**-don), a town in northeastern Boeotia, under the control of Orchomenos (*Il.* 2) 77

Asteropaios, the ambidextrous leader of the Paeonians, killed by Achilles (*Il.* 12, 17, 21, 23) 288, 407, 411, 482, 483, 533, 541

Astyanax (as-**tī**-a-naks), "king of the city, "son of Hector and Andromachê, known as Skamandrios to his parents (*Il.* 6, 22, 24) 172, 173, 513, 514, 567

Astyochê (as-**tī**-o-kë), "city-holder," daughter of the king of Orchomenos, mother by Ares to Askalaphos and Ialmenos, leaders of the Orchomenos contingent (*Il.* 2, 15) 39, 77

Astyocheia (as-tī-o-**kē**-a), mother by Herakles of Tlepolemos (*Il.* 2) 82

atê (**a**-tä), "madness, delusion, blindness," which clouds the minds of gods and men 200, 212, 215, 227, 449

Atreus (**ā**-trūs), king of Mycenae, son of Pelops, brother of Thyestes, father of Agamemnon and Menelaus (*Il.* 1–11, 13–14, 16–17, 19, 22–24) *passim*

Atymnios, a Trojan ally killed by Antilochos (*Il.* 5, 16) 145, 381

Augeiai (ow-**jē**-ē), two different towns, one in Locris, one in Lacedaemon (*Il.* 2) 79

Augeias (ow-**jē**-as), king of the Epeians in the days of Nestor's father Neleus (Homer does not mention the famous episode where Herakles cleaned his stables) (*Il.* 11, 23) 280, 281, 535

Aulis (**ow**-lis), port in Boeotia from which the Trojan expedition set sail 4, 24; (*Il.* 2, 9) 70, 76–77, 216

Autolykos (ow-**tol**-i-kos), "true wolf," rogue and thief, son of Hermes, father of Antikleia, grandfather of Odysseus (*Il.* 10) 243

Automedon (ow-**tom**-i-don), "self-ruler," the charioteer of Patroklos and Achilles (*Il.* 9, 16, 17, 19, 23, 24) 218–219, 376, 378, 380, 386, 392, 399, 413–417, 458, 459, 533, 558, 562, 564

Axios, a river in Paeonia and the god of that river (*Il.* 2, 16, 21, 23) 90, 380, 482, 533

B

Baal (**bā**-al), "lord," a Levantine storm god, 14

Bellerophon (bel-**ler**-o-fon), Corinthian hero, grandson of Sisyphos, tamed Pegasos and killed the Chimaira 8; (*Il.* 6, 7, 13, 16) 163–166, 182, 313, 381

Bias (**bi**-as), (1) one of the five commanders from Pylos (*Il.* 4) 117; (2) an Athenian warrior (*Il.* 13) 325, 326

Boagrios (bo-**ag**-ri-os), a stream in Locris (*Il.* 2) 77

Boeotia (bē-**ō**-sha), "cow-land," region north of Attica where Thebes was situated (*Il.* 2, 5, 7, 9, 12–19) *passim*

Boibê (**bē**-be), a city in Thessaly (*Il.* 2) 84

Boros, (1) a Maeonian, father of Phaistos, whom Idomeneus kills (*Il.* 5) 128; (2) a Myrmidon, who gave a lot of money to Peleus to marry his daughter Polydora (*Il.* 16) 377

Boudeion, a city over which Epeigeus, Patroklos' friend, ruled (*Il.* 16) 389

Bouprasion, a city in Elis where Amarynkeus was buried (*Il.* 2) 80

Briareos (bri-**ar**-e-os), one of the Hecatonchires, the "Hundredhanders," who came to Zeus's aid when other gods wished to bind him (*Il.* 1) 54

Briseïs (brī-**sē**-is), Achilles' war-captive, taken by Agamemnon, 27, 29; (*Il.* 1, 2, 19) 45, 46, 51, 52, 54, 67, 83, 173, 215, 457, 458, 459

Bronze Age, c. 3000–1200 BC, 20, 21, 23, 25, 27, 77, 140, 169, 224, 257, 442

Byzantium, Greek colony at the entrance to the Bosporus (= later Constantinople), 6, 17

C

caduceus (ka-**dū**-se-us), a wand with two intertwined snakes, carried by Hermes (*Il.* 16) 393

Carians, Trojan allies from south of the Troad (*Il.* 2, 10) 91, 250

Centaurs (**sen**-towrs), half-human, half-horse creatures (*Il.* 1, 2, 4, 11, 14, 16, 19) 49, 85, 86, 115, 164, 285, 289, 313, 341

Chalcis, "bronze," "copper," 4 (1) the principal settlement (with Eretria) on the island of Euboea
(*Il.* 2) 77; (2) a coastal settlement in Aetolia (*Il.* 2) 77

Charis, "charm," personification of that quality, the wife of Hephaistos (*Il.* 5, 18) 138, 436

Charites (**kar**-i-tes), the Graces, imparters of feminine charm (*Il.* 5, 14) 138, 338

Charops, (1) a Trojan killed by Odysseus (*Il.* 11) 271; (2) an Achaean, leader of the troops
from Symê (*Il.* 2) 83

Cheiron (**kī**-ron), "hand," the wise Centaur, "the most just of the Centaurs" (*Il.* 4, 9, 11, 16, 19) 115,
226, 284, 285, 376, 458

Chimaira (ki-**mēr**-a), "she-goat," offspring of Typhoeus and Echidna, with a lion's body, snake's tail,
and goat's head protruding from the back, killed by Bellerophon (*Il.* 6, 16) 164, 165, 381

Chios (**kē**-os), Greek island near Asia Minor, often claimed as Homer's birthplace, 3 (*Il.* 2, 7, 8, 13,
15, 16) 83, 183, 184, 204, 310, 317, 325, 357, 358, 384

Chryseïs (krī-**sē**-is), daughter of Chryses, given as booty to Agamemnon (*Il.* 1, 6, 9, 16, 23) 27, 45,
46, 50, 53–55, 173, 218, 376, 541

Chryses (**krī**-sēz), father of Chryseïs, a priest of Apollo whom Agamemnon insulted, 27, 28, 33;
(*Il.* 1) 41–42, 44–45, 53, 55

Chrysothemis (kri-**so**-the-mis), a daughter of Agamemnon and Klytaimnestra (*Il.* 9) 216, 222

Cilicia (si-**lish**-a), region in southeastern Asia Minor (*Il.* 6) 173

Cilicians, the people of Eëtion, the father of Andromachê, who ruled in Thebes under Plakos in the
Troad (*Il.* 6) 173

Corinth (**kor**-inth), city on isthmus between central Greece and the Peloponnesus (*Il.* 2, 6, 9, 13, 14,
15, 23) 76, 78, 163, 225, 313, 324, 341, 344, 364, 535

Crete, largest island in the Aegean 4, 9, 19–21, 37; (*Il.* 2, 3, 9, 10, 13, 14, 16, 17) 76, 82, 100, 101, 212,
243, 318, 325, 341, 390, 419

Cumae (**kū**-mē), site of earliest Greek colony in Italy, north of the bay of Naples, 4

Cyclades (**sik**-la-dēz), "circle islands," around Delos in the Aegean Sea (*Il.* 2) 66, 76, 83

Cyprus, large island in eastern Mediterranean, home of Aphrodite (*Il.* 5, 11) 138, 256

Cythera (**sith**-e-ra), island south of the Peloponnesus, sometimes said to be the
birthplace of Aphrodite (*Il.* 10, 14, 15) 243, 341, 360

D

dactylic hexameter, the meter of Homer, six feet per line 2, 15, 38, 278

Daidalos (**dēd**-a-los), Athenian craftsman who built a dancing place for Ariadnê (*Il.* 18) 443, 445

Danaäns (**dān**-a-anz), descendants of Danaös, one of Homer's name for the Greeks along with
Argives and Achaeans (*Il.* 1–24) *passim*

Danaë (**dān**-a-ē), daughter of Akrisios, mother of Perseus, whom Zeus possessed (*Il.* 14) 340

Dardanelles (= Hellespont), straits between the Aegean Sea and the Propontis (= Sea of Marmora),
4 (*Il.* 6, 11) 158, 264

Dardanians, the inhabitants of Dardania, near Troy (*Il.* 2, 3, 7, 8, 11, 13, 15, 17, 18) 89, 107, 188–190,
197, 198, 210, 266, 308, 360, 363, 406, 429

Dardanos (**dar**-da-nos), (1) early king of Troy, son of Zeus, father of Erichthonios, grandfather
of Tros, after whom the Trojans were called Dardanians (*Il.* 2, 3, 5, 10, 11, 13, 20, 24) 89, 102, 132,
249, 262, 269, 315, 468, 471, 550, 555, 564; (2) a Trojan killed by Achilles (*Il.* 20), 476

Dares the Phrygian (AD fifth century?), alleged author of a book about the Trojan War
127, 128, 132

Dark Ages of Greece, c. 1150–800 BC, 21

Deïopites (de-i-o-pi-tēz), a Trojan killed by Odysseus at the Battle over the Wall (*Il.* 11) 271

Deïphobos (dē-**if**-o-bos), brother of Hector and Paris (who took up with Helen after Paris' death) (*Il.* 12, 13, 22, 24) 26, 288, 308, 312, 316–320, 322, 327, 328, 504, 506, 552

Deïpyros (de-**ip**-i-ros), an Achaean, a leader of the night watch, killed by Helenos (*Il.* 9, 13) 214, 305, 319, 322

Delos (**dē**-los), "clear," tiny island in the center of the Cyclades, where Apollo and Artemis were born (*Il.* 14) 4, 341

Delphi (**del**-fï), sanctuary of Apollo at foot of Mount Parnassus (*Il.* 2, 6, 9, 17) 77, 174, 225, 410

Demeter (de-**mēt**-er), daughter of Kronos and Rhea, mother of Persephonê (*Il.* 2, 5, 13, 14, 21, 23) 77, 83, 143, 314, 340, 341, 480, 526

Deukalion (dū-**kāl**-i-on), (1) son of Minos, father of Idomeneus, king of Crete (*Il.* 13) 313, 318; (2) an obscure Trojan killed by Achilles (*Il.* 20) 476

Diokles (**dī**-o-klēz), rich king of Messenian Pherai, whose sons Orsilochos and Krethos were killed by Aeneas (*Il.* 5) 144, 145

Diomedê (dī-o-**mē**-dê), a daughter of the king of Lesbos, a war-captive and concubine of Achilles (*Il.* 9) 233

Diomedes (dī-ō-**mēd** ēz), son of Tydeus (who fought in the Seven Against Thebes), a principal Greek warrior at Troy (*Il.* 2–23) *passim*

Dionê (dī-**ō**-nê), feminine form of "Zeus," a consort of Zeus, mother of Aphrodite (*Il.* 5) 139, 141

Dionysos, son of Zeus and Semelê, god of ritual ecstasy (never wine in the *Iliad*) (*Il.* 6, 14) 162, 340, 341

Diores, (1) a leader of the Epeians (*Il.* 2) 80; (2) father of Automedon (*Il.* 17) 413, 415

Dioscuri (dī-os-**kūr**-ê), "sons of Zeus" and Leda, Kastor and Polydeukes (= Roman Pollux), brothers of Helen (*Il.* 3) 96, 100

Dodona (do-**dōn**-a), site of oracular shrine of Zeus in northwestern Greece (*Il.* 2, 5, 16) 85, 139, 378, 379

Dolon (**dō**-lon), Trojan spy captured by Odysseus and Diomedes (*Il.* 10) 245–251, 255

Dolops, (1) a tribe in Thessaly (*Il.* 9) 227; (2) a Trojan, cousin of Hector, killed by Menelaos (*Il.* 15) 364, 365; (3) an Achaean killed by Hector (*Il.* 11) 267

Doulichion, one of the Ionian Islands (*Il.* 2, 5, 10, 11, 13, 15, 19, 23) 80, 129, 238, 280, 325, 364, 453, 535, 536

E

Echepolos (e-**ke**-po-los), (1) a Trojan, the first casualty of the *Iliad* (*Il.* 4) 122, 123; (2) an Achaean, a rich resident of Sikyon who gave Agamemnon a mare instead of going to the war (*Il.* 23) 524

Eëtion (ē-**et**-i-on), (1) father of Andromachê 27, 39; (*Il.* 1, 9, 16, 23) 53, 218, 376, 541; (2) of Imbros, guest-friend of Priam, ransomed Lykaon (*Il.* 21) 479, 480; (3) a Trojan (*Il.* 17) 418

Eileithyia (ē-lē-**thī**-ya), "she who comes," goddess of childbirth (*Il.* 11, 16, 19) 266, 377, 450

Elatos (**el**-a-tos), a Trojan killed by Agamemnon (*Il.* 6) 159

Eleon (**el**-e-on), one of the communities providing the Boeotian contingent in the Catalog of Ships (*Il.* 10) 243

Elephenor (el-ef-**ē**-nor), a leader of the Abantes from Euboea, killed by Agenor in the first battle of the *Iliad* (*Il.* 2, 4) 77, 123

Elis, a territory in the northwest Peloponnesus (*Il.* 2, 4, 5, 11, 13, 15, 17, 22, 23) 80, 126, 145, 277, 279, 280, 282, 309, 325, 364, 404, 423, 512, 535

Elonê (el-ō-nē), a town in northeastern Thessaly, led by Lapiths (*Il.* 2) 85

Emathia (e-**math**-i-a), "sandy," the same as Macedonia (*Il.* 14) 336, 337

Eneti (**en**-e-tī), a Paphlagonian tribe, allies of Troy (*Il.* 2) 90

Enkidu (**en**-ki-dū), Gilgamesh's rival and companion, 25

Enlil (**en**-lēl), "lord of wind," Sumerian storm-god, 35

Ennomos (**en**-no-mos), (1) an augur and leader of the Mysians (*Il.* 2) 90; (2) a Trojan killed by
  Odysseus in the Battle at the Wall (*Il.* 11) 271

Enopê (**en**-o-pē), one of the seven towns that Agamemnon offers Achilles if he will return to the
  fight (*Il.* 9) 216, 222

Enyalios (en-**yal**-i-os), a name for Ares (*Il.* 2, 5, 7, 8, 13, 17, 18, 20, 22) 82, 138, 182, 202, 320,
  407, 408, 434, 464, 501

Enyo, a minor goddess of war (*Il.* 5) 138

Epeians, population of Elis, on the one hand (also called Eleians), and of Doulichion and the
  Echinades Islands, on the other (*Il.* 10, 11, 13, 15, 23) 238, 279–281, 309, 325, 364, 535

Epeigeus (e-**pē**-jūs), a Myrmidon killed by Hector (*Il.* 16) 389

Epeios (e-**pē**-os), a boxer, builder of the Trojan Horse (*Il.* 23) 536, 537, 542

Ephialtes (ef-i-**al**-tēz), a giant who with his brother Otos imprisoned Ares in a jar (*Il.* 5) 139, 140

Ephyra (**e**-fir-a), (1) another name for Corinth (*Il.* 6) 163, 166; (2) a city on the Selleïs River in
  Thresprotia (*Il.* 2, 15) 82, 364

epic, a long poem on a heroic topic, 7, 9, 11, 12, 19, 21, 24

Epidaurus (e-pi-**dow**-rus), city in the northeast Peloponnesus (*Il.* 2) 78

Epigoni (e-**pig**-o-nē), "descendants," sons of the Seven Against Thebes, led by Alcmeon, whose
  attack was successful (*Il.* 4, 6) 121, 158

Epistrophos (e-**pis**-tro-fos), "turning back," (1) a son of Iphitos, leader of the Phocians (*Il.* 2) 77;
  (2) among the Trojan forces, a leader of the Halizones (*Il.* 2) 90; (3) a Trojan, son of Euenos,
  killed by Achilles in the sack of Lyrnessos (*Il.* 2) 83

Erechtheus (e-**rek**-thūs), an early king of Athens (*Il.* 2) 78

Ereuthalion, an Arcadian killed by Nestor when Nestor was young (*Il.* 4, 7) 118, 181

Erichthonios (er-ik-**thōn**-i-os), "he of the earth," ancient king of Troy, son of Dardanos, father of
  Tros (*Il.* 2, 20) 89, 468

Erinys (**er**-i-nis), or plural, Erinyes (er-**in**-yes), the underworld punisher(s) of broken oaths; the
  fulfillers of a curse; also called the Furies (*Il.* 9, 19, 21) 230, 449, 490

Eriopis (er-i-**ō**-pis), wife of Oïleus, mother of Little Ajax (*Il.* 13, 15) 325, 357

Eris, "strife," sister and companion to Ares, who rouses men to battle (*Il.* 1, 3–6, 8–24) *passim*

Erythinoi (er-i-**thēn**-oi), one of the five towns of the Paphlagonians, probably on the southern shore
  of the Black Sea (*Il.* 2) 90

Erythrai (er-**ith**-rē), a town in southern Boeotia (*Il.* 2) 76

Eteokles (e-**tē**-o-klēz), son of Oedipus, killed brother Polyneikes in attack of Seven
  Against Thebes (*Il.* 4) 120

Eteonos (e-te-**ō**-nos), city in Boeotia (*Il.* 2) 76

Euboea (yū-**bē**-a), long island east of Attica, site of vigorous Iron Age community where the alpha-
  bet may have been invented; 3–5, 12, 14, 16, 24–25, (*Il.* 2, 4, 8, 9, 14) 76, 77, 123, 196, 233, 338

Euchenor (yū-**kēn**-or), "praying man," an Achaean, son of Polyidos ("much-knowing"), killed by an
  arrow from Paris (*Il.* 13) 324

Eudoros (yū-**dō**-ros), one of the five captains of the Myrmidons led into battle by Patroklos, a son of Hermes (*Il.* 16) 377, 385

Euenos (yū-**ē**-nos), (1) king of Lyrnessos whose two sons Achilles killed (*Il.* 2) 83; an Aetolian, father of Marpessa, wooed by Apollo and Idas (*Il.* 9) 230

Eumelos (yū-**mē**-los), son of Admetos and Alkestis, led a contingent of Thessalians (*Il.* 2, 23) 84, 87, 524, 526, 527, 529, 530, 532, 533, 535

Euneos (yū-**nē**-os), "good with ships," a king of Lemnos, son of Jason and Hypsipylê (*Il.* 7) 191

Euphorbos (yu-**forb**-os), a Trojan, first man to wound Patroklos (*Il.* 16, 17) 397, 398, 400–404

Euripides (yū-**rip**-i-dēz) (480–406 BC), Athenian playwright 21; (*Il.* 6, 10) 162, 163, 235, 253

Euryalos (yū-**rī**-a-los), one of the commanders of the contingent from Argos, with Diomedes and Sthenelos (*Il.* 2, 6, 23) 78, 158, 537

Eurybates (yū-**rib**-a-tēz), Odysseus' herald (*Il.* 1, 2, 9) 51, 67, 217

Eurydamas (yū-rī-**dā**-mas), Trojan dream-interpreter killed by Diomedes (*Il.* 5) 131

Eurymedon (yū-**rim**-e-don), "wide ruling," (1) Agamemnon's charioteer (*Il.* 4) 116; (2) Nestor's charioteer (*Il.* 8, 11) 196, 277

Eurynomê, daughter of Ocean, mother-in-law of Hephaistos who cared for him when he was thrown from heaven (*Il.* 18) 437

Eurypylos (yū-**rip**-i-los), (1) a Thessalian leader, whom Patroklos attended to when wounded (*Il.* 2, 5, 6, 7, 11, 15) 129, 159, 182, 202, 275, 276, 279, 283–286, 359, 371, 375; (2) legendary king of Kos (*Il.* 2) 83, 85

Eurystheus (yu-**ris**-thūs), cousin and tormentor of Herakles, great-grandson of Zeus (*Il.* 8, 15, 19) 206, 367, 368, 450

Eurytos (**yū**-ri-tos), (1) a king of Oichalia, father of Iphitos, famous bowman (*Il.* 2) 79, 84; (2) a leader of the Epeians (*Il.* 2) 80

Eutresis (yu-**trā**-sis), a town in Boeotia (*Il.* 2) 76

Evans, Sir Arthur (1851–1941), British archaeologist, 20

F

Fates, *see* Moerae

formula, a building block in the formation of oral verse 10–13, 24, 36, 85, 215, 262, 278, 557

G

Gaia (**jē**-a), the goddess Earth, consort of Ouranos, Sky (*Il.* 2, 20) 91, 473, 474

Ganymede (**gan**-i-mēd), son of Tros, beloved of Zeus, cupbearer of the gods (*Il.* 2, 5, 20, 23) 89, 133, 135, 466, 468, 469, 526

Gargaros, the highest peak of Mt. Ida (*Il.* 8, 14, 15) 194, 340, 341, 351

geras (**ger**-as), "prize," the outward and visible representation of a hero's honor (*timê*), 26, 27, 30, 44

Gerenian (jer-ē-ni-an), obscure epithet applied to Nestor (*Il.* 4, 7, 8, 9, 10, 11, 14, 15) 118, 182, 195–197, 217, 238–241, 254, 274, 279, 285, 332, 368

Gilgamesh, Mesopotamian hero, 25

Glaukos (**glow**-kos), a co-leader of the Lycians, with Sarpedon (*Il.* 2, 5–8, 11–17) *passim*

Glisas (**gli**-sas), a town in Boeotia (*Il.* 2) 76

Gorgon, terrifying head of Medusa (*Il.* 5, 6, 8, 11, 20, 24) 151, 165, 206, 258, 462, 559

Gorgythion, a son of Priam by a secondary wife, killed by Teucer (*Il.* 8) 203

Gortyn, city in south-central Crete (*Il.* 2) 82

Gouneus (**gou**-nūs), leader of peoples from around Dodona in northwest Greece (*Il.* 2) 85

Graces, attendants of Aphrodite, imparters of feminine charm; *see* Charites (*Il.* 5, 14, 17, 18) 138, 338, 401, 426, 436, 437

Graia (**grē**-a), "old lady," town in Boeotia (*Il.* 2) 76

Gyrtonê (gir-**tō**-nē), a town in Thessaly led by the Lapiths (*Il.* 2) 85

H

Hades (**hā**-dēz), "unseen," lord of the underworld, son of Kronos and Rhea (*Il.* 1, 3, 5–9, 11–16, 20–24) *passim*

Haimon (**hē**-mon), "skilled, eager," (1) a Pylian of high rank, comrade of Nestor (*Il.* 4) 117; (2) father of the only Theban to survive the ambush on Tydeus in war of the Seven Against Thebes (*Il.* 4) 220; (3) a Myrmidon (*Il.* 17) 414

Haliartos, a town in Boeotia (*Il.* 2) 76

Halios, "of the sea," a Lycian killed by Odysseus (*Il.* 5) 149

Halizones, a people of central Anatolia, allies of Troy (*Il.* 2, 5, 10) 76, 90, 128, 250

Harma, "chariot," a town in Boeotia (*Il.* 2) 76

Harpalion, son of Pylaimenes, king of the Paphlagonians, killed by Meriones and transported to Troy accompanied by his father Pylaimenes, who was killed in an earlier book (*Il.* 13) 323, 324

Harpies, "snatchers," wind-spirits; a harpy sired Achilles' horses on West Wind (*Il.* 16) 376

Hebê (**hēb**-ē), "youth," married to Herakles on Olympos (*Il.* 4, 5) 108, 151, 157

Hector, greatest of the Trojan warriors, married to Andromachê, killed by Achilles (*Il.* 1–24) *passim*

Hekabê (**hek**-a-bē), wife of Priam, queen of Troy, mother of Hector (*Il.* 6, 15, 16, 22, 23, 24) 169, 174, 355, 394, 500, 504, 510, 550, 553, 567

Hekamedê (hek-a-**mē**-dē), Nestor's maid-servant (*Il.* 11, 14) 277, 330

Helen, daughter of Zeus and Leda, husband of Menelaos, lover of Paris (*Il.* 1–9, 11–15, 19, 22–24) *passim*

Helenos (**hel**-e-nos), (1) Trojan prophet, brother of Hector (*Il.* 6, 7, 12, 24) 160, 174, 198, 288, 552; (2) an Achaean cut down by Hector (*Il.* 5) 150

Helikê (**hel**-i-kē), a town in the northeast Peloponnesus in the territory of Agamemnon (*Il.* 2, 8, 20) 79, 199, 474

Helios, sun god (*Il.* 8, 14, 16, 19) 194, 209, 341, 395, 452, 455

Hellas, "land of the Hellenes," at first a territory in southern Thessaly near Phthia, later all of Greece (*Il.* 2, 9, 16) 77, 83, 224, 226, 227, 379, 389, 390

Hellenes (**hel**-ēnz), at first the inhabitants of Hellas, later all the Greeks, 26 (*Il.* 2, 16) 77, 83, 379

Hellenistic, referring to Greek culture between Alexander's death in 323 BC and the ascendancy of Rome in 30 BC, 21

Hellespont, straits between the Aegean Sea and the Propontis (Sea of Marmora) (*Il.* 2, 4, 7, 9, 11, 12, 15, 17, 18, 21, 23, 24) 4, 90, 125, 179, 223, 268, 286, 288, 354, 365, 413, 430, 479, 515, 555, 561

Helos (**hē**-los), "marsh-meadow," (1) a town in Lacedaemon on the sea (*Il.* 2) 79; (2) a town in Messenia (*Il.* 2) 79

Hephaistos (he-**fēs**-tos), Greek god of smiths, son of Zeus and Hera or Hera alone (*Il.* 1, 2, 5, 8, 9, 14–23) *passim*

Hera, "mistress(?)," daughter of Kronos and Rhea, wife and sister of Zeus (*Il.* 1–5, 7–21, 23, 24) *passim*

Herakles, son of Zeus and Alkmenê, the strongest man who ever lived (*Il.* 2, 4, 5, 7, 8, 11, 14, 15, 18, 19, 20) *passim*

Hermes, "he of the stone heap," son of Zeus and Maia, a trickster god who presides over boundaries, a guide who leads Priam to Achilles' tent at night (*Il.* 2, 5, 14, 15, 16, 20, 21, 24) *passim*

Hermionê (her-**mī**-o-nē), a town on the Argive plain in the realm of Big Ajax (*Il.* 2) 78

Hermos River, in Lydia, rises in Phrygia, flows into the sea near Smyrna (*Il.* 20) 474

Herodotus (c. 484–425 BC), Greek historian 5, 21, 302, 324

Hesiod (**hēs**-i-od), Greek poet, eighth century BC, composer of *Works and Days* and *Theogony* 15–17, 21, 54, 139, 157, 336, 338, 426, 436, 437, 517, 536

hieros gamos, "holy marriage," ritual sexual union to enhance fertility, 341

Hiketaon (hik-e-**tā**-on), Trojan elder, brother of Priam (*Il.* 3, 15, 20) 96, 365, 366, 468

Hippodameia (hip-po-da-**mē**-a), "horse-tamer," (1) wife of Peirithoös and mother of Polypoites, who led a contingent of Thessalians (*Il.* 2) 85; (2) daughter of Anchises, half-sister of Aeneas (*Il.* 13) 317, 319

Hippolochos (hip-**pol**-o-kos), (1) a Lycian son of Bellerophon, father of Glaukos (*Il.* 6) 162, 163, 166, 177; (2) a Trojan killed by Agamemnon (*Il.* 11) 261, 262

Hippothoös (hip-**o**-tho-os), (1) a leader of the Pelasgians, killed by Big Ajax (*Il.* 2, 17) 90, 407, 409, 410; (2) a son of Priam (*Il.* 24) 552

Hippotion (hip-**pot**-i-on), a Trojan warrior from Askania, killed by Meriones (*Il.* 13, 14) 328, 347

Hirê (**hir**-ē), a town in Messenia promised to Achilles if he will return to the fight (*Il.* 9) 216, 222

Histiaia (his-ti-ē-a), a city of the Abantes in northern Euboea (*Il.* 2) 77

Hittites (**hit**-ītz), Indo-European Bronze Age warrior people in central Anatolia; their capital was Hattusas near modern Ankara, 23, 34

Homeric Hymns, c. seventh to fifth centuries BC, oral dictated texts celebrating the gods, 3

Homeric Question, really "Homeric Investigation," into the origin of Homer's texts, 5, 10

hoplites (**hop**-lītz), "shield-bearers," heavy-armed Greek warriors of Classical Period 104, 124, 205, 298, 403

Hyades (**hī**-a-dēz), "rainers," a star cluster (*Il.* 18) 440

Hyampolis, a town in Phocis (*Il.* 2) 77

Hydê (**hī**-dē), a prosperous Maeonian town at the foot of Mt. Tmolos (perhaps Sardis) (*Il.* 20) 473, 474

Hylê (**hī**-lē), a town of uncertain location, perhaps in Boeotia (*Il.* 2, 5, 7) 76, 150, 184

Hyllos (**hī**-los), a river in Lydia, a tributary of the Hermos (*Il.* 20) 473, 474

Hypereia (hi-per-ē-a), "upper spring," a spring in Thessaly and perhaps a spring of the same name in the Peloponnesus (*Il.* 2, 6) 85, 174

Hyperenor (hi-per-ē-nor), a Trojan, son of Panthoös, killed by Menelaos (*Il.* 14, 17) 347, 400

Hyperion (hi-**per**-ion), "moving on high," a Titan, father or epithet of Helios (*Il.* 8, 19) 209, 458

Hypsenor (hip-**sē**-nor), "lofty man," (1) Trojan priest of the Skamandros River, killed by Eurypylos (*Il.* 5) 129; (2) an Achaean killed by Deïphobos; though dead he "groaned" when carried away (*Il.* 13) 316, 318, 319

Hypsipylê (hip-**sip**-i-lē), queen of Lemnos, mother of Euneos by Jason (*Il.* 7) 191

Hyrminê (hir-**mī**-nē), an unidentified place in Elis (*Il.* 2) 80

I

Ialmenos (i-**al**-me-nos), a son of Ares, co-leader of the contingent from Orchomenos (*Il.* 2, 9, 16) 77, 214, 385

Ialysos (i-**al**-i-sos), city on Rhodes that sends troops under Tlepolemos, a son of Herakles (*Il.* 2) 82

Iapetos (i-**ap**-e-tos), a Titan, father of Prometheus, Epimetheus, and Atlas (*Il.* 8) 209

Iasos (**i**-a-sos), a captain of the Athenians, killed by Aeneas (*Il.* 15) 357, 358

ichor (**i**-kor), "undying," the fluid in the veins of the gods (*Il.* 5) 138, 141

Ida (**ī**-da), Mount, a mountain near Troy (*Il.* 1–24) *passim*

Idaios (i-**dē**-os), (1) Priam's herald (*Il.* 3, 7, 24) 100, 185, 554, 558; (2) son of a priest of Hephaistos, who rescues him from Diomedes (*Il.* 5) 127

Idas (**ī**-das), brother of Lynceus, an Argonaut who competed with Apollo for Marpessa (*Il.* 9) 230

Idomeneus (ī-**dom**-i-nūs), grandson of Minos, leader of the Cretan contingent at Troy (*Il.* 1–23) *passim*

Ilioneus (il-**ī**-o-nūs), a Trojan killed at the Battle of the Ships (*Il.* 14) 346, 347

Ilion, another name for Troy (*Il.* 1–24) *passim*

Ilos (**ī**-los), early king of Troy, son of Tros, grandfather of Priam; his tomb was a landmark on the plain (*Il.* 2, 5, 7, 10, 11, 17, 20, 21, 23, 24) 14, 28, 89, 135, 191, 249, 262, 269, 403, 468, 495, 531, 552, 555

Imbrios, a Trojan killed at the Battle of the Ships by Teucer, then beheaded (*Il.* 13) 309, 310

Imbros, island in the northeast Aegean (*Il.* 6, 13, 14, 17, 21, 24) 4, 162, 302, 303, 309, 338, 418, 479, 547, 567

Inanna (in-**an**-a), Sumerian fertility goddess, related to Aphrodite, 34

Iolkos (ī-**olk**-us), city in southeastern Thessaly, home of Jason, at the head of the Gulf of Pagasae (= modern Volo) (*Il.* 2) 84, 85

Ionia, the west coast of Asia Minor, 3–4, 14, 76, 91, 118, 325

Ionians, a division of the Greek people, 91, 325

Iphianassa (if-i-a-**nas**-a), "powerful queen," one of Agamemnon's three daughters, offered in marriage to Achilles (*Il.* 9) 216, 222

Iphidamas (if-i-**dā**-mas), "mighty subduer," a Trojan, reared in Thrace, killed by Agamemnon (*Il.* 11) 264, 265

Iphiklos (**if**-i-klos), Thessalian father of Protesilaos, a fast runner (*Il.* 2, 13, 23) 84, 326, 535

Iphis (**i**-fis), Patroklos' concubine captured by Achilles on Skyros (*Il.* 9) 233

Iris (**ī**-ris), "rainbow," messenger of Zeus (*Il.* 2, 3, 5, 8, 11, 12, 13, 15, 18, 22, 23, 24) *passim*

Ishtar, Akkadian fertility goddess (= Sumerian Inanna), 34

Ithaca, off the northwest coast of Greece, home of Odysseus, one of the Ionian Islands 4; (*Il.* 2, 3, 4, 5, 13) 67, 76, 80, 99, 118, 120, 129, 325

Ithomê (ith-**ō**-mē), city in northwestern Thessaly at the foot of the Pindus range, its contingent led by Machaon and Podaleirios (*Il.* 2) 84

Iton (**ī**-ton), a city in Thessaly, its contingent led by Protesilaos (*Il.* 2, 4) 83, 125

Ixion (ik-**sī**-on), a Lapith king, father of the Centaurs, tried to rape Hera, married to the woman (Dia) on whom Zeus fathered Peirithoös (*Il.* 13, 14) 313, 340, 341

K

Kadmos (**kad**-mos), "man of the East," founder of Thebes, eponym of the Kadmeians, the inhabitants of Thebes (*Il.* 23) 537

Kaineus (**kē**-nūs), a Lapith, one of the powerful warriors who destroyed the Centaurs (*Il.* 2) 85

Kalchas (**kal**-kas), prophet of the Greek forces at Troy (*Il.* 1, 2, 11, 13) 28, 31, 43, 44, 70, 71, 303, 305, 306

Kallikolonê (kal-i-ko-**lō**-nē), "pleasant hill," a landmark on the Trojan plain (*Il.* 20) 463

Kalydon (**kal**-i-don), main city in Aetolia in southwestern mainland Greece, home of Meleager, site of the Kalydonian Boar Hunt (*Il.* 2, 9, 13, 14) 82, 228–231, 310, 333

Kameiros (ka-**mē**-ros), one of the three cities on Rhodes that sent a contingent under Tlepolemos (*Il.* 2, 11) 82, 258

Kapaneus (**kap**-a-nūs), one of the Seven Against Thebes, struck down by Zeus as he climbed its walls, father of Sthenelos (*Il.* 2, 4, 5) 78, 120, 130, 134, 136

Kardamylê (kar-**dam**-i-lê), one of the seven cities promised to Achilles by Agamemnon (*Il.* 9) 216, 222

Karpathos (kar-**pā**-thos), an island in the southeastern Aegean, its contingent led by sons of Thessalos (*Il.* 2) 83

Karystos (kar-**is**-tos), a city of the Abantes on the southwestern coast of Euboea (*Il.* 2) 77

Kasos (**kā**-sos), an island between Crete and Karpathos in the southwestern Aegean Sea, part of the contingent of Kos (*Il.* 2) 83

Kassandra, beautiful daughter of Priam and Hekabê, a priestess of Apollo (*Il.* 24) 566

Kastor, *see* Dioscuri

Kaukones (kau-**kō**-nēz), two obscure groups fighting on the Trojan side (*Il.* 10, 20) 250, 472

Kaystrios (ka-**is**-tri-os), a river in Asia Minor, 4; (*Il.* 2) 75

Kebriones (keb-ri-**ō**-nēz), half-brother of Hector, one of his charioteers (*Il.* 8, 11, 12, 16) 204, 274, 288, 396

Keladon, "murmuring," a river in Elis or Arcadia (*Il.* 7) 181

Kephallenians (kef-al-**ēn**-i-ans), the contingent of Odysseus, from the Ionian Islands (*Il.* 2, 4) 80, 118

Kephisos, a river in Boeotia that flowed into Lake Copaïs (*Il.* 2) 77

Kerinthos, city of Abantes on the eastern shore of Euboea (*Il.* 2) 77

Killa, a town on the western coast of the Troad (*Il.* 1) 42, 55

Kinyras (**kin**-i-ras), "lyre-man(?)," a ruler on Cyprus who gave a corselet to Agamemnon as a guest-gift when he heard that the Greeks were planning to sail to Troy (*Il.* 11) 256

Kleitos (**klē**-tos), "famous," a Trojan, charioteer of Poulydamas (*Il.* 15) 362

Kleonai (kle-**ō**-nē), a town between Corinth and Argos, in the realm of Agamemnon (*Il.* 2) 78

Kleopatra, wife of Meleager, daughter of Idas and Marpessa (*Il.* 9) 220–231

kleos, "fame," what a warrior hopes to win through martial achievement, 26; (*Il.* 11) 265

Klonios, one of the five captains of the Boeotians, killed by Agenor (*Il.* 2, 15) 76, 357

Klymenê (**klī**-me-nē), "famous," (1) one of Helen's maidservants (*Il.* 3) 96; (2) one of the thirty-three Nereids who lament Patroklos (*Il.* 18) 426

Klytaimnestra, "famed for her suitors," or "famed for her cunning," daughter of Tyndareos and Leda, sister of Helen, wife of Agamemnon (*Il.* 1) 44

Knossos (**knos**-sos), principal Bronze Age settlement in Crete, where labyrinthine ruins have been found, associated with Minos and Daidalos (*Il.* 2, 18) 82, 433

Koiranos, "ruler," (1) a Lycian killed by Odysseus (*Il.* 5) 149; (2) a Cretan, charioteer of Meriones, killed by Hector (*Il.* 17) 419

Koön, Trojan son of Antenor, killed by Agamemnon (*Il.* 11, 19) 265, 448

Kopreus (**kop**-rūs), "dungman," herald of Eurystheus (*Il.* 15) 367

Koroneia (kor-o-**nē**-a), a city in Boeotia (*Il.* 2) 76

Kos (**kōs**), Greek island near Asia Minor, whose contingent was led by grandsons of Herakles (*Il.* 14, 15) 337, 348

Kreon (**krē**-on), "ruler," a king of Thebes, brother of Oedipus' wife Epikastê, father of Lykomedes (*Il.* 9, 19) 214, 453

Krisa (**krē**-sa), a city near Delphi (*Il.* 2) 77

Krokyleia (krok-i-**lē**-a), a location on or near Ithaca (*Il.* 2) 80

Kromna (**krōm**-na), one of the five cities of the Paphlagonians (*Il.* 2) 90

Kronos, child of Ouranos and Gaia, husband of Rhea, overthrown by his son Zeus, who imprisoned him in Tartaros (*Il.* 15) 353

Kteatos (**ktē**-a-tos), an Epeian, one of the Aktorionê (or Molionê), sons of Aktor (really Poseidon), later said with his brother Eurytos to be a Siamese twin (*Il.* 2, 13) 80, 309

Kuretes (kur-ē-**tēz**), "young men," an Aetolian tribe inhabiting Pleuron ten miles west of Kalydon (*Il.* 9) 228, 230, 231

Kyllenê (ki-**lēn**-ê), mountain in Arcadia, where Hermes was born (*Il.* 15) 364

Kynos (**kī**-nos), apparently a seaport in Locris (*Il.* 2) 77

Kyparissos, a town of uncertain location, perhaps in Phocis (*Il.* 2) 77

Kypris, "the lady of Cyprus," a name for Aphrodite (*Il.* 5) 138, 141, 142, 152, 156

Kytoros (ki-**tō**-ros), a city of the Paphlagonians on the southern shore of the Black Sea (*Il.* 2) 90

L

Lacedaemon (las-e-**dēm**-on), the Eurotas furrow in the southern Peloponnesus, bounded by Mt. Taygetos in the west and Mt. Parnes in the east (*Il.* 2, 3) 79, 100, 105, 107

Lampos, "shiner," (1) Trojan elder (*Il.* 3) 96; (2) one of Hector's horses (*Il.* 8) 198

Laodameia (lā-o-da-**mē**-a), daughter of Bellerophon, mother of Sarpedon by Zeus (*Il.* 6) 166

Laodikê (lā-**o**-di-kē), (1) daughter of Priam and Hekabê, sister of Hector and Paris (*Il.* 3, 6) 95, 167; (2) one of the daughters of Agamemnon offered to Achilles in marriage (*Il.* 9) 216, 222

Laodokos (lā-**o**-do-kos), (1) a Trojan son of Antenor (*Il.* 4) 110; (2) an Achaean, charioteer to Antilochos (*Il.* 17) 421

Laomedon (lā-**om**-e-don), early king of Troy, father of Priam; 34, 35 (*Il.* 2, 3, 5, 6, 7, 8, 10, 11, 15, 21, 23, 24) 89, 100, 135, 148, 149, 159, 191, 202, 210, 249, 256, 360, 364, 491, 526, 545

Laothoê (lā-**oth**-o-ê), a secondary wife of Priam, mother of Polydoros and Lykaon (*Il.* 21, 22) 480, 499

Lapiths (**lap**-iths), Thessalian tribe, led by Peirithoös, that defeated the Centaurs (*Il.* 2, 3, 12, 23) 85, 86, 96, 289–291, 542

Larisa, a place of uncertain location associated with the Trojan allies the Pelasgians (*Il.* 2, 17) 90, 409

Leïtos (**lē**-i-tos), one of the five captains of the Boeotians (*Il.* 2, 6, 13, 17) 76, 159, 305, 419

Lekton, a promontory of Mt. Ida near the sea, where there was a temple to Apollo Smintheus (*Il.*14) 338

Leleges (**le**-le-jēz), allies of the Trojans who lived in Lyrnessos and Pedasos (*Il.* 10, 20, 21) 250, 464, 480

Lemnos, island in the northern Aegean, associated with Hephaistos, where Philoktetes was abandoned (*Il.* 1, 2, 7, 8, 13, 14, 21, 23, 24) 59, 60, 84, 191, 200, 325, 337, 338, 479, 480, 539, 567

Leonteus (le-**on**-tūs), with Polypoites leader of the Lapiths (*Il.* 2, 12, 23) 85, 289, 291, 542

Lesbos, island in the Aegean, near Troy (*Il.* 9, 13, 18, 24) 4, 216, 221, 233, 302, 437, 561

Leto (**lē**-tō), mother of Apollo and Artemis, supporter of Troy (*Il.* 1, 2, 5, 13, 14, 15, 16, 17, 20, 21, 24) 21, 33, 35, 41, 42, 82, 91, 142,

Likymnios, Herakles' uncle, killed by Tlepolemos (*Il.* 2) 82

Lilaia (li-**lē**-a), a Phocian city north of Mt. Parnassos (*Il.* 2) 77

Lindos, one of the three cities on Rhodes whose contingent was led by Tlepolemos (*Il.* 2) 82

Linos (**lī**-nus), a mythical musician (*Il.* 18) 443

Lord, Albert B. (1912–1991), student and assistant to Milman Parry, author of *The Singer of Tales* (1960), 11, 12

Lycia (**lish**-a), region in southwest Anatolia, home to the Trojan hero Glaukos (*Il.* 2, 4, 5, 6, 7, 8, 10, 11, 12, 13, 14, 15, 16, 17) *passim*

Lydia, a region in western Anatolia centered on Sardis, 4; (*Il.* 2, 21, 24) 75, 483, 563

Lykaon (li-**kā**-on), (1) a son of Priam killed by Achilles in the river (*Il.* 21) 479–481; (2) the father of the Trojan Pandaros (*Il.* 2, 5) 89, 130, 132, 135

Lykomedes (li-ko-**mē**-dēz), a Boeotian warrior, one of the seven captains who went to guard the Achaean wall (*Il.* 9, 12, 17) 214, 297, 411

Lykourgos (lī-**kur**-gos), "who keeps wolves at bay," (1) Thracian king, opposed Dionysos, eaten by horses (*Il.* 6) 162; (2) an Arcadian who killed Areïthoös the mace-man in a narrow passage and took his armor according to the reminiscences of Nestor (*Il.* 7) 181

Lyktos, city in central Crete, home of Meriones (*Il.* 2) 82

Lyrnessos, a city in the Troad sacked by Achilles (*Il.* 2, 19) 83, 448

M

Machaon (ma-**kā**-on), leader from Thessaly, son of Asklepios physician at Troy, wounded by Paris (*Il.* 2, 4, 5, 11, 14, 16) 85, 115, 137, 273, 274, 276, 277, 279, 285, 330, 371

Maeonians, inhabited the territory around Mt. Tmolos (the Lydians of classical times) (*Il.* 10) 250

Magnesia (mag-**nēz**-i-a), a territory in northern Greece around the Gulf of Pagasae, whose capital was Iolcus (*Il.* 2) 85

Maion (**mē**-on), a Theban, son of Haimon (only survivor of the ambush on Tydeus) (*Il.* 4) 120, 121

Maira (**mē**-ra), a Nereid (*Il.* 18) 426

Makar, the legendary colonizer of Lesbos (*Il.* 24) 561

Mantinea, city in southeast Arcadia (*Il.* 2) 80

Marpessa (mar-**pes**-a), beloved of Apollo and Idas, she chose Idas (*Il.* 9) 230

Mases (**ma**-sēz), a town on the Argive plain in the realm of Diomedes (*Il.* 2) 78

Medeon, a town in Boeotia (*Il.* 2) 76

Medesikastê (med-es-i-**kas**-tē), a daughter of Priam born to a concubine (*Il.* 13) 309

Medon (**me**-dōn), (1) half-brother of Little Ajax who replaced Philoktetes, killed by Aeneas (*Il.* 13, 15) 302, 325, 357; (2) a Trojan (*Il.* 17) 407

Meges (**me**-jēz), leader of the contingent from Doulichion and a leader of the mainland Epeians (*Il.* 2, 5, 10, 11, 13, 15, 16, 19, 23) 80, 129, 238, 280, 325, 364, 365, 381, 453, 535

Mejedovich, Avdo (1875–1953), M. Parry's best guslar, dictated a song as long as the *Odyssey,* 37

Mekisteus (me-**kis**-tūs), (1) brother of Adrastos, competed at the funeral games of Oedipus (*Il.* 2, 23) 78, 537; (2) an Achaean, carried out wounded Teucer, killed by Poulydamas (*Il.* 8, 13, 15) 204, 317, 357, 358

Melas, an Aetolian, ancestor of Diomedes (*Il.* 14) 333

Meleager (mel-ē-**ā**-jer), "he who cares for the hunt," Aetolian hero, brother of Deianeira, killed Kalydonian Boar (*Il.* 2, 9) 82, 228, 230, 231

Meliboia (mel-i-**bē**-a), "caring for cows," a town in Thessaly, part of the contingent of Philoktetes (*Il.* 2) 84

Menelaos (men-e-**lā**-os), "supporter of the people," king of Sparta, son of Atreus, husband of Helen, brother of Agamemnon (*Il.* 1–23) *passim*

Menestheus (men-**es**-thūs), leader of Athenians at Troy (*Il.* 2, 12, 13, 15) 78, 296, 297, 300, 310, 325, 357, 358

Menesthios, a Boeotian killed by Paris (*Il.* 7) 177

Menoitios (men-**ē**-ti-os), son of Aktor, father of Patroklos (*Il.* 1, 9, 11, 12, 16–24) *passim*

Mentes (**men**-tēz), a leader of the Ciconians in whose guise Apollo speaks to Hector (*Il.* 17) 402

Mentor, "advisor," a Trojan killed by Teucer (*Il.* 13) 309

Meriones (mer-i-**ō**-nēz), an archer, aide to Idomeneus, second in command of the Cretan contingent (*Il.* 2, 4, 7–10, 13–23) *passim*

Merops, a Trojan seer from Perkotê who predicted death for his sons, who were killed by Diomedes (*Il.* 2, 11) 89, 268

Mesopotamia, "land between the rivers," the Euphrates and the Tigris; modern Iraq 16, 20, 21, 25, 31, 33–36, 336

Messê (**mes**-sē), a city in Lacedaemon (*Il.* 2) 79

Mesthles (**mes**-thlēz), leader of the Maeonians (*Il.* 2, 17) 91, 407

Mestor (**mēs**-tor), a dead son of Priam (*Il.* 24) 552

Methonê (mē-**thō**-nē), a city on the west side of the Magnesian peninsula subject to Philoktetes (*Il.* 2) 84

Mideia (mi-**dē**-a), a city in Boeotia (*Il.* 2) 76

Miletos, a cultural center in Ionia, inhabited by Carians (*Il.* 2) 82, 91

Minoans, Bronze Age inhabitants of Crete, 20, 21

Minos (**mī**-nos), Cretan king of Knossos, son of Zeus and Europa, husband of Pasiphaë, judge in the underworld, 20; (*Il.* 13, 14) 313, 318, 340, 341

Minotaur (**mīn**-o-tar), "bull of Minos," half-man, half-bull offspring of Pasiphaë and a bull (*Il.* 18) 445

Minyans, inhabitants of Orchomenus (*Il.* 2) 77

Minyeïos (min-**ye**-i-os), an unknown river mentioned in Nestor's reminiscences (*Il.* 11) 281

Morys, a Trojan ally killed by Meriones (*Il.* 13) 328

Moulios, (1) an Epeian leader killed by the young Nestor (*Il.* 11) 281; (2) a Trojan killed by Achilles (*Il.* 20) 476

Mouseion, "temple of the Muses," in Alexandria, Egypt, 6

Muses, the inspirers of oral song, a personification of the oral tradition 6, 426, 443 (*Il.* 1, 2, 11, 14, 16, 18) 60, 75, 79, 264, 347, 374

Mycenae (mī-**sē**-nē), largest Bronze Age settlement in the Argive plain, home of the house of Atreus (*Il.* 2, 4, 6, 7, 9, 10, 11, 13, 15, 17, 18) *passim*

Mycenaean Age, between c. 1600 and 1150 BC, 21

Mydon (**mī**-dōn), (1) a Paphlagonian killed by Antilochos (*Il.* 5) 145, 146; (2) a Paeonian killed by Achilles (*Il.* 21) 484

Mygdon, a Phrygian king who fought the Amazons (*Il.* 3) 97

Mykalê (**mik**-a-lē), a mountain ridge on the western coast of Asia Minor opposite Samos (*Il.* 2) 76, 91

Mykalessos (mi-kal-**es**-sos), a town in northern Boeotia (*Il.* 2) 76

Mynes (**mi**-nēz), king of Lyrnessos, killed by Achilles (*Il.* 2, 19) 83, 455

Myrmidons (**mir**-mi-dons), "ants," followers of Achilles (*Il.* 1, 2, 7, 9, 11, 13, 16–24) *passim*

Myrsinos (**mir**-si-nos), the furthermost point of the territory of the Epeians (*Il.* 2) 80

Mysians, people from the territory to south and east of the Troad (*Il.* 2, 10, 13, 14, 24) 90, 250, 302, 347, 553

N

Naples, "new city," a Greek colony in southern Italy 4, 278

Neleus (**nē**-lūs), son of Poseidon and Tyro, father of Nestor, founder of royal house of Pylos (*Il.* 11) 274, 276, 280, 281

Neoptolemos (nē-op-**tol**-e-mos), "new-fighter," son of Achilles (*Il.* 19) 456

Nereids (**nē**-re-idz), "daughters of Nereus," nymphs of the sea (*Il.* 18) 426–428, 430

Nestor, king of Pylos, garrulous septuagenarian Greek at Troy, who owned a famous elaborate cup (*Il.* 1–19, 23) *passim*

Niobê (**nī**-o-bē), daughter of Tantalos, wife of Amphion, whose sons and daughters were killed by Artemis and Apollo (*Il.* 24) 563

Nireus (**nī**-rūs), the most handsome man at Troy, from the small island of Symê near Kos (*Il.* 2) 83

Nisa (**nī**-sa), city in Boeotia (*Il.* 2) 76

Nisyros (**ni**-si-ros), a small island near Kos (*Il.* 2) 83

Noëmon (no-ē-mon), "thoughtful," (1) a Lycian killed by Odysseus (*Il.* 5) 149; (2) an Achaean comrade of Antilochos (*Il.* 23) 534

nymphs, "young women," spirits of nature (*Il.* 6, 14, 24) 173, 345, 563

Nysa (**nī**-sa), mythical land that received the infant Dionysos (*Il.* 6) 162

O

Oedipus (ē-di-pus, or **e**-di-pus), "swellfoot," son of Laios and Jocasta, buried at Thebes (*Il.* 23) 537

Oichalia (ē-**kāl**-i-a), a city in northwest Thessaly, home of the bowman Eurytos (*Il.* 2) 79, 84

Oïleus (o-**ī**-lūs) (1) father of Little Ajax, king of Locris (*Il.* 2, 13) 77, 84, 260; (2) a Trojan killed by Agamemnon (*Il.* 11) 202

Oineus (ē-nūs), "wine-man," king of Kalydon in southwest mainland Greece two generations before the Trojan War, father of Meleager, Tydeus, and Deianeira, grandfather of Diomedes (*Il.* 6, 9, 14) 166, 228, 321

Oinomaos (ē-nō-**mā**-os), (1) an Aetolian, killed by Hector (*Il.* 5) 150; (2) a Trojan killed by Idomeneus (*Il.* 12, 13) 289, 319

Oitylos (**ē**-ti-los), a town in Lacedaemon (*Il.* 2) 79

Okalea (ō-**kal**-e-a), a town in Boeotia (*Il.* 2) 76

Ocean, a Titan, husband of Tethys, the river that encircles the earth (*Il.* 5, 16, 18) 127, 376, 440

Olenos (**ō**-le-nos), a town in Aetolia near Pleuron (*Il.* 2) 82

Olizon (**ol**-i-zon), town in Magnesia in the realm of Philoktetes (*Il.* 2) 84

Olympos, the highest mountain in Greece, in northern Thessaly, home of the gods (*Il.* 1–24) *passim*

Onchestos, town in Boeotia with a shrine to Poseidon (*Il.* 2) 76

Onetor (o-**nē**-tor), "beneficial," Trojan priest of Idaean Zeus (*Il.* 16) 390

Ophelestes (of-el-**es**-tēz), (1) Trojan killed by Teucer (*Il.* 8) 202; (2) a Paeonian killed by Achilles (*Il.* 21) 484

Opheltios, (1) Trojan killed by Euryalos (*Il.* 6) 158; (2) an Achaean killed by Hector (*Il.* 11) 267

Opoeis (**op**-o-ēs), principal city in Locris, birthplace of Patroklos (*Il.* 18) 435

Orchomenos (or-**kom**-en-os), major Bronze Age site in northern Boeotia (*Il.* 2) 77, 79

Orestes (or-**es**-tēz), son of Agamemnon and Klytaimnestra (*Il.* 9) 216

Orion (ō-**rī**-on), a hunter, lover of Dawn, turned into a constellation (*Il.* 18) 440

Orsilochos (or-**sil**-o-kos), "well-skilled in all ways of battle," (1) a Messenian killed by Aeneas (*Il.* 5) 144, 145; (2) a Trojan killed by Teucer (*Il.* 8) 202

Ortilochos (or-**til**-o-kos), chieftain of Pherai in Messenia (*Il.* 5) 145

Othryoneus (oth-**rī**-o-nūs), Trojan ally killed by Idomeneus (*Il.* 13) 315, 328

Otos (**ō**-tos), (1) with his brother Ephialtes imprisoned Ares in a jar (*Il.* 5) 139; (2) an Epeian leader killed by Poulydamas (*Il.* 15) 364

Oukalegon (ou-**ka**-le-gon), "not-caring," one of the Trojan elders (*Il.* 3) 96

Ouranos (**ou**-ra-nos), "sky," consort of Gaia/Earth," castrated by his son Kronos (*Il.* 5) 139, 157

P

Paiëon (pē-**ē**-on), Greek god of healing, not yet equated with Apollo (*Il.* 5) 140, 157

Paeonians, a northern Aegean tribe, allies of the Trojans (*Il.* 2, 10, 12, 16, 21) 90, 250, 288, 380, 482, 483

Palamedes (pal-a-**mēd**-ēz), son of Nauplius, clever enemy of Odysseus in postHomeric tradition, perhaps the name of the inventor of the Greek alphabet, 14–16

Pallas (**pal**-as), an epithet for Athena (*Il.* 1, 4, 5, 6, 10, 15, 18, 20, 21, 22, 23) *passim*

Pammon, a son of Priam (*Il.* 24) 552

Panathenaic (pan-ath-en-**ē**-ik) Festival, annual festival to Athena at Athens where the *Iliad* and the *Odyssey* were performed, 9

Panopeus, (1) a town in Phocis (*Il.* 2, 17) 77, 410; (2) an Achaean, father of Epeios (the builder of the Trojan Horse) (*Il.* 23) 536

Panthoös, "all-swift," a Trojan elder, father of Poulydamas (*Il.* 3, 13, 14, 15, 16, 17, 18) 96, 327, 345, 362, 364, 388, 397, 400–402, 433

Paphlagonians, a people of northern Asia Minor, allies of the Trojans (*Il.* 2, 10, 13) 90, 250, 324

Paphos (**pāf**-os), city in Cyprus, sacred to Aphrodite (*Il.* 5) 138

Paris, son of Priam and Hekabê, lover of Helen; *see also* Alexandros (*Il.* 1–24) *passim*

Parrhasia (par-**ras**-i-a), district of Arcadia (*Il.* 2) 80

Parry, Milman (1902–1935), American classicist, creator of the oral-formulaic theory of Homeric composition, 10–14, 37–38

Parthenios, a river in Paphlagonia (*Il.* 2) 90

Patroklos (pa-**trok**-los), son of Menoitios, Achilles' best friend, killed by Hector (*Il.* 1, 4, 5, 8, 9, 11, 12, 15–24) *passim*

Pedasos (**pē**-da-sos), (1) a Trojan killed by Diomedes (*Il.* 6) 158, 173; (2) a horse that Achilles stole from Thebes, killed in battle (*Il.* 16) 376, 386; (3) a town near Mt. Ida (*Il.* 6, 20, 21) 159, 464, 480; (4) one of the towns that Agamemnon offers to Achilles (*Il.* 9) 216, 222

Peiraios (pē-**rē**-os), Achaean grandfather of Agamemnon's charioteer Eurymedon (*Il.* 4) 116

Peirithoös (pē-**rith**-o-os), son of Zeus by Ixion's wife, king of the Lapiths, foe of the Centaurs, friend of Theseus (*Il.* 1, 14) 49, 340, 341

Peiroös (pē-**ro**-os), a Thracian killed by Achilles (*Il.* 2, 4) 90, 125, 126

Peisenor (pē-**sē**-nor), a Trojan killed by Teucer (*Il.* 15) 362

Pelagon (**pe**-la-gon), (1) a Pylian, one of the commanders of Nestor's forces (*Il.* 4) 117; (2) a Lycian friend of Sarpedon (*Il.* 5) 150

Pelasgians, "peoples of the sea," allies of the Trojans (*Il.* 2) 90

Pelegon (**pē**-le-gon), Paeonian father of the ambidextrous Asteropaios (*Il.* 21) 482

Peleus (**pē**-lūs), grandson of Zeus, son of Aiakos, husband of Thetis, father of Achilles (*Il.* 1, 2, 4, 7–11, 13, 15–24) *passim*

Pelias (**pel**-i-as), son of Poseidon and Tyro, twin of Neleus, father of Alkestis (*Il.* 2) 84

Pelion, coastal mountain on the Magnesian peninsula in southeastern Thessaly near Iolcus, abode of the Centaurs (*Il.* 2, 5, 16, 19) 85, 140, 376, 458

Peloponnesus (pel-o-po-**nē**-sus), "island of Pelops," the southern portion of mainland Greece linked to the north by the narrow Isthmus of Corinth (*Il.* 1, 2, 4, 5, 7, 8, 10, 11, 13, 14, 15, 23, 24) *passim*

Pelops (**pē**-lops), son of Tantalos, father of Atreus and Thyestes, grandfather of Agamemnon and Menelaos, eponymous hero of the Peloponessus (*Il.* 2) 65

Peneios (pe-**nē**-os), a river in Thessaly that rises in the Pindos and enters the Aegean between Ossa and Olympos (*Il.* 2) 85

Peneleos (pē-**nel**-e-os), an Achaean leader of the Boeotians (*Il.* 13, 14, 16, 17, 18) 305, 346, 347, 382, 418, 419, 433

Pergamos, "tower," the highest point of the citadel of Troy where there was a temple to Apollo (*Il.* 4, 5, 6, 7, 24) 125, 142, 176, 177, 566

Periboia (per-i-**bē**-a), Thracian grandmother of the ambidextrous Asteropaios (*Il.* 21) 482

Perimedes (per-i-**mē**-dēz), father of a leader of the Phocians (*Il.* 15) 364

Periphas (**per**-i-fas), (1) an Aetolian killed by Ares (*Il.* 5) 155; (2) a Trojan whose form Apollo took to urge Aeneas to fight (*Il.* 17) 410

Periphetes (per-i-**fē**-tēz), (1) probably a Mysian, killed by Teucer (*Il.* 14) 347; (2) Mycenaean son of Kopreus, killed by Hector (*Il.* 15) 367, 368

Perkotê (per-**kō**-tē), a city on the Hellespont (*Il.* 2, 11, 15) 89, 90, 264, 268, 365

Persephonê (per-**sef**-o-nē), daughter of Demeter, wife of Hades (*Il.* 9) 226

Perseus (**per**-sūs), "destroyer(?)," son of Zeus and Danaë, founded Mycenae (*Il.* 14, 19) 340, 450

Peteos (**pet**-e-ōs), father of the Athenian leader Menestheus (*Il.* 2, 4, 12, 13) 78, 118, 119, 296, 325

Phainops (**fī**-nops), (1) Trojan father of two sons killed by Diomedes (*Il.* 5) 131; (2) Trojan whose form Apollo takes to exhort Hector (*Il.* 17) 418; (3) Phrygian victim of Big Ajax (*Il.* 17) 410

Phaistos (**fes**-tos), city in south central Crete (*Il.* 2) 82

Phalkes (**fal**-kēz), a Phrygian killed by Antilochos (*Il.* 13, 14) 328, 347

Pherai (**fer**-ē), (1) in Messenia, one of the towns that Agamemnon offers to Achilles (*Il.* 9) 216; (2) in Thessaly, a city whose contingent was led by Eumelos, son of Admetos and Alkestis (*Il.* 2) 84

Phereklos (**fer**-e-klos), a Trojan, killed by Meriones, who built the ship that carried Helen from Sparta (*Il.* 5) 129

Philoktetes (fi-lok-**tēt**-ēz), inherited the bow of Herakles, bit by a serpent and abandoned on Lemnos, killer of Paris according to later tradition (*Il.* 2) 84

Phlegyes (**fleg**-yēz), a mysterious warlike tribe mentioned in a simile (*Il.* 13) 313

Phocis (**fō**-sis), region in central Greece where Delphi is located (*Il.* 2) 76

Phoenicians, "red-men," from the dye that stained their hands, a Semitic seafaring people living on the coast of the northern Levant, 14; (*Il.* 23) 539

Phoinix (**fē**-niks), (1) tutor to Achilles (*Il.* 9, 16, 17, 19) 217, 219, 225, 226, 231, 234, 377, 417, 456; (2) king of Tyre, father to Europa (*Il.* 14) 340, 341

Phorbas, "fodder," (1) a king in Lesbos, father of Achilles' concubine Diomedê (*Il.* 9) 233; (2) a Trojan killed by Peneleos (*Il.* 14) 346

Phorkys (**for**-kis), a Phrygian killed by Big Ajax (*Il.* 2, 17) 91, 407, 409, 410

Phrontis, Trojan wife of Panthoös (*Il.* 17) 401

Phrygia (**frij**-a), region in Asia Minor east of the Troad (*Il.* 3, 10, 16, 18, 24) 97, 105, 106, 250, 394, 434, 561

Phrygians, Anatolian allies of the Trojans (*Il.* 2, 3, 10) 91, 97, 250

Phthia (**thī**-a), region in southern Thessaly, home of Achilles (*Il.* 1, 2, 7, 9, 11, 13, 15, 16, 19, 23) *passim*

Phthires (**thir**-ēz), a mountain near Miletos (*Il.* 2) 91

Phylakê (**fil**-a-kê), a city in Thessaly, homeland of Protesilaos (*Il.* 2, 13, 15) 83, 84, 325, 326, 357

Phylakos (**fil**-a-kos), (1) Thessalian father of Iphiklos, grandfather of Protesilaos (*Il.* 13) 326; (2) a Trojan killed by Leïtos (*Il.* 6) 159

Phyleus (**fil**-ūs), father of Meges the leader of the Epeians (*Il.* 2, 10, 11, 13, 15, 16, 19, 23) 80, 238, 240, 280, 325, 364, 381, 453, 535

Pieria (pi-**er**-i-a), "fat," region in Thessaly near Mt. Olympos, home of the Muses, where the gods land when coming down from Olympos (*Il.* 2, 14) 87, 336, 337

Peisistratos (pi-**sis**-tra-tus) (sixth century BC–527 BC), tyrant of Athens, 9

Pittheus (**pit**-thūs), king of Troezen, host to Aegeus, father of Aithra (*Il.* 3) 96

Pityeia (pit-**yē**-a), a town in the Troad (*Il.* 2) 89

Plakos (**plā**-kos), a mountain in the Troad (*Il.* 6) 173, 174

Plataia (pla-**tē**-a), a town in southern Boeotia (*Il.* 2) 76

Plato (428–348 BC), Greek philosopher, 7, 17, 21

Pleuron (**plu**-rōn), a town in Aetolia, part of the contingent of Thoas (*Il.* 2, 9, 13, 14, 23) 82, 228, 310, 333, 535

Podaleirios (pod-a-**lēr**-i-os), son of Asklepios, brother of the physician Machaon (*Il.* 2, 11) 84, 273, 285

Podargos (pod-**arg**-os), "whitefoot," or "fleetfoot," (1) one of Hector's horses (*Il.* 8) 198; (2) one of the horses of Menelaos in the chariot race (*Il.* 23) 524

Podarkes (pod-**ark**-ēz), "swift-foot," Thessalian brother of Protesilaos (*Il.* 2, 13, 20, 23) 84, 325, 326, 466, 535

Podes (**pōd**-ēz), Trojan killed by Menelaos (*Il.* 17) 418

Polites (pol-**ī**-tēz), a son of Priam, carried Deïphobos from battle (*Il.* 2, 13, 15, 24) 88, 320, 357, 552

Polydora, "of many gifts," daughter of Peleus, mother of Menesthios (a leader of the Myrmidons) (*Il.* 16) 377

Polydoros, (1) an Epeian defeated by Nestor in the funeral games of Amarynkeus (*Il.* 23) 535, 536; (2) the youngest son of Priam, killed by Achilles (*Il.* 20) 474

Polyktor, "much-possessing," alleged father of the Myrmidon impersonated by Hermes when he appears to Priam (*Il.* 24) 556

Polypoites (pol-i-**pē**-tēz), a Lapith, son of Peirithoös, leader of the Thessalians (*Il.* 2, 12, 23) 85, 289, 291, 542

Polyxeinos (pol-ik-**sēn**-os), grandson of Augeias, one of the four leaders of the Epeians (*Il.* 2) 80

Porson, Richard (1759–1808), British classical scholar, 17, 18

Portheus (**por**-thūs), "sacker," ancient Aetolian king of Kalydon, grandfather of Tydeus, great-grandfather of Diomedes (*Il.* 14) 333

Poseidon (po-**sīd**-on), son of Kronos and Rhea, god of the sea (*Il.* 1, 2, 5, 7, 8, 11–15, 17, 19–21, 23, 24) *passim*

Poulydamas (po-li-**dā**-mas), prominent Trojan fighter who repeatedly warns Hector against rash action (*Il.* 11–18, 22) *passim*

Praktios, a river near Abydos in the Hellespont (*Il.* 2) 90

Priam (**prī**-am), king of Troy, son of Laomedon, husband of Hekabê, father of Hector and Paris (*Il.* 1–24) *passim*

Proitos (**prē**-tos), king of Tiryns, whose wife Anteia attempted to seduce Bellerophon (*Il.* 6) 163, 164

Promachos (**prom**-a-kos), "fighting in front," a Boeotian, killed by Akamas at the Battle at the Ships (*Il.* 14) 346, 347

Propontis (prō-**pon**-tis), sea between the Aegean and the Black Sea (= Sea of Marmara) (*Il.* 13) 302

Protesilaos (pro-tes-i-**lā**-os), son of Iphiklos, ruler of Phylakê in Thessaly, first man to die at Troy (*Il.* 2, 13, 15, 16) 83, 84, 325, 326, 369, 380

Prothoös (**pro**-tho-os), "running forward," an Achaean, leader of the Magnesians (*Il.* 2) 83, 84

Ptolemies, Macedonian/Greek dynasty who ruled Egypt from 334 to 30 BC, 6

Pylaimenes (pi-**lē**-me-nēz), "standing fast at the gate," leader of the Paphlagonians , killed by Menelaos (*Il.* 2, 5) 90, 145, then alive to accompany his dead son Harpalion into Troy (*Il.* 13) 323, 324

Pylartes (pi-**lar**-tēz), "gate-fastener," (1) a Trojan killed by Ajax (*Il.* 11) 273 (2) a Trojan killed by Patroklos (*Il.* 16) 392

Pylos (**pī**-los), Bronze Age settlement in the southwest Peloponnesus, kingdom of Nestor where important archaeological remains have been found (*Il.* 1, 2, 4–13, 15–17, 21, 23, 24) *passim*

Pyraichmes (pir-**ēk**-mēz), "fire-spear," leader of Paeonians, killed by Patroklos (*Il.* 2, 16) 90, 380

Pyrasos (pir-**ā**-sos), a city in Thessaly in the contingent of Protesilaos (*Il.* 2, 11) 83, 273

Pytho, Homer's name for Delphi (*Il.* 2, 9) 77, 225

R

Rhadamanthys (rad-a-**man**-this), brother of Minos, judge in the underworld (*Il.* 14) 340, 341

rhapsode, "staff-singer," performer who memorized written poetry, especially Homer (contrast with *aoidoi*), 9

Rhea (**rē**-a), a Titaness, wife of Kronos (*Il.* 6, 12, 14, 15) 173, 287, 336, 352

Rhesos, (1) a Thracian ally of Troy (*Il.* 10) 250–254; (2) a river in the Troad (*Il.* 12) 286

Rhipê (**rip**-ē), a town in Arcadia (*Il.* 2) 80

Rhodes (rōdz), Aegean island near southwestern tip of Asia Minor, whose contingent was led by Tlepolemos, son of Herakles, killed by Sarpedon (*Il.* 2) 82, 83

Rhytion (**rit**-i-on), a city in south central Crete (*Il.* 2) 82

S

Salamis (**sal**-a-mis), island near the port of Athens (*Il.* 2, 7) 78, 183

Samothrace, island in the north Aegean, 4, 6, 8; (*Il.* 12, 24) 302, 547, 567

Sangarius, river in northeast Asia Minor, flowing through Phrygia to the Black Sea (*Il.* 3) 97

Sarpedon (sar-**pēd**-on), son of Zeus, Lycian prince, ally of Troy, killed by Patroklos, 32; (*Il.* 2, 5, 6, 11, 12, 14, 15, 16, 17, 23) *passim*

Satnioeis (sat-**ni**-o-ēs), a river in the Troad (*Il.* 6, 14, 21) 159, 345, 480

Scaean (**skē**-an) Gates, "left" or "western" gates, the principal gate at Troy (*Il.* 3, 6, 9, 11, 16, 18, 22) 96, 100, 167, 169, 173, 174, 223, 262, 394, 397, 438, 498, 503, 509

Schedios, (1) son of Iphitos, leader of the Phocians, killed by Hector (*Il.* 2, 17) 77, 410; (2) son of Perimedes, another leader of the Phocians, killed by Hector (*Il.* 15) 364

Schliemann, Heinrich (1822–1890), German archaeologist, 21–23

Schoinos (**skē**-nos), a town in Boeotia (*Il.* 2) 76

scholia, "little lesson," marginal notations in literary texts that explicate points of interest, 8

Selloi, interpreters of the oracle of Zeus at Dodona (*Il.* 16) 378, 379 *sêmata lugra*, "ruinous signs," inscribed on a tablet given to Bellerophon, the only reference to writing in Homer, 8

Semelê (**sem**-e-lē), daughter of Kadmos and Harmonia, beloved by Zeus, mother to Dionysos, destroyed by lightning (*Il.* 14) 340

Semites, "descendants of Shem," a son of Noah, peoples of the Near East speaking a language with triconsonantal roots, including Assyrians, Babylonians, Hebrews, Phoenicians 14, 169

Sestos, a city opposite Abydos on the Hellespont (*Il.* 2) 90

shame culture, where social sanctions are external, 30

Sidon (**sī**-don), Phoenician city in the Levant, 4, 14; (*Il.* 6, 23) 168, 169, 539

Sidonians, a Homeric word for the Phoenicians (*Il.* 6, 23) 169, 539

simile, when one thing is said to be like another, 4, 17, 25, 37, 94, 143, 212, 252, 259, 261, 267, 275, 290, 356

Simoeis (**sim**-o-ēs), a river in the Troad (*Il.* 4, 5, 6) 123, 152, 158

Sintians, early inhabitants of the island of Lemnos who took care of Hephaistos when he was thrown from heaven (*Il.* 1, 18) 60, 437

Sipylos (**sip**-i-los), mountain in Asia Minor, where Niobê was turned to stone (*Il.* 24) 563

Sisyphos (**sis**-i-fos), son of Aiolos, punished in the underworld (*Il.* 6) 163

Skamandrios, (1) an alternate name for Astyanax (*Il.* 6) 173; (2) a Trojan killed by Menelaos (*Il.* 5) 128

Skamandros, the main river in the Troad, called Xanthos by the gods (*Il.* 2–22) *passim*

Skolos (**skō**-los), a village in Boeotia (*Il.* 2) 76

Skyros (**skir**-os), island west of Euboea where Neoptolemos was raised (*Il.* 9, 19) 233, 456

Smintheus, "mouse-god(?)" an epithet of Apollo, 33; (*Il.* 1) 42

Sokos, a Trojan killed by Odysseus, whom Sokos wounded (*Il.* 11) 271, 272

Solymi (**sol**-i-mē), a tribe of warriors in Lycia defeated by Bellerophon (*Il.* 6) 164, 166

Sophocles (496–406 BC), Greek playwright, 21, 84, 162, 537

Sparta, city in Lacedaemon in the southern Peloponnesus (*Il.* 2, 3, 4, 8, 9) 79, 96, 109, 201, 216, 229

Spercheios (sper-**kē**-os), a river in Thessaly (*Il.* 1, 16, 23) 45, 377, 519

Stentor, a man whose voice was as loud as fifty men (*Il.* 5) 154

Sthenelos, (1) one of the commanders of the Argos contingent (*Il.* 2, 5, 8, 23) 78, 130, 134–136, 155, 196, 532, 537; (2) son of Perseus and Andromeda, father of Eurystheus (*Il.* 19) 450

Stichios, a leader of the Athenians, killed by Hector (*Il.* 13, 15) 310, 325, 357, 358

Stymphalos (**stim**-fa-los), a city in Arcadia beside the Stymphalian lake where Heracles killed the Stymphalian birds (*Il.* 2) 80

Styra, a city on the west coast of Euboea (*Il.* 2) 77

Styx (stiks), "hate," a river in the underworld (*Il.* 2, 8, 14, 15) 85, 206, 338, 349

Symê (**sim**-ē), an island near Rhodes ruled by Nireus (*Il.* 2) 83

T

Talaimenes (tal-ī-men-ēz), a ruler of the Maeonians (*Il.* 2) 91

Talaos (ta-**lā**-os), ancient king of Argos, father of Adrastos, grandfather of Euryalos (one of the leaders of the Argos contingent) (*Il.* 2, 23) 78, 537

Talthybios (tal-**thib**-i-os), the herald of Agamemnon (*Il.* 1, 2, 3, 4, 7, 9, 19, 23) 51, 52, 67, 95, 115, 185, 217, 452, 453, 455, 543

Tarnê, a city in Maeonia, perhaps Sardis (*Il.* 5) 128

Tartaros, place for punishment in the underworld (*Il.* 5, 8, 14) 157, 193, 209, 338

Tegea (**tej**-e-a), a city in Arcadia (*Il.* 2) 80

Telamon (**tel**-a-mon), son of Aiakos, half-brother or friend of Peleus, father of Big Ajax and Teucer (*Il.* 2–18, 20, 23) *passim*

Telemachos (tel-**em**-a-kos), "far-fighter," son of Odysseus and Penelopê (*Il.* 2, 4) 69, 119

Tenedos (**ten**-e-dos), an Aegean island near Troy (*Il.* 1, 11, 13) 42, 55, 277, 303

Tereia (ter-**ē**-a), a mountain in the Troad (*Il.* 2) 89

Tethys (**tē**-this), a deformation of Tiamat, a Titan, wife of Ocean, mother of the Oceanids (*Il.* 14) 336, 340

Teucer (**tū**-ser), half-brother to Big Ajax, a great bowman (*Il.* 6, 8, 12, 13, 14, 15, 16, 17, 20, 23) *passim*

Teuthras, (1) an Achaean killed by Hector (*Il.* 5) 150; (2) a Trojan killed by Diomedes (*Il.* 6) 158

Thalpios, one of the leaders of the Epeians (*Il.* 2) 80

Thamyris (tha-**mi**-ris), a legendary singer from Thrace (*Il.* 2) 79

Theano (the-**an**-o), wife of Antenor and priestess of Athena (*Il.* 5, 6, 11) 129, 169, 264

Thebes (**thēbz**), (1) principal city in Boeotia, unsuccessfully attacked by seven heroes, destroyed by their sons (*Il.* 4, 19) 120, 449; (2) city in the Troad destroyed by Achilles (*Il.* 2, 6, 23) 76, 78, 83, 166, 526, 537; (3) capital of New Kingdom Egypt (*Il.* 9) 218

Themis (**them**-is), "what is laid down," "law," a Titan, early consort of Zeus (*Il.* 9, 15, 20) 216, 222, 350, 461

Thersilochos, a Paeonian ally of Troy, killed by Achilles (*Il.* 20, 21) 407, 484

Thersites (ther-**sīt**-ēz), the ugliest man who went to Troy, opposes Agamemnon, 36; (*Il.* 2) 68, 69

Theseus (**thē**-sūs), son of Poseidon and Aithra (*Il.* 1, 3) 49, 96

Thespeia, a community in Boeotia, probably same as classical Thespiae (*Il.* 2) 76

Thessalos, a son of Herakles, whose sons led the contingent from Kos (*Il.* 2) 83

Thessaly, region in Greece south of Mt. Olympos, 4, 24 (*Il.* 1, 2) 45, 76

Thestor, (1) father of Kalchas (*Il.* 1) 43; an Achaean killed by Sarpedon (*Il.* 12) 297

Thetis (**thē**-tis), a daughter of Nereus, wife of Peleus, mother of Achilles (*Il.* 1, 16, 17, 18, 19, 23, 24) 54, 372, 378, 389, 399, 426–430, 435–439, 446–448, 456, 467, 515, 545, 547–549

Thisbê, a city in Boeotia (*Il.* 2) 76

Thoas, (1) a leader of the Aetolians (*Il.* 2, 4, 7, 13, 15, 19) 82, 126, 182, 305, 310, 311, 356, 453; (2) a Trojan killed by Menelaos (*Il.* 16) 381; (3) an early king of Lemnos (*Il.* 14) 337

Thoön, (1) a Trojan killed by Diomedes (*Il.* 5) 131; (2) a Trojan, killed by Antilochos (*Il.* 12, 13) 289, 321

Thrace, region northeast of Greece, 4, 6, 8; (*Il.* 2, 6, 9, 13, 14, 20, 24) 79, 162, 212, 302, 337, 476, 547, 567

Thrasymedes (thras-i-**mē**-dēz), a son of Nestor (*Il.* 9, 10, 14, 16, 17) 214, 240, 242, 330, 381, 412, 421

Thucydides (c. 460–395 BC), Athenian historian, 5, 18, 21, 26, 27

Thyestes (thī-**es**-tēz), son of Pelops, father of Aigisthos, brother of Atreus, uncle of Agamemnon and Menelaos (*Il.* 2) 65

Thymbrê (**thim**-brē), a town in the Troad (*Il.* 10) 250

Tiamat (**tē**-a-mat), a Babylonian monster of chaos (*Il.* 1) 54

timê (**tē**-mā), "value, worth," the honor for which a hero strives 26–29, 44

Tiryns (**tir**-inz), Bronze Age city in Argive plain, part of the kingdom of Diomedes, associated with Herakles (*Il.* 2, 10) 78, 82, 244

Titanos (**tit**-a-nos), "white earth," a mountain in Thessaly in the domain of Eurypylos (*Il.* 2) 85

Titans (**tī**-tans), offspring of Ouranos and Gaia, the generation of the gods before the Olympians (*Il.* 14) 338

Tithonos (ti-**thōn**-os), brother of Priam, beloved of Dawn, given eternal life without eternal youth (*Il.* 20) 468

Tlepolemos (tlē-**pol**-e-mos), a son of Herakles, leader of the Rhodian contingent (*Il.* 2) 82

Trachis (**trā**-kis), "rough," a city in Thessaly near Thermopylae, scene of Herakles' death, under Achilles' command (*Il.* 2) 83

Tritogeneia (trit-o-ghen-ē-a), an obscure epithet of Athena (*Il.* 4, 8, 22) 125, 194, 503

Troad, the area around Troy at the entrance to the Dardanelles, 4, 27, 33; (*Il.* 9, 21) 223, 487

Troezen (**trē**-zen), city in the Argolid in the realm of Diomedes (*Il.* 2, 3) 78, 90, 96

Tros (trōs), (1) eponymous founder of the Trojan race, son of Erichthonios, king of Troy, father of Ilos and Ganymede (*Il* 20) 468; (2) a Trojan killed by Achilles (*Il.* 20) 476

Troy, Bronze Age city in northwestern Asia Minor (*Il.* 1–24) *passim*

Turkey, 3, 22, 27, 205, 292, 298

Tychios (**tik**-i-os), "maker," the man who made Ajax's body shield (*Il.* 7) 183, 184

Tydeus (**tī**-dūs), son of Oineus, father of Diomedes, fought at Thebes (*Il.* 4, 5, 14) 119–121, 127, 129–136, 138, 139, 141, 142, 154, 155, 156, 333, 342

Typhoeus (tī-**fō**-ūs), or Typhon, monstrous offspring of Gaea overcome by Zeus (*Il.* 2) 87

U

Ugarit, Bronze Age emporium in the northern Levant, destroyed c. 1200 BC, 14

V

Venetus A, the oldest complete manuscript of the *Iliad*, c. AD 1000, 8, 10

Vergil (70–19 BC), Roman poet, 8, 20, 137, 318, 471

vulgate, "common," designates the medieval text of Homer based on the Alexandrian text, our modern text of Homer, 6–7, 10, 20

W

Wolf, Friedrich August (1759–1824), German classicist who formulated the modern Homeric Question, 8, 9, 15

X

xenia (ksen-ē-a), "guest friendship," the conventions that govern relationships between host and guest (*Il.* 2, 4, 5) 89, 111, 133

Z

Zakynthos, the most southerly of the Ionian Islands (*Il.* 2) 80

Zeleia (zel-ē-a), a city in the Troad, homeland of Pandaros (*Il.* 2, 4) 89, 111

Zenodotus (zen-**od**-o-tus) (third century BC), Alexandrian commentator on Homer, 6

Zeus, Greek storm-god, father of gods and men, son of Kronos and Rhea, husband of Hera (i–24) *passim*